The Boats of the
"Glen Carrig"
and Other
Nautical
Adventures

The Boats of the "Glen Carrig" and Other Nautical Adventures

Being The First Volume of
The Collected Fiction of William Hope Hodgson

Edited by Jeremy Lassen

Night Shade Books · New York · 2017

Visit our website at www.nightshadebooks.com.

10 9 8 7 6 5 4 3 2

Library of Congress Cataloging-in-Publication Data is available on file.

ISBN: 978-1-59780-920-7
Ebook ISBN: 978-1-59780-367-0
Hardcover ISBN: 978-1-89238-939-8

Cover and interior artwork © 2003 by Jason Van Hollander
Interior layout and design by Jeremy Lassen
Introduction © 2003 by Jeremy Lassen
A Note on the Texts © 2003 by Jeremy Lassen

Printed in the United States of America

This series is dedicated to the readers, editors, publishers and scholars who have worked tirelessly since William Hope Hodgson's death to ensure that his work would not be lost or forgotten. Without their efforts, these volumes would not be possible.

In particular, the editor would like to thank S. T. Joshi, Mike Ashley, Jack Adrian and George Locke for their generous support.

Contents

Contents

Unreality and the Borderlands of Human Existence

Mr. Hodgson is perhaps second only to Algernon Blackwood in his serious treatment of unreality – H. P. Lovecraft

Among those fiction writers who have elected to deal with the shadowlands and borderlands of human existence, William Hope Hodgson surely merits a place with the very few that inform their treatment of such themes with a sense of authenticity. – Clark Ashton Smith

IT GOES WITHOUT SAYING that William Hope Hodgson was one of the great fantasists of the 20th century. However, the purpose of this introduction is not to sing the praises of William Hope Hodgson, nor to provide critical analysis of the successes or failures of his fiction. Many have done so far more eloquently and insightfully than can be done in this limited forum. The purpose of this essay is to introduce the materials that make up this, the first volume of *The Collected Fiction of William Hope Hodgson*.

It was Hodgson's nautical fiction that first captured his contemporary readers' imaginations. His experiences of life at sea gave this nautical fiction a grounding in reality which, when combined with his weird and cosmic sensibilities, created balanced and remarkably effective narratives. Even his non-weird sea fiction benefited from this dynamic: His realistically detailed backgrounds served to make the dramatic flourishes of his adventure fiction seem less outlandish. His popular success encouraged editors to give him top billing in the premier fiction magazines of the day, and encouraged Hodgson to further develop his peculiar cosmic vision.

The opening novel in this collection, *The Boats of the "Glen Carrig"*, was Hodgson's first published book, and is the cornerstone of his "Sargasso Sea" cycle of stories. The novel was first published in England by Chapman & Hall in 1907. A year earlier, Hodgson's first Sargasso Sea story, "From the Tideless Sea," was published in the April 1906 issue of America's *The Monthly Story*. On Hodgson's side of the Atlantic, the editors of *The London Magazine* made "From the Tideless Sea" their lead story in the May 1907 issue. July of 1907 saw the publication of "The Mystery of the Derelict," which was the second Sargasso Sea story. "More News From the *Homebird*," (a sequel to "From the Tideless Sea") was published in August, 1907. This initial flurry of Sargasso Sea stories almost certainly helped stir interest in *The Boats of the* "Glen Carrig", which was released to unanimous praise in October 1907.

Immediately following these publications, Hodgson wrote some of his most well-known weird sea fiction, but he would not return to the Sargasso Sea until 1912, when "The Thing in the Weeds" appeared in *Story-teller*. Just over a year later, "The Finding of the *Graiken*" was published in *The Red Magazine*, and would become the last Sargasso Sea story published during Hodgson's lifetime.

During the years following his death, Hodgson's wife, Bessie, worked tirelessly to keep her husband's work in print, and to find homes for his unpublished stories. In November 1920, *The Premier* published "The Voice in the Dawn," which was William Hope Hodgson's final Sargasso Sea story. Arkham House reprinted this story in *Deep Waters* in 1947, under the title "The Call in the Dawn."

One of William Hope Hodgson's most commercially successful creations was his series of stories featuring the British smuggler, Captain Gault. These stories were written during 1914 and 1915, prior to his commission in England's Royal Field Artillery. All but one were published between 1914 and 1917 in *The London Magazine*. In September of 1917, Eveleigh Nash published ten of these stories in the collection *Captain Gault*. "The Painted Lady" was probably omitted from this collection because it had been published in his earlier Eveleigh Nash collection *The Luck of the Strong* (in a slightly different form) as "Captain Gumbolt Charity and the Painted Lady." "Trading With the Enemy" appeared in the October 1917 issue of *The London Magazine*, which was too late to allow its inclusion in the Eveleigh Nash collection. "The Plans of the Reefing Bi-Plane" was a rejected Captain Gault story that was not published until 1996 in *Terrors From the Sea*. This volume brings together for the first time all thirteen Captain Gault stories.

Hodgson's earlier commercial successes with his supernatural detective Carnaki may have encouraged him to develop a serial adventure character: Captain Jat was the first such attempt. Though not as commercially successful as Captain Gault, the two Captain Jat stories are excellent combinations of humor and horror, and feature a classic Hodgson stand-in character, Pibby Tawles—a cabin boy who always manages to end up better off than his captain. This image of an apprentice getting his revenge upon or tricking his abusive superiors is a re-occurring theme in Hodgson's fiction that reflected his own love/hate relationship with life at sea. Both Captain Jat stories were published in *The Red Magazine* in 1912 and reprinted in his collection, *The Luck of the Strong*.

The DCO Cargunka stories are another example of Hodgson's search for a commercially-viable series character. The Cargunka stories were published in *The Red Magazine* in 1914 and 1915—the same venue that had earlier published his Captain Jat stories. "The Bells of the 'Laughing Sally,'" and an abridgment of "The Adventures with the Claim Jumpers," were printed in *Cargunka and Poems and Anecdotes* (Harold and Paget, New York, 1914). This unusual publication contained abridgments of several Captain Gault stories and abridged versions of his well known sea fiction, as well as summaries of several of his stories that were not published until after his death("The Sharks of the St. Elmo," and "Eloi, Eloi Lama Sabachthani," among others). This odd collection of summaries and abridgments is mixed together with Hodgson's verse in an almost stream-of-consciousness style. Complete versions of both Cargunka stories were later reprinted in *The Luck of the Strong*.

The stories in this first volume of *Collected Fiction* are the kind of stories that helped Hodgson achieve commercial success. These stories were often published in the highest paying fiction markets of his day, and demonstrate his wide-ranging narrative talents: from the weird and fantastic, to the humorous, to straight adventure stories. Today's readers of Hodgson may be more familiar with his stunningly-original novels of cosmic vision, such as *The House on the Borderlands* or *The Night Land*, but it is his narratives of the sea that first captured the attention of the reading public. Most importantly, however, it was in that weed-choked Sargasso Sea where Hodgson first began to explore unreality, and the borderlands of human existence.

Jeremy Lassen
San Francisco
Februrary, 2003

The Boats of the "Glen Carrig"

Being an account of their Adventures in the Strange Places of the Earth, after the foundering of the good ship *Glen Carrig* through striking upon a hidden rock in the unknown seas to the Southward. As told by John Winterstraw, Gent., to his Son James Winterstraw, in the year 1757, and by him committed very properly and legibly to manuscript.

Madre Mia

People may say thou art no longer young
   And yet, to me, thy youth was yesterday,
     A yesterday that seems
   Still mingled with my dreams.
Ah! how the years have o'er thee flung
   Their soft mantilla, grey.

And e'en to them thou art not over old;
   How could'st thou be! Thy hair
     Hast scarcely lost its deep old glorious dark
   Thy face is scarcely lined. No mark
Destroys its calm serenity. Like gold
   Of evening light, when winds scarce stir,
   The soul-light of thy face is pure as prayer.

Table of Contents

I

The Land of Lonesomeness

ⁿOW WE HAD BEEN five days in the boats, and in all this
time made no discovering of land. Then upon the morning of the
sixth day came there a cry from the bo'sun, who had the command
of the lifeboat, that there was something which might be land afar
upon our larboard bow; but it was very low lying, and none could tell
whether it was land or but a morning cloud. Yet, because there was
the beginning of hope within our hearts, we pulled wearily towards
it, and thus, in about an hour, discovered it to be indeed the coast of
some flat country.

Then, it might be a little after the hour of midday, we had come
so close to it that we could distinguish with ease what manner of land
lay beyond the shore, and thus we found it to be of an abominable
flatness, desolate beyond all that I could have imagined. Here and there
it appeared to be covered with clumps of queer vegetation; though
whether they were small trees or great bushes, I had no means of
telling; but this I know, that they were like unto nothing which ever
I had set eyes upon before.

So much as this I gathered as we pulled slowly along the coast,
seeking an opening whereby we could pass inward to the land; but a
weary time passed ere we came upon that which we sought. Yet, in
the end, we found it—a slimy-banked creek, which proved to be the
estuary of a great river, though we spoke of it always as a creek. Into
this we entered, and proceeded at no great pace upwards along its
winding course; and as we made forward, we scanned the low banks
upon each side, perchance there might be some spot where we could
make to land; but we found none—the banks being composed of a vile
mud which gave us no encouragement to venture rashly upon them.

Now, having taken the boat something over a mile up the great
creek, we came upon the first of that vegetation which I had chanced to

notice from the sea, and here, being within some score yards of it, we were the better able to study it. Thus I found that it was indeed composed largely of a sort of tree, very low and stunted, and having what might be described as an unwholesome look about it. The branches of this tree, I perceived to be the cause of my inability to recognise it from a bush, until I had come close upon it; for they grew thin and smooth through all their length, and hung towards the earth; being weighted thereto by a single, large cabbage-like plant which seemed to sprout from the extreme tip of each.

Presently, having passed beyond this this clump of the vegetation, and the banks of the river remaining very low, I stood me upon a thwart, by which means I was enabled to scan the surrounding country. This I discovered, so far as my sight could penetrate, to be pierced in all directions with innumerable creeks and pools, some of these latter being very great of extent; and, as I have before made mention, everywhere the country was low set—as it might be a great plain of mud; so that it gave me a sense of dreariness to look out upon it. It may be, all unconsciously, that my spirit was put in awe by the extreme silence of all the country around; for in all that waste I could see no living thing, neither bird nor vegetable, save it be the stunted trees, which, indeed, grew in clumps here and there over all the land, so much as I could see.

This silence, when I grew fully aware of it, was the more uncanny; for my memory told me that never before had I come upon a country which contained so much quietness. Nothing moved across my vision—not even a lone bird soared up against the dull sky; and, for my hearing, not so much as the cry of a sea-bird came to me—no! nor the croak of a frog, nor the plash of a fish. It was as though we had come upon the Country of Silence, which some have called the Land of Lonesomeness.

Now three hours had passed whilst we ceased not to labour at the oars, and we could no more see the sea; yet no place fit for our feet had come to view, for everywhere the mud, grey and black, surrounded us—encompassing us veritably by a slimy wilderness. And so we were fain to pull on, in the hope that we might come ultimately to firm ground.

Then, a little before sundown, we halted upon our oars, and made a scant meal from a portion of our remaining provisions; and as we ate, I could see the sun sinking away over the wastes, and I had some slight diversion in watching the grotesque shadows which it cast from the trees into the water upon our larboard side; for we had come to a pause opposite a clump of the vegetation. It was at this time, as I remember, that it was borne in upon me afresh how very silent was the land; and that this was not due to my imagination, I remarked that the men both in our own and in the bo'sun's boat, seemed uneasy because of it; for none spoke save in undertones, as though they had fear of breaking it.

And it was at this time, when I was awed by so much solitude, that there came the first telling of life in all that wilderness. I heard it first in the far distance, away inland—a curious, low, sobbing note it was, and the rise and the fall of it was like to the sobbing of a lonesome wind through a great forest. Yet was there no wind. Then, in a moment, it had died, and the silence of the land was awesome by reason of the contrast. And I looked about me at the men, both in the boat in which I was and that which the bo'sun commanded; and not one was there but held himself in a posture of listening. In this wise a minute of quietness passed, and then one of the men gave out a laugh, born of the nervousness which had taken him.

The bo'sun muttered to him to hush, and, in the same moment, there came again the plaint of that wild sobbing. And abruptly it sounded away on our right, and immediately was caught up, as it were, and echoed back from some place beyond us afar up the creek. At that, I got me upon a thwart, intending to take another look over the country about us; but the banks of the creek had become higher; moreover the vegetation acted as a screen, even had my stature and elevation enabled me to overlook the banks.

And so, after a little while, the crying died away, and there was another silence. Then, as we sat each one harking for what might next befall, George, the youngest 'prentice boy, who had his seat beside me, plucked me by the sleeve, inquiring in a troubled voice whether I had any knowledge of that which the crying might portend; but I shook my head, telling him that I had no knowing beyond his own; though, for his comfort, I said that it might be the wind. Yet, at that, he shook his head; for indeed, it was plain that it could not be by such agency, for there was a stark calm.

Now, I had scarce made an end of my remark, when again the sad crying was upon us. It appeared to come from far up the creek, and from far down the creek, and from inland and the land between us and the sea. It filled the evening air with its doleful wailing, and I remarked that there was in it a curious sobbing, most human in its despairful crying. And so awesome was the thing that no man of us spoke; for it seemed that we harked to the weeping of lost souls. And then, as we waited fearfully, the sun sank below the edge of the world, and the dusk was upon us.

And now a more extraordinary thing happened; for, as the night fell with swift gloom, the strange wailing and crying was hushed, and another sound stole out upon the land—a far, sullen growling. At the first, like the crying, it came from far inland; but was caught up speedily on all sides of us, and presently the dark was full of it. And it increased in volume, and strange trumpetings fled across it. Then, though with slowness, it fell away to a low, continuous growling, and in it there was that which I can only describe as an insistent, hungry snarl. Aye! no other word of which I have knowledge so well describes it as that—a note of *hunger*, most awesome to the ear. And this, more than all the rest of those incredible voicings, brought terror into my heart.

Now as I sat listening, George gripped me suddenly by the arm, declaring in a shrill whisper that something had come among the clump of trees upon the left-hand bank. Of the truth of this, I had immediately a proof; for I caught the sound of a continuous rustling among them, and then a nearer note of growling, as though a wild beast purred at my elbow. Immediately upon this, I caught the bo'sun's voice, calling in a low tone to Josh, the eldest 'prentice, who had the charge of our boat, to come alongside of him; for he would have the boats together. Then got we out the oars and laid the boats together in the midst of the creek; and so we watched through the night, being full of fear, so that we kept our speech low; that is, so low as would carry our thoughts one to the other through the noise of the growling.

And so the hours passed, and naught happened more than I have told, save that once, a little after midnight, the trees opposite to us seemed to be stirred again, as though some creature, or creatures, lurked among them; and there came, a little after that, a sound as of something stirring the water up against the bank; but it ceased in a while and the silence fell once more.

Thus, after a weariful time, away Eastwards the sky began to tell of the coming of the day; and, as the light grew and strengthened, so did that insatiable growling pass hence with the dark and the shadows. And so at last came the day, and once more there was borne to us the sad wailing that had preceded the night. For a certain while it lasted, rising and falling most mournfully over the vastness of the surrounding wastes, until the sun was risen some degrees above the horizon; after which it began to fail, dying away in lingering echoes, most solemn to our ears. And so it passed, and there came again the silence that had been with us in all the daylight hours.

Now, it being day, the bo'sun bade us make such sparse breakfast as our provender allowed; after which, having first scanned the banks to discern if any fearful thing were visible, we took again to our oars, and proceeded on our upward journey; for we hoped presently to come upon a country where life had not become extinct, and where we could put foot to honest earth. Yet, as I have made mention earlier, the vegetation, where it grew, did flourish most luxuriantly; so that I am scarce correct when I speak of life as being extinct in that land. For, indeed, now I think of it, I can remember that the very mud from which it sprang seemed veritably to have a fat, sluggish life of its own, so rich and viscid was it.

Presently it was midday; yet was there but little change in the nature of the surrounding wastes; though it may be that the vegetation was something thicker, and more continuous along the banks. But the banks were still of the same thick, clinging mud; so that nowhere could we effect a landing; though, had we, the rest of the country beyond the banks seemed no better.

And all the while, as we pulled, we glanced continuously from bank to bank; and those who worked not at the oars were fain to rest a hand by their sheath-knives; for the happenings of the past night were continually in our minds, and we were in great fear; so that we had turned back to the sea but that we had come so nigh to the end of our provisions.

II
The Ship In The Creek

THEN, IT WAS NIGH on to evening, we came upon a creek opening into the greater one through the bank upon our left. We had been like to pass it—as, indeed, we had passed many throughout the day—but that the bo'sun, whose boat had the lead, cried out that there was some craft lying-up, a little beyond the first bend. And, indeed, so it seemed; for one of the masts of her—all jagged, where it had carried away—stuck up plain to our view.

Now, having grown sick with so much lonesomeness, and being in fear of the approaching night, we gave out something near to a cheer, which, however, the bo'sun silenced, having no knowledge of those who might occupy the stranger. And so, in silence, the bo'sun turned his craft toward the creek, whereat we followed, taking heed to keep quietness, and working the oars warily. So, in a little, we came to the shoulder of the bend, and had plain sight of the vessel some little way beyond us. From the distance she had no appearance of being inhabited; so that after some small hesitation, we pulled towards her, though still being at pains to keep silence.

The strange vessel lay against that bank of the creek which was upon our right, and over above her was a thick clump of the stunted trees. For the rest, she appeared to be firmly imbedded in the heavy mud, and there was a certain look of age about her which carried to me a doleful suggestion that we should find naught aboard of her fit for an honest stomach.

We had come to a distance of maybe some ten fathoms from her starboard bow—for she lay with her head down towards the mouth of the little creek—when the bo'sun bade his men to back water, the which Josh did regarding our own boat. Then, being ready to fly if we had been in danger, the bo'sun hailed the stranger; but got no reply, save that some echo of his shout seemed to come back at us. And so he sung out again to her, chance there might be some below decks who had not caught his first hail; but, for the second time, no answer came to us, save the low echo—naught, but that the silent trees took on a little quivering, as though his voice had shaken them.

At that, being confident now within our minds, we laid alongside, and, in a minute had shinned up the oars and so gained her decks. Here, save that the glass of the skylight of the main cabin had been broken, and some portion of the framework shattered, there was no extraordinary litter; so that it appeared to us as though she had been no great while abandoned.

So soon as the bo'sun had made his way up from the boat, he turned aft toward the scuttle, the rest of us following. We found the leaf of the scuttle pulled forward to within an inch of closing, and so much effort did it require of us to push it back, that we had immediate evidence of a considerable time since any had gone down that way.

However, it was no great while before we were below, and here we found the main cabin to be empty, save for the bare furnishings. From it there opened off two state-rooms at the forrard end, and the Captain's cabin in the after part, and in all of these we found matters of clothing and sundries such as proved that the vessel had been deserted apparently in haste. In further proof of this we found, in a drawer in the Captain's room, a considerable quantity of loose gold, the which it was not to be supposed would have been left by the free-will of the owner.

Of the state-rooms, the one upon the starboard side gave evidence that it had been occupied by a woman—no doubt a passenger. The other, in which there were two bunks, had been shared, so far as we could have any certainty, by a couple of young men; and this we gathered by observation of various garments which were scattered carelessly about.

Yet it must not be supposed that we spent any great time in the cabins; for we were pressed for food, and made haste—under the directing of the bo'sun—to discover if the hulk held victuals whereby we might be kept alive.

To this end, we removed the hatch which led down to the lazarette, and, lighting two lamps which we had with us in the boats, went down to make a search. And so, in a little while, we came upon two casks which the bo'sun broke open with a hatchet. These casks were sound and tight, and in them was ship's biscuit, very good and fit for food. At this, as may be imagined, we felt eased in our minds, knowing that there was no immediate fear of starvation. Following this, we found a barrel of molasses; a cask of rum; some cases of dried fruit—these were mouldy and scarce fit to be eaten; a cask of salt beef, another of pork;

a small barrel of vinegar; a case of brandy; two barrels of flour—one of which proved to be damp-struck; and a bunch of tallow dips.

In a little while we had all these things up in the big cabin, so that we might come at them the better to make choice of that which was fit for our stomachs, and that which was otherwise. Meantime, whilst the bo'sun overhauled these matters, Josh called a couple of the men, and went on deck to bring up the gear from the boats, for it had been decided that we should pass the night aboard the hulk.

When this was accomplished, Josh took a walk forward to the fo'cas'le; but found nothing beyond two seamen's chests; a sea-bag, and some odd gear. There were, indeed, no more than ten bunks in the place; for she was but a small brig, and had no call for a great crowd. Yet Josh was more than a little puzzled to know what had come to the odd chests; for it was not to be supposed that there had been no more than two—and a sea-bag—among ten men. But to this, at that time, he had no answer, and so, being sharp for supper, made a return to the deck, and thence to the main cabin.

Now while he had been gone, the bo'sun had set the men to clearing out the main cabin; after which, he had served out two biscuits apiece all round, and a tot of rum. To Josh, when he appeared, he gave the same, and, in a little, we called a sort of council; being sufficiently stayed by the food to talk.

Yet, before we came to speech, we made shift to light our pipes; for the bo'sun had discovered a case of tobacco in the Captain's cabin, and after this we came to the consideration of our position.

We had provender, so the bo'sun calculated, to last us for the better part of two months, and this without any great stint; but we had yet to prove if the brig held water in her casks, for that in the creek was brackish, even so far as we had penetrated from the sea; else we had not been in need. To the charge of this, the bo'sun set Josh, along with two of the men. Another, he told to take charge of the galley, so long as we were in the hulk. But for that night, he said we had no need to do aught; for we had sufficient of water in the boats' breakers to last us till the morrow. And so, in a little, the dusk began to fill the cabin; but we talked on, being greatly content with our present ease and the good tobacco which we enjoyed.

In a little while, one of the men cried out suddenly to us to be silent, and, in that minute, all heard it—a far, drawn-out wailing; the same which had come to us in the evening of the first day. At that we looked at one another through the smoke and the growing dark, and, even as we looked, it became plainer heard, until, in a while, it was all about us—aye! it seemed to come floating down through the broken framework of the skylight as though some weariful, unseen thing stood and cried upon the decks above our heads.

Now through all that crying, none moved; none, that is, save Josh and the bo'sun, and they went up into the scuttle to see whether anything was in sight; but they found nothing, and so came down to us; for there was no wisdom in exposing ourselves, unarmed as we were, save for our sheath-knives.

And so, in a little, the night crept down upon the world, and still we sat within the dark cabin, none speaking, and knowing of the rest only by the glows of their pipes.

All at once there came a low, muttered growl, stealing across the land; and immediately the crying was quenched in its sullen thunder. It died away, and there was a full minute of silence; then, once more it came, and it was nearer and more plain to the ear. I took my pipe from my mouth; for I had come again upon the great fear and uneasiness which the happenings of the first night had bred in me, and the taste of the smoke brought me no more pleasure. The muttered growl swept over our heads and died away into the distance, and there was a sudden silence.

Then, in that quietness, came the bo'sun's voice. He was bidding us haste every one into the Captain's cabin. As we moved to obey him, he ran to draw over the lid of the scuttle; and Josh went with him, and, together, they had it across; though with difficulty. When we had come into the Captain's cabin, we closed and barred the door, piling two great sea-chests up against it; and so we felt near safe; for we knew that no thing, man nor beast, could come at us there. Yet, as may be supposed, we felt not altogether secure; for there was that in the growling which now filled the darkness, that seemed demoniac, and we knew not what horrid Powers were abroad.

And so through the night the growling continued, seeming to be mighty near unto us—aye! almost over our heads, and of a loudness far surpassing all that had come to us on the previous night; so that I thanked the Almighty that we had come into shelter in the midst of so much fear.

III
The Thing That Made Search

NOW AT TIMES, I fell upon sleep, as did most of the others; but, for the most part, I lay half sleeping and half waking—being unable to attain to true sleep by reason of the everlasting growling above us in the night, and the fear which it bred in me. Thus, it chanced that just after midnight, I caught a sound in the main cabin beyond the door, and immediately I was fully waked. I sat me up and listened, and so became aware that something was fumbling about the deck of the main cabin. At that, I got to my feet and made my way to where the bo'sun lay, meaning to waken him, if he slept; but he caught me by the ankle, as I stooped to shake him, and whispered to me to keep silence; for he too had been aware of that strange noise of something fumbling beyond in the big cabin.

In a little, we crept both of us so close to the door as the chests would allow, and there we crouched, listening; but could not tell what manner of thing it might be which produced so strange a noise. For it was neither shuffling, nor treading of any kind, nor yet was it the whirr of a bat's wings, the which had first occurred to me, knowing how vampires are said to inhabit the nights in dismal places. Nor yet was it the slurr of a snake; but rather it seemed to us to be as though a great wet cloth were being rubbed everywhere across the floor and bulkheads. We were the better able to be certain of the truth of this likeness, when, suddenly, it passed across the further side of the door behind which we listened: at which, you may be sure, we drew backwards both of us in fright; though the door, and the chests, stood between us and that which rubbed against it.

Presently, the sound ceased, and, listen as we might, we could no longer distinguish it. Yet, until the morning, we dozed no more; being troubled in mind as to what manner of thing it was which had made search in the big cabin.

Then in time the day came, and the growling ceased. For a mournful while the sad crying filled our ears, and then at last the eternal silence that fills the day hours of that dismal land fell upon us.

So, being at last in quietness, we slept, being greatly aweary. About seven in the morning, the bo'sun waked me, and I found that they had opened the door into the big cabin; but though the bo'sun and I made careful search, we could nowhere come upon anything to tell us aught concerning the thing which had put us so in fright. Yet, I know not if I am right in saying that we came upon nothing; for, in several places, the bulkheads had a *chafed* look; but whether this had been there before that night, we had no means of telling.

Of that which we had heard, the bo'sun bade me make no mention, for he would not have the men put more in fear than need be. This I conceived to be wisdom, and so held my peace. Yet I was much troubled in my mind to know what manner of thing it was which we had need to fear, and more—I desired greatly to know whether we should be free of it in the daylight hours; for there was always with me, as I went hither and thither, the thought that IT—for that is how I designated it in my mind—might come upon us to our destruction.

Now after breakfast, at which we had each a portion of salt pork, besides rum and biscuit (for by now the fire in the caboose had been set going), we turned-to at various matters, under the directing of the bo'sun. Josh and two of the men made examination of the water casks, and the rest of us lifted the main hatch-covers, to make inspection of her cargo; but lo! we found nothing, save some three feet of water in her hold.

By this time, Josh had drawn some water off from the casks; but it was most unsuitable for drinking, being vile of smell and taste. Yet the bo'sun bade him draw some into buckets, so that the air might haply purify it; but though this was done, and the water allowed to stand through the morning, it was but little better.

At this, as might be imagined, we were exercised in our minds as to the manner in which we should come upon suitable water; for by now we were beginning to be in need of it. Yet though one said one thing, and another said another, no one had wit enough to call to mind any method by which our need should be satisfied. Then, when we had made an end of dining, the bo'sun sent Josh, with four of the men, upstream, perchance after a mile or two the water should prove of sufficient freshness to meet our purpose. Yet they returned a little before sundown having no water; for everywhere it was salt.

Now the bo'sun, foreseeing that it might be impossible to come upon water, had set the man whom he had ordained to be our cook, to boiling the creek water in three great kettles. This he had ordered to be done soon after the boat left; and over the spout of each, he had hung a great pot of iron, filled with cold water from the hold—this being cooler than that from the creek—so that the steam from each kettle impinged upon the cold surface of the iron pots, and being by this means condensed, was caught in three buckets placed beneath them upon the floor of the caboose. In this way, enough water was collected to supply us for the evening and the following morning; yet it was but a slow method, and we had sore need of a speedier, were we to leave the hulk so soon as I, for one, desired.

We made our supper before sunset, so as to be free of the crying which we had reason to expect. After that, the bo'sun shut the scuttle, and we went every one of us into the Captain's cabin, after which we barred the door, as on the previous night; and well was it for us that we acted with this prudence.

By the time that we had come into the Captain's cabin, and secured the door, it was upon sunsetting, and as the dusk came on, so did the melancholy wailing pass over the land; yet, being by now somewhat inured to so much strangeness, we lit our pipes, and smoked; though I observed that none talked; for the crying without was not to be forgotten.

Now, as I have said, we kept silence; but this was only for a time, and our reason for breaking it was a discovery made by George, the younger apprentice. This lad, being no smoker, was fain to do something to while away the time, and with this intent, he had raked out the contents of a small box, which had lain upon the deck at the side of the forrard bulkhead.

The box had appeared filled with odd small lumber of which a part was a dozen or so grey paper wrappers, such as are used, I believe, for carrying samples of corn; though I have seen them put to other purposes, as, indeed, was now the case. At first George had tossed these aside; but it growing darker the bo'sun lit one of the candles which we had found in the lazarette. Thus, George, who was proceeding to tidy back the rubbish which was cumbering the place, discovered something which caused him to cry out to us his astonishment.

Now, upon hearing George call out, the bo'sun bade him keep silence, thinking it was but a piece of boyish restlessness; but George drew the candle to him, and bade us to listen; for the wrappers were covered with fine handwriting after the fashion of a woman's.

Even as George told us of that which he had found we became

aware that the night was upon us; for suddenly the crying ceased, and in place thereof there came out of the far distance the low thunder of the night-growling, that had tormented us through the past two nights. For a space, we ceased to smoke, and sat—listening; for it was a very fearsome sound. In a very little while it seemed to surround the ship, as on the previous nights; but at length, using ourselves to it, we resumed our smoking, and bade George to read out to us from the writing upon the paper wrappers.

Then George, though shaking somewhat in his voice, began to decipher that which was upon the wrappers, and a strange and awesome story it was, and bearing much upon our own concerns:—

"Now, when they discovered the spring among the trees that crown the bank, there was much rejoicing; for we had come to have much need of water. And some, being in fear of the ship (declaring, because of all our misfortune and the strange disappearances of their messmates and the brother of my lover, that she was haunted by a devil), declared their intention of taking their gear up to the spring, and there making a camp. This they conceived and carried out in the space of one afternoon; though our Captain, a good and true man, begged of them, as they valued life, to stay within the shelter of their living-place. Yet, as I have remarked, they would none of them hark to his counselling, and, because the Mate and the bo'sun were gone he had no means of compelling them to wisdom—"

At this point, George ceased to read, and began to rustle among the wrappers, as though in search for the continuation of the story.

Presently he cried out that he could not find it, and dismay was upon his face.

But the bo'sun told him to read on from such sheets as were left; for, as he observed, we had no knowledge if more existed; and we were fain to know further of that spring, which, from the story, appeared to be over the bank near to the vessel.

George, being thus adjured, picked up the topmost sheet; for they were, as I heard him explain to the bo'sun, all oddly numbered, and having but little reference one to the other. Yet we were mightily keen to know even so much as such odd scraps might tell unto us. Whereupon, George read from the next wrapper, which ran thus:—

"Now, suddenly, I heard the Captain cry out that there was something in the main cabin, and immediately my lover's voice calling to me to lock my door, and on no condition to open it. Then the door of the Captain's cabin slammed, and there came a silence, and the silence was broken by a *sound*. Now, this was the first time that I had heard the Thing make search through the big cabin; but, afterwards, my lover told me it had happened aforetime, and they had told me naught, fearing to frighten me needlessly; though now I understood why my lover had bidden me never to leave my stateroom door unbolted in the nighttime. I remember also, wondering if the noise of breaking glass that had waked me somewhat from my dreams a night or two previously, had been the work of this indescribable Thing; for on the morning following that night, the glass in the skylight had been smashed. Thus it was that my thoughts wandered out to trifles, while yet my soul seemed ready to leap out from my bosom with fright.

"I had, by reason of usage, come to ability to sleep despite of the fearsome growling; for I had conceived its cause to be the mutter of spirits in the night, and had not allowed myself to be unnecessarily frightened with doleful thoughts; for my lover had assured me of our safety, and that we should yet come to our home. And now, beyond my door, I could hear that fearsome sound of the Thing searching—"

George came to a sudden pause; for the bo'sun had risen and put a great hand upon his shoulder. The lad made to speak; but the bo'sun beckoned to him to say no word, and at that we, who had grown to nervousness through the happenings in the story, began every one to listen. Thus we heard a sound which had escaped us in the noise of the growling without the vessel, and the interest of the reading.

For a space we kept very silent, no man doing more than let the breath go in and out of his body, and so each one of us knew that something moved without, in the big cabin. In a little, something touched upon our door, and it was, as I have mentioned earlier, as though a great swab rubbed and scrubbed at the woodwork. At this, the men nearest unto the door came backwards in a surge, being put in sudden fear by reason of the Thing being so near; but the bo'sun held up a hand, bidding them, in a low voice, to make no unneedful noise. Yet, as though the sounds of their moving had been heard, the door was shaken with such violence that we waited, everyone, expecting to see it torn from its hinges; but it stood, and we hasted to brace it by means of the bunk-boards, which we placed between it and the two great chests, and upon these we set a third chest, so that the door was quite hid.

Now, I have no remembrance whether I have put down that when we came first to the ship, we had found the stern window upon the larboard side to be shattered; but so it was, and the bo'sun had closed it by means of a teak-wood cover which was made to go over it in stormy weather, with stout battens across, which were set tight with wedges. This he had done upon the first night, having fear that some evil thing might come upon us through the opening, and very prudent was this same action of his, as shall be seen. Then George cried out that something was at the cover of the larboard window, and we stood back, growing ever more fearful because that some evil creature was so eager to come at us. But the bo'sun, who was a very courageous man, and calm withal, walked over to the closed window, and saw to it that the battens were secure; for he had knowledge sufficient to be sure, if this were so, that no creature with strength less than that of a whale could break it down, and in such case its bulk would assure us from being molested.

Then, even as he made sure of the fastenings, there came a cry of fear from some of the men; for there had come at the glass of the unbroken window, a reddish mass, which plunged up against it, sucking upon it, as it were. Then Josh, who was nearest to the table, caught up the candle, and held it towards the Thing; thus I saw that it had the appearance of a many-flapped thing shaped as it might be, out of raw beef—*but it was alive.*

At this, we stared, everyone being too bemused with terror to do aught to protect ourselves, even had we been possessed of weapons. And as we remained thus, an instant, like silly sheep awaiting the butcher, I heard the framework creak and crack, and there ran splits all across the glass. In another moment, the whole thing would have been torn away, and the cabin undefended, but that the bo'sun, with a great curse at us for our land-lubberly lack of use, seized the other cover, and clapped it over the window. At that, there was more help than could be made to avail, and the battens and wedges were in place in a trice. That this was no sooner accomplished than need be, we had immediate proof; for there came a rending of wood and a splintering of glass, and after that a strange yowling out in the dark, and the yowling rose above and drowned the continuous growling that filled the night. In a little, it died away, and in the brief silence that seemed to ensue, we heard a slobby fumbling at the teak cover; but it was well secured, and we had no immediate cause for fear.

IV
The Two Faces

OF THE REMAINDER OF that night, I have but a confused memory. At times we heard the door shaken behind the great chests; but no harm came to it. And, odd whiles, there was a soft thudding and rubbing upon the decks over our heads, and once, as I recollect, the Thing made a final try at the teak covers across the windows; but the day came at last, and found me sleeping. Indeed, we had slept beyond the noon, but that the bo'sun, mindful of our needs, waked us, and we removed the chests. Yet, for perhaps the space of a minute, none durst open the door, until the bo'sun bid us stand to one side. We faced about at him then, and saw that he held a great cutlass in his right hand.

He called to us that there were four more of the weapons, and made a backward motion with his left hand towards an open locker. At that, as might be supposed, we made some haste to the place to which he pointed, and found that, among some other gear, there were three more weapons such as he held; but the fourth was a straight cut-and-thrust, and this I had the good fortune to secure.

Being now armed, we ran to join the bo'sun; for by this he had the door open, and was scanning the main cabin. I would remark here how a good weapon doth seem to put heart into a man; for I, who but a few, short hours since had feared for my life, was now right full of lustiness and fight; which, mayhap, was no matter for regret.

From the main cabin, the bo'sun led up on to the deck, and I remember some surprise at finding the lid of the scuttle even as we had left it the previous night; but then I recollected that the skylight was broken, and there was access to the big cabin that way. Yet, I questioned within myself as to what manner of thing it could be which ignored the convenience of the scuttle, and descended by way of the broken skylight.

We made a search of the decks and fo'cas'le, but found nothing, and, after that, the bo'sun stationed two of us on guard, whilst the rest went about such duties as were needful. In a little, we came to breakfast, and, after that, we prepared to test the story upon the sample wrappers and see perchance whether there was indeed a spring of fresh water among the trees.

Now between the vessel and the trees, lay a slope of the thick mud, against which the vessel rested. To have scrambled up this bank had been next to impossible, by reason of its fat richness; for, indeed, it looked fit to crawl; but that Josh called out to the bo'sun that he had come upon a ladder, lashed across the fo'cas'le head. This was brought, also several hatch covers. The latter were placed first upon the mud, and the ladder laid upon them; by which means we were enabled to pass up to the top of the bank without contact with the mud.

Here, we entered at once among the trees; for they grew right up to the edge; but we had no trouble in making a way; for they were nowhere close together; but standing, rather, each one in a little open space by itself.

We had gone a little way among the trees, when, suddenly, one who was with us cried out that he could see something away on our right, and we clutched everyone his weapon the more determinedly, and went towards it. Yet it proved to be but a seaman's chest, and a space further off, we discovered another. And so, after a little walking, we found the camp; but there was small semblance of a camp about it; for the sail of which the tent had been formed, was all torn and stained, and lay muddy upon the ground. Yet the spring was all we had wished, clear and sweet, and so we knew we might dream of deliverance.

Now, upon our discovery of the spring, it might be thought that we should set up a shout to those upon the vessel; but this was not so; for there was something in the air of the place which cast a gloom upon our spirits, and we had no disinclination to return unto the vessel.

Upon coming to the brig, the bo'sun called to four of the men to go down into the boats, and pass up the breakers: also, he collected all the buckets belonging to the brig, and forthwith each of us was set to our work. Some, those with the weapons, entered into the wood, and gave down the water to those stationed upon the bank, and these, in turn, passed it to those in the vessel. To the man in the galley, the bo'sun gave command to fill a boiler with some of the most select pieces of the pork and beef from the casks and get them cooked so soon as might be, and so we were kept at it; for it had been determined—now that we had come upon water—that we should stay not an hour longer in

that monster-ridden craft, and we were all agog to get the boats revict-
ualled, and put back to the sea, from which we had too gladly escaped.

So we worked through all that remainder of the morning, and right
on into the afternoon; for we were in mortal fear of the coming dark.
Towards four o'clock, the bo'sun sent the man, who had been set to
do our cooking, up to us with slices of salt meat upon biscuits, and
we ate as we worked, washing our throats with water from the spring,
and so, before the evening, we had filled our breakers, and near every
vessel which was convenient for us to take in the boats. More, some of
us snatched the chance to wash our bodies; for we were sore with brine,
having dipped in the sea to keep down thirst as much as might be.

Now, though it had not taken us so great a while to make a finish
of our water-carrying if matters had been more convenient; yet because
of the softness of the ground under our feet, and the care with which
we had to pick our steps, and some little distance between us and the
brig, it had grown later than we desired, before we had made an end.
Therefore, when the bo'sun sent word that we should come aboard,
and bring our gear, we made all haste. Thus, as it chanced, I found that
I had left my sword beside the spring, having placed it there to have
two hands for the carrying of one of the breakers. At my remarking
my loss, George, who stood near, cried out that he would run for it,
and was gone in a moment, being greatly curious to see the spring.

Now, at this moment, the bo'sun came up, and called for George;
but I informed him that he had run to the spring to bring me my
sword. At this, the bo'sun stamped his foot, and swore a great oath,
declaring that he had kept the lad by him all the day; having a wish to
keep him from any danger which the wood might hold, and knowing
the lad's desire to adventure there. At this, a matter which I should
have known, I reproached myself for so gross a piece of stupidity, and
hastened after the bo'sun, who had disappeared over the top of the
bank. I saw his back as he passed into the wood, and ran until I was
up with him; for, suddenly, as it were, I found that a sense of chilly
dampness had come among the trees; though a while before the place
had been full of the warmth of the sun. This, I put to the account of
evening, which was drawing on apace; and also, it must be borne in
mind, that there were but the two of us.

We came to the spring; but George was not to be seen, and I saw
no sign of my sword. At this, the bo'sun raised his voice, and cried out
the lad's name. Once he called, and again; then at the second shout
we heard the boy's shrill halloo, from some distance ahead among the
trees. At that, we ran towards the sound, plunging heavily across the

ground, which was everywhere covered with a thick scum, that clogged the feet in walking. As we ran, we hallooed, and so came upon the boy, and I saw that he had my sword.

The bo'sun ran towards him, and caught him by the arm, speaking with anger, and commanding him to return with us immediately to the vessel.

But the lad, for reply, pointed with my sword, and we saw that he pointed at what appeared to be a bird against the trunk of one of the trees. This, as I moved closer, I perceived to be a part of the tree, and no bird; but it had a very wondrous likeness to a bird; so much so that I went up to it, to see if my eyes had deceived me. Yet it seemed no more than a freak of nature, though most wondrous in its fidelity; being but an excrescence upon the trunk. With a sudden thought that it would make me a curio, I reached up to see whether I could break it away from the tree; but it was above my reach, so that I had to leave it. Yet, one thing I discovered; for, in stretching towards the protuberance, I had placed a hand upon the tree, and its trunk was soft as pulp under my fingers, much after the fashion of a mushroom.

As we turned to go, the bo'sun inquired of George his reason for going beyond the spring, and George told him that he had seemed to hear someone calling to him among the trees, and there had been so much pain in the voice that he had run towards it; but been unable to discover the owner. Immediately afterwards he had seen the curious, bird-like excrescence upon a tree nearby. Then we had called, and of the rest we had knowledge.

We had come nigh to the spring on our return journey, when a sudden low whine seemed to run among the trees. I glanced towards the sky, and realised that the evening was upon us. I was about to re-mark upon this to the bo'sun, when, abruptly, he came to a stand, and bent forward to stare into the shadows to our right. At that, George and I turned ourselves about to perceive what matter it was which had attracted the attention of the bo'sun; thus we made out a tree some twenty yards away, which had all its branches wrapped about its trunk, much as the lash of a whip is wound about its stock. Now this seemed to us a very strange sight, and we made all of us toward it, to learn the reason of so extraordinary a happening.

Yet, when we had come close upon it, we had no means of arriv-ing at a knowledge of that which it portended; but walked each of us around the tree, and were more astonished, after our circumnavigation of the great vegetable than before.

Now, suddenly, and in the distance, I caught the far wailing that came before the night, and abruptly, as it seemed to me, the tree wailed at us. At that I was vastly astonished and frightened; yet, though I retreated, I could not withdraw my gaze from the tree; but scanned it the more intently; and, suddenly, I saw a brown, human face peering at us from between the wrapped branches. At this, I stood very still, being seized with that fear which renders one shortly incapable of movement. Then, before I had possession of myself, I saw that it was of a part with the trunk of the tree; for I could not tell where it ended and the tree began.

Then I caught the bo'sun by the arm, and pointed; for whether it was a part of the tree or not, it was a work of the devil; but the bo'sun, on seeing it, ran straightway so close to the tree that he might have touched it with his hand, and I found myself beside him. Now, George, who was on the bo'sun's other side, whispered that there was another face, not unlike to a woman's, and, indeed, so soon as I perceived it, I saw that the tree had a second excrescence, most strangely after the face of a woman. Then the bo'sun cried out with an oath, at the strangeness of the thing, and I felt the arm, which I held, shake somewhat, as it might be with a deep emotion. Then, far away, I heard again the sound of the wailing and, immediately, from among the trees about us, there came answering wails and a great sighing. And before I had time to be more than aware of these things, the tree wailed again at us. And at that, the bo'sun cried out suddenly that he knew; though of what it was that he *knew* I had at that time no knowledge. And, immediately, he began with his cutlass to strike at the tree before us, and to cry upon God to blast it; and lo! at his smiting a very fearsome thing happened, for the tree did bleed like any live creature. Thereafter, a great yowling came from it, and it began to writhe. And, suddenly, I became aware that all about us the trees were a-quiver.

Then George cried out, and ran round upon my side of the bo'sun, and I saw that one of the great cabbage-like things pursued him upon its stem, even as an evil serpent; and very dreadful it was, for it had become blood red in colour; but I smote it with the sword, which I had taken from the lad, and it fell to the ground.

Now from the brig I heard them hallooing, and the trees had become like live things, and there was a vast growling in the air, and hideous trumpetings. Then I caught the bo'sun again by the arm, and shouted to him that we must run for our lives; and this we did, smiting with our swords as we ran; for there came things at us, out from the growing dusk.

Thus we made the brig, and, the boats being ready, I scrambled after the bo'sun into his, and we put straightway into the creek, all of us, pulling with so much haste as our loads would allow. As we went I looked back at the brig, and it seemed to me that a multitude of things hung over the bank above her, and there seemed a flicker of things moving hither and thither aboard of her. And then we were in the great creek up which we had come, and so, in a little, it was night.

All that night we rowed, keeping very strictly to the center of the big creek, and all about us bellowed the vast growling, being more fearsome than ever I had heard it, until it seemed to me that we had waked all that land of terror to a knowledge of our presence. But, when the morning came, so good a speed had we made, what with our fear, and the current being with us, that we were nigh upon the open sea; whereat each one of us raised a shout, feeling like freed prisoners.

And so, full of thankfulness to the Almighty, we rowed outward to the sea.

V
The Great Storm

NOW, AS I HAVE said, we came at last in safety to the open sea, and so for a time had some degree of peace; though it was long ere we threw off all of the terror which the Land of Lonesomeness had cast over our hearts.

And one more matter there is regarding that land, which my memory recalls. It will be remembered that George found certain wrappers upon which there was writing. Now, in the haste of our leaving, he had given no thought to take them with him; yet a portion of one he found within the side pocket of his jacket, and it ran somewhat thus:—

"But I hear my lover's voice wailing in the night, and I go to find him; for my loneliness is not to be borne. May God have mercy upon me!"

And that was all.

For a day and a night we stood out from the land towards the North, having a steady breeze to which we set our lug sails, and so made very good way, the sea being quiet, though with a slow, lumbering swell from the Southward.

It was on the morning of the second day of our escape that we met with the beginnings of our adventure into the Silent Sea, the which I am about to make as clear as I am able.

The night had been quiet, and the breeze steady until near on to the dawn, when the wind slacked away to nothing, and we lay there waiting, perchance the sun should bring the breeze with it. And this it did; but no such wind as we did desire; for when the morning came upon us, we discovered all that part of the sky to be full of a fiery redness, which presently spread away down to the South, so that an entire quarter of the heavens was, as it seemed to us, a mighty arc of blood-coloured fire.

Now, at the sight of these omens, the bo'sun gave orders to prepare the boats for the storm which we had reason to expect, looking for it in the South, for it was from that direction that the swell came rolling upon us. With this intent, we roused out so much heavy canvas as the boats contained, for we had gotten a bolt and a half from the hulk in the creek; also the boat covers which we could lash down to the brass studs under the gunnels of the boats. Then, in each boat, we mounted the whaleback—which had been stowed along the tops of the thwarts—also its supports, lashing the same to the thwarts below the knees. Then we laid two lengths of the stout canvas the full length of the boat over the whaleback, overlapping and nailing them to the same, so that they sloped away down over the gunnels upon each side as though they had formed a roof to us. Here, whilst some stretched the canvas, nailing its lower edges to the gunnel, others were employed in lashing together the oars and the mast, and to this bundle they secured a considerable length of new three-and-a-half-inch hemp rope, which we had brought away from the hulk along with the canvas. This rope was then passed over the bows and in through the painter ring, and thence to the forrard thwarts, where it was made fast, and we gave attention to parcel it with odd strips of canvas against danger of chafe. And the same was done in both of the boats, for we could not put our trust in the painters, besides which they had not sufficient length to secure safe and easy riding.

Now by this time we had the canvas nailed down to the gunnel around our boat, after which we spread the boat-cover over it, lacing it down to the brass studs beneath the gunnel. And so we had all the boat covered in, save a place in the stern where a man might stand to wield the steering oar, for the boats were double bowed. And in each boat we made the same preparation, lashing all movable articles, and preparing to meet so great a storm as might well fill the heart with terror; for the sky cried out to us that it would be no light wind, and further, the great swell from the South grew more huge with every hour that passed; though as yet it was without virulence, being slow and oily and black against the redness of the sky.

Presently we were ready, and had cast over the bundle of oars and the mast, which was to serve as our sea-anchor, and so we lay waiting. It was at this time that the bo'sun called over to Josh certain advice with regard to that which lay before us. And after that the two of them sculled the boats a little apart; for there might be a danger of their being dashed together by the first violence of the storm.

And so came a time of waiting, with Josh and the bo'sun each of them at the steering oars, and the rest of us stowed away under the coverings. From where I crouched near the bo'sun, I had sight of Josh away upon our port side: he was standing up black as a shape of night against the mighty redness, when the boat came to the foamless crowns of the swells, and then gone from sight in the hollows between.

Now midday had come and gone, and we had made shift to eat so good a meal as our appetites would allow; for we had no knowledge how long it might be ere we should have chance of another, if, indeed, we had ever need to think more of such. And then, in the middle part of the afternoon, we heard the first cryings of the storm—a far-distant moaning, rising and falling most solemnly.

Presently, all the Southern part of the horizon so high up, maybe, as some seven to ten degrees, was blotted out by a great black wall of cloud, over which the red glare came down upon the great swells as though from the light of some vast and unseen fire. It was about this time, I observed that the sun had the appearance of a great full moon, being pale and clearly defined, and seeming to have no warmth nor brilliancy; and this, as may be imagined, seemed most strange to us, the more so because of the redness in the South and East.

And all this while the swells increased most prodigiously; though without making broken water: yet they informed us that we had done well to take so much precaution; for surely they were raised by a very great storm. A little before evening, the moaning came again, and then a space of silence; after which there rose a very sudden bellowing, as of wild beasts, and then once more the silence.

About this time, the bo'sun making no objection, I raised my head above the cover until I was in a standing position; for, until now, I had taken no more than occasional peeps; and I was very glad of the chance to stretch my limbs; for I had grown mightily cramped. Having stirred the sluggishness of my blood, I sat me down again; but in such position that I could see every part of the horizon without difficulty. Ahead of us, that is to the South, I saw now that the great wall of cloud had risen some further degrees, and there was something less of the redness; though, indeed, what there was left of it was sufficiently terrifying; for it appeared to crest the black cloud like red foam, seeming, it might be, as though a mighty sea made ready to break over the world.

Towards the West, the sun was sinking behind a curious red-tinted haze, which gave it the appearance of a dull red disk. To the North, seeming very high in the sky, were some flecks of cloud lying motionless, and of a very pretty rose colour. And here I may remark that all the sea to the North of us appeared as a very ocean of dull red fire; though, as might be expected, the swells, coming up from the South, against the light were so many exceeding great hills of blackness.

It was just after I had made these observations that we heard again the distant roaring of the storm, and I know not how to convey the exceeding terror of that sound. It was as though some mighty beast growled far down towards the South; and it seemed to make very clear to me that we were but two small craft in a very lonesome place. Then, even while the roaring lasted, I saw a sudden light flare up, as it were from the edge of the Southern horizon. It had somewhat the appearance of lightning; yet vanished not immediately, as is the wont of lightning; and more, it had not been my experience to witness such spring up from out of the sea, but, rather, down from the heavens. Yet I have little doubt but that it was a form of lightning; for it came many times after this, so that I had chance to observe it minutely. And frequently, as I watched, the storm would shout at us in a most fearsome manner.

Then, when the sun was low upon the horizon, there came to our ears a very shrill, screaming noise, most penetrating and distressing, and, immediately afterwards the bo'sun shouted out something in a hoarse voice, and commenced to sway furiously upon the steering oar. I saw his stare fixed upon a point a little on our larboard bow, and perceived that in that direction the sea was all blown up into vast clouds of dust-like froth, and I knew that the storm was upon us. Immediately afterwards a cold blast struck us; but we suffered no harm, for the bo'sun had gotten the boat bows-on by this. The wind passed us, and there was an instant of calm. And now all the air above us was full of a continuous roaring, so very loud and intense that I was like to be deafened. To windward, I perceived an enormous wall of spray bearing down upon us, and I heard again the shrill screaming, pierce through the roaring. Then, the bo'sun whipped in his oar under the cover, and, reaching forward, drew the canvas aft, so that it covered the entire boat, and he held it down against the gunnel upon the starboard side, shouting in my ear to do likewise upon the larboard. Now had it not been for this forethought on the part of the bo'sun we had been all dead men; and this may be the better believed when I explain that we felt the water falling upon the stout canvas overhead, tons and tons, though so beaten to froth as to lack solidity to sink or crush us. I have said "felt;" for I would make it so clear as may be, here once and for all, that so intense was the roaring and screaming of the elements, there could no sound have penetrated to us, no! not the pealing of mighty thunders. And so for the space of maybe a full minute the boat quivered and shook most vilely, so that she seemed like to have been shaken in pieces, and from a dozen places between the gunnel and the covering canvas, the water spurted in upon us. And here one other thing I would make mention of: During that minute, the boat had ceased to rise and fall upon the great swell, and whether this was because the sea was flattened by the first rush of the wind, or that the excess of the storm held her steady, I am unable to tell; and can put down only that which we felt.

Now, in a little, the first fury of the blast being spent, the boat began to sway from side to side, as though the wind blew now upon the one beam, and now upon the other; and several times we were stricken heavily with the blows of solid water. But presently this ceased, and we returned once again to the rise and fall of the swell, only that now we received a cruel jerk every time that the boat came upon the top of a sea. And so a while passed.

Towards midnight, as I should judge, there came some mighty flames of lightning, so bright that they lit up the boat through the double covering of canvas; yet no man of us heard aught of the thunder; for the roaring of the storm made all else a silence.

And so to the dawn, after which, finding that we were still, by the mercy of God, possessed of our lives, we made shift to eat and drink; after which we slept.

Now, being extremely wearied by the stress of the past night, I slumbered through many hours of the storm, waking at some time between noon and evening. Overhead, as I lay looking upwards, the canvas showed of a dull leadenish colour, blackened completely at whiles by the dash of spray and water. And so, presently, having eaten again, and feeling that all things lay in the hands of the Almighty, I came once more upon sleep.

Twice through the following night was I wakened by the boat being hurled upon her beam-ends by the blows of the seas; but she righted easily, and took scarce any water, the canvas proving a very roof of safety. And so the morning came again.

Being now rested, I crawled after to where the bo'sun lay, and, the noise of the storm lulling odd instants, shouted in his ear to know whether the wind was easing at whiles. To this he nodded, whereat I felt a most joyful sense of hope pulse through me, and ate such food as could be gotten, with a very good relish.

In the afternoon, the sun broke out suddenly, lighting up the boat most gloomily through the wet canvas; yet a very welcome light it was, and bred in us a hope that the storm was near to breaking. In a little, the sun disappeared; but, presently, it coming again, the bo'sun beckoned to me to assist him, and we removed such temporary nails as we had used to fasten down the after part of the canvas, and pushed back the covering a space sufficient to allow our heads to go through into the daylight. On looking out, I discovered the air to be full of spray, beaten as fine as dust, and then, before I could note aught else, a little gout of water took me in the face with such force as to deprive me of breath; so that I had to descend beneath the canvas for a little while.

So soon as I was recovered, I thrust forth my head again, and now I had some sight of the terrors around us. As each huge sea came towards us, the boat shot up to meet it, right up to its very crest, and there, for the space of some instants, we would seem to be swamped in a very ocean of foam, boiling up on each side of the boat to the height of many feet. Then, the sea passing from under us, we would go swooping dizzily down the great, black, froth-splotched back of the wave, until the oncoming sea caught us up most mightily. Odd whiles, the crest of a sea would hurl forward before we had reached the top, and though the boat shot upward like a veritable feather, yet the water would swirl right over us, and we would have to draw in our heads most suddenly; in such cases the wind flapping the cover down so soon as our hands were removed. And, apart from the way in which the boat met the seas, there was a very sense of terror in the air; the continuous roaring and howling of the storm; the *screaming* of the foam, as the frothy summits of the briny mountains hurled past us, and the wind that tore the breath out of our weak human throats, are things scarce to be conceived.

Presently, we drew in our heads, the sun having vanished again, and nailed down the canvas once more, and so prepared for the night.

From here on until the morning, I have very little knowledge of any happenings; for I slept much of the time, and, for the rest, there was little to know, cooped up beneath the cover. Nothing save the interminable, thundering swoop of the boat downwards, and then the halt and upward hurl, and the occasional plunges and surges to larboard or starboard, occasioned, I can only suppose, by the indiscriminate might of the seas.

I would make mention here, how that I had little thought all this while for the peril of the other boat, and, indeed, I was so very full of our own that it is no matter at which to wonder. However, as it proved, and as this is a most suitable place in which to tell it, the boat that held Josh and the rest of the crew came through the storm with safety; though it was not until many years afterwards that I had the good fortune to hear from Josh himself how that, after the storm, they were picked up by a homeward-bound vessel, and landed in the Port of London.

And now, to our own happenings.

VI
The Weed-choked Sea

I T WAS SOME LITTLE while before midday that we grew conscious that the sea had become very much less violent; and this despite the wind roaring with scarce abated noise. And, presently, everything about the boat, saving the wind, having grown indubitably calmer, and no great water breaking over the canvas, the bo'sun beckoned me again to assist him lift the after part of the cover. This we did, and put forth our heads to inquire the reason of the unexpected quietness of the sea; not knowing but that we had come suddenly under the lee of some unknown land. Yet, for a space, we could see nothing, beyond the surrounding billows; for the sea was still very furious, though no matter to cause us concern, after that through which we had come.

Presently, however, the bo'sun, raising himself, saw something, and, bending, cried in my ear that there was a low bank which broke the force of the sea; but he was full of wonder to know how that we had passed it without shipwreck. And whilst he was still pondering the matter I raised myself, and took a look on all sides of us, and so I discovered that there lay another great bank upon our larboard side, and this I pointed out to him. Immediately afterwards, we came upon a great mass of seaweed swung up on the crest of a sea, and, presently, another. And so we drifted on, and the seas grew less with astonishing rapidity, so that, in a little, we stript off the cover so far as the midship thwart; for the rest of the men were sorely in need of the fresh air, after so long a time below the canvas-covering.

It was after we had eaten, that one of them made out that there was another low bank astern upon which we were drifting. At that, the bo'sun stood up and made an examination of it, being much exercised in his mind to know how we might come clear of it with safety. Presently, however, we had come so near to it that we discovered it to be composed of seaweed, and so we let the boat drive upon it, making no doubt but that the other banks, which we had seen, were of a similar nature.

In a little, we had driven in among the weed; yet, though our speed was greatly slowed, we made some progress, and so in time came out upon the other side, and now we found the sea to be near quiet, so that we hauled in our sea anchor—which had collected a great mass of weed about it—and removed the whaleback and canvas-coverings, after which we stepped the mast, and set a tiny storm-foresail upon the boat; for we wished to have her under control, and could set no more than this, because of the violence of the breeze.

Thus we drove on before the wind, the bo'sun steering, and avoiding all such banks as showed ahead, and ever the sea grew calmer. Then, when it was near on to evening, we discovered a huge stretch of the weed that seemed to block all the sea ahead, and, at that, we hauled down the foresail, and took to our oars, and began to pull, broadside on to it, towards the West. Yet so strong was the breeze, that we were being driven down rapidly upon it. And then, just before sunset, we opened out the end of it, and drew in our oars, very thankful to set the little foresail, and run off again before the wind.

And so, presently, the night came down upon us, and the bo'sun made us take turn and turn about to keep a look-out; for the boat was going some knots through the water, and we were among strange seas; but *he* took no sleep all that night, keeping always to the steering oar.

I have memory, during my time of watching, of passing odd floating masses, which I make no doubt were weed, and once we drove right atop of one; but drew clear without much trouble. And all the while, through the dark to starboard, I could make out the dim outline of that enormous weed extent lying low upon the sea, and seeming without end. And so, presently, my time to watch being at an end, I returned to my slumber, and when next I waked it was morning.

Now the morning discovered to me that there was no end to the weed upon our starboard side; for it stretched away into the distance ahead of us so far as we could see; while all about us the sea was full of floating masses of the stuff. And then, suddenly, one of the men cried out that there was a vessel in among the weed. At that, as may be imagined, we were very greatly excited, and stood upon the thwarts that we might get better view of her. Thus I saw her a great way in from the edge of the weed, and I noted that her foremast was gone near to the deck, and she had no main topmast; though, strangely enough, her mizzen stood unharmed. And beyond this, I could make out but little, because of the distance; though the sun, which was upon our larboard side, gave me some sight of her hull, but not much, because of the weed in which she was deeply embedded; yet it seemed to me that her sides were very weather-worn, and in one place some glistening brown object, which may have been a fungus, caught the rays of the sun, sending off a wet sheen.

There we stood, all of us, upon the thwarts, staring and exchanging opinions, and were like to have overset the boat; but that the bo'sun ordered us down. And after this we made our breakfast, and had much discussion regarding the stranger, as we ate.

Later, towards midday, we were able to set our mizzen; for the storm had greatly modified, and so, presently, we hauled away to the West, to escape a great bank of the weed which ran out from the main body. Upon rounding this, we let the boat off again, and set the main lug, and thus made very good speed before the wind. Yet though we ran all that afternoon parallel with the weed to starboard, we came not to its end. And three separate times we saw the hulks of rotting vessels, some of them having the appearance of a previous age, so ancient did they seem.

Now, towards evening, the wind dropped to a very little breeze, so that we made but slow way, and thus we had better chance to study the weed. And now we saw that it was full of crabs; though for the most part so very minute as to escape the casual glance; yet they were not all small, for in a while I discovered a swaying among the weed, a little way in from the edge, and immediately I saw the mandible of a very great crab stir amid the weed. At that, hoping to obtain it for food, I pointed it out to the bo'sun, suggesting that we should try and capture it. And so, there being by now scarce any wind, he bade us get out a couple of the oars, and back the boat up to the weed. This we did, after which he made fast a piece of salt meat to a bit of spun yarn, and bent this on to the boat-hook. Then he made a running bowline, and slipped the loop on to the shaft of the boat-hook, after which he held out the boat-hook, after the fashion of a fishing-rod, over the place where I had seen the crab. Almost immediately, there swept up an enormous claw, and grasped the meat, and at that, the bo'sun cried out to me to take an oar and slide the bowline along the boat-hook, so that it should fall over the claw, and this I did, and immediately some of us hauled upon the line, taughtening it about the great claw. Then the bo'sun sung out to us to haul the crab aboard, that we had it most securely; yet on the instant we had reason to wish that we had been less successful; for the creature, feeling the tug of our pull upon it, tossed the weed in all directions, and thus we had full sight of it, and discovered it to be so great a crab as is scarce conceivable—a very monster. And further, it was apparent to us that the brute had no fear of us, nor intention to escape; but rather made to come at us; whereat the bo'sun, perceiving our danger, cut the line, and bade us put weight upon the oars, and so in a moment we were in safety, and very determined to have no more meddlings with such creatures.

Presently, the night came upon us, and, the wind remaining low, there was everywhere about us a great stillness, most solemn after the continuous roaring of the storm which had beset us in the previous days. Yet now and again a little wind would rise and blow across the sea, and where it met the weed, there would come a low, damp rustling, so that I could hear the passage of it for no little time after the calm had come once more all about us.

Now it is a strange thing that I, who had slept amid the noise of the past days, should find sleeplessness amid so much calm; yet so it was, and presently I took the steering oar, proposing that the rest should sleep, and to this the bo'sun agreed, first warning me, however, most particularly to have care that I kept the boat off the weed (for we had still a little way on us), and, further, to call him should anything unforeseen occur. And after that, almost immediately he fell asleep, as indeed did the most of the men.

From the time that I relieved the bo'sun, until midnight, I sat upon the gunnel of the boat, with the steering oar under my arm, and watched and listened, most full of a sense of the strangeness of the seas into which we had come. It is true that I had heard tell of seas choked up with weed—seas that were full of stagnation, having no tides; but I had not thought to come upon such a one in my wanderings; having, indeed, set down such tales as being bred of imagination, and without reality in fact.

Then, a little before the dawn, and when the sea was yet full of darkness, I was greatly startled to hear a prodigious splash amid the weed, mayhaps at a distance of some hundred yards from the boat. Then, as I stood full of alertness, and knowing not what the next moment might bring forth, there came to me across the immense waste of weed, a long, mournful cry, and then again the silence. Yet, though I kept very quiet, there came no further sound, and I was about to re-seat myself, when, afar off in that strange wilderness, there flashed out a sudden flame of fire.

Now upon seeing fire in the midst of so much lonesomeness, I was as one amazed, and could do naught but stare. Then, my judgement returning to me, I stooped and waked the bo'sun; for it seemed to me that this was a matter for his attention. He, after staring at it awhile, declared that he could see the shape of a vessel's hull beyond the flame; but, immediately, he was in doubt, as, indeed, I had been all the while. And then, even as we peered, the light vanished, and though we waited for the space of some minutes; watching steadfastly, there came no further sight of that strange illumination.

From now until the dawn, the bo'sun remained awake with me, and we talked much upon that which we had seen; yet could come to no satisfactory conclusion; for it seemed impossible to us that a place of so much desolation could contain any living being. And then, just as the dawn was upon us, there loomed up a fresh wonder—the hull of a great vessel maybe a couple or three score fathoms in from the edge of the weed. Now the wind was still very light, being no more than an occasional breath, so that we went past her at a drift, thus the dawn had strengthened sufficiently to give to us a clear sight of the stranger, before we had gone more than a little past her. And now I perceived that she lay full broadside on to us, and that her three masts were gone close down to the deck. Her side was streaked in places with rust, and in others a green scum overspread her; but it was no more than a glance that I gave at any of those matters; for I had spied something which drew all my attention—great leathery arms splayed all across her side, some of them crooked inboard over the rail, and then, low down, seen just above the weed, the huge, brown, glistening bulk of so great a monster as ever I had conceived. The bo'sun saw it in the same instant and cried out in a hoarse whisper that it was a mighty devil-fish, and then, even as he spoke, two of the arms flickered up into the cold light of the dawn, as though the creature had been asleep, and we had waked it. At that, the bo'sun seized an oar, and I did likewise, and, so swiftly as we dared, for fear of making any unneedful noise, we pulled the boat to a safer distance. From there and until the vessel had become indistinct by reason of the space we put between us, we watched that great creature clutched to the old hull, as it might be a limpet to a rock.

Presently, when it was broad day, some of the men began to rouse up, and in a little we broke our fast, which was not displeasing to me, who had spent the night watching. And so through the day we sailed with a very light wind upon our larboard quarter. And all the while we kept the great waste of weed upon our starboard side, and apart from the mainland of the weed, as it were, there were scattered about an uncountable number of weed islets and banks, and there were thin patches of it that appeared scarce above the water, and through these later we let the boat sail; for they had not sufficient density to impede our progress more than a little.

And then, when the day was far spent, we came in sight of another wreck amid the weeds. She lay in from the edge perhaps so much as the half of a mile, and she had all three of her lower masts in, and her lower yards squared. But what took our eyes more than aught else was a great superstructure which had been built upward from her rails, almost half-way to her main tops, and this, as we were able to perceive, was supported by ropes let down from the yards; but of what material the superstructure was composed, I have no knowledge; for it was so over-grown with some form of green stuff—as was so much of the hull as showed above the weed—as to defy our guesses. And because of this growth, it was borne upon us that the ship must have been lost to the world a very great age ago. At this suggestion, I grew full of solemn thought; for it seemed to me that we had come upon the cemetery of the oceans.

Now, in a little while after we had passed this ancient craft, the night came down upon us, and we prepared for sleep, and because the boat was making some little way through the water, the bo'sun gave out that each of us should stand our turn at the steering-oar, and that he was to be called should any fresh matter transpire. And so we settled down for the night, and owing to my previous sleeplessness, I was full weary, so that I knew nothing until the one whom I was to relieve shook me into wakefulness. So soon as I was fully waked, I perceived that a low moon hung above the horizon, and shed a very ghostly light across the great weed world to starboard. For the rest, the night was exceeding quiet, so that no sound came to me in all that ocean, save the rippling of the water upon our bends as the boat forged slowly along. And so I settled down to pass the time ere I should be allowed to sleep; but first I asked the man whom I had relieved, how long a time had passed since moon-rise; to which he replied that it was no more than the half of an hour, and after that I questioned whether he had seen aught strange amid the weed during his time at the oar; but he had seen nothing, except that once he had fancied a light had shown in the midst of the waste; yet it could have been naught save a humour of the imagination; though apart from this, he had heard a strange crying a little after midnight, and twice there had been great splashes among the weed. And after that he fell asleep, being impatient at my questioning.

Now it so chanced that my watch had come just before the dawn;

for which I was full of thankfulness, being in that frame of mind when the dark breeds strange and unwholesome fancies. Yet, though I was so near to the dawn, I was not to escape free of the eerie influence of that place; for, as I sat, running my gaze to and fro over its grey immensity, it came to me that there were strange movements among the weed, and I seemed to see vaguely, as one may see things in dreams, dim white faces peer out at me here and there; yet my common sense assured me that I was but deceived by the uncertain light and the sleep in my eyes; yet for all that, it put my nerves on the quiver.

A little later, there came to my ears the noise of a very great splash amid the weed; but though I stared with intentness, I could nowhere discern aught as likely to be the cause thereof. And then, suddenly, between me and the moon, there drove up from out of that great waste a vast bulk, flinging huge masses of weed in all directions. It seemed to be no more than a hundred fathoms distant, and, against the moon, I saw the outline of it most clearly—a mighty devil-fish. Then it had fallen back once more with a prodigious splash, and so the quiet fell again, finding me sore afraid, and no little bewildered that so monstrous a creature could leap with such agility. And then (in my fright I had let the boat come near to the edge of the weed) there came a subtle stir opposite to our starboard bow, and something slid down into the water. I swayed upon the oar to turn the boat's head outward, and with the same movement leant forward and sideways to peer, bringing my face near to the boat's rail. In the same instant, I found myself looking down into a white demoniac face, human save that the mouth and nose had greatly the appearance of a beak. The thing was gripping at the side of the boat with two flickering hands—gripping the bare, smooth outer surface, in a way that woke in my mind a sudden memory of the great devil-fish which had clung to the side of the wreck we had passed in the previous dawn. I saw the face come up towards me, and one misshapen hand fluttered almost to my throat, and there came a sudden, hateful reek in my nostrils—foul and abominable. Then, I came into possession of my faculties, and drew back with great haste and a wild cry of fear. And then I had the steering-oar by the middle, and was smiting downward with the loom over the side of the boat; but the thing was gone from my sight. I remember shouting out to the bo'sun and to the men to awake, and then the bo'sun had me by the shoulder, was calling in my ear to know what dire thing had come about. At that, I cried out that I did not know, and, presently, being somewhat calmer, I told them of the thing that I had seen; but even as I told of it, there seemed to be no truth in it, so that they were all at a loss to know whether I had fallen asleep, or that I had indeed seen a devil.

And presently the dawn was upon us.

VII
The Island In The Weed

IT WAS AS WE were all discussing the matter of the devil face that had peered up at me out of the water, that Job, the ordinary seaman, discovered the island in the light of the growing dawn, and, seeing it, sprang to his feet, with so loud a cry that we were like for the moment to have thought he had seen a second demon. Yet when we made discovery of that which he had already perceived, we checked our blame at his sudden shout; for the sight of land, after so much desolation, made us very warm in our hearts.

Now at first the island seemed but a very small matter; for we did not know at that time that we viewed it from its end; yet despite this, we took to our oars and rowed with all haste towards it, and so, coming nearer, were able to see that it had a greater size than we had imagined. Presently, having cleared the end of it, and keeping to that side which was further from the great mass of the weed-continent, we opened out a bay that curved inward to a sandy beach, most seductive to our tired eyes. Here, for the space of a minute, we paused to survey the prospect, and I saw that the island was of a very strange shape, having a great hump of black rock at either end, and dipping down into a steep valley between them. In this valley there seemed to be a deal of a strange vegetation that had the appearance of mighty toadstools; and down nearer the beach there was a thick grove of a kind of very tall reed, and these we discovered afterwards to be exceeding tough and light, having something of the qualities of the bamboo.

Regarding the beach, it might have been most reasonably supposed that it would be very thick with the driftweed; but this was not so, at least, not at that time; though a projecting horn of the black rock which ran out into the sea from the upper end of the island, was thick with it.

And now, the bo'sun having assured himself that there was no appearance of any danger, we bent to our oars, and presently had the

41

boat aground upon the beach, and here, finding it convenient, we made our breakfast. During this meal, the bo'sun discussed with us the most proper thing to do, and it was decided to push the boat off from the shore, leaving Job in her, whilst the remainder of us made some exploration of the island.

And so, having made an end of eating, we proceeded as we had determined, leaving Job in the boat, ready to scull ashore for us if we were pursued by any savage creature, while the rest of us made our way towards the nearer hump, from which, as it stood some hundred feet above the sea, we hoped to get a very good idea of the remainder of the island. First, however, the bo'sun handed out to us the two cutlasses and the cut-and-thrust (the other two cutlasses being in Josh's boat), and, taking one himself, he passed me the cut-and-thrust, and gave the other cutlass to the biggest of the men. Then he bade the others keep their sheath-knives handy, and was proceeding to lead the way, when one of them called out to us to wait a moment, and, with that, ran quickly to the clump of reeds. Here, he took one with both his hands and bent upon it; but it would not break, so that he had to notch it about with his knife, and thus, in a little, he had it clear. After this, he cut off the upper part, which was too thin and lissom for his purpose, and then thrust the handle of his knife into the end of the portion which he had retained, and in this wise he had a most serviceable lance or spear. For the reeds were very strong, and hollow after the fashion of bamboo, and when he had bound some yarn about the end into which he had thrust his knife, so as to prevent it splitting, it was a fit enough weapon for any man.

Now the bo'sun, perceiving the happiness of the fellow's idea, bade the rest make to themselves similar weapons, and whilst they were busy thus, he commended the man very warmly. And so, in a little, being now most comfortably armed, we made inland towards the nearer black hill, in very good spirits. Presently, we were come to the rock which formed the hill, and found that it came up out of the sand with great abruptness, so that we could not climb it on the seaward side. At that, the bo'sun led us round a space towards that side where lay the valley, and here there was under-foot neither sand nor rock; but ground of strange and spongy texture, and then suddenly, rounding a jutting spur of the rock, we came upon the first of the vegetation—an incredible mushroom; nay, I should say toadstool; for it had no healthy look about it, and gave out a heavy, mouldy odor. And now we perceived that the valley was filled with them, all, that is, save a great circular patch where nothing appeared to be growing; though we were not yet at a sufficient height to ascertain the reason of this.

Presently, we came to a place where the rock was split by a great fissure running up to the top, and showing many ledges and convenient shelves upon which we might obtain hold and footing. And so we set-to about climbing, helping one another so far as we had ability, until, in about the space of some ten minutes, we reached the top, and from thence had a very fine view. We perceived now that there was a beach upon that side of the island which was opposed to the weed; though, unlike that upon which we had landed, it was greatly choked with weed which had drifted ashore. After that, I gave notice to see what space of water lay between the island and the edge of the great weed-continent, and guessed it to be no more than maybe some ninety yards, at which I fell to wishing that it had been greater, for I was grown much in awe of the weed and the strange things which I conceived it to contain.

Abruptly, the bo'sun clapped me upon the shoulder, and pointed to some object that lay out in the weed at a distance of not much less than the half of a mile from where we stood. Now, at first, I could not conceive what manner of thing it was at which I stared, until the bo'sun, remarking my bewilderment, informed me that it was a vessel all covered in, no doubt as a protection against the devil-fish and other strange creatures in the weed. And now I began to trace the hull of her amid all that hideous growth; but of her masts, I could discern nothing; and I doubted not but that they had been carried away by some storm ere she was caught by the weed; and then the thought came to me of the end of those who had built up that protection against the horrors which the weed-world held hidden amid its slime.

Presently, I turned my gaze once more upon the island, which was very plain to see from where we stood. I conceived, now that I could see so much of it, that its length would be near to half a mile, though its breadth was something under four hundred yards; thus it was very long in proportion to its width. In the middle part it had less breadth than at the ends, being perhaps three hundred yards at its narrowest, and a hundred yards wider at its broadest.

Upon both sides of the island, as I have made already a mention, there was a beach, though this extended no great distance along the shore, the remainder being composed of the black rock of which the hills were formed. And now, having a closer regard to the beach upon the weed-side of the island, I discovered amid the wrack that had been cast ashore, a portion of the lower mast and topmast of some great ship, with rigging attached; but the yards were all gone. This find, I pointed out to the bo'sun, remarking that it might prove of use for firing; but he smiled at me, telling me that the dried weed would make a very abundant fire, and this without going to the labour of cutting the mast into suitable logs.

And now, he, in turn, called my attention to the place where the huge fungi had come to a stop in their growing, and I saw that in the centre of the valley there was a great circular opening in the earth, like to the mouth of a prodigious pit, and it appeared to be filled to within a few feet of the mouth with water, over which spread a brown and horrid scum. Now, as may be supposed, I stared with some intentness at this; for it had the look of having been made with labour, being very symmetrical, yet I could not conceive but that I was deluded by the distance, and that it would have a rougher appearance when viewed from a nearer standpoint.

From contemplating this, I looked down upon the little bay in which our boat floated. Job was sitting in the stern, sculling gently with the steering oar and watching us. At that, I waved my hand to him in friendly fashion, and he waved back, and then, even as I looked, I saw something in the water under the boat—something dark coloured that was all of a-move. The boat appeared to be floating over it as over a mass of sunk weed, and then I saw that, whatever it was, it was rising to the surface. At this a sudden horror came over me, and I clutched the bo'sun by the arm, and pointed, crying out that there was something under the boat. Now the bo'sun, so soon as he saw the thing, ran forward to the brow of the hill and, placing his hands to his mouth after the fashion of a trumpet, sang out to the boy to bring the boat to the shore and make fast the painter to a large piece of rock. At the bo'sun's hail, the lad called out "I, I," and, standing up, gave a sweep with his oar that brought the boat's head round towards the beach. Fortunately for him he was no more than some thirty yards from the shore at this time, else he had never come to it in this life; for the next moment the moving brown mass beneath the boat shot out a great tentacle and the oar was torn out of Job's hands with such power as to throw him right over on to the starboard gunnel of the boat. The oar itself was drawn down out of sight, and for the minute the boat was left untouched. Now the bo'sun cried out to the boy to take another oar, and get ashore while still he had chance, and at that we all called out various things, one advising one thing, and another recommending some other; yet our advice was vain, for the boy moved not, at which some cried out that he was stunned. I looked now to where the brown thing had been, for the boat had moved a few fathoms from the spot, having got some way upon her before the oar was snatched, and thus I discovered that the monster had disappeared, having, I conceived, sunk again into the depths from which it had risen; yet it might re-appear at any moment, and in that case the boy would be taken before our eyes.

At this juncture, the bo'sun called to us to follow him, and led the way to the great fissure up which we had climbed, and so, in a minute, we were, each of us, scrambling down with what haste we could make towards the valley. And all the while as I dropped from ledge to ledge, I was full of torment to know whether the monster had returned.

The bo'sun was the first man to reach the bottom of the cleft, and he set off immediately round the base of the rock to the beach, the rest of us following him as we made safe our footing in the valley. I was the third man down; but, being light and fleet of foot, I passed the second man and caught up with the bo'sun just as he came upon the sand. Here, I found that the boat was within some five fathoms of the beach, and I could see Job still lying insensible; but of the monster there was no sign.

And so matters were, the boat nearly a dozen yards from the shore, and Job lying insensible in her; with, somewhere near under her keel (for all that we knew) a great monster, and we helpless upon the beach.

Now I could not imagine how to save the lad, and indeed I fear he had been left to destruction—for I had deemed it madness to try to reach the boat by swimming—but for the extraordinary bravery of the bo'sun, who, without hesitating, dashed into the water and swam boldly out to the boat, which, by the grace of God, he reached without mishap, and climbed in over the bows. Immediately, he took the painter and hove it to us, bidding us tail on to it and bring the boat to shore without delay, and by this method of gaining the beach he showed wisdom; for in this wise he escaped attracting the attention of the monster by unneedful stirring of the water, as he would surely have done had he made use of an oar.

Yet, despite his care, we had not finished with the creature; for, just as the boat grounded, I saw the lost steering oar shoot up half its length out of the sea, and immediately there was a mighty splather in the water astern, and the next instant the air seemed full of huge, whirling arms. At that, the bo'sun gave one look behind, and, seeing the thing upon him, snatched the boy into his arms, and sprang over the bows on to the sand. Now, at sight of the devil-fish, we had all made for the back of the beach at a run, none troubling even to retain the painter, and because of this, we were like to have lost the boat; for the great cuttle-fish had its arms all splayed about it, seeming to have a mind to drag it down into the deep water from whence it had risen, and it had possibly succeeded, but that the bo'sun brought us all to our senses; for, having laid Job out of harm's way, he was the first to seize the painter, which lay trailed upon the sand, and, at that, we got back our courage and ran to assist him.

Now there happened to be convenient a great spike of rock, the same, indeed, to which the bo'sun had bidden Job tie the boat, and to this we ran the painter, taking a couple of turns about it and two half-hitches, and now, unless the rope carried away, we had no reason to fear the loss of the boat; though there seemed to us to be a danger of the creature's crushing it. Because of this, and because of a feeling of natural anger against the thing, the bo'sun took up from the sand one of the spears which had been cast down when we hauled the boat ashore. With this, he went down so far as seemed safe, and prodded the creature in one of its tentacles—the weapon entering easily, at which I was surprised, for I had understood that these monsters were near to invulnerable in all parts save their eyes. At receiving this stab, the great fish appeared to feel no hurt for it showed no signs of pain, and, at that, the bo'sun was further emboldened to go nearer, so that he might deliver a more deadly wound; yet scarce had he taken two steps before the hideous thing was upon him, and, but for an agility wonderful in so great a man, he had been destroyed. Yet, spite of so narrow an escape from death, he was not the less determined to wound or destroy the creature, and, to this end, he despatched some of us to the grove of reeds to get half a dozen of the strongest, and when we returned with these, he bade two of the men lash their spears securely to them, and by this means they had now spears of a length of between thirty and forty feet. With these, it was possible to attack the devil-fish without coming within reach of its tentacles. And now being ready, he took one of the spears, telling the biggest of the men to take the other. Then he directed him to aim for the right eye of the huge fish whilst he would attack the left.

Now since the creature had so nearly captured the bo'sun, it had ceased to tug at the boat, and lay silent, with its tentacles spread all about it, and its great eyes appearing just over the stern, so that it presented an appearance of watching our movements; though I doubt if it saw us with any clearness; for it must have been dazed with the brightness of the sunshine.

And now the bo'sun gave the signal to attack, at which he and the man ran down upon the creature with their lances, as it were, in rest. The bo'sun's spear took the monster truly in its left eye; but the one wielded by the man was too bendable, and sagged so much that it struck the stern-post of the boat, the knifeblade snapping off short. Yet it mattered not; for the wound inflicted by the bo'sun's weapon was so frightful, that the giant cuttle-fish released the boat, and slid back into deep water, churning it into foam, and gouting blood.

For some minutes we waited to make sure that the monster had indeed gone, and after that, we hastened to the boat, and drew her up so far as we were able; after which we unloaded the heaviest of her contents, and so were able to get her right clear of the water.

And for an hour afterwards the sea all about the little beach was stained black, and in places red.

VIII
The Noises In the Valley

NOW, SO SOON AS we had gotten the boat into safety, the which we did with a most feverish haste, the bo'sun gave his attention to Job; for the boy had not yet recovered from the blow which the loom of the oar had dealt him beneath the chin when the monster snatched at it. For awhile, his attentions produced no effect; but presently, having bathed the lad's face with water from the sea, and rubbed rum into his chest over the heart, the youth began to show signs of life, and soon opened his eyes, whereupon the bo'sun gave him a stiff jorum of the rum, after which he asked him how he seemed in himself. To this Job replied in a weak voice that he was dizzy and his head and neck ached badly; on hearing which, the bo'sun bade him keep lying until he had come more to himself. And so we left him in quietness under a little shade of canvas and reeds; for the air was warm and the sand dry, and he was not like to come to any harm there.

At a little distance, under the directing of the bo'sun, we made to prepare dinner, for we were now very hungry, it seeming a great while since we had broken our fast. To this end, the bo'sun sent two of the men across the island to gather some of the dry seaweed; for we intended to cook some of the salt meat, this being the first cooked meal since ending the meat which we had boiled before leaving the ship in the creek.

In the meanwhile, and until the return of the men with the fuel, the bo'sun kept us busied in various ways. Two he sent to cut a bundle of the reeds, and another couple to bring the meat and the iron boiler, the latter being one that we had taken from the old brig.

Presently, the men returned with the dried seaweed, and very curious stuff it seemed, some of it being in chunks near as thick as a man's body; but exceeding brittle by reason of its dryness. And so in a little, we had a very good fire going, which we fed with the seaweed

48

and pieces of the reeds, though we found the latter to be but indifferent fuel, having too much sap, and being troublesome to break into convenient size.

Now when the fire had grown red and hot, the bo'sun half filled the boiler with sea water, in which he placed the meat; and the pan, having a stout lid, he did not scruple to place it in the very heart of the fire, so that soon we had the contents boiling merrily.

Having gotten the dinner under way, the bo'sun set about preparing our camp for the night, which we did by making a rough framework with the reeds, over which we spread the boat's sails and the cover, pegging the canvas down with tough splinters of the reed. When this was completed, we set-to and carried there all our stores, after which the bo'sun took us over to the other side of the island to gather fuel for the night, which we did, each man bearing a great double armful.

Now by the time that we had brought over, each of us, two loads of the fuel, we found the meat to be cooked, and so, without more to-do, set ourselves down and made a very good meal off it and some biscuits, after which we had each of us a sound tot of the rum. Having made an end of eating and drinking, the bo'sun went over to where Job lay, to inquire how he felt, and found him lying very quiet, though his breathing had a heavy touch about it. However, we could conceive of nothing by which he might be bettered, and so left him, being more hopeful that Nature would bring him to health than any skill of which we were possessed.

By this time it was late afternoon, so that the bo'sun declared we might please ourselves until sunset, deeming that we had earned a very good right to rest; but that from sunset till the dawn we should, he told us, have each of us to take turn and turn about to watch; for though we were no longer upon the water, none might say whether we were out of danger or not, as witness the happening of the morning; though, certainly, he apprehended no danger from the devil-fish so long as we kept well away from the water's edge.

And so from now until dark most of the men slept; but the bo'sun spent much of that time in overhauling the boat, to see how it might chance to have suffered during the storm, and also whether the struggles of the devil-fish had strained it in any way. And, indeed, it was speedily evident that the boat would need some attention; for the plank in her bottom next but one to the keel, upon the starboard side, had been burst inwards; this having been done, it would seem, by some rock in the beach hidden just beneath the water's edge, the devil-fish having, no doubt, ground the boat down upon it. Happily, the damage was not great; though it would most certainly have to be carefully repaired before the boat would be again seaworthy. For the rest, there seemed to be no other part needing attention.

Now I had not felt any call to sleep, and so had followed the bo'sun to the boat, giving him a hand to remove the bottom-boards, and finally to slue her bottom a little upwards, so that he might examine the leak more closely. When he had made an end with the boat, he went over to the stores, and looked closely into their condition, and also to see how they were lasting. And, after that, he sounded all the water-breakers; having done which, he remarked that it would be well for us if we could discover any fresh water upon the island.

By this time it was getting on towards evening, and the bo'sun went across to look at Job, finding him much as he had been when we visited him after dinner. At that, the bo'sun asked me to bring across one of the longer of the bottom-boards, which I did, and we made use of it as a stretcher to carry the lad into the tent. And afterwards, we carried all the loose woodwork of the boat into the tent, emptying the lockers of their contents, which included some oakum, a small boat's hatchet, a coil of one-and-a-half-inch hemp line, a good saw, an empty, colza-oil tin, a bag of copper nails, some bolts and washers, two fishing-lines, three spare tholes, a three-pronged grain without the shaft, two balls of spun yarn, three hanks of roping-twine, a piece of canvas with four roping-needles stuck in it, the boat's lamp, a spare plug, and a roll of light duck for making boat's sails.

And so, presently, the dark came down upon the island, at which the bo'sun waked the men, and bade them throw more fuel on to the fire, which had burned down to a mound of glowing embers much shrouded in ash. After that, one of them part filled the boiler with fresh water, and soon we were occupied most pleasantly upon a supper of cold, boiled salt-meat, hard biscuits, and rum mixed with hot water. During supper, the bo'sun made clear to the men regarding the watches, arranging how they should follow, so that I found I was set down to take my turn from midnight until one of the clock. Then, he explained to them about the burst plank in the bottom of the boat, and how that it would have to be put right before we could hope to leave the island, and that after that night we should have to go most strictly with the victuals; for there seemed to be nothing upon the island, that we had up till then discovered, fit to satisfy our bellies. More than this, if we could find no fresh water, he should have to distil some to make up for that which we had drunk, and this must be done before leaving the island.

Now by the time that the bo'sun had made an end of explaining these matters, we had ceased from eating, and soon after this we made each one of us a comfortable place in the sand within the tent, and lay down to sleep. For a while, I found myself very wakeful, which may have been because of the warmth of the night, and, indeed, at last I got up and went out of the tent, conceiving that I might the better find sleep in the open air. And so it proved; for, having lain down at the side of the tent, a little way from the fire, I fell soon into a deep slumber, which at first was dreamless. Presently, however, I came upon a very strange and unsettling dream; for I dreamed that I had been left alone on the island, and was sitting very desolate upon the edge of the brown-scummed pit. Then I was aware suddenly that it was very dark and very silent, and I began to shiver; for it seemed to me that something which repulsed my whole being had come quietly behind me. At that I tried mightily to turn and look into the shadows among the great fungi that stood all about me; but I had no power to turn. And the thing was coming nearer, though never a sound came to me, and I gave out a scream, or tried to; but my voice made no stir in the rounding quiet; and then something wet and cold touched my face, and slithered down and covered my mouth, and paused there for a vile, breathless moment. It passed onward and fell to my throat—and stayed there....

Someone stumbled and fell over my feet, and at that, I was suddenly awake. It was the man on watch making a walk round the back of the tent, and he had not known of my presence till he fell over my boots. He was somewhat shaken and startled, as might be supposed; but steadied himself on learning that it was no wild creature crouched there in the shadow; and all the time, as I answered his inquiries, I was full of a strange, horrid feeling that something had left me at the moment of my awakening. There was a slight, hateful odour in my nostrils that was not altogether unfamiliar, and then, suddenly, I was aware that my face was damp and that there was a curious sense of tingling at my throat. I put up my hand and felt my face, and the hand when I brought it away was slippery with slime, and at that, I put up my other hand, and touched my throat, and there it was the same, only, in addition, there was a slight swelled place a little to one side of the wind-pipe, the sort of place that the bite of a mosquito will make; but I had no thought to blame any mosquito.

Now the stumbling of the man over me, my awakening, and the discovery that my face and throat were be-slimed, were but the happenings of some few, short instants; and then I was upon my feet, and following him round to the fire; for I had a sense of chilliness and a great desire not to be alone. Now, having come to the fire, I took some of the water that had been left in the boiler, and washed my face and neck, after which I felt more my own man. Then I asked the man to look at my throat, so that he might give me some idea of what manner of place the swelling seemed, and he, lighting a piece of the dry seaweed to act as a torch, made examination of my neck; but could see little, save a number of small ring-like marks, red inwardly, and white at the edges, and one of them was bleeding slightly. After that, I asked him whether he had seen anything moving round the tent; but he had seen nothing during all the time that he had been on watch; though it was true that he had heard odd noises; but nothing very near at hand. Of the places on my throat he seemed to think but little, suggesting that I had been bitten by some sort of sand-fly; but at that, I shook my head, and told him of my dream, and after that, he was as anxious to keep near me as I to him. And so the night passed onward, until my turn came to watch.

For a little while, the man whom I had relieved sat beside me; having, I conceived, the kindly intent of keeping me company; but so soon as I perceived this, I entreated him to go and get his sleep, assuring him that I had no longer any feelings of fear—such as had been mine upon awakening and discovering the state of my face and throat—; and, upon this, he consented to leave me, and so, in a little, I sat alone beside the fire.

For a certain space, I kept very quiet, listening; but no sound came to me out of the surrounding darkness, and so, as though it were a fresh thing, it was borne in upon me how that we were in a very abominable place of lonesomeness and desolation. And I grew very solemn.

Thus as I sat, the fire, which had not been replenished for a while, dwindled steadily until it gave but a dullish glow around. And then, in the direction of the valley, I heard suddenly the sound of a dull thud, the noise coming to me through the stillness with a very startling clearness. At that, I perceived that I was not doing my duty to the rest, nor to myself, by sitting and allowing the fire to cease from flaming; and immediately reproaching myself, I seized and cast a mass of the dry weed upon the fire, so that a great blaze shot up into the night, and afterwards I glanced quickly to right and to left, holding my cut-and-thrust very readily, and most thankful to the Almighty that I had brought no harm to any by reason of my carelessness, which I incline me to believe was that strange inertia which is bred by fear. And then, even as I looked about me, there came to me across the silence of the beach a fresh noise, a continual soft slithering to and fro in the bottom of the valley, as though a multitude of creatures moved stealthily. At this, I threw yet more fuel upon the fire, and after that I fixed my gaze in the direction of the valley: thus in the following instant it seemed to me that I saw a certain thing, as it might be a shadow, move on the outer borders of the firelight. Now the man who had kept watch before me had left his spear stuck upright in the sand convenient to my grasp, and, seeing something moving, I seized the weapon and hurled it with all my strength in its direction; but there came no answering cry to tell that I had struck anything living, and immediately afterwards there fell once more a great silence upon the island, being broken only by a far splash out upon the weed.

It may be conceived with truth that the above happenings had put a very considerable strain upon my nerves, so that I looked to and fro continually, with ever and anon a quick glance behind me; for it seemed to me that I might expect some demoniac creature to rush upon me at any moment. Yet, for the space of many minutes, there came to me neither any sight nor sound of living creature; so that I knew not what to think, being near to doubting if I had heard aught beyond the common.

And then, even as I made halt upon the threshold of doubt, I was assured that I had not been mistaken; for, abruptly, I was aware that all the valley was full of a rustling, scampering sort of noise, through which there came to me occasional soft thuds, and anon the former slithering sounds. And at that, thinking a host of evil things to be upon us, I cried out to the bo'sun and the men to awake.

Immediately upon my shout, the bo'sun rushed out from the tent, the men following, and every one with his weapon, save the man who had left his spear in the sand, and that lay now somewhere beyond the light of the fire. Then the bo'sun shouted, to know what thing had caused me to cry out; but I replied nothing, only held up my hand for quietness, yet when this was granted, the noises in the valley had ceased; so that the bo'sun turned to me, being in need of some explanation; but I begged him to hark a little longer, which he did, and, the sounds recommencing almost immediately, he heard sufficient to know that I had not waked them all without due cause. And then, as we stood each one of us staring into the darkness where lay the valley, I seemed to see again some shadowy thing upon the boundary of the firelight; and, in the same instant, one of the men cried out and cast his spear into the darkness. But the bo'sun turned upon him with a very great anger; for in throwing his weapon, the man had left himself without, and thus brought danger to the whole; yet, as will be remembered, I had done likewise but a little since.

Presently, there coming again a quietness within the valley, and none knowing what might be toward, the bo'sun caught up a mass of the dry weed, and, lighting it at the fire, ran with it towards that portion of the beach which lay between us and the valley. Here he cast it upon the sand, singing out to some of the men to bring more of the weed, so that we might have a fire there, and thus be able to see if anything made to come at us out of the deepness of the hollow.

Presently, we had a very good fire, and by the light of this the two spears were discovered, both of them stuck in the sand, and no more than a yard one from the other, which seemed to me a very strange thing.

Now, for a while after the lighting of the second fire, there came no further sounds from the direction of the valley; nothing indeed to break the quietness of the island, save the occasional lonely splashes that sounded from time to time out in the vastness of the weed-continent. Then, about an hour after I had waked the bo'sun, one of the men who had been tending the fires came up to him to say that we had come to the end of our supply of weed-fuel. At that, the bo'sun looked very blank, the which did the rest of us, as well we might; yet there was no help for it, until one of the men bethought him of the remainder of the bundle of reeds which we had cut, and which, burning but poorly, we had discarded for the weed. This was discovered at the back of the tent, and with it we fed the fire that burned between us and the valley; but the other we suffered to die out, for the reeds were not sufficient to support even the one until the dawn.

At last, and whilst it was still dark, we came to the end of our fuel, and as the fire died down, so did the noises in the valley recommence. And there we stood in the growing dark, each one keeping a very ready weapon, and a more ready glance. And at times the island would be mightily quiet, and then again the sounds of things crawling in the valley. Yet, I think the silences tried us the more.

And so at last came the dawn.

IX
What Happened In The Dusk

NOW WITH THE COMING of the dawn, a lasting silence stole across the island and into the valley, and, conceiving that we had nothing more to fear, the bo'sun bade us get some rest, whilst he kept watch. And so I got at last a very substantial little spell of sleep, which made me fit enough for the day's work.

Presently, after some hours had passed, the bo'sun roused us to go with him to the further side of the island to gather fuel, and soon we were back with each a load, so that in a little we had the fire going right merrily.

Now for breakfast, we had a hash of broken biscuit, salt meat and some shell-fish which the bo'sun had picked up from the beach at the foot of the further hill; the whole being right liberally flavoured with some of the vinegar, which the bo'sun said would help keep down any scurvy that might be threatening us. And at the end of the meal he served out to us each a little of the molasses, which we mixed with hot water, and drank.

The meal being ended, he went into the tent to take a look at Job, the which he had done already in the early morning; for the condition of the lad preyed somewhat upon him; he being, for all his size and top-roughness, a man of surprisingly tender heart. Yet the boy remained much as on the previous evening, so that we knew not what to do with him to bring him into better health. One thing we tried, knowing that no food had passed his lips since the previous morning, and that was to get some little quantity of hot water, rum and molasses down his throat; for it seemed to us he might die from very lack of food; but though we worked with him for more than the half of an hour, we could not get him to come-to sufficiently to take anything, and without that we had fear of suffocating him. And so, presently, we had perforce to leave him within the tent, and go about

55

our business; for there was very much to be done.

Yet, before we did aught else, the bo'sun led us all into the valley, being determined to make a very thorough exploration of it, perchance there might be any lurking beast or devil-thing waiting to rush out and destroy us as we worked, and more, he would make search that he might discover what manner of creatures had disturbed our night.

Now in the early morning, when we had gone for the fuel, we had kept to the upper skirt of the valley where the rock of the nearer hill came down into the spongy ground, but now we struck right down into the middle part of the vale, making a way amid the mighty fungi to the pit-like opening that filled the bottom of the valley. Now though the ground was very soft, there was in it so much of springiness that it left no trace of our steps after we had gone on a little way, none, that is, save that in odd places, a wet patch followed upon our treading. Then, when we got ourselves near to the pit, the ground became softer, so that our feet sank into it, and left very real impressions; and here we found tracks most curious and bewildering; for amid the slush that edged the pit—which I would mention here had less the look of a pit now that I had come near to it—were multitudes of markings which I can liken to nothing so much as the tracks of mighty slugs amid the mud, only that they were not altogether like to that of slugs'; for there were other markings such as might have been made by bunches of eels cast down and picked up continually, at least, this is what they suggested to me, and I do but put it down as such.

Apart from the markings which I have mentioned, there was everywhere a deal of slime, and this we traced all over the valley among the great toadstool plants; but, beyond that which I have already remarked, we found nothing. Nay, but I was near to forgetting, we found a quantity of this thin slime upon those fungi which filled the end of the little valley nearest to our encampment, and here also we discovered many of them fresh broken or uprooted, and there was the same mark of the beast upon them all, and now I remember the dull thuds that I had heard in the night, and made little doubt but that the creatures had climbed the great toadstools so that they might spy us out; and it may be that many climbed upon one, so that their weight broke the fungi, or uprooted them. At least, so the thought came to me.

And so we made an end of our search, and after that, the bo'sun set each one of us to work. But first he had us all back to the beach to give a hand to turn over the boat, so that he might get to the damaged part. Now, having the bottom of the boat full to his view, he made discovery that there was other damage beside that of the burst plank;

for the bottom plank of all had come away from the keel, which seemed to us a very serious matter; though it did not show when the boat was upon her bilges. Yet the bo'sun assured us that he had no doubts but that she could be made seaworthy; though it would take a greater while than hitherto he had thought needful.

Having concluded his examination of the boat, the bo'sun sent one of the men to bring the bottom-boards out of the tent; for he needed some planking for the repair of the damage. Yet when the boards had been brought, he needed still something which they could not supply, and this was a length of very sound wood of some three inches in breadth each way, which he intended to bolt against the starboard side of the keel, after he had gotten the planking replaced so far as was possible. He had hopes that by means of this device he would be able to nail the bottom plank to this, and then caulk it with oakum, so making the boat almost so sound as ever.

Now hearing him express his need for such a piece of timber, we were all adrift to know from whence such a thing could be gotten, until there came suddenly to me a memory of the mast and topmast upon the other side of the island, and at once I made mention of them. At that, the bo'sun nodded, saying that we might get the timber out of it, though it would be a work requiring some considerable labour, in that we had only a hand-saw and a small hatchet. Then he sent us across to be getting it clear of the weed, promising to follow when he had made an end of trying to get the two displaced planks back into position.

Having reached the spars, we set-to with a very good will to shift away the weed and wrack that was piled over them, and very much entangled with the rigging. Presently we had laid them bare, and so we discovered them to be in remarkably sound condition, the lower-mast especially being a fine piece of timber. All the lower and topmast standing rigging was still attached, though in places the lower rigging was stranded so far as half-way up the shrouds; yet there remained much that was good and all of it quite free from rot, and of the very finest quality of white hemp, such as is to be seen only in the best found vessels.

About the time that we had finished clearing the weed, the bo'sun came over to us, bringing with him the saw and the hatchet. Under his directions, we cut the lanyards of the topmast rigging, and after that sawed through the topmast just above the cap. Now this was a very tough piece of work, and employed us a great part of the morning, even though we took turn and turn at the saw, and when it was done we were mightily glad that the bo'sun bade one of the men go over with some weed and make up the fire for dinner, after which he was to put on a piece of the salt meat to boil.

In the meanwhile, the bo'sun had started to cut through the top-mast, about fifteen feet beyond the first cut, for that was the length of the batten he required; yet so wearisome was the work, that we had not gotten more than half through with it before the man whom the bo'sun had sent, returned to say that the dinner was ready. When this was dispatched, and we had rested a little over our pipes, the bo'sun rose and led us back; for he was determined to get through with the topmast before dark.

Presently, relieving each other frequently, we completed the second cut, and after that the bo'sun set us to saw a block about twelve inches deep from the remaining portion of the topmast. From this, when we had cut it, he proceeded to hew wedges with the hatchet. Then he notched the end of the fifteen-foot log, and into the notch he drove the wedges, and so, towards evening, as much, maybe, by good luck as good management, he had divided the log into two halves—the split running very fairly down the centre.

Now, perceiving how that it drew near to sundown, he bade the men haste and gather weed and carry it across to our camp; but one he sent along the shore to make a search for shell-fish among the weed; yet he himself ceased not to work at the divided log, and kept me with him as helper. Thus, within the next hour, we had a length, maybe some four inches in diameter, split off the whole length of one of the halves, and with this he was very well content; though it seemed but a very little result for so much labour.

By this time the dusk was upon us, and the men, having made an end of weed carrying, were returned to us, and stood about, waiting for the bo'sun to go into camp. At this moment, the man the bo'sun had sent to gather shell-fish, returned, and he had a great crab upon his spear, which he had spitted through the belly. This creature could not have been less than a foot across the back, and had a very formidable appearance; yet it proved to be a most tasty matter for our supper, when it had been placed for a while in boiling water.

Now so soon as this man was returned, we made at once for the camp, carrying with us the piece of timber which we had hewn from the topmast. By this time it was quite dusk, and very strange amid the great fungi as we struck across the upper edge of the valley to the opposite beach. Particularly, I noticed that the hateful, mouldy odour of these monstrous vegetables was more offensive than I had found it to be in the daytime; though this may be because I used my nose the more, in that I could not use my eyes to any great extent.

We had gotten half way across the top of the valley, and the gloom was deepening steadily, when there stole to me upon the calmness of the evening air, a faint smell; something quite different from that of the surrounding fungi. A moment later I got a great whiff of it, and was near sickened with the abomination of it; but the memory of that foul thing which had come to the side of the boat in the dawn-gloom, before we discovered the island, roused me to a terror beyond that of the sickness of my stomach; for, suddenly, I knew what manner of thing it was that had be-slimed my face and throat upon the previous night, and left its hideous stench lingering in my nostrils. And with the knowledge, I cried out to the bo'sun to make haste, for there were demons with us in the valley. And at that, some of the men made to run; but he bade them, in a very grim voice, stay where they were, and keep well together, else would they be attacked and overcome, straggled all among the fungi in the dark. And this, being, I doubt not, as much in fear of the rounding dark as of the bo'sun, they did, and so we came safely out of the valley; though there seemed to follow us a little lower down the slope an uncanny slithering.

Now so soon as we reached the camp, the bo'sun ordered four fires to be lit—one on each side of the tent, and this we did, lighting them at the embers of our old fire, which we had most foolishly allowed to die down. When the fires had been got going, we put on the boiler, and treated the great crab as I have already mentioned, and so fell-to upon a very hearty supper; but, as we ate, each man had his weapon stuck in the sand beside him; for we had knowledge that the valley held some devilish thing, or maybe many; though the knowing did not spoil our appetites.

And so, presently, we came to an end of eating, whereat each man pulled out his pipe, intending to smoke; but the bo'sun told one of the men to get him upon his feet and keep watch, else might we be in danger of surprise, with every man lolling upon the sand; and this seemed to me very good sense; for it was easy to see that the men, too readily, deemed themselves secure, by reason of the brightness of the fires about them.

Now, whilst the men were taking their ease within the circle of the fires, the bo'sun lit one of the dips which we had out of the ship in the creek, and went in to see how Job was, after the day's rest. At that, I rose up, reproaching myself for having forgotten the poor lad, and followed the bo'sun into the tent. Yet, I had but reached the opening, when he gave out a loud cry, and held the candle low down to the sand. At that, I saw the reason for his agitation, for, in the place where we had left Job, there was nothing. I stepped into the tent, and, in the same instant, there came to my nostrils the faint odour of the horrible stench which had come to me in the valley, and before then from the thing that came to the side of the boat. And, suddenly, I knew that Job had fallen prey of those foul things, and, knowing this, I called out to the bo'sun that *they* had taken the boy, and then my eyes caught the smear of slime upon the sand, and I had proof that I was not mistaken.

Now, so soon as the bo'sun knew all that was in my mind; though indeed it did but corroborate that which had come to his own, he came swiftly out from the tent, bidding the men to stand back; for they had come all about the entrance, being very much discomposed at that which the bo'sun had discovered. Then the bo'sun took from a bundle of the reeds, which they had cut at the time when he had bidden them gather fuel, several of the thickest, and to one of these he bound a great mass of the dry weed; whereupon the men, divining his intention, did likewise with the others, and so we had each of us the wherewithal for a mighty torch.

So soon as we had completed our preparations, we took each man his weapon, and, plunging our torches into the fires, set off along the track which had been made by the devil-things and the body of poor Job; for now that we had suspicion that harm had come to him, the marks in the sand, and the slime, were very plain to be seen, so that it was a wonder that we had not discovered them earlier.

Now the bo'sun led the way, and, finding the marks led direct to the valley, he broke into a run, holding his torch well above his head. At that, each of us did likewise; for we had a great desire to be together, and further than this, I think with truth I may say, we were all fierce to avenge Job, so that we had less of fear in our hearts than otherwise had been the case.

In less than the half of a minute we had reached the end of the valley; but here, the ground being of a nature not happy in the revealing of tracks, we were at fault to know in which direction to continue. At that, the bo'sun set up a loud shout to Job, perchance he might be yet alive; but there came no answer to us, save a low and uncomfortable echo. Then the bo'sun, desiring to waste no more time, ran straight down towards the centre of the valley, and we followed, and kept our eyes very open about us. We had gotten perhaps half way, when one of the men shouted that he saw something ahead; but the bo'sun had seen it earlier; for he was running straight down upon it, holding his torch high and swinging his great cutlass. Then, instead of smiting, he fell upon his knees beside it, and the following instant we were up with him, and in that same moment it seemed to me that I saw a number of white shapes melt swiftly into the shadows further ahead: but I had no thought for these when I perceived that by which the bo'sun knelt; for it was the stark body of Job, and no inch of it but was covered with the little ringed marks that I had discovered upon my throat, and from every place there ran a trickle of blood, so that he was a most horrid and fearsome sight.

At the sight of Job so mangled and be-bled, there came over us the sudden quiet of a mortal terror, and in that space of silence, the bo'sun placed his hand over the poor lad's heart; but there was no movement, though the body was still warm. Immediately upon that, he rose to his feet, a look of vast wrath upon his great face. He plucked his torch from the ground, into which he had plunged the haft, and stared round into the silence of the valley; but there was no living thing in sight, nothing save the giant fungi and the strange shadows cast by our great torches, and the loneliness.

At this moment, one of the men's torches, having burnt near out, fell all to pieces, so that he held nothing but the charred support, and immediately two more came to a like end. Upon this, we became afraid that they would not last us back to the camp, and we looked to the bo'sun to know his wish; but the man was very silent, and peering everywhere into the shadows. Then a fourth torch fell to the ground in a shower of embers, and I turned to look. In the same instant there came a great flare of light behind me, accompanied by the dull thud of a dry matter set suddenly alight. I glanced swiftly back to the bo'sun, and he was staring up at one of the giant toadstools which was in flames all along its nearer edge, and burning with an incredible fury, sending out spirits of flame, and anon giving out sharp reports, and at each report, a fine powder was belched in thin streams; which, getting into our throats and nostrils, set us sneezing and coughing most lamentably; so that I am convinced, had any enemy come upon us at that moment, we had been undone by reason of our uncouth helplessness.

Now whether it had come to the bo'sun to set alight this first of the fungi, I know not; for it may be that his torch coming by chance against it, set it afire. However it chanced, the bo'sun took it as a veritable hint from Providence, and was already setting his torch to one a little further off, whilst the rest of us were near to choking with our coughings and sneezings. Yet, that we were so suddenly overcome by the potency of the powder, I doubt if a full minute passed before we were each one busied after the manner of the bo'sun; and those whose torches had burned out, knocked flaming pieces from the burning fungus, and with these impaled upon their torch-sticks, did so much execution as any.

And thus it happened that within five minutes of this discovery of Job's body, the whole of that hideous valley sent up to heaven the reek of its burning; whilst we, filled with murderous desires, ran hither and thither with our weapons, seeking to destroy the vile creatures that had brought the poor lad to so unholy a death. Yet nowhere could we discover any brute or creature upon which to ease our vengeance, and so, presently, the valley becoming impassable by reason of the heat, the flying sparks and the abundance of the acrid dust, we made back to the body of the boy, and bore him thence to the shore.

And during all that night no man of us slept, and the burning of the fungi sent up a mighty pillar of flame out of the valley, as out of the mouth of a monstrous pit, and when the morning came it still burned. Then when it was daylight, some of us slept, being greatly awearied; but some kept watch.

And when we waked there was a great wind and rain upon the island.

X
The Light In The Weed

NOW THE WIND WAS very violent from the sea, and threatened to blow down our tent, the which, indeed, it achieved at last as we made an end of a cheerless breakfast. Yet, the bo'sun bade us not trouble to put it up again; but spread it out with the edges raised upon props made from the reeds, so that we might catch some of the rain water; for it was become imperative that we should renew our supply before putting out again to sea. And whilst some of us were busied about this, he took the others and set up a small tent made of the spare canvas, and under this he sheltered all of our matters like to be harmed by the rain.

In a little, the rain continuing very violent, we had near a breaker-full of water collected in the canvas, and were about to run it off into one of the breakers, when the bo'sun cried out to us to hold, and first taste the water before we mixed it with that which we had already. At that, we put down our hands and scooped up some of the water to taste, and thus we discovered it to be brackish and quite undrinkable, at which I was amazed, until the bo'sun reminded us that the canvas had been saturated for many days with salt water, so that it would take a great quantity of fresh before all the salt was washed out. Then he told us to lay it flat upon the beach, and scour it well on both sides with the sand, which we did, and afterwards let the rain rinse it well, whereupon the next water that we caught we found to be near fresh; though not sufficiently so for our purpose. Yet when we had rinsed it once more, it became clear of the salt, so that we were able to keep all that we caught further.

And then, something before noon, the rain ceased to fall, though coming again at odd times in short squalls; yet the wind died not, but blew steadily, and continued so from that quarter during the remainder of the time that we were upon the island.

Upon the ceasing of the rain, the bo'sun called us all together, that we might make a decent burial of the unfortunate lad, whose remains had lain during the night upon one of the bottom-boards of the boat. After a little discussion, it was decided to bury him in the beach; for the only part where there was soft earth was in the valley, and none of us had a stomach for that place. Moreover, the sand was soft and easy to dig, and as we had no proper tools, this was a great consideration. Presently, using the bottom-boards and the oars and the hatchet, we had a place large and deep enough to hold the boy, and into this we placed him. We made no prayer over him; but stood about the grave for a little space, in silence. Then, the bo'sun signed to us to fill in the sand; and, therewith, we covered up the poor lad, and left him to his sleep.

And, presently, we made our dinner, after which the bo'sun served out to each one of us a very sound tot of the rum; for he was minded to bring us back again to a cheerful state of mind.

After we had sat awhile, smoking, the bo'sun divided us into two parties to make a search through the island among the rocks, perchance we should find water, collected from the rain, among the hollows and crevasses; for though we had gotten some, through our device with the sail, yet we had by no means caught sufficient for our needs. He was especially anxious for haste, in that the sun had come out again; for he was feared that such small pools as we should find would be speedily dried up by its heat.

Now the bo'sun headed one party, and set the big seaman over the other, bidding all to keep their weapons very handy. Then he set out to the rocks about the base of the nearer hill, sending the others to the farther and greater one, and in each party we carried an empty breaker slung from a couple of the stout reeds, so that we might put all such driblets as we should find, straight away into it, before they had time to vanish into the hot air; and for the purpose of bailing up the water, we had brought with us our tin pannikins, and one of the boat's bailers.

In a while, and after much scrambling amid the rocks, we came upon a little pool of water that was remarkably sweet and fresh, and from this we removed near three gallons before it became dry; and after that we came across, maybe, five or six others; but not one of them near so big as the first; yet we were not displeased; for we had near three parts filled the breaker, and so we made back to the camp, having some wonder as to the luck of the other party.

When we came near the camp, we found the others returned before us, and seeming in a very high content with themselves; so that we had no need to call to them as to whether they had filled their breaker. When they saw us, they set out to us at a run to tell us that they had come upon a great basin of fresh water in a deep hollow a third of the distance up the side of the far hill, and at this the bo'sun bade us put down our breaker and make all of us to the hill, so that he might examine for himself whether their news was so good as it seemed.

Presently, being guided by the other party, we passed around to the back of the far hill, and discovered it to go upward to the top at an easy slope, with many ledges and broken places, so that it was scarce more difficult than a stair to climb. And so, having climbed perhaps ninety or a hundred feet, we came suddenly upon the place which held the water, and found that they had not made too much of their discovery; for the pool was near twenty feet long by twelve broad, and so clear as though it had come from a fountain; yet it had considerable depth, as we discovered by thrusting a spear shaft down into it.

Now the bo'sun, having seen for himself how good a supply of water there was for our needs, seemed very much relieved in his mind, and declared that within three days at the most we might leave the island, at which we felt none of us any regret. Indeed, had the boat escaped harm, we had been able to leave that same day; but this could not be; for there was much to be done before we had her seaworthy again.

Having waited until the bo'sun had made complete his examination, we turned to descend, thinking that this would be the bo'sun's intention; but he called to us to stay, and, looking back, we saw that he made to finish the ascent of the hill. At that, we hastened to follow him; though we had no notion of his reason for going higher. Presently, we were come to the top, and here we found a very spacious place, nicely level save that in one or two parts it was crossed by deepish cracks, maybe half a foot to a foot wide, and perhaps three to six fathoms long; but, apart from these and some great boulders, it was, as I have mentioned, a spacious place; moreover it was bone dry and pleasantly firm under one's feet, after so long upon the sand.

I think, even thus early, I had some notion of the bo'sun's design; for I went to the edge that overlooked the valley, and peered down, and, finding it nigh a sheer precipice, found myself nodding my head, as though it were in accordance with some part formed wish. Presently, looking about me, I discovered the bo'sun to be surveying that part which looked over towards the weed, and I made across to join him. Here, again, I saw that the hill fell away very sheer, and after that we went across to the seaward edge, and there it was near as abrupt as on the weed side.

Then, having by this time thought a little upon the matter, I put it straight to the bo'sun that here would make indeed a very secure camping place, with nothing to come at us upon our sides or back; and our front, where was the slope, could be watched with ease. And this I put to him with great warmth; for I was mortally in dread of the coming night.

Now when I had made an end of speaking, the bo'sun disclosed to me that this was, as I had suspicion, his intent, and immediately he called to the men that we should haste down, and ship our camp to the top of the hill. At that, the men expressed their approbation, and we made haste every one of us to the camp, and began straightway to move our gear to the hill-top.

In the meanwhile, the bo'sun, taking me to assist him, set-to again upon the boat, being intent to get his batten nicely shaped and fit to the side of the keel, so that it would bed well to the keel, but more particularly to the plank which had sprung outward from its place. And at this he laboured the greater part of that afternoon, using the little hatchet to shape the wood, which he did with surprising skill; yet when the evening was come, he had not brought it to his liking. But it must not be thought that he did naught but work at the boat; for he had the men to direct, and once he had to make his way to the top of the hill to fix the place for the tent. And after the tent was up, he set them to carry the dry weed to the new camp, and at this he kept them until near dusk; for he had vowed never again to be without a sufficiency of fuel. But two of the men he sent to collect shell-fish—putting two of them to the task, because he would not have one alone upon the island, not knowing but that there might be danger, even though it were bright day; and a most happy ruling it proved; for, a little past the middle of the afternoon, we heard them shouting at the other end of the valley, and, not knowing but that they were in need of assistance, we ran with all haste to discover the reason of their calling, passing along the right-hand side of the blackened and sodden vale. Upon reaching the further beach, we saw a most incredible sight; for the two men were running towards us through the thick masses of the weed, while, no more than four or five fathoms behind, they were pursued by an enormous crab. Now I had thought the crab we had tried to capture before coming to the island, a prodigy unsurpassed; but this creature was more than treble its size, seeming as though a prodigious table were a-chase of them, and moreover, spite of its monstrous bulk, it made better way over the weed than I should have conceived to be possible—running almost sideways, and with one enormous claw raised near a dozen feet into the air.

Now whether, omitting accidents, the men would have made good their escape to the firmer ground of the valley, where they could have attained to a greater speed, I do not know; but suddenly one of them tripped over a loop of the weed, and the next instant lay helpless upon his face. He had been dead the following moment, but for the pluck of his companion, who faced round manfully upon the monster, and ran at it with his twenty-foot spear. It seemed to me that the spear took it about a foot below the overhanging armour of the great back shell, and I could see that it penetrated some distance into the creature, the man having, by the aid of Providence, stricken it in a vulnerable part. Upon receiving this thrust, the mighty crab ceased at once its pursuit, and clipped at the haft of the spear with its great mandible, snapping the weapon more easily than I had done the same thing to a straw. By the time we had raced up to the men, the one who had stumbled was again upon his feet, and turning to assist his comrade; but the bo'sun snatched his spear from him, and leapt forward himself; for the crab was making now at the other man. Now the bo'sun did not attempt to thrust the spear into the monster; but instead he made two swift blows at the great protruding eyes, and in a moment the creature had curled itself up, helpless, save that the huge claw waved about aimlessly. At that, the bo'sun drew us off, though the man who had attacked the crab desired to make an end of it, averring that we should get some very good eating out of it; but to this the bo'sun would not listen, telling him that it was yet capable of very deadly mischief, did any but come within reach of its prodigious mandible.

And after this, he bade them look no more for shellfish; but take out the two fishing-lines which we had, and see if they could catch aught from some safe ledge on the further side of the hill upon which we had made our camp. Then he returned to his mending of the boat.

It was a little before the evening came down upon the island, that the bo'sun ceased work; and, after that, he called to the men, who, having made an end of their fuel carrying, were standing near, to place the full breakers—which we had not thought needful to carry to the new camp on account of their weight—under the upturned boat, some holding up the gunnel whilst the others pushed them under. Then the bo'sun laid the unfinished batten along with them, and we lowered the boat again over all, trusting to its weight to prevent any creature from meddling with aught.

After that, we made at once to the camp, being wearifully tired, and with a hearty anticipation of supper. Upon reaching the hilltop, the men whom the bo'sun had sent with the lines, came to show him a very fine fish, something like to a huge king-fish, which they had caught a few minutes earlier. This, the bo'sun, after examining, did not hesitate to pronounce fit for food; whereupon they set-to and opened and cleaned it. Now, as I have said, it was not unlike a great king-fish, and like it, had a mouth full of very formidable teeth; the use of which I understood the better when I saw the contents of its stomach, which seemed to consist of nothing but the coiled tentacles of squid or cuttle-fish, with which, as I have shown, the weed-continent swarmed. When these were upset upon the rock, I was confounded to perceive the length and thickness of some of them; and could only conceive that this particular fish must be a very desperate enemy to them, and able successfully to attack monsters of a bulk infinitely greater than its own.

After this, and whilst the supper was preparing, the bo'sun called to some of the men to put up a piece of the spare canvas upon a couple of the reeds, so as to make a screen against the wind, which up there was so fresh that it came near at times to scattering the fire abroad. This they found not difficult; for a little on the windward side of the fire there ran one of the cracks of which I have made previous mention, and into this they jammed the supports, and so in a very little time had the fire screened.

Presently, the supper was ready, and I found the fish to be very fair eating; though somewhat coarse; but this was no great matter for concern with so empty a stomach as I contained. And here I would remark, that we made our fishing save our provisions through all our stay on the island. Then, after we had come to an end of our eating, we lay down to a most comfortable smoke; for we had no fear of attack, at that height, and with precipices upon all sides save that which lay in front. Yet, so soon as we had rested and smoked a while, the bo'sun set the watches; for he would run no risk through carelessness.

By this time the night was drawing on apace; yet it was not so dark but that one could perceive matters at a very reasonable distance. Presently, being in a mood that tended to thoughtfulness, and feeling a desire to be alone for a little, I strolled away from the fire to the leeward edge of the hill-top. Here, I paced up and down awhile, smoking and meditating. Anon, I would stare out across the immensity of the vast continent of weed and slime that stretched its incredible desolation out beyond the darkening horizon, and there would come the thought to me of the terror of men whose vessels had been entangled among its strange growths, and so my thoughts came to the lone derelict that lay out there in the dusk, and I fell to wondering what had been the end of her people, and at that I grew yet more solemn in my heart. For it seemed to me that they must have died at last by starvation, and if not by that, then by the act of some one of the devil-creatures which inhabited that lonely weed-world. And then, even as I fell upon this thought, the bo'sun clapt me upon the shoulder, and told me in a very hearty way to come to the light of the fire, and banish all melancholy thoughts; for he had a very penetrating discernment, and had followed me quietly from the camping place, having had reason once or twice before to chide me for gloomy meditations. And for this, and many other matters, I had grown to like the man, the which I could almost believe at times, was his regarding of me; but his words were too few for me to gather his feelings; though I had hope that they were as I surmised.

And so I came back to the fire, and presently, it not being my time to watch until after midnight, I turned into the tent for a spell of sleep, having first arranged a comfortable spread of some of the softer portions of the dry weed to make me a bed.

Now I was very full of sleep, so that I slept heavily, and in this wise heard not the man on watch call the bo'sun; yet the rousing of the others waked me, and so I came to myself and found the tent empty, at which I ran very hurriedly to the doorway, and so discovered that there was a clear moon in the sky, the which, by reason of the cloudiness that had prevailed, we had been without for the past two nights, Moreover, the sultriness had gone, the wind having blown it away with the clouds; yet though, maybe, I appreciated this, it was but in a half-conscious manner; for I was put about to discover the whereabouts of the men, and the reason of their leaving the tent. With this purpose, I stepped out from the entrance, and the following instant discovered them all in a clump beside the leeward edge of the hill-top. At that, I held my tongue; for I knew not but that silence might be their desire; but I ran hastily over to them, and inquired of the bo'sun what manner of thing it was which called them from their sleep, and he, for answer, pointed out into the greatness of the weed-continent.

At that, I stared out over the breadth of the weed, showing very ghostly in the moonlight; but, for the moment, I saw not the thing to which he purposed to draw my attention. Then, suddenly, it fell within the circle of my gaze—a little light out in the lonesomeness. For the space of some moments, I stared with bewildered eyes; then it came to me with abruptness that the light shone from the lone derelict lying out in the weed, the same that, upon that very evening, I had looked with sorrow and awe, because of the end of those who had been in her—and now, behold, a light burning, seemingly within one of her after cabins; though the moon was scarce powerful enough to enable the outline of the hulk to be seen clear of the rounding wilderness.

And from this time, until the day, we had no more sleep; but made up the fire, and sat round it, full of excitement and wonder, and getting up continually to discover if the light still burned. This it ceased to do about an hour after I had first seen it; but it was the more proof that some of our kind were no more than the half of a mile from our camp.

And at last the day came.

XI

The Signals From The Ship

NOW SO SOON AS it was clearly light, we went all of us to the leeward brow of the hill to stare upon the derelict, which now we had cause to believe no derelict, but an inhabited vessel. Yet though we watched her for upwards of two hours, we could discover no sign of any living creature, the which, indeed, had we been in cooler minds, we had not thought strange, seeing that she was all so shut in by the great superstructure; but we were hot to see a fellow creature, after so much lonesomeness and terror in strange lands and seas, and so could not by any means contain ourselves in patience until those aboard the hulk should choose to discover themselves to us.

And so, at last, being wearied with watching, we made it up together to shout when the bo'sun should give us the signal, by this means making a good volume of sound which we conceived the wind might carry down to the vessel. Yet though we raised many shouts, making as it seemed to us a very great noise, there came no response from the ship, and at last we were fain to cease from our calling, and ponder some other way of bringing ourselves to the notice of those within the hulk.

For awhile we talked, some proposing one thing, and some another; but none of them seeming like to achieve our purpose. And after that we fell to marvelling that the fire which we had lit in the valley had not awakened them to the fact that some of their fellow creatures were upon the island; for, had it, we could not suppose but that they would have kept a perpetual watch upon the island until such time as they should have been able to attract our notice. Nay! more than this, it was scarce credible that they should not have made an answering fire, or set some of their bunting above the superstructure, so that our gaze should be arrested upon the instant we chanced to glance towards the hulk. But so far from this, there appeared even a purpose to shun our attention;

for that light which we had viewed in the past night was more in the way of an accident, than of the nature of a purposeful exhibition.

And so, presently, we went to breakfast, eating heartily; our night of wakefulness having given us mighty appetites; but, for all that, we were so engrossed by the mystery of the lonesome craft, that I doubt if any of us knew what manner of food it was with which we filled our bellies. For first one view of the matter would be raised, and when this had been combated, another would be broached, and in this wise it came up finally that some of the men were falling in doubt whether the ship was inhabited by anything human, saying rather that it might be held by some demoniac creature of the great weed-continent. At this proposition, there came among us a very uncomfortable silence; for not only did it chill the warmth of our hopes; but seemed like to provide us with a fresh terror, who were already acquainted with too much. Then the bo'sun spoke, laughing with a hearty contempt at our sudden fears, and pointed out that it was just as like that they aboard the ship had been put in fear by the great blaze from the valley, as that they should take it for a sign that fellow creatures and friends were at hand. For, as he put it to us, who of us could say what fell brutes and demons the weed-continent did hold, and if we had reason to know that there were very dread things among the weed, how much the more must they, who had, for all that we knew, been many years beset around by such. And so, as he went on to make clear, we might suppose that they were very well aware there had come some creatures to the island; yet, maybe, they desired not to make themselves known until they had been given sight of them, and because of this, we must wait until they chose to discover themselves to us.

Now when the bo'sun had made an end, we felt each one of us greatly cheered; for his discourse seemed very reasonable. Yet still there were many matters that troubled our company; for, as one put it, was it not mightily strange that we had not had previous sight of their light, or, in the day, of the smoke from their galley fire? But to this the bo'sun replied that our camp hitherto had lain in a place where we had not sight, even of the great world of weed, leaving alone any view of the derelict. And more, that at such times as we had crossed to the opposite beach, we had been occupied too sincerely to have much thought to watch the hulk, which, indeed, from that position showed only her great superstructure. Further, that, until the preceding day, we had but once climbed to any height; and that from our present camp the derelict could not be viewed, and to do so, we had to go near to the leeward edge of the hill-top.

And so, breakfast being ended, we went all of us to see if there were yet any signs of life in the hulk; but when an hour had gone, we were no wiser. Therefore, it being folly to waste further time, the bo'sun left one man to watch from the brow of the hill, charging him very strictly to keep in such position that he could be seen by any aboard the silent craft, and so took the rest down to assist him in the repairing of the boat. And from thence on, during the day, he gave the men a turn each at watching, telling them to wave to him should there come any sign from the hulk. Yet, excepting the watch, he kept every man so busy as might be, some bringing weed to keep up a fire which he had lit near the boat; one to help him turn and hold the batten upon which he laboured; and two he sent across to the wreck of the mast, to detach one of the futtock shrouds, which (as is most rare) were made of iron rods. This, when they brought it, he bade me heat in the fire, and afterwards beat out straight at one end, and when this was done, he set me to burn holes with it through the keel of the boat, at such places as he had marked, these being for the bolts with which he had determined to fasten on the batten.

In the meanwhile, he continued to shape the batten until it was a very good and true fit according to his liking. And all the while he cried out to this man and to that one to do this or that; and so I perceived that, apart from the necessity of getting the boat into a seaworthy condition, he was desirous to keep the men busied; for they were become so excited at the thought of fellow creatures almost within hail, that he could not hope to keep them sufficiently in hand without some matter upon which to employ them.

Now, it must not be supposed that the bo'sun had no share of our excitement; for I noticed that he gave ever and anon a glance to the crown of the far hill, perchance the watchman had some news for us. Yet the morning went by, and no signal came to tell us that the people in the ship had design to show themselves to the man upon watch, and so we came to dinner. At this meal, as might be supposed, we had a second discussion upon the strangeness of the behaviour of those aboard the hulk; yet none could give any more reasonable explanation than the bo'sun had given in the morning, and so we left it at that.

Presently, when we had smoked and rested very comfortably, for the bo'sun was no tyrant, we rose at his bidding to descend once more to the beach. But at this moment, one of the men having run to the edge of the hill to take a short look at the hulk, cried out that a part of the great superstructure over the quarter had been removed, or pushed back, and that there was a figure there, seeming, so far as his unaided sight could tell, to be looking through a spy-glass at the island. Now it would be difficult to tell of all our excitement at this news, and we ran eagerly to see for ourselves if it could be as he informed us. And so it was; for we could see the person very clearly; though remote and small because of the distance. That he had seen us, we discovered in a moment; for he began suddenly to wave something, which I judged to be the spy-glass, in a very wild manner, seeming also to be jumping up and down. Yet, I doubt not but that we were as much excited; for suddenly I discovered myself to be shouting with the rest in a most insane fashion, and moreover I was waving my hands and running to and fro upon the brow of the hill. Then, I observed that the figure on the hulk had disappeared; but it was for no more than a moment, and then it was back and there were near a dozen with it, and it seemed to me that some of them were females; but the distance was over great for surety. Now these, all of them, seeing us upon the brow of the hill, where we must have shown up plain against the sky, began at once to wave in a very frantic way, and we, replying in like manner, shouted ourselves hoarse with vain greetings. But soon we grew wearied of the unsatisfactoriness of this method of showing our excitement, and one took a piece of the square canvas, and let it stream out into the wind, waving it to them, and another took a second piece and did likewise, while a third man rolled up a short bit into a cone and made use of it as a speaking trumpet; though I doubt if his voice carried any the further because of it. For my part, I had seized one of the long bamboo-like reeds which were lying about near the fire, and with this I was making a very brave show. And so it may be seen how very great and genuine was our exaltation upon our discovery of these poor people shut off from the world within that lonesome craft.

Then, suddenly, it seemed to come to us to realise that *they* were among the weed, and *we* upon the hill-top, and that we had no means of bridging that which lay between. And at this we faced one another to discuss what we should do to effect the rescue of those within the hulk. Yet it was little that we could even suggest; for though one spoke of how he had seen a rope cast by means of a mortar to a ship that lay off shore, yet this helped us not, for we had no mortar; but here the same man cried out that they in the ship might have such a thing, so that they would be able to shoot the rope to us, and at this we thought more upon his saying; for if they had such a weapon, then might our difficulties be solved. Yet we were greatly at a loss to know how we should discover whether they were possessed of one, and further to explain our design to them. But here the bo'sun came to our help, and bade one man go quickly and char some of the reeds in the fire, and whilst this was doing he spread out upon the rock one of the spare lengths of canvas; then he sung out to the man to bring him one of the pieces of charred reed, and with this he wrote our question upon the canvas, calling for fresh charcoal as he required it. Then, having made an end of writing, he bade two of the men take hold of the canvas by the ends and expose it to the view of those in the ship, and in this manner we got them to understand our desires. For, presently, some of them went away, and came back after a little, and held up for us to see, a very great square of white, and upon it a great "NO," and at this were we again at our wits' ends to know how it would be possible to rescue those within the ship; for, suddenly, our whole desire to leave the island, was changed into a determination to rescue the people in the hulk, and, indeed, had our intentions not been such we had been veritable curs; though I am happy to tell that we had no thought at this juncture but for those who were now looking to us to restore them once more to the world to which they had been so long strangers.

Now, as I have said, we were again at our wits' ends to know how to come at those within the hulk, and there we stood all of us, talking together, perchance we should hit upon some plan, and anon we would turn and wave to those who watched us so anxiously. Yet, a while passed, and we had come no nearer to a method of rescue. Then a thought came to me (waked perchance by the mention of shooting the rope over to the hulk by means of a mortar) how that I had read once in a book, of a fair maid whose lover effected her escape from a castle by a similar artifice, only that in his case he made use of a bow in place of a mortar, and a cord instead of a rope, his sweetheart hauling up the rope by means of the cord.

Now it seemed to me a possible thing to substitute a bow for the mortar, if only we could find the material with which to make such a weapon, and with this in view, I took up one of the lengths of the bamboo-like reed, and tried the spring of it, which I found to be very good; for this curious growth, of which I have spoken hitherto as a reed, had no resemblance to that plant, beyond its appearance; it being extraordinarily tough and woody, and having considerably more nature than a bamboo. Now, having tried the spring of it, I went over to the tent and cut a piece of sampson-line which I found among the gear, and with this and the reed I contrived a rough bow. Then I looked about until I came upon a very young and slender reed which had been cut with the rest, and from this I fashioned some sort of an arrow, feathering it with a piece of one of the broad, stiff leaves, which grew upon the plant, and after that I went forth to the crowd about the leeward edge of the hill. Now when they saw me thus armed, they seemed to think that I intended a jest, and some of them laughed, conceiving that it was a very odd action on my part; but when I explained that which was in my mind, they ceased from laughter, and shook their heads, making that I did but waste time; for, as they said, nothing save gunpowder could cover so great a distance. And after that they turned again to the bo'sun with whom some of them seemed to be in argument. And so for a little space I held my peace, and listened; thus I discovered that certain of the men advocated the taking of the boat—so soon as it was sufficiently repaired—and making a passage through the weed to the ship, which they proposed to do by cutting a narrow canal. But the bo'sun shook his head, and reminded them of the great devil-fish and crabs, and the worse things which the weed concealed, saying that those in the ship would have done it long since had it been possible, and at that the men were silenced, being robbed of their unreasoning ardour by his warnings.

Now just at this point there happened a thing which proved the wisdom of that which the bo'sun contended; for, suddenly, one of the men cried out to us to look, and at that we turned quickly, and saw that there was a great commotion among those who were in the open place in the superstructure; for they were running this way and that, and some were pushing to the slide which filled the opening. And then, immediately, we saw the reason for their agitation and haste; for there was a stir in the weed near to the stern of the ship, and the next instant, monstrous tentacles were reached up to the place where had been the opening; but the door was shut, and those aboard the hulk in safety. At this manifestation, the men about me who had proposed to make use of the boat, and the others also, cried out their horror of the vast creature, and, I am convinced, had the rescue depended upon their use of the boat, then had those in the hulk been forever doomed.

Now, conceiving that this was a good point at which to renew my importunities, I began once again to explain the probabilities of my plan succeeding, addressing myself more particularly to the bo'sun. I told how that I had read that the ancients made mighty weapons, some of which could throw a great stone so heavy as two men, over a distance surpassing a quarter of a mile; moreover, that they compassed huge catapults which threw a lance, or great arrow, even further. On this, he expressed much surprise, never having heard of the like; but doubted greatly that we should be able to construct such a weapon, Yet, I told him that I was prepared; for I had the plan of one clearly in my mind, and further I pointed out to him that we had the wind in our favour, and that we were a great height up, which would allow the arrow to travel the farther before it came so low as the weed.

Then I stepped to the edge of the hill, and, bidding him watch, fitted my arrow to the string, and, having bent the bow, loosed it, whereupon, being aided by the wind and the height on which I stood, the arrow plunged into the weed at a distance of near two hundred yards from where we stood, that being about a quarter of the distance on the road to the derelict. At that, the bo'sun was won over to my idea; though, as he remarked, the arrow had fallen nearer had it been drawing a length of yarn after it, and to this I assented; but pointed out that my bow-and-arrow was but a rough affair, and, more, that I was no archer; yet I promised him, with the bow that I should make, to cast a shaft clean over the hulk, did he but give me his assistance, and bid the men to help.

Now, as I have come to regard it in the light of greater knowledge, my promise was exceeding rash; but I had faith in my conception, and was very eager to put it to the test; the which, after much discussion at supper, it was decided I should be allowed to do.

XII
The Making Of The Great Bow

CHE FOURTH NIGHT UPON the island was the first to pass without incident. It is true that a light showed from the hulk out in the weed; but now that we had made some acquaintance with her inmates, it was no longer a cause for excitement, so much as contemplation. As for the valley where the vile things had made an end of Job, it was very silent and desolate under the moonlight; for I made a point to go and view it during my time on watch; yet, for all that it lay empty, it was very eerie, and a place to conjure up uncomfortable thoughts, so that I spent no great time pondering it.

This was the second night on which we had been free from the terror of the devil-things, and it seemed to me that the great fire had put them in fear of us and driven them away; but of the truth or error of this idea, I was to learn later.

Now it must be admitted that, apart from a short look into the valley, and occasional starings at the light out in the weed, I gave little attention to aught but my plans for the great bow, and to such use did I put my time, that when I was relieved, I had each particular and detail worked out, so that I knew very well just what to set the men doing so soon as we should make a start in the morning.

Presently, when the morning had come, and we had made an end of breakfast, we turned-to upon the great bow, the bo'sun directing the men under my supervision. Now, the first matter to which I bent attention, was the raising, to the top of the hill, of the remaining half of that portion of the topmast which the bo'sun had split in twain to procure the batten for the boat. To this end, we went down, all of us, to the beach where lay the wreckage, and, getting about the portion which I intended to use, carried it to the foot of the hill; then we sent a man to the top to let down the rope by which we had moored the boat to the sea anchor, and when we had bent this on securely to the piece of timber, we returned to the hill-top, and tailed on to the rope, and so, presently, after much weariful pulling, had it up.

The next thing I desired was that the split face of the timber should be rubbed straight, and this the bo'sun understood to do, and whilst he was about it, I went with some of the men to the grove of reeds, and here, with great care, I made a selection of some of the finest, these being for the bow, and after that I cut some which were very clean and straight, intending them for the great arrows. With these we returned once more to the camp, and there I set-to and trimmed them of their leaves, keeping these latter, for I had a use for them. Then I took a dozen reeds and cut them each to a length of twenty-five feet, and afterwards notched them for the strings. In the meanwhile, I had sent two men down to the wreckage of the masts to cut away a couple of the hempen shrouds and bring them to the camp, and they, appearing about this time, I set to work to unlay the shrouds, so that they might get out the fine white yarns which lay beneath the outer covering of tar and blacking. These, when they had come at them, we found to be very good and sound, and this being so, I bid them make three-yarn sennit; meaning it for the strings of the bows. Now, it will be observed that I have said bows, and this I will explain. It had been my original intention to make one great bow, lashing a dozen of the reeds together for the purpose; but this, upon pondering it, I conceived to be but a poor plan; for there would be much life and power lost in the rendering of each piece through the lashings, when the bow was released. To obviate this, and further, to compass the bending of the bow, the which had, at first, been a source of puzzlement to me as to how it was to be accomplished, I had determined to make twelve separate bows, and these I intended to fasten at the end of the stock one above the other, so that they were all in one plane vertically, and because of this conception, I should be able to bend the bows one at a time, and slip each string over the catch-notch, and afterwards frap the twelve strings together in the middle part so that they would be but one string to the butt of the arrow. All this, I explained to the bo'sun, who, indeed, had been exercised in his own mind as to how we should be able to bend such a bow as I intended to make, and he was mightily pleased with my method of evading this difficulty, and also one other, which, else, had been greater than the bending, and that was the *stringing* of the bow, which would have proved a very awkward work.

Presently, the bo'sun called out to me that he had got the surface of the stock sufficiently smooth and nice; and at that I went over to him; for now I wished him to burn a slight groove down the centre, running from end to end, and this I desired to be done very exactly; for upon it depended much of the true flight of the arrow. Then I went back to my own work; for I had not yet finished notching the bows. Presently, when I had made an end of this, I called for a length of the sennit, and, with the aid of another man, contrived to string one of the bows. This, when I had finished, I found to be very springy, and so stiff to bend that I had all that I could manage to do so, and at this I felt very satisfied.

Presently, it occurred to me that I should do well to set some of the men to work upon the line which the arrow was to carry; for I had determined that this should be made also from the white hemp yarns, and, for the sake of lightness, I conceived that one thickness of yarn would be sufficient; but so that it might compass enough of strength, I bid them split the yarns and lay the two halves up together, and in this manner they made me a very light and sound line; though it must not be supposed that it was finished at once; for I needed over half a mile of it, and thus it was later finished than the bow itself.

Having now gotten all things in train, I set me down to work upon one of the arrows; for I was anxious to see what sort of a fist I should make of them, knowing how much would depend upon the balance and truth of the missile. In the end, I made a very fair one, feathering it with its own leaves, and trueing and smoothing it with my knife; after which I inserted a small bolt in the forrard end, to act as a head, and, as I conceived, give it balance; though whether I was right in this latter, I am unable to say. Yet, before I had finished my arrow, the bo'sun had made the groove, and called me over to him, that I might admire it, the which I did; for it was done with a wonderful neatness.

Now I have been so busy with my description of how we made the great bow, that I have omitted to tell of the flight of time, and how we had eaten our dinner this long while since, and how that the people in the hulk had waved to us, and we had returned their signals, and then written upon a length of the canvas the one word, "WAIT." And, besides all this, some had gathered our fuel for the coming night.

And so, presently, the evening came upon us; but we ceased not to work; for the bo'sun bade the men to light a second great fire, beside our former one, and by the light of this we worked another long spell; though it seemed short enough, by reason of the interest of the work. Yet, at last, the bo'sun bade us to stop and make supper, which we did, and after that, he set the watches, and the rest of us turned in; for we were very weary.

In spite of my previous weariness, when the man whom I relieved called me to take my watch, I felt very fresh and wide awake, and spent a great part of the time, as on the preceding night, in studying over my plans for completing the great bow, and it was then that I decided finally in what manner I would secure the bows athwart the end of the stock; for until then I had been in some little doubt, being divided between several methods. Now, however, I concluded to make twelve grooves across the sawn end of the stock, and fit the middles of the bows into these, one above the other, as I have already mentioned; and then to lash them at each side to bolts driven into the sides of the stock. And with this idea I was very well pleased; for it promised to make them secure, and this without any great amount of work.

Now, though I spent much of my watch in thinking over the details of my prodigious weapon, yet it must not be supposed that I neglected to perform my duty as watchman; for I walked continually about the top of the hill, keeping my cut-and-thrust ready for any sudden emergency. Yet my time passed off quietly enough; though it is true that I witnessed one thing which brought me a short spell of disquiet thought. It was in this wise:— I had come to that part of the hill-top which overhung the valley, and it came to me, abruptly, to go near to the edge and look over. Thus, the moon being very bright, and the desolation of the valley reasonably clear to the eye, it appeared to me, as I looked, that I saw a movement among certain of the fungi which had not burnt, but stood up shrivelled and blackened in the valley. Yet by no means could I be sure that it was not a sudden fancy, born of the eeriness of that desolate-looking vale; the more so as I was like to be deceived because of the uncertainty which the light of the moon gives. Yet, to prove my doubts, I went back until I had found a piece of rock easy to throw, and this, taking a short run, I cast into the valley, aiming at the spot where it had seemed to me that there had been a movement. Immediately upon this, I caught a glimpse of some moving thing, and then, more to my right, something else stirred, and at this, I looked towards it; but could discover nothing. Then, looking back at the clump at which I had aimed my missile, I saw that the slime-covered pool, which lay near, was all a-quiver, or so it seemed. Yet the next instant I was just as full of doubt; for, even as I watched it, I perceived that it was quite still. And after that, for some time, I kept a very strict gaze into the valley; yet could nowhere discover aught to prove my suspicions, and, at last, I ceased from watching it; for I feared to grow fanciful, and so wandered to that part of the hill which overlooked the weed.

Presently, when I had been relieved, I returned to sleep, and so till the morning. Then, when we had made each of us a hasty breakfast—for all were grown mightily keen to see the great bow completed—we set-to upon it, each at our appointed task. Thus, the bo'sun and I made it our work to make the twelve grooves athwart the flat end of the stock, into which I proposed to fit and lash the bows, and this we accomplished by means of the iron futtock-shroud, which we heated in its middle part, and then, each taking an end (protecting our hands with canvas), we went one on each side and applied the iron until at length we had the grooves burnt out very nicely and accurately. This work occupied us all the morning; for the grooves had to be deeply burnt; and in the meantime the men had completed near enough sennit for the stringing of the bows; yet those who were at work on the line which the arrow was to carry, had scarce made more than half, so that I called off one man from the sennit to turn-to, and give them a hand with the making of the line.

When dinner was ended, the bo'sun and I set-to about fitting the bows into their places, which we did, and lashed them to twenty-four bolts, twelve a side, driven into the timber of the stock, about twelve inches in from the end. After this, we bent and strung the bows, taking very great care to have each bent exactly as the one below it; for we started at the bottom. And so, before sunset, we had that part of our work ended.

Now, because the two fires which we had lit on the previous night had exhausted our fuel, the bo'sun deemed it prudent to cease work, and go down all of us to bring up a fresh supply of the dry seaweed and some bundles of the reeds. This we did, making an end of our journeyings just as the dusk came over the island. Then, having made a second fire, as on the preceding night, we had first our supper, and after that another spell of work, all the men turning to upon the line which the arrow was to carry, whilst the bo'sun and I set-to, each of us, upon the making of a fresh arrow; for I had realised that we should have to make one or two flights before we could hope to find our range and make true our aim.

Later, maybe about nine of the night, the bo'sun bade us all to put away our work, and then he set the watches, after which the rest of us went into the tent to sleep; for the strength of the wind made the shelter a very pleasant thing.

That night, when it came my turn to watch, I minded me to take a look into the valley; but though I watched at intervals through the half of an hour, I saw nothing to lead me to imagine that I had indeed seen aught on the previous night, and so I felt more confident in my mind that we should be troubled no further by the devil-things which had destroyed poor Job. Yet I must record one thing which I saw during my watch; though this was from the edge of the hill-top which overlooked the weed-continent, and was not in the valley, but in the stretch of clear water which lay between the island and the weed. As I saw it, it seemed to me that a number of great fish were swimming across from the island, diagonally towards the great continent of weed: they were swimming in one wake, and keeping a very regular line; but not breaking the water after the manner of porpoises or black fish. Yet, though I have mentioned this, it must not be supposed that I saw any very strange thing in such a sight, and indeed, I thought nothing more of it than to wonder what sort of fish they might be; for, as I saw them indistinctly in the moonlight, they made a queer appearance, seeming each of them to be possessed of two tails, and further, I could have thought I perceived a flicker as of tentacles just beneath the surface; but of this I was by no means sure.

Upon the following morning, having hurried our breakfast, each of us set-to again upon our tasks; for we were in hopes to have the great bow at work before dinner. Soon, the bo'sun had finished his arrow, and mine was completed very shortly after, so that there lacked nothing now to the completion of our work, save the finishing of the line, and the getting of the bow into position. This latter, assisted by the men, we proceeded now to effect, making a level bed of rocks near the edge of the hill which overlooked the weed. Upon this we placed the great bow, and then, having sent the men back to their work at the line, we proceeded to the aiming of the huge weapon. Now, when we had gotten the instrument pointed, as we conceived, straight over the hulk, the which we accomplished by squinting along the groove which the bo'sun had burnt down the centre of the stock, we turned-to upon the arranging of the notch and trigger, the notch being to hold the strings when the weapon was set, and the trigger—a board bolted on loosely at the side just below the notch—to push them upwards out of this place when we desired to discharge the bow. This part of the work took up no great portion of our time, and soon we had all ready for our first flight. Then we commenced to set the bows, bending the bottom one first, and then those above in turn, until all were set; and, after that, we laid the arrow very carefully in the groove. Then I took two pieces of spun yarn and frapped the strings together at each end of the notch, and by this means I was assured that all the strings would act in unison when striking the butt of the arrow. And so we had all things ready for the discharge; whereupon, I placed my foot upon the trigger, and, bidding the bo'sun watch carefully the flight of the arrow, pushed downwards. The next instant, with a mighty twang, and a quiver that made the great stock stir on its bed of rocks, the bow sprang to its lesser tension, hurling the arrow outwards and upwards in a vast arc. Now, it may be conceived with what mortal interest we watched its flight, and so in a minute discovered that we had aimed too much to the right, for the arrow struck the weed ahead of the hulk—but *beyond* it. At that, I was filled near to bursting with pride and joy, and the men who had come forward to witness the trial, shouted to acclaim my success, whilst the bo'sun clapt me twice upon the shoulder to signify his regard, and shouted as loud as any.

And now it seemed to me that we had but to get the true aim, and the rescue of those in the hulk would be but a matter of another day or two; for, having once gotten a line to the hulk, we should haul across a thin rope by its means, and with this a thicker one; after which we should set this up so taut as possible, and then bring the people in the hulk to the island by means of a seat and block which we should haul to and fro along the supporting line.

Now, having realised that the bow would indeed carry so far as the wreck, we made haste to try our second arrow, and at the same time we bade the men go back to their work upon the line; for we should have need of it in a very little while. Presently, having pointed the bow more to the left, I took the frappings off the strings, so that we could bend the bows singly, and after that we set the great weapon again. Then, seeing that the arrow was straight in the groove, I replaced the frappings, and immediately discharged it. This time, to my very great pleasure and pride, the arrow went with a wonderful straightness towards the ship, and, clearing the superstructure, passed out of our sight as it fell behind it. At this, I was all impatience to try to get the line to the hulk before we made our dinner; but the men had not yet laid-up sufficient; there being then only four hundred and fifty fathoms (which the bo'sun measured off by stretching it along his arms and across his chest). This being so, we went to dinner, and made very great haste through it; and, after that, every one of us worked at the line, and so in about an hour we had sufficient; for I had estimated that it would not be wise to make the attempt with a less length than five hundred fathoms.

Having now completed a sufficiency of the line, the bo'sun set one of the men to flake it down very carefully upon the rock beside the bow, whilst he himself tested it at all such parts as he thought in any way doubtful, and so, presently, all was ready. Then I bent it on to the arrow, and, having set the bow whilst the men were flaking down the line, I was prepared immediately to discharge the weapon.

Now, all the morning, a man upon the hulk had observed us through a spy-glass, from a position that brought his head just above the edge of the superstructure, and, being aware of our intentions—having watched the previous flights—he understood the bo'sun, when he beckoned to him, that we had made ready for a third shot, and so, with an answering wave of his spy-glass, he disappeared from our sight. At that, having first turned to see that all were clear of the line, I pressed down the trigger, my heart beating very fast and thick, and so in a moment the arrow was sped. But now, doubtless because of the weight of the line, it made nowhere near so good a flight as on the previous occasion, the arrow striking the weed some two hundred yards short of the hulk, and at this, I could near have wept with vexation and disappointment.

Immediately upon the failure of my shot, the bo'sun called to the men to haul in the line very carefully, so that it should not be parted through the arrow catching in the weed; then he came over to me, and proposed that we should set-to at once to make a heavier arrow, suggesting that it had been lack of weight in the missile which had caused it to fall short. At that, I felt once more hopeful, and turned-to at once to prepare a new arrow; the bo'sun doing likewise; though in his case he intended to make a lighter one than that which had failed; for, as he put it, though the heavier one fell short, yet might the lighter succeed, and if neither, then we could only suppose that the bow lacked power to carry the line, and in that case, we should have to try some other method.

Now, in about two hours, I had made my arrow, the bo'sun having finished his a little earlier, and so (the men having hauled in all the line and flaked it down ready) we prepared to make another attempt to cast it over the hulk. Yet, a second time we failed, and by so much that it seemed hopeless to think of success; but, for all that it appeared useless, the bo'sun insisted on making a last try with the light arrow, and, presently, when we had gotten the line ready again, we loosed upon the wreck; but in this case so lamentable was our failure, that I cried out to the bo'sun to set the useless thing upon the fire and burn it; for I was sorely irked by its failure, and could scarce abide to speak civilly of it.

Now the bo'sun, perceiving how I felt, sung out that we would cease troubling about the hulk for the present, and go down all of us to gather reeds and weed for the fire; for it was drawing nigh to evening.

And this we did, though all in a disconsolate condition of mind; for we had seemed so near to success, and now it appeared to be further than ever from us. And so, in a while, having brought up a sufficiency of fuel, the bo'sun sent two of the men down to one of the ledges which overhung the sea, and bade them see whether they could not secure a fish for our supper. Then, taking our places about the fire, we fell-to upon a discussion as to how we should come at the people in the hulk.

Now, for a while there came no suggestion worthy of notice, until at last there occurred to me a notable idea, and I called out suddenly that we should make a small fire balloon, and float off the line to them by such means. At that, the men about the fire were silent a moment; for the idea was new to them, and moreover they needed to comprehend just what I meant. Then, when they had come fully at it, the one who had proposed that they should make spears of their knives, cried out to know why a kite would not do, and at that I was confounded, in that so simple an expedient had not occurred to any before; for, surely, it would be but a little matter to float a line to them by means of a kite, and, further, such a thing would take no great making.

And so, after a space of talk, it was decided that upon the morrow we should build some sort of kite, and with it fly a line over the hulk, the which should be a task of no great difficulty with so good a breeze as we had continually with us.

And, presently, having made our supper off a very fine fish, which the two fishermen had caught whilst we talked, the bo'sun set the watches, and the rest turned-in.

XIII
The Weed Men

NOW, ON THAT NIGHT, when I came to my watch, I discovered that there was no moon, and, save for such light as the fire threw, the hill-top was in darkness; yet this was no great matter to trouble me; for we had been unmolested since the burning of the fungi in the valley, and thus I had lost much of the haunting fear which had beset me upon the death of Job. Yet, though I was not so much afraid as I had been, I took all precautions that suggested themselves to me, and built up the fire to a goodly height, after which I took my cut-and-thrust, and made the round of the camping place. At the edges of the cliffs which protected us on three sides, I made some pause, staring down into the darkness, and listening; though this latter was of but small use because of the strength of the wind which roared continually in my ears. Yet though I neither saw nor heard anything, I was presently possessed of a strange uneasiness, which made me return twice or thrice to the edge of the cliffs; but always without seeing or hearing anything to justify my superstitions. And so, presently, being determined to give way to no fancifulness, I avoided the boundary of cliffs, and kept more to that part which commanded the slope, up and down which we made our journeys to and from the island below.

Then, it would be near half way through my time of watching, there came to me out of the immensity of weed that lay to leeward, a far distant sound that grew upon my ear, rising and rising into a fearsome screaming and shrieking, and then dying away into the distance in queer sobs, and so at last to a note below that of the wind's. At this, as might be supposed, I was somewhat shaken in myself to hear so dread a noise coming out of all that desolation, and then, suddenly, the thought came to me that the screaming was from the ship to leeward of us, and I ran immediately to the edge of the cliff overlooking the weed, and stared into the darkness; but now I perceived, by a light which burned in the hulk, that the screaming had come from some place a great distance to the right of her, and more, as my sense assured me, it could by no means have been possible for those in her to have sent their voices to me against such a breeze as blew at that time.

And so, for a space, I stood nervously pondering, and peering away into the blackness of the night; thus, in a little, I perceived a dull glow upon the horizon, and, presently, there rose into view the upper edge of the moon, and a very welcome sight it was to me; for I had been upon the point of calling the bo'sun to inform him regarding the sound which I had heard; but I had hesitated, being afraid to seem foolish if nothing should befall. Then, even as I stood watching the moon rise into view, there came again to me the beginning of that screaming, somewhat like to the sound of a woman sobbing with a giant's voice, and it grew and strengthened until it pierced through the roar of the wind with an amazing clearness, and then slowly, and seeming to echo and echo, it sank away into the distance, and there was again in my ears no sound beyond that of the wind.

At this, having looked fixedly in the direction from which the sound had proceeded, I ran straightway to the tent and roused the bo'sun; for I had no knowledge of what the noise might portend, and this second cry had shaken from me all my bashfulness. Now the bo'sun was upon his feet almost before I had made an end of shaking him, and catching up his great cutlass which he kept always by his side, he followed me swiftly out on to the hill-top. Here, I explained to him that I had heard a very fearsome sound which had appeared to proceed out of the vastness of the weed-continent, and that, upon a repetition of the noise, I had decided to call him; for I knew not but that it might signal to us of some coming danger. At that, the bo'sun commended me; though chiding me in that I had hesitated to call him at the first occurrence of the crying, and then, following me to the edge of the leeward cliff, he stood there with me, waiting and listening, perchance there might come again a recurrence of the noise.

For perhaps something over an hour we stood there very silent and listening; but there came to us no sound beyond the continuous noise of the wind, and so, by that time, having grown somewhat impatient of waiting, and the moon being well risen, the bo'sun beckoned to me to make the round of the camp with him. Now, just as I turned away, chancing to look downward at the clear water directly below, I was amazed to see that an innumerable multitude of great fish, like unto those which I had seen on the previous night, were swimming from the weed-continent towards the island. At that, I stepped nearer the edge; for they came so directly towards the island that I expected to see them close inshore; yet I could not perceive one; for they seemed all of them to vanish at a point some thirty yards distant from the beach, and at that, being amazed both by the numbers of the fish and their strangeness, and the way in which they came on continually, yet never reached the shore, I called to the bo'sun to come and see; for he had gone on a few paces. Upon hearing my call, he came running back; whereat I pointed into the sea below. At that, he stooped forward and peered very intently, and I with him; yet neither one of us could discover the meaning of so curious an exhibition, and so for a while we watched, the bo'sun being quite so much interested as I.

Presently, however, he turned away, saying that we did foolishly to stand here peering at every curious sight, when we should be looking to the welfare of the camp, and so we began to go the round of the hill-top. Now, whilst we had been watching and listening, we had suffered the fire to die down to a most unwise lowness, and consequently, though the moon was rising, there was by no means the same brightness that should have made the camp light. On perceiving this, I went forward to throw some fuel on to the fire, and then, even as I moved, it seemed to me that I saw something stir in the shadow of the tent. And at that, I ran towards the place, uttering a shout, and waving my cut-and-thrust; yet I found nothing, and so, feeling somewhat foolish, I turned to make up the fire, as had been my intention, and whilst I was thus busied, the bo'sun came running over to me to know what I had seen, and in the same instant there ran three of the men out of the tent, all of them waked by my sudden cry. But I had naught to tell them, save that my fancy had played me a trick, and had shown me something where my eyes could find nothing, and at that, two of the men went back to resume their sleep; but the third, the big fellow to whom the bo'sun had given the other cutlass, came with us, bringing his weapon; and, though he kept silent, it seemed to me that he had gathered something of our uneasiness; and for my part I was not sorry to have his company.

Presently, we came to that portion of the hill which overhung the valley, and I went to the edge of the cliff, intending to peer over; for the valley had a very unholy fascination for me. Yet, no sooner had I glanced down than I started, and ran back to the bo'sun and plucked him by the sleeve, and at that, perceiving my agitation, he came with me in silence to see what matter had caused me so much quiet excitement. Now, when he looked over, he also was astounded, and drew back instantly; then, using great caution, he bent forward once more, and stared down, and, at that, the big seaman came up behind, walking upon his toes, and stooped to see what manner of thing we had discovered. Thus we each of us stared down upon a most unearthly sight; for the valley all beneath us was a-swarm with moving creatures, white and unwholesome in the moonlight, and their movements were somewhat like the movements of monstrous slugs, though the things themselves had no resemblance to such in their contours; but minded me of naked humans, very fleshy and crawling upon their stomachs; yet their movements lacked not a surprising rapidity. And now, looking a little over the bo'sun's shoulder, I discovered that these hideous things were coming up out from the pit-like pool in the bottom of the valley, and, suddenly, I was minded of the multitudes of strange fish which we had seen swimming towards the island; but which had all disappeared before reaching the shore, and I had no doubt but that they entered the pit through some natural passage known to them beneath the water. And now I was made to understand my thought of the previous night, that I had seen the flicker of tentacles; for these things below us had each two short and stumpy arms; but the ends appeared divided into hateful and wriggling masses of small tentacles, which slid hither and thither as the creatures moved about the bottom of the valley, and at their hinder ends, where they should have grown feet, there seemed other flickering bunches; but it must not be supposed that we saw these things clearly.

Now it is scarcely possible to convey the extraordinary disgust which the sight of these human slugs bred in me; nor, could I, do I think I would; for were I successful, then would others be like to retch even as I did, the spasm coming on without premonition, and born of very horror. And then, suddenly, even as I stared, sick with loathing and apprehension, there came into view, not a fathom below my feet, a face like to the face which had peered up into my own on that night, as we drifted beside the weed-continent. At that, I could have screamed, had I been in less terror; for the great eyes, so big as crown pieces, the bill like to an inverted parrot's, and the slug-like undulating of its white and slimy body, bred in me the dumbness of one mortally stricken. And, even as I stayed there, my helpless body bent and rigid, the bo'sun spat a mighty curse into my ear, and, leaning forward, smote at the thing with his cutlass; for in the instant that I had seen it, it had advanced upward by so much as a yard. Now, at this action of the bo'sun's, I came suddenly into possession of myself, and thrust downward with so much vigour that I was like to have followed the brute's carcass; for I overbalanced, and danced giddily for a moment upon the edge of eternity; and then the bo'sun had me by the waistband, and I was back in safety; but in that instant through which I had struggled for my balance, I had discovered that the face of the cliff was near hid with the number of the things which were making up to us, and I turned to the bo'sun, crying out to him that there were thousands of them swarming up to us. Yet, he was gone already from me, running towards the fire, and shouting to the men in the tent to haste to our help for their very lives, and then he came racing back with a great armful of the weed, and after him came the big seaman, carrying a burning tuft from the camp fire, and so in a few moments we had a blaze, and the men were bringing more weed; for we had a very good stock upon the hill-top; for which the Almighty be thanked.

Now, scarce had we lit one fire, when the bo'sun cried out to the big seaman to make another, further along the edge of the cliff, and, in the same instant, I shouted, and ran over to that part of the hill which lay towards the open sea; for I had seen a number of moving things about the edge of the seaward cliff. Now here there was a deal of shadow; for there were scattered certain large masses of rock about this part of the hill, and these held off both the light of the moon, and that from the fires. Here, I came abruptly upon three great shapes moving with stealthiness towards the camp, and, behind these, I saw dimly that there were others. Then, with a loud cry for help, I made at the three, and, as I charged, they rose up on end at me, and I found that they overtopped me, and their vile tentacles were reached out at me. Then I was smiting, and gasping, sick with a sudden stench, the stench of the creatures which I had come already to know. And then something clutched at me, something slimy and vile, and great mandibles champed in my face; but I stabbed upward, and the thing fell from me, leaving me dazed and sick, and smiting weakly. Then there came a rush of feet behind, and a sudden blaze, and the bo'sun crying out encouragement, and, directly, he and the big seaman thrust themselves in front of me, hurling from them great masses of burning weed, which they had borne, each of them, up a long reed. And immediately the things were gone, slithering hastily down over the cliff edge.

And so, presently, I was more my own man, and made to wipe from my throat the slime left by the clutch of the monster: and afterwards I ran from fire to fire with weed, feeding them, and so a space passed, during which we had safety; for by that time we had fires all about the top of the hill, and the monsters were in mortal dread of fire, else had we been dead, all of us, that night.

Now, a while before the dawn, we discovered, for the second time since we had been upon the island, that our fuel could not last us the night at the rate at which we were compelled to burn it, and so the bo'sun told the men to let out every second fire, and thus we staved off for a while the time when we should have to face a spell of darkness, and the things which, at present, the fires held off from us. And so at last, we came to the end of the weed and the reeds, and the bo'sun called out to us to watch the cliff edges very carefully, and smite on the instant that any thing showed; but that, should he call, all were to gather by the central fire for a last stand. And, after that, he blasted the moon which had passed behind a great bank of cloud. And thus matters were, and the gloom deepened as the fires sank lower and lower. Then I heard a man curse, on that part of the hill which lay towards the weed-continent, his cry coming up to me against the wind, and the bo'sun shouted to us to all have a care, and directly afterwards I smote at something that rose silently above the edge of the cliff opposite to where I watched.

Perhaps a minute passed, and then there came shouts from all parts of the hill-top, and I knew that the weed men were upon us, and in the same instant there came two above the edge near me, rising with a ghostly quietness, yet moving lithely. Now the first, I pierced somewhere in the throat, and it fell backward; but the second, though I thrust it through, caught my blade with a bunch of its tentacles, and was like to have snatched it from me; but that I kicked it in the face, and at that, being, I believe, more astonished than hurt, it loosed my sword, and immediately fell away out of sight. Now this had taken, in all, no more than some ten seconds; yet already I perceived so many as four others coming into view a little to my right, and at that it seemed to me that our deaths must be very near, for I knew not how we were to cope with the creatures, coming as they were so boldly and with such rapidity. Yet, I hesitated not, but ran at them, and now I thrust not; but cut at their faces, and found this to be very effectual; for in this wise disposed I of three in as many strokes; but the fourth had come right over the cliff edge, and rose up at me upon its hinder parts, as had done those others when the bo'sun had succoured me. At that, I gave way, having a very lively dread; but, hearing all about me the cries of conflict, and knowing that I could expect no help, I made at the brute: then as it stooped and reached out one of its bunches of tentacles, I sprang back, and slashed at them, and immediately I followed this up by a thrust in the stomach, and at that it collapsed into a writhing white ball, that rolled this way and that, and so, in its agony, coming to the edge of the cliff, it fell over, and I was left, sick and near helpless with the hateful stench of the brutes.

Now by this time all the fires about the edges of the hill were sunken into dull glowing mounds of embers; though that which burnt near to the entrance of the tent was still of a good brightness; yet this helped us but little, for we fought too far beyond the immediate circle of its beams to have benefit of it. And still the moon, at which now I threw a despairing glance, was no more than a ghostly shape behind the great bank of cloud which was passing over it. Then, even as I looked upward, glancing as it might be over my left shoulder, I saw, with a sudden horror, that something had come anigh me, and upon the instant, I caught the reek of the thing, and leapt fearfully to one side, turning as I sprang. Thus was I saved in the very moment of my destruction; for the creature's tentacles smeared the back of my neck as I leapt, and then I had smitten, once and again, and conquered.

Immediately after this, I discovered something to be crossing the dark space that lay between the dull mound of the nearest fire, and that which lay further along the hill-top, and so, wasting no moment of time, I ran towards the thing, and cut it twice across the head before ever it could get upon its hind parts, in which position I had learned greatly to dread them. Yet, no sooner had I slain this one, than there came a rush of maybe a dozen upon me; these having climbed silently over the cliff edge in the meanwhile. At this, I dodged, and ran madly towards the glowing mound of the nearest fire, the brutes following me almost so quick as I could run; but I came to the fire the first, and then, a sudden thought coming to me, I thrust the point of my cut-and-thrust among the embers and switched a great shower of them at the creatures, and at that I had a momentary clear vision of many white, hideous faces stretched out towards me, and brown, champing mandibles which had the upper beak shutting into the lower; and the clumped, wriggling tentacles were all a-flutter. Then the gloom came again; but immediately, I switched another and yet another shower of the burning embers towards them, and so, directly, I saw them give back, and then they were gone. At this, all about the edges of the hill-top, I saw the fires being scattered in like manner; for others had adopted this device to help them in their sore straits.

For a little after this, I had a short breathing space, the brutes seeming to have taken fright; yet I was full of trembling, and I glanced hither and thither, not knowing when some one or more of them would come upon me. And ever I glanced towards the moon, and prayed the Almighty that the clouds would pass quickly, else should we be all dead men; and then, as I prayed, there rose a sudden very terrible scream from one of the men, and in the same moment there came something over the edge of the cliff fronting me; but I cleft it or ever it could rise higher, and in my ears there echoed still the sudden scream which had come from that part of the hill which lay to the left of me: yet I dared not to leave my station; for to have done so would have been to have risked all, and so I stayed, tortured by the strain of ignorance, and my own terror.

Again, I had a little spell in which I was free from molestation; nothing coming into sight so far as I could see to right or left of me; though others were less fortunate, as the curses and sounds of blows told to me, and then, abruptly, there came another cry of pain, and I looked up again to the moon, and prayed aloud that it might come out to show some light before we were all destroyed; but it remained hid. Then a sudden thought came into my brain, and I shouted at the top of my voice to the bo'sun to set the great cross-bow upon the central fire; for thus we should have a big blaze—the wood being very nice and dry. Twice I shouted to him, saying:— "Burn the bow! Burn the bow!" And immediately he replied, shouting to all the men to run to him and carry it to the fire; and this we did and bore it to the centre fire, and then ran back with all speed to our places. Thus in a minute we had some light, and the light grew as the fire took hold of the great log, the wind fanning it to a blaze. And so I faced outwards, looking to see if any vile face showed above the edge before me, or to my right or left. Yet, I saw nothing, save, as it seemed to me, once a fluttering tentacle came up, a little to my right; but nothing else for a space.

Perhaps it was near five minutes later, that there came another attack, and, in this, I came near to losing my life, through my folly in venturing too near to the edge of the cliff; for, suddenly, there shot up out from the darkness below, a clump of tentacles, and caught me about the left ankle, and immediately I was pulled to a sitting posture, so that both my feet were over the edge of the precipice, and it was only by the mercy of God that I had not plunged head foremost into the valley. Yet, as it was, I suffered a mighty peril; for the brute that had my foot, put a vast strain upon it, trying to pull me down; but I resisted, using my hands and seat to sustain me, and so, discovering that it could not compass my end in this wise, it slacked somewhat of the stress, and bit at my boot, shearing through the hard leather, and nigh destroying my small toe; but now, being no longer compelled to use both hands to retain my position, I slashed down with great fury, being maddened by the pain and the mortal fear which the creature had put upon me; yet I was not immediately free of the brute; for it caught my sword blade; but I snatched it away before it could take a proper hold, mayhaps cutting its feelers somewhat thereby; though of this I cannot be sure, for they seemed not to grip around a thing, but to *suck* to it; then, in a moment, by a lucky blow, I maimed it, so that it loosed me, and I was able to get back into some condition of security.

And from this onwards, we were free from molestation; though we had no knowledge but that the quietness of the weed men did but portend a fresh attack, and so, at last, it came to the dawn; and in all this time the moon came not to our help, being quite hid by the clouds which now covered the whole arc of the sky, making the dawn of a very desolate aspect.

And so soon as there was a sufficiency of light, we examined the valley; but there were nowhere any of the weed men, no! nor even any of their dead for it seemed that they had carried off all such and their wounded, and so we had no opportunity to make an examination of the monsters by daylight. Yet, though we could not come upon their dead, all about the edges of the cliffs was blood and slime, and from the latter there came ever the hideous stench which marked the brutes; but from this we suffered little, the wind carrying it far away to leeward, and filling our lungs with sweet and wholesome air.

Presently, seeing that the danger was past, the bo'sun called us to the centre fire, on which burnt still the remnants of the great bow, and here we discovered for the first time that one of the men was gone from us. At that, we made search about the hill-top, and afterwards in the valley and about the island; but found him not.

XIV

In Communication

NOW OF THE SEARCH which we made through the valley for the body of Tompkins, that being the name of the lost man, I have some doleful memories. But first, before we left the camp, the bo'sun gave us all a very sound tot of the rum, and also a biscuit apiece, and thereafter we hasted down, each man holding his weapon readily. Presently, when we were come to the beach which ended the valley upon the seaward side, the bo'sun led us along to the bottom of the hill, where the precipices came down into the softer stuff which covered the valley, and here we made a careful search, perchance he had fallen over, and lay dead or wounded near to our hands. But it was not so, and after that, we went down to the mouth of the great pit, and here we discovered the mud all about it to be covered with multitudes of tracks, and in addition to these and the slime, we found many traces of blood; but nowhere any signs of Tompkins. And so, having searched all the valley, we came out upon the weed which strewed the shore nearer to the great weed-continent; but discovered nothing until we had made up towards the foot of the hill, where it came down sheer into the sea. Here, I climbed on to a ledge—the same from which the men had caught their fish— thinking that, if Tompkins had fallen from above, he might lie in the water at the foot of the cliff, which was here, maybe, some ten to twenty feet deep; but, for a little space, I saw nothing. Then, suddenly, I discovered that there was something white, down in the sea away to my left, and, at that, I climbed farther out along the ledge.

In this wise I perceived that the thing which had attracted my notice was the dead body of one of the weed men. I could see it but dimly, catching odd glimpses of it as the surface of the water smoothed at whiles. It appeared to me to be lying curled up, and somewhat upon its right side, and in proof that it was dead, I saw a mighty wound that had come near to shearing away the head; and so, after a further glance, I came in, and told what I had seen. At that, being convinced by this time that Tompkins was indeed done to death, we ceased our search; but first, before we left the spot, the bo'sun climbed out to get a sight of the dead weed man and after him the rest of the men, for they were greatly curious to see clearly what manner of creature it was that had attacked us in the night. Presently, having seen so much of the brute as the water would allow, they came in again to the beach, and afterwards were returned to the opposite side of the island, and so, being there, we crossed over to the boat, to see whether it had been harmed; but found it to be untouched. Yet, that the creatures had been all about it, we could perceive by the marks of slime upon the sand, and also by the strange trail which they had left in the soft surface. Then one of the men called out that there had been something at Job's grave, which, as will be remembered, had been made in the sand some little distance from the place of our first camp. At that, we looked all of us, and it was easy to see that it had been disturbed, and so we ran hastily to it, knowing not what to fear; thus we found it to be empty; for the monsters had digged down to the poor lad's body, and of it we could discover no sign. Upon this, we came to a greater horror of the weed men than ever; for we knew them now to be foul ghouls who could not let even the dead body rest in the grave.

Now after this, the bo'sun led us all back to the hill-top, and there he looked to our hurts; for one man had lost two fingers in the night's fray; another had been bitten savagely in the left arm; whilst a third had all the skin of his face raised in wheals where one of the brutes had fixed its tentacles. And all of these had received but scant attention, because of the stress of the fight, and, after that, through the discovery that Tompkins was missing. Now, however, the bo'sun set-to upon them, washing and binding them up, and for dressings he made use of some of the oakum which we had with us, binding this on with strips torn from the roll of spare duck, which had been in the locker of the boat.

For my part, seizing this chance to make some examination of my wounded toe, the which, indeed, was causing me to limp, I found that I had endured less harm than seemed to me; for the bone of the toe was untouched, though showing bare; yet when it was cleansed, I had not overmuch pain with it; though I could not suffer to have the boot on, and so bound some canvas about my foot, until such time as it should be healed.

Presently, when our wounds were all attended to, the which had taken time, for there was none of us altogether untouched, the bo'sun bade the man whose fingers were damaged, to lie down in the tent, and the same order he gave also to him that was bitten in the arm. Then, the rest of us he directed to go down with him and carry up fuel; for that the night had shown him how our very lives depended upon a sufficiency of this; and so all that morning we brought fuel to the hill-top, both weed and reeds, resting not until midday, when he gave us a further tot of the rum, and after that set one of the men upon the dinner. Then he bade the man, Jessop by name, who had proposed to fly a kite over the vessel in the weed, to say whether he had any craft in the making of such a matter. At that, the fellow laughed, and told the bo'sun that he would make him a kite that would fly very steadily and strongly, and this without the aid of a tail. And so the bo'sun bade him set-to without delay, for that we should do well to deliver the people in the hulk, and afterwards make all haste from the island, which was no better than a nesting place of ghouls.

Now hearing the man say that his kite would fly without a tail, I was mightily curious to see what manner of thing he would make; for I had never seen the like, nor heard that such was possible. Yet he spoke of no more than he could accomplish; for he took two of the reeds and cut them to a length of about six feet; then he bound them together in the middle so that they formed a Saint Andrew's cross, and after that he made two more such crosses, and when these were completed, he took four reeds maybe a dozen feet long, and bade us stand them upright in the shape of a square, so that they formed the four corners, and after that he took one of the crosses, and laid it in the square so that its four ends touched the four uprights, and in this position he lashed it. Then he took the second cross and lashed it midway between the top and bottom of the uprights, and after that he lashed the third at the top, so that the three of them acted as spreaders to keep the four longer reeds in their places as though they were for the uprights of a little square tower. Now, when he had gotten so far as that, the bo'sun called out to us to make our dinners, and this we did, and afterwards had a short time in which to smoke, and whilst we were thus at our ease the sun came out, the which it had not done all the day, and at that we felt vastly brighter; for the day had been very gloomy with clouds until that time, and what with the loss of Tompkins, and our own fears and hurts, we had been exceeding doleful, but now, as I have said, we became more cheerful, and went very alertly to the finishing of the kite.

At this point it came suddenly to the bo'sun that we had made no provision of cord for the flying of the kite, and he called out to the man to know what strength the kite would require, at which Jessop answered him that maybe ten-yarn sennit would do, and this being so, the bo'sun led three of us down to the wrecked mast upon the further beach, and from this we stripped all that was left of the shrouds, and carried them to the top of the hill, and so, presently, having unlaid them, we set-to upon the sennit, using ten yarns; but plaiting two as one, by which means we progressed with more speed than if we had taken them singly.

Now, as we worked, I glanced occasionally towards Jessop, and saw that he stitched a band of the light duck around each end of the framework which he had made, and these bands I judged to be about four feet wide, in this wise leaving an open space between the two, so that now the thing looked something like to a Punchinello show, only that the opening was in the wrong place, and there was too much of it. After that he bent on a bridle to two of the uprights, making this of a piece of good hemp rope which he found in the tent, and then he called out to the bo'sun that the kite was finished. At that, the bo'sun went over to examine it, the which did all of us; for none of us had seen the like of such a thing, and, if I misdoubt not, few of us had much faith that it would fly; for it seemed so big and unwieldy. Now, I think that Jessop gathered something of our thoughts; for, calling to one of us to hold the kite, lest it should blow away, he went into the tent, and brought out the remainder of the hemp line, the same from which he had cut the bridle. This, he bent on to it, and, giving the end into our hands, bade us go back with it until all the slack was taken up, he, in the meanwhile, steadying the kite. Then, when we had gone back to the extent of the line, he shouted to us to take a very particular hold upon it, and then, stooping, caught the kite by the bottom, and threw it into the air, whereupon, to our amazement, having swooped somewhat to one side, it steadied and mounted upwards into the sky like a very bird.

Now at this, as I have made mention, we were astonished, for it appeared like a miracle to us to see so cumbrous a thing fly with so much grace and persistence, and further, we were mightily surprised at the manner in which it pulled upon the rope, tugging with such heartiness that we were like to have loosed it in our first astonishment, had it not been for the warning which Jessop called to us.

And now, being well assured of the properness of the kite, the bo'sun bade us to draw it in, the which we did only with difficulty, because of its bigness and the strength of the breeze. And when we had it back again upon the hill-top, Jessop moored it very securely to a great piece of rock, and, after that, having received our approbation, he turned-to with us upon the making of the sennit.

Presently, the evening drawing near, the bo'sun set us to the building of fires about the hill-top, and after that, having waved our goodnights to the people in the hulk, we made our suppers, and lay down to smoke, after which, we turned-to again at our plaiting of the sennit, the which we were in very great haste to have done. And so, later, the dark having come down upon the island, the bo'sun bade us take burning weed from the centre fire, and set light to the heaps of weed that we had stacked round the edges of the hill for that purpose, and so in a few minutes the whole of the hill-top was very light and cheerful, and afterwards, having put two of the men to keep watch and attend to the fires, he sent the rest of us back to our sennit making, keeping us at it until maybe about ten of the clock, after which he arranged that two men at a time should be on watch throughout the night, and then he bade the rest of us turn-in, so soon as he had looked to our various hurts.

Now, when it came to my turn to watch, I discovered that I had been chosen to accompany the big seaman, at which I was by no means displeased; for he was a most excellent fellow, and moreover a very lusty man to have near, should anything come upon one unawares. Yet, we were happy in that the night passed off without trouble of any sort, and so at last came the morning.

So soon as we had made our breakfast, the bo'sun took us all down to the carrying of fuel; for he saw very clearly that upon a good supply of this depended our immunity from attack. And so for the half of the morning we worked at the gathering of weed and reeds for our fires. Then, when we had obtained a sufficiency for the coming night, he set us all to work again upon the sennit, and so until dinner, after which we turned-to once more upon our plaiting. Yet it was plain that it would take several days to make a sufficient line for our purpose, and because of this, the bo'sun cast about in his mind for some way in which he could quicken its production. Presently, as a result of some little thought, he brought out from the tent the long piece of hemp rope with which we had moored the boat to the sea anchor, and proceeded to unlay it, until he had all three strands separate. Then he bent the three together, and so had a very rough line of maybe some hundred and eighty fathoms in length, yet, though so rough, he judged it strong enough, and thus we had this much the less sennit to make.

Now, presently, we made our dinner, and after that for the rest of the day we kept very steadily to our plaiting, and so, with the previous day's work, had near two hundred fathoms completed by the time that the bo'sun called us to cease and come to supper. Thus it will be seen that counting all, including the piece of hemp line from which the bridle had been made, we may be said to have had at this time about four hundred fathoms towards the length which we needed for our purpose, this having been reckoned at five hundred fathoms.

After supper, having lit all the fires, we continued to work at the plaiting, and so, until the bo'sun set the watches, after which we settled down for the night, first, however, letting the bo'sun see to our hurts. Now this night, like to the previous, brought us no trouble; and when the day came, we had first our breakfast, and then set-to upon our collecting of fuel, after which we spent the rest of the day at the sennit, having manufactured a sufficiency by the evening, the which the bo'sun celebrated by a very rousing tot of the rum. Then, having made our supper, we lit the fires, and had a very comfortable evening, after which, as on the preceding nights, having let the bo'sun attend our wounds, we settled for the night, and on this occasion the bo'sun let the man who had lost his fingers, and the one who had been bitten so badly in the arm, take their first turn at the watching since the night of the attack.

Now when the morning came we were all of us very eager to come to the flying of the kite; for it seemed possible to us that we might effect the rescue of the people in the hulk before the evening. And, at the thought of this, we experienced a very pleasurable sense of excitement; yet, before the bo'sun would let us touch the kite, he insisted that we should gather our usual supply of fuel, the which order, though full of wisdom, irked us exceedingly, because of our eagerness to set about the rescue. But at last this was accomplished, and we made to get the line ready, testing the knots, and seeing that it was all clear for running. Yet, before setting the kite off, the bo'sun took us down to the further beach to bring up the foot of the royal and t'gallant mast, which remained fast to the topmast, and when we had this upon the hill-top, he set its ends upon two rocks, after which he piled a heap of great pieces around them, leaving the middle part clear. Round this he passed the kite line a couple or three times, and then gave the end to Jessop to bend on to the bridle of the kite, and so he had all ready for paying out to the wreck.

And now, having nothing to do, we gathered round to watch, and, immediately, the bo'sun giving the signal, Jessop cast the kite into the air, and, the wind catching it, lifted it strongly and well, so that the bo'sun could scarce pay out fast enough. Now, before the kite had been let go, Jessop had bent to the forward end of it a great length of the spun yarn, so that those in the wreck could catch it as it trailed over them, and, being eager to witness whether they would secure it without trouble, we ran all of us to the edge of the hill to watch. Thus, within five minutes from the time of the loosing of the kite, we saw the people in the ship wave to us to cease veering, and immediately afterwards the kite came swiftly downwards, by which we knew that they had the tripping-line, and were hauling upon it, and at that we gave out a great cheer, and afterwards we sat about and smoked, waiting until they had read our instructions, which we had written upon the covering of the kite.

Presently, maybe the half of an hour afterwards, they signalled to us to haul upon our line, which we proceeded to do without delay, and so, after a great space, we had hauled in all of our rough line, and come upon the end of theirs, which proved to be a fine piece of three-inch hemp, new and very good; yet we could not conceive that this would stand the stress necessary to lift so great a length clear of the weed, as would be needful, or ever we could hope to bring the people of the ship over it in safety. And so we waited some little while, and, presently, they signalled again to us to haul, which we did, and found that they had bent on a much greater rope to the bight of the three-inch hemp, having merely intended the latter for a hauling-line by which to get the heavier rope across the weed to the island. Thus, after a weariful time of pulling, we got the end of the bigger rope up to the hill-top, and discovered it to be an extraordinarily sound rope of some four inches diameter, and smoothly laid of fine yarns round and very true and well spun, and with this we had every reason to be satisfied.

Now to the end of the big rope they had tied a letter, in a bag of oilskin, and in it they said some very warm and grateful things to us, after which they set out a short code of signals by which we should be able to understand one another on certain general matters, and at the end they asked if they should send us any provision ashore; for, as they explained, it would take some little while to get the rope set taut enough for our purpose, and the carrier fixed and in working order. Now, upon reading this letter, we called out to the bo'sun that he should ask them if they would send us some soft bread; the which he added thereto a request for lint and bandages and ointment for our hurts. And this he bade me write upon one of the great leaves from off the reeds, and at the end he told me to ask if they desired us to send them any fresh water. And all of this, I wrote with a sharpened splinter of reed, cutting the words into the surface of the leaf. Then, when I had made an end of writing, I gave the leaf to the bo'sun, and he enclosed it in the oilskin bag, after which he gave the signal for those in the hulk to haul on the smaller line, and this they did.

Presently, they signed to us to pull in again, the which we did, and so, when we had hauled in a great length of their line, we came to the little oilskin bag, in which we found lint and bandages and ointment, and a further letter, which set out that they were baking bread, and would send us some so soon as it was out from the oven.

Now, in addition to the matters for the healing of our wounds, and the letter, they had included a bundle of paper in loose sheets, some quills and an inkhorn, and at the end of their epistle, they begged very earnestly of us to send them some news of the outer world; for they had been shut up in that strange continent of weed for something over seven years. They told us then that there were twelve of them in the hulk, three of them being women, one of whom had been the Captain's wife; but he had died soon after the vessel became entangled in the weed, and along with him more than half of the ship's company, having been attacked by giant devil-fish, as they were attempting to free the vessel from the weed, and afterwards they who were left had built the superstructure as a protection against the devil-fish, and the *devil-men*, as they termed them; for, until it had been built, there had been no safety about the decks, neither day nor night.

To our question as to whether they were in need of water, the people in the ship replied that they had a sufficiency, and, further, that they were very well supplied with provisions; for the ship had sailed from London with a general cargo, among which there was a vast quantity of food in various shapes and forms. At this news we were greatly pleased, seeing that we need have no more anxiety regarding a lack of victuals, and so in the letter which I went into the tent to write, I put down that we were in no great plentitude of provisions, at which hint I guessed they would add somewhat to the bread when it should be ready. And after that I wrote down such chief events as my memory recalled as having occurred in the course of the past seven years, and then, a short account of our own adventures, up to that time, telling them of the attack which we had suffered from the weed men, and asking such questions as my curiosity and wonder prompted.

Now whilst I had been writing, sitting in the mouth of the tent, I had observed, from time to time, how that the bo'sun was busied with the men in passing the end of the big rope round a mighty boulder, which lay about ten fathoms in from the edge of the cliff which overlooked the hulk. This he did, parcelling the rope where the rock was in any way sharp, so as to protect it from being cut; for which purpose he made use of some of the canvas. And by the time that I had the letter completed, the rope was made very secure to the great piece of rock, and, further, they had put a large piece of chafing gear under that part of the rope where it took the edge of the cliff.

Now having, as I have said, completed the letter, I went out with it to the bo'sun; but, before placing it in the oilskin bag he bade me add a note at the bottom, to say that the big rope was all fast, and that they could heave on it so soon as it pleased them, and after that we dispatched the letter by means of the small line, the men in the hulk hauling it off to them so soon as they perceived our signals.

By this, it had come well on to the latter part of the afternoon, and the bo'sun called us to make some sort of a meal, leaving one man to watch the hulk, perchance they should signal to us. For we had missed our dinner in the excitement of the day's work, and were come now to feel the lack of it. Then, in the midst of it, the man upon the look-out cried out that they were signalling to us from the ship, and, at that, we ran all of us to see what they desired, and so, by the code which we had arranged between us, we found that they waited for us to haul upon the small line. This did we, and made out presently that we were hauling something across the weed, of a very fair bulk, at which we warmed to our work, guessing that it was the bread which they had promised us, and so it proved, and done up with great neatness in a long roll of tarpaulin, which had been wrapped around both the loaves and the rope, and lashed very securely at the ends, thus producing a taper shape convenient for passing over the weed without catching. Now, when we came to open this parcel, we discovered that my hint had taken very sound effect; for there were in the parcel, besides the loaves, a boiled ham, a Dutch cheese, two bottles of port well padded from breakage, and four pounds of tobacco in plugs. And at this coming of good things, we stood all of us upon the edge of the hill, and waved our thanks to those in the ship, they waving back in all good will, and after that we went back to our meal, at which we sampled the new victuals with very lusty appetites.

There was in the parcel, one other matter, a letter, most neatly indited, as had been the former epistles, in a feminine hand-writing, so that I guessed they had one of the women to be their scribe. This epistle answered some of my queries, and, in particular, I remember that it informed me as to the probable cause of the strange crying which preceded the attack by the weed men, saying that on each occasion when they in the ship had suffered their attacks, there had been always this same crying, being evidently a summoning call or signal to the attack, though how given, the writer had not discovered; for the weed *devils*—this being how they in the ship spoke always of them—made never a sound when attacking, not even when wounded to the death, and, indeed, I may say here, that we never learnt the way in which that lonesome sobbing was produced, nor, indeed, did they, or we, discover more than the merest tithe of the mysteries which that great continent of weed holds in its silence.

Another matter to which I had referred was the consistent blowing of the wind from one quarter, and this the writer told me happened for as much six months in the year, keeping up a very steady strength. A further thing there was which gave me much interest; it was that the ship had not been always where we had discovered her; for at one time they had been so far within the weed, that they could scarce discern the open sea upon the far horizon; but that at times the weed opened in great gulfs that went yawning through the continent for scores of miles, and in this way the shape and coasts of the weed were being constantly altered; these happenings being for the most part at the change of the wind.

And much more there was that they told us then and afterwards, how that they dried weed for their fuel, and how the rains, which fell with great heaviness at certain periods, supplied them with fresh water; though, at times, running short, they had learnt to distill sufficient for their needs until the next rains.

Now, near to the end of the epistle, there came some news of their present actions, and thus we learnt that they in the ship were busy at staying the stump of the mizzen-mast, this being the one to which they proposed to attach the big rope, taking it through a great iron-bound snatch-block, secured to the head of the stump, and then down to the mizzen-capstan, by which, and a strong tackle, they would be able to heave the line so taut as was needful.

Now, having finished our meal, the bo'sun took out the lint, bandages and ointment, which they had sent us from the hulk, and proceeded to dress our hurts, beginning with him who had lost his fingers, which, happily, were making a very healthy heal. And afterwards we went all of us to the edge of the cliff, and sent back the look-out to fill such crevices in his stomach as remained yet empty; for we had passed him already some sound hunks of the bread and ham and cheese, to eat whilst he kept watch, and so he had suffered no great harm.

It may have been near an hour after this, that the bo'sun pointed out to me that they in the ship had commenced to heave upon the great rope, and so I perceived, and stood watching it; for I knew that the bo'sun had some anxiety as to whether it would take-up sufficiently clear of the weed to allow those in the ship to be hauled along it, free from molestation by the great devil-fish.

Presently, as the evening began to draw on, the bo'sun bade us go and build our fires about the hill-top, and this we did, after which we returned to learn how the rope was lifting, and now we perceived that it had come clear of the weed, at which we felt mightily rejoiced, and waved encouragement, chance there might be any who watched us from the hulk. Yet, though the rope was up clear of the weed, the bight of it had to rise to a much greater height, or ever it would do for the purpose for which we intended it, and already it suffered a vast strain, as I discovered by placing my hand upon it; for, even to lift the slack of so great a length of line meant the stress of some tons. And later I saw that the bo'sun was growing anxious; for he went over to the rock around which he had made fast the rope, and examined the knots, and those places where he had parcelled it, and after that he walked to the place where it went over the edge of the cliff, and here he made a further scrutiny; but came back presently, seeming not dissatisfied.

Then, in a while, the darkness came down upon us, and we lighted our fires and prepared for the night, having the watches arranged as on the preceding nights.

XV
Aboard The Hulk

ꞢOW WHEN IT CAME to my watch, that which I took in company with the big seaman, the moon had not yet risen, and all the island was vastly dark, save the hill-top, from which the fires blazed in a score of places, and very busy they kept us, supplying them with fuel. Then, when maybe the half of our watch had passed, the big seaman, who had been to feed the fires upon the weed side of the hill-top, came across to me, and bade me come and put my hand upon the lesser rope; for that he thought they in the ship were anxious to haul it in so that they might send some message across to us. At his words, I asked him very anxiously whether he had perceived them waving a light, the which we had arranged to be our method of signalling in the night, in the event of such being needful; but, to this, he said that he had seen naught; and, by now, having come near the edge of the cliff, I could see for myself, and so perceived that there was none signalling to us from the hulk. Yet, to please the fellow, I put my hand upon the line, which we had made fast in the evening to a large piece of rock, and so, immediately, I discovered that something was pulling upon it, hauling and then slackening, so that it occurred to me that the people in the vessel might be indeed wishful to send us some message, and at that, to make sure, I ran to the nearest fire, and, lighting a tuft of weed, waved it thrice; but there came not any answering signal from those in the ship, and at that I went back to feel at the rope, to assure myself that it had not been the pluck of the wind upon it; but I found that it was something very different from the wind, something that plucked with all the sharpness of a hooked fish, only that it had been a mighty great fish to have given such tugs, and so I knew that some vile thing out in the darkness of the weed was fast to the rope, and at this there came the fear that it might break it, and then a second thought that something might be climbing up to us along the rope, and so I bade the big seaman stand ready with his great cutlass, whilst I ran and waked the bo'sun. And this I did, and explained to him how that something meddled with the lesser rope, so that he came immediately to see for himself how this might be, and when he had put his hand upon it, he bade me go and call the rest of the men, and let them stand round by the fires; for that there was something abroad in the night, and we might be in danger of attack; but he and the big seaman stayed by the end of the rope, watching, so far as the darkness would allow, and ever and anon feeling the tension upon it.

Then, suddenly, it came to the bo'sun to look to the second line, and he ran, cursing himself for his thoughtlessness; but because of its greater weight and tension, he could not discover for certain whether anything meddled with it or not; yet he stayed by it, arguing that if aught touched the smaller rope then might something do likewise with the greater, only that the small line lay along the weed, whilst the greater one had been some feet above it when the darkness had fallen over us, and so might be free from any prowling creatures.

And thus, maybe, an hour passed, and we kept watch and tended the fires, going from one to another, and, presently, coming to that one which was nearest to the bo'sun, I went over to him, intending to pass a few minutes in talk; but as I drew nigh to him, I chanced to place my hand upon the big rope, and at that I exclaimed in surprise; for it had become much slacker than when last I had felt it in the evening, and I asked the bo'sun whether he had noticed it, whereat he felt the rope, and was almost more amazed than I had been; for when last he had touched it, it had been taut, and humming in the wind. Now, upon this discovery, he was in much fear that something had bitten through it, and called to the men to come all of them and pull upon the rope, so that he might discover whether it was indeed parted; but when they came and hauled upon it, they were unable to gather in any of it, whereat we felt all of us mightily relieved in our minds; though still unable to come at the cause of its sudden slackness.

And so, a while later, there rose the moon, and we were able to examine the island and the water between it and the weed-continent, to see whether there was anything stirring; yet neither in the valley, nor on the faces of the cliffs, nor in the open water could we perceive aught living, and as for anything among the weed, it was small use trying to discover it among all that shaggy blackness. And now, being assured that nothing was coming at us, and that, so far as our eyes could pierce, there climbed nothing upon the ropes, the bo'sun bade us get turned-in, all except those whose time it was to watch. Yet, before I went into the tent, I made a careful examination of the big rope, the which did also the bo'sun, but could perceive no cause for its slackness; though this was quite apparent in the moonlight, the rope going down with greater abruptness than it had done in the evening. And so we could but conceive that they in the hulk had slacked it for some reason; and after that we went to the tent and a further spell of sleep.

In the early morning we were waked by one of the watchmen, coming into the tent to call the bo'sun; for it appeared that the hulk had moved in the night, so that its stern was now pointed somewhat towards the island. At this news, we ran all of us from the tent to the edge of the hill, and found it to be indeed as the man had said, and now I understood the reason of that sudden slackening of the rope; for, after withstanding the stress upon it for some hours, the vessel had at last yielded, and slewed its stern towards us, moving also to some extent bodily in our direction.

And now we discovered that a man in the look-out place in the top of the structure was waving a welcome to us, at which we waved back, and then the bo'sun bade me haste and write a note to know whether it seemed to them likely that they might be able to heave the ship clear of the weed, and this I did, greatly excited within myself at this new thought, as, indeed, was the bo'sun himself and the rest of the men. For could they do this, then how easily solved were every problem of coming to our own country. But it seemed too good a thing to have come true, and yet I could but hope. And so, when my letter was completed, we put it up in the little oilskin bag, and signalled to those in the ship to haul in upon the line. Yet, when they went to haul, there came a mighty splather amid the weed, and they seemed unable to gather in any of the slack, and then, after a certain pause, I saw the man in the look-out point something, and immediately afterwards there belched out in front of him a little puff of smoke, and, presently, I caught the report of a musket, so that I knew that he was firing at something in the weed. He fired again, and yet once more, and after that they were able to haul in upon the line, and so I perceived that his fire had proved effectual; yet we had no knowledge of the thing at which he had discharged his weapon.

Now, presently, they signalled to us to draw back the line, the which we could do only with great difficulty, and then the man in the top of the superstructure signed to us to vast hauling, which we did, whereupon he began to fire again into the weed; though with what effect we could not perceive. Then, in a while he signalled to us to haul again, and now the rope came more easily; yet still with much labour, and a commotion in the weed over which it lay and, in places, sank. And so, at last, as it cleared the weed because of the lift of the cliff, we saw that a great crab had clutched it, and that we hauled it towards us; for the creature had too much obstinacy to let go.

Perceiving this, and fearing that the great claws of the crab might divide the rope, the bo'sun caught up one of the men's lances, and ran to the cliff edge, calling to us to pull in gently, and put no more strain upon the line than need be. And so, hauling with great steadiness, we brought the monster near to the edge of the hill, and there, at a wave from the bo'sun, stayed our pulling. Then he raised the spear, and smote at the creature's eyes, as he had done on a previous occasion, and immediately it loosed its hold, and fell with a mighty splash into the water at the foot of the cliff. Then the bo'sun bade us haul in the rest of the rope, until we should come to the packet, and, in the meantime, he examined the line to see whether it had suffered harm through the mandibles of the crab; yet, beyond a little chafe, it was quite sound.

And so we came to the letter, which I opened and read, finding it to be written in the same feminine hand which had indited the others. From it we gathered that the ship had burst through a very thick mass of the weed which had compacted itself about her, and that the Second Mate, who was the only officer remaining to them, thought there might be good chance to heave the vessel out; though it would have to be done with great slowness, so as to allow the weed to part gradually, otherwise the ship would but act as a gigantic rake to gather up weed before it, and so form its own barrier to clear water. And after this there were kind wishes and hopes that we had spent a good night, the which I took to be prompted by the feminine heart of the writer, and after that I fell to wondering whether it was the Captain's wife who acted as scribe. Then I was waked from my pondering, by one of the men crying out that they in the ship had commenced to heave again upon the big rope, and, for a time, I stood and watched it rise slowly, as it came to tautness.

I had stood there a while, watching the rope, when, suddenly, there came a commotion amid the weed, about two-thirds of the way to the ship, and now I saw that the rope had freed itself from the weed, and clutching it, were, maybe, a score of giant crabs. At this sight, some of the men cried out their astonishment, and then we saw that there had come a number of men into the look-out place in the top of the superstructure, and, immediately, they opened a very brisk fire upon the creatures, and so, by ones and twos they fell back into the weed, and after that, the men in the hulk resumed their heaving, and so, in a while, had the rope some feet clear of the surface.

Now, having tautened the rope so much as they thought proper, they left it to have its due effect upon the ship, and proceeded to attach a great block to it; then they signalled to us to slack away on the little rope until they had the middle part of it, and this they hitched around the neck of the block, and to the eye in the strop of the block they attached a bo'sun's chair, and so they had ready a carrier, and by this means we were able to haul stuff to and from the hulk without having to drag it across the surface of the weed; being, indeed, the fashion in which we had intended to haul ashore the people in the ship. But now we had the bigger project of salvaging the ship herself, and, further, the big rope, which acted as support for the carrier, was not yet of a sufficient height above the weed-continent for it to be safe to attempt to bring any ashore by such means; and now that we had hopes of saving the ship, we did not intend to risk parting the big rope, by trying to attain such a degree of tautness as would have been necessary at this time to have raised its bight to the desired height.

Now, presently, the bo'sun called out to one of the men to make breakfast, and when it was ready we came to it, leaving the man with the wounded arm to keep watch; then when we had made an end, he sent him, that had lost his fingers, to keep a look-out whilst the other came to the fire and ate his breakfast. And in the meanwhile, the bo'sun took us down to collect weed and reeds for the night, and so we spent the greater part of the morning, and when we had made an end of this, we returned to the top of the hill, to discover how matters were going forward; thus we found, from the one at the look-out, that they, in the hulk, had been obliged to heave twice upon the big rope to keep it off the weed, and by this we knew that the ship was indeed making a slow sternway towards the island—slipping steadily through the weed, and as we looked at her, it seemed almost that we could perceive that she was nearer; but this was no more than imagination; for, at most, she could not have moved more than some odd fathoms. Yet it cheered us greatly, so that we waved our congratulations to the man who stood in the look-out in the superstructure, and he waved back.

Later, we made dinner, and afterwards had a very comfortable smoke, and then the bo'sun attended to our various hurts. And so through the afternoon we sat about upon the crest of the hill overlooking the hulk, and thrice had they in the ship to heave upon the big rope, and by evening they had made near thirty fathoms towards the island, the which they told us in reply to a query which the bo'sun desired me to send them, several messages having passed between us in the course of the afternoon, so that we had the carrier upon our side. Further than this, they explained that they would tend the rope during the night, so that the strain would be kept up, and, more, this would keep the ropes off the weed.

And so, the night coming down upon us, the bo'sun bade us light the fires about the top of the hill, the same having been laid earlier in the day, and thus, our supper having been dispatched, we prepared for the night. And all through it there burned lights aboard the hulk, the which proved very companionable to us in our times of watching; and so, at last came the morning, the darkness having passed without event. And now, to our huge pleasure, we discovered that the ship had made great progress in the night; being now so much nearer that none could suppose it a matter of imagination; for she must have moved nigh sixty fathoms nearer to the island, so that now we seemed able almost to recognise the face of the man in the look-out; and many things about the hulk we saw with greater clearness, so that we scanned her with a fresh interest. Then the man in the look-out waved a morning greeting to us, the which we returned very heartily, and, even as we did so, there came a second figure beside the man, and waved some white matter, perchance a handkerchief, which is like enough, seeing that it was a woman, and at that, we took off our head coverings, all of us, and shook them at her, and after this we went to our breakfast; having finished which, the bo'sun dressed our hurts, and then, setting the man, who had lost his fingers, to watch, he took the rest of us, excepting him that was bitten in the arm, down to collect fuel, and so the time passed until near dinner.

When we returned to the hill-top, the man upon the look-out told us that they in the ship had heaved not less than four separate times upon the big rope, the which, indeed, they were doing at that present minute; and it was very plain to see that the ship had come nearer even during the short space of the morning. Now, when they had made an end of tautening the rope, I perceived that it was, at last, well clear of the weed through all its length, being at its lowest part nigh twenty feet above the surface, and, at that, a sudden thought came to me which sent me hastily to the bo'sun; for it had occurred to me that there existed no reason why we should not pay a visit to those aboard the hulk. But when I put the matter to him, he shook his head, and, for awhile, stood out against my desire; but, presently, having examined the rope, and considering that I was the lightest of any in the island, he consented, and at that I ran to the carrier which had been hauled across to our side, and got me into the chair. Now, the men, so soon as they perceived my intention, applauded me very heartily, desiring to follow; but the bo'sun bade them be silent, and, after that, he lashed me into the chair, with his own hands, and then signalled to those in the ship to haul upon the small rope; he, in the meanwhile, checking my descent towards the weeds, by means of our end of the hauling-line.

And so, presently, I had come to the lowest part, where the bight of the rope dipped downward in a bow towards the weed, and rose again to the mizzen mast of the hulk. Here I looked downward with somewhat fearful eyes; for my weight on the rope made it sag somewhat lower than seemed to me comfortable, and I had a very lively recollection of some of the horrors which that quiet surface hid. Yet I was not long in this place; for they in the ship, perceiving how the rope let me nearer to the weed than was safe, pulled very heartily upon the hauling-line, and so I came quickly to the hulk.

Now, as I drew nigh to the ship, the men crowded upon a little platform which they had built in the superstructure somewhat below the broken head of the mizzen, and here they received me with loud cheers and very open arms, and were so eager to get me out of the bo'sun's chair, that they cut the lashings, being too impatient to cast them loose. Then they led me down to the deck, and here, before I had knowledge of aught else, a very buxom woman took me into her arms, kissing me right heartily, at which I was greatly taken aback; but the men about me did naught but laugh, and so, in a minute, she loosed me, and there I stood, not knowing whether to feel like a fool or a hero; but inclining rather to the latter. Then, at this minute, there came a second woman, who bowed to me in a manner most formal, so that we might have been met in some fashionable gathering, rather than in a cast-away hulk in the lonesomeness and terror of that weed-choked sea; and at her coming all the mirth of the men died out of them, and they became very sober, whilst the buxom woman went backward for a piece, and seemed somewhat abashed. Now, at all this, I was greatly puzzled, and looked from one to another to learn what it might mean; but in the same moment the woman bowed again, and said something in a low voice touching the weather, and after that she raised her glance to my face, so that I saw her eyes, and they were so strange and full of melancholy, that I knew on the instant why she spoke and acted in so unmeaning a way; for the poor creature was out of her mind, and when I learnt afterwards that she was the Captain's wife, and had seen him die in the arms of a mighty devil-fish, I grew to understand how she had come to such a pass.

Now for a minute after I had discovered the woman's madness, I was so taken aback as to be unable to answer her remark; but for this there appeared no necessity; for she turned away and went aft towards the saloon stairway, which stood open, and here she was met by a maid very bonny and fair, who led her tenderly down from my sight. Yet, in a minute, this same maid appeared, and ran along the decks to me, and caught my two hands, and shook them, and looked up at me with such roguish, playful eyes, that she warmed my heart, which had been strangely chilled by the greeting of the poor mad woman. And she said many hearty things regarding my courage, to which I knew in my heart I had no claim; but I let her run on, and so, presently, coming more to possession of herself, she discovered that she was still holding my hands, the which, indeed, I had been conscious of the while with a very great pleasure; but at her discovery she dropped them with haste, and stood back from me a space, and so there came a little coolness into her talk: yet this lasted not long; for we were both of us young, and, I think, even thus early we attracted one the other; though, apart from this, there was so much that we desired each to learn, that we could not but talk freely, asking question for question, and giving answer for answer. And thus a time passed, in which the men left us alone, and went presently to the capstan, about which they had taken the big rope, and at this they toiled awhile; for already the ship had moved sufficiently to let the line fall slack.

Presently, the maid, whom I had learnt was niece to the Captain's wife, and named Mary Madison, proposed to take me the round of the ship, to which proposal I agreed very willingly; but first I stopped to examine the mizzen stump, and the manner in which the people of the ship had stayed it, the which they had done very cunningly, and I noted how that they had removed some of the superstructure from about the head of the mast, so as to allow passage for the rope, without putting a strain upon the superstructure itself. Then when I had made an end upon the poop, she led me down on to the main-deck, and here I was very greatly impressed by the prodigious size of the structure which they had built about the hulk, and the skill with which it had been carried out, the supports crossing from side to side and to the decks in a manner calculated to give great solidity to that which they upheld. Yet, I was very greatly puzzled to know where they had gotten a sufficiency of timber to make so large a matter; but upon this point she satisfied me by explaining that they had taken up the 'tween decks, and used all such bulkheads as they could spare, and, further, that there had been a good deal among the dunnage which had proved usable.

And so we came at last to the galley, and here I discovered the buxom woman to be installed as cook, and there were in with her a couple of fine children, one of whom I guessed to be a boy of maybe some five years, and the second a girl, scarce able to do more than toddle. At this I turned and asked Mistress Madison whether these were her cousins; but in the next moment I remembered that they could not be; for, as I knew, the Captain had been dead some seven years; yet it was the woman in the galley who answered my question; for she turned and, with something of a red face, informed me that they were hers, at which I felt some surprise; but supposed that she had taken passage in the ship with her husband; yet in this I was not correct; for she proceeded to explain that, thinking they were cut off from the world for the rest of this life, and falling very fond of the carpenter, they had made it up together to make a sort of marriage, and had gotten the Second Mate to read the service over them. She told me then, how that she had taken passage with her mistress, the Captain's wife, to help her with her niece, who had been but a child when the ship sailed; for she had been very attached to them both, and they to her. And so she came to an end of her story, expressing a hope that she had done no wrong by her marriage, as none had been intended. And to this I made answer, assuring her that no de-cent-minded man could think the worse of her; but that I, for my part, thought rather the better, seeing that I liked the pluck which she had shown. At that she cast down the soup ladle, which she had in her fist, and came towards me, wiping her hands; but I gave back, for I shamed to be hugged again, and before Mistress Mary Madison, and at that she came to a stop and laughed very heartily; but, all the same, called down a very warm blessing upon my head; for which I had no cause to feel the worse. And so I passed on with the Captain's niece.

Presently, having made the round of the hulk, we came aft again to the poop, and discovered that they were heaving once more upon the big rope, the which was very heartening, proving, as it did, that the ship was still a-move. And so, a little later, the girl left me, having to attend to her aunt. Now whilst she was gone, the men came all about me, desiring news of the world beyond the weed-continent, and so for the next hour I was kept very busy, answering their questions. Then the Second Mate called out to them to take another heave upon the rope, and at that they turned to the capstan, and I with them, and so we hove it taut again, after which they got about me once more, questioning; for so much seemed to have happened in the seven years in which they had been imprisoned. And then, after a while, I turned-to and questioned them on such points as I had neglected to ask Mistress Madison, and they discovered to me their terror and sickness of the weed-continent, its desolation and horror, and the dread which had beset them at the thought that they should all of them come to their ends without sight of their homes and countrymen.

Now, about this time, I became conscious that I had grown very empty; for I had come off to the hulk before we had made our dinner, and had been in such interest since, that the thought of food had escaped me; for I had seen none eating in the hulk, they, without doubt, having dined earlier than my coming. But now, being made aware of my state by the grumbling of my stomach, I inquired whether there was any food to be had at such a time, and, at that, one of the men ran to tell the woman in the galley that I had missed my dinner, at which she made much ado, and set-to and prepared me a very good meal, which she carried aft and set out for me in the saloon, and after that she sent me down to it.

Presently, when I had come near to being comfortable, there chanced a lightsome step upon the floor behind me, and, turning, I discovered that Mistress Madison was surveying me with a roguish and somewhat amused air. At that, I got hastily to my feet; but she bade me sit down, and therewith she took a seat opposite, and so bantered me with a gentle playfulness that was not displeasing to me, and at which I played so good a second as I had ability. Later, I fell to questioning her, and, among other matters, discovered that it was she who acted as scribe for the people in the hulk, at which I told her that I had done likewise for those on the island. After that, our talk became somewhat personal, and I learnt that she was near on to nineteen years of age, whereat I told her that I had passed my twenty-third. And so we chatted on, until, presently, it occurred to me that I had better be preparing to return to the island, and I rose to my feet with this intention; yet feeling that I had been very much happier to have stayed, the which I thought, for a moment, had not been displeasing to her, and this I imagined, noting somewhat in her eyes when I made mention that I must be gone. Yet it may be that I flattered myself.

Now when I came out on deck, they were busied again in heaving taut the rope, and, until they had made an end, Mistress Madison and I filled the time with such chatter as is wholesome between a man and maid who have not long met, yet find one another pleasing company. Then, when at last the rope was taut, I went up to the mizzen staging, and climbed into the chair, after which some of the men lashed me in very securely. Yet when they gave the signal to haul me to the island, there came for awhile no response, and then signs that we could not understand; but no movement to haul me across the weed. At that, they unlashed me from the chair, bidding me get out, whilst they sent a message to discover what might be wrong. And this they did, and, presently, there came back word that the big rope had stranded upon the edge of the cliff, and that they must slacken it somewhat at once, the which they did, with many expressions of dismay. And so, maybe an hour passed, during which we watched the men working at the rope, just where it came down over the edge of the hill, and Mistress Madison stood with us and watched; for it was very terrible, this sudden thought of failure (though it were but temporary) when they were so near to success. Yet, at last there came a signal from the island for us to loose the hauling-line, the which we did, allowing them to haul across the carrier, and so, in a little while, they signalled back to us to pull in, which, having done, we found a letter in the bag lashed to the carrier, in which the bo'sun made it plain that he had strengthened the rope, and placed fresh chafing gear about it, so that he thought it would be so safe as ever to heave upon; but to put it to a less strain. Yet he refused to allow me to venture across upon it, saying that I must stay in the ship until we were clear of the weed; for if the rope had stranded in one place, then had it been so cruelly tested that there might be some other points at which it was ready to give. And this final note of the bo'sun's made us all very serious; for, indeed, it seemed possible that it was as he suggested; yet they reassured themselves by pointing out that, like enough, it had been the chafe upon the cliff edge which had frayed the strand, so that it had been weakened before it parted; but I, remembering the chafing gear which the bo'sun had put about it in the first instance, felt not so sure; yet I would not add to their anxieties.

And so it came about that I was compelled to spend the night in the hulk; but, as I followed Mistress Madison into the big saloon, I felt no regret, and had near forgotten already my anxiety regarding the rope.

And out on deck there sounded most cheerily the clack of the capstan.

XVI
Freed

NOW, WHEN MISTRESS MADISON had seated herself, she invited me to do likewise, after which we fell into talk, first touching upon the matter of the stranding of the rope, about which I hastened to assure her, and later to other things, and so, as is natural enough with a man and maid, to ourselves, and here we were very content to let it remain.

Presently, the Second Mate came in with a note from the bo'sun, which he laid upon the table for the girl to read, the which she beckoned me to do also, and so I discovered that it was a suggestion, written very rudely and ill-spelt, that they should send us a quantity of reeds from the island, with which we might be able to ease the weed somewhat from around the stern of the hulk, thus aiding her progress. And to this the Second Mate desired the girl to write a reply, saying that we should be very happy for the reeds, and would endeavour to act upon his hint, and this Mistress Madison did, after which she passed the letter to me, perchance I desired to send any message. Yet I had naught that I wished to say, and so handed it back, with a word of thanks, and, at once, she gave it to the Second Mate, who went, forthwith, and dispatched it.

Later, the stout woman from the galley came aft to set out the table, which occupied the centre of the saloon, and whilst she was at this, she asked for information on many things, being very free and unaffected in her speech, and seeming with less of deference to my companion, than a certain motherliness; for it was very plain that she loved Mistress Madison, and in this my heart did not blame her. Further, it was plain to me that the girl had a very warm affection for her old nurse, which was but natural, seeing that the old woman had cared for her through all the past years, besides being companion to her, and a good and cheerful one, as I could guess.

Now a while I passed in answering the buxom woman's questions, and odd times such occasional ones as were slipt in by Mistress Madison; and then, suddenly there came the clatter of men's feet overhead, and, later, the thud of something being cast down upon the deck, and so we knew that the reeds had come. At that, Mistress Madison cried out that we should go and watch the men try them upon the weed; for that if they proved of use in easing that which lay in our path, then should we come the more speedily to the clear water, and this without the need of putting so great a strain upon the hawser, as had been the case hitherto.

When we came to the poop, we found the men removing a portion of the superstructure over the stern, and after that they took some of the stronger reeds, and proceeded to work at the weed that stretched away in a line with our taffrail. Yet that they anticipated danger, I perceived; for there stood by them two of the men and the Second Mate, all armed with muskets, and these three kept a very strict watch upon the weed, knowing, through much experience of its terrors, how that there might be a need for their weapons at any moment. And so a while passed, and it was plain that the men's work upon the weed was having effect; for the rope grew slack visibly, and those at the capstan had all that they could do, taking fleet and fleet with the tackle, to keep it anywhere near to tautness, and so, perceiving that they were kept so hard at it, I ran to give a hand, the which did Mistress Madison, pushing upon the capstan-bars right merrily and with heartiness. And thus a while passed, and the evening began to come down upon the lonesomeness of the weed-continent. Then there appeared the buxom woman, and bade us come to our suppers, and her manner of addressing the two of us was the manner of one who might have mothered us; but Mistress Madison cried out to her to wait, that we had found work to do, and at that the big woman laughed, and came towards us threateningly, as though intending to remove us hence by force.

And now, at this moment, there came a sudden interruption which checked our merriment; for, abruptly, there sounded the report of a musket in the stern, and then came shouts, and the noise of the two other weapons, seeming like thunder, being pent by the over-arching superstructure. And, directly, the men about the taffrail gave back, running here and there, and so I saw that great arms had come all about the opening which they had made in the superstructure, and two of these flickered in-board, searching hither and thither; but the stout woman took a man near to her, and thrust him out of danger, and after that, she caught Mistress Madison up in her big arms, and ran down on to the main-deck with her, and all this before I had come to a full knowledge of our danger. But now I perceived that I should do well to get further back from the stern, the which I did with haste, and, coming to a safe position, I stood and stared at the huge creature, its great arms, vague in the growing dusk, writhing about in vain search for a victim. Then returned the Second Mate, having been for more weapons, and now I observed that he armed all the men, and had brought up a spare musket for my use, and so we commenced, all of us, to fire at the monster, whereat it began to lash about most furiously, and so, after some minutes, it slipped away from the opening and slid down into the weed. Upon that several of the men rushed to replace those parts of the superstructure which had been removed, and I with them; yet there were sufficient for the job, so that I had no need to do aught; thus, before they had made up the opening, I had been given chance to look out upon the weed, and so discovered that all the surface which lay between our stern and the island, was moving in vast ripples, as though mighty fish were swimming beneath it, and then, just before the men put back the last of the great panels, I saw the weed all tossed up like to a vast pot a-boil, and then a vague glimpse of thousands of monstrous arms that filled the air, and came towards the ship.

And then the men had the panel back in its place, and were hasting to drive the supporting struts into their positions. And when this was done, we stood awhile and listened; but there came no sound above that of the wail of the wind across the extent of the weed-continent. And at that, I turned to the men, asking how it was that I could hear no sounds of the creatures attacking us, and so they took me up into the look-out place, and from there I stared down at the weed; but it was without movement, save for the stirring of the wind, and there was nowhere any sign of the devil-fish. Then, seeing me amazed, they told me how that anything which moved the weed seemed to draw them from all parts; but that they seldom touched the hulk unless there was something visible to them which had movement. Yet, as they went on to explain, there would be hundreds and hundreds of them lying all about the ship, hiding in the weed; but that if we took care not to show ourselves within their reach, they would have gone most of them by the morning. And this the men told me in a very matter-of-fact way; for they had become inured to such happenings.

Presently, I heard Mistress Madison calling to me by name, and so descended out of the growing darkness, to the interior of the superstructure, and here they had lit a number of rude slush-lamps, the oil for which, as I learned later, they obtained from a certain fish which haunted the sea, beneath the weed, in very large schools, and took near any sort of bait with great readiness. And so, when I had climbed down into the light, I found the girl waiting for me to come to supper, for which I discovered myself to be in a mightily agreeable humour.

Presently, having made an end of eating, she leaned back in her seat and commenced once more to bait me in her playful manner, the which appeared to afford her much pleasure, and in which I joined with no less, and so we fell presently to more earnest talk, and in this wise we passed a great space of the evening. Then there came to her a sudden idea, and what must she do but propose that we should climb to the look-out, and to this I agreed with a very happy willingness. And to the lookout we went. Now when we had come there, I perceived her reason for this freak; for away in the night, astern the hulk, there blazed half-way between the heaven and the sea, a mighty glow, and suddenly, as I stared, being dumb with admiration and surprise, I knew that it was the blaze of our fires upon the crown of the bigger hill; for, all the hill being in shadow, and hidden by the darkness, there showed only the glow of the fires, hung, as it were, in the void, and a very striking and beautiful spectacle it was. Then, as I watched, there came, abruptly a figure into view upon the edge of the glow, showing black and minute, and this I knew to be one of the men come to the edge of the hill to take a look at the hulk, or test the strain on the hawser. Now, upon my expressing admiration of the sight to Mistress Madison, she seemed greatly pleased, and told me that she had been up many times in the darkness to view it. And after that we went down again into the interior of the superstructure, and here the men were taking a further heave upon the big rope, before settling the watches for the night, the which they managed, by having one man at a time to keep awake and call the rest whenever the hawser grew slack.

Later Mistress Madison showed me where I was to sleep, and so, having bid one another a very warm good-night, we parted, she going to see that her aunt was comfortable, and I out on to the main-deck to have a chat with the man on watch. In this way, I passed the time until midnight, and in that while we had been forced to call the men thrice to heave upon the hawser, so quickly had the ship begun to make way through the weed. Then, having grown sleepy, I said good-night, and went to my berth, and so had my first sleep upon a mattress, for some weeks.

Now when the morning was come, I waked, hearing Mistress Madison calling upon me from the other side of my door, and rating me very saucily for a lie-a-bed, and at that I made good speed at dressing, and came quickly into the saloon, where she had ready a breakfast that made me glad I had waked. But first, before she would do aught else, she had me out to the lookout place, running up before me most merrily and singing in the fullness of her glee, and so, when I had come to the top of the superstructure, I perceived that she had very good reason for so much merriment, and the sight which came to my eyes, gladdened me most mightily, yet at the same time filling me with a great amazement; for, behold! in the course of that one night, we had made near unto two hundred fathoms across the weed, being now, with what we had made previously, no more than some thirty fathoms in from the edge of the weed. And there stood Mistress Madison beside me, doing somewhat of a dainty step-dance upon the flooring of the look-out, and singing a quaint old lilt that I had not heard that dozen years, and this little thing, I think, brought back more clearly to me than aught else how that this winsome maid had been lost to the world for so many years, having been scarce of the age of twelve when the ship had been lost in the weed-continent. Then, as I turned to make some remark, being filled with many feelings, there came a hail, from far above in the air, as it might be, and, looking up, I discovered the man upon the hill to be standing along the edge, and waving to us, and now I perceived how that the hill towered a very great way above us, seeming, as it were, to overhang the hulk though we were yet some seventy fathoms distant from the sheer sweep of its nearer precipice. And so, having waved back our greeting, we made down to breakfast, and, having come to the saloon, set-to upon the good victuals, and did very sound justice thereto.

Presently, having made an end of eating, and hearing the clack of the capstan-pawls, we hurried out on deck, and put our hands upon the bars, intending to join in that last heave which should bring the ship free out of her long captivity, and so for a time we moved round about the capstan, and I glanced at the girl beside me; for she had become very solemn, and indeed it was a strange and solemn time for her; for she, who had dreamed of the world as her childish eyes had seen it, was now, after many hopeless years, to go forth once more to it—to live in it, and to learn how much had been dreams, and how much real; and with all these thoughts I credited her; for they seemed such as would have come to me at such a time, and, presently, I made some blundering effort to show to her that I had understanding of the tumult which possessed her, and at that she smiled up at me with a sudden queer flash of sadness and merriment, and our glances met, and I saw something in hers, which was but newborn, and though I was but a young man, my heart interpreted it for me, and I was all hot suddenly with the pain and sweet delight of this new thing; for I had not dared to think upon that which already my heart had made bold to whisper to me, so that even thus soon I was miserable out of her presence. Then she looked downward at her hands upon the bar; and, in the same instant, there came a loud, abrupt cry from the Second Mate, to vast heaving, and at that all the men pulled out their bars and cast them upon the deck, and ran, shouting, to the ladder that led to the look-out, and we followed, and so came to the top, and discovered that at last the ship was clear of the weed, and floating in the open water between it and the island.

Now at the discovery that the hulk was free, the men commenced to cheer and shout in a very wild fashion, as, indeed, is no cause for wonder, and we cheered with them. Then, suddenly, in the midst of our shouting, Mistress Madison plucked me by the sleeve and pointed to the end of the island where the foot of the bigger hill jutted out in a great spur, and now I perceived a boat, coming round into view, and in another moment I saw that the bo'sun stood in the stern, steering; thus I knew that he must have finished repairing her whilst I had been on the hulk. By this, the men about us had discovered the nearness of the boat, and commenced shouting afresh, and they ran down, and to the bows of the vessel, and got ready a rope to cast. Now when the boat came near, the men in her scanned us very curiously; but the bo'sun took off his head-gear, with a clumsy grace that well became him; at which Mistress Madison smiled very kindly upon him, and, after that, she told me with great frankness that he pleased her, and, more, that she had never seen so great a man, which was not strange seeing that she had seen but few since she had come to years when men become of interest to a maid.

After saluting us the bo'sun called out to the Second Mate that he would tow us round to the far side of the island, and to this the officer agreed, being, I surmised, by no means sorry to put some solid matter between himself and the desolation of the great weed-continent; and so, having loosed the hawser, which fell from the hill-top with a prodigious splash, we had the boat ahead, towing. In this wise we opened out, presently, the end of the hill; but feeling now the force of the breeze, we bent a kedge to the hawser, and, the bo'sun carrying it seawards, we warped ourselves to windward of the island, and here, in forty fathoms, we vast heaving, and rode to the kedge.

Now when this was accomplished they called to our men to come aboard, and this they did, and spent all of that day in talk and eating; for those in the ship could scarce make enough of our fellows. And then, when it had come to night, they replaced that part of the superstructure which they had removed from about the head of the mizzen-stump, and so, all being secure, each one turned-in and had a full night's rest, of the which, indeed, many of them stood in sore need.

The following morning, the Second Mate had a consultation with the bo'sun, after which he gave the order to commence upon the removal of the great superstructure, and to this each one of us set himself with vigour. Yet it was a work requiring some time, and near five days had passed before we had the ship stripped clear. When this had been accomplished, there came a busy time of routing out various matter of which we should have need in jury-rigging her; for they had been so long in disuse, that none remembered where to look for them. At this a day and a half was spent, and after that we set-to about fitting her with such jury-masts as we could manage from our material.

Now, after the ship had been dismasted, all those seven years gone, the crew had been able to save many of her spars, these having remained attached to her, through their inability to cut away all of the gear; and though this had put them in sore peril at the time, of being sent to the bottom with a hole in their side, yet now had they every reason to be thankful; for, by this accident, we had now a foreyard, a topsail-yard, a main t'gallant-yard, and the fore-topmast. They had saved more than these; but had made use of the smaller spars to shore up the superstructure, sawing them into lengths for that purpose. Apart from such spars as they had managed to secure, they had a spare topmast lashed along under the larboard bulwarks, and a spare t'gallant and royal-mast lying along the starboard side.

Now, the Second Mate and the bo'sun set the carpenter to work upon the spare topmast, bidding him make for it some trestle-trees and bolsters, upon which to lay the eyes of the rigging; but they did not trouble him to shape it. Further, they ordered the same to be fitted to the fore-topmast and the spare t'gallant and royal-mast. And in the meanwhile, the rigging was prepared, and when this was finished, they made ready the shears to hoist the spare topmast, intending this to take the place of the main lower-mast. Then, when the carpenter had carried out their orders, he was set to make three partners with a step cut in each, these being intended to take the heels of the three masts, and when these were completed, they bolted them securely to the decks at the fore part of each one of the stumps of the three lower-masts. And so, having all ready, we hove the main-mast into position, after which we proceeded to rig it. Now, when we had made an end of this, we set-to upon the foremast, using for this the fore-topmast which they had saved, and after that we hove the mizzen-mast into place, having for this the spare t'gallant and royal-mast.

Now the manner in which we secured the masts, before ever we came to the rigging of them, was by lashing them to the stumps of the lower-masts, and after we had lashed them, we drove dunnage and wedges between the masts and the lashings, thus making them very secure. And so, when we had set up the rigging, we had confidence that they would stand all such sail as we should be able to set upon them. Yet, further than this, the bo'sun bade the carpenter make wooden caps of six inch oak, these caps to fit over the *squared* heads of the lower-mast stumps, and having a hole, each of them, to embrace the jury-mast, and by making these caps in two halves, they were abled to bolt them on after the masts had been hove into position.

And so, having gotten in our three jury lower-masts, we hoisted up the foreyard to the main, to act as our mainyard, and did likewise with the topsail-yard to the fore, and after that, we sent up the t'gallant-yard to the mizzen. Thus we had her sparred, all but a bowsprit and jibboom; yet this we managed by making a stumpy, spike bowsprit from one of the smaller spars which they had used to shore up the superstructure, and because we feared that it lacked strength to bear the strain of our fore and aft stays, we took down two hawsers from the fore, passing them in through the hawse-holes and setting them up there. And so we had her rigged, and, after that, we bent such sail as our gear abled us to carry, and in this wise had the hulk ready for sea.

Now, the time that it took us to rig the ship, and fit her out, was seven weeks, saving one day. And in all this time we suffered no molestation from any of the strange habitants of the weed-continent; though this may have been because we kept fires of dried weed going all the night about the decks, these fires being lit on big flat pieces of rock which we had gotten from the island. Yet, for all that we had not been troubled, we had more than once discovered strange things in the water swimming near to the vessel; but a flare of weed, hung over the side, on the end of a reed, had sufficed always to scare away such unholy visitants.

And so at last we came to the day on which we were in so good a condition that the bo'sun and the Second Mate considered the ship to be in a fit state to put to sea—the carpenter having gone over so much of her hull as he could get at and found her everywhere very sound; though her lower parts were hideously overgrown with weed, barnacles and other matters; yet this we could not help, and it was not wise to attempt to scrape her, having consideration to the creatures which we knew to abound in those waters.

Now in those seven weeks, Mistress Madison and I had come very close to one another, so that I had ceased to call her by any name save Mary, unless it were a dearer one than that; though this would be one of my own invention, and would leave my heart too naked did I put it down here.

Of our love one for the other, I think yet, and ponder how that mighty man, the bo'sun, came so quickly to a knowledge of the state of our hearts; for he gave me a very sly hint one day that he had a sound idea of the way in which the wind blew, and yet, though he said it with a half-jest, methought there was something wistful in his voice, as he spoke, and at that I just clapt my hand in his, and he gave it a very huge grip. And after that he ceased from the subject.

XVII
How We Came To Our
Own Country

NOW WHEN THE DAY came on which we made to leave the nearness of the island, and the waters of that strange sea, there was great lightness of heart among us, and we went very merrily about such tasks as were needful. And so, in a little, we had the kedge tripped, and had cast the ship's head to starboard, and presently, had her braced up upon the larboard tack, the which we managed very well; though our gear worked heavily, as might be expected. And after that we had gotten under way, we went to the lee side to witness the last of that lonesome island, and with us came the men of the ship, and so, for a space, there was a silence among us; for they were very quiet, looking astern and saying naught; but we had sympathy with them, knowing somewhat of those past years.

And now the bo'sun came to the break of the poop, and called down to the men to muster aft, the which they did, and I with them; for I had come to regard them as my very good comrades; and rum was served out to each of them, and to me along with the rest, and it was Mistress Madison herself who dipped it out to us from the wooden bucket; though it was the buxom woman who had brought it up from the lazarette. Now, after the rum, the bo'sun bade the crew to clear up the gear about the decks, and get matters secured, and at that I turned to go with the men, having become so used to work with them; but he called to me to come up to him upon the poop, the which I did, and there he spoke respectfully, remonstrating with me, and reminding me that now there was need no longer for me to toil; for that I was come back to my old position of passenger, such as I had been in the *Glen Carrig*, ere she foundered. But to this talk of his, I made reply that I had as good a right to work my passage home as any other among us; for though I had paid for a passage in the *Glen*

Carrig, I had done no such thing regarding the *Seabird*—this being the name of the hulk—; and to this, my reply, the bo'sun said little; but I perceived that he liked my spirit, and so from thence until we reached the Port of London, I took my turn and part in all seafaring matters, having become by this quite proficient in the calling. Yet, in one matter, I availed myself of my former position; for I chose to live aft, and by this was abled to see much of my sweetheart, Mistress Madison.

Now after dinner upon the day on which we left the island, the bo'sun and the Second Mate picked the watches, and thus I found myself chosen to be in the bo'sun's, at which I was mightly pleased. And when the watches had been picked, they had all hands to 'bout ship, the which, to the pleasure of all, she accomplished; for under such gear and with so much growth upon her bottom, they had feared that we should have to veer, and by this we should have lost much distance to leeward, whereas we desired to edge so much to windward as we could, being anxious to put space between us and the weed-continent. And twice more that day we put the ship about, though the second time it was to avoid a great bank of weed that lay floating athwart our bows; for all the sea to windward of the island, so far as we had been able to see from the top of the higher hill, was studded with floating masses of the weed, like unto thousands of islets, and in places like to far-spreading reefs. And, because of these, the sea all about the island remained very quiet and unbroken, so that there was never any surf, no, nor scarce a broken wave upon its shore, and this, for all that the wind had been fresh for many days.

When the evening came, we were again upon the larboard tack, making, perhaps, some four knots in the hour; though, had we been in proper rig, and with a clean bottom, we had been making eight or nine, with so good a breeze and so calm a sea. Yet, so far, our progress had been very reasonable; for the island lay, maybe, some five miles to leeward, and about fifteen astern. And so we prepared for the night. Yet, a little before dark, we discovered that the weed-continent trended out towards us; so that we should pass it, maybe, at a distance of something like half a mile, and, at that, there was talk between the Second Mate and the bo'sun as to whether it was better to put the ship about, and gain a greater sea-room before attempting to pass this promontory of weed; but at last they decided that we had naught to fear; for we had fair way through the water, and further, it did not seem reasonable to suppose that we should have aught to fear from the habitants of the weed-continent, at so great a distance as the half of a mile. And so we stood on; for, once past the point, there was much likelihood of the weed trending away to the Eastward, and if this were so, we could square-in immediately and get the wind upon our quarter, and so make better way.

Now it was the bo'sun's watch from eight of the evening until midnight, and I, with another man, had the look-out until four bells. Thus it chanced that, coming abreast of the point during our time of watching, we peered very earnestly to leeward; for the night was dark, having no moon until nearer the morning; and we were full of unease in that we had come so near again to the desolation of that strange continent. And then, suddenly, the man with me clutched my shoulder, and pointed into the darkness upon our bow, and thus I discovered that we had come nearer to the weed than the bo'sun and the Second Mate had intended; they, without doubt, having miscalculated our leeway. At this, I turned and sang out to the bo'sun that we were near to running upon the weed, and, in the same moment, he shouted to the helmsman to luff, and directly afterwards our starboard side was brushing against the great outlying tufts of the point, and so, for a breathless minute, we waited. Yet the ship drew clear, and so into the open water beyond the point; but I had seen something as we scraped against the weed, a sudden glimpse of white, gliding among the growth, and then I saw others, and, in a moment, I was down on the main-deck, and running aft to the bo'sun; yet midway along the deck a horrid shape came above the starboard rail, and I gave out a loud cry of warning. Then I had a capstan-bar from the rack near, and smote with it at the thing, crying all the while for help, and at my blow the thing went from my sight, and the bo'sun was with me, and some of the men.

Now the bo'sun had seen my stroke, and so sprang upon the t'gallant rail, and peered over; but gave back on the instant, shouting to me to run and call the other watch, for that the sea was full of the monsters swimming off to the ship, and at that I was away at a run, and when I had waked the men, I raced aft to the cabin and did likewise with the Second Mate, and so returned in a minute, bearing the bo'sun's cutlass, my own cut-and-thrust, and the lantern that hung always in the saloon. Now when I had gotten back, I found all things in a mighty scurry—men running about in their shirts and drawers, some in the galley bringing fire from the stove, and others lighting a fire of dry weed to leeward of the galley, and along the starboard rail there was already a fierce fight, the men using capstan-bars, even as I had done. Then I thrust the bo'sun's cutlass into his hand, and at that he gave a great shout, part of joy, and part of approbation, and after that he snatched the lantern from me, and had run to the larboard side of the deck, before I was well aware that he had taken the light; but now I followed him, and happy it was for all of us in the ship that he had thought to go at that moment; for the light of the lantern showed me the vile faces of three of the weed men climbing over the larboard rail; yet the bo'sun had cleft them or ever I could come near; but in a moment I was full busy; for there came nigh a dozen heads above the rail a little aft of where I was, and at that I ran at them, and did good execution; but some had been aboard, if the bo'sun had not come to my help. And now the decks were full of light, several fires having been lit, and the Second Mate having brought out fresh lanterns; and now the men had gotten their cutlasses, the which were more handy than the capstan-bars; and so the fight went forward, some having come over to our side to help us, and a very wild sight it must have seemed to any onlooker; for all about the decks burned the fires and the lanterns, and along the rails ran the men, smiting at hideous faces that rose in dozens into the wild glare of our fighting lights. And everywhere drifted the stench of the brutes. And up on the poop, the fight was as brisk as elsewhere; and here, having been drawn by a cry for help, I discovered the buxom woman smiting with a gory meat-axe at a vile thing which had gotten a clump of its tentacles upon her dress; but she had dispatched it, or ever my sword could help her, and then, to my astonishment, even at that time of peril, I discovered the Captain's wife, wielding a small sword, and the face of her was like to the face of a tiger; for her mouth was drawn, and showed her teeth clenched; but she uttered no word nor cry, and I doubt not but that she had some vague idea that she worked her husband's vengeance.

Then, for a space, I was as busy as any, and afterwards I ran to the buxom woman to demand the whereabouts of Mistress Madison, and she, in a very breathless voice, informed me that she had locked her in her room out of harm's way, and at that I could have embraced the woman; for I had been sorely anxious to know that my sweetheart was safe.

And, presently, the fight diminished, and so, at last, came to an end, the ship having drawn well away from the point, and being now in the open. And after that I ran down to my sweetheart, and opened her door, and thus, for a space, she wept, having her arms about my neck; for she had been in sore terror for me, and for all the ship's company. But, soon, drying her tears, she grew very indignant with her nurse for having locked her into her room, and refused to speak to that good woman for near an hour. Yet I pointed out to her that she could be of very great use in dressing such wounds as had been received, and so she came back to her usual brightness, and brought out bandages, and lint, and ointment, and thread, and was presently very busy.

Now it was later that there rose a fresh commotion in the ship; for it had been discovered that the Captain's wife was a-missing. At this, the bo'sun and the Second Mate instituted a search; but she was nowhere to be found, and, indeed, none in the ship ever saw her again, at which it was presumed that she had been dragged over by some of the weed men, and so come upon her death. And at this, there came a great prostration to my sweetheart so that she would not be comforted for the space of nigh three days, by which time the ship had come clear of those strange seas, having left the incredible desolation of the weed-continent far under our starboard counter.

And so, after a voyage which lasted for nine and seventy days since getting under weigh, we came to the Port of London, having refused all offers of assistance on the way.

Now here, I had to say farewell to my comrades of so many months and perilous adventures; yet, being a man not entirely without means, I took care that each of them should have a certain gift by which to remember me.

And I placed monies in the hands of the buxom woman, so that she could have no reason to stint my sweetheart, and she having—for the comfort of her conscience—taken her good man to the church, set up a little house upon the borders of my estate; but this was not until Mistress Madison had come to take her place at the head of my hall in the County of Essex.

Now one further thing there is of which I must tell. Should any, chancing to trespass upon my estate, come upon a man of very mighty proportions, albeit somewhat bent by age, seated comfortably at the door of his little cottage, then shall they know him for my friend the bo'sun; for to this day do he and I fore-gather, and let our talk drift to the desolate places of this earth, pondering upon that which we have seen—the weed-continent, where reigns desolation and the terror of its strange habitants. And, after that, we talk softly of the land where God hath made monsters after the fashion of trees. Then, maybe, my children come about me, and so we change to other matters; for the little ones love not terror.

The Sargasso Sea Stories

From the Tideless Sea Part One

THE CAPTAIN OF THE schooner leant over the rail, and stared for a moment, intently.

"Pass us them glasses, Jock," he said, reaching a hand behind him.

Jock left the wheel for an instant, and ran into the little companionway. He emerged immediately with a pair of marine-glasses, which he pushed into the waiting hand.

For a little, the Captain inspected the object through the binoculars. Then he lowered them, and polished the object glasses.

"Seems like er water-logged barr'l as sumone's been doin' fancy paintin' on," he remarked after a further stare. "Shove ther 'elm down er bit, Jock, an' we'll 'ave er closer look at it."

Jock obeyed, and soon the schooner bore almost straight for the object which held the Captain's attention. Presently, it was within some fifty feet, and the Captain sung out to the boy in the caboose to pass along the boathook.

Very slowly, the schooner drew nearer, for the wind was no more than breathing gently. At last the cask was within reach, and the Captain grappled at it with the boathook. It bobbed in the calm water, under his ministrations; and, for a moment, the thing seemed likely to elude him. Then he had the hook fast in a bit of rotten-looking rope which was attached to it. He did not attempt to lift it by the rope; but sung out to the boy to get a bowline round it. This was done, and the two of them hove it up on to the deck.

The Captain could see now, that the thing was a small water-breaker, the upper part of which was ornamented with the remains of a painted name.

"H—M—E—B—" spelt out the Captain with difficulty, and

scratched his head. " 'ave er look at this 'ere, Jock. See wot you makes of it."

Jock bent over from the wheel, expectorated, and then stared at the breaker. For nearly a minute he looked at it in silence.

"I'm thinkin' some of the letterin's washed awa'," he said at last, with considerable deliberation. "I have ma doots if ye'll be able to read it.

"Hadn't ye no better knock in the end?" he suggested, after a further period of pondering. "I'm thinkin' ye'll be lang comin' at them contents otherwise."

"It's been in ther water er thunderin' long time," remarked the Captain, turning the bottom side upwards. "Look at them barnacles!"

Then, to the boy:—

"Pass erlong ther 'atchet outer ther locker." Whilst the boy was away, the Captain stood the little barrel on end, and kicked away some of the barnacles from the underside. With them, came away a great shell of pitch. He bent, and inspected it.

"Blest if ther thing ain't been pitched !" he said. "This 'ere's been put afloat er purpose, an' they've been mighty anxious as ther stuff, in it shouldn't be 'armed."

He kicked away another mass of the barnacle—studded pitch. Then, with a sudden impulse, he picked up the whole thing and shook it violently. It gave out a light, dull, thudding sound, as though something soft and small were within. Then the boy came with the hatchet.

"Stan' clear!" said the Captain, and raised the implement. The next instant, he had driven in one end of the barrel. Eagerly, he stooped forward. He dived his hand down and brought out a little bundle stitched up in oilskin.

"I don' spect as it's anythin' of valley," he remarked. "But I guess as there's sumthin' 'ere as'll be worth tellin' 'bout w'en we gets 'ome."

He slit up the oilskin as he spoke. Underneath, there was another covering of the same material, and under that a third. Then a longish bundle done up in tarred canvas. This was removed, and a black, cylindrical shaped case disclosed to view. It proved to be a tin canister, pitched over. Inside of it, neatly wrapped within a last strip of oilskin, was a roll of papers, which, on opening, the Captain found to be covered with writing. The Captain shook out the various wrappings; but found nothing further. He handed the MS. across to Jock.

"More 'n your line 'n mine, I guess," he remarked. "Jest you read it up, an' I'll listen."

He turned to the boy.

"Fetch ther dinner erlong 'ere. Me an' ther Mate'll 'ave it comfertable up 'ere, an' you can take ther wheel. Now then, Jock!"

And, presently, Jock began to read.

"The Losing of the *Homebird*"

"The *'Omebird*!" exclaimed the Captain. "Why, she were lost w'en I wer' quite a young feller. Let me see—seventy-three. That were it. Tail end er seventy-three w'en she left 'ome, an' never 'eard of since; not as I knows. Go a'ead with ther yarn, Jock."

"It is Christmas eve. Two years ago today, we became lost to the world. Two years! It seems like twenty since I had my last Christmas in England. Now, I suppose, we are already forgotten—and this ship is but one more among the missing! My God! to think upon our loneliness gives me a choking feeling, a tightness across the chest!

"I am writing this in the saloon of the sailing ship, *Homebird*, and writing with but little hope of human eye ever seeing that which I write; for we are in the heart of the dread Sargasso Sea—the Tideless Sea of the North Atlantic. From the stump of our mizzen mast, one may see, spread out to the far horizon, an interminable waste of weed—a treacherous, silent vastitude of slime and hideousness!

"On our port side, distant some seven or eight miles, there is a great, shapeless, discoloured mass. No one, seeing it for the first time, would suppose it to be the hull of a long lost vessel. It bears but little resemblance to a sea-going craft, because of a strange superstructure which has been built upon it. An examination of the vessel herself, through a telescope, tells one that she is unmistakably ancient. Probably a hundred, possibly two hundred, years. Think of it! Two hundred years in the midst of this desolation! It is an eternity.

"At first we wondered at that extraordinary superstructure. Later, we were to learn its use—and profit by the teaching of hands long withered. It is inordinately strange that we should have come upon this sight for the dead! Yet, thought suggests, that there may be many such, which have lain here through the centuries in this World of Desolation. I had not imagined that the earth contained so much loneliness, as is held within the circle, seen from the stump of our shattered mast. Then comes the thought that I might wander a hundred miles in any direction—and still be lost.

"And that craft yonder, that one break in the monotony, that monument of a few men's misery, serves only to make the solitude the more atrocious; for she is a very effigy of terror, telling of tragedies in the past, and to come!

"And now to get back to the beginnings of it. I joined the *Homebird*, as a passenger, in the early part of November. My health was not quite the thing, and I hoped the voyage would help to set me up. We had a lot of dirty weather for the first couple of weeks out, the wind dead ahead. Then we got a Southerly slant, that carried us down through the forties; but a good deal more to the Westward than we desired. Here we ran right into a tremendous cyclonic storm. All hands were called to shorten sail, and so urgent seemed our need, that the very officers went aloft to help make up the sails, leaving only the Captain (who had taken the wheel) and myself upon the poop. On the maindeck, the cook was busy letting go such ropes as the Mates desired.

"Abruptly, some distance ahead, through the vague sea-mist, but rather on the port bow, I saw loom up a great black wall of cloud.

" 'Look, Captain!' I exclaimed; but it had vanished before I had finished speaking. A minute later it came again, and this time the Captain saw it.

" 'O, my God!' he cried, and dropped his hands from the wheel. He leapt into the companionway, and seized a speaking trumpet. Then out on deck. He put it to his lips.

" 'Come down from aloft! Come down! Come down!' he shouted. And suddenly I lost his voice in a terrific mutter of sound from somewhere to port. It was the voice of the storm—shouting. My God! I had never heard anything like it! It ceased as suddenly as it had begun, and, in the succeeding quietness, I heard the whining of the kicking-tackles through the blocks. Then came a quick clang of brass upon the deck, and I turned quickly. The Captain had thrown down the trumpet, and sprung back to the wheel. I glanced aloft, and saw that many of the men were already in the rigging, and racing down like cats.

"I heard the Captain draw his breath with a quick gasp.

" 'Hold on for your lives!' he shouted, in a hoarse, unnatural voice.

"I looked at him. He was staring to windward with a fixed stare of painful intentness, and my gaze followed his. I saw, not four hundred yards distant, an enormous mass of foam and water coming down upon us. In the same instant, I caught the hiss of it, and immediately it was a shriek, so intense and awful, that I cringed impotently with sheer terror.

"The smother of water and foam took the ship a little foreside of the beam, and the wind was with it. Immediately, the vessel rolled over on to her side, the sea-froth flying over her in tremendous cataracts.

"It seemed as though nothing could save us. Over, over we went, until I was swinging against the deck, almost as against the side of a house; for I had grasped the weather rail at the Captain's warning. As I swung there, I saw a strange thing. Before me was the port quarter boat. Abruptly, the canvas-cover was flipped clean off it, as though by a vast, invisible hand.

"The next instant, a flurry of oars, boats' masts and odd gear flittered up into the air, like so many feathers, and blew to leeward and was lost in the roaring chaos of foam. The boat, herself, lifted in her chocks, and suddenly was blown clean down on to the main-deck, where she lay all in a ruin of white-painted timbers.

"A minute of the most intense suspense passed; then, suddenly, the ship righted, and I saw that the three masts had carried away. Yet, so hugely loud was the crying of the storm, that no sound of their breaking had reached me.

"I looked towards the wheel; but no one was there. Then I made out something crumpled up against the lee rail. I struggled across to it, and found that it was the Captain. He was insensible, and queerly limp in his right arm and leg. I looked round. Several of the men were crawling aft along the poop. I beckoned to them, and point-ed to the wheel, and then to the Captain. A couple of them came towards me, and one went to the wheel. Then I made out through the spray the form of the Second Mate. He had several more of the men with him, and they had a coil of rope, which they took forrard. I learnt afterwards that they were hastening to get out a sea-anchor, so as to keep the ship's head towards the wind.

"We got the Captain below, and into his bunk. There, I left him in the hands of his daughter and the steward, and returned on deck.

"Presently, the Second Mate came back, and with him the re-mainder of the men. I found then that only seven had been saved in all. The rest had gone.

"The day passed terribly—the wind getting stronger hourly; though, at its worst, it was nothing like so tremendous as that first burst.

"The night came—a night of terror, with the thunder and hiss of the giant seas in the air above us, and the wind bellowing like some vast Elemental beast.

"Then, just before the dawn, the wind lulled, almost in a moment; the ship rolling and wallowing fearfully, and the water coming aboard—hundreds of tons at a time. Immediately afterwards it caught us again; but more on the beam, and bearing the vessel over on to her side, and this only by the pressure of the element upon the stark hull. As we came head to wind again, we righted, and rode, as we had for hours, amid a thousand fantastic hills of phosphorescent flame.

"Again the wind died—coming again after a longer pause, and then, all at once, leaving us. And so, for the space of a terrible half hour, the ship lived through the most awful, windless sea that can be imagined. There was no doubting but that we had driven right into the calm centre of the cyclone—calm only so far as lack of wind, and yet more dangerous a thousand times than the most furious hurricane that ever blew.

"For now we were beset by the stupendous Pyramidal Sea; a sea once witnessed, never forgotten; a sea in which the whole bosom of the ocean is projected towards heaven in monstrous hills of water; not leaping forward, as would be the case if there were wind; but hurling upwards in jets and peaks of living brine, and falling back in a continuous thunder of foam.

"Imagine this, if you can, and then have the clouds break away suddenly overhead, and the moon shine down upon that hellish turmoil, and you will have such a sight as has been given to mortals but seldom, save with death. And this is what we saw, and to my mind there is nothing within the knowledge of man to which I can liken it.

"Yet we lived through it, and through the wind that came later. But two more complete days and nights had passed, before the storm ceased to be a terror to us, and then, only because it had carried us into the seaweed laden waters of the vast Sargasso Sea.

"Here, the great billows first became foamless; and dwindled gradually in size as we drifted further among the floating masses of weed. Yet the wind was still furious, so that the ship drove on steadily, sometimes between banks, and other times over them.

"For a day and a night we drifted thus; and then astern I made out a great bank of weed, vastly greater than any which hitherto we had encountered. Upon this, the wind drove us stern foremost, so that we over-rode it. We had been forced some distance across it, when it occurred to me that our speed was slackening. I guessed presently that the sea-anchor, ahead, had caught in the weed, and was holding. Even as I surmised this, I heard from beyond the bows a faint, droning, twanging sound, blending with the roar of the wind. There came an indistinct report, and the ship lurched backwards through the weed. The hawser, connecting us with the sea-anchor, had parted.

"I saw the Second Mate run forrard with several men. They hauled in upon the hawser, until the broken end was aboard. In the meantime, the ship, having nothing ahead to keep her "bows on," began to slew broadside towards the wind. I saw the men attach a chain to the end of the broken hawser; then they paid it out again, and the ship's head came back to the gale.

"When the Second Mate came aft, I asked him why this had been done, and he explained that so long as the vessel was end-on, she would travel over the weed. I inquired why he wished her to go over the weed, and he told me that one of the men had made out what appeared to be clear water astern, and that—could we gain it—we might win free.

"Through the whole of that day, we moved rearwards across the great bank; yet, so far from the weed appearing to show signs of thinning, it grew steadily thicker, and, as it became denser, so did our speed slacken, until the ship was barely moving. And so the night found us.

"The following morning discovered to us that we were within a quarter of a mile of a great expanse of clear water—apparently the open sea; but unfortunately the wind had dropped to a moderate breeze, and the vessel was motionless, deep sunk in the weed; great tufts of which rose up on all sides, to within a few feet of the level of our main-deck.

"A man was sent up the stump of the mizzen, to take a look round. From there, he reported that he could see something, that might be weed, across the water; but it was too far distant for him to be in any way certain. Immediately afterwards, he called out that there was something, away on our port beam; but what it was, he could not say, and it was not until a telescope was brought to bear, that we made it out to be the hull of the ancient vessel I have previously mentioned.

"And now, the Second Mate began to cast about for some means by which he could bring the ship to the clear water astern. The first thing which he did, was to bend a sail to a spare yard, and hoist it to the top of the mizzen stump. By this means, he was able to dispense with the cable towing over the bows, which, of course, helped to prevent the ship from moving. In addition, the sail would prove helpful to force the vessel across the weed. Then he routed out a couple of kedges. These, he bent on to the ends of a short piece of cable, and, to the bight of this, the end of a long coil of strong rope.

"After that, he had the starboard quarter boat lowered into the weed, and in it he placed the two kedge anchors. The end of another length of rope, he made fast to the boat's painter. This done, he took four of the men with him, telling them to bring chain-hooks, in addition to the oars—his intention being to force the boat through the weed, until he reached the clear water. There, in the marge of the weed, he would plant the two anchors in the thickest clumps of the growth; after which we were to haul the boat back to the ship, by means of the rope attached to the painter.

" 'Then,' as he put it, 'we'll take the kedge-rope to the capstan, and heave her out of this blessed cabbage heap!'

"The weed proved a greater obstacle to the progress of the boat, than, I think, he had anticipated. After half an hour's work, they had gone scarcely more than some two hundred feet from the vessel; yet, so thick was the stuff, that no sign could we see of them, save the movement they made among the weed, as they forced the boat along.

"Another quarter of an hour passed away, during which the three men left upon the poop, paid out the ropes as the boat forged slowly ahead. All at once, I heard my name called. Turning, I saw the Captain's daughter in the companionway, beckoning to me. I walked across to her.

" 'My father has sent me up to know, Mr. Philips, how they are getting on?'

" 'Very slowly, Miss Knowles,' I replied. 'Very slowly indeed. The weed is so extraordinarily thick.'

"She nodded intelligently, and turned to descend; but I detained her a moment.

" 'Your father, how is he?' I asked.

"She drew her breath swiftly.

" 'Quite himself,' she said; 'but so dreadfully weak. He—'

"An outcry from one of the men, broke across her speech:—

" 'Lord 'elp us, mates! Wot were that!'

"I turned sharply. The three of them were staring over the taff-rail. I ran towards them, and Miss Knowles followed.

" 'Hush!' she said, abruptly. 'Listen!'

"I stared astern to where I knew the boat to be. The weed all about it was quaking queerly—the movement extending far beyond the radius of their hooks and oars. Suddenly, I heard the Second Mate's voice:—

" 'Look out, lads! My God, look out!'

"And close upon this, blending almost with it, came the hoarse scream of a man in sudden agony.

"I saw an oar come up into view, and descend violently, as though someone struck at something with it. Then the Second Mate's voice, shouting: " 'Aboard there! Aboard there! Haul in on the rope! Haul in on the rope—!' It broke off into a sharp cry.

As we seized hold of the rope, I saw the weed hurled in all directions, and a great crying and choking swept to us over the brown hideousness around.

" 'Pull!' I yelled, and we pulled. The rope tautened; but the boat never moved.

" 'Tek it ter ther capsting!' gasped one of the men.

"Even as he spoke, the rope slackened.

" 'It's coming!' cried Miss Knowles. 'Pull! Oh! Pull!'

"She had hold of the rope along with us, and together we hauled, the boat yielding to our strength with surprising ease.

" 'There it is!' I shouted, and then I let go of the rope. There was no one in the boat.

"For the half of a minute, we stared, dumfounded. Then my gaze wandered astern to the place from which we had plucked it. There was a heaving movement among the great weed masses. I saw something waver up aimlessly against the sky; it was sinuous, and it flickered once or twice from side to side; then sank back among the growth, before I could concentrate my attention upon it.

"I was recalled to myself by a sound of dry sobbing. Miss Knowles was kneeling upon the deck, her hands clasped round one of the iron uprights of the rail. She seemed momentarily all to pieces.

" 'Come! Miss Knowles,' I said, gently. 'You must be brave. We cannot let your father know of this in his present state.'

"She allowed me to help her to her feet. I could feel that she was trembling badly. Then, even as I sought for words with which to reassure her, there came a dull thud from the direction of the companionway. We looked round. On the deck, face downward, lying half in and half out of the scuttle, was the Captain. Evidently, he had witnessed everything. Miss Knowles gave out a wild cry, and ran to her father. I beckoned to one of the men to help me, and, together, we carried him back to his bunk. An hour later, he recovered from his swoon. He was quite calm, though very weak, and evidently in considerable pain.

"Through his daughter, he made known to me that he wished me to take the reins of authority in his place. This, after a slight demur, I decided to do; for, as I reassured myself, there were no duties required of me, needing any special knowledge of ship-craft. The vessel was fast; so far as I could see, irrevocably fast. It would be time to talk of freeing her, when the Captain was well enough to take charge once more.

"I returned on deck; and made known to the men the Captain's wishes. Then I chose one to act as a sort of bo'sun over the other two, and to him I gave orders that everything should be put to rights before the night came. I had sufficient sense to leave him to manage matters in his own way; for, whereas my knowledge of what was needful, was fragmentary, his was complete.

"By this time, it was near to sunsetting, and it was with melancholy feelings that I watched the great hull of the sun plunge lower. For awhile, I paced the poop, stopping ever and anon to stare over the dreary waste by which we were surrounded. The more I looked about, the more a sense of lonesomeness and depression and fear assailed me. I had pondered much upon the dread happening of the day, and all my ponderings led to a vital questioning:— What was there among all that quiet weed, which had come upon the crew of the boat, and destroyed them? And I could not make answer, and the weed was silent—dreadly silent!

"The sun had drawn very near to the dim horizon, and I watched it, moodily, as it splashed great clots of red fire across the water that lay stretched into the distance across our stern. Abruptly, as I gazed, its perfect lower edge was marred by an irregular shape. For a moment, I stared, puzzled. Then I fetched a pair of glasses from the holdfast in the companion. A glance through these, and I knew the extent of our fate. That line, blotching the round of the sun, was the conformation of another enormous weed bank.

"I remembered that the man had reported something as showing across the water, when he was sent up to the top of the mizzen stump in the morning; but, what it was, he had been unable to say. The thought flashed into my mind that it had been only just visible from aloft in the morning, and now it was in sight from the deck. It occurred to me that the wind might be compacting the weed, and driving the bank which surrounded the ship, down upon a larger portion. Possibly, the clear stretch of water had been but a temporary rift within the heart of the Sargasso Sea. It seemed only too probable.

"Thus it was that I meditated, and so, presently, the night found me. For some hours further, I paced the deck in the darkness, striving to understand the incomprehensible; yet with no better result than to weary myself to death. Then, somewhere about midnight, I went below to sleep.

"The following morning, on going on deck, I found that the stretch of clear water had disappeared entirely, during the night, and now, so far as the eye could reach, there was nothing but a stupendous desolation of weed.

"The wind had dropped completely, and no sound came from all that weed-ridden immensity. We had, in truth, reached the Cemetery of the Ocean!

"The day passed uneventfully enough. It was only when I served out some food to the men, and one of them asked whether they could have a few raisins, that I remembered, with a pang of sudden misery, that it was Christmas day. I gave them the fruit, as they desired, and they spent the morning in the galley, cooking their dinner. Their stolid indifference to the late terrible happenings, appalled me somewhat, until I remembered what their lives were, and had been. Poor fellows! One of them ventured aft at dinner time, and offered me a slice of what he called 'plum duff.' He brought it on a plate which he had found in the galley and scoured thoroughly with sand and water. He tendered it shyly enough, and I took it, so graciously as I could, for I would not hurt his feelings; though the very smell of the stuff was an abomination.

"During the afternoon, I brought out the Captain's telescope, and made a thorough examination of the ancient hulk on our port beam. Particularly did I study the extraordinary superstructure around her sides; but could not, as I have said before, conceive of its use.

"The evening, I spent upon the poop, my eyes searching wearily across that vile quietness, and so, in a little, the night came—Christmas night, sacred to a thousand happy memories. I found myself dreaming of the night a year previous, and, for a little while, I forgot what was before me. I was recalled suddenly—terribly. A voice rose out of the dark which hid the main-deck. For the fraction of an instant, it expressed surprise; then pain and terror leapt into it. Abruptly, it seemed to come from above, and then from somewhere beyond the ship, and so in a moment there was silence, save for a rush of feet and the bang of a door forrard.

"I leapt down the poop ladder, and ran along the main-deck, towards the fo'cas'le. As I ran, something knocked off my cap. I scarcely noticed it then. I reached the fo'cas'le, and caught at the latch of the port door. I lifted it and pushed; but the door was fastened.

" 'Inside there!' I cried, and banged upon the panels with my clenched fist.

"A man's voice came, incoherently.

" 'Open the door!' I shouted. 'Open the door!'

" 'Yes, Sir—I'm com-ming, Sir,' said one of them, jerkily.

"I heard footsteps stumble across the planking. Then a hand fumbled at the fastening, and the door flew open under my weight.

"The man who had opened to me, started back. He held a flaring slush-lamp above his head, and, as I entered, he thrust it forward. His hand was trembling visibly, and, behind him, I made out the face of one of his mates, the brow and dirty, clean-shaven upper lip drenched with sweat. The man who held the lamp, opened his mouth, and gabbered at me; but, for a moment, no sound came.

" 'Wot—wot were it? Wot we-ere it?' he brought out at last, with a gasp.

"The man behind, came to his side, and gesticulated.

" 'What was what?' I asked sharply, and looking from one to the other. 'Where's the other man? What was that screaming?'

"The second man drew the palm of his hand across his brow; then flirted his fingers deckwards.

" 'We don't know, Sir! We don't know! It were Jessop! Somethin's took 'im just as we was comin' forrid! We—we—He—he—HARK!'

"His head came forward with a jerk as he spoke, and then, for a space, no one stirred. A minute passed, and I was about to speak, when, suddenly, from somewhere out upon the deserted main-deck, there came a queer, subdued noise, as though something moved stealthily hither and thither. The man with the lamp caught me by the sleeve, and then, with an abrupt movement, slammed the door and fastened it.

" 'That's *it*, Sir!' he exclaimed, with a note of terror and conviction in his voice.

"I bade him be silent, while I listened; but no sound came to us through the door, and so I turned to the men and told them to let me have all they knew.

"It was little enough. They had been sitting in the galley, yarning, until, feeling tired, they had decided to go forrard and turn-in. They extinguished the light, and came out upon the deck, closing the door behind them. Then, just as they turned to go forrard, Jessop gave out a yell. The next instant they heard him screaming in the air above their heads, and, realising that some terrible thing was upon them, they took forthwith to their heels, and ran for the security of the fo'cas'le.

"Then I had come.

"As the men made an end of telling me, I thought I heard something outside, and held up my hand for silence. I caught the sound again. Someone was calling my name. It was Miss Knowles. Likely enough she was calling me to supper—and she had no knowledge of the dread thing which had happened. I sprang to the door. She might be coming along the main-deck in search of me. And there was Something out there, of which I had no conception—something unseen, but deadly tangible!

" 'Stop, Sir!' shouted the men, together; but I had the door open.

" 'Mr. Philips!' came the girl's voice at no great distance. 'Mr. Philips!'

" 'Coming, Miss Knowles!' I shouted, and snatched the lamp from the man's hand.

"The next instant, I was running aft, holding the lamp high, and glancing fearfully from side to side. I reached the place where the mainmast had been, and spied the girl coming towards me.

" 'Go back!' I shouted. 'Go back!'

"She turned at my shout, and ran for the poop ladder. I came up with her, and followed close at her heels. On the poop, she turned and faced me.

" 'What is it, Mr. Philips?'

"I hesitated. Then:—

" 'I don't know!' I said.

" 'My father heard something,' she began. 'He sent me. He—'

"I put up my hand. It seemed to me that I had caught again the sound of something stirring on the main-deck.

" 'Quick!' I said sharply. 'Down into the cabin!' And she, being a sensible girl, turned and ran down without waste of time. I followed, closing and fastening the companion-doors behind me.

"In the saloon, we had a whispered talk, and I told her everything. She bore up bravely, and said nothing; though her eyes were very wide, and her face pale. Then the Captain's voice came to us from the adjoining cabin.

" 'Is Mr. Philips there, Mary?'

" 'Yes, father.'

" 'Bring him in.'

"I went in.

" 'What was it, Mr. Philips?' he asked, collectedly.

"I hesitated; for I was willing to spare him the ill news; but he looked at me with calm eyes for a moment, and I knew that it was useless attempting to deceive him.

" 'Something has happened, Mr. Philips,' he said, quietly. 'You need not be afraid to tell me.'

"At that, I told him so much as I knew, he listening, and nodding his comprehension of the story.

" 'It must be something big,' he remarked, when I had made an end. 'And yet you saw nothing when you came aft?'

" 'No,' I replied.

" 'It is something in the weed,' he went on. 'You will have to keep off the deck at night.'

"After a little further talk, in which he displayed a calmness that amazed me, I left him, and went presently to my berth.

"The following day, I took the two men, and, together, we made a thorough search through the ship; but found nothing. It was evident to me that the Captain was right. There was some dread Thing hidden within the weed. I went to the side and looked down. The two men followed me. Suddenly, one of them pointed.

" 'Look, Sir!' he exclaimed. 'Right below you, Sir! Two eyes like blessed great saucers! Look!'

"I stared; but could see nothing. The man left my side, and ran into the galley. In a moment, he was back with a great lump of coal.

" 'Just there, Sir,' he said, and hove it down into the weed immediately beneath where we stood.

"Too late, I saw the thing at which he aimed—two immense eyes, some little distance below the surface of the weed. I knew instantly to what they belonged; for I had seen large specimens of the octopus some years previously, during a cruise in Australasian waters.

" 'Look out, man!' I shouted, and caught him by the arm. 'It's an octopus! Jump back!' I sprang down on to the deck. In the same instant, huge masses of weed were hurled in all directions, and half a dozen immense tentacles whirled up into the air. One lapped itself about his neck. I caught his leg; but he was torn from my grasp, and I tumbled backwards on to the deck. I heard a scream from the other man as I scrambled to my feet. I looked to where he had been; but of him there was no sign. Regardless of the danger, in my great agitation, I leapt upon the rail, and gazed down with frightened eyes. Yet, neither of him nor his mate, nor the monster, could I perceive a vestige.

"How long I stood there staring down bewilderedly, I cannot say; certainly some minutes. I was so bemazed that I seemed incapable of movement. Then, all at once, I became aware that a light quiver ran across the weed, and the next instant, something stole up out of the depths with a deadly celerity. Well it was for me that I had seen it in time, else should I have shared the fate of those two—and the others. As it was, I saved myself only by leaping backwards on to the deck. For a moment, I saw the feeler wave above the rail with a certain apparent aimlessness; then it sank out of sight, and I was alone.

"An hour passed before I could summon a sufficiency of courage to break the news of this last tragedy to the Captain and his daughter, and when I had made an end, I returned to the solitude of the poop; there to brood upon the hopelessness of our position.

"As I paced up and down, I caught myself glancing continuously at the nearer weed tufts. The happenings of the past two days had shattered my nerves, and I feared every moment to see some slender death-grapple searching over the rail for me. Yet, the poop, being very much higher out of the weed than the main-deck, was comparatively safe; though only comparatively.

"Presently, as I meandered up and down, my gaze fell upon the hulk of the ancient ship, and, in a flash, the reason for that great superstructure was borne upon me. It was intended as a protection against the dread creatures which inhabited the weed. The thought came to me that I would attempt some similar means of protection; for the feeling that, at any moment, I might be caught and lifted out into that slimy wilderness, was not to be borne. In addition, the work would serve to occupy my mind, and help me to bear up against the intolerable sense of loneliness which assailed me.

"I resolved that I would lose no time, and so, after some thought as to the manner in which I should proceed, I routed out some coils

of rope and several sails. Then I went down on to the main-deck and
brought up an armful of capstan bars. These I lashed vertically to the
rail all round the poop. Then I knotted the rope to each, stretching
it tightly between them, and over this framework stretched the sails,
sewing the stout canvas to the rope, by means of twine and some
great needles which I found in the Mate's room.

"It is not to be supposed that this piece of work was accomplished immediately. Indeed, it was only after three days of hard
labour that I got the poop completed. Then I commenced work
upon the main-deck. This was a tremendous undertaking, and a
whole fortnight passed before I had the entire length of it enclosed;
for I had to be continually on the watch against the hidden enemy.
Once, I was very nearly surprised, and saved myself only by a quick
leap. Thereafter, for the rest of that day, I did no more work;
being too greatly shaken in spirit. Yet, on the following morning, I
recommenced, and from thence, until the end, I was not molested.

"Once the work was roughly completed, I felt at ease to begin
and perfect it. This I did, by tarring the whole of the sails with
Stockholm tar; thereby making them stiff, and capable of resisting
the weather. After that, I added many fresh uprights, and much
strengthening ropework, and finally doubled the sailcloth with additional sails, liberally smeared with the tar.

"In this manner, the whole of January passed away, and a part of
February. Then, it would be on the last day of the month, the Captain sent for me, and told me, without any preliminary talk, that he
was dying. I looked at him; but said nothing; for I had known long
that it was so. In return, he stared back with a strange intentness, as
though he would read my inmost thoughts, and this for the space
of perhaps two minutes.

" 'Mr. Philips,' he said at last, 'I may be dead by this time tomorrow. Has it ever occurred to you that my daughter will be alone
with you?'

" 'Yes, Captain Knowles,' I replied, quietly, and waited.

"For a few seconds, he remained silent; though, from the changing expressions of his face, I knew that he was pondering how best
to bring forward the thing which it was in his mind to say.

" 'You are a gentleman—' he began, at last.

" 'I will marry her,' I said, ending the sentence for him.

"A slight flush of surprise crept into his face.

" 'You—you have thought seriously about it?'

" 'I have thought very seriously,' I explained.

" 'Ah!' he said, as one who comprehends. And then, for a little, he lay there quietly. It was plain to me that memories of past days were with him. Presently, he came out of his dreams, and spoke, evidently referring to my marriage with his daughter.

" 'It is the only thing,' he said, in a level voice.

"I bowed, and after that, he was silent again for a space. In a little, however, he turned once more to me:—

" 'Do you—do you love her?'

"His tone was keenly wistful, and a sense of trouble lurked in his eyes.

" 'She will be my wife,' I said, simply; and he nodded.

" 'God has dealt strangely with us,' he murmured, presently, as though to himself.

"Abruptly, he bade me tell her to come in.

"And then he married us.

"Three days later, he was dead, and we were alone.

"For a while, my wife was a sad woman; but gradually time eased her of the bitterness of her grief.

"Then, some eight months after our marriage, a new interest stole into her life. She whispered it to me, and we, who had borne our loneliness uncomplainingly, had now this new thing to which to look forward. It became a bond between us, and bore promise of some companionship as we grew old. Old! At the idea of age, a sudden flash of thought darted like lightning across the sky of my mind:— *FOOD!* Hitherto, I had thought of myself, almost as of one already dead, and had cared naught for anything beyond the immediate troubles which each day forced upon me. The loneliness of the vast Weed World had become an assurance of doom to me, which had clouded and dulled my faculties, so that I had grown apathetic. Yet, immediately, as it seemed, at the shy whispering of my wife, was all this changed.

"That very hour, I began a systematic search through the ship. Among the cargo, which was of a 'general' nature, I discovered large quantities of preserved and tinned provisions, all of which I put carefully on one side. I continued my examination until I had ransacked the whole vessel. The business took me near upon six months to complete, and when it was finished, I seized paper, and made calculations, which led me to the conclusion that we had sufficient food in the ship to preserve life in three people for some fifteen to seventeen years. I could not come nearer to it than this; for I had no means of computing the quantity the child would need year by year. Yet it is sufficient to show me that seventeen years *must* be the limit. Seventeen years! And then——

"Concerning water, I am not troubled; for I have rigged a great sailcloth tun-dish, with a canvas pipe into the tanks; and from every rain, I draw a supply, which has never run short.

"The child was born nearly five months ago. She is a fine little girl, and her mother seems perfectly happy. I believe I could be quietly happy with them, were it not that I have ever in mind the end of those seventeen years. True! we may be dead long before then; but, if not, our little girl will be in her teens—and it is a hungry age.

"If one of us died—but no! Much may happen in seventeen years. I will wait.

"My method of sending this clear of the weed is likely to succeed. I have constructed a small fireballoon, and this missive, safely enclosed in a little barrel, will be attached. The wind will carry it swiftly hence.

"Should this ever reach civilised beings, will they see that it is forwarded to:— "

(Here followed an address, which, for some reason, had been roughly obliterated. Then came the signature of the writer)

"Arthur Samuel Philips."

The Captain of the schooner looked over at Jock, as the man made an end of his reading.

"Seventeen years pervisions," he muttered thoughtfully. "An' this 'ere were written sumthin' like twenty-nine years ago!" He nodded his head several times. "Poor creetures!" he exclaimed. "It'd be er long while, Jock—a long while!"

From the Tideless Sea Part Two: Further News of the Homebird

IN THE AUGUST OF 1902, Captain Bateman, of the schoner *Agnes*, picked up a small barrel, upon which was painted a half obliterated word; which, finally, he succeeded in deciphering as "Homebird," the name of a full-rigged ship, which left London in the November of 1873, and from thenceforth was heard of no more by any man.

Captain Bateman opened the barrel, and discovered a packet of Manuscript, wrapped in oilskin. This, on examination, proved to be an account of the losing of the *Homebird* amid the desolate wastes of the Sargasso Sea. The papers were written by one Arthur Samuel Philips, a passenger in the ship; and, from them, Captain Bateman was enabled to gather that the ship, mastless, lay in the very heart of the dreaded Sargasso; and that all of the crew had been lost; some in the storm which drove them thither, and some in attempts to free the ship from the weed, which locked them in on all sides.

Only Mr. Philips and the Captain's daughter had been left alive, and they two, the dying Captain had married. To them had been born a daughter, and the papers ended with a brief but touching allusion to their fear that, eventually, they must run short of food.

There is need to say but little more. The account was copied into most of the papers of the day, and caused widespread comment. There was even some talk of fitting out a rescue expedition; but this fell through, owing chiefly to lack of knowledge of the whereabouts of the ship in all the vastness of the immense Sargasso Sea. And so, gradually, the matter has slipped into the background of the Public's memory.

Now, however, interest will be once more excited in the lonesome fate of this lost trio; for a second barrel, identical, it would seem, with that found by Captain Bateman, has been picked up by a Mr. Bolton, of Baltimore, master of a small brig, engaged in the South American coast-trade. In this barrel was enclosed a further message from Mr.

Philips—the fifth that he has sent abroad to the world; but the second, third and fourth, up to this time, have not been discovered.

This "fifth message" contains a vital and striking account of their lives during the year 1879, and stands unique as a document informed with human lonesomeness and longing. I have seen it, and read it through, with the most intense and painful interest. The writing, though faint, is very legible; and the whole manuscript bears the impress of the same hand and mind that wrote the piteous account of the losing of the *Homebird*, of which I have already made mention, and with which, no doubt, many are well acquainted.

In closing this little explanatory note, I am stimulated to wonder whether, somewhere, at some time, those three missing messages ever shall be found. And then there may be others. What stories of human, strenuous fighting with Fate may they not contain. We can but wait and wonder. Nothing more may we ever learn; for what is this one little tragedy among the uncounted millions that the silence of the sea holds so remorselessly. And yet, again, news may come to us out of the Unknown—out of the lonesome silences of the dread Sargasso Sea—the loneliest and the most inaccessible place of all the lonesome and inaccessible places of this earth.

And so I say, let us wait. W.H.H.

THE FIFTH MESSAGE

"This is the fifth message that I have sent abroad over the loathsome surface of this vast Weed-World, praying that it may come to the open sea, ere the lifting power of my fire-balloon begone, and yet, if it come there—the which I could now doubt—how shall I be the better for it? Yet write I must, or go mad, and so I choose to write, though feeling as I write that no living creature, save it be the giant octopi that live in the weed about me, will ever see the thing I write.

"My first message I sent out on Christmas Eve, 1875, and since then, each eve of the birth of Christ has seen a message go skywards upon the winds, towards the open sea. It is as though this approaching time, of festivity and the meeting of parted loved ones, overwhelms me, and drives away the half apathetic peace that has been mine through spaces of these years of lonesomeness; so that I seclude myself from my wife and the little one, and with ink, pen, and paper, try to ease my heart of the pent emotions that seem at times to threaten to burst it.

"It is now six completed years since the Weed-World claimed us from the World of the Living—six years away from our brothers and sisters of the human and living world—It has been six years of living in a grave! And there are all the years ahead! Oh! My God! My God! I dare not think upon them! I must control myself—

"And then there is the little one, she is nearly four and a half now, and growing wonderfully, out among these wilds. Four and a half years, and the little woman has never seen a human face besides ours—think of it! And yet, if she lives four and forty years, she will never see another…. Four and forty years! It is foolishness to trouble about such a space of time; for the future, for us, ends in ten years—eleven at the utmost. Our food will last no longer than that…. My wife does not know; for it seems to me a wicked thing to add unnecessarily to her punishment. She does but know that we must waste no ounce of food-stuff, and for the rest she imagines that the most of the cargo is of an edible nature. Perhaps, I have nurtured this belief. If anything happened to me, the food would last a few extra years; but my wife would have to imagine it an accident, else would each bite she took sicken her.

"I have thought often and long upon this matter, yet I fear to leave them; for who knows but that their very lives might at any time depend upon my strength, more pitifully, perhaps, than upon the food which they must come at last to lack. No, I must not bring upon them, and myself, a near and certain calamity, to defer one that, though it seems to have but little less certainty, is yet at a further distance.

"Until lately, nothing has happened to us in the past four years, if I except the adventures that attended my mad attempt to cut away through the surrounding weed to freedom, and from which it pleased God that I and those with me should be preserved[1]. Yet, in the latter part of this year, an adventure, much touched with grimness, came to us most unexpectedly, in a fashion quite unthought of—an adventure that has brought into our lives a fresh and more active peril; for now I have learned that the weed holds other terrors besides that of the giant octopi.

"Indeed, I have grown to believe this world of desolation capable of holding any horror, as well it might. Think of it—an interminable stretch of dank, brown loneliness in all directions, to the distant horizon; a place where monsters of the deep and the weed have undisputed reign; where never an enemy may fall upon them; but from

---

[1] This is evidently a reference to something which Mr. Philips has set forth in an earlier message—one of the three lost messages—W. H. H.

which they may strike with sudden deadliness! No human can ever bring an engine of destruction to bear upon them, and the humans whose fate it is to have sight of them, do so only from the decks of lonesome derelicts, whence they stare lonely with fear, and without ability to harm.

"I cannot describe it, nor can any hope ever to imagine it! When the wind falls, a vast silence holds us girt, from horizon to horizon, yet it is a silence through which one seems to feel the pulse of hidden things all about us, watching and waiting—waiting and watching; waiting but for the chance to reach forth a huge and sudden death-grapple.... It is no use! I cannot bring it home to any; nor shall I be better able to convey the frightening sound of the wind, sweeping across these vast, quaking plains—the shrill whispering of the weed-fronds, under the stirring of the winds. To hear it from beyond our canvas screen, is like listening to the uncounted dead of the mighty Sargasso wailing their own requiems. Or again, my fancy, diseased with much loneliness and brooding, likens it to the advancing rustle of armies of the great monsters that are always about us—waiting.

"And so to the coming of this new terror:—

"It was in the latter end of October that we first had knowledge of it—a tapping in the night time against the side of the vessel, below the water-line; a noise that came distinct, yet with a ghostly strangeness in the quietness of the night. It was on a Monday night when first I heard it. I was down in the lazarette, overhauling our stores, and suddenly I heard it—tap—tap—tap—against the outside of the vessel upon the starboard side, and below the water-line. I stood for a while listening; but could not discover what it was that should come a-tapping against our side, away out here in this lonesome world of weed and slime. And then, as I stood there listening, the tapping ceased, and so I waited, wondering, and with a hateful sense of fear, weakening my manhood, and taking the courage out of my heart....

"Abruptly, it recommenced; but now upon the opposite side of the vessel, and as it continued, I fell into a little sweat; for it seemed to me that some foul thing out in the night was tapping for admittance. Tap—tap—tap—it went, and continued, and there I stood listening, and so gripped about with frightened thoughts, that I seemed without power to stir myself; for the spell of the WeedWorld, and the fear bred of its hidden terrors and the weight and dreeness of its loneliness have entered into my marrow, so that I could, then and now, believe in the likelihood of matters which, ashore and in the midst of my fellows, I might laugh at in contempt. It is the dire lonesomeness of this strange world into which I have entered, that serves so to take the heart out of a man.

"And so, as I have said, I stood there listening, and full of frightened, but undefined, thoughts; and all the while the tapping continued, sometimes with a regular insistence, and anon with a quick spasmodic tap, tap, tap-a-tap, as though some Thing, having Intelligence, signalled to me.

"Presently, however, I shook off something of the foolish fright that had taken me, and moved over to the place from which the tapping seemed to sound. Coming near to it, I bent my head down, close to the side of the vessel, and listened. Thus, I heard the noises with greater plainness, and could distinguish easily, now, that something knocked with a hard object upon the outside of the ship, as though someone had been striking her ironside with a small hammer.

"Then, even as I listened, came a thunderous blow close to my ear, so loud and astonishing, that I leaped sideways in sheer fright. Directly afterwards there came a second heavy blow, and then a third, as though someone had struck the ship's side with a heavy sledge-hammer, and after that, a space of silence, in which I heard my wife's voice at the trap of the lazaretto, calling down to me to know what had happened to cause so great a noise.

" 'Hush, My Dear!' I whispered; for it seemed to me that the thing outside might hear her; though this could not have been possible, and I do but mention it as showing how the noises had set me off my natural balance.

"At my whispered command, my wife turned her about and came down the ladder into the semidarkness of the place.

" 'What is it, Arthur?' she asked, coming across to me, and slipping her hand between my arm and side.

"As though in reply to her query, there came against the outside of the ship, a fourth tremendous blow, filling the whole of the lazarette with a dull thunder.

"My wife gave out a frightened cry, and sprang away from me; but the next instant, she was back, and gripping hard at my arm.

" 'What is it, Arthur? What is it?' she asked me; her voice, though no more than a frightened whisper, easily heard in the succeeding silence.

" 'I don't know, Mary,' I replied, trying to speak in a level tone. 'It's—

" 'There's something again,' she interrupted, as the minor tapping noises recommenced.

"For about a minute, we stood silent, listening to those eerie taps. Then my wife turned to me:—

" 'Is it anything dangerous, Arthur—tell me? I promise you I shall be brave.'

" 'I can't possibly say, Mary,' I answered. 'I can't say; but I'm going up on deck to listen... Perhaps,' I paused a moment to think; but a fifth tremendous blow against the ship's side, drove whatever I was going to say, clean from me, and I could do no more than stand there, frightened and bewildered, listening for further sounds. After a short pause, there came a sixth blow. Then my wife caught me by the arm, and commenced to drag me towards the ladder.

" 'Come up out of this dark place, Arthur,' she said. 'I shall be ill if we stay here any longer.   Perhaps the—the thing outside can hear us, and it may stop if we go upstairs.'

"By this, my wife was all of a shake, and I but little better, so that I was glad to follow her up the ladder. At the top, we paused for a while to listen, bending down over the open hatchway. A space of, maybe, some five minutes passed away in silence; then there commenced again the tapping noises, the sounds coming clearly up to us where we crouched. Presently, they ceased once more, and after that, though we listened for a further space of some ten minutes, they were not repeated. Neither were there any more of the great bangs.

"In a little, I led my wife away from the hatch, to a seat in the saloon; for the hatch is situated under the saloon table. After that, I returned to the opening, and replaced the cover. Then I went into our cabin—the one which had been the Captain's, her father, and brought from there a revolver, of which we have several. This, I loaded with care, and afterwards placed in my side pocket.

"Having done this, I fetched from the pantry, where I have made it my use to keep such things at hand, a bull's-eye lantern, the same having been used on dark nights when clearing up the ropes from the decks. This, I lit, and afterwards turned the dark-slide to cover the light. Next, I slipped off my boots; and then, as an afterthought, I reached down one of the long-handled American axes from the rack about the mizzenmast—these being keen and very formidable weapons.

"After that, I had to calm my wife and assure her that I would run no unnecessary risks, if, indeed, there were any risks to run; though, as may be imagined, I could not say what new peril might not be upon us. And then, picking up the lantern, I made my way silently on stockinged feet, up the companion way. I had reached the top, and was just stepping out on to the deck, when something caught my arm. I turned swiftly, and perceived that my wife had followed me up the steps, and from the shaking of her hand upon my arm, I gathered that she was very much agitated.

" 'Oh, My Dear, My Dear, don't go! don't go!' she whispered, eagerly. 'Wait until it is daylight. Stay below tonight. You don't know what may be about in this horrible place.'

"I put the lantern and the axe upon the deck beside the companion; then bent towards the opening, and took her into my arms, soothing her, and stroking her hair; yet with ever an alert glance to and fro along the indistinct decks. Presently, she was more like her usual self, and listened to my reasoning, that she would do better to stay below, and so, in a little, left me, having made me promise afresh that I would be very wary of danger.

"When she had gone, I picked up the lantern and the axe, and made my way cautiously to the side of the vessel. Here, I paused and listened very carefully, being just above that spot upon the port side where I had heard the greater part of the tapping, and all of the heavy bangs; yet, though I listened, as I have said, with much attention, there was no repetition of the sounds.

"Presently, I rose and made my way forrard to the break of the poop. Here, bending over the rail which ran across, I listened, peering along the dim main-decks; but could neither see nor hear anything; not that, indeed, I had any reason for expecting to see or hear ought unusual *aboard* of the vessel; for all of the noises had come from over the side, and, more than that, from beneath the water-line. Yet in the state of mind in which I was, I had less use for reason than fancy; for that strange thudding and tapping, out here in the midst of this world of loneliness, had set me vaguely imagining unknowable terrors, stealing upon me from every shadow that lay upon the dimly-seen decks.

"Then, as still I listened, hesitating to go down on to the main-deck, yet too dissatisfied with the result of my peerings, to cease from my search, I heard, faint yet clear in the stillness of the night, the tapping noises recommence.

"I took my weight from off the rail, and listened; but I could no longer hear them, and at that, I leant forward again over the rail, and peered down on to the main-deck. Immediately, the sounds came once more to me, and I knew now, that they were borne to me by the medium of the rail, which conducted them to me through the iron stanchions by which it is fixed to the vessel.

"At that, I turned and went aft along the poop-deck, moving very warily and with quietness. I stopped over the place where first I had heard the louder noises, and stooped, putting my ear against the rail. Here, the sounds came to me with great distinctness.

"For a little, I listened; then stood up, and slid away that part of the tarred canvas-screen which covers the port opening through which we dump our refuse; they being made here for convenience, one upon each side of the vessel. This, I did very silently; then, leaning forward through the opening, I peered down into the dimness of the weed. Even as I did so, I heard plainly below me a heavy thud, muffled and dull by reason of the intervening water, against the iron side of the ship. It seemed to me that there was some disturbance amid the dark, shadowy masses of the weed. Then I had opened the dark-slide of my lantern, and sent a clear beam of light down into the blackness. For a brief instant, I thought I perceived a multitude of things moving. Yet, beyond that they were oval in shape, and showed white through the weed fronds, I had no clear conception of anything; for with the flash of the light, they vanished, and there lay beneath me only the dark, brown masses of the weed—demurely quiet.

"But an impression they did leave upon my over excited imagination—an impression that might have been due to morbidity, bred of too much loneliness; but nevertheless it seemed to me that I had seen momentarily a multitude of dead white faces, upturned towards me among the meshes of the weed.

"For a little, I leant there, staring down at the circle of illumined weed; yet with my thoughts in such a turmoil of frightened doubts and conjectures, that my physical eyes did but poor work, compared with the orb that looks inward. And through all the chaos of my mind there rose up weird and creepy memories—ghouls, the un-dead. There seemed nothing improbable, in that moment, in associating the terms with the fears that were besetting me. For no man may dare to say what terrors this world holds, until he has become lost to his brother men, amid the unspeakable desolation of the vast and slimy weed-plains of the Sargasso Sea.

"And then, as I leaned there, so foolishly exposing myself to those dangers which I had learnt did truly exist, my eyes caught and subconsciously noted the strange and subtle undulation which always foretells the approach of one of the giant octopi. Instantly, I leapt back, and whipped the tarred canvas-cover across the opening, and so stood alone there in the night, glancing frightenedly before and behind me, the beam from my lamp casting wavering splashes of light to and fro about the decks. And all the time, I was listening—listening; for it seemed to me that some Terror was brooding in the night, that might come upon us at any moment and in some unimagined form.

"Then, across the silence, stole a whisper, and I turned swiftly towards the companionway. My wife was there, and she reached out her arms to me, begging me to come below into safety. As the light from my lantern flashed upon her, I saw that she had a revolver in her right hand, and at that, I asked her what she had it for; whereupon she informed me that she had been watching over me, through the whole of the time that I had been on deck, save for the little while that it had taken her to get and load the weapon.

"At that, as may be imagined, I went and embraced her very heartily, kissing her for the love that had prompted her actions; and then, after that, we spoke a little together in low tones—she asking that I should come down and fasten up the companion-doors, and I demurring, telling her that I felt too unsettled to sleep; but would rather keep watch about the poop for a while longer.

"Then, even as we discussed the matter, I motioned to her for quietness. In the succeeding silence, she heard it, as well as I, a slow—tap! tap! tap! coming steadily along the dark main-decks. I felt a swift vile fear, and my wife's hold upon me became very tense, despite that she trembled a little. I released her grip from my arm, and made to go towards the break of the poop; but she was after me instantly, praying me at least to stay where I was, if I would not go below.

"Upon that, I bade her very sternly to release me, and go down into the cabin; though all the while I loved her for her very solicitude. But she disobeyed me, asserting very stoutly, though in a whisper, that if I went into danger, she would go with me; and at that I hesitated; but decided, after a moment, to go no further than the break of the poop, and not to venture on to the maindeck.

"I went very silently to the break, and my wife followed me. From the rail across the break, I shone the light of the lantern; but could neither see nor hear anything; for the tapping noise had ceased. Then it recommenced, seeming to have come near to the port side of the stump of the mainmast. I turned the lantern towards it, and, for one brief instant, it seemed to me that I saw something pale, just beyond the brightness of my light. At that, I raised my pistol and fired, and my wife did the same, though without any telling on my part. The noise of the double explosion went very loud and hollow sounding along the decks, and after the echoes had died away, we both of us thought we heard the tapping going away forrard again.

"After that, we stayed awhile, listening and watching; but all was quiet, and, presently, I consented to go below and bar up the companion, as my wife desired; for, indeed, there was much sense in her plea of the futility of my staying up upon the decks.

"The night passed quietly enough, and on the following morning, I made a very careful inspection of the vessel, examining the decks, the weed outside of the ship, and the sides of her. After that, I removed the hatches, and went down into the holds; but could nowhere find anything of an unusual nature.

"That night, just as we were making an end of our supper, we heard three tremendous blows given against the starboard side of the ship, whereat, I sprang to my feet, seized and lit the dark-lantern, which I had kept handy, and ran quickly and silently up on to the deck. My pistol, I had already in my pocket, and as I had soft slippers upon my feet, I needed not to pause to remove my footgear. In the companionway, I had left the axe, and this I seized as I went up the steps.

"Reaching the deck, I moved over quietly to the side, and slid back the canvas door; then I leant out and opened the slide of the lantern, letting its light play upon the weed in the direction from which the bangs had seemed to proceed; but nowhere could I perceive anything out of the ordinary, the weed seeming undisturbed. And so, after a little, I drew in my head, and slid-to the door in the canvas-screen; for it was but wanton folly to stand long exposed to any of the giant octopi that might chance to be prowling near, beneath the curtain of the weed.

"From then, until midnight, I stayed upon the poop, talking much in a quiet voice to my wife, who had followed me up into the companion. At times, we could hear the knocking; sometimes against one side of the ship, and again upon the other. And, between the louder knocks, and accompanying them, would sound the minor tap, tap, tap-a-tap, that I had first heard.

"About midnight, feeling that I could do nothing, and no harm appearing to result to us from the unseen things that seemed to be encircling us, my wife and I made our way below to rest, securely barring the companion-doors behind us.

"It would be, I should imagine, about two o'clock in the morning, that I was aroused from a somewhat troubled sleep, by the agonised screaming of our great boar, away forrard. I leant up upon my elbow, and listened, and so grew speedily wide awake. I sat up, and slid from my bunk to the floor. My wife, as I could tell from her breathing, was sleeping peacefully, so that I was able to draw on a few clothes without disturbing her.

"Then, having lit the dark-lantern, and turned the slide over the light, I took the axe in my other hand, and hastened towards the door that gives out of the forrard end of the saloon, on to the maindeck, beneath the shelter of the break of the poop. This door, I had locked before turning-in, and now, very noiselessly, I unlocked it, and turned the handle, opening the door with much caution. I peered out along the dim stretch of the main-deck; but could see nothing; then I turned on the slide of the lamp, and let the light play along the decks; but still nothing unusual was revealed to me.

"Away forrard, the shrieking of the pig had been succeeded by an absolute silence, and there was nowhere any noise, if I except an occasional odd tap-a-tap, which seemed to come from the side of the ship. And so, taking hold of my courage, I stepped out on to the main-deck, and proceeded slowly forrard, throwing the beam of light to and fro continuously, as I walked.

"Abruptly, I heard away in the bows of the ship a sudden multitudinous tapping and scraping and slithering; and so loud and near did it sound, that I was brought up all of a round-turn, as the saying is. For, perhaps, a whole minute, I stood there hesitating, and playing the light all about me, not knowing but that some hateful thing might leap upon me from out of the shadows.

"And then, suddenly, I remembered that I had left the door open behind me, that led into the saloon, so that, were there any deadly thing about the decks, it might chance to get in upon my wife and child as they slept. At the thought, I turned and ran swiftly aft again, and in through the door to my cabin. Here, I made sure that all was right with the two sleepers, and after that, I returned to the deck, shutting the door, and locking it behind me.

"And now, feeling very lonesome out there upon the dark decks, and cut off in a way from a retreat, I had need of all my manhood to aid me forrard to learn the wherefore of the pig's crying, and the cause of that manifold tapping. Yet go I did, and have some right to be proud of the act; for the dreeness and lonesomeness and the cold fear of the WeedWorld, squeeze the pluck out of one in a very woeful manner.

"As I approached the empty fo'cas'le, I moved with all wariness, swinging the light to and fro, and holding my axe very handily, and the heart within my breast like a shape of water, so in fear was I. Yet, I came at last to the pig-sty, and so discovered a dreadful sight. The pig, a huge boar of twenty-score pounds, had been dragged out on to the deck, and lay before the sty with all his belly ripped up, and stone dead. The iron bars of the sty—great bars they are too—had been torn apart, as though they had been so many straws; and, for the rest, there was a deal of blood both within the sty and upon the decks.

"Yet, I did not stay then to see more; for, all of a sudden, the realisation was borne upon me that this was the work of some monstrous thing, which even at that moment might be stealing upon me; and, with the thought, an overwhelming fear leapt upon me, overbearing my courage; so that I turned and ran for the shelter of the saloon, and never stopped until the stout door was locked between me and that which had wrought such destruction upon the pig. And as I stood there, quivering a little with very fright, I kept questioning dumbly as to what manner of wild-beast thing it was that could burst asunder iron bars, and rip the life out of a great boar, as though it were of no more account than a kitten. And then more vital questions:— How did it get aboard, and where had it hidden? And again:— *What was it?* And so in this fashion for a good while, until I had grown something more calmed.

"But through all the remainder of that night, I slept not so much as a wink.

"Then in the morning when my wife awoke, I told her of the happenings of the night; whereat she turned very white, and fell to reproaching me for going out at all on to the deck, declaring that I had run needlessly into danger, and that, at least, I should not have left her alone, sleeping in ignorance of what was towards. And after that, she fell into a fit of crying, so that I had some to-do comforting her. Yet, when she had come back to calmness, she was all for accompanying me about the decks, to see by daylight what had indeed befallen in the night-time. And from this decision, I could not turn her; though I assured her I should have told her nothing, had it not been that I wished to warn her from going to and fro between the saloon and the galley, until I had made a thorough search about the decks. Yet, as I have remarked, I could not turn her from her purpose of accompanying me, and so was forced to let her come, though against my desire.

"We made our way on deck through the door that opens under the break of the poop, my wife carrying her loaded revolver half-clumsily in both hands, whilst I had mine held in my left, and the long-handled axe in my right—holding it very readily.

"On stepping out on to the deck, we closed the door behind us, locking it and removing the key; for we had in mind our sleeping child. Then we went slowly forrard along the decks, glancing about warily. As we came fore-side of the pig-sty, and my wife saw that which lay beyond it, she let out a little exclamation of horror, shuddering at the sight of the mutilated pig, as, indeed, well she might.

"For my part, I said nothing; but glanced with much apprehension about us; feeling a fresh access of fright; for it was very plain to me that the boar had been molested since I had seen it—the head having been torn, with awful might, from the body; and there were, besides, other new and ferocious wounds, one of which had come nigh to severing the poor brute's body in half. All of which was so much additional evidence of the formidable character of the monster, or Monstrosity, that had attacked the animal.

"I did not delay by the pig, nor attempt to touch it; but beckoned my wife to follow me up on to the fo'cas'le head. Here, I removed the canvas-cover from the small skylight which lights the fo'cas'le beneath; and, after that, I lifted off the heavy top, letting a flood of light down into the gloomy place. Then I leant down into the opening, and peered about; but could discover no signs of any lurking thing, and so returned to the maindeck, and made an entrance into the fo'cas'le through the starboard doorway. And now I made a more minute search; but discovered nothing, beyond the mournful array of sea-chests that had belonged to our dead crew.

"My search concluded, I hastened out from the doleful place, into the daylight, and after that made fast the door again, and saw to it that the one upon the port side was also securely locked. Then I went up again on to the fo'cas'le head, and replaced the skylight-top and the canvas-cover, battening the whole down very thoroughly.

"And in this wise, and with an incredible care, did I make my search through the ship, fastening up each place behind me, so that I should be certain that no Thing was playing some dread game of hide and seek with me.

"Yet I found *nothing*, and had it not been for the grim evidence of the dead and mutilated boar, I had been like to have thought nothing more dreadful than an over vivid Imagination had roamed the decks in the darkness of the past night.

"That I had reason to feel puzzled, may be the better understood, when I explain that I had examined the whole of the great, tarred canvas-screen, which I have built about the ship as a protection against the sudden tentacles of any of the roaming giant octopi, without discovering any torn place such as must have been made if any conceivable monster had climbed aboard out of the weed. Also, it must be borne in mind that the ship stands many feet out of the weed, presenting only her smooth iron sides to anything that desires to climb aboard.

"And yet there was the dead pig, lying brutally torn before its empty sty! An undeniable proof that, to go out upon the decks after dark, was to run the risk of meeting a horrible and mysterious death!

"Through all that day, I pondered over this new fear that had come upon us, and particularly upon the monstrous and unearthly power that had torn apart the stout iron bars of the sty, and so ferociously wrenched off the head of the boar. The result of my pondering was that I removed our sleeping belongings that evening from the cabin to the iron half-deck—a little, four-bunked house, standing fore-side of the stump of the mainmast, and built entirely of iron, even to the single door, which opens out of the after end.

"Along with our sleeping matters, I carried forrard to our new lodgings, a lamp, and oil, also the dark-lantern, a couple of the axes, two rifles, and all of the revolvers, as well as a good supply of ammunition. Then I bade my wife forage out sufficient provisions to last us for a week, if need be, and whilst she was so busied, I cleaned out and filled the water breaker which belonged to the half-deck.

"At half-past six, I sent my wife forrard to the little iron house, with the baby, and then I locked up the saloon and all of the cabin doors, finally locking after me the heavy, teak door that opened out under the break of the poop.

"Then I went forrard to my wife and child, and shut and bolted the iron door of the half-deck for the night. After that, I went round and saw to it that all of the iron storm-doors, that shut over the eight ports of the house, were in good working order, and so we sat down, as it were, to await the night.

"By eight o'clock, the dusk was upon us, and before half-past, the night hid the decks from my sight. Then I shut down all the iron portflaps, and screwed them up securely, and after that, I lit the lamp.

"And so a space of waiting ensued, during which I whispered reassuringly to my wife, from time to time, as she looked across at me from her seat beside the sleeping child, with frightened eyes, and a very white face; for somehow there had come upon us within the last hour, a sense of chilly fright, that went straight to one's heart, robbing one vilely of pluck.

"A little later, a sudden sound broke the impressive silence—a sudden dull thud against the side of the ship; and, after that, there came a succession of heavy blows, seeming to be struck all at once upon every side of the vessel; after which there was quietness for maybe a quarter of an hour.

"Then, suddenly, I heard, away forrard, a tap, tap, tap, and then a loud rattling, slurring noise, and a loud crash. After that, I heard many other sounds, and always that tap, tap, tap, repeated a hundred times, as though an army of wooden-legged men were busied all about the decks at the fore end of the ship.

"Presently, there came to me the sound of something coming down the deck, tap, tap, tap, it came. It drew near to the house, paused for nigh a minute; then continued away aft towards the saloon:— tap, tap, tap. I shivered a little, and then, fell half consciously to thanking God that I had been given wisdom to bring my wife and child forrard to the security of the iron deckhouse.

"About a minute later, I heard the sound of a heavy blow struck somewhere away aft; and after that a second, and then a third, and seeming by the sounds to have been against iron—the iron of the bulkshead that runs across the break of the poop. There came the noise of a fourth blow, and it blended into the crash of broken wood-work. And therewith, I had a little tense quivering inside me; for the little one and my wife might have been sleeping aft there at that very moment, had it not been for the Providential thought which had sent us forrard to the half-deck.

"With the crash of the broken door, away aft, there came, from forrard of us, a great tumult of noises; and, directly, it sounded as though a multitude of wooden-legged men were coming down the decks from forrard. Tap, tap, tap; tap-a-tap, the noises came, and drew abreast of where we sat in the house, crouched and holding our breaths, for fear that we should make some noise to attract that which was without. The sounds passed us, and went tapping away aft, and I let out a little breath of sheer easement. Then, as a sudden thought came to me, I rose and turned down the lamp, fearing that some ray from it might be seen from beneath the door. And so, for the space of an hour, we sat wordless, listening to the sounds which came from away aft, the thud of heavy blows, the occasional crash of wood, and, presently the tap, tap, tap, again, coming forrard towards us.

"The sounds came to a stop, opposite the starboard side of the house, and, for a full minute, there was quietness. Then suddenly, "Boom!" a tremendous blow had been struck against the side of the house. My wife gave out a little gasping cry, and there came a second blow; and, at that, the child awoke and began to wail, and my wife was put to it, with trying to soothe her into immediate silence.

"A third blow was struck, filling the little house with a dull thunder of sound, and then I heard the tap, tap, tap, move round to the after end of the house. There came a pause, and then a great blow right upon the door. I grasped the rifle, which I had leant against my chair, and stood up; for I did not know but that the thing might be upon us in a moment, so prodigious was the force of the blows it struck. Once again it struck the door, and after that went tap, tap, tap, round to the port side of the house, and there struck the house again; but now I had more ease of mind for it was its direct attack upon the door, that had put such horrid dread into my heart.

"After the blows upon the port side of the house, there came a long spell of silence, as though the thing outside were listening; but, by the mercy of God, my wife had been able to soothe the child, so that no sound from us, told of our presence.

"Then, at last, there came again the sounds:— tap, tap, tap, as the voiceless thing moved away forrard. Presently, I heard the noises cease aft; and, after that, there came a multitudinous tapa-tapping, coming along the decks. It passed the house without so much as a pause, and receded away forrard.

"For a space of over two hours, there was an absolute silence; so that I judged that we were now no longer in danger of being molested. An hour later, I whispered to my wife; but, getting no reply, knew that she had fallen into a doze, and so I sat on, listening tensely; yet making no sort of noise that might attract attention.

"Presently, by the thin line of light from beneath the door, I saw that the day was breaking; and, at that, I rose stiffly, and commenced to unscrew the iron port-covers. I unscrewed the forrard ones first, and looked out into the wan dawn; but could discover nothing unusual about so much of the decks as I could see from there.

"After that, I went round and opened each, as I came to it, in its turn; but it was not until I had uncovered the port which gave me a view of the port side of the after main-deck, that I discovered any-thing extraordinary. Then I saw, at first dimly, but more clearly as the day brightened, that the door, leading from beneath the break of the poop into the saloon, had been broken to flinders, some of which lay scattered upon the deck, and some of which still hung from the bent hinges; whilst more, no doubt, were strewed in the passage beyond my sight.

"Turning from the port, I glanced towards my wife, and saw that she lay half in and half out of the baby's bunk, sleeping with her head besides the child's, both upon one pillow. At the sight, a great wave of holy thankfulness took me, that we had been so wonderfully spared from the terrible and mysterious danger that had stalked the decks in the darkness of the preceding night. Feeling thus, I stole across the floor of the house, and kissed them both very gently, being full of tenderness, yet not minded to waken them. And, after that, I lay down in one of the bunks, and slept until the sun was high in the heaven.

"When I awoke, my wife was about and had tended to the child and prepared our breakfast, so that I had naught to do but tumble out and set to, the which I did with a certain keenness of appetite, induced, I doubt not, by the stress of the night. Whilst we ate, we discussed the peril through which we had just passed; but without coming any the nearer to a solution of the weird mystery of the Terror.

"Breakfast over, we took a long and final survey of the decks, from the various ports, and then prepared to sally out. This we did with instinctive caution and quietness, both of us armed as on the previous day. The door of the half-deck we closed and locked behind us, thereby ensuring that the child was open to no danger whilst we were in other parts of the ship.

"After a quick look about us, we proceeded aft towards the shattered door beneath the break of the poop. At the doorway, we stopped, not so much with the intent to examine the broken door, as because of an instinctive and natural hesitation to go forward into the saloon, which but a few hours previous had been visited by some incredible monster or monsters. Finally, we decided to go up upon the poop and peer down through the skylight. This we did, lifting the sides of the dome for that purpose; yet though we peered long and earnestly, we could perceive no signs of any lurking thing. But broken woodwork there appeared to be in plenty, to judge by the scattered pieces.

"After that, I unlocked the companion, and pushed back the big, over-arching slide. Then, silently, we stole down the steps and into the saloon. Here, being now able to see the big cabin through all its length, we discovered a most extraordinary scene; the whole place appeared to be wrecked from end to end; the six cabins that line each side had their bulksheading driven into shards and slivers of broken wood in places. Here, a door would be standing untouched, whilst the bulkshead beside it was in a mass of flinders—There, a door would be driven completely from its hinges, whilst the surrounding woodwork was untouched. And so it was, wherever we looked.

"My wife made to go towards our cabin; but I pulled her back, and went forward myself. Here the desolation was almost as great. My wife's bunk-board had been ripped out, whilst the supporting side-batten of mine had been plucked forth, so that all the bottom-boards of the bunk had descended to the floor in a cascade.

"But it was neither of these things that touched us so sharply, as the fact that the child's little swing cot had been wrenched from its standards, and flung in a tangled mass of white-painted ironwork across the cabin. At the sight of that, I glanced across at my wife, and she at me, her face grown very white. Then down she slid to her knees, and fell to crying and thanking God together, so that I found myself beside her in a moment, with a very humble and thankful heart.

"Presently, when we were more controlled, we left the cabin, and finished our search. The pantry, we discovered to be entirely untouched, which, somehow, I do not think was then a matter of great surprise to me; for I had ever a feeling that the things which had broken a way into our sleeping cabin, had been looking for us.

"In a little while, we left the wrecked saloon and cabins, and made our way forrard to the pigsty; for I was anxious to see whether the carcass of the pig had been touched. As we came round the corner of the sty, I uttered a great cry; for there, lying upon the deck, on its back, was a gigantic crab, so vast in size that I had not conceived so huge a monster existed. Brown it was in colour, save for the belly part, which was of a light yellow.

"One of its pincer-claws, or mandibles, had been torn off in the fight in which it must have been slain (for it was all disembowelled). And this one claw weighed so heavy that I had some to-do to lift it from the deck; and by this you may have some idea of the size and formidableness of the creature itself.

"Around the great crab, lay half a dozen smaller ones, no more than from seven or eight to twenty inches across, and all white in colour, save for an occasional mottling of brown. These had all been killed by a single nip of an enormous mandible, which had in every case smashed them almost into two halves. Of the carcass of the great boar, not a fragment remained.

"And so was the mystery solved; and, with the solution, departed the superstitious terror which had suffocated me through those three nights, since the tapping had commenced. We had been attacked by a wandering shoal of giant crabs, which, it is quite possible, roam across the weed from place to place, devouring aught that comes in their path.

"Whether they had ever boarded a ship before, and so, perhaps, developed a moustrous lust for human flesh, or whether their attack had been prompted by curiosity, I cannot possibly say. It may be that, at first, they mistook the hull of the vessel for the body of some dead marine monster, and hence their blows upon her sides, by which, possibly, they were endeavouring to pierce through our somewhat unusually tough hide!

"Or, again, it may be that they have some power of scent, by means of which they were able to smell our presence aboard the ship; but this (as they made no general attack upon us in the deckhouse) I feel disinclined to regard as probable. And yet—I do not know. Why their attack upon the saloon, and our sleeping-cabin? As I say, I cannot tell, and so must leave it there.

"The way in which they came aboard, I discovered that same day; for, having learned what manner of creature it was that had attacked us, I made a more intelligent survey of the sides of the ship; but it was not until I came to the extreme bows, that I saw how they had managed. Here, I found that some of the gear of the broken bowsprit and jibboom, trailed down on to the weed, and as I had not extended the canvas-screen across the heel of the bowsprit, the monsters had been able to climb up the gear, and thence aboard, without the least obstruction being opposed to their progress.

"This state of affairs, I very speedily remedied; for, with a few strokes of my axe, I cut through the gear, allowing it to drop down among the weed; and, after that, I built a temporary breastwork of wood across the gap, between the two ends of the screen; later on making it more permanent.

"Since that time, we have been no more molested by the giant crabs; though for several nights afterwards, we heard them knocking strangely against our sides. Maybe, they are attracted by such refuse as we are forced to dump overboard, and this would explain their first tappings being aft, opposite to the lazarette; for it is from the openings in this part of the canvas-screen that we cast our rubbish.

"Yet, it is weeks now since we heard aught of them, so that I have reason to believe that they have betaken themselves elsewhere, maybe to attack some other lonely humans, living out their short span of life aboard some lone derelict, lost even to memory in the depth of this vast sea of weed and deadly creatures.

"I shall send this message forth on its journey, as I have sent the other four, within a well-pitched barrel, attached to a small fire-balloon. The shell of the severed claw of the monster crab, I shall enclose[2], as evidence of the terrors that beset us in this dreadful place. Should this message, and the claw, ever fall into human hands, let

---

[2] Captain Bolton makes no mention of the claw, in the covering letter which he has enclosed with the MS.—W.H.H.

them, contemplating this vast mandible, try to imagine the size of the other crab or crabs that could destroy so formidable a creature as the one to which this claw belonged.

"What other terrors does this hideous world hold for us?

"I had thought of inclosing, along with the claw, the shell of one of the white smaller crabs. It must have been some of these moving in the weed that night, that set my disordered fancy to imagining of ghouls and the Un-Dead. But, on thinking it over, I shall not; for to do so would be to illustrate nothing that needs illustration, and it would but increase needlessly the weight which the balloon will have to lift.

"And so I grow wearied of writing. The night is drawing near, and I have little more to tell. I am writing this in the saloon, and, though I have mended and carpentered so well as I am able, nothing I can do will hide the traces of that night when the vast crabs raided through these cabins, searching for—what?

"There is nothing more to say. In health, I am well, and so is my wife and the little one, but....

"I must have myself under control, and be patient. We are beyond all help, and must bear that which is before us, with such bravery as we are able. And with this, I end; for my last word shall not be one of complaint.

"ARTHUR SAMUEL PHILIPS.

"Christmas Eve, 1879."

The Mystery of the Derelict

ALL THE NIGHT HAD the four-masted ship, *Tarawak*, lain motionless in the drift of the Gulf Stream; for she had run into a "calm patch"—into a stark calm which had lasted now for two days and nights.

On every side, had it been light, might have been seen dense masses of floating gulf-weed, studding the ocean even to the distant horizon. In places, so large were the weed-masses that they formed long, low banks, that, by daylight, might have been mistaken for low-lying land.

Upon the lee side of the poop, Duthie, one of the 'prentices, leaned with his elbows upon the rail, and stared out across the hidden sea, to where in the Eastern horizon showed the first pink and lemon streamers of the dawn—faint, delicate streaks and washes of colour.

A period of time passed, and the surface of the leeward sea began to show—a great expanse of grey, touched with odd, wavering belts of silver. And everywhere the black specks and islets of the weed.

Presently, the red dome of the sun protruded itself into sight above the dark rim of the horizon; and, abruptly, the watching Duthie saw something—a great, shapeless bulk that lay some miles away to starboard, and showed black and distinct against the gloomy red mass of the rising sun.

"Something in sight to looard, Sir," he informed the Mate, who was leaning, smoking, over the rail that ran across the break of the poop. "I can't just make out what it is."

The Mate rose from his easy position, stretched himself, yawned, and came across to the boy.

"Whereabouts, Toby?" he asked, wearily, and yawning again.

"There, Sir," said Duthie—alias Toby— "broad away on the beam, and right in the track of the sun. It looks something like a big houseboat, or a haystack."

173

The Mate stared in the direction indicated, and saw the thing which puzzled the boy, and immediately the tiredness went out of his eyes and face.

"Pass me the glasses off the skylight, Toby," he commanded, and the youth obeyed.

After the Mate had examined the strange object through his binoculars for, maybe, a minute, he passed them to Toby, telling him to take a "squint," and say what he made of it.

"Looks like an old powder-hulk, Sir," exclaimed the lad, after a while, and to this description the Mate nodded agreement.

Later, when the sun had risen somewhat, they were able to study the derelict with more exactness. She appeared to be a vessel of an exceedingly old type, mastless, and upon the hull of which had been built a roof-like superstructure; the use of which they could not determine. She was lying just within the borders of one of the weedbanks, and all her side was splotched with a greenish growth.

It was her position, within the borders of the weed, that suggested to the puzzled Mate, how so strange and unseaworthy looking a craft had come so far abroad into the greatness of the ocean. For, suddenly, it occurred to him that she was neither more nor less than a derelict from the vast Sargasso Sea—a vessel that had, possibly, been lost to the world, scores and scores of years gone, perhaps hundreds. The suggestion touched the Mate's thoughts with solemnity, and he fell to examining the ancient hulk with an even greater interest, and pondering on all the lonesome and awful years that must have passed over her, as she had lain desolate and forgotten in that grim cemetery of the ocean.

Through all that day, the derelict was an object of the most intense interest to those aboard the *Tarawak*, every glass in the ship being brought into use to examine her. Yet, though within no more than some six or seven miles of her, the Captain refused to listen to the Mate's suggestions that they should put a boat into the water, and pay the stranger a visit; for he was a cautious man, and the glass warned him that a sudden change might be expected in the weather; so that he would have no one leave the ship on any unnecessary business. But, for all that he had caution, curiosity was by no means lacking in him, and his telescope, at intervals, was turned on the ancient hulk through all the day.

Then, it would be about six bells in the second dog watch, a sail was sighted astern, coming up steadily but slowly. By eight bells they were able to make out that a small barque was bringing the wind with her; her yards squared, and every stitch set. Yet the night had advanced apace, and it was nigh to eleven o'clock before the wind reached those aboard the *Tarawak*. When at last it arrived, there was a slight rustling and quaking of canvas, and odd creaks here and there in the darkness amid the gear, as each portion of the running and standing rigging took up the strain.

Beneath the bows, and alongside, there came gentle rippling noises, as the vessel gathered way; and so, for the better part of the next hour, they slid through the water at something less than a couple of knots in the sixty minutes.

To starboard of them, they could see the red light of the little barque, which had brought up the wind with her, and was now forging slowly ahead, being better able evidently than the big, heavy *Tarawak* to take advantage of so slight a breeze.

About a quarter to twelve, just after the relieving watch had been roused, lights were observed to be moving to and fro upon the small barque, and by midnight it was palpable that, through some cause or other, she was dropping astern.

When the Mate arrived on deck to relieve the Second, the latter officer informed him of the possibility that something unusual had occurred aboard the barque, telling of the lights about her decks,[1] and how that, in the last quarter of an hour, she had begun to drop astern.

On hearing the Second Mate's account, the First sent one of the 'prentices for his night-glasses, and, when they were brought, studied the other vessel intently, that is, so well as he was able through the darkness; for, even through the night-glasses, she showed only as a vague shape, surmounted by the three dim towers of her masts and sails.

Suddenly, the Mate gave out a sharp exclamation; for, beyond the barque, there was something else shown dimly in the field of vision. He studied it with great intentness, ignoring for the instant, the Second's queries as to what it was that had caused him to exclaim.

All at once, he said, with a little note of excitement in his voice:—

"The derelict! The barque's run into the weed around that old hooker!"

The Second Mate gave a mutter of surprised assent, and slapped the rail.

"That's it!" he said. "That's why we're passing her. And that explains the lights. If they're not fast in the weed, they've probably run

---

[1] Unshaded lights are never allowed about the decks at night, as they are likely to blind the vision of the officer of the watch.—W.H.H.

slap into the blessed derelict!"

"One thing," said the Mate, lowering his glasses, and beginning to fumble for his pipe, "she won't have had enough way on her to do much damage."

The Second Mate, who was still peering through his binoculars, murmured an absent agreement, and continued to peer. The Mate, for his part, filled and lit his pipe, remarking meanwhile to the unhearing Second, that the light breeze was dropping.

Abruptly, the Second Mate called his superior's attention, and in the same instant, so it seemed, the failing wind died entirely away, the sails settling down into runkles, with little rustles and flutters of sagging canvas.

"What's up?" asked the Mate, and raised his glasses.

"There's something queer going on over yonder," said the Second. "Look at the lights moving about, and—Did you see *that?*"

The last portion of his remark came out swiftly, with a sharp accentuation of the last word.

"What?" asked the Mate, staring hard.

"They're shooting," replied the Second. "Look! There again!"

"Rubbish!" said the Mate, a mixture of unbelief and doubt in his voice.

With the falling of the wind, there had come a great silence upon the sea. And, abruptly, from far across the water, sounded the distant, dullish thud of a gun, followed almost instantly by several minute, but sharply defined, reports, like the cracking of a whip out in the darkness.

"Jove!" cried the Mate, "I believe you're right." He paused and stared. "There!" he said. "I saw the flashes then. They're firing from the poop, I believe.... I must call the Old Man." He turned and ran hastily down into the saloon, knocked on the door of the Captain's cabin, and entered. He turned up the lamp, and, shaking his superior into wakefulness, told him of the thing he believed to be happening aboard the barque:—

"It's mutiny, Sir; they're shooting from the poop. We ought to do something—" The Mate said many things, breathlessly; for he was a young man; but the Captain stopped him, with a quietly lifted hand.

"I'll be up with you in a minute, Mr. Johnson," he said, and the Mate took the hint, and ran up on deck.

Before the minute had passed, the Skipper was on the poop, and staring through his night-glasses at the barque and the derelict. Yet now, aboard of the barque, the lights had vanished, and there showed no more the flashes of discharging weapons—only there remained the dull, steady red glow of the port sidelight; and, behind it, the night-glasses showed the shadowy outline of the vessel.

The Captain put questions to the Mates, asking for further details.

"It all stopped while the Mate was calling you, Sir," explained the Second. "We could hear the shots quite plainly."

They seemed to be using a gun as well as their revolvers," interjected the Mate, without ceasing to stare into the darkness.

For a while the three of them continued to discuss the matter, whilst down on the main-deck the two watches clustered along the starboard rail, and a low hum of talk rose, fore and aft.

Presently, the Captain and the Mates came to a decision. If there had been a mutiny, it had been brought to its conclusion, whatever that conclusion might be, and no interference from those aboard the *Tarawak*, at that period, would be likely to do good. They were utterly in the dark—in more ways than one—and, for all they knew, there might not even have been any mutiny. If there had been a mutiny, and the mutineers had won, then they had done their worst; whilst if the officers had won, well and good. They had managed to do so without help. Of course, if the *Tayawak* had been a man-of-war with a large crew, capable of mastering any situation, it would have been a simple matter to send a powerful, armed boat's crew to inquire; but as she was merely a merchant vessel, undermanned, as is the modern fashion, they must go warily. They would wait for the morning, and signal. In a couple of hours it would be light. Then they would be guided by circumstances.

The Mate walked to the break of the poop, and sang out to the men:—

"Now then, my lads, you'd better turn in, the watch below, and have a sleep; we may be wanting you by five bells."

There was a muttered chorus of "Aye, Aye, Sir," and some of the men began to go forrard to the fo'cas'le; but others of the watch below remained, their curiosity overmastering their desire for sleep.

On the poop, the three officers leaned over the starboard rail, chatting in a desultory fashion, as they waited for the dawn. At some little distance hovered Duthie, who, as eldest 'prentice just out of his time, had been given the post of acting Third Mate.

Presently, the sky to starboard began to lighten with the solemn coming of the dawn. The light grew and strengthened, and the eyes of those in the *Tayawak* scanned with growing intentness that portion of the horizon where showed the red and dwindling glow of the barque's sidelight.

Then, it was in that moment when all the world is full of the silence of the dawn, something passed over the quiet sea, coming out of the East—a very faint, long-drawn-out, screaming, piping noise. It might almost have been the cry of a little wind wandering out of the dawn across the sea—a ghostly, piping skirl, so attenuated and elusive was it; but there was in it a weird, almost threatening note, that told the three on the poop it was no wind that made so dree and inhuman a sound.

The noise ceased, dying out in an indefinite, mosquito-like shrilling, far and vague and minutely shrill. And so came the silence again.

"I heard that, last night, when they were shooting," said the Second Mate, speaking very slowly, and looking first at the Skipper and then at the Mate. "It was when you were below, calling the Captain," he added.

"Ssh!" said the Mate, and held up a warning hand; but though they listened, there came no further sound; and so they fell to disjointed questionings, and guessed their answers, as puzzled men will. And ever and anon, they examined the barque through their glasses; but without discovering anything of note, save that, when the light grew stronger, they perceived that her jibboom had struck through the superstructure of the derelict, tearing a considerable gap therein.

Presently, when the day had sufficiently advanced, the Mate sung out to the Third, to take a couple of the 'prentices, and pass up the signal flags and the code book. This was done, and a "hoist" made; but those in the barque took not the slightest heed; so that finally the Captain bade them make up the flags and return them to the locker.

After that, he went down to consult the glass, and when he reappeared, he and the Mates had a short discussion, after which, orders were given to hoist out the starboard life-boat. This, in the course of half an hour, they managed; and, after that, six of the men and two of the 'prentices were ordered into her.

Then half a dozen rifles were passed down, with ammunition, and the same number of cutlasses. These were all apportioned among the men, much to the disgust of the two apprentices, who were aggrieved that they should be passed over; but their feelings altered when the Mate descended into the boat, and handed them each a loaded revolver, warning them, however, to play no "monkey tricks" with the weapons.

Just as the boat was about to push off, Duthie, the eldest 'prentice, came scrambling down the side ladder, and jumped for the after thwart. He landed, and sat down, laying the rifle which he had brought, in the stern; and, after that, the boat put off for the barque.

There were now ten in the boat, and all well armed, so that the Mate had a certain feeling of comfort that he would be able to meet any situation that was likely to arise.

After nearly an hour's hard pulling, the heavy boat had been brought within some two hundred yards of the barque, and the Mate sung out to the men to lie on their oars for a minute. Then he stood up and shouted to the people on the barque; but though he repeated his cry of "Ship ahoy!" several times, there came no reply.

He sat down, and motioned to the men to give way again, and so brought the boat nearer the barque by another hundred yards. Here, he hailed again; but still receiving no reply, he stooped for his binoculars, and peered for a while through them at the two vessels—the ancient derelict, and the modern sailing-vessel.

The latter had driven clean in over the weed, her stern being perhaps some two score yards from the edge of the bank. Her jib-boom, as I have already mentioned, had pierced the green-blotched superstructure of the derelict, so that her cutwater had come very close to the grass-grown side of the hulk.

That the derelict was indeed a very ancient vessel, it was now easy to see; for at this distance the Mate could distinguish which was hull, and which superstructure. Her stern rose up to a height considerably above her bows, and possessed galleries, coming round the counter. In the window frames some of the glass still remained; but others were securely shuttered, and some missing, frames and all, leaving dark holes in the stern. And everywhere grew the dank, green growth, giving to the beholder a queer sense of repulsion. Indeed, there was that about the whole of the ancient craft, that repelled in a curious way—something elusive—a remoteness from humanity, that was vaguely abominable.

The Mate put down his binoculars, and drew his revolver, and, at the action, each one in the boat gave an instinctive glance to his own weapon. Then he sung out to them to give-way, and steered straight for the weed. The boat struck it, with something of a sog;

and, after that, they advanced slowly, yard by yard, only with considerable labour.

They reached the counter of the barque, and the Mate held out his hand for an oar. This, he leaned up against the side of the vessel, and a moment later was swarming quickly up it. He grasped the rail, and swung himself aboard; then, after a swift glance fore and aft, gripped the blade of the oar, to steady it, and bade the rest follow as quickly as possible, which they did, the last man bringing up the painter with him, and making it fast to a cleat.

Then commenced a rapid search through the ship. In several places about the main-deck they found broken lamps, and aft on the poop, a shotgun, three revolvers, and several capstan-bars lying about the poop-deck. But though they pried into every possible corner, lifting the hatches, and examining the lazaretto, not a human creature was to be found—the barque was absolutely deserted.

After the first rapid search, the Mate called his men together; for there was an uncomfortable sense of danger in the air, and he felt that it would be better not to straggle. Then, he led the way forrard, and went up on to the t'gallant fo'cas'le head. Here, finding the port sidelight still burning, he bent over the screen, as it were mechanically, lifted the lamp, opened it, and blew out the flame; then replaced the affair on its socket.

After that, he climbed into the bows, and out along the jibboom, beckoning to the others to follow, which they did, no man saying a word, and all holding their weapons handily; for each felt the oppressiveness of the Incomprehensible about them.

The Mate reached the hole in the great superstructure, and passed inside, the rest following. Here they found themselves in what looked something like a great, gloomy barracks, the floor of which was the deck of the ancient craft. The superstructure, as seen from the inside, was a very wonderful piece of work, being beautifully shored and fixed; so that at one time it must have possessed immense strength; though now it was all rotted, and showed many a gape and rip. In one place, near the centre, or midships part, was a sort of platform, high up, which the Mate conjectured might have been used as a "look-out"; though the reason for the prodigious superstructure itself, he could not imagine.

Having searched the decks of this craft, he was preparing to go below, when, suddenly, Duthie caught him by the sleeve, and whispered to him, tensely, to listen. He did so, and heard the thing that had attracted the attention of the youth—it was a low, continuous, shrill whining that was rising from out of the dark hull beneath their feet, and, abruptly, the Mate was aware that there was an intensely disagreeable animal-like smell in the air. He had noticed it, in a sub-conscious fashion, when entering through the broken superstructure; but now, suddenly, he was *aware* of it.

Then, as he stood there hesitating, the whining noise rose all at once into a piping, screaming squeal, that filled all the space in which they were inclosed, with an awful, inhuman and threatening clamour. The Mate turned and shouted at the top of his voice to the rest, to retreat to the barque, and he, himself, after a further quick nervous glance round, hurried towards the place where the end of the barque's jibboom protruded in across the decks.

He waited, with strained impatience, glancing ever behind him, until all were off the derelict, and then sprang swiftly on to the spar that was their bridge to the other vessel. Even as he did so, the squealing died away into a tiny shrilling, twittering sound, that made him glance back; for the suddenness of the quiet was as effective as though it had been a loud noise. What he saw, seemed to him in that first instant so incredible and monstrous, that he was almost too shaken to cry out. Then he raised his voice in a shout of warning to the men, and a frenzy of haste shook him in every fibre, as he scrambled back to the barque, shouting ever to the men to get into the boat. For in that backward glance, he had seen the whole decks of the derelict a-move with living things—giant rats, thousands and tens of thousands of them; and so in a flash had come to an understanding of the disappearance of the crew of the barque.

He had reached the fo'cas'le head now, and was running for the steps, and behind him, making all the long slanting length of the jibboom black, were the rats, racing after him. He made one leap to the main-deck, and ran. Behind, sounded a queer, multitudi-nous pattering noise, swiftly surging upon him. He reached the poop steps, and as he sprang up them, felt a savage bite in his left calf. He was on the poop-deck now, and running with a stagger. A score of great rats leapt around him, and half a dozen hung grimly to his back, whilst the one that had gripped his calf, flogged madly from side to side as he raced on. He reached the rail, gripped it, and vaulted clean over and down into the weed.

The rest were already in the boat, and strong hands and arms hove him aboard, whilst the others of the crew sweated in getting their little craft round from the ship. The rats still clung to the Mate; but a few blows with a cutlass eased him of his murderous burden. Above them, making the rails and half-round of the poop black and alive, raced thousands of rats.

The boat was now about an oar's length from the barque, and, suddenly, Duthie screamed out that *they* were coming. In the same instant, nearly a hundred of the largest rats launched themselves at the boat. Most fell short, into the weed; but over a score reached the boat, and sprang savagely at the men, and there was a minute's hard slashing and smiting, before the brutes were destroyed.

Once more the men resumed their task of urging their way through the weed, and so in a minute or two, had come to within some fathoms of the edge, working desperately. Then a fresh terror broke upon them. Those rats which had missed their leap, were now all about the boat, and leaping in from the weed, running up the oars, and scrambling in over the sides, and, as each one got inboard, straight for one of the crew it went; so that they were all bitten and be-bled in a score of places.

There ensued a short but desperate fight, and then, when the last of the beasts had been hacked to death, the men lay once more to the task of heaving the boat clear of the weed.

A minute passed, and they had come almost to the edge, when Duthie cried out, to look; and at that, all turned to stare at the barque, and perceived the thing that had caused the 'prentice to cry out; for the rats were leaping down into the weed in black multitudes, making the great weed-fronds quiver, as they hurled themselves in the direction of the boat. In an incredibly short space of time, all the weed between the boat and the barque, was alive with the little monsters, coming at breakneck speed.

The Mate let out a shout, and, snatching an oar from one of the men, leapt into the stern of the boat, and commenced to thrash the weed with it, whilst the rest laboured infernally to pluck the boat forth into the open sea. Yet, despite their mad efforts, and the death-dealing blows of the Mate's great fourteen-foot oar, the black, living mass were all about the boat, and scrambling aboard in scores, before she was free of the weed. As the boat shot into the clear water, the Mate gave out a great curse, and, dropping his oar, began to pluck the brutes from his body with his bare hands, casting them into the sea. Yet, fast almost as he freed himself, others sprang upon him, so that in another minute he was like to have been pulled down, for the boat was alive and swarming with the pests, but that some of the men got to work with their cutlasses, and literally slashed the brutes to pieces, sometimes killing several with a single blow. And thus, in a while, the boat was freed once more; though it was a sorely wounded and frightened lot of men that manned her.

The Mate himself took an oar, as did all those who were able. And so they rowed slowly and painfully away from that hateful derelict, whose crew of monsters even then made the weed all of a-heave with hideous life.

From the *Tarawak* came urgent signals for them to haste; by which the Mate knew that the storm, which the Captain had feared, must be coming down upon the ship, and so he spurred each one to greater endeavour, until, at last they were under the shadow of their own vessel, with very thankful hearts, and bodies, bleeding, tired and faint.

Slowly and painfully, the boat's crew scrambled up the side-ladder, and the boat was hoisted aboard; but they had no time then to tell their tale; for the storm was upon them.

It came half an hour later, sweeping down in a cloud of white fury from the Eastward, and blotting out all vestiges of the mysterious derelict and the little barque which had proved her victim. And after that, for a weary day and night, they battled with the storm. When it passed, nothing was to be seen, either of the two vessels or of the weed which had studded the sea before the storm; for they had been blown many a score of leagues to the Westward of the spot, and so had no further chance—nor, I ween, inclination—to investigate further the mystery of that strange old derelict of a past time, and her habitants of rats.

Yet, many a time, and in many fo'cas'les has this story been told; and many a conjecture has been passed as to how came that ancient craft abroad there in the ocean. Some have suggested—as indeed I have made bold to put forth as fact—that she must have drifted out of the lonesome Sargasso Sea. And, in truth, I cannot but think this the most reasonable supposition. Yet, of the rats that evidently dwelt in her, I have no reasonable explanation to offer. Whether they were true ship's rats, or a species that is to be found in the weedhaunted plains and islets of the Sargasso Sea, I cannot say. It may be that they are the descendants of rats that lived in ships long centuries lost in the weed-sea, and which have learned to live among the weed, forming new characteristics, and developing fresh powers and instincts.

Yet, I cannot say; for I speak entirely without authority, and do but tell this story as it is told in the fo'cas'le of many an old-time sailing ship—that dark, brine-tainted place where the young men learn somewhat of the mysteries of the all mysterious sea.

The Thing in the Weeds

I

THIS IS AN EXTRAORDINARY tale. We had come up from the Cape, and owing to the Trades heading us more than usual, we had made some hundreds of miles more westing than I ever did before or since.

I remember the particular night of the happening perfectly. I suppose what occurred stamped it solid into my memory, with a thousand little details that, in the ordinary way, I should never have remembered an hour. And, of course, we talked it over so often among ourselves that this, no doubt, helped to fix it all past any forgetting.

I remember the Mate and I had been pacing the weather side of the poop and discussing various old shellbacks' superstitions. I was Third Mate, and it was between four and five bells in the first watch, i.e. between ten and half-past. Suddenly he stopped in his walk and lifted his head and sniffed several times.

"My word, Mister," he said, "there's a rum kind of stink somewhere about. Don't you smell it?"

I sniffed once or twice at the light airs that were coming in on the beam; then I walked to the rail and leaned over, smelling again at the slight breeze. And abruptly I got a whiff of it, faint and sickly, yet vaguely suggestive of something I had once smelt before.

"I can smell something, Mr. Lammart," I said. "I could almost give it name; and yet somehow I can't." I stared away into the dark to windward. "What do you seem to smell?" I asked him.

"I can't smell anything now," he replied, coming over and standing beside me. "It's gone again. No! By Jove! There it is again. My goodness! Phew!"

The smell was all about us now, filling the night air. It had still that indefinable familiarity about it, and yet it was curiously strange, and, more than anything else, it was certainly simply beastly.

The stench grew stronger, and presently the Mate asked me to go forrard and see whether the look-out man noticed anything. When I reached the break of the fo'c's'le head I called up to the man, to know whether he smelled anything.

"Smell anythin', Sir?" he sang out. "Jumpin' larks! I sh'u'd think I do. I'm fair p'isoned with it."

I ran up the weather steps and stood beside him. The smell was certainly very plain up there, and after savouring it for a few moments I asked him whether he thought it might be a dead whale. But he was very emphatic that this could not be the case, for, as he said, he had been nearly fifteen years in whaling ships, and knew the smell of a dead whale, "like as you would the smell of bad whisky, Sir," as he put it. " 'Tain't no whale yon, but the Lord He knows what 'tis. I'm thinking it's Davy Jones come up for a breather."

I stayed with him some minutes, staring out into the darkness, but could see nothing; for, even had there been something big close to us, I doubt whether I could have seen it, so black a night it was, without a visible star, and with a vague, dull haze breeding an indistinctness all about the ship.

I returned to the Mate and reported that the look-out complained of the smell but that neither he nor I had been able to see anything in the darkness to account for it.

By this time the queer, disgusting odour seemed to be in all the air about us, and the Mate told me to go below and shut all the ports, so as to keep the beastly smell out of the cabins and the saloon.

When I returned he suggested that we should shut the companion doors, and after that we commenced to pace the poop again, discussing the extraordinary smell, and stopping from time to time to stare through our night-glasses out into the night about the ship.

"I'll tell you what it smells like, Mister," the Mate remarked once, "and that's like a mighty old derelict I once went aboard in the North Atlantic. She was a proper old-timer, an' she gave us all the creeps. There was just this funny, dank, rummy sort of century-old bilge-water and dead men an' seaweed. I can't stop thinkin' we're nigh some lonesome old packet out there; an' a good thing we've not much way on us!"

"Do you notice how almighty quiet everything's gone the last half hour or so?" I said a little later. "It must be the mist thickening down."

"It is the mist," said the Mate, going to the rail and staring out. "Good Lord, what's that?" he added.

Something had knocked his hat from his head, and it fell with a sharp rap at my feet. And suddenly, you know, I got a premonition of something horrid.

"Come away from the rail, Sir!" I said sharply, and gave one jump and caught him by the shoulders and dragged him back. "Come away from the side!"

"What's up, Mister?" he growled at me, and twisted his shoulders free. "What's wrong with you? Was it you knocked off my cap?" He stooped and felt around for it, and as he did so I heard something unmistakably fiddling away at the rail which the Mate had just left.

"My God, Sir!" I said, "there's something there. Hark!" The Mate stiffened up, listening; then he heard it. It was for all the world as if something was feeling and rubbing the rail there in the darkness, not two fathoms away from us.

"Who's there?" said the Mate quickly. Then, as there was no answer: "What the devil's this hanky-panky? Who's playing the goat there?" He made a swift step through the darkness towards the rail, but I caught him by the elbow.

"Don't go, Mister!" I said, hardly above a whisper. "It's not one of the men. Let me get a light."

"Quick, then!" he said, and I turned and ran aft to the binnacle and snatched out the lighted lamp. As I did so I heard the Mate shout something out of the darkness in a strange voice. There came a sharp, loud, rattling sound, and then a crash, and immediately the Mate roaring to me to hasten with the light. His voice changed even whilst he shouted, and gave out something that was nearer a scream than anything else. There came two loud, dull blows and an extraordinary gasping sound; and then, as I raced along the poop, there was a tremendous smashing of glass and an immediate silence.

"Mr. Lammart!" I shouted. "Mr. Lammart!" And then I had reached the place where I had left the Mate for forty seconds before; but he was not there.

"Mr. Lammart!" I shouted again, holding the light high over my head and turning quickly to look behind me. As I did so my foot glided on some slippery substance, and I went headlong to the deck with a tremendous thud, smashing the lamp and putting out the light.

I was on my feet again in an instant. I groped a moment for the lamp, and as I did so I heard the men singing out from the main-deck and the noise of their feet as they came running aft. I found the broken lamp and realised it was useless; then I jumped for the companionway, and in half a minute I was back with the big saloon lamp glaring bright in my hands.

I ran forrard again, shielding the upper edge of the glass chimney from the draught of my running, and the blaze of the big lamp seemed to make the weather side of the poop as bright as day, except for the mist, that gave something of a vagueness to things.

Where I had left the Mate there was blood upon the deck, but nowhere any signs of the man himself. I ran to the weather rail and held the lamp to it. There was blood upon it, and the rail itself seemed to have been wrenched by some huge force. I put out my hand and found that I could shake it. Then I leaned out-board and held the lamp at arm's length, staring down over the ship's side.

"Mr. Lammart!" I shouted into the night and the thick mist. "Mr. Lammart! Mr. Lammart!" But my voice seemed to go, lost and muffled and infinitely small, away into the billowy darkness.

I heard the men snuffling and breathing, waiting to leeward of the poop. I whirled round to them, holding the lamp high.

"We heard somethin', Sir," said Tarpley, the leading seaman in our watch. "Is anythin' wrong, Sir?"

"The Mate's gone," I said blankly. "We heard something, and I went for the binnacle lamp. Then he shouted, and I heard a sound of things smashing, and when I got back he'd gone clean." I turned and held the light out again over the unseen sea, and the men crowded round along the rail and stared, bewildered.

"Blood, Sir," said Tarpley, pointing. "There's somethin' almighty queer out there." He waved a huge hand into the darkness. "That's what stinks—"

He never finished; for suddenly one of the men cried out something in a frightened voice: "Look out, Sir! Look out, Sir!" I saw, in one brief flash of sight, something come in with an infernal flicker of movement; and then, before I could form any notion of what I had seen, the lamp was dashed to pieces across the poop-deck. In that instant my perceptions cleared, and I saw the incredible folly of what we were doing; for there we were, standing up against the blank, unknowable night, and out there in the darkness there surely lurked some Thing of monstrousness; and we were at its mercy. I seemed to feel it hovering—hovering over us, so that I felt the sickening creep of gooseflesh all over me.

"Stand back from the rail!" I shouted. "Stand back from the rail!" There was a rush of feet as the men obeyed, in sudden apprehension of their danger, and I gave back with them. Even as I did so I felt some invisible thing brush my shoulder, and an indescribable smell was in my nostrils from something that moved over me in the dark.

"Down into the saloon everyone!" I shouted. "Down with you

all! Don't wait a moment!"

There was a rush along the dark weather deck, and then the men went helter-skelter down the companion steps into the saloon, falling and cursing over one another in the darkness. I sang out to the man at the wheel to join them, and then I followed.

I came upon the men huddled at the foot of the stairs and filling up the passage, all crowding each other in the darkness. The skipper's voice was filling the saloon, and he was demanding in violent adjectives the cause of so tremendous a noise. From the steward's berth there came also a voice and the splutter of a match, and then the glow of a lamp in the saloon itself.

I pushed my way through the men and found the Captain in the saloon in his sleeping gear, looking both drowsy and angry, though perhaps bewilderment topped every other feeling. He held his cabin lamp in his hand, and shone the light over the huddle of men.

I hurried to explain, and told him of the incredible disappearance of the Mate, and of my conviction that some extraordinary thing was lurking near the ship out in the mist and the darkness. I mentioned the curious smell, and told how the Mate had suggested that we had drifted down near some old-time, sea-rotted derelict. And, you know, even as I put it into awkward words, my imagination began to awaken to horrible discomforts; a thousand dreadful impossibilities of the sea became suddenly possible.

The Captain (Jeldy was his name) did not stop to dress, but ran back into his cabin, and came out in a few moments with a couple of revolvers and a handful of cartridges. The Second Mate had come running out of his cabin at the noise, and had listed intensely to what I had to say; and now he jumped back into his berth and brought out his own lamp and a large Smith and Wesson, which was evidently ready loaded.

Captain Jeldy pushed one of his revolvers into my hands, with some of the cartridges, and we began hastily to load the weapons. Then the Captain caught up his lamp and made for the stairway, ordering the men into the saloon out of his way.

"Shall you want them, Sir?" I asked.

"No," he said. "It's no use their running any unnecessary risks." He threw a word over his shoulder: "Stay quiet here, men; if I want you I'll give you a shout; then come spry!"

"Aye, aye, Sir," said the watch in a chorus; and then I was following the Captain up the stairs, with the Second Mate close behind. We came up through the companionway on to the silence of the deserted poop. The mist had thickened up, even during the brief time that I had been below, and there was not a breath of wind. The mist was so dense that it seemed to press in upon us, and the two lamps made a kind of luminous halo in the mist, which seemed to absorb their light in a most peculiar way.

"Where was he?" the Captain asked me, almost in a whisper.

"On the port side, Sir," I said, "a little foreside the charthouse and about a dozen feet in from the rail. I'll show you the exact place."

We went forrard along what had been the weather side, going quietly and watchfully, though, indeed, it was little enough that we could see, because of the mist. Once, as I led the way, I thought I heard a vague sound somewhere in the mist, but was all unsure because of the slow creak, creak of the spars and gear as the vessel rolled slightly upon an odd, oily swell. Apart from this slight sound, and the far-up rustle of the canvas slatting gently against the masts, there was no sound at all throughout the ship. I assure you the silence seemed to me to be almost menacing, in the tense, nervous state in which I was.

"Hereabouts is where I left him," I whispered to the Captain a few seconds later. "Hold your lamp low, Sir. There's blood on the deck."

Captain Jeldy did so, and made a slight sound with his mouth at what he saw. Then, heedless of my hurried warning, he walked across to the rail, holding his lamp high up. I followed him, for I could not let him go alone; and the Second Mate came too, with his lamp. They leaned over the port rail and held their lamps out into the mist and the unknown darkness beyond the ship's side. I remember how the lamps made just two yellow glares in the mist, ineffectual, yet serving somehow to make extraordinarily plain the vastitude of the night and the *possibilities of the dark*. Perhaps that is a queer way to put it, but it gives you the effect of that moment upon my feelings. And all the time, you know, there was upon me the brutal, frightening expectancy of something reaching in at us from out of that everlasting darkness and mist that held all the sea and the night, so that we were just three mist-shrouded, hidden figures, peering nervously.

The mist was now so thick that we could not even see the surface of the water overside, and fore and aft of us the rail vanished away into the fog and the dark. And then, as we stood here staring, I heard something moving down on the main-deck. I caught Captain Jeldy by the elbow.

"Come away from the rail, Sir," I said, hardly above a whisper; and he, with the swift premonition of danger, stepped back and allowed me to urge him well inboard. The Second Mate followed, and the

three of us stood there in the mist, staring round about us and holding
our revolvers handily, and the dull waves of the mist beating in slowly
upon the lamps in vague wreathings and swirls of fog.

"What was it you heard, mister?" asked the Captain after a few
moments.

"Ssst!" I muttered. "There it is again. There's something moving
down on the main-deck!"

Captain Jeldy heard it himself now, and the three of us stood listening intensely. Yet it was hard to know what to make of the sounds.
And then suddenly there was the rattle of a deck ringbolt, and then
again, as if something or someone were fumbling and playing with it.

"Down there on the main-deck!" shouted the Captain abruptly,
his voice seeming hoarse close to my ear, yet immediately smothered
by the fog. "Down there on the main-deck! Who's there?"

But there came never an answering sound. And the three of us
stood there, looking quickly this way and that, and listening—

Abruptly the Second Mate muttered something:

"The look-out, Sir! The look-out!"

Captain Jeldy took the hint on the instant.

"On the look-out there!" he shouted.

And then, far away and muffled-sounding, there came the answering cry of the look-out man from the fo'cas'le head:

"Sir-r-r?" A little voice, long drawn out through unknowable
alleys of fog.

"Go below into the fo'cas'le and shut both doors, an' don't stir out
till you're told!" sung out Captain Jeldy, his voice going lost into the
mist. And then the man's answering "Aye, aye, Sir!" coming to us
faint and mournful. And directly afterwards the clang of a steel door,
hollow-sounding and remote; and immediately the sound of another.

"That puts them safe for the present, anyway," said the Second
Mate. And even as he spoke there came again that indefinite noise
down upon the main-deck of something moving with an incredible
and unnatural stealthiness.

"On the main-deck there!" shouted Captain Jeldy sternly. "If
there is anyone there, answer, or I shall fire!"

The reply was both amazing and terrifying, for suddenly a tremendous blow was stricken upon the deck, and then there came the
dull, rolling sound of some enormous weight going hollowly across
the main-deck. And then an abominable silence.

"My God!" said Captain Jeldy in a low voice, "what was *that*?" And
he raised his pistol, but I caught him by the wrist. "Don't shoot, Sir!"

I whispered. "It'll be no good. That—that—whatever it is I—mean it's something enormous, Sir. I—I really wouldn't shoot—" I found it impossible to put my vague idea into words; but I felt there was a force aboard, down on the maindeck, that it would be futile to attack with so ineffectual a thing as a puny revolver bullet.

And then, as I held Captain Jeldy's wrist, and he hesitated, irresolute there came a sudden bleating of sheep and the sound of lashings being burst and the cracking of wood; and the next instant a huge crash, followed by crash after crash, and the anguished m-aa-a-a-ing of sheep.

"My God!" said the Second Mate, "the sheep-pen's being beaten to pieces against the deck. Good God! What sort of thing could do that?"

The tremendous beating ceased, and there was a splashing over-side; and after that a silence so profound that it seemed as if the whole atmosphere of the night was full of an unbearable, tense quietness. And then the damp slatting of a sail, far up in the night, that made me start—a lonesome sound to break suddenly through that infernal silence upon my raw nerves.

"Get below, both of you. Smartly now!" muttered Captain Jeldy. "There's something run either aboard us or alongside; and we can't do anything till daylight."

We went below and shut the doors of the companionway, and there we lay in the wide Atlantic, without wheel or look-out or officer in charge, and something incredible down on the dark main-deck.

II

For some hours we sat in the Captain's cabin talking the matter over whilst the watch slept, sprawled in a dozen attitudes on the floor of the saloon. Captain Jeldy and the Second Mate still wore their pyjamas, and our loaded revolvers lay handy on the cabin table. And so we watched anxiously through the hours for the dawn to come in.

As the light strengthened we endeavoured to get some view of the sea from the ports, but the mist was so thick about us that it was exactly like looking out into a grey nothingness, that became presently white as the day came.

"Now," said Captain Jeldy, "we're going to look into this."

He went out through the saloon to the companion stairs. At the top he opened the two doors, and the mist rolled in on us, white and impenetrable. For a little while we stood there, the three of us, absolutely silent and listening, with our revolvers handy; but never a sound came to us except the odd, vague slatting of a sail or the slight creaking of the gear as the ship lifted on some slow, invisible swell.

Presently the Captain stepped cautiously out onto the deck; he was in his cabin slippers, and therefore made no sound. I was wearing gum-boots, and followed him silently, and the Second Mate after me in his bare feet. Captain Jeldy went a few paces along the deck, and the mist hid him utterly. "Phew!" I heard him mutter, "the stink's worse than ever!" His voice came odd and vague to me through the wreathing of the mist.

"The sun'll soon eat up all this fog," said the Second Mate at my elbow, in a voice little above a whisper.

We stepped after the Captain, and found him a couple of fathoms away, standing shrouded in the mist in an attitude of tense listening. "Can't hear a thing!" he whispered. "We'll go forrard to the break, as quiet as you like. Don't make a sound."

We went forward, like three shadows, and suddenly Captain Jeldy kicked his shin against something and pitched headlong over it, making a tremendous noise. He got up quickly, swearing grimly, and the three of us stood there in silence, waiting lest any infernal thing should come upon us out of all that white invisibility. Once I felt sure I saw something coming towards me, and I raised my revolver, but saw in a moment that there was nothing. The tension of imminent nervous expectancy eased from us, and Captain Jeldy stooped over the object on the deck.

"The port hencoop's been shifted out here!" he muttered. "It's all stove!"

"That must be what I heard last night when the Mate went," I whispered. "There was a loud crash just before he sang out to me to hurry with the lamp."

Captain Jeldy left the smashed hencoop, and the three of us tiptoed silently to the rail across the break of the poop. Here we leaned over and stared down into the blank whiteness of the mist that hid everything.

"Can't see a thing," whispered the Second Mate; yet as he spoke I could fancy that I heard a slight, indefinite, slurring noise somewhere below us; and I caught them each by an arm to draw them back.

"There's something down there," I muttered. "For goodness' sake come back from the rail."

We gave back a step or two, and then stopped to listen; and even as we did so there came a slight air playing through the mist. "The breeze is coming," said the Second Mate. "Look, the mist is clearing already."

He was right. Already the look of white impenetrability had gone, and suddenly we could see the corner of the after-hatch coamings through the thinning fog. Within a minute we could see as far forrard as the mainmast, and then the stuff blew away from us, clear of the vessel, like a great wall of whiteness, that dissipated as it went.

"*Look!*" we all exclaimed together. The whole of the vessel was now clear to our sight; but it was not at the ship herself that we looked, for, after one quick glance along the empty main-deck, we had seen something beyond the ship's side. All around the vessel there lay a submerged spread of weed, for, maybe, a good quarter of a mile upon every side.

"Weed!" sang out Captain Jeldy in a voice of comprehension. "Weed! Look! By Jove, I guess I know now what got the Mate!" He turned and ran to the port side and looked over. And suddenly he stiffened and beckoned silently over his shoulder to us to come and see. We had followed, and now we stood, one on each side of him, staring.

"Look!" whispered the Captain, pointing. "See the great brute! Do you see it? There! Look!"

At first I could see nothing except the submerged spread of the weed, into which we had evidently run after dark. Then, as I stared intently, my gaze began to separate from the surrounding weed a leathery-looking something that was somewhat darker in hue than the weed itself.

"My God!" said Captain Jeldy. "What a monster! What a monster! Just look at the brute! Look at the thing's eyes! That's what got the Mate. What a creature out of hell itself!"

I saw it plainly now; three of the massive feelers lay twined in and out among the clumpings of the weed; and then, abruptly, I realised that the two extraordinary round disks, motionless and inscrutable, were the creature's eyes, just below the surface of the water. It appeared to be staring, expressionless, up at the steel side of the vessel. I traced, vaguely, the shapeless monstrosity of what must be termed its head. "My God!" I muttered. "It's an enormous squid of some kind! What an awful brute! What—"

The sharp report of the Captain's revolver came at that moment. He had fired at the thing, and instantly there was a most awful commotion alongside. The weed was hove upward, literally in tons. An enormous quantity was thrown aboard us by the thrashing of the monster's great feelers. The sea seemed almost to boil, in one great cauldron of weed and water, all about the brute, and the steel side of the ship resounded with the dull, tremendous blows that the creature gave in its struggle. And into all that whirling boil of tentacles, weed, and seawater the three of us emptied our revolvers as fast as we could fire and reload. I remember the feeling of fierce satisfaction I had in thus aiding to avenge the death of the Mate.

Suddenly the Captain roared out to us to jump back, and we obeyed on the instant. As we did so the weed rose up into a great mound over twenty feet in height, and more than a ton of it slopped aboard. The next instant three of the monstrous tentacles came in over the side, and the vessel gave a slow, sullen roll to port as the weight came upon her, for the monster had literally hove itself almost free of the sea against our port side, in one vast, leathery shape, all wreathed with weed-fronds, and seeming drenched with blood and curious black liquid.

The feelers that had come inboard thrashed round here and there, and suddenly one of them curled in the most hideous, snake-like fashion around the base of the mainmast. This seemed to attract it, for immediately it curled the two others about the mast, and forthwith wrenched upon it with such hideous violence that the whole towering length of spars, through all their height of a hundred and fifty feet, were shaken visibly, whilst the vessel herself vibrated with the stupendous efforts of the brute.

"It'll have the mast down, Sir!" said the Second Mate, with a gasp. "My God! It'll strain her side open! My—"

"One of those blasting cartridges!" I said to Jeldy almost in a shout, as the inspiration took me. "Blow the brute to pieces!"

"Get one, quick!" said the Captain, jerking his thumb towards the companion. "You know where they are."

In thirty seconds I was back with the cartridge. Captain Jeldy took out his knife and cut the fuse dead short; then, with a steady hand, he lit the fuse, and calmly held it, until I backed away, shouting to him to throw it, for I knew it must explode in another couple of seconds.

Captain Jeldy threw the thing like one throws a quoit, so that it fell into the sea just on the outward side of the vast bulk of the monster. So well had he timed it that it burst, with a stunning report, just as it struck the water. The effect upon the squid was amazing. It seemed literally to collapse. The enormous tentacles released themselves from the mast and curled across the deck helplessly, and were drawn inertly over the rail, as the enormous bulk sank away from the ship's side, out of sight, into the weed. The ship rolled slowly to starboard, and then steadied. "Thank God!" I muttered, and looked at the two others. They were pallid and sweating, and I must have been the same.

"Here's the breeze again," said the Second Mate, a minute later. "We're moving." He turned, without another word, and raced aft to the wheel, whilst the vessel slid over and through the weedfield.

"Look where that brute broke up the sheep-pen!" cried Jeldy, pointing. "And here's the skylight of the sail-locker smashed to bits!"

He walked across to it, and glanced down. And suddenly he let out a tremendous shout of astonishment:

"Here's the Mate down here!" he shouted. "He's not overboard at all! He's *here!*"

He dropped himself down through the skylight on to the sails, and I after him; and, surely, there was the Mate, lying all huddled and insensible on a hummock of spare sails. In his right hand he held a drawn sheath-knife, which he was in the habit of carrying, A.B. fashion, whilst his left hand was all caked with dried blood, where he had been badly cut. Afterwards, we concluded he had cut himself in slashing at one of the tentacles of the squid, which had caught him round the left wrist, the tip of the tentacle being still curled tight about his arm, just as it had been when he hacked it through. For the rest, he was not seriously damaged, the creature having obviously flung him violently away through the framework of the skylight, so that he had fallen in a studded condition on to the pile of sails.

We got him on deck, and down into his bunk, where we left the steward to attend to him. When we returned to the poop the vessel had drawn clear of the weed-field, and the Captain and I stopped for a few moments to stare astern over the taffrail.

As we stood and looked, something wavered up out of the heart of the weed—a long, tapering, sinuous thing, that curled and wavered against the dawn-light, and presently sank back again into the demure weed—a veritable spider of the deep, waiting in the great web that Dame Nature had spun for it in the eddy of her tides and currents.

And we sailed away northwards, with strengthening Trades, and left thuat patch of monstrousness to the loneliness of the sea.

The Finding of the Graiken

I

WHEN A YEAR HAD passed, and still there was no news of the full-rigged ship *Graiken*, even the most sanguine of my old chum's friends had ceased to hope perchance, somewhere, she might be above water.

Yet Ned Barlow, in his inmost thoughts, I knew, still hugged to himself the hope that she would win home. Poor, dear old fellow, how my heart did go out towards him in his sorrow!

For it was in the *Graiken* that his sweetheart had sailed on that dull January day some twelve months previously.

The voyage had been taken for the sake of her health; yet since then—save for a distant signal recorded at the Azores—there had been from all the mystery of ocean no voice; the ship and they within her had vanished utterly.

And still Barlow hoped. He said nothing actually, but at times his deeper thoughts would float up and show through the sea of his usual talk, and thus I would know in an indirect way of the thing that his heart was thinking.

Nor was time a healer.

It was later that my present good fortune came to me. My uncle died, and I—hitherto poor—was now a rich man. In a breath, it seemed, I had become possessor of houses, lands, and money; also—in my eyes almost more important—a fine fore-and-aft-rigged yacht of some two hundred tons register.

It seemed scarcely believable that the thing was mine, and I was all in a scutter to run away down to Falmouth and get to sea.

In old times, when my uncle had been more than usually gracious, he had invited me to accompany him for a trip round the coast or elsewhere, as the fit might take him; yet never, even in my most hopeful moments, had it occurred to me that ever she might be mine.

And now I was hurrying my preparations for a good long sea trip—for to me the sea is, and always has been, a comrade.

Still, with all the prospects before me, I was by no means completely satisfied, for I wanted Ned Barlow with me, and yet was afraid to ask him.

I had the feeling that, in view of his overwhelming loss, he must positively hate the sea; and yet I could not be happy at the thought of leaving him, and going alone.

He had not been well lately, and a sea voyage would be the very thing for him if only it were not going to freshen painful memories.

Eventually I decided to suggest it, and this I did a couple of days before the date I had fixed for sailing.

"Ned," I said, "you need a change."

"Yes," he assented wearily.

"Come with me, old chap," I went on, growing bolder. "I'm taking a trip in the yacht. It would be splendid to have—"

To my dismay, he jumped to his feet and came towards me excitedly. "I've upset him now," was my thought. "I *am* a fool!"

"Go to sea!" he said. "My God! I'd give—" He broke off short, and stood opposite to me, his face all of a quiver with suppressed emotion. He was silent a few seconds, getting himself in hand; then he proceeded more quietly: "Where to!"

"Anywhere," I replied, watching him keenly, for I was greatly puzzled by his manner. "I'm not quite clear yet. Somewhere south of here—the West Indies, I have thought. It's all so new, you know—just fancy being able to go just where we like. I can hardly realise it yet."

I stopped, for he had turned from me and was staring out of the window.

"You'll come, Ned?" I cried, fearful that he was going to refuse me.

He took a pace away, and came back.

"I'll come," he said, and there was a look of strange excitement in his eyes that set me off on a tack of vague wonder; but I said nothing, just told him how he had pleased me.

II

We had been at sea a couple of weeks, and were alone upon the Atlantic—at least, so much of it as presented itself to our view.

I was leaning over the taffrail, staring down into the boil of the wake; yet I noticed nothing, for I was wrapped in a tissue of somewhat uncomfortable thought. It was about Ned Barlow.

He had been queer, decidedly queer, since leaving port. His whole attitude mentally had been that of a man under the influence of an all-pervading excitement. I had said that he was in need of change, and had trusted that the splendid tonic of the sea breeze would serve to put him soon to rights mentally and physically; yet here was the poor old chap acting in a manner calculated to cause me anxiety as to his balance.

Scarcely a word had been spoken since leaving the Channel. When I ventured to speak to him, often he would take not the least notice, other times he would answer only by a brief word; but talk—never.

In addition, his whole time was spent on deck among the men, and with some of them he seemed to converse both long and earnestly; yet to me, his chum and true friend, not a word.

Another thing came to me as a surprise—Barlow betrayed the greatest interest in the position of the vessel, and the courses set, all in such a manner as left me no room for doubt but that his knowledge of navigation was considerable.

Once I ventured to express my astonishment at this knowledge, and ask a question or two as to the way in which he had gathered it, but had been treated with such an absurdly stony silence that since then I had not spoken to him.

With all this it may be easily conceived that my thoughts, as I stared down into the wake, were troublesome.

Suddenly I heard a voice at my elbow:

"I should like to have a word with you, Sir." I turned sharply. It was my skipper, and something in his face told me that all was not as it should be.

"Well, Jenkins, fire away."

He looked round, as if afraid of being overheard; then came closer to me.

"Someone's been messing with the compasses, Sir," he said in a low voice.

"What?" I asked sharply.

"They've been meddled with, Sir. The magnets have been shifted and by someone who's a good idea of what he's doing."

"What on earth do you mean?" I inquired. "Why should anyone mess about with them? What good would it do them? You must be mistaken."

"No, Sir, I'm not. They've been touched within the last forty-eight hours, and by someone that understands what he's doing."

I stared at him. The man was so certain. I felt bewildered.

"But why should they?"

"That's more than I can say, Sir; but it's a serious matter, and I want to know what I'm to do. It looks to me as though there were something funny going on. I'd give a month's pay to know just who it was, for certain."

"Well," I said, "if they have been touched, it can only be by one of the officers. You say the chap who has done it must understand what he is doing."

He shook his head. "No, Sir—" he began, and then stopped abruptly. His gaze met mine. I think the same thought must have come to us simultaneously. I gave a little gasp of amazement.

He wagged his head at me. "I've had my suspicions for a bit, Sir," he went on; "but seeing that he's—he's—" He was fairly struck for the moment.

I took my weight off the rail and stood upright.

"To whom are you referring?" I asked curtly.

"Why, Sir, to him—Mr. Ned—"

He would have gone on, but I cut him short.

"That will do, Jenkins!" I cried. "Mr. Ned Barlow is my friend. You are forgetting yourself a little. You will accuse me of tampering with the compasses next!"

I turned away, leaving little Captain Jenkins speechless. I had spoken with an almost vehement over-loyalty, to quiet my own suspicions.

All the same, I was horribly bewildered, not knowing what to think or do or say, so that, eventually, I did just nothing.

III

It was early one morning, about a week later, that I opened my eyes abruptly. I was lying on my back in my bunk, and the daylight was beginning to creep wanly in through the ports.

I had a vague consciousness that all was not as it should be, and feeling thus, I made to grasp the edge of my bunk, and sit up, but failed, owing to the fact that my wrists were securely fastened by a pair of heavy steel handcuffs.

Utterly confounded, I let my head fall back upon the pillow; and then, in the midst of my bewilderment there sounded the sharp report of a pistol-shot somewhere on the decks over my head. There came a second and the sound of voices and footsteps, and then a long spell of silence.

Into my mind had rushed the single word—mutiny! My temples throbbed a little, but I struggled to keep calm and think, and then, all adrift, I fell to searching round for a reason. Who was it? And why?

Perhaps an hour passed, during which I asked myself ten thousand vain questions. All at once I heard a key inserted in the door. So I had been locked in! It turned, and the steward walked into the cabin. He did not look at me, but went to the arm-rack and began to remove the various weapons.

"What the devil is the meaning of all this, Jones?" I roared, getting up a bit on one elbow. "What's happened?"

But the fool answered not a word—just went to and fro carrying out the weapons from my cabin into the next, so that at last I ceased from questioning him, and lay silent, promising myself future vengeance.

When he had removed the arms, the steward began to go through my table drawers, emptying them, so that it appeared to me, of everything that could be used as a weapon or tool.

Having completed his task, he vanished, locking the door after him.

Some time passed, and at last, about seven bells, he reappeared, this time bringing a tray with my breakfast. Placing it upon the table, he came across to me and proceeded to unlock the cuffs from off my wrists. Then for the first time he spoke.

"Mr. Barlow desires me to say, Sir, that you are to have the liberty of your cabin so long as you will agree not to cause any bother. Should you wish for anything, I am under his orders to supply you." He retreated hastily toward the door.

On my part, I was almost speechless with astonishment and rage.

"One minute, Jones!" I shouted, just as he was in the act of leaving the cabin. "Kindly explain what you mean. You said Mr. Barlow. Is it to him that I owe all this?" And I waved my hand towards the irons which the man still held.

"It is by his orders," replied he, and turned once more to leave the cabin.

"I don't understand!" I said, bewildered. "Mr. Barlow is my friend, and this is my yacht! By what right do you dare to take your orders from him? Let me out!"

As I shouted the last command, I leapt from my bunk, and made a dash for the door, but the steward, so far from attempting to bar it, flung it open and stepped quickly through, thus allowing me to see that a couple of the sailors were stationed in the alleyway.

"Get on deck at once!" I said angrily. "What are you doing down here?"

"Sorry Sir," said one of the men. "We'd take it kindly if you'd make no trouble. But we ain't lettin' you out, Sir. Don't make no bloomin' error."

I hesitated, then went to the table and sat down. I would, at least, do my best to preserve my dignity.

After an inquiry as to whether he could do anything further, the steward left me to breakfast and my thoughts. As may be imagined, the latter were by no means pleasant.

Here was I prisoner in my own yacht, and by the hand of the very man I had loved and befriended through many years. Oh, it was too incredible and mad!

For a while, leaving the table, I paced the deck of my room; then, growing calmer, I sat down again and attempted to make some sort of a meal.

As I breakfasted, my chief thought was as to *why* my one-time chum was treating me thus; and after that I fell to puzzling *how* he had managed to get the yacht into his own hands.

Many things came back to me—his familiarity with the men, his treatment of me—which I had put down to a temporary want of balance—the fooling with the compasses; for I was certain now that he had been the doer of that piece of mischief. But *why?* That was the great point.

As I turned the matter over in my brain, an incident that had occurred some six days back came to me. It had been on the very day after the Captain's report to me of the tampering with the compasses.

Barlow had, for the first time, relinquished his brooding and silence, and had started to talk to me, but in such a wild strain that he had made me feel vaguely uncomfortable about his sanity, for he told me some wild yarn of an idea which he had got into his head. And then, in an overbearing way, he demanded that the navigating of the yacht should be put into his hands.

He had been very incoherent, and was plainly in a state of considerable mental excitement. He had rambled on about some derelict, and then had talked in an extraordinary fashion of a vast world of seaweed.

Once or twice in his bewilderingly disconnected speech he had mentioned the name of his sweetheart, and now it was the memory of her name that gave me the first inkling of what might possibly prove a solution of the whole affair.

I wished now that I had encouraged his incoherent ramble of speech, instead of heading him off; but I had done so because I could not bear to have him talk as he had.

Yet, with the little I remembered, I began to shape out a theory. It seemed to me that he might be nursing some idea that he had formed—goodness knows how or when—that his sweetheart (still alive) was aboard some derelict in the midst of an enormous "world," he had termed it, of seaweed.

He might have grown more explicit had I not attempted to reason with him, and so lost the rest. Yet, remembering back, it seemed to me that he must undoubtedly have meant the enormous Sargasso Sea— that great seaweed-laden ocean, vast almost as Continental Europe, and the final resting-place of the Atlantic's wreckage.

Surely, if he proposed any attempt to search through that, then there could be no doubt but that he was temporarily unbalanced. And yet I could do nothing. I was a prisoner and helpless.

IV

Eight days of variable but strongish winds passed, and still I was a prisoner in my cabin. From the ports that opened out astern and on each side—for my cabin runs right across the whole width of the stern—I was able to command a good view of the surrounding ocean, which now had commenced to be laden with great floating patches of Gulf-weed—many of them hundreds and hundreds of yards in length.

And still we held on, apparently towards the nucleus of the Sargasso Sea. This I was able to assume by means of a chart which I had found in one of the lockers, and the course I had been able to gather from the "tell-tale" compass let into the cabin ceiling.

And so another and another day went by, and now we were among weed so thick that at times the vessel found difficulty in forcing her way through, while the surface of the sea had assumed a curious oily appearance, though the wind was still quite strong.

It was later in the day that we encountered a bank of weed so prodigious that we had to up helm and run round it, and after that the same experience was many times repeated; and so the night found us.

The following morning found me at the ports, eagerly peering out across the water. From one of those on the starboard side, I could discern at a considerable distance a huge bank of weed that seemed to be unending, and to run parallel with our broadside. It appeared to rise in places a couple of feet above the level of the surrounding sea.

For a long while I stared, then went across to the port side. Here I found that a similar bank stretched away on our port beam. It was as though we were sailing up an immense river, the low banks of which were formed of seaweed instead of land.

And so that day passed hour by hour, the weed-banks growing more definite and seeming to be nearer. Towards evening something came into sight—a far, dim hulk, the masts gone, the whole hull covered with growth, an unwholesome green, blotched with brown in the light from the dying sun.

I saw this lonesome craft from a port on the starboard side and the sight roused a multitude of questionings and thoughts.

Evidently we had penetrated into the unknown central portion of the enormous Sargasso, the Great Eddy of the Atlantic, and this was some lonely derelict, lost ages ago perhaps to the outside world.

Just at the going down of the sun, I saw another; she was nearer, and still possessed two of her masts, which stuck up bare and desolate into the darkening sky. She could not have been more than a quarter of a mile in from the edge of the weed. As we passed her I craned out my head through the port to stare at her. As I stared the dusk grew out of the abyss of the air, and she faded presently from sight into the surrounding loneliness.

Through all that night I sat at the port and watched, listening and peering; for the tremendous mystery of that inhuman weed-world was upon me.

In the air there rose no sound; even the wind was scarcely more than a low hum aloft among the sails and gear, and under me the oily water gave no rippling noise. All was silence, supreme and unearthly.

About midnight the moon rose away on our starboard beam, and from then until the dawn I stared out upon a ghostly world of noiseless weed, fantastic, silent, and unbelievable, under the moonlight.

On four separate occasions my gaze lit on black hulks that rose above the surrounding weeds—the hulks of long-lost vessels. And once, just when the strangeness of dawn was in the sky, a faint, long-drawn wailing seemed to come floating to me across the immeasurable waste of weed.

It startled my strung nerves, and I assured myself that it was the cry of some lone sea bird. Yet, my imagination reached out for some stranger explanation.

The eastward sky began to flush with the dawn, and the morning light grew subtly over the breadth of the enormous ocean of weed until it seemed to me to reach away unbroken on each beam into the grey horizons. Only astern of us, like a broad road of oil, ran the strange river-like gulf up which we had sailed.

Now I noticed that the banks of weed were nearer, very much nearer, and a disagreeable thought came to me. This vast rift that had allowed us to penetrate into the very nucleus of the Sargasso Sea—suppose it should close!

It would mean inevitably that there would be one more among the missing—another unanswered mystery of the inscrutable ocean. I resisted the thought, and came back more directly into the present.

Evidently the wind was still dropping, for we were moving slowly, as a glance at the ever-nearing weed-banks told me. The hours passed on, and my breakfast when the steward brought it, I took to one of the ports, and there ate; for I would lose nothing of the strange surroundings into which we were so steadily plunging.

And so the morning passed.

V

It was about an hour after dinner that I observed the open channel between the weed-banks to be narrowing almost minute by minute with uncomfortable speed. I could do nothing except watch and surmise.

At times I felt convinced that the immense masses of weed were closing in upon us, but I fought off the thought with the more hopeful one that we were surely approaching some narrowing outlet of the gulf that yawned so far across the seaweed.

By the time the afternoon was half through, the weed-banks had approached so close that occasional outjutting masses scraped the yacht's sides in passing. It was now with the stuff below my face, within a few feet of my eyes, that I discovered the immense amount of life that stirred among all the hideous waste.

Innumerable crabs crawled among the seaweed, and once, indistinctly, something stirred among the depths of a large outlying tuft of weed. What it was I could not tell, though afterwards I had an idea; but all I saw was something dark and glistening. We were past it before I could see more.

The steward was in the act of bringing in my tea, when from above there came a noise of shouting, and almost immediately a slight jolt. The man put down the tray he was carrying, and glanced at me, with startled expression.

"What is it, Jones?" I questioned.

"I don't know, Sir. I expect it's the weed," he replied.

I ran to the port, craned out my head, and looked forward. Our bow seemed to be embedded in a mass of weeds, and as I watched it came further aft.

Within the next five minutes we had driven through it into a circle of sea that was free from the weed. Across this we seemed to drift, rather than sail, so slow was our speed.

Upon its opposite margin we brought up, the vessel swinging

broadside on to the weed, being secured thus with a couple of kedges cast from the bows and stern, though of this I was not aware until later. As we swung, and at last I was able from my port to see ahead, I saw a thing that amazed me.

There, not three hundred feet distant across the quaking weed, a vessel lay embedded. She had been a three-master; but of these only the mizzen was standing. For perhaps a minute I stared, scarcely breathing in my exceeding interest.

All around above her bulwarks, to the height of apparently some ten feet, ran a sort of fencing, formed, so far as I could make out, from canvas, rope and spars. Even as I wondered at the use of such a thing, I heard my chum's voice overhead. He was hailing her:

"*Graiken*, ahoy!" he shouted. "*Graiken*, ahoy!"

At that I fairly jumped. *Graiken!* What could he mean? I stared out of the port. The blaze of the sinking sun flashed redly upon her stern, and showed the lettering of her name and port; yet the distance was too great for me to read.

I ran across to my table to see if there was a pair of binoculars in the drawers. I found one in the first I opened; then I ran back to the port, racking them out as I went. I reached it, and clapped them to my eyes. Yes; I saw it plainly, her name *Graiken* and her port London.

From her name my gaze moved to that strange fencing about her. There was a movement in the aft part. As I watched a portion of it slid to one side, and a man's head and shoulders appeared.

I nearly yelled with the excitement of that movement. I could scarcely believe the thing I saw. The man waved an arm, and a vague hail reached us across the weed; then he disappeared. A moment later a score of people crowded the opening, and among them I made out distinctly the face and figure of a girl.

"He was right, after all!" I heard myself saying out loud in a voice that was toneless through very amazement.

In a minute, I was at the door, beating it with my fists. "Let me out, Ned! Let me out!" I shouted.

I felt that I could forgive him all the indignity that I had suffered. Nay, more; in a queer way I had a feeling that it was I who needed to ask him for forgiveness. All my bitterness had gone, and I wanted only to be out and give a hand in the rescue.

Yet though I shouted, no one came, so that at last I returned quickly to the port, to see what further developments there were.

Across the weed I now saw that one man had his hands up to his mouth shouting. His voice reached me only as a faint, hoarse cry;

the distance was too great for anyone aboard the yacht to distinguish its import.

From the derelict my attention was drawn abruptly to a scene alongside. A plank was thrown down on to the weed and the next moment I saw my chum swing himself down the side and leap upon it.

I had opened my mouth to call out to him that I would forgive all were I but freed to lend a hand in this unbelievable rescue.

But even as the words formed they died, for though the weed appeared so dense, it was evidently incapable of bearing any considerable weight, and plank, with Barlow upon it, sank down into the weed almost to his waist.

He turned and grabbed at the rope with both hands, and in the same moment he gave a loud cry of sheer terror, and commenced to scramble up the yacht's side.

As his feet drew clear of the weed I gave a short cry. Something was curled about his left ankle—something oily, supple, and tapered. As I stared another rose up out from the weed and swayed through the air, made a grab at his leg, missed, and appeared to wave aimlessly. Others came towards him as he struggled upwards.

Then I saw hands reach down from above and seize Barlow beneath the arms. They lifted him by main force, and with him a mass of weed that enfolded something leathery, from which numbers of curling arms writhed.

A hand slashed down with a sheath-knife, and the next instant the hideous thing had fallen back among the weed.

For a couple of seconds longer I remained, my head twisted upwards; then faces appeared once more over our rail, and I saw the men extending arms and fingers, pointing. From above me there rose a hoarse chorus of fear and wonder, and I turned my head swiftly to glance down and across that treacherous extraordinary weed-world.

The whole of the hitherto silent surface was all of a-move in one stupendous undulation—as though life had come to all that desolation.

The undulatory movement continued, and abruptly, in a hundred places, the seaweed was tossed up into sudden, billowy hillocks. From these burst mighty arms, and in an instant the evening air was full of them, hundreds and hundreds, coming towards the yacht.

"Devil-fishes!" shouted a man's voice from the deck. "Octopuses! My Gord!"

Then I caught my chum shouting.

"Cut the mooring ropes!" he yelled. This must have been done almost on the instant, for immediately there showed between us and the nearest weed a broadening gap of scummy water.

"Haul away, lads!" I heard Barlow shouting; and the same instant I caught the *splash, splash* of something in the water on our port side. I rushed across and looked out. I found that a rope had been carried across to the opposite seaweed, and that the men were now warping us rapidly from those invading horrors.

I raced back to the starboard port, and, lo! as though by magic, there stretched between us and the *Graiken* only the silent stretch of demure weed and some fifty feet of water. It seemed inconceivable that it was a covering to so much terror.

And then speedily the night was upon us, hiding all; but from the decks above there commenced a sound of hammering that continued long throughout the night—long after I, weary with my previous night's vigil, had passed into a fitful slumber, broken anon by that hammering above.

VI

"Your breakfast, Sir," came respectfully enough in the steward's voice; and I woke with a start. Overhead, there still sounded that persistent hammering, and I turned to the steward for an explanation.

"I don't exactly know, Sir," was his reply. "It's something the carpenter's doing to one of the lifeboats." And then he left me.

I ate my breakfast standing at the port, staring at the distant *Graiken*. The weed was perfectly quiet, and we were lying about the center of the little lake.

As I watched the derelict, it seemed to me that I saw a movement about her side, and I reached for the glasses. Adjusting them, I made out that there were several of the cuttlefish attached to her in different parts, their arms spread out almost starwise across the lower portions of her hull.

Occasionally a feeler would detach itself and wave aimlessly. This it was that had drawn my attention. The sight of these creatures, in conjunction with that extraordinary scene the previous evening, enabled me to guess the use of the great screen running about the *Graiken*. It had obviously been erected as a protection against the vile inhabitants of that strange weed-world.

From that my thoughts passed to the problem of reaching and rescuing the crew of the derelict. I could by no means conceive how this was to be effected.

As I stood pondering, whilst I ate, I caught the voices of men chaunteying on deck. For a while this continued; then came Barlow's voice shouting orders, and almost immediately a splash in the water on the starboard side.

I poked my head out through the port, and stared. They had got one of the lifeboats into the water. To the gunnel of the boat they had added a superstructure ending in a roof, the whole somewhat resembling a gigantic dog-kennel.

From under the two sharp ends of the boat rose a couple of planks at an angle of thirty degrees. These appeared to be firmly bolted to the boat and the superstructure. I guessed that their purpose was to enable the boat to override the seaweed, instead of ploughing into it and getting fast.

In the stern of the boat was fixed a strong ringbolt, into which was spliced the end of a coil of one-inch Manilla rope. Along the sides of the boat, and high above the gunnel, the superstructure was pierced with holes for oars. In one side of the roof was placed a trapdoor. The idea struck me as wonderfully ingenious, and a very probable solution of the difficulty of rescuing the crew of the *Graiken*.

A few minutes later one of the men threw over a rope side-ladder, and ran down it on to the roof of the boat. He opened the trap, and lowered himself into the interior. I noticed that he was armed with one of the yacht's cutlasses and a revolver.

It was evident that my chum fully appreciated the difficulties that were to be overcome. In a few seconds the man was followed by four others of the crew, similarly armed; and then Barlow.

Seeing him, I craned out my head as far as possible, and sang out to him.

"Ned! Ned, old man!" I shouted. "Let me come along with you!"

He appeared never to have heard me. I noticed his face, just before he shut down the trap above him. The expression was fixed and peculiar. It had the uncomfortable remoteness of a sleep-walker.

"Confound it!" I muttered, and after that I said nothing; for it hurt my dignity to supplicate before the men.

From the interior of the boat I heard Barlow's voice, muffled. Immediately four oars were passed out through the holes in the sides while from slots in the front and rear of the superstructure were thrust a couple of oars with wooden chocks nailed to the blades.

These, I guessed, were intended to assist in steering the boat, that in the bow being primarily for pressing down the weed before the boat, so as to allow her to surmount it the more easily.

Another muffled order came from the interior of the queer-looking craft, and immediately the four oars dipped, and the boat shot towards the weed, the rope trailing out astern as it was paid out from the deck above me.

The board-assisted bow of the lifeboat took the weed with a sort of squashy surge, rose up, and the whole craft appeared to leap from the water down in among the quaking mass.

I saw now the reason why the oar-holes had been placed so high. For of the boat itself nothing could be seen, only the upper portion of the superstructure wallowing amid the weed. Had the holes been lower, there would have been no handling the oars.

I settled myself to watch. There was the probability of a prodigious spectacle, and as I could not help, I would, at least, use my eyes.

Five minutes passed, during which nothing happened, and the boat made slow progress towards the derelict. She had accomplished perhaps some twenty or thirty yards, when suddenly from the *Graiken* there reached my ears a hoarse shout.

My glance leapt from the boat to the derelict. I saw that the people aboard had the sliding part of the screen to one side, and were waving their arms frantically, as though motioning the boat back.

Amongst them I could see the girlish figure that had attracted my attention the previous evening. For a moment I stared, then my gaze travelled back to the boat. All was quiet.

The boat had now covered a quarter of the distance, and I began to persuade myself that she would get across without being attacked.

Then, as I gazed anxiously, from a point in the weed a little ahead of the boat there came a sudden quaking ripple that shivered through the weed in a sort of queer tremor. The next instant, like a shot from a gun, a huge mass drove up clear through the tangled weed, hurling it in all directions, and almost capsizing the boat.

The creature had driven up rear foremost. It fell back with a mighty splash, and in the same moment its monstrous arms were reached out to the boat. They grasped it, enfolding themselves about it horribly. It was apparently attempting to drag the boat under.

From the boat came a regular volley of revolver shots. Yet, though the brute writhed, it did not relinquish its hold. The shots closed, and I saw the dull flash of cutlass blades. The men were attempting to hack at the thing through the oar-holes, but evidently with little effect.

All at once the enormous creature seemed to make an effort to overturn the boat. I saw the half submerged boat go over to one side, until it seemed to me that nothing could right it, and at the sight I went mad with excitement to help them.

I pulled my head in from the port, and glanced round the cabin.

I wanted to break down the door, but there was nothing with which to do this.

"Then my sight fell upon my bunkboard, which fitted into a sliding groove. It was made of teak wood, and very solid and heavy. I lifted it out, and charged the door with the end of it.

The panels split from top to bottom, for I am a heavy man. Again I struck, and drove the two portions of the door apart. I hove down the bunkboard and rushed through.

There was no one on guard; evidently they had gone on deck to view the rescue. The gunroom door was to my right, and I had the key in my pocket.

In an instant, I had it open, and was lifting down from its rack a heavy elephant gun. Seizing a box of cartridges, I tore off the lid, and emptied the lot into my pocket; then I leapt up the companionway on the deck.

The steward was standing near. He turned at my step; his face was white, and he took a couple of paces towards me doubtfully.

"They're—they're—" he began; but I never let him finish.

"Get out of my way!" I roared and swept him to one side. I ran forward.

"Haul in on that rope!" I shouted. "Tail on to it! Are you going to stand there like a lot of owls and see them drown!"

The men only wanted a leader to show them what to do, and, without showing any thought of insubordination, they tacked on to the rope that was fastened to the stern of the boat, and hauled her back across the weed—cuttle-fish and all.

The strain on the rope had thrown her on an even keel again, so that she took the water safely, though that foul thing was sproddled all across her.

" 'Vast hauling!" I shouted. "Get the doc's cleavers, some of you—anything that'll cut!"

"This is the sort, Sir!" cried the bo'sun; from somewhere he had got hold of a formidable doublebladed whale lance.

The boat, still under the impetus given by our pull, struck the side of the yacht immediately beneath where I was waiting with the gun. Astern of it towed the body of the monster, its two eyes—monstrous orbs of the Profound—staring out vilely from behind its arms.

I leant my elbows on the rail and aimed full at the right eye. As I pulled on the trigger one of the great arms detached itself from the boat, and swirled up towards me. There was a thunderous bang as the heavy charge drove its way through that vast eye, and at the same instant something swept over my head.

There came a cry from behind: "Look out, Sir!" A flame of steel before my eyes, and a truncated something fell upon my shoulder, and thence to the deck.

Down below, the water was being churned to a froth, and three more arms sprang into the air, and then down among us.

One grasped the bo'sun, lifting him like a child. Two cleavers gleamed, and he fell to the deck from a height of some twelve feet, along with the severed portion of the limb.

I had my weapons reloaded again by now, and ran forward along the deck somewhat, to be clear of the flying arms that flailed on the rails and deck.

I fired again into the hulk of the brute, and then again. At the second shot, the murderous din of the creature ceased, and, with an ineffectual flicker of its remaining tentacles, it sank out of sight beneath the water.

A minute later we had the hatch in the roof of the superstructure open, and the men out, my chum coming last. They had been mightily shaken, but otherwise were none the worse.

As Barlow came over the gangway, I stepped up to him and gripped his shoulder. I was strangely muddled in my feelings. I felt that I had no sure position aboard my own yacht. Yet all I said was:

"Thank God, you're safe, old man!" And I meant it from my heart.

He looked at me in a doubtful, puzzled sort of manner, and passed his hand across his forehead. "Yes," he replied; but his voice was strangely toneless, save that some puzzledness seemed to have crept into it. For a couple of moments he stared at me in an unseeing way, and once more I was struck by the immobile, tensed-up expression of his features. Immediately afterwards he turned away—having shown neither friendliness nor enmity—and commenced to clamber back over the side into the boat.

"Come up, Ned!" I cried. "It's no good. You'll never manage it that way. Look!" and I stretched out my arm, pointing. Instead of looking, he passed his hand once more across his forehead, with that gesture of puzzled doubt. Then, to my relief, he caught at the rope ladder, and commenced to make his way slowly up the side.

Reaching the deck, he stood for nearly a minute without saying a word, his back turned to the derelict. Then, still wordless, he walked slowly across to the opposite side, and leant his elbows upon the rail, as though looking back along the way the yacht had come.

For my part, I said nothing, dividing my attention between him and the men with occasional glances at the quaking weed and the—apparently—hopelessly surrounded *Graiken*.

The men were quiet, occasionally turning towards Barlow, as though for some further order. Of me they appeared to take little notice. In this wise, perhaps a quarter of an hour went by; then abruptly Barlow stood upright, waving his arms and shouting:

"It comes! It comes!" He turned towards us, and his face seemed transfigured, his eyes gleaming almost maniacally.

I ran across the deck to his side, and looked away to port, and now I saw what it was that had excited him. The weed-barrier through which we had come on our inward journey was divided, a slowly broadening river of oily water showing clean across it.

Even as I watched it grew broader, the immense masses of weed being moved by some unseen impulsion.

I was still staring, amazed, when a sudden cry went up from some of the men to starboard. Turning quickly, I saw that the yawning movement was being continued to the mass of weed that lay between us and the *Graiken*.

Slowly, the weed was divided, surely as though an invisible wedge were being driven through it. The gulf of weed-clear water reached the derelict, and passed beyond. And now there was no longer anything to stop our rescue of the crew of the derelict.

VII

It was Barlow's voice that gave the order for the mooring ropes to be cast off, and then, as the light wind was right against us, a boat was out ahead, and the yacht was towed towards the ship, whilst a dozen of the men stood ready with their rifles on the fo'c's'le head.

As we drew nearer, I began to distinguish the features of the crew, the men strangely grizzled and old looking. And among them, white-faced with emotion, was my chum's lost sweetheart. I never expect to know a more extraordinary moment.

I looked at Barlow; he was staring at the whitefaced girl with an extraordinary fixidity of expression that was scarcely the look of a sane man.

The next minute we were alongside, crushing to a pulp between our steel sides one of those remaining monsters of the deep that had continued to cling steadfastly to the *Graiken*.

Yet of that I was scarcely aware, for I had turned again to look at Ned Barlow. He was swaying slowly to his feet, and just as the two vessels closed he reached up both his hands to his head, and fell like a log.

Brandy was brought, and later Barlow carried to his cabin; yet we had won clear of that hideous weed-world before he recovered consciousness.

During his illness I learned from his sweetheart how, on a terrible night a long year previously, the *Graiken* had been caught in a tremendous storm and dismasted, and how, helpless and driven by the gale, they at last found themselves surrounded by the great banks of floating weed, and finally held fast in the remorseless grip of the dread Sargasso.

She told me of their attempts to free the ship from the weed, and of the attacks of the cuttlefish. And later of various other matters; for all of which I have no room in this story.

In return I told her of our voyage, and her lover's strange behavior. How he had wanted to undertake the navigation of the yacht, and had talked of a great world of weed. How I had—believing him unhinged—refused to listen to him. How he had taken matters into his own hands, without which she would most certainly have ended her days surrounded by the quaking weed and those great beasts of the deep waters.

She listened with an evergrowing seriousness, so that I had, time and again, to assure her that I bore my old chum no ill, but rather held myself to be in the wrong. At which she shook her head, but seemed mightily relieved.

It was during Barlow's recovery that I made the astonishing discovery that he remembered no detail of his imprisoning of me.

I am convinced now that for days and weeks he must have lived in a sort of dream in a hyper state, in which I can only imagine that he had possibly been sensitive to more subtle understandings than normal bodily and mental health allows.

One other thing there is in closing. I found that the Captain and the two Mates had been confined to their cabins by Barlow. The Captain was suffering from a pistol-shot in the arm, due to his having attempted to resist Barlow's assumption of authority. When I released him he vowed vengeance. Yet Ned Barlow being my chum, I found means to slake both the Captain's and the two Mates' thirst for vengeance, and the slaking, thereof is—well, another story.

The Call In the Dawn

TO THOSE WHO HAVE cast doubt upon the reality of the great Sargasso Sea, asserting that the romantic features of this remarkable sea of weed have been greatly exaggerated, I would point out that this mass of weed lurking in the central parts of the Atlantic Ocean is a fluctuating quantity, not confined strictly to an area, but moving bodily for many hundred of miles according to storms and prevailing winds, though always within certain limits.

Thus it may be that those who have gone in search of it, and not having found it where they expected, have therefore foolishly considered it to be little more than a myth built around those odd patches and small conglomerations of the weed which they may have chanced across. And all the time somewhere to the North or South, East or West, the great shifting bulk of the weed has lain quiet and lonesome and impassable—a cemetery of lost ships and wrack and forgotten things. And so my story will prove to all who read.

I was, at the time of this happening, a passenger in a large barque of eight hundred and ninety tons, bound down to the Barbadoes. We had very fine, light weather for the first twenty days out with the wind variable, giving the men a great deal of work with the yards.

On the twenty-first day, however, we ran into strong weather, and at night-fall Captain Johnson shortened sail right down to the main topsail, and hove the vessel to.

I questioned him concerning his reason for doing this as the wind was not extraordinarily heavy. He took me down into the saloon, and there by the aid of diagrams, showed me that we were within the Eastern fringe of a great cyclone which was coming up Northward from the vicinity of the Line, but trending constantly Westward in its progress. By heaving the vessel to as he had done, he allowed the cyclone to continue its Westward journey, leaving us free. If, however, he had continued to run the ship on, then he would have ended by running us right into the heart of the storm, where we might have been very easily dismasted or even sunk; for the fury of these storms is prodigious if one comes truly within their scope.

The Captain gave me his opinion and reasons for supposing that this storm, of which we felt no more than the fringe, as it were, was a cyclone of quite unusual violence and extent. He assured me also that when daylight came on the morrow there would most probably be a certain proof of this, in the great masses of floating weed and wrack that we should be likely to encounter when once more he put the vessel on her course to the Southward. These weed masses, he informed me, were torn from the great Eddy of the Atlantic Ocean, where enormous quantities of it were gathered, extending—broken and unbroken—for many hundreds of miles. A place to be avoided by all reasonable navigators.

Now, it all turned out as the Captain had foretold. The storm eased hourly through the night as the cyclone drew off into the Westward sea; so that ere the dawn had come, we lay upon water somewhat broken by the swell of the departed storm, yet almost lacking even a light breath of wind.

At midnight I went below for sleep; but was again on deck in a few hours, being restless. I found Captain Johnson there walking with the Mate, and after greeting him I went over to the lee rail to watch the coming of the dawn which even then made some lightness in the Eastward sky. It came with no more than moderate quickness, for we had not yet come into the tropics, and I watched very earnestly because the dawn-light has always held for me a strange attraction.

There grew first in the East a pale shimmering of light, very solemn, coming so quietly into the sky it might have been a ghostlight spying secretly upon the sleeping world. And then, even as I took account of this thing, there went a spreading of gentle rose hues to the Northward, and upon this a dull orange light in the mid-sky. Presently there was a great loom of greenness, most wondrous, in the upper sky, and from this green and aerial splendour of utter quietness there dropped curtains of lemon that enticed the sight to peer through their mystery into the lost distance, so that my thoughts were all very far from this world.

And the lights grew and strengthened as if they had a great pulse, and the wonder of the dawn-lights beat steadily upon the eye, in an ever-continuing brightness, until all the Eastward sky was full of a pale and translucent lemon, flaked athwart with clouds of transparent greyness and gentle silver. And in the end there came a little light upon the sea, very solemn and dreary, making all that vast ocean but a greater mystery.

And surely, as I looked outward upon the sea, there was something that broke the faint looming of light upon the waters, but what it was I could not at first see. Out of the mists of the lost horizon there climbed, presently, a little golden glory, so that I knew the sun had near come out of the dark. And the golden light made a halo in that part of the far world, sending a ray across the mystery of the dark waters. Then I saw somewhat more plainly the thing that had lain upon the sea, between me and the far lights of the dawn. It was a great, low-seeming island in the midst of the loneliness of the ocean. Yet, as I knew well from the charts, there was no proper island in these parts; and I conceived therefore that this thing must be an island of the weed, of which the Captain had spoken the previous day.

"Captain Johnson," I called to him, softly, because there seemed so great a quietness beyond the ship, "Captain Johnson. Bring the glasses." And presently we were spying across the vanishing dark at this floating land of the storm.

Now as we looked earnestly across all that quiet greyness of the sea at the dim seen island, I became doubly filled with the mystery and utter hush of the dawn-time, and of the lights and of the lesson of the morning which is told silently at each dawn over the world. I seemed to hear newly and with great plainness each sound and vague noise that was about me; so that the gentle creaking of the masts and gear was as a harsh calling across that quiet, while the sea made hollow and dank sounds against the wet sides of the ship, and the noise of one walking on the fo'cas'le was a thing that made all the vessel seem to resound emptily.

But when I listened to the far off parts of the sea, even whilst I looked with solemn feelings at that ghostly island half seen in the dawn, it was as if no sound had ever been out there, except it might be some damp wind that wandered forlorn in the distance of the ocean.

And by all this you will understand something of the mood that had come upon me; and indeed, I think this mood was not mine alone; for the Captain was very quiet, and said little, looking constantly towards the grey gloom of the island in the dawn.

And then, as the sun cast the first beam of light clear over the mists of the hid horizon, there came a little thin noise out of all the dawn of the world. It was as if I heard a small voice far off in the miles, coming to me out of an infinite distance:

"Son of Man!

"Son of Man!

"Son of Man!"

I heard it very faint and lost-seeming in all that mystery of the Eastward sea, drifting out of the quiet of the dawn. Towards the East there was only emptiness and greyness, and the quiver of the dawn-shine, and the first rays of the morning upon the silver-grey shimmer of the sea. Only these things, and the low-lying stretch of the weed island, maybe half a mile to the Eastward—a desolate shadow, quiet upon the water.

I set my hand to my ear and listened, looking at the Captain; he likewise listening, having looked first well through his glasses. But now he stared at me, half questioning with his eyes.

The sun stood up over the edge of the grey-glimmering ocean like a roadway of flame, broken midway by the dull stretch of the weed-island. And in that moment the sound came again:

"Son of Man!

"Son of Man!

"Son of Man!"   out of morning light that made glows in the Eastward sea. Far and faint and lonesome was the voice, and so thin and aethereal it might have been a ghost calling vaguely out of the scattering greynesses—the shadow of a voice amid the fleeting shadows.

I started round at all the sea, and surely on every side it was studded with islets of weed, clearly seen upon the silver of the morning sea through the quiet miles into the horizons. As I looked this way and that way with something of astonishment, there came again to my hearing a faint sound, as if I heard a thin, attenuated piping in the East, coming very incredible and far-off sounding and unreal over the hush of the water. Shrill and dree and yet vague it was; and presently I heard it no more.

The Captain and I looked often at one another during this time; and again we searched the width of the Eastward sea, and the desolateness of the long, low island of the weed; but there was nowhere anything that might lead us to an understanding of this thing that bewildered us.

The Mate also had stood near to us listening, and had heard the strange thin, far-off calling and piping; but he, likewise, had no knowledge or understanding by which we might judge the thing.

While we were drinking our morning coffee Captain Johnson

and I discoursed upon this mysterious happening, and could in no-wise come any the nearer to an understanding, unless it was some lone derelict held in the weed of the great island that lay Eastward of us. This was, in truth, a proper enough explanation, if only we might set proof upon it; and to this end the Captain ordered one of the boats to be lowered, and a large crew to man the boat, and each man to be armed with a musket and a cutlass. Moreover, he sent down into the boat two axes and three double-edged whale-pikes or lances, with six feet blades, very keen and as broad as my palm.

To me he dealt a brace of pistols, and likewise a brace to himself, and the two of us had our knives. And by all of these things you can see, as I have told, that he had known previous adventures with the weed, and that he had knowledge of dangers that were peculiar thereto.

We put out presently in the clear morning light towards the great island of the weed that lay to the Eastward. And this island was, maybe, nearly two miles long, and, as we found, something more than half of a mile broadwise, or as the sailors named it "in the beam." We came to it pretty quickly, and Captain Johnson bid the men back-water when we were some twenty fathoms off from the midmost part which was opposite to the ship. Here we lay awhile, and looked through our glasses at the weed, searching it all ways, but saw nowhere any sign of derelict craft, nor aught that spoke of human life.

Yet of the life of sea animals there was no end; for all the weed, upon the outer edges seemed a-crawl with various matters; though at first we had not been able to perceive these because of the similarity in colour with the yellowness of the weed, which was very yellow in the light outward fronds spreading out upon the waters. Inward of the mass of the island I saw that there went a dark and greener shading of the yellow, and there I discovered that this green darkness was the colour of the great weedstems that made up the bulk of the island, like so many great cables and serpents of a yellow green, very dank and gloomy, wandering amid their twistings and turning and vast entanglements that made so huge and dreary a labyrinth.

After we had made a pretty good survey of that part we turned to the Northward, and Captain Johnson bid the men pull slowly along the coast of that great island of weed. In this wise we went a good mile until we came to the end, where we set the boat to the Eastward so as to come round to the other side. And all the while as we went forward the Captain and I made constant observation of the island and of the sea about it, using our glasses to the purpose.

This way I saw a thousand matters to give me cause for interest and wonder; for the weed all about the borders of the island had living creatures a-move within amid the fronds, and the sea showed frequently in this place and the glitter of strange fish, very plentiful and various.

Now I took a particular heed to note the many creatures that lived amid the weed; for I was always interested in the weed-sea from the many accounts which I had heard concerning it, both from Captain Johnson and from other men of the sea that had been ship masters in my voyages. And surely these islands and gatherings together of the weed had been rent from that same great weed-sea which Captain Johnson spoke of always as the Great Eddy. As I have said, I took very good heed to note what manner of creatures lived in the weed, and in this way I perceived presently that there were more crabs than aught else, so far as the power of my glasses could show me; for there were crabs in every place, and all of them yellow in the top parts as the weed. And some were as small as my thumb top, and many were less, I suppose, had I been closer to discover them; but others crawling amid the weed fronds must have spread a great foot across the back, and were all yellow, so that save when they moved they might lie hidden entirely by matching the shades of the weed in which they lived.

We had pulled round the Northward end of the island, and found it, as I have told, something more than the half of a mile wide, or maybe three-quarters for all that we could be sure. And here let me tell concerning the height of the island above the sea, which we judged now, being very low down in the boats and looking upward at the weed, to be about twenty or twenty-five feet good above the ocean, the greatest height being in the middle parts, inland as it were of the island, looking as if it had been a low thick wood with the greater trees in the centre, and all lost in jungle of strange creeping plants. And this is the best likeness I can give of that island to any landward thing.

Having pulled round the North end of the island we made Southward all along the Western coast of the weed, being minded to go entirely about it and chance discovering the cause and the place of that strange calling in the dawn. And indeed it was a dree place to by by; for constantly we would open out some dark, cavern-place of dark green and gloom that went inward of the weed, amid those great stems; and often there seemed to be things moving therein;

and always there was a quietness in all that desolate waste save when some small wind played strangely across it, making the yellow fronds of the weed stir a little in this place and that with little sighings of sound, as if doleful beings lurked in all that mass of quiet darkness. And when the little wind had gone away over the sea there came a double silence by the contrast, so that I was glad that the boat was kept well off from the weed.

In this way, with growing caution and quietness because of the dreeness of that dank and lonesome island which had begun now to affect our spirits somewhat, we went downward to the South along that coast of the Westward side of the island; and as we went a greater and a greater hush and caution came upon us, so that the men scarcely dipped their oars with any sound, but pulled daintily, each one staring very keen and tensely into the shadows within that mighty mass of weed.

It chanced that one of the men ceased suddenly to pull upon his oar, looking very eagerly and fearfully at something that he perceived amid the gloom that lurked among the monstrous stems of the weed. And at that, every man ceased likewise to work upon his oar, and peered fearfully into the dark places of the weed, being assured that the man saw something very dreadful.

The Captain made no attempt to chide the men, but stared himself, as even as I did, to see what manner of thing it was that the man saw. And presently each one discovered the Thing for himself; but at the first it seemed only as if we peered at a great and ugly bunching of the weed-stems, far inward from the edge of the island; but in a little while the thing grew plainer to the eye, and we saw that it was some kind of a devil-fish or octopus lying among the weed, very quiet, and shaded with the same gloom and colour as the weed which was its home. The thing was enormous, as my eyes told me, seeming to spread all ways among the weed.

Captain Johnson got up out of the stern of the boat, and called in a low voice to the men to dip their oars very gently so as to have way upon the boat again; and this they did with great care while the Captain steered the boat outward awhile from the island, and we became presently happier in our minds as we drew afar off from so dreadful and horrible a brute.

In this way we pulled nearly a good mile Southward, keeping well from the shore of the island, and soon we saw the weed come outward in something of a ness or cape from the main body. We came round this with a fair offing, and found the shore of the island ran inward in a deep bay, and in the weed in the bight of the bay we saw something that made us suppose we had discovered the place whence came that unnatural calling in the dawn; for there was the hull of a vessel all mastless in among the weed, near the edge, yet not very plain to be seen, because it was so hidden and smothered by the weed.

We were all vastly excited at this, and the Captain bid the men give way with heartiness; and indeed we lost suddenly the fear of lurking monsters which had before made us so quiet and cautious. And because the men set their strength into the oars, we came very soon to the bight of the bay where lay the derelict ship and found that she was no more than maybe a dozen yards or so inward of the weed which was pretty low and flat in that place around her; but beyond the ship the weed was piled up very dark and gloomy for twenty feet high and more, and growing all over her.

We paused now wondering how we should best come up to the ship; and all the time while the Captain considered, I spied through my glasses at the wreck, having little hope that we should find any aboard of her; for it was plain to me now how old she was and all crumbled with time and weather, and the weed girting her in all parts, seeming to grow through the wood of her sides, though this was very incredible; yet so we found it to be when we came near her. Afterwards I searched the weed all near her to see whether there were any monster fish about; Captain Johnson doing the same; but we found nothing. And the Captain then gave orders to put the boat in among the weed, and we cut our way through the low weed to the side of the ship.

Now as we made way through the weed it amazed us to see how much life had been hidden there, very still; for all the weed now about the boat was a-swarm with small crabs, running along the fronds and smaller stems; while the water that showed between the growths of the weed was full of living things, great shrimps that seemed bigger than prawns, darting a thousand ways at once, and coloured fish that passed very swiftly. From the weed itself numberless insects of a peculiar kind jumped like any flea, only that they were a hundred times greater. And twice and trice as we put the boat through the weed we disturbed great crabs that were lain there sullen or waiting for their prey; one of them as big across the back as a dish-cover, which caught at the oar of one of the men with its pincers, and nipped the thin wood of the blade through quick and cleanly. Afterwards it went away, rough and active, shaking the weed in its passage, which will show you the vigour and strength that was in the creature.

In a few minutes we had cut a way in to the ship, using the axes and the men's knives and the oars; but the cutlasses the Captain would not have used on the weed because they were weapons and to be kept as such.

When we came close in upon the ship we found that the weed grew completely through her side as though the weed had rooted in the wood of her; and we were all somewhat astonished at this thing, and many another which we discovered; for when we came to clamber up her side, we found the wood had gone soft and rotted to a sponginess, so that we could kick our shod toes into the wood, and thereby make each an immediate ladder upwards.

When we came to the top level of the hulk, and could look aboard there was nothing to her but the shell of her sides and of her bows and stern; for all the decks were gone, and the beams that had held the decks were part missing, and few of those which remained were complete. The bottom of the ship was rotted nigh out of her so that the weed came upward in plenty that way with the water showing down below very gloomy and dark. And the weed grew through the sides of the vessel, or over the rails, just as it had seemed to suit the convenience of that strange vegetable, if I may call it so.

It was very dismal looking downward into that desert hull which had been upheld from its sinking by the grip of the weed through a hundred or maybe two hundred years. When I asked the Captain about this he set her age to be something more than four hundred years, speaking learnedly concerning the rotted stern and bow, and the way and set of the frame-timbers; so that it was plain to me that he had considerable knowledge on such matters.

Presently, because there was nothing more to be done, we came down again to the boat, kicking our toes into the soft hull of the old ship for our footholds. And before we left her I broke away a lump of one of her smaller timbers for a memento of the adventure.

And after that we backed out from the weed, glad to be free of it now that the lust of adventure had somewhat died out of us, and the memory of what lurked therein still strong upon us. So we made the complete round of that island which was more than seven good miles in all to circumnavigate. And afterwards we pulled to our own ship with very good appetites for our breakfast, as you may think.

All that day it remained calm, and often I turned my glass upon the weed islets that studded the sea in other parts; but none was very great or high, though I reminded myself that they would have appeared higher had we approached them in a boat. And this we found to be true; for we used that afternoon to go from one small islet to another, in the boat; and crabs and fish and small living things we found in plenty but never any sign of a wreck or of human life. We returned to our ship in the evening, and had much talk upon the strangeness of that calling that had come to us in the dawn; but no reasonable explanation could we make. And presently I went to my bed, being weary by the lack of rest on the night that had passed.

I was waked in the early morn by the Captain shaking me, and when I had come properly to my senses he told me to hasten on deck, that it was still calm and they had heard the voice again in the dawn that was just breaking.

On hearing this I made speed to go with Captain Johnson on deck, and here, upon the poop, I found the Second Mate with his glass, staring Eastward across the sea towards the weed island which was barely seen save as a vague shadow, low upon the water.

The Second Mate held up his hand to us and whispered "Hist!" and we all fell to listening; but there came no sound for a time, and meanwhile I was greatly aware of the very solemn beauty of the dawn; for the Eastward sky seemed lost in waters of quiet emerald, from a strange and apparent green to a translucence of shimmering green that surely stretched to the very borders of the Eternal, in palest lights that carried the consciousness through aethereal deeps of space, until the soul went lost through the glimmering dawn, greeting unknown spirits. And this is but a clumsy wording of the way that the holiness of that dim light and wonder hushed my very being with a silent happiness. Then, even as I came to this condition of mind, out of the Eastward sea and of all that quiet of the dawn, there came again that far attenuated voice:

"Son of Man!

"Son of Man!

"Son of Man!" coming faint and thin and incredible out of the utter stillness of the wonder and silent glamour of the East. The green of the lower sky faded even as we listened, breathless, and upward there stole the stain of purple lights that blended into a growing bloom of fire-clouds in the middle and lower sky, and so to warmer lights and then to the silver-grey paling of the early morning. And still we waited.

Presently, Eastward, there came a golden warmth upward into the pearly-quiet of the lower sky, and the edge of the sun rose up calm and assured out of the mists, casting a roadway of light over the sea. And in that moment the far, lost voice came again:

"Son of Man!

"Son of Man!

"Son of Man!" drifting to us strangely over the hushed sea, seeming to come out of immense and infinite distances—a voice thin and lonesome, as might be thought to be the call of a spirit crying in the morning. As we looked at one another, questioning wordless things, there came a vague, impossible piping far away and away over the sea, to be presently lost again in the quietness. And we were all adrift to know what it might portend.

After breakfast that day Captain Johnson ordered the boat to be lowered, and put a large crew into her, all armed as before. Then we put off to the weed island; but before we left the ship the Captain had dismounted the smaller ship's bell that was upon the poop, and this we had with us in the boat, also his speaking trumpet.

All that morning we spent circumnavigating the great weed island again, and at each hundred fathoms I beat upon the bell, and the Captain sent his voice inland, speaking through the trumpet and asking whether there were any derelict ship with lost humans hid in the heart of the weed. Yet whether his voice carried through the weed or was smothered we could not know, but only of this could we be certain, that there came never an answer out of all that desolation of the weed, neither to the bell nor to our callings.

In this way we went full round about that island, and naught came of it, save once when we were very near inshore I saw a truly monstrous crab, double as big as any I had ever seen, far in among the great weed stems; and the crab was dark hued as though to match the darker colour of that inward weed; and by this I judged that it lived far inward amid the gloom of the centre parts of that strange island. And truly, as I thought, what could we do even though we found a ship far inward of the weed; for how could any man face a monstrous thing like that, and surely there would be multitudes of such brutes in the middle part of the island, taking no count of the devil fish which also inhabited the weed of that desolate and lonesome island.

In the end we came back to our own ship, having passed again that doleful hulk within the edge of the weed island; and I remember how I thought of the long centuries that had gone since that old craft was lost.

When we came back to the ship Captain Johnson went up the

mainmast, and I with him; and from the crosstrees we made a further examination through the glasses of the inward parts of the great
island; but the weed went everywhere in a riot of ugly yellow and in
this place and that the colour changed to a dull greenish hue where
the weed was hidden from the light. And presently we ceased to
spy upon the island; for the over-arching and entanglement of those
monstrous fronds would have hidden with ease a great fleet of ships
if the same had been lacking their masts.

Now whether there was a ship hidden in all that desolation of
weed, who shall say? And if there had been a ship hidden and caught
far inward of that weed and all overgrown with it, how was it likely
that any living being was aboard of her? For you must bear in mind
the human needs of any that would be so held; and further you
must remember the monstrous brutes that roamed in that great bulk
of the weed.... And again if there had been a ship inward of that
weed and a living human still within her, why should he make that
strange crying in the dawn, over the sea and yet give no answer to
our callings? On all this I have pondered a thousand times and oft,
but have no ready answer to myself, save that there might have been
some poor mad soul yet holding off desperately from death through
the lonesome years, in a lost ship hidden within that weed. This is
the only explanation that I have found to come anywhere near the
need of my reasoning. And truly it would be strange if such a one
could be anything but a lonesome madman, greeting each dawn with
wild and meaningless words and singings that might seem to be of
meaning to a poor demented brain.

But whether this was so or whether there was some matter in
the adventure beyond our indifferent knowledge, I cannot altogether decide. I can only tell you that in the dawn of the third day of
that calm, we heard again that far and strange calling, coming to us
through the hush and the greyness, out of the Eastward sea where
the weed island lay. Very thin and lonesome was the cry:

"Son of Man!

"Son of Man!

"Son of Man!" coming to us in a long drawn out attenuation
of sound, as if out of an immense distance. The dawn was ruddy,
showing plain signs of wind; yet before the wind came down upon
us the upward edge of the sun rose above the black-gloomed horizon,
very sombre seeming and bearded with the wind-haze. The sea had
gone leaden, and the sun threw a roadway of crimson light upon us,
very grand yet somewhat dreary, and in that moment we heard the

far, faint voice again for the last time:

"Son of Man!

"Son of Man!

"Son of Man!"

And afterwards that vague, attenuated piping that had grown so weak sounding we scarcely knew whether we heard it or not; for the coming of the wind made a little almost unperceived noise over the sea. And presently the wind darkened the Northward sea, and our sails filled as the yards were swung by the sailors. And we sailed beyond the long desolation of the great weed island, and continued our voyage, leaving the mystery of the voice to the hush of the sea and the companionship of its constant mystery.

The Exploits Of Captain Gault

Contraband of War

S.S. John L. Sullivan,
May 15.

ONE OF THE MAIN-HATCH slings bust again this morning, and lost a lot of heavy crated goods over the side.

This is the second time a sling has parted in the last couple of days.

"Mr. Anwyn," I said to the First Mate, "scrap every one of those
confounded cargo slings at once. You ought never to have lifted
another ton with them, after that one parted yesterday. I'll not have
another thing hoisted out of the holds until you've new slings. Use
some of that new coil of four-inch Manilla; and get some of the men
on the job, smart. We're just wasting money keeping the lighters idle.
You ought not to have needed me to tell you a thing like this!"

I let the Mate see what I felt in the matter, and I said what I had
to say flat out before Mr. Jelloyne, the tally clerk; for there was no
excuse for the thing happening twice, and I had a right to feel warm.

This unloading into lighters is a slow, weary job at best, and it will
take us another week or ten days to clear the cargo out of her.

May 16.

Mr. Jelloyne, the tally clerk, is certainly a bit of a character. He
was talking this morning about the government restrictions on landing
war material, and the difficulty of doing it secretly.

The old chap seems quite what one might call a bit of a sport.

"Would you do it, Mr. Jelloyne, if you got a chance?" I asked him;
for I was more than simply curious to find out how he looked at a
thing of that kind.

He took a glance round, and then came closer to me.

"It all depends, Cap'n," he said. "There's a lot of cash in it; but
getting caught is a serious business."

"But if you were practically *sure* of not being caught?" I suggested.

"Ah!" he said, and winked at me. "Who wouldn't undertake it, under those conditions!"

That was enough for one time, and I said nothing more to him until this afternoon, when we got talking about it again. He was contending that, apart from the disagreeables attendant upon capture, the thing was enormously difficult. He instanced some of the difficulties.

First, an "examination" of the ship's manifest, showing what she was carrying.

Second, the booking down (or "tallying") of every case and article hoisted out of the hold of every ship in the bay, by the clerk sent aboard every ship.

Third, the examination of every lighter-load sent ashore. If any cases went astray between the ship and the shore, a comparison of the tally clerk's tally-book with the Customs officials' checking of the load would show instantly that a case or article was missing.

Fourth, any suspicious-looking case might be opened by the authorities, to verify that its contents were as per ship's manifest.

Fifth, if any vessel tried to unload cargo secretly after dark, she was bound to be discovered, because her hatches were sealed every night by the government official on the last tug, and were broken by him each morning when he came round on the first tug.

Sixth, there was a night patrol boat, which kept an eye on things in general, and especially on any vessel that acted in any way out of the ordinary, or which did any noticeable amount of boat-traffic with the shore, or even with other vessels lying out in the bay.

"Makes it quite a pleasantly interesting mental problem to see how it might be managed," I said. "I don't think it would be very difficult. . . . One might make the tally clerk a present of a hundred quid on a big job, not to 'tally' down a case of contraband every now and again."

Old Mr. Jelloyne shook his head at that.

"No good, Captain!" he said. "No man is going to risk losing his billet for that kind of thing. Why, he'd be at the mercy of anyone who felt like talking."

"Not my notion of a clever job," I told him. "If I were the kind of man who would do things of that sort, Mr. Jelloyne, I'd try to make it interesting to carry out. For instance, one could avoid the sealing of the hatches, by cutting through into the hold from the lazarette under the main cabin. The stuff could be brought up through the cabin without ever touching the sealed hatches. That is one of the big difficulties overcome."

"What about these same cases being missing when we come to compare the tally-book with the ship's manifest?" he asked me.

"That's certainly a difficulty," I admitted; "but it would simply have to be ignored. By the time the cases were proved missing, they'd be away and away-oh, ashore.

"Then, again, I'd avoid the port risks, and minimize the chance of the patrol-boat dropping on me, by moving the ship over nearer to the north shore. There are plenty of lonely bits of quiet beach there, where I could make a quick dash with a boat-load, now and again at night, if I watched when the patrol-boat was over on the other side of the bay."

Mr. Jelloyne grinned at me in his wicked old way.

"It *might* do," he admitted. "It's plain and simple. Perhaps it's just as well you're not in the business, Captain!"

"My goodness!" I wanted to shout, "I've two thousand pounds' worth of rifles to smuggle ashore, if you only knew it!"

But I took jolly good care not to, as you may think.

"As you remarked just now, Mr. Jelloyne," I said, passing him my case, "it's a mighty risky business. And a sea-Captain's like the law: he should be above suspicion."

"Quite right, Captain. Quite right, Captain," he said heartily; and I let it drop at that.

May 17.

We've been riding to one anchor since we've been here; but last night there was a strong breeze from the Southeast that made us drag for nearly a mile. I let her drag; for there's plenty of room, and it suited my purpose. Then I let go the second bower, and that brought her up.

"You've dragged, Cap'n, during the night," said old Mr. Jelloyne, when he came out this morning. "That was a stiff little blow you had out here. I never thought the sea would have been quiet enough for the lighters this morning, and I'd promised myself a day off. But there's no rest for the wicked."

"Yes," I told him. "It was quite a smart little breeze. I'm going to shift over to the north side. It's nearer in, but the holding's better."

When the tug came out with the second string of lighters, I arranged with the Captain to go ahead of us, while we hove up, and then to give us a tow across to the north side, where, as I told Mr. Jelloyne, the holding is admitted to be better. . . . All the same, I had my own notion that we had dragged, simply because we must have fouled our anchor; but I did not elabourate the idea. I have waited a couple of weeks for just such a breeze, and I have been fully aware that our anchor must have been fouled for some days.

By such means as these, I have been able to bring my ship over nearer to the north shore, without exciting any unnecessary comment.

Night.

What old Mr. Jelloyne, the tally clerk, told me about the patrol-boat is quite correct. She was lying near us for some time tonight, out in the darkness, about four or five hundred yards away; I spotted her through my night-glasses. Evidently, her officer in charge wants to make sure there's nothing behind my moving the ship over here. Of course, I've simply watched the boat, and said nothing, except had a quiet sniggle to myself.

May 22.

Tonight is to be the night. I've given the patrol-boat time to get used to my ship being here.

They had the patrol-boat near the ship most of the night of the 17th, and again on the 18th; but I guessed they'd tire of that! I just looked upon it as a mild diversion, watching them through my night-glasses. They must have been fools not to realise that a good pair of glasses must show them up plain on the water!

However, the last three nights they appear to have got settled in their minds that there's no especial need to keep their eyes glued on my ship all night long. And so tonight, the firm ashore being now ready to remove the goods, I'm going to attempt to complete my little investment in rifles. If all goes well, I stand to clear a thousand pounds to my own cheek, and the money is as acceptable as money always is to a man of my somewhat developed tastes. I've rather stretched my finances lately, buying a Guido, which I could not let pass me.

I went ashore this morning, and got into final touch with the consignees. I took elaborate precautions to insure a secrecy as perfect as ever my heart could desire, and I know that there can have been no dangerous information leaking into the wrong quarters.

The arrangements are, that if I decide, last thing, to send the stuff ashore, I am to have the House-Flag checked, when lowering it at sun-set, and re-hoisted, as if the signal haul-yards had fouled and needed clearing. Then the flag can be lowered in the usual way.

This is to be taken to mean that I will bring the boat ashore, with certain cases, any time after eleven o'clock, the exact time being impossible to fix, owing to the chance of the patrol-boat being on my side of the bay at the time.

Just before I leave the ship I am to flash a bull's-eye over the rail—the signal to be two long flashes and two short.

As an additional precaution for the success of my little adventure, I have had the boat I shall use painted a dead-coloured grey, which should make it almost invisible at night; and new leathers on all the oars, to make them quieter in the rowlocks. The rendezvous is a little bit of lonely beach right opposite the ship.

May 23.

From sunset until eleven o'clock I kept an eye for the patrol-boat. She came over to our side of the bay about 10:45 but did not stay more than a few minutes; and as soon as she had gone well away towards the south side I gave word to haul up the boat, which was lying astern, and to hoist into her, four big cases, that have been snugly out of sight down in the lazarette.

It was a very dark, quiet night, and just before giving the flashes with the bull's-eye, I thought I heard somewhere, far away over the water, and vague, the low, dull beat of a petrol-launch.

I told the men to come up out of the boat, and have a smoke for half an hour. Then I went up on to the bridge with my night-glasses, and had a good look to the Southeast; but, so far as I could see, there was no sign of anything moving out in the bay. Then I examined the water between my ship and the shore; but this was quite clear of any craft.

I put in a full half hour, listening and watching the bay; but there was not a single thing to make me uneasy, and at last I sent word for the men to lay aft again into the boat.

I gave the required lamp-flashes; then I went down into the boat, and we pulled out from the ship's side. I headed her for the dip in the cliffs that marked the beach.

"Gently, men, gently! No hurry!" I told them.

All the time, as we moved quietly shorewards, I kept my eyes about me and my ears open; but there was not a thing of any kind to bother me, that I could see or hear; yet all the time I had a vague excitement of expectancy on me, that kept me a little tense, as may be supposed.

"Easy there. In bow!" I gave the word, as we drew in under the shadow of the cliffs. "Get up in the bows with the boathook, Svensen, and stand by to fend her off."

Though I spoke quietly, the words echoed back in a soft, curious echo from the low cliffs.

"That sounded funny, Sir," said the Third Mate, who was sitting by me.

"Only the echo," I told him; and as I spoke, the boat grounded on the soft sand of the beach, and the men were tumbling out on the instant, pell-mell, to haul her up.

"Out with the stuff, men," I said, as I jumped ashore.

As the last of the four big cases was landed on the sand, the Third Mate touched my arm.

"Hark, Sir," he said, quickly. "What was that? . . . Look, Sir, what's that up the beach?"

I bent forward, and stared. As I did so, there was a sharp command out of the darkness up the beach.

"Hands up, or we fire!" shouted the voice.

"Copped, by the Lord!" said the Third Mate, and whirled round instinctively to the boat.

"Stop that, Mister!" I said. "Do you want to get us all filled with lead? The authorities in this part shoot first and inquire afterwards! Put your hands up, men, all of you. And leave the talking to me."

As I spoke, I heard the pom, pom, pom, of petrol engines, and knew it was the sound of the patrol-boat coming full-tilt across the bay to cut off our retreat.

Then there came from up the beach the flash of several police-lanterns; and as the beams of light circled and rested on us, I could see what a confoundedly absurd spectacle we all looked, every man with his hands reached up so earnestly to the black heavens!

"Well," I said, staring, and trying to see the men behind the lanterns, "what the devil's this mean? Are you a hold-up, or what?"

Of course, I knew it was bound to be the authorities, right enough; but I wanted badly to blow off at them, or somebody. It was plain there had been a leakage somewhere.

"Well," I said again, "what is it? What the deuce is it? I can't stand here all night!"

Then, out of the darkness behind the bull's-eye lantern, stepped the Port Officer, and informed me that I and my men were under arrest for attempting to run a cargo of rifles into the country.

"Don't talk rot," I told him. "Keep your hands still, men," I said. "Leave this to me. . . . Don't you think, Officer, you and I could fix this up, without importing my men or your men into it? Let us take a quiet walk up the shore, while I put a proposition to you."

There was a roar of laughter from his own men in the darkness behind the lanterns. But the Port Officer did not laugh.

"Quit your fooling, Captain Gault," he said. "You may find yourself in extra trouble over this job, for attempting bribery, if you don't keep the lid on a bit more. Don't you get imagining you can bribe me or my men. We're not bribable."

"Go and boil your head," I advised, as mildly as the sentiment implied admitted. "You annoy me incredibly. You're troubled with a badly enlarged liver."

"See you," he said, stepping up close to me. "If you don't drop that sort of talk, you're going to get a hammering, right here and now."

"Not by a puffy child like you," I said; for it was part of my intention to aggravate him to the limit. And I did this sooner than I expected; for, without a word further, he hit me with the back of his hand across the mouth, while I stood helpless, with my hands above my head. I am, perhaps rather narrow-mindedly, glad to assert that he was not a countryman of mine. At the time it would not have mattered if he had been.

I just dropped my hands, and hit him as hard and solid as I could, right and left—one flat in the middle of his bread-machinery, and the other equally in the middle of his face—not scientific blows, perhaps; but they were so hearty and soundly-intentioned that he went nearly a dozen paces, spinning on his feet, before he fell.

My men shouted and dropped their hands, and I leaned quickly towards the Third Mate.

"There's going to be a rumpus," I whispered. "While it's on, collar one or two of the men, and shove those cases down into the sea. Quick, now! I don't fancy there'll be any shooting."

I was completely right; for if the Port Officer was no sportsman, his men were splendidly so. Down went their rifles with a crash, and they leaped to meet my men. I fancy there must have been a good many Irishmen among them, from the intoning of their joyous and entirely improper and separate litanies. My men were mostly Scots, and they did very well in the fighting line (as later comparisons showed); but they were less fluent, or perhaps, to be strictly accurate, quite as persistent; but eventually a trifle monotonous!

How the fighting went on for a bit I could not tell; for every lantern had been put out in the first rush; moreover, I was dealing with the Port Officer in a way that I felt should prove memorable. I'll admit that he made lusty objections; but I'm nearer fifteen than fourteen stone, and I never did run to fat.

*　*　*　*

When at last the lanterns were lit again, I found my men all handcuffed in a row, and looking as if they had thoroughly enjoyed themselves.

There were twenty of the government men—big, hefty lads they were, too, and not one of them but had to choke a grin when I assisted the Port Officer politely to his feet.

"Now, Sir," I said, "perhaps you will kindly explain the whole of this business, and the meaning of your unwarrantable and illegal assault upon my person."

The idiot glared at me; but had not a word to say. In any case, a violent loss of teeth does not improve articulation.

"The cases!" he shouted to his men, in a thick voice.

"They've gone clean away, Sir," said one of his men, after a brief search.

He grew frantic.

"Don't you tell me *that* for a yarn, you blind dummies," he shouted. "Look about! Look about! They're bound to be near."

I smiled; for the Third Mate had done very well indeed. Meanwhile, he and his men searched everywhere, more and more bewildered; until at last one of them spotted the corner of one of the cases sticking up above the water, where the Third Mate and one of the men had sunk them, during the row.

It took the Officer and his men half an hour to salvage the cases, and every man was wet through by the time they were hauled ashore.

As the big cases were taken from the sea, the water rushed out of holes that had been bored in them; and one of the men remarked this to the Port Officer, who snatched a lamp and began to examine the cases.

"Knock in the top of one of them!" he said, suddenly.

One of his men brought an axe from up the beach, and in a minute he had the side of one of the boxes laid right open.

"Empty!" shouted every one of his men, and my Third Mate as well; but the Port Officer said not a word. He seemed stunned for a moment.

"The—the others!" he said, at last. "Quick!"

But the other boxes were empty also, as they could tell by lifting them, now that the sea-water had drained out.

"Perhaps now, Sir, you will take that same little stroll along the beach which I requested awhile ago," I said. "If you had courteously acceded to my request, all this melodrama might have been omitted."

He stared at me, a moment, in a kind of dazed sulkiness.

"Meanwhile," I added, "you may as well give orders for my men to be released. I don't fancy it will pay you to keep them longer in that condition; for, as things are, you stand the chances of getting into serious trouble for your action tonight, in assaulting and arresting a body of law-abiding men, who have come ashore for no other object at all than to have a quiet evening's 'gam' on the beach, with a bit of a bonfire made out of these old cases we've brought ashore, and towards which you seem to have exhibited extraordinary covetousness."

"Oh, stow it!" he muttered, wearily. "I'll come with you, and hear what you've got to say."

He beckoned to his sub.

"Unlock them!" he ordered, and turned and followed me twenty or thirty yards up the beach.

"Now," he said, "be quick with what you wanted to tell me!"

"You've already learned, by ocular proof, as I might say, the major portion of it," I told him. "There are, however, one or two details to add. In the first place, I happened to receive information from a friend that old Mr. Jelloyne was 'one of yours,' so I outlined to him just such a little outing as tonight's, only with rifles in those cases instead of air.

"He courteously performed his share of my little plot by detailing my talk to you! I then shifted my ship over to this side, and when all was ready I went ashore and gave information, per telephone, to your office that the S.S. *John L. Sullivan* would make certain signals this evening to inform certain confederates ashore that her Captain would land a consignment of contraband of war secretly tonight.

"I explained exactly what these signals would be, and when you grew too gratefully insistent for the name of the 'man on the 'phone', I told you it was someone who would see you personally, at the right moment, and define his reward. This is, if you will allow me to say so, the right moment.

"There are just one or two minor details unexplained. My men were not in this plot at all. The Third, however, was fooled in exactly the same way that you were; for I told him secretly that there was contraband in the cases. He must have thought it mighty light contraband!

"By the way, don't you think the painting of the boat was a splendid little touch on my part to lend actuality to my, shall I call it, practical joke?

"In many ways, this joke is almost the best part of tonight's work. You see, it was so essential to draw all official attention away from our old berth in the bay; for, some days ago, Mr. Officer, we broke (not quite by accident) a couple of slings, and there fell over the ship's side four cases of rifles, labelled sewing machines.

"These cases had been previously roped together, in couples, to facilitate a grapple finding them, and were picked up tonight (as a lantern signal informed me some fifteen minutes ago) by friends of mine ashore, while you and the patrol-launch have been attending my little burlesque here.

"Don't you think, now, it was all distinctly neat? And I stand to clear quite a thousand on the job.

"Shall we go back now? You see, dear man, there have been no witnesses to this little talk; so you can prove nothing, and certainly nothing to *your credit*, while I can prove a great deal that is not to yours. Shall we call the game even?

"By the way, I can confidently recommend to you a raw beef-steak for black eyes. . . ."

The Diamond Spy

S.S. Montrose,
June 18.

I AM HAVING ENOUGH bother with one or two of the passengers this trip, to make me wish I was running a cargo boat again.

When I went up on the upper bridge this morning, Mr. Wilmet, my First Officer, had allowed one of the passengers, a Mr. Brown, to come up on to the bridge and loose off some prize pigeons. Not only that; but the Third Officer was taking the time for him, by one of the chronometers.

I'm afraid what I said looked a bit as if I had lost my temper.

"Mr. Wilmet," I said, "will you explain to Mr. Brown that this bridge is quite off his beat? And I should like him to remove himself, and ask him please to remember the fact for future reference. If Mr. Brown wants to indulge his taste in pigeon-flying, I've no objections to offer at all; but he'll kindly keep off my bridge!"

I certainly made no effort to spare Mr. Brown; and this is not the first time I have had to pull him up; for he took several of his birds down into the dinner-saloon yesterday, and was showing them off to a lot of his friends—actually letting them fly all about the place; and you know what dirty brutes the birds are! I gave him a smart word or two before all the saloon-full; and I fancy they agreed with me. The man's a bit mad on his pigeon-flying.

Then there's a bore of a travelling colonel, who's always trying to invade my bridge, to smoke and yarn with me. I've had to tell him plainly to keep off the bridge, same as Mr. Brown, only, perhaps, not quite in the same manner. And there are two ladies, an old and a young one, who are always on the bridge-steps, as you might say. I took the opportunity to talk to the oldest about my eighth boy, today. I thought it might cool her off; but it didn't; she's started talking to me now about the dear children; and as I'm not even married, I've lied myself nearly stupid, confound her! And the old lady has let the young one know, *of course!* And the young one has left me now entirely to the old one's mercies. Goodness me!

But the passenger who really bothers me is a Mr. Aglae, a sallow, fat, darkish man, short, and most infernally inquisitive. He seems always to be hanging about; and I've more than a notion he's cultivating a confidential friendship with my servant-lad.

Of course, I've guessed all along he's a diamond spy; and I don't doubt but there's little need for the breed in these boats; for there's a pile to be made in running stones and pearls through the Customs.

I nearly broke loose on him today, and told him, slam out, I knew he was a spy, and that he had better keep his nose out of my cabin and my affairs; and pay a bit more attention to people who had the necessary thousands to deal successfully in his line of goods.

The man was actually peeping into my cabin when I came up behind him; but he was plausible enough. He said he had knocked, and thought I said, "Come in." He had come to ask me to take care of a very valuable diamond, which he brought out of his vest pocket, in a wash-leather bag. He told me he had begun to feel it might be safer if properly locked up. Of course, I explained that his diamond would be taken care of in the usual way; and when he asked my opinion of it, I became astonishingly affable; for it was plainly his desire to get me to talk on the subject.

"A magnificent stone!" I said. "Why, I should think it must be worth thousands. It must be twenty or thirty carats."

I knew perfectly well that the thing was merely a well-cut piece of glass; for I tried it slyly on the tester I carry on the inner edge of my ring; and as for the size, I purposely "out"; for I knew that if it had been a diamond, it would have been well over a hundred carats.

The little fat spy frowned slightly, and I wondered whether I'd shown him that he was getting up the wrong tree; and then, in a moment, I saw by the look in his eyes that he suspected me as much as ever, and was putting me down as being simply *ostentatiously* ignorant of diamonds. After he had gone, I thought him over for a bit, and I got wishing I could give the little toad a lesson.

June 19.

I got a splendid idea during the night. We should dock this evening, and I've just time to work it. The diamond-running talk came up at dinner last night, as is but natural in these boats; and different passengers told some good yarns, some of them old and some new, and a lot of them, very clever dodges that have been worked on the Customs.

One man at my table, told an I.D.B. yarn of how a duck had been induced to gobble up diamonds by bedding them in pellets of bread, and in this way the diamonds had been cunningly hidden, at a very critical moment for the well-being of their "illicit" owner.

This gave me my idea; for that diamond spy has got on my nerves a bit, and if I don't do something to make him look and feel a fool, I shall just get rude; and rudeness to passengers is not a thing that commends itself to owners.

I have a coop of S. African black ring-neck hens, down on the well-deck, which I am taking across to my brother, who makes a hobby of hen-keeping, and has bred some wonderful strains.

I sent my servant for a plateful of new crumb-bread, and then I fished out from the bottom of my sea-chest, a box of what we used to call among the islands "native blazers"—that is, cut-glass imitation diamonds, which certainly cleaned up to a very pretty glitter. I'd had the things with me for years, some left-overs, from a sporting trip I made once that way.

I sat down at my table, and made bread pellets; and then I began to bed each of the "stones" into a pellet. As I did so, I became aware that someone was peeping in the window that looks into the saloon. I glanced into the mirror, across on the opposite bulkhead of my cabin, and saw for an instant the face of my servant. Then he was gone.

This is what I had expected.

"So, ho! my lad!" I said to myself. "I guess this is the last trip you'll take with me; for, though you aren't dangerous now, you may be some other time."

When I had done coating my "diamonds" with bread, I went forrard to my hen-coop, and began to feed the pellets to the birds. As I turned away, from giving the last of the big bread pills, I literally bumped into Mr. Aglae, who had just come round the end of the coop. Obviously, he had received word from my servant, and had been watching me feed diamonds to my hens, so as to hide my illegal jewellery, while the search officers were aboard!

It was rather funny to see the way in which the diamond spy put on a vacant expression, and apologised for his clumsiness, blaming the rolling of the vessel. As a matter of fact, he had no business in that part of the ship at all; and I made a courteous reference to this fact; for I wished him to think that I was disturbed and annoyed at his being there at so (apparently) critical a moment for me.

Later on, when I went into the wireless room, I found Mr. Algae sending a wireless; and I sat down on the lounge to write my own message, while Melson (the operator) was sending.

Instead, however, of writing out my own message, I jotted down the dot and dash iddle-de-umpty of the iggle-de-piggle that the operator was sending, for it was a private code message, and ran: 1 7 a y b o z w r e y a a j g o o a v 0 0 1 0 w t p q 2 2 3 2 1 m v n 6 7 a m n t 8 t s .17. aglae. g.v.n.

I smiled; for it was the latest official cypher, and I had the "key" in my pocket-book. It is desirable to have what is properly called "a friend in high quarters." Only my friend is not very high, at least, not highly paid; though his secretarial position gives him access in a certain government office to papers that help him considerably to make both ends meet.

After Mr. Algae had departed, I took out my "key," and translated the message, while Melson was sending mine. Translated, it was this: "Hens fed on hundreds of diamonds concealed in bread pellets. Better come out in the pilot tug. Shall mark coop. I must not appear in the case at all. Most important capture of years. 17. Algae. g.v.n."

This was sent to a private address, merely as a blind; for Mr. Algae would be of little further use as a diamond spy if he began sending cypher messages to the head office! The 17, just before his name, I knew, must be his official number, and I was interested, and perhaps a little impressed; for I had heard of the unknown "Number 17" before. He had effected some wonderful captures among the diamond smugglers. I wondered what he might look like, minus what I began now to suspect was both a false stomachic appendage, and dyed hair, plus his little, vaguely foreign mannerisms, to suit.

The letters "g.v.n." which followed the signature were the inner "keys" to the message; for the cypher is really clever, in that a long message can be sent with a limited number of symbols, by a triplicate reading, according to the use of the various combinations—the working of which the main "key" explains, and which are indicated by the combination letters, which are always written, in this cypher, after the signature.

As I went out of the wireless room, I had a second splendid idea. I got some bread-crumbs as an excuse, and had another walk down to the well-deck to look at my coop of prize chickens, and I came slam on Number 17 (as I now called him to myself) just strolling off.

Now, I had made it plain to him that he had no business down there, and I called to him to ask him what he was doing again in that part of the ship, after what I had told him in the morning.

I must say that Number 17 has got quite a remarkably sound "nerve" on him.

"I'm sorry, Captain," he said; "but I'd lost my cigarette-holder. I knew I'd had it in my fingers when I tumbled against you this morning, and I thought I might have dropped it then."

He held it out to me, between his finger and thumb.

"I found it lying on the deck here," he explained. "A mercy it was not trodden on. I'm thankful much, for I prize it ver' much."

"That's all right, Mr. Aglae," I said, and hid the smile his tricky little foreign flavor of speech rose in me. As a matter of fact, if what I've heard is correct, the man is Scotch, bred and born and reared. It shows what even a Scotchman can come down to!

After he had gone, with one of his dinky little bows, I overhauled the hen-coop; but in a casual sort of way, so that no one, looking on, could suspect I was doing more than making one of my usual bi-daily visits to my chuck-chucks, and feeding them with bread-crumbs.

If I had not read the cypher message, I should certainly not have discovered the marks that Mr. Aglae had made on the coop; they were merely three small dots in a triangle, like this . · ., with a tiny 17 in the centre. The thing had just been jotted down on one of the legs of the coop with a piece of sharp-pointed chalk, and it could have been covered with a ha'penny.

I grinned to myself and went to the carpenter's shop for a piece of chalk. I made Chips sharpen it to a fine point with a chisel; then I put it in my pocket and continued my afternoon stroll round the decks.

I wanted first to place Mr. Aglae; for it would spoil part of the amusingness of my plot, if he were on the spy, and saw what I was going to do. I found him away aft, in the upper-deck smoke-room, reading *Le Petit Journal*, and looking most subtly foreign and most convincingly innocent.

"You little devil!" I thought; and went right away to the well-deck. Here, in an unobtrusive way, I copied Mr. Aglae's private signature faithfully onto the hen-coop above the one in which I was carrying my brother's black ring-necks. The coop was occupied for the voyage by the bulk of Mr. Brown's confounded pigeons, which, I had insisted, must not be brought again into the saloon.

After I had re-duplicated the mark, I lifted out four of my ring-necks from the bottom coop, and put them into the top one, among Mr. Brown's pigeons. My argument was that, when the searchers boarded us with the pilot, they would find both these coops marked, and both with hens in them, and would act accordingly. They would have to open the upper coop to remove the four hens, and there would be a general exodus of Mr. Brown's pigeons, which would redouble the confusion and general glad devilment of my little plot.

Mr. Brown would be enormously angry and enormously vociferous. I could picture him thundering: "I have never heard of such a thing! Confound you, Sir! I shall write to *The Times* about this."

And then, it seemed to me, Number 17 would have to come and make some kind of semi-public explanation, of what he could never properly explain; and ever after his value as a diamond spy would be decreased something like 25 per cent; for quite a lot of people aboard (maybe some of them in the diamond-running business) would be able to get a good, square look at the famous Number 17, and for all time afterwards, in whatever way he might try to veil his charming personality, he would run chances of being recognised at some awkward and premature moment; at least, from his point of view!

But, of course, at first, Mr. Aglae (Number 17) would be only partly involved in any cheerful little net of difficulties. He would know, all the time, that these curious complications were only trifling; for had he not made the greatest capture of years. Let Mr. Brown be apologised to; even compensated, if such compensation were legally his right. The great thing would be to reduce the black ring-necks to poultry, as speedily as possible, and then to pick his triumph from their gizzards!

I wriggled quietly with pleasure, as I saw it all. And then the official appraiser's brief explanation to the Chief; and the salty flavour of the Chief's explanation to Number 17, that there was no law against a sea-Captain feeding his pet hens with bits of glass, cut or otherwise, for the improvement, or otherwise, of their digestions.

Then there would be the replacing of my five dozen ring-necks, or their equivalent in good, honest dollars, treasury dollars, I presume. I calculated rapidly that even as the prestige of Number 17 must come down, so the price of my hens should as infallibly go up.

I snicked the lesser door of the upper coop shut, and watched my four hens and Mr. Brown's pigeons. The hens clucked, and walked odd paces in the dignified and uncertain fashion affected by all hens of a laying age. The pigeons fluttered a bit, and then resumed their wonted cooing; and after that, all was comfortable in that ark; for the hens discovered pigeon-food to be very good hen-food also, and set to work earnestly to fill the unfillable.

*　*　*　*

The searchers came aboard with the pilot, and after the usual preliminaries, my presence was requested at the opening of the hen-coop. I noticed that Mr. Aglae was still in the upper smoke-room as I passed, and there he appeared intent to stay. I admired his judgment.

The officials gathered on the well-deck, and the Chief explained that they had received certain information which they were acting upon; and asked me formally whether I had any diamonds to declare.

"I'm sorry to say that I've left my diamond investments at home this trip, Mister," I said. "I've nothing I'm setting out to declare, except you've been put on to some mare's nest!"

"We happen to think otherwise, Cap'n," he said. "I've given you your chance, and you've chucked it. Now you've got to take what's coming to you!"

He turned to one of his men.

"Open the lower coop, Ellis," he told him. "Rake out those chick-ens. Hand 'em over to the poulterer."

As each chicken was taken out it was handed to the poulterer, and the man killed it then and there. My little plan was making things unfortunate, of course, for my brother's ring-necks; but, after all, they were fulfilling their name, and I felt that, eventually, I should have nothing personally to grumble about.

But, in spite of this pleasant inward feeling, I protested formally and vigourously against the whole business, and pointed out that someone would have to pay, and keep on paying, for an "outrage" (as I called it) of this kind.

The Chief merely shrugged his shoulders, and told the man to rake out the four hens from the upper coop. The man reached in his hand through the trap; but, of course, the hens sidestepped him in a dignified fashion. Then the man grew a little wrathy, and whipped down the whole front of the coop, and plunged in, head and shoulders, to get them.

Instantly, what I had planned, happened. There was a multitudi-nous, harsh, dry whisper of a hundred pairs of wings; and then, hey! the air was white with pigeons. The man backed out of the coop, with a couple of my ring-necks in each hairy fist; and met the blast of his superior's wrath—

"You clumsy goat!" snarled the Chief— "What—" And then the second thing that I had foreseen, occurred—

"Confound you, Sir!" yelled Mr. Brown, dashing in among us, breathless. "Confound you! Confound you! You've loosed all my pigeons! What the blazes does this mean! What the blazes...."

"You may well ask, Sir, what it means," I answered. "I think these officials have gone mad!"

But Mr. Brown was already, to all appearances, quite oblivious of any one or anything, except his beloved pigeons.

He had lugged out a big gold watch and a notebook, and was making frantic efforts to achieve a lightning-like series of time-notes, staring up with a crick in his neck, trying crazily to identify the directions taken by various of his more particular birds.

He had, of course, to give it up almost at once, for already the bulk of the birds had made their preliminary circles, and were now shooting away for the coast, at various angles.

Then Mr. Brown proved himself more of a man than I had hitherto supposed possible in one who flew pigeons. He attained a height of denunciatory eloquence, which not only brought most of the first-class passengers to the spot; but caused a number, even of the married women, to withdraw hastily.

The Chief made several attempts to pacify him; but it was useless, and he made dumb-show then to the poulterer to set about opening up my brother's five dozen ring-necks, which that man did with admirable skill, until the well-deck looked like a slaughter house. And still Mr. Brown continued to express himself.

At last the Chief sent a messenger, and (evidently much against his will) Mr. Aglae had to come and explain.

Mr. Brown ceased to denunciate for a moment, while Mr. Aglae explained, and the passengers crowded nearer, until the Chief asked me to tell them to retire. But I shrugged my shoulders. It fell in well with my plans for the spy's flattening, to have as many witnesses as possible.

"I never marked your coop, Sir," said Number 17, warmly. "It was the Captain's coop of hens that I marked...."

"Rubbish!" interpolated the Chief; "here's your mark on both coops!"

It struck me, in that moment, that possibly the Chief would not be sorry to weaken Number 17's position; for that man may have been climbing the promotion-ladder a little too rapidly for the Chief's piece of mind, though I knew the Chief would not dare to say much, in case the capture proved as important as Number 17 had described it to be.

I never saw a man look so bewildered as the spy when he saw that both coops were marked. Then he turned and looked straight at me; but I gave him a good healthy back-stare.

"So," I said aloud, for everyone to hear, "you're a beastly spy? I don't wonder I've felt crawly every time you've passed me this trip!"

The little man glared at me, and I thought he was going to lose control, and come for me; but at that moment Mr. Brown, having rested, began again.

During the fluent period that followed, the poulterer worked stolidly and quickly and I saw that he was resurrecting quite a number of my cut-glass ornaments.

They had brought out the official appraiser with them, so important had they considered the case, from Number 17's message; and that man, breaking himself from the charmed circle of Mr. Brown's listeners, walked over to the poulterer, and began to examine the "diamonds."

I watched him, quietly, and saw him test the first one carefully; then frown, and pick up another. At the end of five minutes, both he and the poulterer finished their work almost simultaneously; and I saw the appraiser throw down the last of the "diamonds" contemptuously on to the hatch.

"Mr. Franks," he called aloud, to the Chief, "I have to report that there is not a single diamond in the crops of these—er—poultry. There are a large number of pieces of cut-glass, such as can be bought for ten cents a dozen; but no diamonds. I imagine our Mr. Aglae has made a thumper for once."

I grinned, as I realised that Number 17 was not loved, even by the appraiser. But I laughed outright, when I looked from the Chief's face to Number 17's, and then back again.

Mr. Brown had halted spasmodically, in his fiftieth explanation of the remarkable and unprintable letter that he meant to write to *The Times,* on the subject of his outrage. And now he commenced again, but, by mutual consent, everyone moved away sufficiently far to hear themselves speak; and there and then the Chief said quite some of the things he was thinking, and feeling, about Number 17's "capture."

Number 17 said not a word. He looked stunned. Abruptly, a light came into his eyes, and he threw up his hand, to silence the Chief.

"Good Lord, Sir!" he said, in a high, cracking voice of complete comprehension. "The pigeons! The pigeons! We've been done brown. The hens were a blind, worked off on me to keep me from smelling the pigeon pie. Carrier pigeons, Sir! What a fool I've been!"

I explained that he had no right to make such a libellous and unfounded statement, and Mr. Brown's proposed letter to *The Times* grew in length and vehemence. Eventually, Mr. Aglae had to apologise as publicly as he had slandered both Mr. Brown and me. But that did not prevent us from presenting our bills for compensation for damage done. And what is more, both of us got paid our own figure; for neither the Treasury, nor its officers, were eager for the further publicity which would have inevitably accompanied the fighting of our "bills of costs."

*   *   *   *

It was, maybe, a week later, that Mr. Brown and I had dinner together.

"Pigeons—" said Mr. Brown, meditatively—" I like 'em best with a neat little packet of diamonds fixed under their feathers."

"Same here!" I said, smiling reminiscently. I filled my glass.

"Pigeons!" I said.

"Pigeons!" said Mr. Brown, raising his glass.

And we drank.

The Red Herring

S.S. Calypso,
August 10.

WE DOCKED THIS MORNING, and the Customs gave us the very devil of a turn-out; but they found nothing.

"We shall get you one of these days, Captain Gault," the head of the searchers told me. "We've gone through you pretty carefully; but I'm not satisfied. We've had information that I could swear was sound, but where you've hidden the stuff, I'll confess, stumps me out."

"Don't be so infernally ready to give the dog the bad name, and then add insult to injury by trying to hang him," I said. "You know you've never yet caught me trying to shove stuff through."

The head searcher laughed.

"Don't rub it in, Captain," he said. "That's just it! Take that last little flutter of yours, with the pigeons, and the way you made money both ways, both on the hens and on the diamonds; and all the rest of your devil's tricks. You've got the nerve! You ought to be able to retire by now!"

"I'm afraid I'm neither so fortunate nor so clever as you seem to think, Mr. Anderson," I told him. "You had no right to kill my hens, and I made your man apologise for his abominable suggestion about the pigeons!"

"You did so, Cap'n," he said. "But we'll get you yet. And I'll eat my hat if you get a thing through the gates this time, even if we've missed finding it now. We're bound to get you at last. Good morning, Captain!"

"Good morning, Mr. Anderson!" I said. And he went ashore.

There you have the position. I've got £6000 worth of pearls in a remarkable little hiding-place of my own aboard; and somehow word has been passed to the Customs, and it's going to make the getting of them ashore a deuced difficult thing, that will take some planning. All my old methods, they're up to. Besides, I never try the same plan

249

twice, if I can help it; for it is altogether too risky.

And a lot of them are not so practicable as they appear at first. That carrier pigeon idea, for instance, was both good and bad; but Mr. Brown and I lost nearly a thousand pounds' worth of stones through it; for there's a class of oaf with a gun who would shoot his own mother-in-law if she passed him on wings. Perhaps he'd not be really to blame in such circumstances; but he is certainly to blame when he looses off at a "carrier." Any shooting man should be able to recognise them from the common or garden variety. But I fancy the aforementioned oaf does the recognising cheerfully, and shoots promptly. Some of these gentlemen must have made a haul! That was why we never loosed the pigeons before reaching port. We never meant to trust all that value in the air, except as a last resort.

Anyway, Mr. Anderson and his lot have got it in for me; and I shall have a job to get the stuff safely into the right hands by the 20th, which is the date we sail.

August 11.

I have hit on what I believe is rather a smart notion, and I began to develop it today.

When I went up to the dock gates this morning, with my bag, I was met by a very courteous and superior person of the Customs Department, who invited me to step into his office. Here, I was again invited into quite a snug little cubicle, and there two searchers made a very thorough examination of me (very thorough indeed!), also of my bag; but, as you may imagine, there was nothing dutiable within a hundred yards of me—that is, nothing of mine.

At the conclusion of the search, after the superior and affable personage had departed, pleasingly apologetic, I was left to acquire clothing and mental equilibrium in almost equal quantities, for I can tell you I was a bit wrathy. And then—perhaps it was just because my mental pot was so a-boil—up simmered *the* idea; and I began straight away on the aforementioned developing.

By the time that I had completed my dressing, I had learned not only that the names of the two official searchers were Wentlock and Ewiss, but also the numbers of their respective families, and other pleasing details. I dispensed tact and *bonhomie* with liberality, and eventually suggested an adjournment to the place across the road, for a drink.

But my two new (very new) friends shook their heads at this. The "boss" might see them. It would not do. I nodded a complete comprehension. Would they be off duty tonight? They would, at 6:30 prompt.

"Meet me at the corner at seven o'clock," I said. "I've nothing to do and no one to talk to. We'll make an evening of it."

They smiled cheerfully and expansively, and agreed—well, as only such people do agree!

August 18.

The dinner came off, and was in every way a success, both from their point and my point of view. And I think I may say the same of the two dinners that followed on the 15th and the 17th. That was yesterday.

It is now the evening of the 18th, and I'm jotting down what happened, in due order.

It was last night, at our third little dinner together (which for a change I had aboard), that we got really friendly over some of my liqueur whisky. And I saw the chance had come to ask them straight out if they were open to make a fiver each.

The two men looked at each other for a few moments without speaking.

"Well, Sir, it all depends," said Wentock, the older of the two.

"On what?" I asked.

"We've our place to think of," he said. "It's no use asking us to risk anything, if that's what you mean, Sir."

"There's no risk at all," I told him. "At least, I mean the risk is so infinitesimal as hardly to count at all. What I want you to do is simply this. Tonight, if you agree, I'll hand you over this bag I've got here with me. Take it down to the gates tomorrow, and put it somewhere handy in the office. When I come off from the ship, to come ashore through the gates, I shall be carrying another bag, exactly the same as this in every detail. You see, I've got two of them, made exactly alike.

"Well, I shall be stopped, as usual, at the gates, and taken into the office, and I and my bag will be pretty well turned inside out again; which I can tell you I'm getting sick of, only your people have got it in for me, pretty savage."

The two searchers grinned at this.

"I ain't surprised, Cap'n," said Wentock, "with a reputation like yours. Why, they say as you could retire this minute, with the brass you've made, running in stuff without our smelling out the way you do it."

"Don't be so infernally flattering," I told him. "You mustn't believe half you hear. And I don't want you to get imagining I do this kind of thing regularly. It's just a few trifling little trinkets I want to pass in, as a favor to a friend. Not a habit of mine; but just once in a way."

Both the men burst into roars of laughter. They evidently considered this a great joke.

"Well," I said, "let me tell you just what I want you to do.

"When I go into the office, one of you always takes my bag from me. Well, I simply want you to substitute for it the one I shall give you tonight, and which, of course, you can search then as hard as you like, before the boss. Then, when he goes out, hand me back the unsearched one, and I shall just clear off with it, and the trick is done. No risk for you at all. You've simply to take this bag I have here, with a few shore clothes in it, up to the office tomorrow. When I appear, and am searched, you substitute this Number 1 bag for Number 2, which I shall bring in; and you search this Number 1 as fiercely as you like before the boss. Then, when I am let out you hand me Number 2, and I go. As for Number 1, I'll make you a present of it, as a little souvenir. Now say 'yes,' and I'll hand you the fivers now."

Wentock said "yes" promptly, for the two of them, and I pulled out my pocket-book and handed then each a five-pound note.

"No," said Wentock quickly. "Gold, if you please, Cap'n. Them things is too easy traced."

I laughed, and passed him across ten sovereigns, and took back my notes.

"You're a smart man, Wentock," I said.

"Have to be, Sir, in our business," he replied, grinning in his cheerfully unscrupulous fashion.

August 19. a.m.

I sail tomorrow; so if I don't manage to get the stuff through today, I shall be in a hole; for I promised it faithfully, for not later than the 20th.

Later. p.m.

When I took my bag down to the gates today to go out, it can be easily imagined that I felt a bit of tension. Six thousand pounds is a lot to risk, apart from the possibility of serious trouble if one is nailed.

However, it had to be done; so I went up to the gates, trying to look as cheerful as usual, and made my accustomed protest against searching, to the genial and diplomatic officer who met me, and invited me to my expected *séance* in the cubicle.

As I was entering the doorway of the outer office, a messenger boy came up to me, and touched his cap.

"Are you Cap'n Gault, Sir?" he asked me.

"I am," I said.

"I just been down to the ship, Sir," he explained. "They said you was just off through the gates, and I might catch you if I hurried. I'm to deliver this letter to you, Sir, and to tell you there ain't no answer. Good morning, Sir."

"Good morning," I said, and tipped him a quarter. Then, as I entered the office with my polite official, I opened the letter.

What I found therein could hardly be supposed to decrease my feelings of tension. The note was printed, crudely, so as to disguise the handwriting. It ran exactly thus—

"Captain Gault,

"S.S. *Calypso.*

"Sir,

"Be advised, and do not attempt to smuggle your stuff through the Customs. You will be sold if you do, and some one who cannot help a friendly feeling for you would regret not to have given you this chance to draw back. Pay the duty, even if you lose money. The authorities know far more than you can think. They know absolutely that you bought the 'material' you wish to smuggle through, and they know the price you paid, which was £5997. That is a lot of money to risk losing, apart from fines and imprisonment. So be warned, and pay the duty in the ordinary way. I can do no more for you than this.

"A WELL WISHER."

Now, that was what might really be called a nerve-racker to read, and just after I had entered the very place that the warning begged me to avoid, at least, in what I might call a "smuggling capacity." I could not possibly back out now, for suspicion would be inevitable; also, my plans were all arranged.

I went straight on into the place, looking more comfortable than I felt. I took a quick look round the inner office, and saw the end of a bag, half hidden, under a table. That, at any rate, looked as if Ewiss and Wentock meant to be faithful and carry out the substitution, as arranged. If they had given me away, it might be supposed that the bag I had given them would be now in the hands of their superior officers.

I looked at the problem every way. And all the time, as I puzzled, I kept asking myself not only who *wrote* the warning, but who, of all the people I knew, had the necessary *knowledge of detail* that it showed.

Ewiss and Wentock rose from their desks as I entered the private room, and Wentock came forward and took my bag from me, while Ewiss beckoned me towards the cubicle.

The search they made of me was not drastic; but even had it been I should not have minded, in the circumstances. What I was thinking about all the time was the bags, and whether the two searches meant to be faithful to their part of the bargain.

One thing, at first, I placed as an argument in their favor. It was that the unemotional courtesy of the head official was quite unimpaired; and I could not imagine that even he would be able to remain so absolutely and almost statuesquely calm if my two presumed confederates had given me away to him, and told him that a big capture was on the carpet (it was really linoleum, and cold to the feet!).

There was, however, something disturbing in the attitude of Ewiss. The man seemed almost hang-doggish, in the way he avoided meeting my eye. But I could not say this of Wentock; for that cheerful person was completely his own glad and (as I always felt) unscrupulous self.

While I was dressing, my bag was banged down onto the table, and I knew the instant it was thrown open that Wentock and Ewiss had sold me; for they had not carried out the substitution of the Number 1 bag for the Number 2 which I had just brought in; but had frankly and brutally ignored our whole arrangement, and opened Number 2—the bag that I had bargained with them should not be opened.

As he flung the bag open, Wentock looked up at me and grinned broadly. He considered it evidently a splendid effort of smartness; but it was a faint comfort to my belief in the goodness of human nature that Ewiss looked down at the table and seemed decidedly uncomfortable.

I felt so fierce that I could have given them away, in turn, to their superior for accepting bribes; for it was quite plain now that they had said nothing to him about the plan I had proposed to them to substitute one bag for the other. I could see their way of looking at the whole business. They were not readily bribable; but if people were foolish enough to offer them a bribe it was accepted—as a *present*; and so much the worse for the person who offered it, and so much the better for the officer presented with this kind of—shall I say "honourarium"? I think anyone must admit I had cause to feel bitter.

I did not, of course, think really of giving them away; for there might have been a charge made of bribery and corruption; whilst they, as I was pretty sure, would say nothing, lest they be mulcted of the "presents" I had made them; and also, possibly, have a reprimand for meddling with my proposition in any way at all.

The search Wentock gave that bag was a revelation of drastic thoroughness. I remonstrated once, and said I would put in a claim for a new bag; for Wentock, as he went further and further, and found nothing, seemed almost inclined to rip the bag to pieces, so sure was he that he "had me safe."

At last, he had to give it up, and pronounced it free of all dutiable stuff—which of course it was; for, as I told him later, I had considered the chances of their proving treacherous, and had carefully omitted on this occasion to put anything dutiable into the bag. I told them that it must be regarded as a kind of trial trip, to test their intentions.

This was as soon as the boss had left the cubicle, and then I cut loose on the two of them.

"For a couple of treacherous, grunting human hogs, you two are something to talk about!" I told them. "You take my money with one hand, and try to do me in with the other. Suppose you hand out that cash I gave you!"

Wentock laughed outright at this, as if it were a particularly nutty kind of joke; but I was glad to see that Ewiss looked more uncomfortable than ever.

"Our perquisites, Cap'n," said Wentock. "We're often asked out to a bit of dinner, and we get people who are mighty anxious to hand us nice little cash presents, *ad lib*, as you might say, every once in a while. And we don't say 'no,' do we, Ewiss? Seeing we're both married men with families to bring up, and remembering, Cap'n, how affectionately you've asked after the youngsters, you might remember us again, Cap'n, when you've any odd cash as you don't want, burning holes in your pocket. Likewise we both admired them dinners you stood us uptown. You can do it again, Cap'n, any time you like, and keep on doing it. We're always open. If you can stand it, we can. Now, how would tonight suit you? We're both free and—"

"Go to blazes!" I said, "and stay there. You're a pair of treacherous animals, like all your kind, and you might have ruined me if I hadn't been careful. Give me my bags, and be damned to you! They say never trust a policeman, even if he's your own brother. He'll lock you up first chance he gets for the sake of promotion. And I guess you're the same kind of cheap stuff."

And with that I picked up my bags and walked out, Wentock holding the door for me. But Ewiss was looking as thoroughly miserable and ashamed as a man need look.

"How would tonight suit you, Sir?" called Wentock after me as I passed through the gates.

"Go to the devil!" I said. "And get him to shut your infernal mouth with a red-hot brick."

And with that I boarded a street car and went rather thoughtfully up town.

August 19. Later still.

As it chances, I have invited the men to dinner again—both of them; for I'm not the kind of man who likes taking a fall too quietly.

This is what I wrote, addressing it to Wentock at his office:

"Dear Mr. Wentock,

"I have been thinking things over a bit, and have come to the conclusion that everything was not said at our last meeting that might have been said. I bear no malice at all for the somewhat pungent wit you handed out to me. I guess I was in the position that invited a few jabs.

"I have been thinking that perhaps there is still a way to arrange this affair a little more to my liking, and I can assure you and your friend that you will be the gainers, and without having your strict feelings for high honesty and fairness outraged.

"Will you both meet me at our little restaurant tonight at the usual time, and I will go thoroughly into the matter; for as I start off tomorrow, it is imperative to me to carry through my plan before I sail.

"Remember, I bear no malice at all. Look upon this as an entirely business-like and reasonable friendly little invite.

"Yours sincerely,

"G. Gault."

I sent this by messenger, and tonight I shall be at the restaurant.

August 20.

They both came on time. Wentock as cheerful and unscrupulous as ever. Ewiss looking awkward, and as if he would rather have stopped away.

"Now," I said, as we sat down, "pleasure first and business afterwards." And I reached for the hock.

"One moment, Sir," said Ewiss suddenly, and pushed forward a small roll of paper, which I took from him, feeling a little puzzled.

It contained dollar notes to the approximate value of five pounds. I looked across at Ewiss with a sudden gladness and respect in my heart, for I understood. But what I said was—

"What are these, Mr. Ewiss?"

"It's your brass, Cap'n," he said. "I've thought a deal lately, an' I reckon I can't hold on to it. I'm not grumbling at Mr. Wentock's way of looking at it. Lots of our men look at it that way; but even if you'd no right to try to bribe me, that doesn't say as I'm right to take your brass, an' mean to sell you all the time. If I'm above the job you wanted me to do, I feel I ought to be above taking the brass for it, too. So take it back, Sir; an' after that I shall enjoy my dinner with you as well as any one."

I looked across at Wentock.

"And you?" I asked.

"Well," he said, grinning in his cheerful fashion, "I don't see it that way, Cap'n. Ewiss, here, always was a bit funny on that point. Sometimes I've screwed him up to our general way of looking at it; but in the main he's not built on those lines, and I don't grumble at him, any more than he don't grumble at me. I look at it this way. You, or any man as insults me by tryin' to bribe me, has got to pay for it."

"Good man, Wentock," I said. "It takes a deal of different opinions to oil the different kinds of consciences. I've a brand of my own, and you've a brand of your own, and Mr. Ewiss, there, has his. Anyway, you're welcome to the cash, Mr. Wentock. As for you, Mr. Ewiss, I see you can't take yours; so I'll have it back, and I apologise to you. I think your way is the soundest of the three of us. Now, forgetting all this, let's drop the serious for a time, and we'll have our dinner."

* * * *

It was over the wine that I explained to Wentock the things I had to explain. Ewiss was out of it, though he listened quietly, with the deepest interest, and a flash of a smile now and again that showed he had a sense of humour.

"You see, Wentock," I said, "I never meant to bribe either of you, but only to make you *think* that I did. No man in his senses would risk £6000—to be exact, £5997" (I glanced at Ewiss and smiled; for I had guessed who was my "well-wisher") "on a piffly little bribe like a couple of fivers. If I had seriously meant to buy you, I should have offered something nearer your price, say fifty or a hundred pounds. As it was, I wanted merely, by means of my trifling bribes, to make you think I was going to run the stuff through in the way I explained so carefully. In other words, I wished to focus your entire suspicions upon Number 2 bag, thereby ensuring that the Number 1 bag, which I left in your hands, should receive only the most casual attention; for you would naturally think only of the second bag, which I assured you I did not want searched. Moreover, it would seem self-evident to you that the Number 1 bag, which I handed entirely over to your care, would never have anything dutiable in it; for, had you acted up to your agreement, there was no apparent reason for supposing that I would ever even handle it again. To ensure your subconsciously realising this, I even told you you could keep it once it had served me in the matter of the substitution.

"Of course, had you been faithful to our arrangement, and substituted the Number 1 bag to be searched for the Number 2 bag, which I brought with me, I might have been in a hole. You see, the handle of the Number 1 bag contained the particular, shall we say, trinkets, you were anxious to lay hands on.

"But then, I knew, both from the smallness of my bribe and from my reading of your face, and from the ways of Customs officials in general, that you would go for the big 'cop' you felt sure you were wise to. It might have meant promotion—oh, and quite a number of desirable things, from your point of view.

"After all, Wentock, even you," I said quietly and pleasantly, "will agree that honesty's the best policy!

"And that concludes all I have to say, practically. I planned it all out, even to the burst of anger and the snatching up of both my bags and walking off in that quite superb indignation on discovery of your treachery. I did it well, didn't I?—while you were so pleasingly and wittily inviting yourself to this final little dinner, which I had even then planned, like all the rest of it.

"As I said in my note, you would be the gainers for coming tonight. That is so; for you are the richer for a dinner and an explanation, and Mr. Ewiss for an apology. That is all."

The Case of the Chinese Curio Dealer

S.S. Iolanthe,
October 29.

I MET A RUM sort of customer ashore in 'Frisco today. At least, I was the customer, and he, as a matter of fact, was the shopman. It was one of those Chinese curio shops that have drifted down, somehow, near to the waterfront. By the look of him, he was half Chinaman, a quarter Negro, and the other quarter badly mixed. But his English was quite good, considering.

"You go to England, Cap'n?" he asked me.

"London Town, my lad," I told him. "But you can't come. We don't carry passengers. Try higher up. There's a passenger packet ahead of my ship; you'll see her with the prettily painted funnel."

"I not want to come," he explained. Then he came a step nearer to me, and spoke quieter, taking a look quickly to right and left; but there was no one else in the shop.

"Want to send a blox home, Cap'n—a big long blox. Long as you, Cap'n," he told me, almost in a whisper. "How much you take him for? Send him down tonight, when dark?"

"Who've you been murdering now?" I said, lighting a cigarette. "I should try the bay, and have a good heavy stone or two in the sack. I'm not in the body-biding line."

The man's yellow, dusky face went quite grey, and his eyes set, for an instant, in a look of complete terror. Then some sense of comprehension came into them, and he smiled, in rather a pallid kind of way.

"You mak-a joke, Cap'n," he said. "I not murder anyone. The blox contain a mummy, I have to consign to the town of London."

But I had seen the look on his face, when I let off my careless squib about the corpse; and I know when a man's badly frightened. Also, why did he not consign his box of mummy to London in the ordinary way; and why so anxious to send it aboard after dark? In short, there were quite a number of whys. Too many!

259

The man went to the door, and took a look out up and down the street; then came away, and went to the inner door, which I presumed was his living-room. He drew back and shut the door gently; then took a walk round the backs of the counters, glancing under them. He came out, and walked once or twice up and down the centre of the shop, in a quick, irresolute kind of way, glancing at me earnestly. I could see that his forehead was covered with sweat, and his hands shook a little, as he fumbled his long coat-fixing. I felt sorry for him.

"Now, my son," I said, at last. "what is it? You look as if you badly needed to tell somebody. If you want to hand it on to me, I'll not swear to help you; but I'll hold my tongue solidly afterwards."

"Cap'n, Sir," he said, and seemed unable to get any further. He went again to the shop door and looked out; then once more to the inner door, which he opened quietly. He peeped in; then closed it gently, and turned and walked straight across to me. I could see his mind was pretty well made up. He came close up to me, and touched a charm which I wear on my chain.

"That, Cap'n!" he said. "I too!" And he pulled aside a flap of his coat-robe, and showed me a similar one.

"They can be bought for a couple of dollars, anywhere," I said, looking him slam in the eyes. As I said so, he answered a sign I had made.

"Brother," he said. "Greatly good is God to have send you in my distress;" and he answered my second sign.

"Brother," I said, as I might have spoken to my own brother, "let us prove this thing completely." And, in a minute, I could no longer doubt at all. This stranger, part Chinese, part Negro and part other things, was a member of the same brotherhood to which I belong. Those who are also my brothers will be able to name it.

"Now," I said, "tell me all your tale, and if it is not against common decency to help you, you may depend on me." I smiled at him encouragingly.

The man simply broke down, and cried a few moments into his loose sleeve.

"You take the blox, Cap'n Brother," he said, at last. "I pay you a t'ousand dollars now this moment."

"No," I told him. "Tell me all about it, first. If it is murder, I can't help you, unless there are things to excuse you; for if you have murdered, you have no longer any call on me, as a brother."

"I not done murder, Cap'n Brother," he said. "I tell you all. You then take blox for t'ousand dollars?"

"If you're clear of anything ugly in this matter," I said, "I'll take you box into hell and out again, if necessary, and there'll be no talk of pay between us. Now get going."

He beckoned to me, and took me round the counter. Here was a long box, a huge affair, very strongly made, and with a hinged lid. He took hold of the lid, and lifted it.

"The mummy!" I exclaimed, for the thing was plain there before my eyes, in its long, painted casing—a huge man or woman it must have been, too.

"My son, Cap'n Brother," said the Chinaman.

"What?"

"Him, there." said the Chinaman.

"What! Now?" I asked again, staring.

He nodded and glanced around the shop, anxiously.

"Dead?" I said. "Is he embalmed?"

"No, Cap'n Brother," he said. "The mummy-case empty. My son under there, hiding. Him sleep with much opium I give him. I ship him to you tonight. First I tell you why—

"I belong to the Nameless Ones, we call them. They are a brotherhood also, an' have lived for two t'ousand years. I belong also with two other brotherhood; for in China I have importance by family and relation. But this have to do with the brotherhood of the Nameless Ones. My son a little wild. Him drink Engleesh spirit, an' him come home drunk, an' there three of the Nameless Ones brotherhood speak secret with me; but him drunk, an' not heed nothing. Him come in an' sit down an' laugh. The Number 7, that is the President, order him to go out, an' him put the thumb to his nose—so! The President have a great anger; but hold it; for I am old in the brotherhood, an' the young man is my son; but not of the brotherhood.

"The President again order my son to go; an' my son, in the badness of his great drunk, him" (the man bent, and literally whispered the terrible detail to me) "him *pull* the hair tail of the President, an' the tail a false one, which I not know before, an' the tail come away in the hand of my son, an' the President naked there before us.

"The President wish to kill my son immediately; but I had great speech with him, an' reasoned much, an' he consent the young man grow first sober, an' afterward be tried by the Second Sixty of the brotherhood of the Nameless Ones that have live two t'ousand year.

"That was yesterday, an' when they gone away, I put my son to grow sober, an' I prepare the mummy-case to hold him, an' when him sober, I tell him, an' him nearly die with great fear; for they will take out his heart, an' hang it in a gold ball over the door of our great Hall; for memory of so great a rude to the President of the brotherhood that is older in all China than all.

"When I tell my son, I have escape planned for him. I give him strong opium drink an' put him in the mummy-case.

"In the night they come for my son; but I tell them him not here. Him away to drink again. They say I hide him. If they find I hide him, they dis-bowel me for a false brother. I say I not hide him. I tell them search house. They search all house, but not think of mummy-case, for mummy long in my shop, an' real; but I burn mummy when I prepare case for my son, an' mummy cost five t'ousand dollars. But I care not, for it save my son.

"They have brothers that make a search all drink saloon in 'Frisco. They have a hundred, two hundred to look for my son that make rude to the President of the Nameless Ones that have lived for two t'ousand year. But they find him not.

"Then they put a brother here in my house to keep watch, an' a brother in the street, an' how shall I save the life of my son?

"Then you come in, Cap'n Brother, an' I see the sign upon your coat, an' you Engleesh, an' I have a new courage, an' I tell you. An' all you now know."

"Good Lord!" I said. "I've heard of the Nameless Ones; but you don't tell me they'll kill a lad, just for pulling the pigtail of their beastly old President?"

"Hush, Cap'n Brother!" said the man, white with fear, and staring first at the door behind him, and then at the outer doorway. "You not speak so, Cap'n. You go now. I not want them to see me talk to you. I send blox down tonight when dark."

"I'll go when I've satisfied myself on one or two points, brother," I said. I walked straight across the room, and gently opened the in-ner door and peeped. I wished to test this extraordinary tale. It sounded so unreasonable to my West-built brain and constitution; though I knew there was a good chance of it being every word true.

Well, what I saw in there quite satisfied me. There was the biggest Chinaman I ever saw in my life, sitting cross-legged on a cushion on the floor, and across his knees he held the longest and ugliest-looking knife I've ever set eyes on, before or since.

I shut the door, even quieter than I opened it, and when I turned to my new friend, his face was like a grey mask, and he couldn't speak for nearly a minute.

"It's all right, brother," I said; "he never saw me. I'd got to double-prove that tale of yours, before I got mixed up with it. I believe it now, right enough; only it's hard to understand there's a live devil, and this kind of deviltry going on, not twenty fathoms away from my own ship."

"You—you take him, Cap'n Brother? You promise true?" he managed to get out at last, his one thought for that son of his.

"Yes," I said; "but you've not got to bring him aboard tonight. Why, if what you say is right, they'd guess in half a tick; and then it would be too late, except to bury him. You leave it to me, I'll think out a way. I'll send my Second Mate up later to buy one of those bamboo curio sticks of yours. He'll give you a note, telling you what I want you to do. You can read English?"

He nodded, and pointed to the open doorway, at the same time staring in a stiff sort of terror over his shoulder at the closed door.

The handle of the closed door was being revolved slowly and noiselessly; and I thought it best to get outside at once; for if that big devil inside had grown suspicious, it would increase my difficulties, if he got a sufficient sight of my face to be able to recognise me again.

Later, that same day.

My ship is almost across the road, as you might say, from the Chinaman's shop. I'm not eighty yards away, in a direct line; but there's puffing-billy tracks in between—an amusing little way they have here of running their railway lines along the open street!

When I came aboard, I went to my chart house, on the bridge, and reached down a pair of decent glasses, that I got from the Board of Trade for a little life-saving stunt I was once mixed up in. I'll say this for them, they're good glasses, and I suppose I couldn't match them under sixteen guineas. Anyway, they showed me what I wanted; for I unscrewed a couple of the port lights on the shore side of the chart house, and a couple forrard and aft; and I kept a watch on that curiosity shop the whole blessed afternoon, into the evening, from two to eight.

Standing inside there, I was able to stare all I wanted without being seen; and here is what my afternoon's work told me.

First of all, Mr. Hual Miggett was the name above the door of my newfound brother of mixed nationalities. Second, Mr. Hual Miggett had evidently no idea of the elabourateness of the watch that was being kept upon his premises. Apparently there was no doubt at all but that the famous brotherhood of the Nameless Ones deprecated strongly the tonsorial attentions of Master Hual Miggett; for they were out in force. Through my glasses, I counted more than a dozen Chinamen in the street, some lounging about, others walking at the normal Chinese patter pace, and crossing and recrossing one another.

There were two private cars also in the street, drawn up, each with a Chinese driver. (There are some rich men in this affair, I can see that.)

I was easily able to test that these men were on the watch; for they never left the street; also, from time to time, I caught odd vague signs, passing between this one and that. There was obviously *purpose* behind it all.

It came on dusk before seven-thirty; and I noticed that there were more Chinamen in the street, and also there were now three open cars, all driven by Chinamen. I still could not see the need for all this fuss over the President's false pigtail; but, as I explained to myself, there's no accounting for a Chinaman's way of looking at things.

The electrics had been turned on at 7 p.m., and the street was pretty light; though there were plenty of shadows in places, and wherever there was a shadow there seemed to be a Chinaman.

A devil of a lot of chance there would have been to cart that box out of the shop and aboard, I thought to myself! The man must have been made foolish with terror to think it could be done *that* way. Why, it is evident these men will keep watch all night, for a week of Sundays, until they get what they're after.

At a quarter to eight, I sent the Second Mate ashore with a note to Hual Miggett. I told the Chinaman that if he watched the street for a bit, he'd find there was a round score of the "Nameless" devils eyeing his house; and that if he wanted to bury his son without delay, he had only to send him across in the mummy-case, whenever he liked! I suggested, though, that if he wished to save the life of his amateur barber, he had better keep his son comfortably in the shop, drugged according to need, and wait for me in the morning, when I would come along in, and propose a plan by which he might be gotten safely aboard.

I explained sufficient to my Second Mate to insure his not making a mess of things. I told him that he had better take a cut up into the city first, and come down on the shop from another direction. Then hand over the note, buy a curio stick, and come out at once. After which he had better put in an hour or two at one of the music halls, before returning to the ship, for I do not want that crowd of Chinks in the street to connect me with the shop over the way, as the pork butcher said.

October 30.

I watched the street last night again, from nine up to one o'clock this morning; and there were Chinamen there, either walking past each other or standing about. And every once in a while a car would drive up and stop for an hour at a time, by the corner of the next block, where they could see Hual Miggett's shop.

The Second Mate got aboard, just before I turned in. I had seen him enter and leave the shop, a little after nine, and through my glasses I had traced a couple of Chinamen following him right up the street, after he came out of the shop; but they had turned back, at last, evidently satisfied that he was simply a normal customer.

I asked the Second Mate whether anyone had been in the shop when he delivered the note. He said no; but that the biggest Chi-naman in the world had suddenly shoved his head in through a doorway at the back of the shop, while he was buying the stick, and stared steadily at him for nearly a minute.

"I could have thought he wasn't right in his head!" the Second Mate told me. "If he'd been a bit smaller I should have asked him what the devil he wanted. But he was such an almighty great brute that I took no notice. Do you reckon he'd be the man you saw in the back parlour with the big knife on his lap?"

"I shouldn't be surprised," I said.

"Just what I thought," remarked the Second. "If I were you, Sir, I'd drop the whole business. They're a murdering lot of devils, are Chinamen! Think nothing at all of cutting a throat!"

"I agree with your reading of 'em," I said. "But I'll see this difficulty through."

Later on today, I went up into the city, where I arranged one or two things; then I went into Jell's, the costumiers, and got them to fix me up with a dye and a little careful face paint. Also, they lent me a suit of clothes to match. I'm getting pretty earnest now in this particular bit of business.

When I went in, I was my ordinary self—hair a little brightish; not red. I'm not really what an unpredjudiced man would call red. My eyebrows are a couple of shades lighter; and skin fair, reddish. I was dressed in serge, with uniform buttons, and a peak hat. When I came out, my hair and eyebrows were dyed black (washable dye, of course). My skin was a good tawny brown, and I had on a check suit that was a chess-knot in every sense of the word; also a crush hat, and spats on my boots. I was the American conception of a certain type of English tourist. Heaven help the type. They would need it.

I called in at a book-shop, and bought a 'Frisco guide, one of those pretty little flip-flap things that ripple out a fathom long, all pictures of Telegraph Hill and the waterfront and the ferry boats, with glimpses of the bay and a "peep at Oakland"; not forgetting even the mud flats across the bay, where the wind-jammers used to lie up by the dozen and wait for a rise in the grain freights.

Then I made a line for the waterfront, with my "guide" draped over my hands, staring at it like a five-year-old laddie.

Presently, as I went along, I stopped outside the Chinaman's shop. I stared in at the lacquer boxes; the bamboo walking sticks, the josses… Birmingham delightful variations of certain heathen deities. I was profoundly impressed. At least, I hope I looked like it. Secretly, I was even more amused; for I know just sufficient about what I might call "godology" to recognise the fantastic impossibilities that ignorance had produced, and inflicted daily upon the unwary. There were gods there, whose every "line" should have told a tale, or made a hidden (often obscene) suggestion to the less Ignorant; but the "lines" or gagules were meaningless and confused; exactly as an ignorant Negro's attempts to reproduce the handwriting of a letter written in English would probably seem to our comprehending eyes. Yet not all was Brummagem.

I have mentioned my staring at the gods; because it was while doing so that I got the first clear idea of how to deal with a certain phase of the situation in which Hual Miggett found himself.

I walked into the shop, and Hual Miggett came forward to serve me. He looked a bilious, dusky yellow, and as if he were at the end of his tether of endurance.

"I would like to look at some of those gods in your window," I said, in a rather high-pitched voice. "I'm always interested in things of that kind."

The mixed-breed crossed to the window, without a word, and drew back the glass partition. I could see that, temporarily at any rate, he had lost all the money-craving of the salesman, and was, for the time being, little more than a living automaton.

As he pulled back the partition, he made a gesture with his hand, inviting me to look at the gods, and take my choice. He appeared still too stupefied and weary and stonily depressed to use any sort of art to make a sale.

I followed his invitation, and picked up first one god and then another, looking curiously at their Birmingham craftsmanship. Finally, I lifted a bronze goat god that had first attracted me. It is rare, and should be worth something. I glanced up at Hual Miggett, but he was not even looking at me. He seemed to be listening, with a frightened, half-desperate look on his flattish face. Then, with a muttered ex-cuse, he stepped across the shop and went behind the counter. I guessed he had heard, or fancied he had heard, a sound from his son in the mummy-case.

While he was away, I examined the gagules, or "lines," on the goat god. They told me many decidedly unprintable things, which were extremely interesting, though repellent to the more restrained individuality of the modern and balanced person.

I examined the "lines" round the base of the figure, and found the old secret sign "to open," with a chased diminishing device of double lessening circles, leading the eye towards the locations of the concealed catches. I concluded that the boss of the human ankle bone, above the goat's foot, and the significant inturned thumb of the third hand, might be worth investigating. I pressed on the boss of the protruding ankle-bone, and pulled the thumb, first to me, then pressed it away. As I did so, the bottom of the figure fell away into my hand, and showed an opening into the god, easily big enough to contain my head; for the god is nearly three feet high, and quite two in breadth.

There was nothing in the cavity, and I pressed back the "lid" into place, where it snapped home with a faint double click. As I did so, Hual Miggett came round the counter again into sight, looking a little less anxious. As he walked towards me, I made a certain sign to him, and he stopped and shivered a little, in bewilderment and doubt. Then he answered the sign.

"Brother," I said, speaking quietly in my natural voice; and I gave him a further sign. And so, in a moment, he knew me.

I said nothing to him about the secret opening into the goat god. If Hual Miggett did not know his business well enough to read the gagules, it was to no interest of mine to teach him. I continued to turn the god about, as if examining it; but all the time I did so, I was speaking, telling him my plan.

"Tonight," I said, "you must give no more than a little opium to your son. In the morning I will enter with a lady on my arm. The lady and I will examine your curios. Presently she will throw off her dress and hat and veil. Underneath she, or, rather, he, for it will be a man, will appear dressed in a suit of your son's, which you must get for me now. When all is ready we will make sufficient noise in the shop to bring out the big Chinaman with the knife, who keeps watch in you inner room. Before, however, he can reach this man, who will seem to him your son, the man (who is an athlete) will race out of your shop; run straight across to the waterside, and jump into a racing launch which will be there, with her engines running. The big man will be sure to follow him, and every one of the watchers will do the same.

The man, however, will be already on his way to Oakland, across the water, and, barring accidents, should be over long before any of them are able to get another launch.

"Meanwhile, we shall have pulled your son out of the mummy-case, and while he is behind the counter, we will get him into the woman's dress, and put the hat and veil on him. I will then take him out of the shop, on my arm, and across to my vessel, while everyone's attention is taken up by the escape of the trained runner they imagine to be your son.

"Your son will be weak, with the drugging he has undergone; but he will have my arm; and the distance to my ship in not great. Am I clear?"

"Clear as the moon, Cap'n Brother, when there are no clouds," said the Chinaman. "Truly—"

"One moment," I said. "Perhaps your ecstasy may be calmed a little by learning that this business will cost you not one cent less than a thousand dollars, plus the price of your son's passage to England. The man who takes the risk will not do it for less. I have already paid him five hundred on account, and the second five hundred I am to pay him tomorrow, if all goes well."

Hual Miggett made no bones about the money. He pulled a wad of bills out of his coat-robe; and counted me out one thousand dollars.

"His passage money will run a hundred and fifty," I said. "That's what the company charged last trip to a German hoodoo, who took the voyage home with us."

He paid me this also, while I continued to revolve the goat god in my hands, as if I were really in doubts whether to buy it, or not. This was in case we were watched. Finally, I asked him seriously what he wanted for it, as I have a weakness for that kind of thing.

As I spoke I saw the money-greed show momentarily in his eyes.

"One t'ousand dollars," he said.

It was worth, perhaps, five or six hundred, and as much more as he could get for it, as per Curio Dealers' Creed; but I did not bother to argue with him. His sudden touch of meanness, considering the trouble and risk I was taking for his sake, sickened me a bit; and I simply put the god back on the shelf without a word.

"The suit of clothes," I said, and Hual Miggett went out of the shop. As he did so I slipped across and looked into the box at the mummy-case. It belonged evidently to the 18th Dynasty. It was black, with crossed hands carved in relief upon the breast, and the mask was a dull red.

I lifted the lid quickly, and looked inside, and in that moment I believed that Hual Miggett's son was not hidden in the mummy-case at all; for instead of the living body of a young Chinaman, I found, apparently, the thoroughly dead body of a mummy, all wound round and round eternally with age-browned bandages. The head and face of the mummy were wrapped tightly with the same brown ban-dages, in a way that precluded any idea of a living, breathing being within.

And then, as I stared, I realised that the thing was alive. The breast was stirred ever so faintly under its swathings. It gave me a simply beastly feeling, for a moment, to watch it. Then, suddenly, I saw how the whole thing had been worked and I stooped and caught at one of the tightly stretched, age-stiffened folds of the encircling bandag-es. I lifted, and the whole of the bandages came away, in a life-size half-model of the human body.

Cunning Hual Miggett! I saw how he had managed this most clever method of suggesting that the figure below the bandages was really *wrapped* in them. You see, if you take a mummy, and, with a sharp knife, very carefully cut through the bandages down each side, working right round the mummy, from head to feet, it is possible sometimes to work the brown, ancient bandages free from the mummy so that they come away in two half-shells (back and front) which, having become stiffened by age and olden spices, are a veri-table and exact model of the mummy they have so long enwrapped.

Clever Hual Miggett! He had cut the bandages free from what I might term their original owner, in two full length halves, then, hav-ing, as he had informed me, destroyed the mummy, he had laid his son in the lower half of the hardened shape of the wrappings, and placed the other half upon the top of him, so that it appeared to any-one looking into the mummy-case that it enclosed only an in-credibly olden figure, wrapped in bandages untouched for many and many a forgotten century.

Breathing had been arranged for by a few hidden slits, and the mummy-case and outer box had been similarly doctored.

No wonder the searching Chinese had never "tumbled" to his hiding-place, when they searched the shop!

I lifted the body-shaped skin of brown bandages right out of the case, and looked in. There was a sallow young Chinese-looking man inside, lying in a heavily drugged and extremely unwashed condition. The shaped shell of bandages was long, much longer than the young Chinaman, and in the space at his feet, under a piece of fancy sacking, there was the most magnificent carving I could ever have dreamed of, in old amber, of the nameless god, Kuch, of the Blood Lust.

There is no actual name for this monstrosity; which is, indeed, indicated only by a curious, ugly guttural. It is known literally as the Nameless One. There is no real equivalent in the letter sounds of any nation for the guttural which indicates this embodiment of the most dreadful of the Desires—the elemental appeal of the Blood Lust—a lust that has been atrophying through weary centuries, under the effects of the Codes of Restraint, which are more popularly termed Religion.

As I have said, there is no symbol, or written equivalent, in any language for the indicating guttural of this truly terrible deifying of the most monstrous of the primitive Desires; so that the crudely phonetic "Kuch" has become, literally, the name by which Western writers have alluded to it, in dealing with the frightful lore which concerns this embodiment of all that is behind every brutish impulse of man.

And here, before my eyes, was a marvelously wonderful representation of the Blood Monster, carved from one enormous lump of yellow amber; with every last detail of typified vileness, reproduced with an amazingly wonderful and horrible skill of workmanship.

*   *   *   *

I replaced the various covers quickly, and hurried outside the counter again; for I had heard a sound that might have been the big brute of a Chinaman moving in the inner room.

I resumed my broken inspection of the big, bronze goat god; and presently, as I turned it this way and that, I was aware that the handle of the door of the inner room was turning quietly. Then the door slowly opened, and the enormous head of the big Chinaman came forward into the shop, staring round. He stared like a great animal; and moved his monstrous, ugly head and flat, brutish face from side to side, just as I have seen a dangerous bull swing his head, before charging.

I had a feeling that the man reminded me of something; and suddenly I realised that his face, in some uncomfortable, unnatural way, suggested that of the god I had discovered at the feet of the man in the mummy-case. And it was just then, in that instant, that I comprehended the full extent, shape and quality of the dangerous business into which I was poking my Western nose.

"Oh, you rotten liar, Hual Miggett!" I said to myself. "You rotten liar, to have let me in for all this!"

It had come like a flash; but I had been pretty sure, since discovering the abnormal excitement among the Chinamen (made evident in the number and type of those who watched the house), that there was something more troubling them than what I might term pulled pigtail.

It was this suspicion which had made me step across to the mummy-case as soon as Hual Miggett had gone for a suit of his son's Chinese garments. The god, the Nameless One, was the real hub about which the chief excitement was twiddling. I wondered I had not seen it on the instant; but it was plain enough now—the brotherhood of the Nameless Ones; and the Nameless god! It was, at once, so obvious what the brotherhood was named after! And the representation of the "Kuch" in yellow amber was undoubtedly the amazingly valued possession of the brotherhood.

The pulling of the President's pigtail was all a clever but outrageous lie (oh, you liar, Hual Miggett!). The young Miggett had evidently displayed no such tonsorial learnings as his father had suggested. Burglary (preferably of valuable "godlike" curios) was evidently his *forte!* Being so confoundedly mixed of birth, I presume he had no special fears of a god so essentially Chinese in conception!

And I had been hauled into the business, as a sort of *édition de luxe* of the Cat's Paw.... Not much! I can understand Hual Miggett, senior, being so eager to send mummy-case, and all, abroad. But if I save his son tomorrow, the god shall certainly not come with us. I guess he deserves the worry of it!

At this point, much to my relief, the considerably overgrown member of the brotherhood withdrew himself as noiselessly as he had intruded. I wondered what dreadful things the brute could tell of untellable Rites; and while I was wondering this, Hual Miggett returned.

I took the two garments and the funny little cap from him, and nodded towards the inner door.

"Monsieur the High Chief Executioner of the brotherhood just stuck his ugly head into the shop," I told him.

The man went ghastly in colour, and stared at me, as if I were something superhuman. I began to think my shot must have got a bull's-eye.

"I don't know what you're doing mixed up with people of that kind," I told him. Then I stuffed the garments (they were very thin material) into my inside pockets, and the cap I folded small and slipped under my belt; for I was not going out of that shop, carrying any parcel of a size sufficiently large to make the watchers suspect me of being used as a vehicle for the conveying of their beastly god to some other place. I guessed I should have a bad accident, before I had gone the length of the street, if any of them got thinking that!

"Tomorrow, about ten in the morning," I said, and went out of the shop, without saying another word.

They're rum hogs, some of these mixed breeds, I thought to myself; and walked comfortably up into the city, quite pleasantly aware that a couple of the watching Chinamen were following me. They dropped back, however, near the end of the street, apparently satisfied that I was no one they were looking for.

October 31.

At ten o'clock this morning, I entered Hual Miggett's shop, with a lanky-looking "female" upon my arm.

Hual Miggett came forward; and, for a time, the "lady" and I looked at this thing and that, and bought one or two trifles. I observed that the Mixed Breed seemed enormously depressed, and scarcely spoke. He appeared to be pondering something, to the ex-clusion of everything else. Well, he certainly had enough troubles to make a man think!

After a few minutes, I beckoned Hual Miggett to take a look up and down the street. Then I told him to see what the big Chinaman was doing. He opened the inner door boldly, and went in, as if to fetch something. When he came back, he told me that the man with the knife was sleeping on the floor.

"Strip off smart now, Billy!" I said to the "woman" I had brought in.

The hat and veil came off instantly, and the very ample dress followed. The result was a typical *seeming* young Chinaman, but lean and exceedingly muscular.

"Over there, behind the counter!" I said. "Smart now, before you're seen. Keep your gun handy; but for the Lord's sake don't use it unless you're absolutely cornered."

I had a brace of heavy Colts in my own pockets; for I was taking quite some risks myself, during the next couple of minutes.

"Now, Miggett," I said, "get moving, if you want any of us to come through this with a whole skin. Out with that son of yours!"

I had the dress up, ready in my hands, and Hual Miggett literally dragged the dazed lad out of the mummy-shell. Before he was firmly on his feet, I was pulling the dress over his head. Without waiting to fasten it, I dived for the hat and veil, to get his give-away head and face hidden. In a moment I had crammed the hat onto him, and dragged the veil over and round his face; then I hurried to fasten the dress. I made my fingers fly! If we had been caught in that minute by the big Chinaman, I should certainly have had to shoot; and then there would have been fifty of the brutes into the shop in no time; and the results would have puzzled our greatest friends to identify; for the beggars have an extraordinary *penchant,* as I might term it, for knife-work.

About a minute later, I was outside the counter again, still with a female-seeming creature upon my arm. A dress and a veil may cover a multitude, well not exactly a multitude; but certainly they make most things look alike!

"Are you ready there, Billy?" I called softly to the sporting runner, crouching behind the counter.

"Sure," he said.

"Then look out now," I told him. "I'm going to bring out that big brute. Just let him see you, and then get away smart, or there'll be murder done right here. Ready?"

"I guess so," was the confident kind of answer that pleased me. "The bigger the guy is, the better. It's not him *I'm* botherin' about; it's the devils in the street."

I turned to the counter, and picked up a porcelain Mallet vase, which I looked at with great interest, and suddenly let slip, with an enormous crash on to the floor, where it broke into quite some pieces. I hoped it was valuable. Anyway, it did what I meant it to do; for the inner door opened swiftly, and the great bulk of the big Chinaman filled the doorway, as he stared into the shop.

At the exact instant Billy Johnson, the runner, glided out from below the end of the counter nearest to the street, and tiptoed noiselessly towards the door, in full view of the big Chinaman.

There was a hideous, inarticulate bull roar from the inner doorway, and I glanced towards the great, flat, swaying face. The eyes were glaring, like two greenish slits; and a little froth had blown out over the coarse, walrus-like moustache. There was a crashing of falling gear, as he leaped forward; for he had literally ripped one of the projecting counters clean over on to its side as he made his rush. Then the huge bulk of the great Chinaman dashed past me at a speed that was amazing, considering his size. As he thundered by me, I saw that he had in his hand a great four-foot-long knife. The dull blue glint of the steel shone just for one fraction on my eye; then man and knife were out of the door, with a second crash; for his great shoulder had struck and burst one of the wooden door-posts clean off.

But Billy Johnson was away, thirty yards ahead, running like a deer, with a swift, beautiful, strong *pat, pat, pat,* of entirely capable feet.

From all sides, as we crowded in the doorway and stared, there were converging upon him ever increasing numbers of Chinamen, seeming to come literally out of nowhere.

The huge Chinaman was still, however, nearer to Johnson than any one else, and running with a grim intentness; his great head held curiously low.

I saw Johnson take the tracks in half a dozen swift steps, and then he was heading straight for the water-side. I heard the sudden, deep *brrp! brrp!* of the racing launch's exhaust, distinct above the roar of the growing crowd.

Suddenly the big Chinaman flung up his right hand, and I saw the dull gleam of the yard-long blade. Then, still running, he threw, and I could not help shouting; though, of course, no one could have heard me in the din that was now going on.

"Missed him!" I yelled; for the big knife had gone slap over Johnson's shoulder, missing him by no more than an inch or two. Evidently the big Chinaman had understood suddenly the plan by which the runner hoped to escape. A number of the other pursuers must also have discovered it on the instant, for there came an irregular ripple of revolver firing; but gun practise is apt to be off the target, when both parties are running.

Then Johnson was at the quay side.

"Safe!" I yelled again, as I saw him jump. "Good man, Johnson! Good man!

"I guess, Miggett, that's cheap at a thousand dollars," I told him.

There was firing from the dense and increasing bunch of men at the waterside; and from all down the street there was a sound of running feet, as hundreds of American citizens ran up to discover the wherefore-ness of so much powder and noise.

A city marshal (a big Irishman by the looks of him) raced by limberly, white-helmeted and superb in summer uniform. I saw him laying about him, cheerfully, on the heads and shoulders (chiefly the heads) of a num-ber of interested and unoffending citizens, who appeared, however, to consider his attentions as the natural order of things.

There was a deal of further gun firing from the quay front; but already I could see the racing launch, away out in the bay, half a mile or more from the quay.

Up the street, there was a crash of horses' hoofs, as a squad of mounted marshals swept bang around a corner. They roared past the shop—big Irishmen, most of them, joyous and holding their guns with a pleasurable expectancy.

"Great sport, Hual Miggett," I said, "over one solitary pigtail!"

The crowd on the water front was fading—literally vanishing; for the mounted marshals are so inexpressibly and cheerfully effective.

And, after all, a bullet fired with a smile . . . almost as one might say, as a jest, is quite as deadly as those dispatched in a more serious spirit.

I glanced at Hual Miggett, and wondered what he was thinking. Possibly quite as much of the yellow god, which had caused all this trouble, as the torpid, cheerless "female" by my side.

"I guess we'd better depart in the confusion," I added. "Come along, sweet maid."

We moved out of the shop, pleasingly unobserved, and reached my ship within the space of two uneventful minutes.

November 1.

We sail tonight, and I went across to see Hual Miggett this morning. I thought that I deserved the reward of virtue; for I had a genuine hankering for that goat god. But hear the essential meanness of the Mixed Breed.

I found him very glum; but I wasted no pity on him.

"How much for this?" I asked, slapping the goat god on its capable, bronze shoulder.

"A t'ousand dollars, Cap'n Brother," he said.

"A thousand cents," I answered and walked towards the door.

"Eight hundred dollars, Cap'n Brother," he called out. "I lose many dollars to you, gladly, for your great goodness to me, Cap'n Brother."

"I don't want you to lose," I said. "We'll drop all talk of what I've done, or haven't done. You're not able to pay me, anyway, even if I'd let you. I'll give you your thousand for the thing, simply because I want it, and I won't have you patting yourself on that weevily mean back of yours, and thinking you've done *me* a favour. This thing is worth not a cent more than five or six hundred. Here are the notes. Give me a receipt, or you'll be swearing I've not paid you, next. Oh, don't talk. I'm just a bit sick of you!" I told him.

He tried to excuse himself; but I simply held out the notes and waited for the receipt. Then, without bothering to fall on his neck and say good-bye, I walked out of the shop, with the old bronze goat god tucked under my arm.

Anyway, I thought to myself, it will be something to remember this little affair by.

Down in my cabin, however, having locked the door, I worked the secret opening in the base of the god, and then, gently and tenderly, I slid from the hollow interior the amber god (the Kuch) which I had taken from the mummy-case and hidden inside the Goat god, when I sent Hual Miggett for a suit of his son's clothing.

I keep wondering, rather pleasantly, what the mean-souled Mixture thought when he found the yellow god had vanished. Possibly superstition (being no longer deadened by the drug of greed) has helped him to some impossible explanation. In any case, he could not very well (after his gorgeous yarn of the Presi-dent's pigtail) enlarge upon his loss to me. His glumness yesterday and today is, perhaps, understandable. The stealing of the amber god cannot have proved a profitable investment of time or labour, not to mention money.

As I look at the wonderful carving of the amber atrocity, I cannot help feeling enormously satisfied with my course of action in this matter. Hual Miggett deserves punishment for a number of undesirable things. Moreover, like Hual Miggett, I also know a collector who will pay a good, hefty price for the little yellow monster.

The Drum of Saccharine

S.S. Adriatic,
May 23.

MR. ARMES, MY FIRST Mate, and Mr. James, the second, had a row today. They clubbed together in port and bought a hundred pounds of saccharine.

The duty on it, going into England, is considerable—sevenpence an ounce, upwards. In this case the duty will amount to about fifteen shillings a pound, as the stuff is over "proof," as I might say, and the duty varies according to strength. I think the two of them are rather aghast at their own daring; they've been planning, all the way home, how they're going to get the "goods" through the Customs.

Mr. Armes mentioned to me the proposition he and the Second Mate had in mind. This was after they'd bought the stuff, and I told him it would not interfere with anything I was doing, and they could go ahead. Only, if the Customs dropped on the saccharine, they must own up and pay the fine themselves. For I was not going to have the ship fined.

This was on the bridge, and he grinned at me, warningly.

"Sst! Remember the man at the wheel, Sir!" he said.

The row they had today came about through Mr. Armes proposing to hide the stuff in a big, empty paint-drum, which was to be made watertight and then lowered over the side before the searchers came aboard. They would sink it on the end of a line and buoy the end with a casual bit of cork. Then, when the search was over, they would only have to get hold of the inconspicuous little float and haul the stuff up again.

The Second Mate's notion was to hang the stuff down inside the hollow steel mainmast with a thin wire, the end of which could be fixed by jamming it under one of the nuts that held down the lid that covers the top of every mast that isn't a spike mast.

It was in this morning's watch that they got squabbling about the thing—each wanting his own way and each sure that his method of hiding the stuff was the best.

Finally, they came up to me to ask my opinion. I was on the bridge at the time, and I had to keep telling them to speak quieter; for I could see that Sedwell, the man at the wheel, was curious.

When my two officers had explained their ideas, I told them how I felt in the matter. I said that possibly the Second Mate's plan was quite as good as the Mate's; but it was no better, and certainly not as safe; for if the stuff were found outside the ship neither they nor the ship could be fined, as long as there were no witnesses, and they would lose only the price they had paid for the stuff—though, of course, this would be bad enough, for the two of them had spent a year's savings on their "speculation."

But I made clear to them that I left the choice entirely with them. I preferred the First Mate's method, chiefly because it would keep the ship free; and I fancy we want to let things rest a bit; for I can tell lately, by the thoroughness of the official search after every voyage, that we are somewhat under a cloud! Perhaps we have deserved it; for certainly I've had some very good luck lately.

"But, mind you," I said, "I stand out of this business altogether. Do it your own way, and, profit or loss, you must take the responsibility. I merely advise the two of you to take the First Mate's plan of sinking the stuff to a small float alongside just before the searchers come aboard...."

"Sshh, Sir! Not too loud!" said Mr. James, the Second Mate, holding up his hand, quickly.

I stopped at once; for I had certainly spoken a little louder, in my intention to make it clear that I stood entirely out of the business, lock, stock and barrel, as you might say.

I glanced over at Sedwell, at the wheel. It struck me that the man was plainly trying to hear what we were saying, and I stepped over quickly to look at the compass. I found that he had indeed been taking more notice of the two officers' argument than of his steering; for the vessel was nearly two points off her course. I suggested to Sedwell that our ideas of steering were not, perhaps, quite identical. I endeavoured to fuse this suggestion into him in as few words as possible, and returned to where the two Mates were standing.

"He was certainly trying to hear," I told them; "but I'm pretty sure he's heard nothing that matters. In fact, I'm *sure* he's heard nothing that could give your plans away."

"So are we, Sir," said the Second Mate, Mr. James. "We both tried to catch the few carefully chosen phrases you dealt out to him" (they both grinned); "but we could only just hear the more vigourous portion!"

May 24.

We docked this evening, and I was certainly interested to see whether the two of them got the stuff through; for a hundred pounds of saccharine is a hefty quantity to try to smuggle casually into port and afterwards ashore through the officers at the dock gates.

Apparently, the First Mate's plan was the one they'd chosen, for they disappeared below with the biggest empty paint-drum we've got in the ship. I stayed on the bridge all the morning, so as to give them full liberty; and they fixed and caulked the thing up in my cabin, where no one could see them.

Just before the officers came aboard, the Mate slipped away aft, to where he had previously slung the paint-drum over the quarter. He took a look round, then lowered it rapidly away, and let go the end of the line, to which he had fastened a piece of rough cork, that looked as if it were nothing but a bit of old stuff that was just floating about in the water.

It was Sedwell's wheel again, as it chanced; and when I turned from having a quick look to see how the Mate had managed I caught Sedwell also staring aft, over his shoulder, at the Mate.

I explained to Sedwell that, as a variant, he might as well take a look ahead, now and then, to see that we made some show of following in the wake of the tug.

When the Customs came up over the side, we were already a hundred feet ahead of the place where the Mate had let go the buoyed paint-drum; and I felt that the thing should succeed; for we were going slowly ahead all the time.

Yet, I was a little anxious about Sedwell, in one or two ways. The man plainly had some suspicion; but as we moved steadily farther and farther away, I felt safer about the saccharine.

It would be impossible for him to get away from the ship before dark. I could see to that! And then he could do no harm, for the two Mates would have had ample time, by then, to deal with the stuff themselves.

The officers reported themselves to me; but before we went down into the cabin, to go through the usual preliminaries, I excused myself a moment and had a word with Mr. Armes.

"That man, Sedwell, is on to the game," I told him. "Watch him."

"Very good," said the Mate, "I'll certainly watch him, Sir!"

Down in my cabin, the officers struck me as being most perfunctory in their work. I asked them to take a look through my gear, as I wanted to get ashore as soon as possible. Here again, their attitude was most peculiar. Instead of the exact and elabourate search-methods that have been lately wasted on my ship, they simply made believe to look over my belongings, and were actually out of the cabin within five minutes.

This made me form certain conclusions, and when I went up on deck again I had word with my two officers.

"They've done my place already," I told them. "They hardly looked at a thing!"

"Same with us, Sir," said the two Mates. "Looks as if we were getting to be considered a reformed character, as one might say."

"Rather rich, after the way you cleared all that stuff safely last trip, Sir!" said Mr. James, my Second.

The two of them grinned at me; but I pulled them up.

"You'll grin on the other side," I told them, "if this business of yours goes wrong! Have you kept an eye on Sedwell?"

"Yes, Sir," said the First Mate.

"Excuse me, Sir, shoving in cheeky like," said the bo'sun, coming up to me at this moment; "but I been watchin' that Sedwell. I knows as you got a little flutter on wiv' the Customs people, an' I sees the Mate dump the stuff astern; an' then I sees that yon Sedwell 'ad seen it, same as me. Well, I didn't know as that mattered, till the search officers come up on the bridge to see you, Sir, an' you goes down to speak to the First Mate. But then I got suspicious; for I seen the officers swappin' quick talk with Sedwell, quiet like; and then, when you went up again on the bridge, they made as if they'd never seen 'im. An' now, look at 'em, they ain't more than pretendin' to search the ship. I 'ope you don't mind my shoving in like this, Sir; but I'd lay my pay-day to a marlin-spike, as yon Sedwell's split."

"Thank you, Bo'sun," I said. "I'll remember this. Keep an eye on Sedwell while you're about the deck."

As the bo'sun walked away I looked at the two Mates, and they looked at me.

"This will need some pondering about," I said, gravely.

"What do you think they will do?" asked Mr. Armes. And the two of them stared at me.

"Exactly what you'd expect them to do," I said. "They'll send out a boat to find the buoy. Then they'll set a watch then, until you go for the stuff. Then they'll arrest you, and there'll be something more than the usual bother. You see, it's a reasonable little haul is a hundred pounds of saccharine; though what'll make them hot will be to nab us for our past flutters. I should leave it strickly alone. They can't possibly *prove* anything against you; for there's no mark on the paint-drum that Sedwell can swear to; and unless they catch you in the act of hauling it up, you can just keep mum and smile at them. Of course, you'll have to lose all that valuable stuff!"

The two Mates grinned at me in what, by a suspicious onlooker, might have been considered a sickly fashion.

"It's better, anyway, than anything else you can do," I said, "except come up to the hotel tonight, and I'll stand you both to a good dinner to cheer you up."

They both agreed that I was right, and accepted my invitation. After all, there was no other course for them to steer.

A little later, a shore-boat signalled us ahead and hooked on alongside as we came up. A messenger boy had brought an express letter from the owners, asking me to go ashore at once on important business. As I was reading it, the Chief of the Customs came up to see me, before going ashore, and I had to have a few words with him.

He and his men had certainly done their work in record time. It was quite plain to me, that the "A.B." Sedwell was a Customs spy, who had shipped for the voyage out and home with us, to try to get a case against the ship or the officers. This is sometimes done (though never admitted) where the authorities have begun to be suspicious of smuggling in a particular vessel, yet cannot fix any proof on her.

"Perhaps you won't mind putting me ashore in your launch?" I asked the Chief, as we shook hands. "The owners want to see me at once."

He agreed cordially, and I shouted to the steward to bring out my portmanteaux, which he had just been packing.

"I'll leave you to see her made fast, Mister," I called to the First Mate. "As soon as I've done my business, I shall take rooms at the *Gwalia*."

This was to let him know where to pick me up before going out to the dinner I had promised him and the Second Mate.

Twenty minutes later I was ashore. I shared a taxi, part of the way up from the docks, with our genial but dangerous enemy, the Chief of the search officers. As I dropped him, I could not help wondering whether their boat had already gone out to find the buoyed saccharine.

It is strange, this almost amicable cut-and-thrust, that is none the less deadly because of the quietness and courtesy with which the thrust may be given. Here was I, seated in a taxi, sharing it with the well and pleasant-mannered man on the seat alongside of me, who would, on the first opportunity, do his best to get me into serious trouble, even as I have undoubtedly got him certain ratings from his superiors if office, owing to my wits having, up to the present, out-matched his, as he and they know very well, but cannot prove.

I thought his eyes twinkled over some secret thought, as he jumped down and shook hands. No doubt he anticipated that the lure of the sunk saccharine would be bound to bring us straight into his hands that very night.

Maybe my own eyes twinkled as I said good-bye. He might watch a long time, so far, at least, as I was concerned, before the big, sunk paint-drum had a visitor. If only he knew just how much I knew! I thought to myself as I sat back, smiling.

Then I lapsed into serious thought—a hundred pounds of saccharine represents a certain amount of money. It was a lot for my two Mates to have staked on a single throw of the Customs dice, as one might say.

Well! Well!... I turned my thoughts on a space, to dinner. At least, I could promise that it should be made a cheering function.

* * * *

We had dinner in a private room at the *Cecil*.

"Certainly, Mr. Armes and Mr. James," I told them, as I handed them a fat little bank-note each, "the occasion demands joy, and I think this slight celebration is almost morally justified."

My two officers smiled at me, and I raised my glass.

"Here's my toast," I said—

> " 'To the flour that lies in the paint-drum,
> To the spy that we spotted at once,
> To the two portmanteaux that carried the stuff
> While the Customs swallowed out jolly good bluff
> That we worked on the dunce,
> Viz., Sedwell the bum—
> A right proper bum of a Customs House watcher,
> Who heard, ah! I fear,
> What he has wanted to hear,
> Just that, and no more!
> Let us drink to the dear!' "

I had put this into shape while I was waiting for them; and, really, I think it explains all that there is to explain.

We all drank; and as we drank, I doubt not that out on the dark waters of the river, a number of Customs officials kept a shivery and lurid watch for the smugglers who came not.

From Information Received

Sailing ship Alice Saunders,
September 4.

"THIS SHIPPING INTO A windjammer is a bit of a come-down for me, Sir," said my new Second Mate when I signed him on at the beginning of the voyage.

"Is it!" I said. "Well, Mister, there's men nearly as good as you made the change. I'm one of them; and let me tell you it has its compensations, as I'll show you, if you're the man I take you to be."

In a way, he was right! This is a bit of a come-down from passenger-carrying, but it has its good points. There's less palaver, less starch and more rest—quite decidedly there's more rest! And, incidentally, more cash.

This may sound a bit funny, after my late forty-a-month, while now I'm getting only fourteen-ten; but I was too much watched—a deuced sight too much watched! In the last three trips I was passenger-shunting I never cleared more than an odd hundred, over and above my pay.

September 9.

I've been too long out of sailing ships; and I'm forgetting their little ways. I told Mr. Parkins, the Second Mate, to keep the sail on her, as I didn't want to be a year on the passage. If he wanted to shorten down he'd got to give me a call first. There's been too much shortening down, to my mind! I suppose I've got used to steam and a steady number of knots per hour.

Anyway, Parkins carried on, to orders, and now I've a sprung main-topmast. That'll mean a fortnight's work when we get into port and a new spare topmast. Meanwhile, I've put a "bandage" round the spar and am carrying less sail and a little less cocksureness about things in general.

September 15. In Port (Havana).

283

I'm on to a problem that I hope may prove good. The problem resolves itself into something quite simple—to talk about! That is, how to transfer two hundred thousand first-class cigars from this tight little island bang into the warehouse of Messrs. — & Co., Liverpool.... No names mentioned! My share of the transaction to be most of the work and all the risk (as usual)! Incidentally I'm to have half the profits. What they will be you can easily reckon out, if you will calculate the duty on two thousand boxes of a certain half-crown cigar you no doubt often smoke, as I do always.

I make nothing on the freight; neither do Messrs. — nor Messrs. — ; for this sailing packet is the owners', and they run it for profit, not for my pleasure; therefore they shall receive full feightage, though I shall pay it under the heading of personal sundries, with weight and cubic details to match!

September 18.

I've risked it and shipped the lot; but I'm still in a bit of a haze, how I'm going to get these sixteen hefty cases of contraband slap into the warhouse of Messrs. — & Co., right in the heart of Liverpool City. The details are more than I've been able to imagine, yet.

Meanwhile, I've got my other troubles, in the shape of rigging the new main-topmast. Chips has got it shaped out, and I've got a couple of new spares from ashore, and, generally, we're in a devil of a muddle.

October 13th. At sea again.

I've been putting in a lot of thought how to get this contraband stuff through safely. It's no joke putting through sixteen big cases of cigars right under the noses of the Customs, as you can imagine; but I've got the major part of the plot all fixed, and, provided the Customs at Liverpool are not tipped off to make a special search, I've very good hopes of getting the stuff through; for the hiding-place I've got is cute enough to hide Charles the Second from a dozen hefty Cromwells.

October 28. Off Liverpool.

Did anyone ever hear the like! I've just had a cypher wireless from the agent ashore, to tell me that there's been a leakage. The Customs have got hold of the fact that I shipped two hundred thousand cigars in Havana, and they're just waiting to pounce on me as soon as they get aboard. Did anyone ever hear such a thing! The fact that they know the exact quantity shows that they've got firsthand information from some sneak-eye somewhere the other end. And they'll be abroad inside of two hours!

The agent insists that I must declare the stuff, and his firm will supply me privately with the cash to pay the duty. I can see he's in a proper funk! But if I pay the duty there'll not be a cent in the business for me.

Also, there's too much that's irregular about the whole thing for me to expect to come off scot-free! If I'd not been out to smuggle the stuff, why did I ship it secretly, and then hide it—well, in the queer place where it is hidden and where it's not too easy to get at?

I guess it's easy to talk. I'm going to have a shot to run the stuff through yet. I must think; for there's got to be a mighty big alteration in all my little plans.

October 29. Liverpool.

I thought hard for a bit; then I went over to my "sender," for I have a two-hundred-mile radius installation, which I have fitted at my own expense. I sent a return cypher to the Agent, with one or two plain, healthy, vigourous words to help it along!

After that I went up on deck, and got hold of Mr. Allison, the First Mate.

I set out the situation to him and the Second Mate and made them both "interested" in the stuff getting safely ashore.

"Come along down with me and start to hide cigars for all you're worth!" I told the First Mate.

To the Second Mate I gave instructions to rig the cargo-gear, and to get gantlines up on the three masts, and start sending down the upper yards; for we're going up the ship canal, and the upper spars will have to come down, to go under the bridges.

"The busier we are at ship's work," I told him, "the more honest we'll look when the Custom sharks get aboard. So make things hum, Mister!"

Then the First Mate and I went below to hide cigars. I hauled out boxes of cigars, and burst them open.

"Load as many up the inside of the stove flue, as you can," I told the Mate. "It's an excellant place! I'll be unscrewing the top of the saloon table. There's a famous well underneath, the size of the whole tabletop, and big enough to hold three layers of cigars at least. It should hold thousands, at a pinch."

Just then the Steward poked his head into the saloon.

"Get out of here, Steward, and keep out!" I told him. "Shut the door!"

"Can you trust him, Sir?" asked the Mate, from where he knelt, packing half-crown cigars up the flue, which, however, was as clean inside as salt water and elbow grease could make it.

"Trust no one in this wicked world!" I told him. "I guess he's more to lose by chewing out any suspicions he's suffering from than by holding his tongue. The worst thing I know against him, is he's a deuce of a thief. He bought a box of rotten cigars in port, and he's smoked mine all the way home, and swears they're some of those he bought; but I can smell the difference the length of the decks. If the Customs happen to drop on any of the hidden cigars I'll swear I hid them from the Steward. It may sound a bit thin; but I'll declare a dozen boxes, just to cover the odd finds they're liable to make. Then they can't touch me, unless, of course, they find more than I've declared!"

I grinned at him.

"As for the Steward, whatever he suspects, he *knows* nothing that can do much harm. Not even you or the Second Mate knew about the stuff till I told you."

"That's the truth, Sir," said the Mate.

Jove! how we worked! I kept breaking open boxes of cigars, and as I emptied them I chucked the empty boxes out through the stern portholes into the river; for we were now in the estuary of the Mersey.

When, at last, I had loaded as many into the concealed "well," under the tabletop, as I thought wise, I put the top back, and began to screw it down again.

"Get up on deck, Mister," I said to the Mate, for we had put in a solid hour and a half's labour. "See if you can spot the Customs launch coming off. I'll finish here."

"Very good, Sir," he said, and put on his coat, and went up on to the poop.

In less than ten seconds he came down the companion stairs with a jump.

"They're here, Sir!" he called out, quickly, shoving his head in through the saloon doorway. "They're alongside!"

"All right!" I said. "Don't get excited, for goodness' sake. I've got to bluff them. I'll swear they've got hold of a mare's nest. Now get up on to the poop and stand around handy. Tell the officer in charge that I'm down here."

"Very good, Sir," said my First Mate, and raced up again on to the poop.

A minute later, I heard the tramp of feet on the poop-deck above me, and I slung the screwdriver I had been using under the table.

"Good morning, Captain Gault," said the head officer of the Customs, as he came into the saloon. He was a man I didn't know; for I've not been into this port of late.

"Morning," I said, "will you come into my cabin, Mister?"

As I spoke, I saw that he was shooting glances all round the place. And then, suddenly, as if to catch me unexpectedly, he whipped round on me with a sharp—

"Anything to declare, Cap'n Gault?"

He began to reel off the usual list, but I checked him.

"It's all right!" I said. "I know it all by heart. I've got twelve boxes of a hundred cigars each to declare, and nothing more of any kind."

I said it with a bit of a snap; for the beggar had something about him that put my back up.

He turned to the two men who had followed him down, and nodded; and then he came round me again.

"You stick to that, Captain Gault, do you?" he asked.

"Certainly," I said. "What is more, allow me to explain that I dislike your manners, your method of pronouncing your words, and your breath. The last is particularly displeasing. You should smoke better cigars!"

The man stared at me, as if he thought I was mad; but before he could get out any expression of easement I concluded—

"Perhaps, Mister," I said, "you'll finish your examination of the cabins as quick as you can, and get out of here. You're in my way. I've declared twelve hundred cigars, and they're for my own smoking" (which last fact was strictly true). "Now get on with your searching, or you'll not be done today. You've all the rest of the ship to attend to yet!"

"Confound your impudence!" he sung out. "I never heard the like of you before. I declare you're—" But what other qualities of mine he was going to praise I can't say, for at that moment one of his two men caught his arm, and as he turned I heard the man say, quite distinctly, in an excited whisper—

"They're down here, Sir. Jock's just had a word with the Steward."

The Customs officer came round on me again.

"Now, my man," he began; but I pulled him up sharp.

"Say, 'Sir,' " I told him, "or 'Captain Gault'!"

He went quite white at that in his attempt to hold back the temper I had risen in him.

"I'll make you eat humble-pie in half a moment!" he said, in a quiet voice that was, yet, actually husky with the temper I'd prodded into healthy activity. "Now, quit your confounded fooling. You've declared twelve hundred cigars, but *we* happen to know you've two hundred thousand aboard. They're down here, and we're going to find them. You may as well own up!"

"You're on a mare's nest!" I told him. "I've got just twelve one-hundred boxes of cigars."

"Where are they?" he snapped back at me. "Out with them!"

"All right!" I said; and then I saw the Steward looking in over the shoulders of the two men.

"Get out of here, Steward!" I said. "And you others, too, while I get out my cigars. I'll not have any one know where I choose to hide my stuff. Take the Steward out with you, and shut the door. I'll call out when you're to come in. I'll not have the Steward see where they are. He's a thief—"

"You're a liar!" shouted the Steward, at the top of his voice. "A confounded liar!"

And at that, I went for him; but the officer and his two men got hold of me, and for a moment I nearly lost my temper!

I took no more direct notice of the Steward; but spoke again to the officer.

"Let go of my jacket! Confound your infernal insolence!" I said. "I've twelve hundred cigars to declare—do you hear me? Twelve hundred cigars! Get that into your thick head! Twelve hundred cigars!" I shouted it in their faces, at the top of my voice. "Here! If you don't believe me, get out of here!... On deck there! On deck there!" I yelled. "On deck, there!"

There was a sudden running of feet, and the Mate came crashing and clattering down the stairs into the saloon. He carried a heavy capstan-bar in his fists.

One of the Customs men loosed me and jumped at him. He caught him round the body, and started to wrestle with him lustily, and with all his might; while the office lugged out a big silver whistle, on the end of a chain, and whistled, till the saloon rang and piped again with the shrill sound.

There was a rush of feet along the poop-deck, and several Customs officals came racing down the companionway stairs into the saloon.

"Arrest these two for obstruction!" yelled the head officer.

"Obstruction be jiggered!" I shouted. "Obstruction be jiggered! I'm obstructing nobody. Do you hear me? I'm obstructing nobody. I've stated that I've twelve hundred cigars to declare, and I've declared them till I've got a sore throat. Do you hear me? I've declared twelve hundred— Here! let go of me!"

"Hold him!" shouted the head officer. "Hold them both! Peters, down with that funnel——"

"If you'll get out of here, and take the Steward with you," I called out, "I'll get you the cigars myself, without your breaking or unshipping anything. But I'll not let the Steward see where I keep my stuff. I've missed over fifty on the trip home——"

"You're a liar, Sir!" shouted the Steward's voice fiercely, from the doorway.

"Hold your tongue!" sung out the Mate. "If I put my hands on you, I'll learn you manners to the Cap'n!"

"Silence!" shouted the head officer. Then, as the Mate began to fight his way towards the Steward, there was quite a dust-up in the saloon, until about four of them went down in a heap on him.

"Get at that table, Jackson," said the head officer. "It's screwed."

"Suppose some of you get off the Mate's head!" I called out. "There's plenty of chairs in the place. You might let him breathe, now and then, for a change!"

"Silence!" shouted the officer. Then to the men: "Let him get up, but keep hold of him."

As the First Mate got to his feet, and saw that they had started to unscrew the top of the saloon table, he swore!

"Yes!" said the head officer, grimly. "We've got you where we want you, this time. We've been tipped off that you've tried a big speculation, but it's impossible to do that kind of thing now-a-days; as you should know, if you'd the sense of sheep.... Billy, hand me out those boxes we picked up. I told you to shove 'em in the Steward's pantry, handy for when we wanted them."

The man Billy loosed the Mate, and stepped out into the pantry. He came back in a few moments, with a great stack of empty cigar-boxes, that still dripped salt water. I recognised them, and stared at the Mate. He stared back at me, silent.

"You see, you're done, finished—knocked out!" said the head officer. "You'll do time for this bit of business. You'll——"

"It's a lie!" sung out the First Mate. "It's some lie that Steward's been stuffing you with."

"That's it!" I said. "A thief's bound to be a liar."

"Liar yourself, Cap'n!" sung out the Steward, obviously insolent, because he knew he was safe. "You got thousands and millions of ceegars; and maybe I'd not have split, only you was that stingy. I don't mind a bit of smuggling, not on principle; but I expects to have *my* share, and if I don't get it, I guess I does the other thing. . . . It's your own fault, Cap'n. I'd have stuck by you if you'd have give me my share. I would—"

"What's all that?" called out the officer. "You be careful what you're saying, my lad, or you'll be in chokee along with the Captain and the Mate."

He turned to his own men.

"That'll do, Billy and Saunders," he said. "You two can go up on deck, and finish there; we'll be able to manage these two now, I guess."

Saunders was one of the men who were holding me; and as soon as he let go, I made one dive for the Steward, who was playing Tunes of Insolence, in which his nose and right thumb made a displeasing conjunction.

"Let's lamn the animal, Sir!" I heard the Mate shout, as I made my charge; and I knew that the two of us were truly bent to a single purpose.

"Hold them!" I heard the officer shout. "Hold them!" And then his men were hanging on to me like a lot of rats, and there was quite some energy adrift in the saloon.

During the hullabaloo, the man who was working at the tabletop continued stolidly to unscrew screws; and presently, when the Mate and I decided on a mutual rest, the man sung out to someone to come and give him a lift.

As the tabletop came off, there was a mutter of exclamation from the Customs men, to see the cigars lying there in a brown layer. Immediately afterwards, the man with the screwdriver, who had pushed his fingers down into the shallow well, called out that there weren't above eight or nine hundred.

"I told you that I declared only twelve boxes of a hundred each!" I said. "Did you suppose they were going to have young ones? The others are up the flue. And you'll not find another, if you hang on to my jacket till you turn grey!"

Neither did they find one, though they turned the saloon and the cabin upside down, and finally the lazarette underneath.

Eventually, the Second Mate came down into the saloon, to ask whether he was supposed to be in sole charge of the ship, or what. And, at that, the head officer had to give orders to his men to release us. A precious fool he must have felt; and, as I explained to him, I was not at all sure that I had not got a case against him for assault and false imprisonment! For he had certainly made prisoners of the Mate and me in my own saloon.

However, I told him that I was inclined to mercy; and that, no doubt, when he was older, he would look back with gratitude to the old sea-Captain who was too soft-hearted to ruin the career of a young, though insolent, Customs officer, merely to gratify a feeling of indignation, however righteous! Finally, I insisted on shaking hands with him, which he submitted to in a stupefied sort of way.

"What's your name, Mister?" I asked him.

"Grey," he answered, still in a dazed kind of fashion. You see, he'd been so certain sure of finding the stuff down aft; and, I daresay, my friendly way rather staggered him!

"Well, Mr. Grey," I said, "away and do your duty. There's all the rest of the ship to search yet; and as you say I've two hundred thousand cigars aboard, you shouldn't have much trouble in locating them!

"When you come to think of it, two hundred thousand cigars would take up a lot of room; why, they'd pretty well fill a whole cabin from deck to deck—eh? Now, don't you see, Mister, the whole foolishness of what you've been told? No ship-master, in his senses, would try to run a cabinful of cigars through the Customs. It couldn't be done. Some joker's been pulling your leg! But if you still think I'm clever enough to magic wholesale orders of that kind past you, why, just turn to on the ship again; and afterwards, when you've found nothing (for I'm betting that's all you will find!), come along aft, and own up you've been fooled!"

But my little talk never stopped him one bit. He seemed to get a fresh notion, and went racing up on deck to test it, and I went after him, to see what it was.

As you know, I'd given the Second Mate orders to start sending down the upper yards, so as to be ready for out trip up the ship canal. Well, what did your Mister Customs Officer do but have the plugs taken out of all the hollow steel yards that had been lowered, to make sure that I'd not packed them with cigars.

Of course, there was nothing in them; but that didn't satisfy him. He sent his men aloft, and they took out the cross-bolts and worked out the plugs from the ends of every yard aloft. And when they found nothing there, they examined the hollow steel topmasts and lower masts. Then they came down to the hull again, and tried the spare wooden topmast and royal masts, that were lashed along under the bulwarks. But they were just plain, sound natural wood.

They were still at it last evening, when we tied up in Ellesmere Port, in the Canal. I could see that the Customs must have had pretty certain information, to waste time like that.

Last night they kept a watch of two men aboard; and today they've had more men down, to tackle the three holds, and they're simply *proving* to themselves that the cigars are not aboard.

November 3, Evening.

The Customs have at last assured themselves that I'm neither as illegal as a magician nor as big a liar as the man who cabled them misleading cigar-shaped news from Havana.

They gave up the search last night, after three agitated days of it. During these three days I've got quite friendly with the head officer; and when he gave me a clean sheet, and called his men off to something more useful, I invited myself ashore with him, for I was going into Liverpool for the evening.

"Look here," I said, as we climbed out at Liverpool, "you're off duty, now, aren't you?"

"Yes," he replied, "my time's my own now, till tomorrow— Why?"

"Well," I told him, "if you're off duty, I guess we can bury the hatchet. So come and have a quiet dinner with me, and I'll tell you a bit of a yarn, as between man and man."

He came, and this is the yarn I told him, over the wine—

"A friend of mine, just a plain, ordinary seafaring man, shipped two hundred thousand cigars aboard, on the strict Q.T. When he reached England, he got word that the Customs had received 'certain information'; the said information being horribly correct.

"My friend thought for a while; then he acted. He broke open a number of cigar boxes, and hid all his personal smokes in the saloon. He pitched the boxes out through the after port-holes, for he knew that sharp eyes were sure to be watching his ship; but he left nothing to chance. He had a quiet word or two with his Steward.

"'Steward,' he said, 'when the Customs House officers come aboard, you can let them know, in a friendly sort of way, that there are possibly some cigars hidden in the saloon. Also, if I should chance to tell you to your face just what a damned thief you are, you need not bother to be as polite as courage might suggest. Got that?'

"'Yes, Sir,' said the Steward. 'I s'pose there'll be something in it for me if I does it all right and proper?'

"'Five quid, my lad,' he told him.

"'I'll earn 'em, Sir,' said the Steward fervently.

"And so, it happened that when the Customs officers boarded my friend's ship, they had not only the information which the floating cigar-boxes had given them of cigars hastily hidden, but they were aided in their search by timely suggestions from the Steward.

"My friend was careful to declare the exact number of cigars that the officers would be likely to find, and offered to produce them, if they would vacate the saloon for a while; which, of course, he knew they would not do.

"He then shouted for his First Mate, who had been carefully primed. The First Mate came racing down into the saloon, without waiting even to drop the capstan-bar which he had in his hands. This studied omission imparted a warlike effect to him; yet there was no intention of (or need for) violence; but the head officer of the Customs searchers saw intentions to offer fight, and he whistled for all his men to come to his rescue.

"They did so, and my friend and his First Mate were somewhat roughly handled. They received further rough treatment when they evinced an unnatural desire to chastise the insolence of the Steward.

"But finally, when no cigars were discovered, over and above those which had been declared, the Customs House officer had to order the release of my friend and his First Mate.

"For three days the Customs infested the vessel; and at last had to admit that there was no such thing as a secret consignment of cigars aboard, and that they had been misled, through acting upon 'uncertain' information!

"And yet the two hundred thousand cigars *were* aboard.

"You will remember that my friend acted peculiarly in the cabin, hiding no more cigars than he intended to declare. Also, his calling for the First Mate was curious, and their united and earnest desire to hammer the Steward was also somewhat, shall I say, abnormal.

"You will be able to understand the plot better when I tell you that, at the very moment when my friend and his First Mate and Steward were 'entertaining' the whole of the Customs officials in the saloon, the two hundred thousand cigars were being hoisted over the side, under the superintendence of the Second Mate, into a launch, which my friend had arranged to run alongside on a given signal from the deck.

"You will see now that *all* that went on in the saloon was nothing more than a lure and a ruse, intended to get all the Customs men aboard below, and keep them interested there whilst the two hundred thousand cigars were being transhipped to the launch.

"You might ask, however, how it was that none of the watchful eyes ashore noticed this somewhat unusual act of unloading. And would not the Engineer who was left in the Customs launch think there was something wrong?

"The explanation is simple. My friend was safe from suspicion, either from those ashore, or from the Customs Engineer, through the following causes: First, because the official watchers ashore would not suspect a vessel which had the Customs launch alongside, and the officers actually aboard. Second, the Engineer never saw the other launch, because it came up on the opposite side of the vessel. Third, because no cases were lowered over the side; for the two hundred thousand cigars were all hidden, in sixteen tin cases, inside a dummy 'spare' topmast, in which they were actually shipped aboard out abroad. And as the Second Mate was lowering spars from aloft, there was nothing particularly noteworthy of the fact that one of the spars at the end of his tackle happened to be that genuine-looking, but exceedingly valuable, spare topmast.

"And, of course, as soon as it was in the water, the launch took it in tow, and went off, away and away-oh!

"Neat of my friend, wasn't it?" I asked.

"You cunning devil!" said the Customs Officer.

The German Spy

S.S. Galatea, July 22.

"THERE'S ONE THING ABOUT taking charge of a tramp steamer," I said yesterday to Mr. MacWhirr, the Chief Engineer, "one does get some variety; and if the pay is rather watery, there are little ways of making ends meet!"

This was when I was explaining what I wanted him to do.

I am drawing just seventeen-ten a month in this boiler, and that's a rise on the last Skipper, who was getting only fourteen-ten; but I stuck at that!

I told Mr. Johnson, our owner, it wouldn't pay my washing, tobacco, and wine bills. He laughed at the joke, as he thought it; but there's more truth in it than he could ever understand.

The little commissioned piece of work I was talking over with MacWhirr comes off tonight. I am just jotting this down, while I have a quiet smoke, before getting busy.

We shall be off Toulon at 10:30. La Seyne comes after that, and I reckon to be off Sanary before 11:30. That's the place where I've got the £500 commission. There's a German ashore there, one of those spies, I suppose; and he's got plans that I'm to buy from him for the tidy sum of £2,000, in English bank-notes. And how I do hate the spy brand, that haven't even the decency to spy for their own Fatherland; but do the dirty work of any confounded country that'll pay them a good figure.

I've my own idea what the plans are, and I shall keep an eye skinned for them, too.

I'm to get the German aboard and land him safe in Spain. I'm to meet him (his name is Herr Fromach) on the Point Issol at 12:30, exactly. If he is not there I am to wait half an hour. If he has not turned up then, I am free to come away, as it may be presumed (from what I can understand) that Herr Fromach will by then have been captured,

295

and will be probably inspecting the inside of some kind of French lock-up. I expect he'll get a private leathering, too, from the men who catch him; for I understand it is generally known ashore that the plans have been stolen by this same Herr, and feeling is running high among the Frenchmen; and there are search parties loose on all the mountains round Sanary, for they've got word he's hiding somewhere about there.

If I don't get him tonight, he'll almost certainly be caught; but I've given my word to do my best; and £500 isn't to be sniffed at!

There will be some risk attached, as people don't offer five-hundred-pound commis-sions merely for the trouble of embarking a casual passenger aboard a cargo tramp!

* * * *

I had a wireless tonight from a "mutual friend" ashore. (I have fitted up a two-hundred-mile-radius installation aboard here at my own expense.) He warned me, as a friend, that the search is getting so hot and close I had better drop the whole business and not come ashore at all; for there has been a leakage somewhere, and the authorities know that Herr Fromach is to attempt an escape from Sanary Bay tonight.

All this was, of course, in cypher, and I replied, in cypher, that I had promised to be on the Point Issol, near the Old Mill, from 12:30 midnight to one o'clock, and that nothing short of a gun-boat would stop me from being there. I nearly told him that seventeen-ten a month was badly needed supplementing, or else I should have to go unlaundried; but I thought it better not to muddle him; for it might prove a puzzling point of view to French minds.

He wirelessed me again, remonstrating; but I told him that Herr Fromach, acting upon instructions, had previously left the Bandol *arrondissement* (or district), where he had been hiding while the Sanary district was being searched, and had passed into the Sanary district, before the route de Bandol was closed, by the search parties.

All this I received by wireless yesterday, from another "mutual friend." And I made it clear that now the news had leaked out that Herr Fromach was certainly in the Sanary *arrondissement*, he must be got off tonight, or he would inevitably be captured, probably before morning. I explained that we might pretend to have a break-down in the engine-room, and this would account for our hanging about, off Sanary, if any official inquiry should be made. I had to repeat this, twice, before the strength of my reasoning was fully appreciated; and after that, I suggested that perhaps it would be safer to stop "sending" until I had either got my man away, or failed. I asked him first, though, about the landing on the point, and the position of the mill.

He replied that the Point Issol came down into the Mediterranean on the western side of the Sanary Bay (which, of course, I knew from the chart!), and that it "concluded" (which amused me) in a long, low snout of black rock, which could be boarded, as the night was calm, right at the point end, with a little scrambling. The mill, he told me, lay right up on the brow of the point.

He went on to remind me (as if I did not know!) that there was practically no tide in the Mediterranean, as along the shores of "Angleterre," and so I need make no "mathematics" of this—in which I agreed with him!

After climbing upon the Point, I must go up the "snout" until I came among the trees, and here I would find a central road, which would lead me right down into Sanary. The rest, he must leave to me; but if I gave any "vocal" signal, he would advise the croaking of a bull-frog, which is sufficiently common not to attract undue attention.

I replied that Herr Fromach had already arranged with me, to answer the howl of a dog, three times repeated, for dogs, I understand, are plentiful among the farms on the land side, and so this kind of signal will not be noticeable.

*   *   *   *

July 23.

We arrived off Sanary last night, at 11:15, and I went below into the engine-room to interview Mister MacWhirr.

"Have you arranged that breakdown, Mac?" I asked him.

"Is it Mister MacWhirr you're askin', or plain MacTullarg, the greaser, ow'r yonder?" he questioned. That's just the way of him, and we understand each other very well.

"*Mister* MacWhirr," I shouted, in a way that made the engine-room ring, "have you fixed up that—"

Mr. MacWhirr thrust out an oily hand at me.

"Whist! For all sakes, whist, mon!" he whispered. "Do ye want to tell all the stokehold what we've gotten planned?"

"That's better, Mac," I said. "If you're ready, I am. We're off Sanary now, and you'd better hurry the breakdown. What's it to be?"

"I'm thinking," whispered MacWhirr, over the back of his hand, "as yon bar-iron as I've leaned so casual like near by the valve guide of the low pressure'll maybe shift with the vessel rollin' so heavy" (the vessel was as steady as a rock!). "An' the guide'll sure get a wee bent. Oh, aye, we've a spare; but I'll no charge it to the ship, Captain; for I'm not thinkin' as yon would be justice to Mr. Johnson, as is a fair man to work for, an' a countryman though I'm not sayin' as he's not a wee inclined to meaness, for a Scotsman. But I'll no ha' yon on ma conscience. If the guide's to go ashore to be straightened, then the cost must be shared by yon an' me, Cap'n, in the proportion of oor shares o' the siller we make this night."

"That's all right, Mac," I said, laughing a little. "Your conscience shall be kept pure and undefiled. I'm going up on the bridge now, so get a move on with the accident."

I went up on to the bridge, and I had been there scarcely more than a minute when there was a muffled jar from the engine-room, and the screw stopped turning. I'm pretty sure that Mac had throttled down handsomely, before he let the "rolling of the vessel" roll the bar-iron into the guides, so as to ensure the gentlest sort of "accident" possible.

I heard him now, shouting at the top of his voice, cursing and making the very kind of a hullaballoo that he would never have made had there been much the matter.

"Which of ye left yon bar-iron there?" I heard him roaring. "I'd gie ma heid to know; for I'd bash the man into hell an' oot again, I wad that!... Mac, away doon, an' tak' two of the men an' rouse out the spare guide, an' get a move on ye. There's two an' maybe three hours' work here for us!"

I ran down off the bridge, and met MacWhirr at the foot of the ladder.

"I'm feared ye'll ha' to anchor, Cap'n," he said, in a voice you could have heard fore and aft. "There's yon fool greaser, though he'll no own to it, made a store closet o' ma engine-room, an' stood a two-inch bar of mild steel on end in a corner, like you might in a fittin' shop ashore; an' the ship's juist rolled it slam into the valve guide o' the low pressure an' we'll ha' two, or maybe three, hours' work to fit the spare. Heard ye ever the like o' such damned aggravatingness, Cap'n!"

I assured him that I hadn't, and ran forrard to put the anchor over.

Now, I had scarcely done this, and the sound of our chain cable ceased echoing across the quiet water, when there was a hail out of the darkness, and a voice, speaking fair English, though with a strong French accent, asked—

"What vessel is that?"

"What the devil's has that to do with you?" I asked. "Who are you, anyway?"

"I'm Lieutenant Brengae, of the destroyer *Gaul,*" said the voice. "You are not very civil, Captain, are you? It is the Captain, is it?"

"I apologise, Monsieur Brengae," I said hur-riedly.... (It was evident that there was a warship in the Bay itself!) "But Monsieur will understand that I am annoyed, when I explain that we have just had a breakdown in our engine-room."

I could have fancied that I heard the Lieutenant, down in the darkness, stifle a vague exclamation. There followed a few moments of absolute silence, during which I ran over all sorts of possibilities in my mind.... All the probabilities and possibilities of his suspecting us of being there for any other reason than I had given. At last he spoke—

"I am sorry, Captain, to hear of your misfortune," he said. Then, with a charming air of friendliness, he went on: "Our Second Mechanician (Engineer, you call him), Lieutenant Cagnes, is with me in the boat; we are enjoying a promenade. We will come aboard, Captain, if you will invite us, and have the pleasure of a talk. I will polish my poor English upon you; and my friend will be pleased to assist your mechanician in any way he can. Lieutenant Cagnes never can resist the call of the machinery. It will be for him a pleasure most great to be of assistance. And for me, Captain, perhaps, if you weary of your own ship, you will come across to *La Gaul,* and split (is not that the idiom) a bottle of our friend Cassis with me?"

I did not hesitate an instant in my reply; for I had thought like lightning, as the Lieutenant was speaking, and it was plain that he had strong suspicions of the reality of our accident.

"Come aboard, Monsieur, by all means," I said. "Your offer is downright good *entente cordiale*! I dare say my Chief Engineer, Mr. MacWhirr, will pal on with your friend; but for me, I fear I shall have to decline with regrets, for I have certain letters which I must get off at this opportunity. Perhaps, Monsieur would cause them to be posted for me tomorrow."

My reasoning had shown me that it was most necessary that they should see at once that we were genuinely disabled; and I could tell, by the change of tone in the Lieutenant's voice, that he was half-way to doubting he had any cause for seriously suspecting us. Also, by getting him to post the letters, I hoped I should be able to get rid of him early.

I had a ladder put over, and they came aboard at once, and a couple of active young men they seemed, too. I took them, myself, down to the engine-room, and left them with Mac, explaining that I was no Engineer, so could not explain the nature of the trouble; but that doubtless Mister MacWhirr would be able to give all particulars.

I smiled to myself. I could picture MacWhirr giving them particulars in broad Scots.

As I left, I heard Mac begin:

"I'd ha' ye to unnerstan', gentlemen, as that's noo Engineers the like o' the Scottish in this worrld. I mind me when I wer' in the *Agyptian Queen,* runnin' fro' Belfast to Glasga——"

That was as far as I heard, before I reached the decks. I stopped there to laugh. Mac would certainly polish his *English* for him!

Then I went round the decks, to make sure there were no give-away things about. I found everything correct; for I had previously had the aerial wires, of my wireless installation, unrigged; for a tramp steamer, in the circumstances, was better without the display of such luxuries.

Half an hour later, Jales (the steward) knocked at my cabin door. "Them two Frenchies is going off in their boat, Sir," he told me. "One of 'em says as you wanted him to post some letters."

"Thank you, Jales," I said, raking my letters together. "I'll come up myself."

I found the two officers standing ready by the side ladder. They seemed to me almost apologetic in their manner, as if they were ashamed for having suspected me. It was obvious that my plan of allowing them to invite themselves aboard had produced exactly the effect I had hoped for. Moreover, as I had expected, half an hour of Mac's Scots version of the English language had proved sufficient to stunt both their desires for more exact information, either on the cause of our accident or on the finer glazes that may be given to our English speech.

"Monsieur MacWheer has been very gracious," said Lieutenant Brengae. "But he will not allow my friend to *salir* his paws—is not that the idiom, Captain? So we will take your letters and return; for we have a slumber most great upon us."

"That's certainly a complaint that calls for hammock treatment, Messieurs les Lieutenants," I said. "Many thanks for offering to post my letters. Don't apologize for inviting yourselves aboard. I'm sure we're always open to give instruction in Scots English and Engineering at any hour of the night. Mind the step!—as we have it in our idiom. Good night!"

And I bowed them both down over the side, in a somewhat puzzled state of mind, while one of the watch held a lantern over the ladder, to light them.

This showed their boat; and I could not help thinking it curious that two French lieutenants should go "promenading" with a fully manned gig of six oars, with each man of the crew armed. There is, of course, no accounting for tastes. But to me, it looked less like "promenading," than doing a sort of glorified sentry-go.

I stood and listened to the sounds of their oars die away into the distance across the bay; then I gave the word to lower the dinghy, which we carry on davits across the stern. It is a light, convenient boat, and pulls well with two men.

I did not have the oars muffled; for I would not put myself into the position of allowing the men to suspect that I was mixed up in anything irregular; also, if we were discovered, prior to reaching the point, there would be no material for evidence to prove that I was not also indulging in the favourite water "promenading" of the south coast. All I did to quiet the sounds of the oars was to tell the men to "pull easy."

I took my night-glasses with me and studied the end of the long, low point on our port bow, which I knew, from its position, must be the Point Issol. It was a simply perfect night, so quiet that from some place, far in the bight of the bay to the eastward, I could hear the constant, interminable *karr, karr, karr,* of the bull-frogs, in some unseen marshland ashore.

Presently we had come so close in that I could see the stark outline of the low snout of rock, black against the clear night sky to the westward.

"Gently! Gently!" I said to my men; and then, after a minute. "'Vast pulling! Back starboard!" and the boat's gunnel was rubbing gently against the rocky end of the snout. I climbed out of the boat, and fumbled my way up on to the rock. Then I turned to the men.

"Lie off a couple of lengths," I said. "Don't smoke. Chew, if you want to, and keep your ears open for my hail."

"Aye, aye, Sir," they said, and I turned to go up the black slope of the point.

I went slowly for about ten fathoms, listening, as I went, and doing my best, for obvious reasons, not to stumble on the sharp edges of the rock surface. Then I stopped and adjusted my night-glasses and made as thorough an examination as possible, all round me.

So far as my glasses showed me, there was no kind of shrubbery or cover anywhere near—nothing but just the bare mass of the back of the long snout, in which the point ended.

Farther up the slope, however, I could see the vague straggle of odd small trees, and above them, a squat tower showed, black and silent against the night. This I presumed to be the mill, near which I was to signal to Herr Fromach that I had come for him.

I put my glasses in my pocket, and continued slowly and carefully; but in spite of my care, I slipped twice, and the second time, I sent a small lump of rock rolling and clattering down the right-hand side of the point. The "plunk" it made, as it entered the calm water, seemed to me to be loud enough to be heard half across the absolute silence of the bay.

I stood for nearly a minute listening, but there was not a sound anywhere, and I knew that there was no reason, in the ordinary course of things, for me to trouble about the noise made by a smallish piece of rock tumbling into the water. But my state of mind was naturally a little tensed up by the situation.

I began to go upwards again towards the old mill, and presently I had come among the first of the odd trees. They were small, and I could tell by their smell that they were pines.

Presently, I was quite close to the old mill. It stood about twenty to thirty feet high, in a clear space, near the brow, to the right hand, where the point sloped down into the Bay of Sanary. But ahead of me, I could see vaguely that the pine trees grew thicker, and seemed to cover most of the landward portion of the point. To my left, the rock sloped away broadly into a small bay, and I could see numbers of stunted trees here and there, scattered oddly.

I literally tiptoed up to the side of the mill, and there I squatted low down, silently, and stared round through my night-glasses for maybe two or three minutes. Once, I thought I saw something move among the odd trees on the left-hand slope of the point; but after looking fixedly for a time, I could not be sure I had seen anything.

I stood up then, and walked quietly round the mill; and after about a dozen steps, I found that I had come opposite an open doorway, with a small pile of rubble just tumbled loosely across the old threshold. I had a sudden thought to step inside; but a feeling of repugnance of the unknown possibilities of the old place, stopped me, and I stood absolutely still again to listen.

It seemed to me that I never was in such a silent part of the world; for, except for the vague and monotonous *karr, karr, karr* of the bull-frogs, somewhere in the bight of the long bay, and the occasional far-off howling of dogs among the hidden farms, there seemed no other sound at all.

Then I heard a faint noise near me; that made me listen the more intently. I could not locate it at first, and I drew back out, of a line with the dark, open doorway, and squatted down once more, so as to be hidden. Also, as anyone knows, who has ever done any "night work," one can generally see objects better, the nearer the ground one gets.

I squatted still for quite a minute, and heard the slight noise twice. And then, as I looked up, I found the cause; for a length of broken wire was swinging gently, as an occasional slight air of wind moved it. I could only see it when it swung idly, between me and the night sky.

I stood up noiselessly and reached for it. I had a sudden vague, perhaps absurd, suspicion of a trap, in my mind, and I thought I would make sure the wire was no more than a broken end, swinging from the old structure. I caught the end, and gave it a good hard tug, and fortunate it was for me that the night was no darker, or I should not have seen in time to jump; for there was a vague rumble above me, and then I saw something revolve against the sky. I made one jump to the side, and as I did so, some heavy mass fell close to me, with a crash that seemed to echo through miles of the quiet night. I ran several steps, like a cat; then stopped and listened. But there was no sound anywhere, and I began to realise what an ass I had been; for I had pulled at some hanging bit of wire, which had probably been fixed at some time or other to some woodwork of the old mill.

I walked quietly over to the fallen mass and felt it. I was right in my supposition; for I had simply pulled down a large portion of a rotten beam, and come very near to making my night's work thoroughly unprofitable in every sense of the word.

I guessed that I had better get done with my business, and be off. I held my wristwatch out in the starlight, and managed to see that it was just on the half-past twelve. As I did so, a clock, somewhere along the shore, struck the half-hour, and I raised my hands to my lips and howled three times like a dog. The sounds were most horribly mournful in that lonely sort of place, and I could almost have given myself the creeps, with the way the last of the infernal sounds seemed to die away and away, among the black masses of the trees that lay all along inland of where I stood.

I waited for about five minutes, listening; but there came never an answer; and then I howled once more, and I felt that if I had to make the beastly noises again, I should want twice the cash that was coming to me. I had not thought a man could have made so weird and horrible a cry, so infernally able to disturb about ten miles of silent night. I felt that half the people of Sanary would be getting out of their beds, to stare up at the black bulk of the Point Issol, to discover the cause.

Yet, still there came no answer; and presently, after waiting a little longer, I thought I would walk quietly a short distance from the old mill, along the inland portion of the point.

I went very carefully, looking round me, every moment or two, and I found, after about twenty or thirty steps, that I was in a kind of gloomy little road, with the small pine trees thick on each side of me, and the night full of their rich, oily smell.

Presently, I went a little further along the road, which had begun to lead down towards the hidden town. And all the time, as I went, I stared to right and left; for I was quite sure, on two separate occasions, that I had heard some further sound, almost as if something were following me among the trees; but on which side I could not be sure.

Abruptly, as I stared down the slope to my right, I saw distinctly a vague movement among the dark boles of the trees. I felt I was not mistaken, and I squatted down again near the ground, and stared. For quite five minutes I remained like this, and there was not a single noise, or movement of any kind, to suggest that there was anyone near me. Then, as I stood upright, I saw something move again among the trees; and the suggestion came to me, like a flash, that I should make quite sure it was not Herr Fromach dodging me in turn, waiting for me to give the signal again. So, without waiting a moment, I just clapped my hands to my mouth, and let go the first of the three howls. As I did so, a most extraordinary thing happened. I heard someone turn in the path, not thirty yards before me, and begin to walk hurriedly away. I howled again, and the walk became a run; and then suddenly there was a rush of feet, and a loud crying in the night, about a hundred yards away, and a sound of scuffling and muffled cries and a fall and a voice shouting: *"Attrapé! Attrapé! Attrapé!"*

There came a number of voices shouting, and then a quick command, which was followed by a silence, in which I heard a man's voice protesting monotonously.

There rang out, far and clear, three or four notes on a bugle, and immediately the whole night was filled with enormous beams of light, that circled and poised and then rested immovably along the length of the point. I saw the tops of the pine trees shine like ten million fronds of silver against the light; and down among the trunks of the trees on the right-hand slope, there burned great silent splashes of light.

Behind me, up on the highest brow of the point, the old mill stood like a chunk of white fire, every edging of broken stone or mortar picked out with the great blazes that beat in on every side; and in the light, standing immovable in a silent row, as if they were statues, was a long line of French man-of-war's men, with rifles and fixed bayonets. They were drawn clean across the point, the ends of the line vanishing among the trees on each side.

I comprehended thoroughly the perfectness of the trap into which I had walked. In some way, a complete knowledge of what I had sent by wireless, must have been obtained by the authorities. There were warships lying in the bay, and it had been easy to arrange every-thing. The two lieutenants, probably with a score of other officers and boats, had patrolled the mouth of the bay, and kept a watch for every vessel that came "near in." They had come aboard, apparently in casual friendly fashion; and when they had left, they had evidently been confirmed in their own minds, that my ship was the one they were looking for. Possibly the whole of the Point Issol had been silently invested, in readiness, for some hours, and every step of my way, even up the "snout," and my little adventure with the old beam, must all have had their silent onlookers.

A rare bit of drama I had been providing the fleet with! And there had obviously been orders not to interfere with me in any way; but to give every chance to the German to meet me, for it was not me they wanted, but the German, Herr Fromach, with (as I had already guessed) the almost priceless plans of the new additions to the great Fortress of Toulon.

As I stared, fascinated, at the line of silent man-of-war's men, with the blaze making their bayonets shine like spikes of fire, someone touched my shoulder gently, and I whirled round.

Monsieur Brengae was standing close to me, saying something, which I did not hear; for over his shoulder, down the slope, among the trees, there were vaguely seen movements of hundreds of men among the shadows.

"Monsieur the Captain has come ashore for a promenade?" I realised that the lieutenant was saying, in the most courteous fashion possible.

"Good Lord!" I said, staring. "That you, Monsieur?.... What are your men doing? Is it an execution?"

"The men!" he said, looking at me, in a mild kind of way. "But what is Monsieur's remark? What men?"

"Why!" I said, and turned up the brow towards the old mill. But there was not a man visible, of all the silent guards who had stood a moment before across the breadth of the point, between me and the sea.

I laughed, as I looked at the Lieutenant. Evidently they were acknowledging nothing unusual, except a searchlight display.

"Remarkably fine show!" I said, staring down at Lieutenant Brengae.

"A little welcome, shall we say?" said the Lieutenant, smiling; but his lips came back a bit too much from his teeth, and quite spoilt the friendly tone of his preceding words.

"Perhaps, Monsieur the Captain had an assignation," he said, still in his gentle way. "... No?"

"Certainly not, Monsieur," I answered.

"Ah!" he said, smiling still; but now the way his lips left his teeth was almost a sneer. "Perhaps Monsieur came ashore to sample the cheese of the country, or maybe it was a foreign cheese... perhaps Monsieur has a fondness for cheese, shall we say, Roquefort? But I fear the shops are shut tonight!"

I'm not much of a French scholar, but I knew enough to remember that *fromage* goes for cheese, and that the little Lieutenant was rotting me; he was simply punning on the German's name. But I only laughed, as good naturedly as I could, in the circumstances.

"I fear Monsieur disbelieves me?" I said.

"Perhaps as the shops have closed up," said the Lieutenant, looking at me fixedly, "Monsieur the Captain will not want to buy any cheese tonight?"

I thought of the scuffle I had heard, and it was plain that he was telling me that Herr Fromach had been caught.

"Promotion, Monsieur Lieutenant, is a glory for the young man," I said. "I perceive that Monsieur is in the cheese business, and hopes to make a profit!"

He stared at me, half fierce as he wrestled dumbly to shred out my exact meaning. Then he shrugged his shoulders; but was still at a loss how to get even with me for the way in which I had levelled him up, in his own little word-game of quiet cut-and-thrust.

However, I saw no reason for giving him time to mature a reply, and, raising my cap, I said *Bon soir*, and turned seawards.

Lieutenant Brengae accompanied me to the end of the snout of rock, and stood silently by me, while I whistled for my boat.

As I got in, he murmured: "Good night, Monsieur the Captain. I have cheesed it for you, is not that the idiom?"

This was evidently a great and successful effort, and he threw his chest out, with a queer little swaggering motion.

I laughed quietly, as I answered him—

"Perhaps, in the circumstances, Monsieur, I must accept your idiom as correct," I said. "Good night, Monsieur le Lieutenant."

"Good-night, Monsieur the Captain," he said. And so we parted.

When I got aboard, Mac had everything ready, and I up anchor and away, at once, as any one can imagine.

The searchlights of the warships followed me, as if in a silent unison of jeers at my night's imbroglio, until the Point la Cride hid me.

July 28.

I went ashore today at Gib., where I posted the following letter to my friend, Lieutenant Brengae, of the destroyer *Gaul—*

"MY DEAR LIEUTENANT,

"I felt at our last brief meeting it would have been out of place to attempt to force upon you the truth that I did not go ashore on the Point Issol to meet the German, Herr Fromach. It was not, in any way, a fitting moment to insist upon the truth of my statement. But the time has come when I must do so, in the hope that you will now, of your natural courtesy, accord me belief in my word, which I fear you were once inclined to discredit.

"I did not go ashore on the Point Issol to meet the German; for at the moment that I went ashore, my Second Mate, in one of our life-boats, was embarking Herr Fromach in the Bay of Bandol, some miles away. My little excursion to the Point Issol was planned solely to direct attention to that one spot; and my wireless messages (of a cypher too easy to be secret!) were purely bogus; for I myself sent both my queries and my replies; repeating them courteously, until I felt sure that the warships in the Bay of Sanary could not have failed to assimilate them. Need I explain more! Except that I landed Herr Fromach at Algeciras, not more than two hours ago.

"I have often wondered who was the innocent and unfortunate visitor you 'captured' on the point that night. He must have been almost as bewildered as you were later, when you discovered that, after all, your investment in, shall we say, Roquefort, on the Point Issol, failed to prove a profitable speculation!

"I trust you will admire the smartness of my little plot, in the same courteous spirit in which you and the Admiralty genially assisted me to carry it out.

"Believe me, dear Lieutenant Brenage,
"Yours faithfully,
"G. GAULT—
"*Master.*

"P.S.—There is just something more I must add, in closing. I do not believe in spying, and, incidentally, I've no particular use for

Germans.

"Further, I'm an Englishman; and as this war between Germany and France (our friend) seems now to be a certainty, I think that you will be pleased to hear that Herr Fromach went ashore minus his plans. When he comes to open the envelope which contained them, he will find some really first-class blank paper.

"I was offered five hundred pounds to pick up the respected Herr and land him safely in Algeciras. I accepted the contract, and have fulfilled it faithfully; for it is my fixed principle always to carry out any engagement I undertake. As I have said, I landed him two hours ago in Algeciras, and my commission is honestly earned.

"The plans, however, are another matter. And, to go into details, they are, at this moment of writing, *en route* to the Governor of Toulon, in a registered package, with my compliments. Let us shake hands, my dear Lieutenant. As you would yourself phrase it, in excellent idiom: 'I have Herr Fromach on buttered toast.' In England we should not, perhaps, be so particular about the butter; we should account just plain, dry toast sufficient.

"Shake hands, old man.

"G. GAULT."

The Problem of the Pearls

S.S. Zurich,
June 17.

"IF I'D ONLY HAD the sense to stay ashore when I was a boy and play the fiddle or the flute, I'd have made my fortune," I told Mister Gamp, my First Mate, this morning.

Gamp's got the morals of a virago and the tongue of an Irishman. Oh, I mean it that way! If a virago were moral, she'd hold her tongue and stop being a virago; and if an Irishman held his tongue, he'd stop being an Irishman. So there you are! Any way, Gamp wasn't complimentary; but he granted it helped a man to think; and somehow the way he admitted even that much wasn't nice.

We're away and away-o across the Western Ocean, bound for little old New York; and I fiddle and flute a bit, as you might say, to keep my hand in, and likewise to help me think.

You see, I've cause to think. I undertook a little private contract, when we were in Amsterdam. I bought six pearls for the respectable sum of £12,375 from a merchant I know there. I supplied the judgement, and a friend of mine, in the jewel trade in New York, supplied the cash. My job now is to hand these over to my friend in New York without undergoing the, shall we call it, formalities of paying the ridiculous duty which the Customs attempt to enforce?

Unfortunately, I am not unknown to the New York Customs; though, with my hand on my heart, I assure you there had never been anything so vulgar as a, shall I say, *débâcle* on my part? During the last few years, I have turned an honest dollar or two in this pretty game of wits wit who can; but there! Why give way to naughty vanity? It comes too often before the aforementioned *débâcle* to be a safe vice for a jewel runner.

Now, because of past episodes with the people across the way (I refer to the New York Customs) I have been subjected to flattering attentions from their agents, who keep an unobtrusive eye upon the jewel marts of Amsterdam and other places, with or without dams, where the precious "pills" and "pebbles" are on sale.

Because of this *espionnage* (a most suitable and fashionable phrase!) I took particular care to "arrange" my transaction with the merchant in Amsterdam. I 'phoned him from a public cabaret; and only when I had him on the wire did I give my name, and such other particulars as were necessary. I told him to meet me on the dam, on the palace side, away from the cafés.

I drove round to the back of the palace, in a taxi, and told the driver to wait, while I had a walk on to the big square. Here I found my business acquaintance, and took him back to my taxi, and told the man to drive out to the model cheese farms.

"You indrested mit cheese, Cap'n?" asked my acquaintance, smiling.

"Nix!" I told him, in the vernacular. "I want to get away from the cafés. We've not got to be seen together. When we get out there, I'll leave you in the taxi and come back by tram. I guess you'll have to pay the taxi. If I'm seen with you, there'll go a message to New York, and they'll be waiting for me with open arms, as you might say.... I'd have the very devil then to get the stuff through."

He nodded; and we turned to business.

By the time we reached the cheese farms, we had done business to the tune of the aforementioned £12,375; and I had paid him in cold cash. In return, I had six really wonderful pearls; and the whole transaction was finished.

"I'm off, now," I said, and stopped the cabby. "I think we're safe; but it's better to part here."

"Shoost so," he agreed, and I jumped out.

"Back to the dam," I told the driver, and stood away, while he turned, feeling thankful that I had managed the thing so neatly.

And then, just as the driver let in his clutch again, the ass of a merchant shoved his fat, round face out of the taxi—

"Goot voyage, Cap'n!" he said, beaming like a full moon. "Und I pe glad to know you ged all safe trou de Gusdoms."

"Shove your head in, you idiot!" I said. "Quick!"

He looked started, and his face went back into the taxi with considerable speed, for so fat a man. I saw the vehicle lurch as he sat down; and then it gathered way and presently vanished in the distance.

I turned round from watching it, and pulled out a cigarette. As I did so, I saw a man step back rather hastily, into one of the small village shops, a little way up the short street. There was something at once familiar and suspicious about the thing I had seen. Why should a man seem to dodge back into one of the shops? And why had I that vague sense of something familiar?

I walked up to the door of the shop, one of those Dutch shops that seem to overflow with innumerable broods of brass candlesticks, unnameable pottery and unashamedly "antique" furniture, lying in wait to ensnare the expectedly asinine tourist.

I went right into the shop, and stared, for maybe a full minute, at a back that I seemed to know. It was *very* "touristy," in the worst "British" style, by means of which continental tailors vent upon Britain the venom of centuries. But I was sure I knew what I might call "the Man in the Check Coat"—and trousers, of course; not to forget the stockings that would have put to shame a full-blooded Cockney.

I am sure the man's interest in the impossible plaque he was studying was due to the fact that it offered so good an excuse to withdraw from me the light of his countenance.

But I persisted in my exposition of patience; and because I stood so calmly behind him, the woman in the shop did not press me to buy a fumed-oak cradle for the babe that I have not; being evidently under the impression that I was a friend of the man in the checked coat, and was no more than waiting for him—which was a just and exact estimate of what I was doing.

At last, the plaque afforded no longer any pretext for silence and study; and the man, evidently embarrassed, unhung it, and presented it to the woman, with a dumb gesture of: "How much?"

"Twenty florins?" said the woman, without changing colour.

The unfortunate man paid the money, grabbed the plaque, and walked out hastily, tumbling over a cradle and upsetting half a dozen Birmingham candlesticks, in his anxiety to go out with his back turned to me, and yet to appear as if he were not badly deformed or mentally deficient.

But I knew who it was; for I had got one good square look at his side face. It was James Atkinson, one of the most active of the Customs' agents on the European side of the pond.

And now, as I fiddle and flute, here in my chart-house, I am eternally asking myself: Did he see *who* I was with, in the taxi? That's the question! If he did, then good-bye to my getting the pearls ashore, without the devil's own trouble!

I know the New York Customs! They're IT—when it comes to acting on sure information. They'll turn the ship inside out, and afterwards skin her alive, before they'll let these six wee jewels of the sea get past their infernal hawks'-eyes! Gracious me! I wish I knew!

Do you wonder that I fiddle and flute, flute and fiddle, and that Mr. Gamp looks sourer and sourer, and wears ostentatious pads of cotton wool in his somewhat oversized ears? I'm sure I don't blame him. It's as absurd to blame a man for having no soul for music, as it is to blame a man for being born without legs. You don't *blame* him?

Meanwhile, what *did* that infernal Atkinson-Paul-pry see or suspect?

New York, June 29.

"I'd like a word with you in the cabin, Captain Gault."

Those were the words I got from MacAllister, the chief searcher, when he came aboard this morning, as we were docking. I knew then that the agent in Amsterdam *had* seen who was in the taxi; and if he had seen that much, there was a good certainty he'd followed up the clue. . . . Well, it was no use cursing; so I went below with the searcher.

"Look here, old man," he said, in his friendly way, when we reached the cabin, "we *know* you've got pearls. We know you paid £12,375 for six of them. Is that enough to show you it's no use playing tricks and getting yourself into trouble? Be a sensible man and *don't* try to run 'em through. You can't do it; for we're alive to what you're up to.

"Now, I've warned you fair!" he went on; "so you're getting a square chance. I ask you now, formally, Captain Gault, have you anything to declare?"

"Nothing, dear man," I said.

"I'm sorry," he replied. "I've given you every chance; and now I tell you plainly that if the boss can nail you, he'll do it, and he'll not spare you, either. You've had things too much your own way, and you think you can't get caught. Now you'll see!"

"Excuse me one moment, Mac," I said. "But I thought I heard someone outside the door."

I stepped across smartly, as I spoke, and flung it open; but there was no one there.

"Funny!" I said. "I could have sworn I heard something."

"So could I," said MacAllister, looking puzzled. "Anyway, there's no one; and I guess now I'd better get up and put my men on to the job of rooting out where you've hid the pills. You're an owl, old man, to butt into trouble like this!"

New York, July 3.

Well, that was something of a search! Though I wasn't afraid they'd ever find the place where I've hid the stuff. They'd have to take the ship to pieces, first; but they did their best! They kept thirty men on the job, for seventy-two hours, changing them every eight hours. They simply mapped the vessel out into sections, and went over every available foot of her; but there are many unavailable feet in a vessel; and six pearls can lie in a very small place indeed. I need hardly add that they searched me also, and my personal belongings. They found nothing.

They searched everybody and everything that came near the ship, so it seemed to me; also they've got one of their men aboard all the time, to keep a general eye on things. The final trouble was a pompous Treasury official, who came down and tried to bully me—

"We know you've got the pearls," he told me. "We know it, because we know all about you, and all you did in Amsterdam. You bought six pearls from Van Lumb, and you paid £12,375 for them. That means that somewhere in this ship there are hidden over sixty thousand dollars' worth of pearls. And we mean to have them. Where are they?"

"Now, Sir," I said, "you've asked me a leading question, and I'll answer it as frankly as it was asked. I'm a bit of a ladies' man, like I've heard you say you are yourself, when your wife's gone South.

"Well, I guess you'll feel in sympathy with me when I tell you I bought those pearls for a lady friend of mine, and she's got them this present moment."

"Don't talk nonsense," he said, getting warm. "Your ship sailed direct here from Amsterdam. You were watched every hour in Holland, after you bought the pearls."

"It was since then," I explained. "My dear man, do be a bit more helpful. These—er—affairs are somewhat delicate to talk about, as you should know; but I suppose I had better forget my finer feelings. In short, Sir, the lady was one we met on the trip across."

"What!" he said. "You have neither touched anywhere nor boarded any vessel since leaving the continent of Europe. What do you mean by this stupidity? There are no ladies floating loose about on the North Atlantic!"

"Well, you see," I continued, "I was not right in calling her a lady— as a matter of honest fact she was only a mere maid—or I believe it is fashionable to omit the second 'e'!"

He got up then, and went. I've seen him since; and I've felt him, often, or rather the effects of him, for the way I'm searched each time I go ashore is nothing short of immodest.

The first time I went ashore I was stopped by the Customs, and taken into a comfortable enough office, with a room at the back of it that I know too well by now, for I've been there before. It has a big skylight overhead, plus windows all round, except where a cubicle stands in one corner.

There were two officers in the place, and I was invited to step into the cubicle and strip. The two officers then took my clothes out into the room and examined every square inch of them, also my boots; they were very particular about the heels; but they found everything all right. Then they started on me, and gave me a similar course of treatment. It was very embarrassing; but life has its thorny places; so I made the best of things.

They found nothing, of course, for I wasn't risking sixty thousand dollars, odd, on the chance of getting through, unsearched. After they had searched me, they examined the floor and walls of the cubicle, to be sure I had not dropped anything, or stuck anything up above the eye "level" with a bit of chewing gum. They were up to all the dodges!

Then they introduced me to a new fakement, an upright grey panel, that I had to stand against, with a pattern of big brass balls, on a framework, the other side of me. They pulled a switch and flared off a criss-cross of great violet coloured sparks, that went jumping and cracking across and across the curious framework of brass balls.

I saw then that they were trying some kind of X-ray test on me. They repeated this, elabourately; then told me I might dress.

When I was finished I went out into the big, well-lighted room, and here I found the two officers, with MacAllister and a man with an apron on and bare-armed, who I supposed might be a photographer. They were all examining a number of big, oblong pieces of paper, which I saw must be some kind of paper negative. It was most extraordinary to see the hidden parts of my own anatomy brazening their shadows there for every one of their callous eyes to examine.

MacAllister, the chief searcher, turned to me.

"Sorry, Captain Gault, to have to put you through it like this," he said, speaking a little formally before the three men. "But we know you've got those pearls, and I guess we're going to have them. You've only yourself to thank for putting us to all this trouble. I assure you, we ain't keen on it! But it's what you're liable to get each time you come ashore. And it's what anyone else is liable to get, if we see anything that looks like you're trying to use anyone else to put the pills past us."

"Any further questions, or may I go now?" I asked. "You certainly are the limit on this side of the pond!"

"As I've said, Captain Gault, I'm sorry; but you've brought it on yourself," he replied, as friendly as ever. "We *know* you've diddled the U.S.A. Customs to the tune of thousands, only we've not been able to *prove* it yet. You've put it over on us that much we'll be getting superstitious if we don't hand you out a take-down before long. Why, man, you're the swellest Contrabandist this side of Jerusalem!"

"You've no right to make such a statement!" I said. "If you care to come outside and say a thing of that sort before witnesses who aren't your own men, I'll have a writ on you for libel before forty-eight hours are out."

McAllister laughed.

"I don't doubt it, Captain Gault," he said. "In fact, I'm sure of it. You're the Wonder Unlimited! The way you put it over us with that cigarful of pearls last trip— Well!"

"Look here!" I warned him. "That's a proved libel; so be careful. I won my case against the Treasury on that same statement, and they had to bail up on it—"

The chief searcher roared.

"I know it, old man," he called out, shaking all over, and forgetting any attempt at formality in his exuberance. "All little old New York knows it... You're *the* classic!"

Everybody in the room appeared to be laughing, and I laughed with them. Then, in the midst of our laughter, a voice spoke from the doorway leading out into the office—

"What's the meaning of this? Mr. MacAllister, are you making free with that smuggling scoundrel there?"

I recognised the voice, even as I turned. It was the Treasury official who had been vanquished by my tale of the mere maid who wasn't a lady.

I glanced at MacAllister, and saw that he was annoyed at his superior's manner. The two other officers and the photographer looked as if they had never laughed in their lives. They bent, all of them, over the paper negatives, and it was I who answered His Mightiness.

"Were you referring to me, Sir?" I asked him.

"I have no wish to bandy words with you!" he said, speaking like a "comic" Englishman out of an American "best-seller." He turned to MacAllister again—

"Have you searched this person?" he asked the chief searcher.

"Sure," said MacAllister, tersely. "If it's Captain Gault you mean." He looked at me—

"I guess you can pass out, Sir," he said, and nodded towards the doorway.

"Thanks," I replied. "Good morning."

At the doorway, however, the uncivil personage from the Treasury forgot his commendable intention not to speak to me.

"Look here, you—you smuggling scamp," he said. "I've given orders that you're to be searched every time you come ashore. We shall have those pearls, never fear! We shall have them. You will never bring them ashore past *my* men!" He stamped his foot. "We shall catch you before may days are past; and I will see that you suffer bitterly—bitterly. You are an unmitigated, thieving scoundrel. You are a—"

"Ah!" I said, blandly interrupting him. "Let me see your tongue." I slipped my forefinger under his scraggy and dyspeptic chin and tilted his face up gently but firmly. "Ah!" I said. "I thought so! Your eyes tell a sad tale, my dear Sir. Liver! Undoubtedly liver! Try a course of Epsoms, my dear Sir. Magnificent thing, Epsoms. A sure tonic, Sir. You will hardly recognise yourself afterwards. Your friends certainly won't. A great improver of a coarse complexion and coarse manners, Sir. Try it."

And with the last word I took my finger from under the little man's chin and passed out. As I went I thought the dead silence of the inner room was broken by sounds that suggested the kind of agony men feel who stifle a large and natural laughter.

July 5.

I invited MacAllister aboard last night, to have a smoke and a yarn with me. As I pointed out to him, I could not be getting into mischief if he were with me, and I wanted someone to talk to. I told him, also, there was something I wanted to speak to him about, whereat I believe he scented regeneration! Also, I added that he could have some music, if he liked. And here, let me say, that my fiddling and fluting is not quite so bad as Mr. Gamp's attitude might suggest to a stranger.

MacAllister agreed, and we had a very pleasant evening. He plays the fiddle a bit, and I accompanied him with the flute. Between whiles, we smoked and yarned; and it was understood that, for that one evening, pearls were strictly taboo.

However, just when he was leaving, I made the protest that had been in my mind all evening.

"Look here, dear man," I said, "I don't think it's the thing for the man you've got aboard to keep an eye on things, to go round on a private search-stunt of his own, among my personal belongings. If he wants to search my gear, I'm reasonably willing, at any reasonable time, provided I'm present; but it's bad cricket doing that sort of thing when I'm ashore!"

MacAllister was simply astonished, genuinely; but he asked me to send Pelter, my steward, for the man at once.

When he came, MacAllister turned on him, and asked what the deuce he meant by exceeding instructions. But the man swore he had done nothing more than keep a general eye on things. He had never once been into my cabin, except during the time of the search of the vessel. He stuck to this statement, and, at last, MacAllister sent him away.

"Are you sure?" he asked me. "What makes you sure there's been anyone among your gear?"

"Things disarranged; one lock forced and another jammed through someone tackling it too roughly with a key that didn't fit!" I told him.

He nodded.

"Proof enough, old man!" he said. "I'm puzzled. Yet I'm inclined to believe our man, Quill. He's a straight one, or we shouldn't have put him on to this job. What about your man, Pelter, the steward? He may be looking out for the pills himself. However, that's your lookout!

"I guess, anyway, he know he's on to a safe thing, if it's him. You see, if he gets them from you, you daren't put the police on him; for then we'd drop on you for the duty, and we'd confiscate the pearls as well, even if the police got them back from Pelter. No! I guess you're in a corner, if he or any one else can put a finger on them.

"As a friend, I should advise you to keep your eyes skinned. As a Customs official, I say it'll serve you right if you get done.

"Now let's drop the subject. Only remember, it's bound to get round the place that you've over 60,000 dollars' worth of pearls hidden aboard, as we're bound to believe; and if that tale goes round, look out for crooks! It'll be enough to bring all the man-eaters in New York trying to pay you a night visit. Well, so long, old man! The way of transgressors isn't exactly macadam, is it?"

You can imagine that what he had told me set me thinking after he had gone. I had never suspected the steward; for I had imagined that no one on the American side, either ashore or aboard, knew about the pearls, except the Customs and myself. Even then, I could not see how he could have heard anything definite; for the Customs officers are not in the habit of blabbing all round the place.

Suddenly, I slapped my knee. I remembered the first day in port, when I took MacAllister into my cabin, and both of us thought we heard someone at the door. That was Pelter, right enough. It couldn't very well be anyone else; for both of my Mates were on deck at the time, and only the Steward could have entered the after cabin without being noticed.

I determined to lay a trap and began my preparations accordingly, the first of which was to secure a number of eggs from the pantry, some roping-twine from a locker, a bottle of sepia and a camel-hair brush.

I made a tiny hole in each end of each egg, after which I blew them. When they were empty, I painted, with sepia, the brief legend "PEARLS" on each of the empty eggshells. Then I strung the six of them together on the piece of roping-twine.

I went, then, into my cabin and shut the door; but instead of locking it I made fast one end of a piece of fine cotton to the hook-eye at the top of the door, and led the free end over a long wire guide, which I arranged above my pillow.

To this end of the cotton I lashed a slightly wetted sponge, which was thus suspended directly above where my face would be when I was lying down. Whoever opened the door would, automatically, lower the wet sponge onto my face and so waken me without a sound.

Fortunately, we have the luxury of a dynamo, so that I could have the cabin lit up at any moment I wished by means of the bunk-switch, which was just to my hand, as I lay in my bunk. The "pearl" legended string of eggs I hung on the knob of the switch.

After seeing that all was in working order, I took a revolver from my lock-up drawer and pushed it under my pillow as a handy adjunct in case of any unpleasantness. Then I turned in and went promptly to sleep. The wet sponge was my night watch.

I woke suddenly, with the chill of an impossible, cold, wet thing upon my face. I reached up swiftly and caught the sponge—and remembered.

Without moving, I stared at the door and saw by the dim light from the saloon beyond that it was being slowly and gently closed. It shut without a sound, and there was an absolute darkness in my cabin, then the vague, soft sound of a bare foot upon the floor, and I knew that someone was in my cabin with me, and was tiptoeing silently towards my bunk.

Very quietly I reached up in the darkness to the switch with my left hand. I unhooked the string of empty eggshells off the knob of the switch and transferred them to my right hand. Then I put up my left again to the switch and waited.

Suddenly I felt something touch me. A hand was feeling gently down my chest, towards my waist. It stopped there and began with infinite gentleness and an equally infinite patience to work at the buckles of my money-belt, which I find it advisable, in my wanderings among the "wits" of humanity, to wear next to my skin.

I waited awhile, lying silent. There was evidently no thought of putting anything so uncomfortable as a knife between my ribs, so I thought it safe to pander somewhat to my curiosity. Possibly, whoever was in my cabin had the impression that I slept with sixty thousand dollars' worth of pearls round my waist! The thought tickled me.

For maybe a quarter of an hour I lay there, extremely awake and very curious to discover how the person in the dark would attempt to get the belt from under me after he had undone all the buckles. There are three of these to the belt, and I counted them as the hidden personage worked them adrift.

As the last buckle was loosed, I was tickled to death, in more ways than one, to find out how I was to be made roll over off the belt; for the infernal and silent personage in the dark reached down one hand to my feet and proceeded gently to tickle the sole of my left foot. I bit my lip to keep from laughing and found that he certainly knew his business; for I instinctively rolled away from him.

Doubtless the plan is known by sneak-thieves to work perfectly on a sleeping person; but I was awake and found myself unable to hold back any longer.

I let out one enormous yell of laughter and in the same instant switched on the light and sat up, holding out the string of blown egg-shells to—Pelter, my Steward!

Yes, it was Pelter, right enough, and he shrivelled where he stood. He backed, quaking, his eyes staring at me, his face the colour of chalk, and all his body arched half sideways, in a very tension of the agony of complete and dreadful surprise. And there I sat in my bunk and roared, still holding out the string of eggshells to him—those "pearls" that made no secret of the fact!

"Ah, Pelter," I said at last, still shaking, "they are yours, with my compliments. I have been expecting you to call." And I held the gorgeous necklace towards him, while his body arched more and more tensely towards the door, with the blind instinct of retreat.

Abruptly, his wit came back into him, and he turned and jumped for the door, tore it open, dashed through and slammed it.

*   *   *   *

This morning I discovered that I am Pelterless!

*   *   *   *

In a way, things are looking a bit serious. I've been searched every time I've gone ashore, and each time they've been pretty near as drastic as the first time. I fancy Monsieur the Treasury Johnny, has his knife especially deep into me. Anyway, if I'd had the pearls on me I should have been caught, as sure as nuts are nuts.

I've done my best, up to the present, to keep my temper, but this kind of thing gets on one's nerves; and it's less the cash now that is keeping me fixed to run the pearls through, as the determination to get the better of the little comic Treasury man. I believe he's begun to dream of me at night. He's been in at the office several times lately and superintended the search himself, which I can see has annoyed McAllister no end. I suppose the only thing is to keep on smiling!

Evening of July 5.

When I went ashore today, I took the six blown eggshells with me, as I knew Mac would be interested, after his warning to keep an eye on Pelter.

"I've brought the six pearls," I said, as soon as I was ushered into the inner room, and I hauled out the string of egg-shells and held them up, so that Mac and the two officers could read the legend on each. Everyone laughed, but they roared when I told them of the way I had treated the Steward. Yet, for all that they were so jolly and friendly, they searched me just as mercilessly as ever.

As I was going to leave the office, after my usual undress rehearsal, the little Treasury official came in.

I looked at MacAllister and winked; then turned towards the doorway.

"Good morning, Sir," I said to the little man as he stood and glared at me. "You were a prophet. Your men have discovered six pearls of unsurpassable size upon me."

"What!" he shouted, and I heard the subordinate officials striving manfully with an inconvenient laughter.

"Where are the pearls, Mr. MacAllister?" called out the high official. "I knew we should catch the scoundrel if we searched him properly every time he went ashore. Let me see them.... You are under arrest!" (This last to me!) "Have you got all six, Mr. MacAllister? Let me see them at once."

"Here they are, Sir," I said. "Not exactly pearls of great price, but undoubtedly of wonderful size and shape!" And I drew out the six blown eggshells and held them out, so that he might admire the fine black inscription on each.

"Allow me!" I said and stepped up to him. But as I made to wreathe the "necklace" about his elderly neck, he lost control and made as if he would strike me.

"The gift is not acceptable?" I asked. "Gratitude is not in you, Sir! Bye-bye!"

And I left, just as MacAllister and the subordinate officials proved unable to rise to sufficiently heroic heights to die silently upon their feet. They crowed, all of them, like a farmyard, and then roared in hopeless unison. I could still hear them roaring as I boarded a street car to go uptown.

As I was coming aboard again this evening I met MacAllister.

"You shouldn't do it, old man!" he said. "You shouldn't, and that's a sure thing! We laughed till we nearly fell down, and then old Andrew Akbotham fell on us. He's got a tongue that would make sulphur taste like cane sugar."

"Sorry," I said. "Where's he live? I'll write and smooth him down a bit."

He gave me the address, and this is the letter I wrote—

"Andrew Akbotham, Esq.,

"Dear Sir,

"I feel that I owe you an apology for my hardly excusable buffoonery towards you. In evidence of my penitence, I beg you to accept as a little proof of my entire freedom from any thought of personal malice towards you the jewel box which accompanies this letter. The contents will interest you the more you examine them. You will find in the box the same six eggshells that I proffered you so uncouthly today. If you look at them closely you will see that they have been cut round the middle very neatly with a sharp razor and afterwards joined again with 'Mells' Lime Cement,' which, being made from ground eggshells, makes a join that is quite invisible, except microscopically.

"If you choose to break open one of the shells you will find inside, attached to the twine which runs through it, a small lump of cobbler's wax. In this, if you examine it, you will find an indentation, such as might be made by a marble, a large pill, or even a fine pearl.

"In each of the eggs you will find a similar pellet of cobbler's wax and a similar indentation—six in all.

"Need I say more, to prove to you the sincerity of my apologies and the truth of my explanations, when I saw that nothing was further from my thoughts than practising mere gratuitous buffoonery upon a man of your years?

"May I beg of you to keep the jewel case and the six eggshells? They have done their work, twice over, as one might say. And I should like to feel that this apology of mine will be remembered long after I, its unworthy author, am forgotten.

"Believe me, dear Sir,

Yours faithfully,

"G. GAULT."

The Painted Lady

S.S. Boston.
April 2nd. Evening.

I HAD A SPLENDID offer made me today. A man came aboard, with what looked like a drawing-board wrapped in brown paper.

He had a letter of introduction from a man who knows me.

"My name's Black, as I guess Mr. Abel's told you in the letter," he said; "I want to talk business with you, Cap'n Gault."

"Go ahead!" I said.

"What I say, goes no further; that's understood, I guess?" he asked. "Mr. Abel gave you a good name, Cap'n, an' he told me a thing or two about you that sounded pretty safe to me."

"I'm mum!" I told him. "If you've murdered someone, it's no concern of mine, and I don't want to hear about it. If it's anything clean, get it off your chest. You'll find me a good listener."

He nodded.

"You know about that 'Mona Lisa' bit of goods?" he asked me.

"The picture?" I said.

He nodded again.

"Well," he said, "they got the wrong one. That's a copy that's been made from the original. It's a mighty good copy. It should be; it cost me over twenty thousand dollars before it was finished. It's so good, you couldn't make 'em believe it isn't the original. I got the original, though, safe and sound; and a patron of mine's mad for it. That's what I came to see you about. I've got to get it taken across and through the U.S.A. customs."

"But you don't tell me that a copy could fool all the art experts who've seen the 'recovered' 'Mona Lisa'?" I said. "Why, the old canvas—"

"Wood, Cap'n," he interpolated.

"It's on wood, is it?" I said. "I'd never realised that. Well, you

323

don't tell me they don't know the kind of wood, and the smell, and the general oldness and the 'seasonedness,' and all the rest of it, of a panel of wood as old as that must be. The very smell of it would be enough to tell them whether it was the original or not.

"And that's not all. Why, the pigments they used, they can't be matched today, so I understand. And how'd you get the 'time tone,' the 'time surface'? Why, man, any one of these things could never be faked properly—not well enough to deceive an expert who knew his business.

"Don't you see, your tale won't wash. All these things put together make a picture as famous as the 'Gioconda' absolutely unforgeable— that is, of course, to an expert."

"Now, Cap'n," he said, "you've had your say, and I will have mine.

"First of all, to get a panel that could not be pronounced anything but genuine, Cap'n, I had the 'Mona Lisa' panel split, using a special machine-saw for the purpose. It was an anxious job, I can promise you. The man who cut it was an expert at his job, and the saw was a specially made ribbon saw, with hair-fine teeth.

"He practised on a dozen model panels before I'd let him split the 'Mona.' Then he put the picture flat on the steel saw-table, and he just skinned off the 'Mona' with no more than an eighth of an inch of wood under her. He did it as easy and smooth as skimming milk; but I just stood and sweated till it was done. He got a hundred dollars for that ten minutes of work, and I guess I got about a hundred extra grey hairs.

"Well, Cap'n, then I took the 'Mona,' and mounted her on a brand-new panel, for she was on a layer of wood so thin that she bent just with picking her up.

"That's how we got the panel for the copy. The copy's painted on the old 'Mona Lisa' panel. Smart, wasn't it? I guess the experts couldn't get past that—what? Not much, Sir!

"Queer, when you come to think of it, Cap'n, that if those French-men only thought to notice it—not that they could, after not seeing the lady for a couple of years—they'd the clue there, in the thinner panel, that the 'Mona's' been doctored!

"Great, I call it! And she'll hang there all through the ages; and people'll come from all parts, and stare and gasp and go away, feeling they've seen only the genuine. And all the time she'll be where all the real stuff's going—in God's own country, Sir—U.S.A.

"And to think a pair of callipers would give the whole show away, if only they'd taken the thickness of the panel *before* a friend of mine lifted her out of the Louvre!"

"That was smart, certainly," I said. "You can spin a good yarn! What about the old pigments, and all the rest of the impossible things, eh?"

"The pigments, Cap'n, cost me exactly fifteen thousand dollars in cold cash. I bought old canvasses of the same period—some of them were not bad, either—and I *scraped* 'em, Sir. Yes, I did, for the pigments that were on 'em. Nearly broke my heart! But this is a big business. Then an old painter I know got the job of his life. He's as clever a man as ever stole a canvas 'cause he hadn't money to pay for it.

"I told him there were five thousand big fat dollars for him the day he'd finished a copy of her on the wooden panel; that's if the copy were so good I couldn't tell one from the other.

"Well, Cap'n, he did it. Three months he took; and when it was finished, *I* couldn't have told one painting from the other, except that the new one wanted 'sunning'—that's a little secret of my own. I do part of it with the sun and coloured glass. I gave her a solid year of that treatment, while she was drying and hardening. Then I'd have defied L. da V. himself to tell one from t'other!"

"But what was the idea of getting this copy made for twenty thousand dollars when you had the real thing?"

"It was for the French government to sneak," he told me.

"What?" I said.

"It was for a plant!" he explained. "It was going to be 'planted' and then an agent of mine was going to approach a picture-dealer and offer to sell it to him—as the real thing, you know.

"And, of course, I knew no dealer on the east side of the duck-pond would look at it. No use to anyone there, except to get 'em into bad trouble. I knew the next thing they'd do would be to lay information, for the sake of the reward and the press notices."

"Well," I asked, "what had you to gain by all that, and what did you gain by getting your agent into the hands of the police?"

"He bungled things!" he told me. "It wasn't my fault he got nabbed."

"But the reason you wanted the authorities to cop the copy you'd spent twenty thousand dollars on?" I asked again. "If you were so anxious for them to have a copy, why didn't you offer to sell it back? They'd have paid a decent sum—quite decent, I should imagine—that's if they couldn't get their hands on you first!"

"That's just the point," he explained. "If I offered to sell back the picture, they'd have approached it in a more suspicious spirit; and I want no blessed suspicions at all, Cap'n. If they thought I was trying to get rid of the original secretly to a dealer, and that they had dropped on me unexpectedly, then their whole frame of mind would be the way I want it to be—see?

"You see, Cap'n, I paid twenty thousand dollars odd to get that copy made, simply for a blind. I'm taking the original out to U.S.A., where I've got a patron for it at five hundred thousand dollars, as I've told you.

"But he won't even look at it, if there's going to be any bother attached. I've to clean up behind me. I'm to let the French government have back what they think is their picture; and then my patron can hang the original in his private gallery, without fear of trouble.

"He's a real collector, and it's sufficient for him to know he's got the original, under his own roof-shades, without wanting to shout the song half across the world, like a society hostess.

"If there are any comments, he'll acknowledge it to be what it isn't—and that's a *copy*. This is bound to go down, as people are convinced the original is clamped up good and solid, back in its old place in the Louvre. Thank God for that sort of collector, I say! They make living possible for people in my business. Now, have you got all the points, Cap'n?"

He grinned so cheerfully, that I had to do the same thing.

"But all the same," I told him, "I'm not available for handling stolen goods, Mr. Black. You'll have to try further up."

"Come now, Cap'n Gault," he said, "and you a good American, too! I guess we've got to have this bit of goods in little old U.S.A. It's too fine for any other nation on earth. You mustn't think it's *only* the dollars I'm thinking of. It it were just the dollars only I'm after, I'd sell it right here, within twenty-four hours, and be shut of all trouble and risk; but it's got to go over to our country, Cap'n, and stay right there till it's acclimatised."

I couldn't help liking the man for that. But I had to stare at him a bit, to size up how much he was honest and how much I was dreaming; but he was honest, right enough; and I felt I'd got to look good and hard, so that I'd not forget what an honest picture-dealer looked like.

"It's a pity you can't put it through, openly, as the original," I said. "You'd have no duty at all to pay then, seeing that it's more than a hundred years old. Anyway, why don't you put the thing through yourself, as a copy? If your customer's going to manage to palm it off to *his* friends (and there's likely to be some experts among 'em) as a copy, why don't you put it through the Customs frankly, as a copy?

There'll be nothing much to bother about in the duty-line on a mere copy by an unknown artist. Shove a fairly good price on it, so they won't think you're trying to 'jew' them, and there you are. Anyway, mister, that'll come a heap cheaper than paying me what I should need, before I'd even look at a job of this sort."

He put his finger to the side of this nose, in French fashion.

"Don't you worry, Cap'n," he replied. "That picture's worth five hundred thousand dollars; and I guess I'm taking no chances at all. You must reckon there's others that guess things about this besides me, and it ain't only the Customs I'm bothering about, but it's a little bunch of crooks that have got to suspecting more than's good for them. And I guess if they can't get a finger in the pie, they're capable of dropping a hint to the New York Customs, just for spite.

"If the Customs put their eyes on the picture, after a hint like that, they'd hold it and communicate with the French authorities, and it'd be all U.P. then, once the two pictures were put together and compared.

"And, anyhow, Cap'n, I reckon there may be a bit of trouble going across, for the gang'll never drop trying until it's 'no go' for them. They'll sail with the picture and me, on the chance of nipping in before we get to the other side. I'd not be surprised if they came across with a proposal to go shares or split, if they can't do me in any other way. Now, what's it to be, Cap'n Gault—are you on, or is it 'no go'?"

I thought for a few seconds, then I answered him.

"I'll do it," I said. "I guess I'd like it to go across to God's country."

"That's good. It's going to belong to the little old U.S.A. What'll your figure be, Cap'n?"

"Five percent," I told him. "That'll be twenty-five thousand dollars."

"Very good, Cap'n," he agreed. "It's a good tough price; but I'll come across all right. I reckon the more you stand to make out of it, the more like you are to do your best. And just what that is I guess every Customs official each side of the pond knows. If you do up to your usual, the New York Customs'll never even smell it. That's why I've come to you; and that's why I don't kick at your figure."

"Where's the picture?" I asked him.

"Here!" he said, almost in a whisper, and patted the wrapped-up drawing-board affair that he held under his arm.

"Bring it along into my cabin, and let's have a look at it," I told him. "I want to see this *smile* that won't come off, that I've heard so much about. Is it anything wonderful?"

"Cap'n," he said, with extraordinary earnestness, "it *is* wonderful!

It's as if one of the old gods had got in some mighty fine work on the panel."

We went along to my cabin, and I shut and locked both doors. Then he unwrapped the thing on the table. I looked at it for a good bit. It was certainly fine and strange.

"It's got something about it that looks as if a clever devil had painted it," I told him. "She's got no eyebrows. That makes her look a bit peculiar and, somehow, slightly abnormal. But it doesn't explain what I mean. It's as if the elemental female smiled out in her face—not what we mean nowadays by the word *woman,* but all that is the essential of the *female.* The smile is conscienceless; not consciously so, but naturally. It's as if the unrestrained female—the 'faun' in the woman—the subtle licence in her—the subtle, yet unbridled, goat-spirit in her was spreading out over her face, like a slow stain. It's the truth about that side of a woman that the best part of a man insists on turning his blind eye to. The painting ought to be called: 'The Uncomfortable Truth!'"

"Cap'n," he said, "for a man that pretends not to understand pictures, you're doing mighty well! I guess you've just put into words a bit that I've felt, but couldn't get unmuddled into plain talk. Anyway, the chief thing that counts just now, is there's five hundred thousand dollars on the table there; and twenty-five thousand of them are yours the day you hand me the painted lady, safe and sound, in Room 86 of the Madison Square Hotel, New York.

"I guess you've got that all plain, Cap'n? Meanwhile, I'll book my passage across with you. I reckon I shall feel easier sleeping in the same ship with her."

"That's all right, Mr. Black," I told him. "If you've got an hour or two to put in, you'll find that chair's comfortable, and that's my brand of whisky in the rack."

"Right you are, Cap'n," he said; and while he was making himself comfortable I began to get out my colours, palette, and brushes.

"You paint, Cap'n?" he asked, over the top of his glass. He seemed surprised.

I nodded towards the oils and water-colours round the bulkheads. He got up with his glass of whisky, and began to go the round, sipping and muttering some astonishment as he journeyed.

"My word, Cap'n!" he said at last, facing round at me, "you sure can paint some! And I guess I'm slinging no cheap flattery. What are you going to do now?"

"I'm going to do an oil sketch of the 'Mona' as a keepsake, right now, and before I hide her for the voyage," I told him. I hauled out a sheet of prepared millboard from my portfolio. "I guess I'd like to remember I once handled the original," I went on; "and I'd like to have a shot at that smile. The trick of it catches me."

"Good for you, Cap'n," he said, quite interested, and set down his whisky, while he propped up the 'Gioconda' in a good light from the glazed skylight above. Then he came round behind me to watch.

I finished the thing—a rough sketch, of course—in about an hour and a half, and Mr. Black seemed to be genuinely impressed.

"Cap'n," he said, "that's good work, you know. You're a mighty queer sort of sea Captain!"

"Mr. Black," I said, as I fetched out my pipe, "you're a mighty queer sort of picture-dealer!"

But he couldn't see it.

April 8th. At sea.

Mr. Black's an interesting man to talk to, but he's got the itch to know where I've hidden his blessed picture. I've explained to him, though, that when a secret *has* to be kept, it's better kept by one head than by any other number you could think of in a month.

Meanwhile, I've found that he's a good taste for other things beside pictures. As he put it:

"Cap'n, I'm no one-horse show in the manner of liking good things. A pretty woman I like, and if she's good, so much the better."

"They're rare," I told him.

"I grant you that, Cap'n," he said. "As rare as a high-pressure man with a sound temper. That's why they're worth finding. Well, I like a pretty woman, a good violin solo, a good whisky, a good picture, and a good patron of art. And I reckon the five mean life!"

I smiled, and I said nothing, but when he came up to my chart-room today I introduced him to a pretty young American of the name of Lanny, who has made a point of palling on with me, and has come up to look at my pictures.

When he came in she was criticising my copy of the 'Gioconda,' and after I had introduced him she hauled him into the discussion, willy-nilly.

"I think that's a fine piece of work of the Captain's," she said. "But you sure ought to see the original in the Louvre, Mr. Black. Captain Gault's done fine, but the original just gives you shivers all done your spine."

"I've seen it, Miss Lanny," he assured her, "and I agree with you. It's a mighty wonderful thing. But Cap'n Gault don't reckon it's good art."

"What!" cried Miss Lanny. "Captain Gault, you don't tell me that?"

"It's not good art, Miss Lanny," I said. "It's true, but it shows the ugly side of a woman's character."

"That's downright insulting, Captain," she said warmly. "I reckon it shows what the great artist meant it to show. It shows the delicate subtlety and refined spirituality of woman. There's more in 'La Gionconda's' smile than in the laughter of a hundred men."

"I hope you're right, Miss Lanny," I said— "for the sake of the hundred men."

This talk occurred this morning, and I put the stopper on them, for it was getting a bit too serious. And, anyway, when there's a pretty girl in one's chart-room, who looks as if she's good as gold and chock-full of hell-fire all in one and the same moment, one is apt to get fidgety.

April 10th. Night. Late.

Great excitement; at least, Mr. Black's in a state.

He's spent most of the last two days spooning Miss Lanny in *my* chart-house, while I've made shots at doing sky effects in water-colours.

I call that cool, to try and cut me out with the young lady—though I can't say that she's seemed backward.

However, this sort of thing has to be paid for.

About an hour ago Mr. Black sent word by a steward, would I come along to his cabin? Lord! The mess! Someone, or several, I should think, had been through his place, and left it like a wooden township after a cyclone.

His box lids had all been ripped off; his bed had been pulled to pieces, and his mattress had been cut open; his wardrobe (he's got a suite de luxe, off the saloons) was ripped away from the bulkhead, and was lying on its side, and the mirror had been broken clean out, and lay on the carpet.

The marble top had been lifted off the washstand, and the carpet had been pulled up in several places, and was ripped across, as if with a pair of shears.

In his dining-room, the Louis XVI sofa had met bad trouble, and yielded up its springs, much tapestry and the ghost, all at once. The writing-table had its top lifted off, and another table had evidently seen trouble. The heavy pile carpet here was divorced both from itself and the floor, and lay in heaps, literally cut to pieces.

In the bathroom, some of the tiles had been forced out, as if the human cyclone had meant to make sure of what lay below; and in the dressing-room things had equally not been neglected.

I sat down on the wreckage of Mr. Black's bed and roared. He just stood and stared.

"You sure see the funny side of a thing, Cap'n!" he said at last.

"This'll pay you for cutting me out with my lady friends!" I told him, when I could breathe again. "I suppose you've been up spooning on the boat-deck, instead of coming down and turning in at a reasonable hour like a Christian."

He looked sheepish enough to please me.

"Providence, Mr. Black," I told him, "is always careful to leave the dustpan on the stairs, when it sees we're getting too 'aughty." Then I got serious. "Missed anything?" I asked him.

"Not a thing yet," he said, "but it'll take a bit of straightening up."

I rang for his servant, and sent a message to the Chief Steward.

Fortunately the next suite was empty, and we moved Mr. Black's gear into it. Just the three of us; for I wanted no talk among the passengers, until the trip is finished. That sort of thing is better kept quiet.

The Chief Steward locked up the whole suite, and we knew then there could be no talk; for Black's servant had not been allowed in to see the place since the trouble.

"Now, Mr. Black," I said, "come along up to my place for a talk."

When we reached my cabin, Mr. Black had a whisky to pick him up, and we talked the thing over; though I saw he didn't see as far into it as I had done already.

"Anyway," I told him, "you've lost nothing; and now they'll leave you alone. They've proved the thing isn't in your possession. If it had been, they'd sure have had it—eh?"

"Sure!" he said soberly. "Are you mighty certain it's safe where you've put it?"

"Safe till the old ship falls to pieces!" I told him. "All the same, they must be a pretty determined lot, whoever they are; and I ex-pect they'll be paying my quarters a visit if they get the half of a show. By Heaven, I'd like 'em to try it on!"

April 11th. Afternoon.

Mr. Black and Miss Lanny spent the morning up with me in my chart-room. The talk turned on a water-colour I was making of the distant wind-on-spray effects, and I hit out once or twice at Miss Lanny's critical remarks.

"That's pretty good, Captain Gault," she said, looking over my shoulder; "but I like your copy of the 'Gioconda' better; though you haven't got the da Vinci ability to peep underneath, and see the abysmal deeps of human nature."

"Dear lady," I said, "may I light a cigarette in your presence, and likewise offer you one?"

She accepted, and Mr. Black also.

"Da Vinci was a great painter," I said.

"I'm sure," she answered.

"But he wasn't a great artist. Understand, I'm judging him just on the 'Mona,' which is the only thing of his I've seen, but which is supposed to be his greatest work."

"What do you mean?"

That was a plain question, and I answered it plainly:

"The da Vinci Johnny was too busy looking out for his abysmal deeps of human nature to remember the heights," I told her. "He was like a painter with his eye glued into a sewer, painting and sweating himself into eternal fame—that is for other perverts like himself; and for the big blind, uncaring crowd that follows the shouting of the perverts, because they don't know enough to shout tosh frankly.

"Now the value of the 'Mona' must be put at a high figure, maybe ten million dollars in the *open* market." (I grinned cheerfully in the back of my mind.) "But if it's worth that, it's worth it as a painting—not as a *complete* work of art! It is the product of a twisted art and a very great handicraft."

"It is a perfect work of great and wondrous art!" said Miss Lanny. "I like to see how piffly little amateurs try to teach the master!"

I laughed at her bad temper.

"Dear lady," I said, "you admit my copy of the 'Gioconda' is not so bad," and I beckoned to where I had hung it on the bulkhead, under the skylight.

"By the side of the original," she smiled at me, "it is as a ginger-pop bottle beside a Venetian glass wonder. You've sure got a hearty, healthy conceit of yourself, Captain! Why, Captain, you've painted your copy with eyebrows!" she added suddenly.

"Yes," I said. "I like the effect better. I've no use for those ab-normal effects. Besides, it's more decent!"

"Goodness!" muttered Mr. Black, "you sure are cracked today, Cap'n."

"'The Mona,'" I asserted once more, "is a twisted fragment of a woman—the produce of a twisted nature. I understand, I guess, because I'm a bit twisted myself; it's only in odd moments that I can fight down the twist in me, which makes me see every woman worse even than she is.

"There, you see! I can't stop slamming at 'em; not even when I'm out to explain."

I had to laugh at myself; and the tension eased out of the two of them. I had watched the softer look of capable feminine interest supersede the incapable critical light in Miss Lanny's eyes, as I had explained my own shortcomings.

"Cap'n Gault's sure running amuck, every time a woman's on the carpet!" said Mr. Black. "I guess, Miss Lanny, he's like a number of men, he's gone and got fond of a bad 'un; some time or other she's scorched the youngness out of his soul. I know!"

He wagged his head at me.

"The only reason he'll talk about the 'Mona' is because she's a woman, bless her," he said. "But, you know, Cap'n, you'll sure have to quit going on the rampage like that, or it'll be getting a habit."

Miss Lanny reached out her hand for another cigarette, and then bent towards me for a light.

"Was she a very bad woman, Captain Gault?" she said, under her breath. "She must have been!" She looked up into my eyes, through the smoke of her cigarette. "I'm sorry you've had that sort of experience of women," she went on, still in an undertone, and still looking into my eyes. "You ought sure to know a really nice woman; she would heal you up."

"Why?" I asked. And then: "Do you reckon you're qualified to act the part of a kind healer, dear lady?"

"I'd not mind trying," she said, still in a low tone.

"Why," I said out loud, so that Mr. Black could hear where he sat, over by the open doorway, "in your way, you're just as bad! You say a thing like that, in a tone to make me think you're a stainless angel of pity and compassionate womanhood, and at bottom you're just another of them! You may be virtuous—I don't say you aren't; I believe you are—but you're up to all the eternal meanness and everlasting deceit of the woman! You come here, posing as my friend, as the friend of Mr. Black, chummy and friendly with us, even to the point of losing your temper, and all the time you're one of a gang of thieves aboard this ship, trying to diddle Mr. Black or me out of a picture you and your pals think is aboard."

As I spoke, she had whitened slowly, until I thought she must surely faint. And she sat there, without saying a word, the smoke curling up from her cigarette between her fingertips, and her eyes looking at me dumbly and big and dark through the thin smoke.

Mr. Black had stood up and taken a quick step towards me, an incredulous anger on his face, as I had proceeded to formulate my charge against Miss Lanny; but he had checked at my mention of the picture, and now he was staring in a stunned sort of way at the girl. We were both looking at her, but she never moved, and she never ceased to look at me in that speechless fashion.

"You allowed Mr. Black to make love to you last night, late, so that you could keep him up on the boat-deck while your friends ransacked his suite. And now, as you realise that Mr. Black has not got the picture, you and your friends suppose that I must have it, and you have been directed to divert your valuable attentions to me. If necessary, I don't doubt that you meant to encourage a little love-making on my part up on the boat-deck or elsewhere tonight while an attempt was made on my cabin.

"But I assure you, dear Madam, that where a lady is concerned, it has been my rule in life to avoid making one of a crowd. Also, as Captain of this vessel, I have facilities for keeping an eye on things which might surprise you and your friends.

"In proof of this, let me mention the names of your gang. They are Messrs. Tillosson, Vrager, Bentley, and finally, Mr. Alross, your husband.

"I had the names of three of them before we had been at sea for twenty-four hours, and now I think I may say I can put my finger on the whole lot of you.

"It is quite within my power to cause the arrest of you and your party, but there is no need.

"Neither Mr. Black nor I have any fear of what your friends can do, for, let me tell you, the only 'Mona Lisa' aboard this ship is my own copy, which you see hanging up there on the bulkhead.

"Surely you did not suppose that if Mr. Black has, or had, a va-lu-able picture to transmit to New York, he would advertise the fact to people of your sort by traveling in the same vessel with it!

"That is almost all I have to say. You had better go now. Provided I receive from your party before tonight the sum of one hundred and two pounds, fifteen shillings (which is the Chief Steward's estimate of the damage done to Mr. Black's suite last night), I shall allow affairs to pass, and your party may land free in New York.

"But, if the money is not delivered before six o'clock tonight, and if afterwards I have any further trouble with Messrs. Tillosson, Vrager, Bentley, Alross or yourself, I shall order the arrest of the en-tire party, and shall hand you all over to the police when we enter New York."

She had spoken not a single word. Only once had she shown any sign of feeling, and that was when I announced my knowledge of her relationship to Mr. Alross, a tall, thin, blonde man, of quiet manners and an unhappy skill at cards. Then the hand which held the cigarette had begun to shake a little; but, beyond this, never a sign of the shock, except the absolutely ghastly whiteness of her face. She certainly is a woman of nerve, and good pluck, too, I grant her.

Then she stood up suddenly, and what do you think she said?

"Captain, your cigarettes are as treacherous as you seem to imagine all women to be. See how it's burnt me while I was listening to your scolding. I must run away now."

And she turned and walked out of the chart-house as calmly as if she had just been if for one of her usual chats.

"How's that for some?" I said to Mr. Black. "Let me tell you, man, I admire that woman. She's got the real female brand of pluck, and full strength at that. She's stunned half dead at the present moment, yet she carried it off."

Mr. Black was all questions, and he wanted to know why I told them the picture wasn't aboard.

"I told them what I told them," I said, "in the gentle hope that they may try to believe it, and so not consider it worthwhile to lay information with the Customs, which is a thing they'd do in a moment, as you know yourself, just to make things ugly for us, and to ease their own petty spite."

"Why not arrest them?" he asked.

"Don't want any unnecessary 'Mona Lisa' talk in New York, do you?"

"My oath; no!" he said.

"And now they know I'm onto the crowd of them, bound to walk a bit like Agag, eh?" I said. "No, I guess we'll have no more trouble with 'em this side of New York. And I bet they pay up within the hour."

April 12th. Night.

I was wrong in one respect and right in the other. The money was sent up to me by a steward inside of half an hour, and I sent back a formal receipt.

But we have not seen the end of our troubles about the picture, for the gang approached Mr. Black quite openly last night, and told him that if he'd let them come in on a quarter share of the profits, they'd hold their tongues and give him all the assistance they could. If he said no, then the New York Customs were going to get the tip as soon as ever the search officers came aboard.

They told him quite plainly that they knew the picture was aboard, and that they were satisfied I was the one who had it hidden away. But, as they put it to him, it was one thing to hide contraband jewels, like small packets of pearls, of which a hundred thousand dollars' worth could go into one cigar, but that I could never hope to hide from the Customs, if they were put on the scent, a thing the size of the 'Mona,' which, being painted on a panel of wood, could not be rolled up small like a picture on canvas, etc.

They quite worked on poor old Mr. Black's feelings. I guess he may be some expert at picture stealing, like any other dealer, but he's out of it when it comes to real nerve—the kind that's wanted for running stuff through the Customs.

However, I've got him pacified, and I guess he'll manage now to keep a stiff upper-lip. I pointed out to him that a twenty-thousand-ton ship is a biggish affair, and there are quite some hiding places aboard of her, and that I know them all.

I told him, in good plain American, that the picture would not be found.

"You needn't fear they'll start to break the ship up looking for it!" I told him. "Ship-breaking is an expensive job. Don't you get fretful. They'll never find her where I've put her!"

April 13th. Evening.

We docked this morning, and the gang did their best to do us down. I reckon they'd guessed I wasn't keen to arrest them; and they just put the Customs wise to the whole business before they went ashore—that is, as far as they had it sized up.

Well, next thing I knew the chief searcher was in my place demanding 'Mona Lisas,' as if they were stock articles; but I disabused him to the best of my ability.

"No, Sir," I told him. "The only 'Mona Lisa' picture we're carrying is the one there on the bulkhead; and I guess you can have that for fifty dollars right now, and take it home. I reckon that's a good painting now, don't you, mister, for an amateur?"

But I couldn't enthuse him; not up to a sale! He was out for big things, it seemed by his talk; so I let him search.

They're still at it, and Mr. Black, last I saw of him as he went ashore, was looking about as anxious as a man who's bet someone else's last dollar on a horse race.

April 14th.

Still searching.

Still searching.

Mr. Black sent a messenger down aboard this morning to ask when "it" was going to come.

I swore; for if that note had got into the wrong hands the game would have been all up. I've warned him to keep away from the ship, and not to communicate with me in any way. I'll act as soon as it's safe.

I decided to give him a heart-flutter as a lesson to be patient.

"Look here," I said to the hotel messenger, and I pulled down the cardboard on which was the copy I'd painted of the 'Mona,' and handed it across to him. "Take this ashore," I told him. "Go to a picture dealer's, and tell them to frame it in a cheap frame, and then send it up to A. Black, Esq., Room 86, Madison Square Hotel, with the compliments of Captain Gault. Tell them to wrap it up well as if it were something valuable. Here's a dollar for you, my son. Tell them he'll pay! When you see Mr. Black, tell him that 'it'—mind you say 'it'—is coming! It is!"

When he had gone, I sat down and roared at poor Black's digestion when he found what "it" amounted to. I guess I'll not be bothered with him now until I'm ready to see him.

I went ashore to see Mr. Black this evening. The Customs nabbed me en route, as usual, and I had a search that would have unmasked and unearthed a postage stamp. But they needn't fear. I'm not carting 'Mona Lisas' ashore in the thick of this hue and cry!

When I saw Mr. Black it was for the first time since he left the ship, and he rushed at me.

"Where is it?" he asked. He looked positively ill.

"Dear man," I said, "I don't hawk the 'Mona' around with me. Perhaps that's what you want"—and I pointed to the copy of the 'Mona' in its cheap frame which stood on the top of a bookcase.

"Quit it!" he snapped, almost ugly; but I only laughed at him.

Then I took out my hanky, and a bottle of solution. I took the picture down and put it on the table, wet my hanky with the solution, and wiped the picture over gently but firmly.

The eyebrows came away; also one of two other parts where I had laid my fake paint on pretty thick.

"There's the 'Mona,' Mr. Black," I said; "and I guess you owe me twenty-five thousand dollars."

He looked; then he yelled; yes, he fairly yelled. First his delight, then his questions. I endured the first, and answered the second.

"You saw me paint a picture, didn't you?" I asked.

"Sure!" he said.

"Well, that's in England, for a *keepsake,*" I said. "Afterwards, I took the 'Mona,' soaking her off the board-backing you had glued her to, and remounted her on cardboard. Then I painted her a pair of eyebrows with fake paint. Also I touched up one or two other parts of the picture, and you and Miss Lanny spent most of the voyage criticising the immortal da Vinci.

"Miss Lanny called him even worse things than I did. She told me, if I remember right, that the painting was like a ginger-pop bottle compared with Venetain glass!

"I think I said he was not a big artist; and as for you, you looked as if you backed up what Miss Lanny said. Altogether, poor old da Vinci had a lot of hard things said against him. And all the time his masterpiece, plus a pair of eyebrows, and some surface polish, was looking down at us from the bulkhead. I offered her to the Customs officer for fifty dollars, but I couldn't get him to bid.

"Yes, Mr. Black, I've some enjoyed myself this trip. That's what I call doing the thing in style.

"Thanks; yes, twenty-five thousand dollars is the figure. I guess we've got to celebrate this—what?"

The Adventure of the Garter

S.S. *Edric,*
January 17.

I'M BACK PASSENGER CARRYING, and I suppose I'm a bit of a fool; but there's a certain young lady aboard, who's managed to twist me round her finger more than I should have imagined possible a few days ago, when we left Southampton.

She's next to me at the head of my table, and we've rather cottoned on to each other. Indeed, I'll admit I like her that well, that I've broken my general rule, never to allow a passenger up on the lower bridge; for she's been up there with me several times lately, and I feel a bit of an ass; for I guess my officers are sure to be poking fun at my expense, among themselves. A ship's Captain should keep his lady friendships ashore, if he hopes to have things run smooth aboard.

She's a dainty little woman, with pretty hands and feet, and heaps of brown hair. Looks about twenty-two; but I'm old enough to know she's probably about thirty. She's too wise for twenty-two. Knows when to keep quiet; and that's a thing; twenty-two is generally too bubbly, or too much of a know-all, as the case may be, to have learnt.

"Captain Gault," she said to me this morning, after we had walked the lower bridge for the better part of two hours, "what's in this little house here, you're always going into?"

"That's my chart-room, Miss Malbrey," I said. "It's where I do most of my nautical work."

"Won't you take me in and show me?" she asked, in a pretty way she has. She hesitated a moment; then she said, a little awkwardly: "There's something I want to talk to you about, Captain Gault. I simply must go somewhere where I can talk to you."

"Well," I replied, "if I can be of any service, I shall be downright pleased. Come along in and look at my working den; and talk as much as you like."

I guess that shows she can wrap me round her finger, more than is

339

good for me; for I've made it a rule for years, to keep my chart-room strictly private and strictly for ships' work. At least, I mean I've tried to!

But there you are! That's what happenes to the best of us, when a lass takes our fancy. They get us on our soft side, and we're like tabbies round a milk saucer. As MacGelt, an old Engineer of mine, used to say: "It's pairfec'ly reediclous; but I canna say nay to a wumman, once she's set me wantin' to gi'e her a bit hug." And there you have the Philosophy of the Ages in a nutshell! At least some of it.

Now see how things came about. We'd no more than got inside the chart-room, than Miss Malbrey asked me to close the door.

"Please turn your back a moment, Captain, will you? I sha'n't be a minute," she said.

The next thing I knew, she called out to me that I could look round. And when I did so, she was shaking her skirt down straight with her right hand, and holding out to me something in her left which I saw at once was a garter, of surprisingly substantial make.

"Take it, Captain," she said, looking up at me, and blushing a little. "I'm going to beg you to do me a very great favour indeed. See! Feel it. Do you feel those cut-out places inside, and the hard things in them?... Surely, Captain, you know what it is."

"Yes," I said, rather soberly. "I know what it is, Miss Malbrey. It's simply a jewel-runner's garter. I'm sorry. I don't like to think of a woman like you doing this sort of thing—"

She waved her hand to me to stop.

"Listen a moment!" she said. "Do listen, Captain Gault. This is to be my very last trip with the sparklers. I've made up my mind to drop it, for good. And I should never have troubled you about it, only there's one of the Treasury spies aboard, and they've spotted me; and I shall simply be caught; and oh, I don't know what to do, if you won't help me, Captain Gault. You're so clever at running the stuff through. You've never been caught. I've heard lots of times about you, and the way the Customs never can catch you with the goods. Won't—won't you just this once, to save me from being caught, run this through for me? I promise you it will be for the last time. I shall never try to run stuff in again. I've made enough to live on quietly; and now I guess I want to end it all. Will you help me, Captain Gault? Promise me you will?"

What else could I do? I promised, and now I'm booked to run this pretty lady's stuff through, willy-nilly; and never a thought does she seem to have that I may get caught, and suffer fine and maybe imprisonment. But I certainly don't mean to get "catched," if you know anything about it!

"Where are you going to hide it, Captain? Do trust me," she said.

"I never show my pet hiding-places to anyone," I told her. "You see, my dear young lady, if ever you have to keep a secret, keep it to yourself; that's my rule. If I told first one person and then another, where I hide some of the trifles I sometimes take ashore duty-free in New York, why I guess I should be in bad trouble pretty soon."

"But I'm a trustable sort of person, aren't I, Captain Gault?" she assured me. "And I *can* keep secrets. Why, if I couldn't, I'd never have put anything over on the U.S.A. Treasury. I've never once been caught and it's only through an accident that I've become suspected. But I don't care. I'm tired of it; and I'm going to stop, really and truly, and be good and settle down. Now do be a dear man, and let me be *the* privileged one person in the world, and let me see your famous hiding-place that all the Customs officers are sure exists; but which they can never find. Now do, Captain."

"Miss Malbrey," I said, "a man's but a poor, weak thing, in the hands of a pretty woman; if you will forgive an honest compliment—"

"Gee!" she interrupted, laughing right away down in the back of her eyes. "I'll forgive you anything, Captain, pretty near, that is, if you'll make me the only other person in the world who knows the truth of the great mystery."

"Well," I said, "you'll have to give me your solemn word you'll keep it a secret till the end of your life."

"Sure, Captain Gault. I'll die on the rack first," she told me, twinkling at my seriousness. "Now be a good man and show me. I declare I'm all on the quiver with wondering where it is. Is it down in the hold, or where?"

"Miss Malbrey," I said slowly, "you're standing within six feet of a human miracle of a hiding-place."

"What? Where, now?" she asked, staring round and round in a way that she surely knew was disturbingly taking to a plain sailor-man.

"See," I answered. "You shall open it yourself. You see that the thin, steel beams over your head are not cased with wood, as they are in the cabins and saloons. They're just plain, small, solid steel T-girders, with no size about them, you would say, to hide anything—eh?

"Well, now," I continued, "look at the 'beam' just above your head, and count the square-headed bolts that go through the flange on the forrard side of the beam, up into the deck that makes the roof of the house. Stand on this chair. I will steady you. Now! The seventh bolt-head. Take it between your finger and thumb and see if you can turn it to your left… Can you?"

"Yes," she said, with a little gasp of effort. "Just a teeny, weeny bit…. But nothing's happened!" she added in a disappointed voice.

"Ah, believe me, dear lady, that's just the beauty of this hiding-place," I said. "If a Customs searcher happened on that bolt-head and twisted it a little, as you have done, he would merely suppose that it was a loose bolt, because nothing would happen to make him think otherwise. But let me help you off the chair. Now come along to the other end of the beam. See, I twist the second bolt-head here, close to the side, and now I can lift out a bit of the steel flange here, right in the center of the beam, with a row of false bolt-heads attached. Look! Do you see the hollow in the deck planks which the flange covers? There's room there to hide a hundred thousand dollars' worth of pearls or stones.

"Now do you realise the cunning of it all? Before this bit of removable steel flange can be shifted, even a hundredth part of an inch, the seventh bolt on the starboard side has to be turned to the left; then one has to go across to port, and turn the second, from the side of the house, to the right. Then one has to come here to the center of the beam, and catch hold of the twenty-fourth bolt from the starboard side, and pull outwards, evenly, and there you are. When it's closed, it is almost microscopically invisible. I tell you, Miss Malbrey, the man who thought out that dodge, and had the old beam taken away, and that doctored one fitted in place of it, was a smart chap, and no mistake!"

"And that man was you, sure enough, Captain Gault," she said, laughing, with her pert little head turned on one side, and clapping her two small hands.

"You flatter me, my dear lady!" I answered her; and refused to tell her whether I was the one who'd had the beams altered, or not. All the same, the notion is a smart one; and I pride myself on it; which is certainly one way of letting the cat out of the bag!

"Ah! Well, Captain Gault, you're sure one smart man!" she told me, when she had helped me hide the "smuggler's garter" in the recess above the beam flange. "I'd never have thought of a notion like that. I guess I'd better run away now, and take Toby for a run, before you get tired of me. Isn't he a darling dearum, now. Kiss me, pet!"

This, perhaps, it may be as well to explain, was not a direct invitation to me; but was addressed to her pet dog, Toby; a toy pom, which had become quite friendly with me; but I've no use for it. I abominate lap-dogs; but I've not said so to the young woman!

"Miss Malbrey," I said, "I'm getting quite jealous of that dog!"

And by this speech you may gather that I had slightly lost my head. I can't say I've quite got it back, even at this present writing. She's a confoundedly taking young woman!

January 18.

Mr. Allan Jarvis, the Chief Steward, came up to see me this morning. He's a man I trust; which is more than I do most people. We both hail from the same town, and when we're alone together we drop the Mr. Jarvis and the Captain Gault. It's just plain Jarvis and Gault, as it should be, between men who are friends and who have helped one another put through more than one odd deal that had money at the bottom of it.

"Look here, Gault," he said, as he lit one of my cigars, "you're going pretty strong with the young lady in Number 4 cabin."

"You don't say, old man," I replied. "Well?"

"It's just this," he told me. "Don't trust her too much. I've a notion she's playing a game with you, that's got more than an odd kiss or so at the bottom of it. Look at this, before you start to cuss me for butting in!"

He handed me across a folded newspaper clipping, headed—

"AMERICA OPENS A NEW PROFESSION FOR WOMEN.

"The Treasury Recruits Twelve Pretty Women to Play I-spy-I on the Trans-Atlantic Jewel-Runners."

"Well!" I said, "what of it? You're not going to suggest to me that Miss Malbrey's one of them—"

"Open the thing, man!" he interrupted. "Unfold it!"

I was doing so, as he spoke, and now I saw what he meant. There, on the cutting, was a photo of a pretty girl, looking at me, and the girl was most extraordinarily like Miss Malbrey (Alicia Malbrey, she's told me is her name).

"It's not her, Jarvis, man," I said. "I'll not believe it. I just won't believe that sort of thing of her. Why, man, look at the face; the eyes are too close for her, and this is a younger woman altogether. And, besides, it's impossible. Why, she's just the opposite to anything of this kind. Why, she's a—"

I pulled up short, for I had nearly told Jarvis that she was as much a smuggler, in a small way, as either he or I.

I pondered a moment, whether I might not tell him; but before I could decide, he chipped in again—

"Poor old chap!" he said. "You sure got it bad!" And that shut me up.

"Have it your own way," I told him. "But I happen to have a special reason for *knowing* that the little lady's all right."

"Ah!" he said, getting up, "I know the special reason well enough, Gault. We all feel that way, when we're a bit gone on some woman. The worst of it is, they've generally too much brutal sense, not to use our little feelings to their own advantage! Ha! Ha! old man! I love to quote your own vinegar sayings against yourself!"

And with that, he left me, taking his beastly cutting with him. All the same, I've had some pretty fierce thinks; but I've decided the *evidence* is quite insufficient to condemn my dainty lady of the laughing eyes. Oh, Lord, haven't I gone and got it properly!

January 19.

"Don't you just love my doggie, Captain Gault?" said Miss Alicia Malbrey, to me this afternoon.

"Well," I answered, "I suppose, Miss Malbrey, there's all sorts of ways of looking at things."

"Now you're just dodging me, Captain, and I won't have it!" she told me. "You do love my Toby boykins, don't you? Tell me honest true."

"No, Miss Malbrey," I replied. "If you want an honest answer, I do not like Toby or any other kind of lap-dog. To my mind, a dog is an unsuitable object for a woman's arms; and a woman who kisses and nurses a dog, cannot, it seems to me, prize herself as highly as she should, or she would shrink from such physical intimacies with what is, after all, simply a stunted little animal, less useful than a cow, and less courageous than a common rat!"

"Captain Gault," she rapped back at me, "you're sure forgetting yourself. Let me tell *you*, a dog's as good as a man, any day!"

"There's no accounting for tastes, Miss Malbrey," I said, smiling a bit. "We men do not hug and kiss our dogs. We consider a woman pleasanter and more suitable."

"I should think so!" she interrupted. "Do you mean to say you'd compare a woman with a dog, Captain Gault?"

"That's just what I refused to do," I said. "You see, dear lady, you began by asking me, did I like lap-dogs—or something to that effect; and now, because I like to think they are inferior to women, you're belabouring me and pretending that I've been saying just the opposite! Oh, woman! Woman! In our hours of ease—! Now, if, instead of asking me what I thought of your lap-dog, you'd asked me what I thought of you—why, then, lady of the winsome face, methinks I would have never ended the nice things I could have said. Why, of all the dainty-faced—"

I paused, to hunt round for words to describe further.

"Yes, Captain Gault?" she prompted.

I looked at her. There was not a sign of anger now in her face; only a sort of *waiting*—I could almost have thought it was a kind of triumphant expectancy.

"Yes?" she said again, scarcely breathing the word.

I looked at her in the eyes, and suddenly I realised that I was being allowed to look right down into them; and a woman only does that when she is either luring or loving.

Was she flirting with me, or did she really care? I put it to the test, so I caught her up in my arms and kissed her full on the lips.

"Oh!" she said, with a gasp.

A minute later, she laughed, breathlessly.

"I knew you'd not be able to hold out against me much longer!" she said.

She laughed again, in her quaint, pretty way.

"Now, shut your eyes a moment, Captain, dear, and see what love will bring you!" she said; and brushed my eyes gently shut with her small hands.

There was a rustle of skirts; the rattle of the bells on Toby's collar; a faint creaking, and than a dainty, mocking laugh—

"That's as much as is good for you for one day, Captain Gault," came her voice; and I opened my eyes just in time to see her closing the door.

New York,
January 20.

My Chief Officer came along to my cabin this morning, after I had interviewed the officer of the Customs. My cabin had just been searched; and I had declared all that I meant to declare!

"I don't know if this concerns you, Sir," he said; "but it seems as if it might. The breeze blew it out of one of the Customs men's hands, and I put my foot on it before they saw where it had got to. I thought you'd better see it at once."

"It does concern me, very much indeed, Mr. Graham," I said grimly, as I read the crumpled note he had handed me.

"Treacherous little devil!" I heard him mutter under his breath;

and I knew that he also guessed who had written the note. It was fairly brief and brutal, and quite comprehensive—

"Look in the Captain's chart-room. Middle beam. Turn seventh bolt, from starboard side, to left; and second bolt from port side, to right. Then catch hold of the twenty-forth bolt, from starboard side, and twenty-ninth, from port side, near the middle of the beam, and pull out sideways. A part of the flange will slide out; and there is a recess cut in the deck flanks above. The diamonds are there in a 'garter.' Remember, I am not to be mentioned in the case at all. He's a slippery customer; but I guess I've got him nailed down solid this time.—No. 7. F."

"Perhaps there's time yet, Sir, to go one better than her," said my Chief Officer aloud. "They'll have to go back to her for fresh instructions, now they've lost this paper. Can't you get up to the chart-room and nobble the stuff, before they get there? You may be in time, yet. Heave the blessed stuff over the side, rather than let them do you in, Sir. That's what I'd do!"

I looked at him. I daresay he thought I was a little dazed. I fancy I shook my head; for this was as bad as my worst suspicions could have suggested it. In that moment, I was thinking far less of the "trap" the Customs had prepared so carefully for me, than of the completeness of the ruin of my faith in women in general.

"Mr. Graham," I said, "a man's a preposterous ass if he hasn't learnt to mistrust any woman, by the time he's thirty!"

"Yes, Sir," he answered, seriously enough. "Unless she's his mother."

"Ah, just so!" I said. "Unless she's mother. But they can't all be our mothers; confound it! I'll get up to my chart-room. No, don't come, Mr. Graham. It's too late now to undo what's been done. . . . The treachery of it! My God! The cold, brutish treachery of it!"

I reached the chart-room, and peeped in through the after window. The Customs were already in the place; four men were in there. And suddenly I heard Miss Malbrey's voice. I could see her now, over by the starboard side, with her back to me. She was directing operations, as cold-bloodedly as you please. Evidently, they had sent for her, now they had lost her note, to explain how to work the secret catches in the steel beam.

"No," I heard her say. "The seventh bolt from the starboard side. Twist it to the left. That's right. Yes. The second from the port side— To the right. Now, Mace, the twenty-fourth from the starboard and twenty-ninth from the port. Do get a move on you. I don't want the Captain to catch me here. Pull—"

I opened the door and stepped inside.

"Sorry if I'm a little premature, Miss Malbrey," I said, "May I ask what you are doing in my chart-room?"

I held the door open for her to pass out. But she took no notice of me; only the cheek and ear that I could see were a burning red. I was grimly pleased that she felt some sort of shame for herself.

"I must ask you to leave my chart-room, Miss Malbrey," I said quietly. "This part of the ship is not open to passengers."

"Aw! Quit it, Cap'n!" said the man she had called Mace, who was standing on my chart-table, lugging clumsily at the bolt-heads. "We've got you at last, I guess, Cap'n; an' you don't come any of that tall stuff over us. . . . Is these two the right ones, Miss?" he finished, looking over his shoulder at Miss Malbrey.

"Yes," she said, not much above a whisper. "Pull out parallel with the deck, evenly—"

"It's coming," said the man. "We sha'n't be long now, Cap'n, before we has you just where we been wantin' you this two years, an' more!"

I said nothing; but walked across to my telephone, and rang up the Chief Stewardess.

"Please come up to my chart-room at once, Miss Allan," I said. "Bring a couple of stewardesses with you."

I hung up the receiver, just as the man on the table worked the sliding portion of the flange clear of its sockets. He put up his forefinger, and ran it along the recess in the deck-planking above, which he had laid bare. He was obviously disappointed, and made it clear to every one.

"Aw!" he said. "Watcher givin' us, Miss! This is sure a bum do! There's nothin'! Just plain nothin' at all!"

"Stop talking foolish!" said Miss Malbrey, in a voice sharp enough to show the kind of metal she was. She made one jump to a chair, and then onto my chart-table. She pushed the man named Mace to one side....

"It's gone!" she called out, suddenly, a moment later, in a voice that was half a scream. "It *was* there! A proper runner's garter. There were five thousand dollars' worth of stones!"

She whirled round on me.

"You wicked man!" she called out, in a thorough little fury. "You thief! You thief! What have you done with my stones...."

"'Ssh!" said one of the other search officers. "There's someone coming. They're the Captain's good we are looking for, Miss. Don't you worry yourself, and talk rash. You mind how you saw Cap'n Gault hide some di'monds; an' you done your duty, like a proper citizen, an' told us."

In a way it was almost laughable, if it had not been for the way this pretty little woman was showing the poor, bad stuff she was built of. It was plain enough to me that the man was prompting her, and trying to steady her down to normal control again, before she gave away more completely the plot they had made to trap me.

But he could not quiet Miss Alicia Malbrey, disgruntled feminine Treasury spy, in that moment of complete failure of all her hours and days of treacherous planning. And then, in the midst of her wild storming at me, as she stood there on the table, the chart-room door opened, and in came the Chief Stewardess, with two strapping looking stewardesses behind her.

"Ah, Miss Allan," I said, "perhaps you would kindly see Miss Malbrey to the passengers' part of the ship. I've tried to explain to her that she is intruding here; but I find that she does not quite comprehend."

"Aw! Quit the tall talk, Cap'n!" growled the man called Mace, in an ugly sort of way. "An' you other leddies, let the young leddy be. It's just more'n *you* dare do, Cap'n, to shove in between our lot, an' what we got to do!"

"Indeed," I said, as gently as a father. "Am I to understand that Miss Malbrey is a Treasury official?"

The man, Mace, hesitated and turned red. He had evidently let his tongue off on the gallop, ahead of instructions. While he paused, just that one moment, one of the other search officers chipped in.

"Go ahead, Cap'n," he said. "You gotter do what you think proper. Only don't try interferin' with us men. I guess the young lady's not one of ours."

He gave Mace a nudge to keep quiet, and I saw that Miss Malbrey was not to "come out into the open" as a full-blown Treasury spy; for then her value, as such, would be enormously lowered. In other vessels, she is evidently to continue her unpleasing profession.

I smiled, with a good deal of bitterness in my heart. Then I nodded to the Chief Stewardess, who went up to Miss Malbrey.

"Come now, Madam," she said quietly. "Let me help you down." Then in a lower voice, I heard her say: "Don't make a scene, Miss Malbrey, for your own sake. Come now, be a wise young lady. You shall come to my own cabin, and tell me all about it."

I smiled again; this time at the genuine humour of the thing. The Chief Stewardess's tact seemed blended with a more than a possible curiosity; but I certainly admired the tact—the result of years of the tradition that "scenes" and passengers must be kept out of sight of each other.

Miss Alicia Malbrey went quietly enough. It seemed incredible that I had held her in my arms within the last twenty-four hours, and that she had kissed me freely, and apparently with some pleasure in the process. I began to doubt the sex of Judas!

As she went past me, I had a strong impression that she would never tell the real facts to the Chief Stewardess, or any one else, for that matter. Even such women as Miss Alicia Malbrey have a way of preferring that people should not credit them in full with the treachery that ripples so naturally and smoothly through their systems.

And, fortunately for me, it had all led to nothing; for kind Nature has blessed me with a certain caution and foresight, and an ability to abide by some of the teachings of Commonsense and Experience. One of these teachings is: Never use two heads to keep one secret! The hiding-place above the beam is one I have long since given up; and I removed the "garter" of stones within half an hour of putting it there; and later, I placed it in another, and even more cutely conceived hiding-place, where it lies at this present moment.

January 27.

By methods of my own, I discovered the address of Miss Alicia Malbrey. And I took a taxi there this morning to have an interview with her, which pride, prejudice, and a number of other things demanded.

I was shown into a pretty sitting-room, and told that Miss Malbrey (though that was not the name given!) would see me in a few minutes.

When, at last, she came in, she stopped in the doorway. She was carrying her pet dog; and she looked pale, and, I could almost have imagined, a little frightened.

"What—what do you want, Captain Gault?" she asked, in a low voice.

"Won't you sit down, Miss Malbrey," I said. "You must not feel worried. I am not here to bully you."

"I—I'm not afraid of you, Captain Gault!" she said, with a little nervous hesitation.

She came across the room, and sank into a small chair.

"What is it you want of me?" she asked again. She was still white and nervous.

"I've come to return you some property of yours, or the government's," I said.

And, with the word, I stooped forward over her, and unbucked

Toby's collar. Taking it by the end, I tore it open lengthways.

"Hold your hand," I said; and I poured a little cascade of diamonds into her palms.

"Oh!" she cried out; and stared at me with very wide opened eyes.

"Do you remember that last day aboard, when you missed Toby's collar?" I said. "Well, I had borrowed it from the little brute. The Chief Steward gave it to you back, later. He told you it had been found on the saloon floor. Well, while I had the collar, I 'loaded' it with your stones. I was practically sure, by then, that you were a Treasury spy; but I kept hoping against hope that you would find it impossible to 'sell' me, when it came to the point. I felt that your womanhood would make that impossible to you. We men have some queer, silly notions, haven't we? No, I'm not going to bully you. I promised you that. Besides, it's not my way."

She had gone a deep burning red of shame. Then the red sank out of her face; and she was whiter than ever.

"But," she said, in a very low voice, staring at me strangely, "if you knew what I was, Captain, why did you do this? Why didn't you keep these stones, as—as spoils of war?" she held out her hand, and stared from me to the diamonds.

"They were not mine," I said. "And I smuggled them ashore for you, just to keep my promise to you—a sort of joke. You see, as I was practically sure you were a Treasury spy, I knew your dog would not be a likely 'suspect.' It is one of my little prides, that I always keep a promise."

"What a strange, strange man you are!" she said, almost under her breath.

I stood up.

"I'll say good-bye now," I said.

At the door, I heard her cry out something in a low, queer voice; but I never looked back. Faith dies hard with me; but it stays dead, when it does die.

In the street, I got into my taxi and drove off. In my hand I still held the ripped-up dog's collar. I rattled the two brass bells and smiled. Then I unscrewed each of the bells, and took out the pea from each. They were big peas, covered with a celluloid skin. I peeled off the skins, and there I held in my hand two magnificent ten-thousand-dollar apiece pearls.

You see, I had made one stone kill two birds, or rather one dog collar carry two lots of smuggled jewelry.

Rather neat, I call it. Look at it every way you like, it was neat—eh?

My Lady's Jewels

London City,
March 4.

WOMEN HAVE A GREAT trick of asking me to help them through the Customs with their jewellery.

I've said "Yes" once or twice, and not always had occasion to regret it. You see, there are women who are more honest than you'd think a woman could be, considering just what a woman is.

I make it a general rule, though, to say "No" to these requests, for it's bad policy to mix up business and pleasure; and I've no use for a woman when it comes to sharing a secret with her. She's so apt to be a bit mixed in her ideas of fair-play.

It's all rot to say a woman can't keep a secret. She can! She could keep a secret till Old Nick gurned grey, begging for it, *if it suited her.* But that's just the trouble! You never know when it's going to stop suiting her to keep mum. If she gets the notion there's more cash for her to talk, than in keeping quiet, she'll pull the lid off and let the secret pop out, regardless of the hole you may get shoved into as a result.

Anyway, I can't help making friends occasionally on the trip across. And there's a Mrs. Ernley, a pretty young widow, American, with heaps of dollars, who's shown a friendly side to me since the first day out.

I spotted her the moment she came aboard, and I gave the Chief Steward word to put her at my table. There are always little compensations, like that, to make up for the long hours, short pay, and big responsibilities of a sea-Captain's life!

We got on splendidly; and as she had no one to look after her, I have done my best ever since.

She was up with me on the lower bridge today, helping me "keep the watch," she called it; though it's not much watch I can keep when she's looking up at me, and saying things, of an "Americanness" beyond belief, and of an artlessness that ought to be beyond propriety, but somehow isn't.

351

"I've bought a heap of stuff in London and Paris," she told me; "and I'm afraid the New York Customs will sure have it in savage for me, Captain Gault."

"I'm afraid so," I said.

I was truly afraid; for that's the way a lot of them lead up to asking me to help them hide the stuff somewhere in the ship, so as to get it safely past the Customs searchers.

"It's a mighty wicked tax," she said. "I wish we women had the vote, we'd alter things. I s'pose you don't think a woman's fit to vote, Captain. But let me tell you, she's a heap fitter than half the men."

"I'm not against the vote," I said, "under conditions that are fair to the men."

"What's fair to one is fair to the other!" she said.

"That's a bit vague," I told her. "The suffrage is largely the modern equivalent of physical force. Women have less of it by nature, than men, and consequently there is a certain artificiality in the situation of a woman voting on equal terms with a man; for it implies that she is *physically* the equal of the man."

"Might's not right!" she said, warmly. "A clever woman has more brains than a labourer. Yet you give *him* the vote!"

"Exactly!" I said, smiling a little at her feminine method of meeting my distinctly masculine argument. "The labouring man has the vote, when you haven't it, because the vote is the modern equivalent of *physical* strength. Nowadays, when a man wants a thing, he votes for it, instead of fighting for it. In the old days, he fought for it, and would today, if his vote were outvoted by a lot of people who were *physically* midgets. The vote is might as well as right. All the same, ethically, the very cows in the field have a right to vote. I wonder how they'd vote on a pure butter question, and the vealing of their calves!"

"I'm not interested one bit about cows having the vote," she said; "but I tell you, Captain, when we women get the vote, we'll wipe this wicked tax on women's jewellery, and pretty things, clean off the slate! If things go on like this, only very rich women will be able to dress at all."

"I hadn't thought of it in that light," I said. "How shocking! There's still always the cheaper sorts of dress stuffs—plain cotton prints look quite pretty. No need really, you know, to allow this man-made tax to achieve its abominable end—"

"Captain," she interrupted, suddenly, "will you do something for me?"

I knew then that I could not delay the fatal moment any longer. She was going to ask me to risk liberty and profession for the sake of her pocket. And being a man, what chance had I?

"Captain Gault," she said, "I bought something enormously expensive when I was in Paris."

"Yes," I asked, rather hopelessly, "was it a necklace or a tiara?"

"Look!" she said, and opened her handbag.

"What did you pay for that?" I asked. "You ought to have it locked up in the strong room. For goodness' sake, don't let anyone aboard know that you've got a thing like that with you. A sea-Captain's responsibilities are bad enough, without adding to them gratuitously. Do shut the bag, please, and take it to the strong room! It'll be much safer there."

"I paid nearly a million dollars for it," she said, looking up at me, "and I guess that's as much as I'm going to pay. I'm going to smuggle it through the Customs. I'm not going to pay a cent of their horrible wicked tax."

"Mrs. Ernley," I said, "it's evident you don't know much about the U.S.A. Customs people. Let me tell you, dear lady, they're smart; and the chances are they know at the present moment that you've bought this neckace, and what you have paid for it."

"No," she said, "they don't just know anything at all about it, Captain. I made up my mind that I wouldn't pay the tax. Why, it would be about six hundred thousand dollars on this one necklace! It's just robbery! And so I made arrangements secretly through a friend, with Monsieur Jervoyn, the jeweller, to meet me at her house, and I bought this lovely thing there, and paid for it in cash. So you see, they can't know!"

"My dear Mrs. Ernley," I remonstrated, "never be sure of anything where the U.S.A. Customs are concerned, except that they're on the job all the time. Americans are like that, as you know. If they go in for graft, they do the thing properly; and if they go in for doing their duty, they do it properly likewise, in about forty different ways at one and the same time. That's the way they're built. They've got to be efficient per pound whatever else they are or are not. And you can bet on this, when the Customs come aboard in New York, they'll know you've got this, and they'll know the name of the man you got it from; and they'll be able to make a shot at what you paid for it."

She shook her head, obstinately. It's a confoundedly pretty little head, and I don't mind whether she shakes it or just nods. It looks nice any way.

"I'm sure they don't know!" she asserted. "I was far, far too careful. I was, now, Captain; and I bet my last dollar they don't even dream I've bought anything much. Not for all their secret agents and things. Oh, I know more of their ways than you think, Captain Gault! I've heard some of my relations talk; and they're in the Treasury, and I know I'm up against something; but I guess I'll get the thing through all right, if you'll help me. You see, I've got it all plotted out, as clever as you like. I've got a proper plan. Will you help me, Captain? Oh, I don't mean that you're to risk things for nothing. I wouldn't have that! I'll pay you a percentage if you will help me. . . . A percentage on what I paid for it, will you, now?"

"Well," I said, after pausing a moment to think, "I might; but I don't like mixing business and friendship. I'm not set on having a percentage."

"That's the only way I'll deal with you, Captain," she told me. "How would five or ten percent suit you?"

"Oh," I said, smiling a little at her casualness, "I guess two and a half percent will suit me very well indeed."

"That's settled, then," she replied. "Now, here's my plan. When I ordered the necklace, I stipulated that they should make me another—and exact facsimile of it, in Carn glass—you know that new glass stuff that looks as good as the best paste?"

"Carn Prism glass, you mean?" I suggested.

She nodded.

"Yes, that's it," she said. "Well, now, I've the two here in my bag, and I can't tell the difference, and wouldn't be able to, Captain, only I've tied a bit of silk round the real one. Now this is my plan, you are to take and hide the real one for me—oh, I know you're a wonderful man at getting things past the Customs! And I shall have the false one in my bag. Then, *if* they've got scent that I've bought a necklace, and search me, they'll find the false one; and they'll reckon they've been misinformed. Then, after I'm searched, you can give me back the real one as soon as things are safe, and I'll give you a cheque for the five percent."

"Two and a half," I corrected her.

"Take me somewhere where I can give you the thing," she went on, unheeding my correction, and I took her into my chart-room. Here she lifted the two necklaces out of her bag. They were certainly wonderful; and, though I could tell one from the other, after an examination, they would easily have deceived lots of men who think they know diamonds "at sight"; and certainly, apart, I should have been puzzled to say which was which, without making a test.

"Very well," I said. "I'll hide it for you in a safe place."

And with that she handed me the real necklace—a regular chain of light—a marvellous thing it was. And I put it away; but refused to let her know how I should hide it.

March 6. Evening.

Women are as much like little girls, as men are like little boys, when it comes to jewellery. Mrs. Ernley coaxes me at least twice a day to let her see and play with her gorgeous necklace. And while she plays with it, sitting on the settee in my chart-room, I sit across on the locker and look at her. She's a remarkably pretty woman!

"Why do you stare so at me, Captain Gault?" she asked, this afternoon, looking across at me, with a touch of mischief.

"I guess it's for the same reason you suppose it is, dear lady," I said, smiling a little at her pretence. "You're good to look at, and you're generally an interesting study for a man of my temperment. I'm wondering what next *trait* will come top in you—weakness or virtue. Frankly, I suspect weakness."

"Don't you make any error, Captain; there's no weakness about me!" she assured me, in her quaint way. "You can sure take that for a conviction!"

"A conviction, dear lady, should be that which is produced by the action of Reason upon Experience!" I told her. "Now my experience of you tells me that you are quite averagely human—a good average mixture of strengths and weaknesses. Up to the present, you've shown me your strong side. Now, Reason, acting upon Experience, bids me to expect the other side of the shield."

"Captain Gault!" she said, "you're going too deep for me. Now be sensible, and look at my shining beauty. Did you ever see the like now? I just had to buy it. I couldn't say no. I'd like to see the woman that could. You'll call that a weakness, I suppose!"

"A weakness that I'm not going to quarrel with, seeing that it's going to put twenty-five thousand dollars into my pocket," I told her. She looked so startled, that I had to explain.

"That's my share, you know. Two and a half percent on a million dollars is twenty-five thousand."

"Oh!" she said, in rather a queer tone. "Yes, of course. I never thought to work it out."

I said nothing; but I could not help wondering whether it was here that the little weakness was going to show out. It was obvious that she'd had a shock, when I explained to her just how much my commission was going to cost her; though, goodness knows, it's cheap enough, when one remembers how much the Customs would have rooked her for. But you never know how women are going to look at things of this kind. Women are extraordinary mixtures of big extravagances and petty economics.

She was pretty silent for the rest of the time she was in the chart-room; and I rallied her mildly on her sudden soberness.

"Dear lady," I said, "if the size of my fee troubleth thee (forgive the *tutoiement*), why I'll e'en hoodwink our common enemy for no more than the joy of the game and good friendship!"

She protested so hotly that this could not be thought of, and had so much good colour in her cheeks, that I had very little doubt but that I had shot true. However, she made it very clear indeed that my fee was mine, and that her word was more truly her bond than if it had been signed and stamped and sealed and lawyered. And all the time she fiddled with the great million-dollar chain-of-light, running it through and through her hands.

Then she handed it back to me, and went away to dress for dinner. And see the nature of woman! She had changed necklaces. She had left with me the imitation, as I knew in a minute, by testing it. And, that it was no accident, I had easy proof; for she had shifted the mark (the piece of silk) from the real necklace to the false.

Truly, it takes some twisting to follow a woman! But there is, in a matter of money, a simple rule to aid a man, with a woman, if he would get at the truth of her motive. For, either her action is prompted by insane generosity or an even more insane meanness. And here it was not difficult to see what had governed her action. She had been shocked to see that out of a million dollars she had pledged herself to pay twenty-five thousand; and she had palmed me the false necklace, meaning to try to run the real one through herself, after all, and so avoid paying me my fee. She had lacked the moral courage to tell me so, honestly; but I suppose, once she is safe through the Customs with the real necklace, she will write me a polite little note, telling me that she decided to run the thing through herself. She may even ask me to keep the glass one as a souvenir; and, being a woman, she will not mean to be cynical. She will really wish me to accept it, in memory of her! Little wonder the simple, straightforward logical male feels at sea; for a woman obeys her impulses, while, all the time, he supposes her to be using her reasoning powers, which, by the way, are generally atrophied.

And now I'm interested to follow her further manoeuvres!

March 9.

"For the last couple of days you've not asked to see your necklace,"
I told her this morning, after I had invited her up on to the lower
bridge. "And you're getting tired of keeping the old sea-dog company!
Confess now, aren't you?"

"No," she answered. "I'm just denying myself. I'm showing you
I can be stronger than you think."

"All women are liars," I whispered solemnly to myself. "I suppose
they can't help it, any more than a man can stop being logical at some
oneelse's expense."

But I said nothing out loud; and for a minute or two we walked
the length of the bridge, without saying a word.

"Being strong isn't just being strong in the way you find easy to
be strong," I said at last.

"That sounds rather difficult," she answered. "Try now if you can't
do something better than that, Captain, or I'll miss what you want
to tell me."

"I mean," I said, "that if I set out, say, not to tell lies, just to prove
how much of a moral athlete I was, it would not prove anything; for
the simple reason that lying is not my particular poison. Of course, if
I've got to, I do it in a finished kind of fashion; but I've no particular
Ananias leanings. Given two ways out of a difficulty, I'd not necessarily
choose the lie. Sumga?"

"Sure I do," she said; "but I don't see what that's to do with my
refraining from coming to see my nec—you and my necklace, I mean.
I wanted badly to see both of you. No, don't get conceited! But I
have kept away. Doesn't that show strength, to keep away from doing
things you're wanting bad to do?"

"Dear lady," I answered. "God made Adam, and the Two of
Them helped to make Eve—I guess that's why the result's been spot
uncertain."

"What do you mean?" she asked.

"Adam should never have been let in on the job," I told her. "A
human is sure some machine. I guess he was too much of an amateur,
and left out the governor—"

"That's rude!" she cracked out at me.

"The truth's generally a bit that way," I said. "I'm not one to shut
my eyes, when it's someone else's sins I'm looking at. I've a strong
fellow-feeling for old Sir Almoth. I consider he justified his name.
He's some marksman."

"What are you talking? Words or sense?" she asked, honestly

bewildered.

"Both," I told her. "If that old amateur, Adam, had only added the governor, Logic, you could have found out all that by yourself. I'll make you a bet, and the amount shall be the sum that you were to have paid me for running your necklace through the Customs—twenty-five thousand dollars."

"What—what do you mean?" she asked, stammering slightly, and turning rather white looking. "What do you want to bet?"

She stared me right in the eyes, closely, and with an intense, expectant attention.

"That you will not manage to run your necklace through by yourself," I said slowly, looking at her steadily. "I did not ask you to pay me any commission; and I halved what you offered me; but had I arranged to do it for a full five percent, it would have been money well spent, from your side of the bargain."

She was as white as a sheet now, and had to catch at the forrard bridge-rail, to help steady herself; but I did not spare her; for if I could crush the meanness in her, with the Hammer of Shame, I meant to do so.

"Why had you not the moral strength to tell me the truth, when I worked out for you how much two and a half percent on a million dollars would come to?" I said. "Why did you not just say, simply, that you had not thought to pay so much? I should have relieved you of the bargain in a moment. What is more, I should have respected you for having the moral strength to tell me the truth; though I should have regretted the *trait* of meanness it would have disclosed—for you are a very wealthy woman, and you could well afford to pay me twice what I agreed to run your necklace through for. I did not, as I have said, ask you to pay me anything. I would have done it for nothing—just for friendliness' sake; but when you turned it into a business proposition, I met you on a business footing. It was to save your pocket some six hundred thousand dollars; and for the risk I took of losing personal liberty, and my situation as Captain of this ship, I consented to accept twenty-five thousand dollars as payment.

"And now you have shown not only meanness, but, a thousand times worse, you have lied to me, lie after lie; and with every lie you hurt me badly; for you blackened not only yourself in my eyes; but, at the same time, you blackened all of your sex; for a man judges women through the goodness or badness of the women he gets to know personally. I tell you frankly, Mrs. Ernley, I wish your necklace had been at the bottom of the sea before you had let it be a lever to further lower my general opinion of all that you stand for!"

"Stop, stop!" she said, quite hoarsely. She had flushed once or twice as I set out my indictment; but now she stood shivering and deadly pale.

"Help—help me down the steps," she said, and I helped her down to the deck.

"Now leave me," she said, almost in a whisper, "I can manage. No, I will not have you with me. I have done wrong. But I cannot bear you near me. You—you have shamed me so!"

I watched her go along the deck, and pass down one of the stairways, then I went back to the bridge. I do not regret what I have done. I am getting a sick fear that every woman I meet is going to turn out mean or treacherous or deceitful or worse. If I have helped one to cure herself, I'm satisfied.

March 19th. Night.

We docked this morning, and Mrs. Ernley has never come near me once of her own free will. And there has been a deuce of a scene with the Customs.

I did not know, at first, whether to say anything about the necklace or not; but finally decided that I had better show it, and say it had been left in my charge by a Mrs. Ernley, one of the First Class passengers. If it served to bluff the Customs into supposing that this was the necklace she had bought, and that she had been swindled into paying real money for a Carn Prism sham set of sparklers, it might serve to lull them from making a drastic search of her. And, goodness knows, I'm willing enough to do the little woman a good turn if I can.

When the Chief of the searchers came along to the chart-house, he asked me a leading question, straight off, which made it sufficiently plain that he knew a good deal about Mrs. Ernley's Paris transaction.

"Captain," he said, "I hear from one of our people, who's been abroad, that you and Mrs. Ernley have got pretty friendly on the trip across, and I want you to be a real friend to her; and do your best to persuade her to show up her necklace, like a wise woman. We know a good deal about it, Captain; so, for the Lord's sake, don't try to do any bluffing, and don't encourage her to, either. It'll mean serious trouble if you do. We *know* it's aboard this ship; and we mean to have it. It's six hundred thousand dollars of duty we're out for, and we're going to have it; but she swears she has no necklace, and my women searchers haven't been able to locate it yet. Now, will you, Captain, wise her up, that she can't put a thing like this over us; and I guess we'll let her down easy for false declaration."

"Mister," I said, "perhaps this is what you are looking for;" and I went across and hauled out the sham necklace from a drawer. "She asked me to take care of this for her."

He gave out a little shout of relief; and snatched at the thing. He ran to the north window, and held it up to the light, then he pulled a magnificent-looking brilliant from his vest pocket, set in the end of a little steel bar, and he began to compare the "stones" with it.

He let out a sudden exclamation; and whipped an eye-microscope from his pocket. He fitted this to his eye, then turned up the other end of the steel bar, and I saw that there was a "tester" set in it. He scratched carefully with this at one of the "stones" in the necklace. Then he gave a shout of disgust, and turned and hove the necklace on to my chart table.

"Careful with the thing, man!" I said. "Anyone would suppose you were *blasé*."

"Careful!" he said. "My oath, Captain, drop it! I don't know whether she's put the blinkers on you too. She may have; though I'm doubting it. But that's not worth more than the platinum setting that mounts the stuff. It's one of those new 'prism' fakes. Though, I'll own I never saw such a good one. Now, Captain, we're going to get the real goods; so don't get up against us. Help us, and we'll make things as pleasant as we can; but butt in on us, and you'll get twisted; and the lady'll get prison; for Judge H— gave it out in court last week that he's going to teach some of these dollar-dames they can't monkey with the U.S.A. laws, and get off the way some of them are doing."

"I'll do my best," I said, "to make things all right. The lady certainly handed me this necklace as the real thing."

I picked it up, and took it across to its drawer; as I did so, there was a knock on the chart-room door, and a Customs officer pushed his head in.

"We've got it, Sir!" he said, in an excited voice. "Miss Synks found it in the ventilator of the lady's cabin. Will you come, Sir? She's making a rumpus down there. Perhaps the Captain had better come too. Some of the passengers seem inclined to make trouble for our people."

The head searcher was already half out through the doorway; but he beckoned to me to follow.

When we got down into the main saloon, off which Mrs. Ernley's cabin opened, I found there was certainly some riot going on!

There was a crowd of First Class passengers round her cabin. The door was open, and over the heads of the passengers I could see Mrs. Ernley and a young, smartly-dressed woman. Mrs. Ernley looked to be dressed ready for going ashore. She was standing in the middle of her cabin, and appeared to be holding something frantically to her breast, which the other woman was trying to take from her.

At this moment, one of the Customs officials entered the cabin, and went to assist the woman searcher in taking from Mrs. Ernley what she held so crazily to her. Mrs. Ernley gave out a scream, and at that there was an ugly growl of sound from the passengers round the doorway.

"Manhandling a lady like that!" I heard one man expostulating, above the sudden murmur of voices.

I reached quickly, and caught the head searcher's elbow.

"For the Lord's sake, sing out to your man to quit mauling the lady," I said, "or there's going to be a lot of unnecessary trouble."

"Svenson," sung out the chief searcher. "Come out of that!"

At his voice, the semi-circle of passengers glanced round quickly; and I took charge.

"Come, ladies and gentlemen," I said. "This is a matter between Mrs. Ernley and the United States Customs. I am sure you do not want to embarrass her more than need be; so please allow matters to arrange themselves. You can trust me to see that the lady will get courteous treatment, while she's aboard my ship."

"That's the tune, Captain!" called out one of the men passengers. "If this sort of thing is necessary, let it be done properly, I say."

"You may be sure that the head officer and I will show all consideration for the lady," I answered. "He must carry out his duty; but he has no wish to make it more unpleasant than need be. Now do, please, all of you go away from the doorway. There is no need for any scene."

They melted like snow, now that their instinctive desire for fair and courteous treatment for a woman in trouble had been assured, and I stepped right in through the doorway, and touched the woman-searcher on the shoulder.

"Allow me one moment," I said. "Perhaps I can get Mrs. Ernley to listen to me without continuing this painful situation."

The woman-searcher glanced over my shoulder at her chief, who must have nodded his assent to my intervention; for she loosed hold of Mrs. Ernley immediately.

"Mrs. Ernley!" I said. "Mrs. Ernley! Please listen to me. You must give the necklace up. You will have to pay the duty; but the chief searcher has kindly assured me that he will not press any charge against you, if you will consent now to let matters go forward, without further trouble." I looked over my shoulder at the head officer.

"I am right in making the lady this promise?" I asked, under my breath. "I have your promise?"

He nodded. I could see that the man was geniunely sorry for her; but he had to do his duty, which was to see that Uncle Sam got his full and necessary pound of meat.

"Now, Mrs. Ernley, please give me the necklace, and end this distressing scene. It is distressing us all. We are all genuinely sorry for you; but you must realise that luxuries must be paid for; and the Customs can favour no one. Come, now." And, very gently, I eased her hands open, and took from her the tightly rolled up glittering string of stones. She stood then, looking not at me, but fixedly at the stones, as I held them out to the head officer. She was trembling from head to foot, and I beckoned suddenly to the woman-searcher to hold her; for I thought she was going to faint.

The head officer let the glimmering string of light swing a time or two in his hands, as if he were, himself, fascinated by the flashes they sent out. Then he turned, and put his head out of the cabin doorway.

"Jim," he called, "slip up and fetch Mr. Malch."

"The official appraiser," he explained, turning back to me. "I'll have him on this job; then there sure can't be any error!"

In about two minutes the man, Jim, returned with Mr. Malch—a long, thin, hard-bitten looking man.

"Hand it across, Soutar," he said, "I'll soon put you wise to the quality of the goods!"

He took it over to the port-hole, and laid it out in the bunk—Mrs. Ernley's own bunk. Then he pulled a case out of his pocket, and bent over the necklace.

I was standing by Mrs. Ernley, talking to her quietly, to try to ease the tension a bit. The woman-searcher, who was evidently the Miss Synks who had found the necklace, had moved behind Mrs. Ernley, ready to support her, if need be. I must say they were downright considerate to her, taking things all round.

Suddenly, the appraiser burst out into a contemptuous laugh.

"For all sakes, Soutar, aren't you wise to know glass from the real thing!" he said, turning round. He held the necklace out to us all. "There's not a diamond there!" he went on. "It's one of those Carn Prism fakes. If the lady bought this for the real goods, she's been done as brown as a coffee bean!"

Mrs. Ernely let out a shrill scream—

"It's real! It's real! I know it's real! I paid a million dollars for it!" She sprang at the man and snatched it from his hand.

"Real glass, Madam!" he said, grimly. "I guess you can take that kind of stuff ashore by the cartload, duty free. We ain't going to object! Of course, the setting's fine. It's real platinum; but I guess we're looking for more than settings!"

Mrs. Ernley let the necklace fall with a sharp little clatter of sound, to the floor. And Miss Synks was just in time to catch her, as she fainted.

I helped her lift her on to the settee; then I picked up the condemned necklace, coiled it up and tossed it on to the table.

"Poor little woman!" said the chief of the searchers. "She's sure been put through a quick-change scene of high-voltage troubles. I guess she's got a sure police-case against that Paris jeweller! That's if they ever put hands on him again, which ain't a likely thing, after clearing up a million as easy as all that!"

Abruptly, a sudden idea came to him; and I saw suspicion flash into his eyes.

"I'll take another look, Captain Gault, at that necklace you've got in charge for the little lady!" he said, with a little curt note in his voice. "Maybe I made a mistake somewhere. We'll have Mr. Malch on the job. He's the man that know the real goods."

"Certainly!" I said. "Come up to the chart-room."

He beckoned to the appraiser, and we all went up to the chart-room. I stepped across to the drawer, and fetched out the first necklace. I handed it to the appraiser without a word. I was getting a heap weary of it all.

"Same sort of prism muck!" said Mr. Malch, shrugging his shoulders contemptuously, after a series of tests. "I guess it's the guy over in Paris that's made the dollars this trip! Come on, Sourtar. Sorry to have bothered you, Cap'n; but I guess it's all in a day's work."

"Just so," I said, as dryly as I could.

After they had gone I went down to see how Mrs. Ernley was. She had come round when I called, and was helping her maid to pack. She looked up at me, very white-faced, and very red-eyed.

"Please go away, Captain Gault," she said. "Thank you for all you've done. I want to get right away and never see anyone again. I've been a very silly, weak woman. Please go away."

And, of course, I had to go.

But this evening, when all my business was done, I dressed, and had a taxi sent down to the ship. I was going up to see Mrs. Ernley, at her big house up Madison Square way. I meant to make the returning of the sham necklace an excuse to call; though I wondered whether she might not still refuse to see me.

However, when I sent my name in to her, I found I was to be

received, and I went in, wondering how I should find her. She was sitting in a pretty boudoir sort of room; and when I entered, she was playing idly and rather sadly with the other necklace; but as I came into the room she threw it on to a chair, and came across to meet me.

"A million dollars is a lot to lose in one lump," I told her, as she sat down again; "even for a rich woman like you."

"Yes," she said quietly. "But I guess that's not what I'm feeling worst about now I've got steadied a bit. I showed that I was poor stuff, didn't I, Captain Gault? I guess I've never been so ashamed of myself in my life as I feel right now."

I nodded.

"I'm glad to hear it," I said. "I fancy you've won more than you've lost, if you feel that way, dear lady."

"Perhaps I have," she answered, rather doubtfully, as she reached out for the necklace she had been playing with. "The police here have cabled across, and I guess they'll do their best to nab that crook, Monsieur Jervoyn, who sold me this rubbish; though I'm not surprised I was taken in. Even the Customs expert couldn't tell they weren't real, first go off, could he?"

I nodded again.

"Mrs. Ernley," I said, "you've come well out of this affair, in many ways, and I think you've taken it as a bit of a lesson, haven't you?"

"Yes," she said slowly. "I don't think I shall ever forget what I've gone through today; and all the voyage, for that matter. I suppose, Captain Gault, you feel just simple contempt for me? You feel I've proved I was weak. You said I should."

She dabbed at her eyes with her handkerchief. "I suppose being rather well-off *does* make one inclined to grow soft, morally," she murmured at last.

"I guess Life is either Training or Degeneration," I told her. "But smuggling diamonds isn't necessarily degeneration. It consists largely of *using* Circumstances. But it's a man's job. A woman's too much given to expecting heads I win, tails you lose. And that's just *dodging* Circumstances. And dodging Circumstances is plain Degeneration."

She nodded.

"I guess you're right, Captain Gault," she said quietly. "A woman's awfully apt to think she ought to be able to eat her macaroons and have them still in her hand. And that's impossible, it seems!"

I stood up, smiling at the pretty, earnest way she mixed her words.

"In this case, dear lady," I said, "the 'plumb impossible' has happened, or something like it. I'll run along now; but you'll like to know that the necklace you've got in your hands is worth just about one million dollars cash, so I'd put it away safe tonight before you turn in."

She had stood up, as I was speaking, and she held the necklace out now in her right hand, and stared first at me, and then back at it, as if she were half dazed with what I had just said to her.

"What?" she asked at last, in a voice that was low and deep, like a man's, with the nerve shock that had half paralysed her and relaxed her vocal chords. "What?"

"Please sit down," I said, and guided her back gently into her chair. . . . "Now you're all right. . . . Sure?"

She nodded speechlessly at me.

"Listen to me, then," I told her. "That's your million-dollar necklace. The actual thing you bought in Paris. It's genuine and quite all right. I saved it for you. Probably you'd like to know, so I'll tell you how.

"When the Customs man came up into my chart-room, I showed him the sham necklace, and he tested it and found that it was sham. Then one of his men came up to say that they had found the real one in your cabin ventilator. I had pretended to put the false one back into one of my chart-room drawers, but really I had coiled it up tight in my hand.

"I followed the chief searcher down, and I coaxed you to hand over the real one, which you had rolled up into a ball in your hands, after you must have snatched it from the woman-searcher.

"Then I handed the Customs man the false necklace, which had been ready in my hand, and kept the real one in its place.

"Of course, they simply found out, for the second time of asking, that the false necklace, was as false as it was! Pretty obvious sort of thing to find. Afterwards, you remember, you snatched it back, when the expert told you it was only Carn glass, and then you fainted and dropped it on the floor. I helped lift you to the settee; then I picked up the false necklace; wrapped it up, and threw it on to your cabin table; but what I actually threw was the real one, and kept the false one again held tight in my hand.

"Now, don't you admire my nerve, chucking down on to the table right in front of the expert, a million-dollar necklace, as if it were just common so-much-a-ton-stuff—eh? Wasn't that a great bluff, dear lady?"

"Sure! Sure! Sure!" she gasped out, her eyes dancing. "And then?"

"And then I guess I sealed the trick. The Customs man got a sudden notion that he would like to have another look at the necklace I had shown him in my chart-room.

"Well, I took him up there, along with the expert, and I went over to the drawer, dipped in my hand, that held the sham necklace, and then pulled the thing out, in a sort of *ad lib* fashion, for them to examine for the third time of asking. They certainly showed some interest in that length of prism sparklers! By the way, I've brought it back for you," and I drew it out of my pocket and laid it on the table.

Mrs. Ernley rose now and went across to a small writing desk. I saw a minute later, that she had started to fill in a cheque; and I guessed it was my commission.

I walked over to her, and put my hand across the cheque-book.

"Dear lady," I said, "I can take no commission for what I did. Our business transaction ended when you changed the necklaces. . . . But, out of curiosity, I should like to know just how much the cheque was going to be?"

"Look!" she said, and I drew away my hand, and looked. It was for a hundred thousand dollars.

"I'm glad!" I told her. "I guess you've stamped pretty solid on the poor streak in you. You're sure going to be one of the few women I can think well of. But I can't take that cheque, dear lady. If you want to go on the way you've begun, send it to the Sailors' Home. They need the cash pretty bad, I know."

Then I shook hands and left; though she begged me to stay; and showed the nicest and best possible side that a woman has to show.

"What a strange man you are, Captain Gault," she said, as I turned and smiled at her in the doorway.

"Maybe," I said. "All humans are a bit strange to others, when you get the lid off some of their soul pots!"

But when I got out into the street I couldn't help thinking how true my notions of woman often are. Her actions are prompted either by insane meanness, or else by an equally insane generosity!

I guess it's right that old Adam left the governor out!

Trading with the Enemy

Oil Ship S.S. Ganymede,
November 5th.

TROUBLE HAS BEEN LOOKING for me today. I met a man ashore in a restaurant this morning who knew too much.

That's the worst of doing the Customs people in the eye! There's bound to be an odd person here and there who gets to know just a little too much for one's comfort, though I can assure you there are not a multitude.

But I'll admit this beggar does know something the U.K. Customs people would pay to have proof of, and he made it pretty clear that he's got the proofs right where he can put his dirty paws on them anytime it suits him.

"Well, mister," I said, "what's the game, anyway? Is it a cash gag you're looking for, or a berth as steward, or what?"

"Neither, Cap'n," he said. "I'd not rob you of the first, and I'd not trust myself afloat with you for the second."

"Well," I told him, "out with it!"

"Cap'n," he remarked. "I don't reck'n you pose as a violent patriot, do you?"

"No, I don't," I said. "I've not time for fancy fireworks. I've got a living to make, and it's a deuce of a job, too!"

"You're taking that old oil boat across to Holland tomorrow night," he remarked in a sort of full-and-bye fashion. "How'd you like to make a thousand pounds, *and* have those letters handed across to you, so I'll have no pull on you anymore, eh, Cap'n?"

I took a good look at him.

"And if I don't?" I said. "What about it?"

"In that case, Cap'n, you can rely on the letters going by registered packet to the U.K. Customs people right away by tonight's post. Also, you ll be short a thousand yellow-boys, and someone else'll do our—my little job, while you spoil your pretty finger-ends on old junk. Like the alternative, Cap'n?"

367

"I don't," I said; "though, mind you, I'm not granting you *could* get me a job picking oakum. All the same, let's hear your proposition. A thousand quid takes a bit of earning these days."

"Come up close," he said, and I hitched my chair right up to the table and leant over a bit, so that he'd not require to shout the business, whatever it was, to the whole crowd in the eating-house.

"You take the old *Ganymede* out tomorrow night," he told me for the second time. "Well, Cap'n, if you want those letters and that thousand quid, I want you to arrange things so that you're off the Texel Light, from midnight to four a.m., on the night of the 8th. You ll have to keep outside the three-mile limit, of course, and I reckon you'll have to fix things up with your Chief Engineer, so as to make a darned slow trip of it, or you'll get there ahead of time."

"Go on," I suggested, "let's have the bunt of it. That's only the earrings!"

"Just so, Cap'n," he said, grinning. "While you're hanging round off the Texel, I shall want you to see that only three of your cabin ports on each side show a light, and the middle port of each three must be covered with a bit of blue celluloid that I'll supply you with.

"Maybe, during the four hours I want you to hang around, you may get a visit from three or four small craft, anxious to buy petrol and oil. If they do, why, I just want you to sell 'em oil and petrol, as much as they want—"

"German submarines!" I interrupted.

"I couldn't swear to it," he said, grinning. "But you never know your luck. And, any case, just to settle your mind a bit, there's at least four of 'em, an' they're expecting you. So if you try to dodge 'em—well, Cap'n, I guess you'll just go right up to heaven on a gasoline fountain. An' it'll be a hot goin'!"

"Quit the threats!" I told him. "You won't get me that way. What about the letters and the cash? Do I have 'em now, or how?"

He shoved a tricky finger to the side of his nose.

"Cap'n," he said, "you gets the cash an' the letters from them as you sells the petrol an' oil to. But just to show I'm talking business, I'll pay you two hundred and fifty right now, provided you agree to be there at the time, an' show those three lighted ports a side, same as I've described. I'll trust your word for that much."

I shrugged my shoulders.

"It's a cleft-stick proposition, it seems to me, all the way," I said. "How do I know they won't hang on to the rest of the cash and all the letters?"

"Cap'n," he began, "I give you my word of honour—"

"Don't!" I said. "Talk sense!"

He looked ugly a moment, then grinned.

"Well, I grant it, Cap'n," he said. "Maybe it's worn a bit thin, but you've just got to take it or leave it, you see. I'm only the agent in this biz. But I've the word of some straight men as you'll get a square deal, if you do what I've put up to you. Be there, with the ports lit up, like I tell you, from midnight to four o'clock on the morning of the 8th. And, anyway, Cap'n, if you don't fall for it, you'll certainly never get across, not all in one piece. And I reckon I know what I'm saying. They'll lay for you, so be a wise guy an' go for the thousand quid an' the letters, an' after that, well, you can call it a hold-up, just to keep your face clean. You won't never have no one smelling a rat, if you go at it like the wise one you're known for."

"Hand over that two-fifty!" I said at last. "I guess it's not as bad as murder, anyway."

"No murder about it, Cap'n," he said. "Just a little business on the way across, and if you hand the Engineer a hundred, he'll never open his talkin' trap, an' that'll mean nine hundred for your own bank-roll. Here you are, Cap'n!"

"And if a British cruiser drops on me while I'm selling gasoline out there across the counter?" I said as I counted and examined the notes. "Pleasant for me! I'll be liable to be shot on sight."

He shrugged his shoulders as he rose from the table.

"Naturally, Cap'n," he said, yawning, "that's your lookout. As you said just now, a thousand quid takes a bit of earning, not to mention those letters! Anyway, I've got your word, and I guess you've been known to keep it."

"Yes," I said, sighing a bit. "I keep my word, Mister, and I'd advise you to keep out of my way from now onward. I don't feel friendly to you, not by a whole lot."

"Ah! Just so," he said, grinning. "I'm not aching to hang round your neck. So long, Cap'n!"

* * * *

There you have the mess I'm into. I hate it like poison, but talk is easy! I'm into it, and I suppose I've got to go through with the business. Darn that sneak-spy! If ever I get my hands on him, after I've got those letters safe, I guess he'll know a thing or two that'll help to fit his soul for the Milky Way.

November 6th, night. North Sea.

We're underway at last. The whole day's been a nightmare, thinking about things. But I can see no way of getting hold of those letters, except by meeting the submarines. And, of course, I've given my word now. I make a point always of sticking to what I promise.

The two circles of blue celluloid were brought down aboard by a messenger-boy just before we cast off. It s pretty plain everything's been cut and dried.

November 7th.

I had to fix things up with old Mac (my Chief Engineer). I just told him the whole business. Honesty's the best policy sometimes, even when you're bucking head-foremost into a mess, like I'm doing. I handed Mac over the whole of the two hundred and fifty I've already drawn, as his share, and he's just arranging things in the engine-room so that no one'll suspect anything. I don't know just what he's done, but he's cut our speed down by a good three knots an hour, and I reckon that should land us off the Texel Light any-where between eleven and twelve tomorrow night. And, meanwhile, I'm feeling a bit easier, for I've been, I'll admit frankly, in the deuce of a funk lest any of the engine-room gang might guess we were cutting her speed down on purpose. And once let them get that notion into their head, they'll be sure to smell a rat, and I guess I can't afford any unneccessary suspicion just now. But once I've got those letters back, and safely burnt, I don't doubt I'll feel different. I was a fool ever to write them, but plotting and planning to go one better than the Customs forces a man to take risks with his personal liberty now and again. After all, it's true enough that a man gets what he's sown. Anyway, that's how I feel this trip.

Same day, evening.

A big British destroyer overhauled us this afternoon and sent a boat aboard to look at our papers. Believe me, I'm sweating still with the cold shivers I got when the lieutenant in charge of the boat's crew asked me what our engine-power was, and remarked that we steamed like she was an old tub.

"She's not steaming up well at all this trip," I told him. "Mr. Mac-Gallen, my Chief Engineer, was only saying this morning that she'll want to have her cylinders re-bored if they're going to keep expenses down and shove her speed up. He's right."

Mac hadn't said anything of the sort, as you will understand, but

I'd got to say something, and anyway, I knew the man wasn't an Engineer officer, or he'd not be doing boarding-duty; so I suppose he'd swallowed it all right, though he was inquisitive enough to take a look into the engine-room and chat a bit with Mac.

When he'd gone, and told us to go ahead again, Mac came along to have a word with me.

"What like was yon chap, Cap'n?" he asked me straight away.

I shrugged my shoulders.

"I guess you know just as much about it as I do, Mac," I told him. "What's at the back of your mind that sets you thinking, my son?"

"Just naethin', Cap'n," he replied. "I were just wonderin' how a plain, ignorant sailorman, same as you'd reckon him to be, come to know sae darned much aboot engines."

"What?" I said. "What's that, Mac? What makes you think he knew anything about engines?"

"Well, Cap'n," said Mac, in his quiet, dry way, "you spun him a little yarn aboot oor needin' oor cylinders re-bored. Ye'd been wiser to ha' left th' leein' to me, I'm thinkin', for it needs an expert. I refer to ma profession, ye'll unnerstan'. Nae ignorant sailorman can lie aboot engines wi oot running risks, and that's what ye were doin', Cap'n, when ye passed oot yon yarn aboot oor needin' oor cylinders re-borin'."

"But what makes you think he knew anything more about engines than any intelligent sailorman is likely to know?" I asked the old beggar, feeling a bit yellow.

Mac, however, was in one of his short moods, and turned away. But after three steps he paused and spoke over his shoulder.

"Sailormen, Cap'n, are just plain ignorant, as any Engineer well kens," he said. "Yon laddie kenned th' relationship between firin' an' boiler-pressure, not to speak o' piston-speed and throttle-openin', juist to mention th' plain alphebeet o' the rudiments o' engin' runnin'. Man, a blind mule could deferentiate between the runnin' o' an engine that needed re-borin' an' one that's pairfectly steam-tight, same as mine. The deeference fair shouts. An' I'm na ower sure yon laddie couldna read the signs. Anyway, if ought happens, ye'll ken it werena' my fault, an' I'm wish-ful ye should ken it richt now."

And with that he left me with a fresh infernal worry to add to all my others.

November 8th, evening.

I'm feeling more comfortable in my mind. This business seems to be going right. I fancy old Mac got fancying things about that naval officer. Anyway, there's nothing in sight now, and we're shaping nicely to be off the Texel by midnight.

This time tomorrow the whole beastly strain will be over, and I shall have those letters if the Germans mean to play straight with me. And there'll be a matter of seven hundred and fifty quid as well. Not to be sneezed at these days!

But I'll not forget the chap that mixed me up with all this. I'll even up with him one of these days, and, meanwhile, the thing is to do what I've got to do without being caught, for that will certainly mean a firing-party, and not even the confounded letters would matter then.

November 9th, early morning.

I kept my promise and saw to it that no light was shown through any of our ports, except three, one each side of my cabin. Also, I fixed the circles of blue celluloid in the middle port on each side.

We were off the Texel Light, about seven miles from the coast, at exactly 11:45 p.m. I rang to dead slow, and then went down and fixed up the ports, as per directions. After that it was just a case of wait.

At 12:25, we were hailed in good English from some vessel on the landward side of us.

"This is the oil ship *Ganymede* from London to the Hook," I sung out. "Who are you?"

I was sweating a bit, for I knew that only a war vessel of some kind would be messing round with no lights showing, and the hail had been in such perfect English, I couldn't swear that it wasn't a British naval officer who was singing out to us. In that moment the last thing in this wide world I wanted to see was a British sea scout. I guess you can imagine my feelings.

And then, you know, I heard something that put heart into me. It was a German voice talking. I knew then (at least, I was practically certain) that it was one of the German submarines that had found us.

Immediately afterwards the man who had hailed us sung out again:

"We're coming alongside. Don't try any tricks, or we'll make a mess of you!"

I said nothing. The thing was so typically German in sentiment that I knew it was meant literally. It came from the heart.

And then from the port side came another hail in English, though this time with a distinct German accent:

"What ship is that?"

"The oil ship *Ganymede*, from London to the Hook," I said. "What do you want?"

"Are you Captain Gault?" asked the voice.

"I am," I answered. "What about it?"

"We're coming alongside, Captain," replied the voice. "Try no tricks, or from the water we shall blow you!"

"Sweet lot!" I said to myself. "They're keen on blowing! Politeness not on the list of extras at their little boarding establishments!"

"That you, Catty?" called the first voice from the submarine on our starboard side. This was in German. Then *sotto voce* to some companions:

"It's Catty, in the S24. We'll make him wait. We got alongside first."

I stirred a bit as I heard what he said, for I knew very well that the "S" submarines are the new 1,200-ton type of sea-going boats just completed by Germany for the express purpose of smashing up our merchantmen and so trying to starve our little British tummies.

Then, simultaneously, both on the port and starboard bows, there came fresh hails, also in English, but both somewhat Germanic:

"Vat sheep is dat?" said the one from broad away on the starboard bow in a long drawn-out hail.

"Gif me ze name of dat sheep!" bellowed the voice on the port bow, but from close at hand.

"It's Schulze and old Grunwald," said the man who had first hailed me, in violently idiomatic German, to his unseen companion; though for that matter, I couldn't see any of 'em. The night was too dark for that, though the sea was as still as a pond, pretty near.

The hails were repeated in a somewhat wrathy fashion, and the first-comer sung out to them, in German, to "Speak English! Herr Captain does not understand you!" This with unkind sarcasm, whereat there was laughter from the sea all round the ship, so it seemed to me; and in the same moment I had two further hails, one of them in first-rate English.

"What ship is that?" they asked.

I repeated my text like a kindergarten school chorus.

"And you?" I asked in turn. "How many of you are there? And what on earth do you want, anyway?"

"I guess we want juice, Cap'n," they told me. "We're willing to pay for it, and maybe we'll be able to make you a present of something you'll be glad to have. But let me tell you straight, if there's any funny biz, we'll blow you out of the water!"

"Good Lord!" I said. "Another blower! For the Lord's sake, quit your threats. What you're all going to do to this old packet of mine, if I happen to breathe without permission, is likely to injure her constitution! I s'pose a German's not happy if he's not blowing up something!"

"You'll find out all about that if you talk too much, Captain Gault," he said in a grim sort of way.

It was queer how they had my name at the ends of their tongues. Shows how the whole thing had been planned from back to front. Some big spying going on around out coasts, that's fairly plain.

"The commodore's here," I heard the first-comer saying to his companion in German.

Then the man who spoke perfect English said:

"We'll come alongside now, three on each beam, Cap'n, and start filling up. We'll be away inside of two hours, if you act sensible and do your part like a wise man. Tell your Engineer to have the gasoline pipes rigged. The sooner we're filled up and away, the better for us and for you, too, Cap'n; so get a move on you!"

Ten minutes later they were all fast alongside, and six different pipes were pumping their petrol-tanks full as hard as our pumping engine could run.

And they could just hold some essence, too, I can tell you! We put a hundred and thirty tons of liquid into each of them (they were all the new ocean-going model "S" boats) before they sang out to us to "cut off" and take the hoses back aboard.

And they ran no risks, either. They drew off and tested the stuff from each tank as we tapped it, drawing a full bucketful of essence through each hose, and trying it for density and "gassing." The last was done with a curious little spray pump and a sparkling contact breaker connected with a dry battery. They were a smart, cute lot of men right enough. But they were painfully uncivil, and I thought once my temper was going to get the better of me, only I needed those letters badly, not to mention my life.

But, to show the breed, they commandeered all my cigars (all, that is, that they could find) and all the liquer whisky in my cabin. Nor did they offer to pay for it when I remonstrated, but had the infernal impudence to tell me that the £750 they were going to hand over to me was sufficient to cover the "smokes and the drinks." I realised then how true is the saying that you can make an efficient man out of a German, but never a gentleman!

However, the six commanders, having drunk the Kaiser's health in my whisky, paid me the £750, as agreed upon, and then the one they called the commodore handed me a packet of letters, which I pounced on. I ripped the cord away and opened and looked them through. Yes, they were the letters all right; but there should have been eight, and I had been given only six.

"Six," I said, turning to the commodore. "There should be eight of these letters. You have given me only six."

The beggar wasn't at all ashamed. He didn't even deny it.

"I've the other two in my pocket, Captain," he said. "We may want your services again in the future, and these" (he slapped the breast of his coat) "may be an inducement to make you run risks where a cash payment alone might fail. Not that Captain Gault has not always got his price, of course."

Now that's the exact place where I nearly let my temper go. The darned measliness of hauling me into a mess like they had done, and then slamming *that* into my face, nearly pulled the lid right off my steam-box. But, fortunately, I kept hold of myself, or I'd not be alive now, I dare swear.

Instead, however, of doing anything rash, I realised that I had worked largely in vain in trying to get hold of those confounded letters. And now the only thing to do was to get the officers out of the ship before I lost control of my temper and started the beginning of a bad mess.

"Gentlemen," I said, as soon as I could keep my voice fairly steady, "you had better be going. Every minute you stay here increases the risks both for yourselves and for me. It is plainly useless to—"

"B-a-n-g!" went the roar of a great gun from somewhere quite near; and then, in the same instant, three successive booms of sound and a great crash of an explosion alongside, which seemed to shake the vessel.

"Mein Gott!" shouted several of the German officers, and there was a dash for the decks.

The whole night seemed to be one blaze of light. There were at least twenty odd searchlights playing on the ship from both port and starboard. Everything aboard of us was as bright as day.

The German officers rushed, shouting, to the sides. I ran to the port side and started over. The foremost submarine was just disappearing in a smother of oil and broken water. She'd been hit. The two others on that side had shut down the hatches of their conning-towers, and were rapidly submerging themselves.

As I stared, there flicked out half a dozen fierce red flashes from below the searchlights to port, and instantly the whole sea roared to the crashes of bursting shells and heavy gunfire, whilst the port side of the old *Ganymede,* forrard of me, seemed to splash into volcanoes of fire and flying iron.

And then—C-R-A-S-H!—the whole of the forrard decks, everything, roared heavenwards in a spout of flame. The shells had slapped right through into the forrard oil containers. The entire fore part of the ship *bumped,* just as if a giant had kicked her from underneath; then she rolled over slowly to starboard, and I saw that already there were about a dozen power launches pelting for us at full speed, plain to see in the tremendous light all about us.

I went tumbling down the slope of the decks, struck the rail with my body, a brute of a thump, and flopped over like a sack into the sea. I was vaguely conscious, as I went, that all about me others were doing the cascading trick in similar style.

I wasn't stunned, or seriously damaged in any way, and as soon as I hit the water, it was so beastly, freezingly, brutal cold, I had all my wits about me in a moment. I ploughed up to the surface at the rate of knots, got the water out of my eyes and nose, and yelled to everybody near me to swim away from the old *Ganymede* before she took the final dip.

Then I did some tall swimming on my own, and in the midst of it, I guess, the *Ganymede* went; for there was a terrific explosion, and showers of burning drops of oil fell all over the sea for hundreds of yard round.

The next thing I knew, a launch was coming for me full speed, and I had to roar at the fools to shut off or steer wide, one or the other.

Two minutes later they hauled me aboard, and just about one hour after that, aboard one of the British light cruisers. I was the centre, or shall I say the vortex, of as lively a bit of moral disagreement as ever I've experienced.

I had been given some rum, a towel, and a change of clothes, and finally, just as a sort of finish to the general *tout ensemble,* I s'pose, a pair of hand-cuffs and a firm invitation to accompany two particularly muscular and hefty-looking gentlemen to the Captain's cabin.

I did not know the name of the cruiser till I entered the cabin; but there I saw it, the *A*— (censored), beautifully inlaid in solid silver on a bronze shield, let into the forrard bulkhead. And, anyway, I was worrying less about that than the things I had to say to the Captain of that particular cruiser.

There were four officers in British naval uniform in the cabin, all sitting round a table; and there were five out of the eight German officers, dressed in undress uniforms which had evidently been lent them by the officers of the cruiser. The chap they had called the commodore was among them, and it was pretty plain that they were being well treated. A good cigar each (I recognised the smell) and *no hand-cuffs*.

I held mine out, so that everyone in the cabin could see them.

"Why *these*, gentlemen?" I said.

"Shut up!" said the biggest of the two aforesaid muscular blue-jackets, speaking as much into my ear as possible.

No one, except the courteous bluejacket, seemed to be even aware that I had spoken, and I decided to wait and see what was going to happen. From the look of the four officers round the table I judged I was in for a solemn time, and that they were simply trying to settle in their minds whether to shoot me with half a dozen rifles or a 6 in. cannon. Disappointing economy, I decide, would preclud-ed the 6 in. method—which should have been a comfort, but wasn't.

They had no difficulty in proving me guilty, right up to the hilt, for it was plainly and obviously what our leading novelists, in their highly original phraseology, term a case of having been caught red-handed.

However, the German officer, who spoke English, seemed deter-mined that I should have no loophole, and he explained how I had voluntarily agreed to meet them and sell them oil for a personal con-sideration of one thousand pounds in cash, plus certain letters of a compromising character. He advised a search through the pockets of the clothes I had worn when picked up, and finally he exhibited the two letters which he had refused to give me just before the catastro-phe, and handed these over to the four solemn-faced officers as a sort of final tombstone for the grave of poor old Master-Mariner Gault.

"That, gentleman," said the English-speaking German, "will sure show you that he's a proper outsider—a proper double-crosser!"

I stared at the man, for it was plain he felt pretty ugly to me. Then I twigged. He'd evidently got some notion into his head that

I'd double-crossed him and brought the cruisers down on his track. The man was a plain fool. Good Heavens! I'd more to fear from the cruisers, and more to lose, than ever he had, in spite of his having been taken prisoner. But anyway, it was no use arguing with that sort of a grouch. I could see that. But he made me crazy to get one good fair punch at him, right into his solar plexus. I didn't give up all hope.

Meanwhile, the officer in charge of the show (a court-martial I believe they called it) was explaining the particulars regarding hour and place, when and where, he meant a number of his men to put daylight through me. In plain English, it appeared plausible that, some morning, daylight and death were to effect an unpleasing conjuction for G. Gault, master-mariner.

This was bad enough in its way, but when he got his beard wagging about my sins, and set out to add insult to arranged injury by pointing out that I was a traitor of so particulary putrid a breed that it would soil the boots of any honest sailor should they adventure to wipe them on me, why, I thought it time to make my little speech—my swan-song, as it were.

Said I, in the little absolute silence that always follows a death sentence:

"Gentlemen, may I ask a question or two?"

They nodded agreement. A condemned man always has special privileges extended to him as soon as he's safely condemned.

"What is it, Captain Gault?" said the senior officer.

"What are we doing?" I asked, and looked up at the tell-tale compass in the deck above my head.

No one answered; they didn't know quite how to take a question of that sort at such a time. So I continued:

"I see we're heading W.S.W. And by the feel of her, and seeing she's a thirty-knot boat, I should say we're doing all that; so we ought to be quite sixty knots W.S.W. of the place where you sunk my ship—"

"I cannot listen to all this talk," the senior officer said quietly. "Have you anything else to say?"

"A lot!" I told him, speaking quietly, too. "Supposing, instead of all this balderdash, and *these*"—I held up the handcuffs—"you 'bout ship and get back again. We should get there just nicely by daylight. And while we're going, give orders to have these taken off—"

"Is that all you have to say?" he interrupted, rising, as a signal that I'd exceeded even the privileges of the condemned.

"There are just two things," I said, and they all paused there about the table, with a sort of deadly, quiet courtesy.

"First of the two is: Am I condemned for this oil 'trade' I've been into?"

"That expresses it," replied the senior officer, and waited for me to finish.

"The second is: Can a submarine do anything, except sink to the bottom or rise to the surface, if her accumulators are played out and her fuel tanks empty?"

"What do you mean, Sir?" asked the senior officer, with a sudden new tone in his voice, and I saw that everyone in the cabin was looking at me queerly.

"I mean," I said, very quietly and very slowly, so as to have the full enjoyment of saying it, "I mean that, as poor old Mac and I pumped salt water solidly for two hours into the tanks of those submarines, they'll not run far; at least"—I turned to the English-speaking German—"perhaps you will tell us whether German submarines *can* run their engines on a saltwater diet?"

My word! But I never got further. The whole cabin was in an uproar. The bluejackets had to leave me unsupported while they subdued the English-speaking German. Then, when quiet came again, I began to explain quite a number of things. And long before I had finished, the senior officer himself had unlocked the handcuffs with his own hands.

"You see," I concluded, "I told poor old Mac the whole of my pickle, and we arranged between us to fix up bypasses to the salt-water pump, and connect these up to the oil-hoppers. When these German officers here drew off their test bucketfuls we gave them good, honest essence. But when we had the pipes into the tanks, we gave them nice, clean, honest enough salt water. And they never guessed. Why should they?

"And now, gentlemen, if you go back there and wait, you'll be bound to get the five you didn't sink when they come up to breathe—eh? Anyway, they're there until the Judgement, unless they can get someone to sell them something stronger than salt water. And that'll not be easy, if you keep a scout there to watch out.

"Meanwhile, I'd like those two letters—I fancy I've earned 'em!"

The Plans of the Reefing Bi-Plane

"LOOK HERE, CAPTAIN GAULT," said Mr. Harpentwater to me at dinner. "I guess we'd better get down to business about your carting my plans and the model—"

He shut up suddenly as I frowned at him, and turned to the butler who had just entered the dining room.

"That will do, Baynes," he said. "I'll ring if I want you."

"Very well, Sir," said the butler, and oiled himself out of the room on the queer frictionless joints that butlers seem to sport. We shut the door, and there was a bit of silence. This was in February of 1915—long before you American boys joined forces with us. I'd docked the old Bendanga in Baltimore harbour, and was dining with my old inventor friend, Harpentwater.

"About this model, Captain," he began again. "What would you consider a fair price to take it and the plans across for me?"

"How big is the model?" I interrupted.

"Goes into a portmanteau, folded," he explained. "Weighs twenty-four pounds, four ounces."

"I'll do the job for a thousand dollars, cash down," I said, after thinking a moment. "I can take it as personal luggage if it's as small as that. No need to charge freightage. I'll lump it down with me, in a taxi."

"You'll never reach your ship alive, Captain," he said, coolly enough. "If it were as simple as all that, I'd never have brought you into the business, but just mailed it across. No, Sir! I'll send it down tomorrow sometime between twelve and one; and no one will know how or when it's going to reach you. It'll be packed and sealed, along with the plans, in a strong case; and all you've got to do is to hand it over to my agents in London. They'll be responsible that it reaches the War Office."

"That sounds all right to me," I told him.

"That's settled then," he agreed. "I'll pay you now and be done."

He hauled out a wad fit to plug a four-inch shot-hole and peeled off ten hundreds, which he pushed across to me. "I'm eternally obliged to you, Captain," he said…. "Just one minute."

He slid noiselessly out of his chair and took four lightning-like strides to the door; caught the knob, and flipped the door open.

"Ah!" he said in a curious voice. "What are you looking for, Baynes?"

"I dropped a cufflink here, Sir," said Baynes' voice. "I'm sorry I made a noise looking for it."

"No noise at all, Baynes," said Mr. Harpentwater, quietly. "Go upstairs and pack your traps. Come to me in ten minutes, and I'll pay you up."

Baynes said nothing, and Mr. Harpentwater came back into the room, closed the door, and returned to the table.

"Listening?" I asked.

"Looked like it," he said. "Anyway, out he goes. I'll have no doubtful servants in my house a moment longer than I've a use for 'em!"

"Quite so," I agreed, and finished my coffee.

An hour later, I left the house, and within five minutes of leaving it, I was tackled by a mob of five hooligans down near the front.

At first I thought I was just what they call a "spec"—i.e., a chance pigeon; but as I lammed at the head of the second man (I'd kicked the first in the stomach), I heard one of men at the back call out:

"Maul the guy good, boys; he's got a thousand bucks on him right now."

That made me think suddenly of the butler. I guess Harpentwater had been wise to give him the long throw; but it looked as if I were to lose out on it also, unless I moved lively; for two more men ran out from a side street and joined in against me.

There followed a vigorous fifty seconds. I dodged two slung-shots that would have made holes in my head; and laid out a third man; but I got two nasty bashes from knuckle-dusters; and then I heard one of them sing out:

"Knives, you guys!"

I knew it was time now to stop scrapping, and begin business.

I slid my Colt automatic out of my wainscoat pocket and let drive: crack—crack—crack—crack!

If you've ever used an "auto," you'll know how they "brrrr" death out mighty easy. Well, there were four downed men right there in front of me inside of three full seconds, each one of 'em shot nice and business-like, not to kill but to hurt a bit. For I saw no use in ending the lives even of that kind of person.

The whole body of 'em left me then, hurriedly; and I came on down to the ship.

Perhaps I ought to explain a few details.

Mr. Harpentwater is the man who invented the American Underswing Sewing Machine and the Apwater Gasoline Engine, as probably you know just as well as I do.

He made, roughly, a million and a half dollars out of the first; and I guess the way things are looking, he's going to top that figure on the second; for the "Apwater Rotator," as they call it over here on the hoardings, "leaves the Gnome gnoming!" This is, of course, pure American; but I believe it is quite true that the Apwater gadget is "some" engine.

Well, the Apwater Rotator naturally chucked old Harpentwater's inventive faculties slam bang into the middle of aeronautics with the consequence that his latest effort is the Harpentwater Reefing Biplane which, briefly, is what the flying people have all been howling about, ever since they started to grow wings, or perhaps, to be more accurate, wing-pains!

Briefly, in simple phrasing, the trouble with all existing flying-planes is that if you want a fast plane, you've got to cut your supporting surfaces down to the "limit." This means that the machine so treated can't leave old terra firma except at a very high rate of speed. Equally, it must land, when it returns, also at a high speed; and landing at a high speed means all sorts of breakages, both to man and machine, unless the God of Luck offers himself continually as a sort of buffer between man and outraged natural laws. So much for fast planes.

And if you feel that life is more valuable to you than speed, and that you prefer to leave earth slowly and return with equal deliberation, you must use large and liberal planes. And large and liberal planes means that speed for you is practically *non est*.... And in *war, speed is, after stability, the most desirable of all things.*

There you have the whole secret at the back of Harpentwater's action in sending for me to discuss taking the plans and the model of his plane across to England; for that hypenated gentleman known as the German-American exists in large quantities on this side of the pond. Further, he has a genius for amalgamating and organizing himself into societies for the furtherence, not of American interests, mind you, but of "dear old Germany."

The remainder is easy to comprehend. Harpentwater's Reefing Bi-plane combines the stability of the machine with large planes, with all its landing advantages, plus the speed of the machine suffering from abridged planes. In other words, the most timid of aviators can go aloft with a Harpentwater Reefing Bi-plane from any old *ploughed* field he happens to have a fancy for. He can also descend gently and precisely onto a field similarly unfitted for aeronautical purposes. And further, while in the air, he can touch speeds that are apt to cause a serious wastage of the enemy's high velocity shells; not to mention uncounted shiploads of steel and nickel, in the shape of rifle-bullets.

And this combination of qualities is achieved (in part, at least) by Mr. Harpentwater's cunning invention, by means of which, as soon as his Reefing Bi-plane has safely mounted into the air, the pilot can, by means of a beautiful worm and wheel piece of mechanism, reduce the planes to something scandalously approaching the vanishing point—the exact degree of vanishment being determined by the engine-speed, and screw-pitch by means of a harnessed governor.

Then, when the aviator wishes to descend, he reverses his worm and wheel gadget, and his planes grow again, as his engine speed and screw-pitch lessen, until, at last, under full plane surface, he floats, soft as the proverbial thistle-down, to rest upon the aforementioned ploughed field, or other aviatory abomination.

There you have the details (at least as many as I'm going to give you) of the Harpentwater Reefing Bi-plane. And even a long-honest Englishman may begin to understand, even though he condemns, something of the lust of possession which had seized upon a very appreciable section of German-Americans.

Now, when you take into account that these gentlemen occupied the old U.S.A. in their millions, and that they were, as I've already said, banded together to help the "old country" (meaning the Fatherland) to the limit, you will realize what old inventor Harpentwater was up against. For certain representatives of these consistently hyphenated millions had called upon him and made him what I must describe as a very handsome offer, if only it had been a little—well, a little, shall I say, less Germanic in tone and spirit. In brief, if he would sell them the secret of the Reefing Bi-plane, they would pay him, cash down, the sum of one million dollars, provided he kept the secret of the invention for six months from that date, from the other allies. After which they were willing that he should take out and negotiate his patents in the usual way, or do anything else he felt drawn to.

A very handsome offer I should have called it, as I've said, had it not as I've already hinted, been made it, a fashion just a little too Germanic to suit the stomach of a completely free-born and typically and wholesomely self-assertive, non-hyphenated American Citizen. In short then, to insure as they fatuously thought, Mr. Harpentwater's swift and unhesitating acceptance of their offer, these misguided, hyphenated gentlemen suggested pleasantly but unmistakably that if he (Mr. Harpentwater) did not close speedily with their very generous offer, they might withdraw it, and invoke the hushed aid of some of their confreres in official positions. To put it even more shortly, they threatened him, even while offering him so much loose cash, with the alternative that if he refused, some of their countrymen in the Foreign Mails Department, would see to it in any case that if he tried to offer the Reefing Bi-plane to the British, French or Russian Governments, they would certainly intercept the plans and the model *en route*.

Naturally, Harpentwater "blew up," violently; and, as I had gathered from him, they "blew out." I can believe it! I should not imagine Harpentwater a pleasant man to threaten. And, of course, they couldn't get the plans out of him now, even with a pair of American dentists' forceps.

However, equally, he's no fool. He sent for his secretary and procured much interesting information and many fathoms of official statistics, and was eventually very solidly satisfied that the hyphenated folk could make good their threat; for his investigations, and the investigations of his secretary, made it quite unpleasantly clear to him that the "hyphenated citizen" occupied in a quite extraordinary number, official positions varying from the blushing (perhaps this is not an exact description!) police forces of the States, to the more lucrative heights (or depths) of the "political posts."

He saw plainly that if he attempted to mail anything of a confidential nature to Europe, it would not long remain confidential. And then, being an inventor, he invented a plan to evade the enemy; but fortunately, he tested it first. He sent his butler, as an old servant, down to the shipping office to book a passage to England.

A boat was sailing that very day, and he ordered the butler to take a couple of portmanteaux aboard and put them in his berth.

The tactic taught him two things; one, that his house was evidently being watched; the other, that the hyphenated-folk would go to quite some lengths to get what they wanted.

The old butler's taxi was rammed by a powerful car on the way to the docks, and the next thing Harpentwater learned was that the butler was in hospital, badly hurt, and that the portmanteaux had vanished.

They were, however, recovered a week later by the police from an empty house in Belles Avenue. Nothing was missing; but the portmanteaux were literally cut to pieces. Evidently someone had searched earnestly for something; and Harpentwater found it easy enough to guess just what that was.

A little later, he engaged a new butler and caught him prying the first day. He said nothing, but kept an eye on him. About that time, my ship hit Baltimore, and a mutual friend reminded him that I have something of a penchant for tackling, shall I say, evasive little jobs. I have always found that if one puts one's mind to it, people are not difficult to deceive. Even the U.S.A. Customs people are not quite so obstinately opposed to this view as they used to be.

Well, Mr. Harpentwater sent for me, and I agreed to tackle the job. The rest you know—or most of it. The evening of that same day saw us at sea.

Harpentwater was promptly on time with his box, but the German organization was a jolly sight more prompt; for about a dozen men (of surprisingly hefty build) came down that forenoon, to take a passage home in the old *Bandanga*, and I couldn't refuse good passage-money; for that wouldn't be fair to my owners. However, you can bet your boots I took one or two little precautions. If they thought to start a rough-house in my ship as soon as we were away to sea, well I just fancy they'd have got hauled up with a round-turn!

The box was brought alongside by a boatman, just before one o'clock, and there was the whole two dozen (twenty-three, to be exact) of those German-American passengers of mine knocking around the decks, trying to seem as if they weren't looking for something. Well, I guess if they thought those plans and the model were theirs, just because their beastly butler-spy put them wise to our little plot, why... well, you'll see, that's all! I could carry that job through comfortably, Germans or no Germans, and I shouldn't need a squad of U.S.A. Militia to help me, either. God helps those who help themselves is as true as ever it was, and truer still if you stop the other fellow helping *himself!* Anyway, I was not going to hand back that thousand dollars. I was going to keep 'em and earn 'em! You bet.

First of all, I had word with my two Mates, Mr. Alty and Mr. Truss, and then I sent for Vinner, the First Engineer, and had a word with him. After that, I went down to my cabin and sat a bit, thinking out the best hiding place for that box of valuables.

Half an hour later I'd hit on the very place, and the box was safe out of sight.

The following day, things were still quiet, but there was mischief brewing, and my two Mates and I were walking about like blessed arsenals! I'd a big Colt automatic in each jacket pocket, in addition to my waist-coat pocket pet; and both Mr. Alty and Mr. Truss sported large-calibre revolvers of old but efficient pattern.

I'd had a further consultation with the Chief, and he and his three Engineers were all carrying guns; not to mention that they'd rigged a steam hose as a sort of "last stand" notion. The Chief told me I could depend on his holding the engine-room, and I believed him; but, all the same, twenty-three armed Germans—and I was quite sure they were armed—was a hefty problem for the seven of us to tackle.

After thinking things over, I sent for Keller, the bo'sun, and told him how matters lay. He begged to get the men and the stokers and join a rush on the Germans; but I pointed out that we could not move a finger until they did something illegal; and that any rushing of them would probably mean simply plain murder to any unarmed shell-back who might try it on.

In fact, as I proceeded to explain to the bo'sun, the reason I'd taken him into my confidence was to make sure of the men's safety. For, if and when the trouble did start, he was to send every man into the fo'cas'le, and make them shut the steel doors and keep out of the way. You see, we had only six A.B.s all told, and they couldn't do much, even if they were armed, which, as I've made clear, they were not. And Vinner's stokers were in the same hole, for there was not a gun in the ship except those that the four Engineers and my two Mates and I were carrying.

What the Germans had got, of course I didn't know; but I guessed from the look of them, they were all trained soldiers in mufti, and they would sprout guns like an arsenal when the time came!

Anyway, I made it clear to the bo'sun that I expected him to run the men and keep them free of any row with the Germans. I instructed him to keep a man at the wheel unless the Germans actually ordered otherwise. But whatever he did there was to be no chance given the enemy to pot the men. I felt sure, if they kept quiet and did not meddle, the Germans would be glad enough to leave them alone.

The trouble came on during the first day watch.

It began when one of the passengers, a Herr Deberswynch came to my cabin and asked for a word with me. After a little humming and hawing around the mulberry bush, he quit all pretense at finesse, and told me he knew the plans and model were aboard, and that he was empowered to offer me five thousand dollars for them cash down, and no trouble.

"There'll be no trouble in any ship I command unless I start it!" I told him.

"There are twenty-three of us, Cap'n!" he said, in a way that was plainly an ugly threat.

"There are, are there!" I answered, and was going to make one jump at him; only right then someone knocked at the door of my cabin, and three more of the passengers shoved in their heads.

"Well, Deberswynch," said one of them, as if I didn't exist, "what's the Cap'n say?"

"He says get out of this cabin and do it *now!*" I ripped out, boiling. "All of you! Get!"

They tried to argue for a minute, but Deberswynch shepherded them out, then turned to me at the door. "We'll give you a few minutes to think it over, Cap'n," he said. "I guess you'll maybe see your way to touching that five thousand dollars, as soon as you get looking hard and plain at all the facts. If not, of course—" he grinned, and slapped his coat pocket in a way that told what was in it. "We're all trained soldiers, you know, Cap'n" he added quietly, "and we mean to have what we want if we have to shoot you all, sink the ship, and go back in one of the boats. That's plain talk."

"Very," I said. "I guess I'd better have a word with my two Mates. I'll give you your answers in ten minutes."

"That's the idea, Cap'n," he agreed. "I thought you'd see it was no use going against us."

Then they all cleared off, and I went up on to the bridge.

My two Mates were both up there, chatting after the "tea relief," and as soon as they heard my step on the bridge, they turned toward me.

I gave a quick look at them; then jerked my head towards my chart-house, which is steel-built, doors and all, and lies just aft of the wheel-house.

"The game's started!" I said, as they came up to me. "Get into the chart-house smart, both of you. Mr. Truss, screw up the steel covers of the after ports, and you, Mr. Alty, phone down to Mr. Vinner and warn him. Tell him to keep the engines going at half-speed unless he hears from me." I jumped for the wheel-house door and pulled it open.

"Pelter," I said to the man at the wheel, "get right forrard and tell the bo'sun the passengers have started ructions. Then take your orders from him till further notice."

"Aye, aye, Sir," said the A.B., but he hesitated, unable at first to comprehend that I meant him actually to leave the wheel untended, even for a minute.

"Smart now!" I said. "You'll have to leave the wheel. The bo'sun'll send you aft again, as soon as you've given him my message."

"Aye, aye, Sir," he said again; then hesitatingly loosed the wheel-spokes and went off on his errand. Probably it was the first time in his life he had ever seen the wheel deserted at sea.

I left the wheel-house and went out on to the bridge again. Away aft there was a bunch of Germans grouped around Herr Deberswynch, who saw me and waved his hand to signify that he was coming for his answer.

He started to come forward, along with the whole lot of them, and I walked to the after side of the bridge. There I waited for them, close to the starboard door of my chart-house, which Mr. Truss, my Second Mate held open, ready for me to bunk to cover.

"Well, Cap'n?" said Herr Deberswynch, as soon as they had all climbed up on to the bridge-deck, just below the after part of the bridge.

"What do you want?" I asked, pretending that I refused to take any notice of what he had said earlier.

"Come off the roof, Cap'n," he replied. "We've come for your answer. Are you going to hand those plans and the model over quietly, or are you going looking for trouble?"

"Don't talk rot," I said. "You couldn't get that box inside of a month's search. And if you think I'm going to help you, you're a bigger owl than you look; and that's putting it strong!"

"Quit that, Cap'n!" he said in a way that showed he was ready to get ugly the next moment. "Just answer out straight; is it peace or war? If it's war, the Lord help you; for inside of five minutes I'll have you down here on your knees, begging like a toy dog. Now then, what is it?"

"Well," I said, speaking very slowly and in a thoughtful-sounding way so as to hide the fact that I was planning to act mighty quick. "Well, Mister Deberswynch, I'm not great on spelling long words... I guess I'll take the three-letter one."

He grabbed my meaning quicker than the rest and hauled out a full-sized Mauser pistol with a quick jerk from inside his coat; but I beat him on the draw, for I had both hands in the side pockets of my coat, gripping my two big Colts, and I fired slam through the pockets... I sounded like a hefty sort of Fifth of November.

My shooting was not half bad, considering the handicap; though, of course, I've practiced that sort of trick-shooting before and burnt many a good coat. I plugged Herr Deberswynch through the right shoulder, and again through the left forearm. And then, before any one of the others could get a gun on me, I'd shoved ten more shots down among their legs. I reckon I got six or seven of 'em between the ankle and the hip.

And then I made one prize jump sideways into the chart-house, and Mr. Truss slammed and bolted the door. As he did so, the whole steel starboard side of the house thudded and pinged with bullets; and for a full half-minute, we couldn't hear each other speak well. "My oath!" I said, when it eased off, "I'm just as well pleased to be in out of the rain!"

"Good Lord, Sir!" said Mr. Truss, "that was cutting it fine. Did you kill many of them?

"Nary a one, Mister," I told him. "And let me make it plain right now that if we can put this business through, minus corpses, home or foreign, it'll be better all round. Shoot to hurt as much as you like, but not for the undertaker. We don't want old Uncle Sam shoving his nose into this business; and I reckon I can tame that little lot outside without killing 'em. They've a deal to learn yet; and I'm going to do the teaching…. Mr. Alt, you phoned Mr. Vinner?"

"Yes, Sir," said the First Mate. "He's waiting for 'em now."

"Get him again," I said, "and tell him not to shoot to kill, if he can avoid it. Tell him I'll get a talk in with him in a bit…. Now, Mr. Truss, give me a hand here with these forrard port-covers before the beggars get at them!" The fusilade had ended now, and while Mr. Alty rang up the Chief Engineer, the Second Mate and I completed the screwing up of the steel port-covers. Then I switched on the lights and told the two Mates not to make a sound, while I listened.

For ten minutes, none of us moved; but we could not hear anything beyond the faint croak of the bulkheads, as the vessel rolled a little.

"Looks as if you'd scared 'em into taking cover," said Mr. Truss. "I s'pose you're sure you didn't make a mistake an' kill 'em all off, Sir?"

As he made his joke, he got his answer, and a pretty rough answer it was, too. There came a thundering crash that made me think, for a moment, the ship had blown up. The whole air of the house seemed literally to *jolt*, and for a second or two I felt a sort of dizzy, head-pressure kind of feeling which cleared and left me feeling rather sick.

"You two all right?" I heard myself saying in a dull-sounding, far-away sort of voice. And then, without seeming to expect them to answer, I stared round at the starboard door. It was bowed in, like a bent sheet of tin that's been kicked. I could see a gap between the lower half of the door-edge and the jamb, big enough to shove my arm through; and up through this a bluish smoke was curling in thin streams.

As I stared, I realized that a queer singing had gone suddenly out of my ears; and in place of it a cotton-wooly sort of quietness. I could hear the odd ship sounds again. I heard the Mate's voice behind me saying, very slowly, and somehow tonelessly:

"I'm all right, Sir."

And then the Second Mate's voice, more alive: "I'm not hurt, Sir. Are you all right? The brutes tried to blow us up. I'd...."

As he spoke, through the bowed-in space between the edge of the bent door and the jamb, I saw a face come into view, very slowly and cautiously, round the after end of the house. I watched it come more and more into sight. Then another came, and then another, and after that a fourth. They tiptoed nearer to the bent door, and I could see them staring with a queer sort of fearful curiosity, more like boys who've been in mischief than grown men.

"It's not fallen in," I heard one of them say.

"Do you think the air-shock will have snuffed them?" said another voice.

"Likely enough!" said someone more to the left. "They're quiet enough, anyhow. Try the door, Dussol."

I got up quickly, tiptoed over to the switch, and put out the lights. I beckoned to the Mates not to move; and then I pulled out my two Colts, put them on the table and started reloading them quietly. There was just enough light coming into the place, through the space round the bent door, to enable me to see what I was doing.

As I did so, I heard the bent door creak and whine where it still hung on its hinges and the upper of the two heavy bolts. The lower bolt-hasp had been blown clean away.

"It's fast yet," said the man who had been called Dussol. "Good stuff to stand that Mark X stuff. Pity we've only another. Anyway, I guess it's put them all to sleep for good; and that's something done."

"Serves the fools right!" said the man who had just spoken. "There's eight of us drilled through the legs and Herr Deberswynch has got all he'll want for a week or two. That guy couldn't half use a gun! Damn him! Try the door again; all of us together now!"

There was much grunting, denoting physical effort, and the door whined and creaked weirdly; but it was good Tyne steel, and it "stayed put."

They gave it up at last.

"Get some of those things that go in the capstans," said the voice of the man who seemed to be giving all the orders. "I'd use that other Mark X canister, but if the box is inside, we might smash it up too much. And anyway, we'll want that to sink the darned ship when we leave her!"

I had finished loading my Colts, and I tiptoed over to where the two Mates sat.

"Mr. Alty," I said to the First Mate, "I'm going out on deck to do a bit of sniping if I can. You keep your eyes on the starboard door, and when they bring those caps'n bars, give it to 'em in the legs. I'll pepper 'em, then run from behind the big ventilator... Mr. Truss, you come and open the port door for me. Stand by it with your guns so as to let me in smart when I sing out. And don't get losing your head and loosing off at me in mistake. Come along!"

The First Mate moved across to where he could cover the big open place along the bolt-edge of the door, and Mr. Truss, the Second Mate, came across and let me out through the port doorway.

There was just the first grey of the dusk in the air, which suited me very well, and I slid down on to my hands and crept quickly along by the coaming of the house until I'd reached the ventilator, which came up in two canvas-covered wire winches.

Here I squatted, pretty safe for the moment, with my guns ready in my fists. I could hear the Germans talking on the other side of the house; and then one of them sung out to the men who had gone for the capstan bars to hurry up.

"Coming right now!" I heard a man singing out, and as he spoke there came a shot from somewhere forrard of me. At first I thought it was the Mate firing through the burst edge of the starboard door; and then there came another shot and shouting down on the main well-deck. And immediately afterwards, a dozen shots, or more, fired in an irregular sort of volley.

"What the deuce is up, down there?" I thought to myself, and the same moment I realized that the Germans on the other side of the chart-house were racing towards the forrard end of the bridge deck to see what was up. Directly after that, there was a whole lot more shooting, and I thought it was time to make myself useful, especially as a way aft I could see four more of the passengers coming forrard along the after well-deck; and all of them showing marked and varied limps. I'm afraid I smiled a little unkindly, but I was careful not to let them see me; for they all had Mauser pistols in their hands, and I knew they'd be hankering to get a good square pot at me. They were obviously coming to take a turn in whatever new trouble was on.

I didn't wait to admire them anymore; but went down on to my hands and knees again, and crept quickly forrard along by the side of the house, until the after break of the bridge-deck hid me from the coming "limpers" on the after main-deck. Then I stood up and ran on tiptoe to the forrard break and looked down on to the fore well-deck.

It was Keller, the bo'sun! I might have known a man with a name like that couldn't keep out of a fight. He was in his little steel half-deck and firing through one of the ports, with what I guessed was an old navy revolver that he must have had in his sea-chest. It had a bark like a four-inch gun; and it was plain that my bo'sun was vastly enjoying himself; though with a lot more courage than brains; for they'd have had him inside of another minute if I hadn't come along right then. But it was an interesting little scene right enough.

Three Germans were lying, taking cover, behind the big main-deck capstan. They each had a capstan bar, and I could see that the bo'sun must have opened his artillery on them just as they were getting the bars, which stood in a rack near the capstan.

The men behind the capstan were not firing back; but staring round the barrel of it at the forrard end of the half-deck, as if they were expecting something. The next instant I saw what it was they were waiting for. All the Germans who had left the chart-house were standing away to port of the half-deck, out of the bo'sun's range; and round the forrard end of the half-deck two of the passengers were cat-walking, keeping flat in close to the house, so that the bo'sun could not see them. When they got close enough, one would grab the bo'sun's outreached revolver, and the other would shoot him through the open port. And then bye-bye bo'sun! Silly owl for disobeying me!

However, I was there, as I've said, and I just let go a one-two, aiming low but carefully.

How those two Germans did run! I merely skinned them; for I was not setting out to do more than punish and frighten the life out of them.

"Keller!" I roared, "shut the port, you fool! They're creeping round the house, flat up against it. Close that port and put that gun away."

Slam! went Keller's port; and the same moment the whole air all round me fairly buzzed with the Mauser bullets those disappointed Germans loosed off at me. I whanged off six shots at them, just to liven them up, and then bolted; for I remembered the four limping Germans in my rear. As it was, I reached the port chart-house door, just as they came up the after ladders; and if the Second Mate hadn't been watching and thrown the door open for me just in the instant, I'd have been perforated; for I heard their bullets whack on the steel door just as it flipped open between their guns and me.

Then I was into the chart-house safe, with the door locked, wondering what the night had for us. I felt sure we could count on a "certain liveline."

Darkness came on without anything fresh happening. Once or twice we caught the sounds of footsteps passing preciously quietly along the bridge-decks to the port of the chart-house. It struck me they were mighty anxious lest we should hear 'em, and try a shot or two from the ports.

By the time it was quite dark, I thought it as well to get going with certain plans I had made; for, I can tell you, I was not aching to stay a minute longer in the chart house than need be. I was anxious about that other Mark X canister I'd heard them talking about. They *might* decide to use it on us after all; and once a day is quite as much blowing up as my constitution will stand.

I thought it as well to have a look out before opening the port door. I guessed it would be more than likely that a guard would have been placed on us, after my little sortie; and I started in to prove my notion by opening one of the after port-covers.

But this proved a deuce of a job to manage quietly; for the screw of the hold-fast squealed like a pig disgorging its soul. Then I remembered there was a hand-load in one of the lockers; and this I rooted out. There was still some tallow left in the lead-hole, as I'd hoped, and with this, I tallowed the infernal screw until it hadn't a squeal left in it. Half a minute later, I had the steel cover back, without a sound.

It was easy to spot our guard by the glow of burning cigars; for there were, in fact, two of them; and when I had treated the glass-cover screw, and got the glass-cover open, I recognized the smell of my own cigars! Confound their gargantuan gip! I guess a German's just a natural-born pirate! I got a notion that if I was going to have a cigar left, it was time I got busy.

First of all, I tackled the hinges of the port door with the tallow, so as to quiet them; and after that I opened one of the port-covers on the starboard side, having first introduced it also to my tallow-treatment. Then I explained to my two Mates just what we were going to do. Mr. Alty, the First Mate, was to stand at the opened porthole on the starboard side of the house, and Mr. Truss was to attend to the port door. When I gave the word, Mr. Alty was to do revolver stunts through the open port, and that would send the German guard over to that side of the deck in a hurry. Meanwhile, Mr. Truss was to have the port door open, and we were all to get out on deck, as quiet as you like, shut the door again, and vamoose to the roof of the wheel-house, where we could lie flat and watch events. The Germans would imagine we were still in the chart-house, and I trusted it would give them much pleasure to keep on guarding it. Whilst, if that second Mark X canister were brought forward to blow the place open, we should be able to do a whole lot of damage before they realised where it was coming from. And, to be frank, if they tried the blowing up dodge again, I felt that I should shoot to hurt.

Well, we carried it out finely. The Mate took his station at the open port, and at the first bang of his revolver, I saw the lights of the burning cigars hustle across to investigate the whereforeness of the gun-fire. Then we all slipped out quietly through the port doorway; we shut the door again, and thirty seconds afterwards, we were all three flat on top of the wheel-house, and no one but ourselves aware of the fact.

Fifteen minutes later, I saw that I had guessed right once more; for those confounded brutes actually tried to place that second Mark X canister on the house. We spotted them doing it, just in time, and the volley we let loose among their legs, must have hurt a whole lot. Anyway, inside of five seconds or a bit less, every one of them had done the grand "bunk;" for they simply didn't know who was hurting them, or how it was done, or anything else, except that it was painful. They ran and crept and rolled away through the darkness, *yelling*! And before they were more than properly gone, I had jumped off the wheel-house roof, and sent the darned canister of high explosive sailing overboard; for I felt I might want to use the chart-house again.

"Now," I said, "we'll go back to our little home again. They can't trouble us much, now we've got shut of that busting-up stuff. I want to get some sleep."

Quite a bit happened the next day. We got our sleep all right, as I'd thought we should; for they'd had quite as much too much of us, as I'd imagined they would, and their damages were quite extensive, as I saw when I woke up in the morning and had a look at them knocking round the decks.

Then I got what I guess they felt was a surprise; for on looking at the tell-tale compass, I found that they'd put the vessel about, sometime during the night, and she was heading back for America at a good steady half-speed. I guessed it was time to start making hay, now or never, and I got Mr. Vinner on the engine-room telephone.

"Stop her right now, Mr. Vinner," I said, "and whatever happens, don't start up your engines again till you hear from me. See? The beggars are heading her for the old U.S.A. again; but if they think they're going to get a free trip back after all this mess and bother, well I guess they don't know *me*, Mr. Vinner."

I heard him laugh over the phone.

"I've a notion they've learnt a bit, Captain," he said; "and they, no doubt, they'll learn the rest between here and the U.S.A. I'll stop her right now, till I hear from you again."

"That's right," I said; "and look out for squalls. By the way, if you're pressed and have to use steam on 'em, don't do any real damage—see? Just give them a deuce of a shake-up, and let them go. They'll not face you again. I never met the man who'd face steam twice!"

"Nor me, Captain," said Vinner. "I'll get busy right now."

"Right!" I said, and rang off.

A minute later the screw stopped turning. Ten minutes after this, there was a German delegation to the engine-room skylight, and much talk; followed, in a bit by threats and, finally, quite a noticable liveliness around Mr. Vinner's skylight.

The gun-firing began at last to sound serious, and I was thinking I'd better get out and take a hand when I caught the roar of the steam jet.

"Vinner's steaming 'em," said Mr. Truss, grinning cheerfully. "That'll fix 'em. They'll not want much of that!"

They didn't. They simply quit; and for a few hours they were slow enough for a funeral.

Then, about four o'clock in the afternoon, they evidently got desperate. I fancy some of them were getting pretty anxious to see a doctor, and they sent a white flag man to talk business with me.

He knocked at the port door and explained his errand through half-an-inch of good steel.

After surveying the decks all round, through the various ports, we opened the door and invited him in; and then the business talk began. He wanted me to order the engines started. I told him the ship's head was pointed just a wee matter of a hundred and eighty degrees off her course. Followed then some more talk; and at last, after I'd explained to him just what I thought of them all, I told him that I was prepared to stay out here till they were all dead of gangrene, unless they paid their passage back; also five thousand dollars to cover damage to the vessel, and finally, ten thousand to be divided between the Engineers, my two Mates and myself, for moral injuries.

To tell the truth, the way he took the news at first was so violent that I felt a little anxious lest they'd not got the cash with them; but I determined to stick out for my price. You see, I was pretty sure they'd brought more than the five thousand dollars they'd offered me, so as to be able to raise their bids for my sinful old soul, if they'd found I was inclined to put a higher price on it. Honestly, I don't believe the poor innocents had ever conceived that the whole world's morality wasn't "made in Germany." Well, I sent him away to his friends, and told him not to bother to come back unless he brought the cash with him.

He returned in an hour with the whole sum in quite a comfortable wad of notes; and as soon as I'd examined them, I phoned down word to Mr. Vinner to start her up again at full lick.

I sent the German away then and told Mr. Truss to take the bridge; but Mr. Alty and I sat guard over that pile of dollars in the chart-house, for I'd not have trusted my precious passengers as far as I could throw each one separately.

Every four hours that night, the two Mates relieved each other, and I made the one off-duty sleep with me in the chart-house. Further, I both shored up the broken starboard door and kept the port one locked. There were altogether too many armed strangers aboard to suit me. However, the night went away all right; though both officers told me they had a feeling there was "gunpowder in the air," as the saying is; and I felt a bit the same way myself.

At midday we sighted land, and two hours later I had the engines stopped; for we were in half a mile of the shore, about ten miles north of Baltimore.

I sent word now to tell the German passengers that I was as close in as I cared to go, and if they wanted to get ashore, they'd have to buy one of the boats; for I wasn't going to trust any of my men or either of my officers alone with that lot away from the ship on a lonely bit of coast. I told this frankly, and I explained through the Second Mate that these details being just so, there would be no one to bring the boat back to the ship again, and therefore I should be forced to charge for her.

Maybe the figure I put on the boat was a little high, for after all, a ship's lifeboat doesn't cost a thousand dollars. I suppose I ought to admit that you could buy one for less than two-hundred-and-fifty; but that does not excuse the attempt they made to steal one of my boats and get her launched and away.

There is, however, a certain technical skill required to hoist a boat out of her chocks and over the side, when a vessel is rolling in a seaway! And when men who are not sailormen attempt to do this sort of thing under the fire of two Colts and four revolvers, the thing becomes ridiculous, as they seemed at last to realise. For the two Mates and I had retired once more to the fortress of the charthouse, from which one can command the ship, fore and aft. And really, I did some very pretty shooting.

Finally, my adventurous passengers gave it up, paid the money, and begged for peace.

Half an hour later the ship was well rid of them, and they and their boat were following the promptings of a certain, popular hymn writer, and pulling for the shore; not cleverly, perhaps, but certainly with determination.

And an hour and a half after they had gone, I discovered another reason why they were so anxious to say good-bye to us and get ashore quickly at any price. For the box *containing both the plans and the model had gone!* They had found it after all!

We reached old England on March 20th, and docked at noon, without having been torpedoed. The first thing I did, after finishing my duties aboard, was to write the following letter to that infernal Herr Deberswynch:

S.S.*Bandaga.*
London Docks.
Dear Herr Deberswynch:

You will not be in a hurry, I daresay, to stop crowing over me. Certainly you got the plans and the model. You paid for them, and you got them. At the same time, I feel that the following details will interest you:

Mr. Harpentwater, the inventor, paid me one thousand dollars to fulfill a certain duty. It was to drag a red herring across your track. I did so, and you apparently liked the smell to the tune of fifteen thousand dollars and the price of the boat (mind you, it was not at all a bad boat, though perhaps the market was inclined to be bullish— eh?). And then, of course, there was the passage money and, finally, quite a healthy number of what I might call Colt-marks—a fine little weapon, properly used.

After all, the figure was rather high to pay for a red herring. You see, as you will presently hear from your aerial experts, the plans and the model you took ashore so feloniously, were not the plans and model of Mr. Harpentwater's Reefing Bi-plane. They were merely a set of fake plans and an experimental model specially boxed up for red herring purposes.

And while you and your superiors were intent upon the chase of the red herring I was carting across the Atlantic, the real plans and the real model of the Reefing Bi-plane were traveling safely to England in a simple looking package consigned to the U.S. Mail, beautifully free from the suspicions of your superiors and the multitude of their spies who use their official position not to further American interests, but German interests.

Rather a neat little plan, don't you think so, my dear Herr?

Yours truly,

G. GAULT
Master

The Adventures of Captain Jat

The Island of the Ud

PIBBY TAWLES, CABIN-BOY and deck-hand stood to lee-ward of the half-poop, and stared silently at the island, incredibly lonely against the translucence of the early dawn—a place of lonesome and mysterious silence, with strange birds of the sea wheeling and crying over it, and making the silence but the more apparent.

A way to wind'ard, Captin Jat, his Master, stood stiff and erect against the growing light, all his leathery length of six feet, five inches, set into a kind of grim attention as he stared at the black shadow upon the sea, that lay off his weather bow.

The minutes passed slowly, and the dawn seemed to dream, stirred to reality only be the far and chill sound of the birds crying so dreely. The small barque crept on, gathering the slight morning airs to her aid, whilst the dawn-shine grew subtly and strengthened up, so that the island darkened the more against it for a little while, and grew stealthily more real. And all the time, above it, the sea birds swung about in noiseless circling against the gold-of-light that hung now in all the lower sky.

Presently, there came the hoarse hail of the lookout man, who must have waked suddenly:—

"Land on the weather bow, Sir!"

But the lean, grim-looking figure to the wind'ard vouchsafed no reply, beyond a low growled "grrrrr!" of contempt.

And all the time, Pibby Tawles, the boy, stared, overwhelmed with strange imaginings—treasure, monsters, lovely women, weirdness unutterable, terror brooding beyond all powers of his imagination to comprehend! He had listened to some marvelously strange things, when Captain Jat had been in drink: for it was often then the Cap-tain's whim to make the boy sit at the table with him, and dip his cup likewise in the toddy-bowl.

And presently, when Captain Jat had drunk his toddy steadily out of the big pewter mug, he would begin to talk; rambling on in garrulous fashion from tale to tale; and, at last, as like as not, mixing them quite inextricably. And as he talked, the long, lean man would throw his glance back over his shoulder suspiciously every minute or so, and perhaps bid the boy go up to the little half-poop, and discover the wherabouts of the officer of the watch, and then into the cabin of the officer whose watch it might chance to be below, and so to make sure that neither of his Mates were attending listening ears on the sly.

"Don't never tell the Mates, boy!" he would say to Pibby Tawles, "Or I'll sure maul you! They'd be wantin' profits."

For that was, in the main, the substance of all his talks—treasure, that is to say. To be exact, treasure and women.

"Never a word boy. I trusts you; but no one else in this packet!"

And truly, Captain Jat did seem to have a trust in the boy; for in his cups, he told him everything that came up in his muddled mind; and always the boy would listen with a vast interest, putting in an odd question this time and that to keep the talk running. And indeed it suited him very well; for though he could never tell how much to believe, or how little, he was very well pleased to be sitting drinking his one cup of toddy slowly in the cabin, instead of being out on the deck, doing ship work.

It is true that the Captain appeared both to like the boy, in his own queer fashion, and to trust him; but for all that, he had with perfect calmness and remorseless intent, shown him the knife with which he would cut his throat, if ever he told a word of anything that his master might say to him during his drinking bouts.

Captain Jat's treatment of the lad was curious in many ways. He had him sleep in a little cabin aback the Mate's where through the open door he could see the boy in his bunk. When he ran out of toddy, he would heave his pewter mug at the lad's head as he lay asleep, and roar to him to turn-out and brew him fresh and stronger; but this trick of the Captain's was no trouble to Pibby; for he rigged a dummy oakum-head to that end of his bunk which showed through the open doorway and slept then the other way about.

And so with this little that I have told you may know something of the life aft in the cabin of the little barque *Gallat*, which vessel belonged stick-and-keel, to Captain Jat; and some pretty rum doings there were aboard of her, first and last, as you may now have chance to judge.

At times, another side of Captain Jat would break out, and he would spend the whole of a watch having a gorgeous pistol-shooting match against Pibby; and a wonderful good shot the boy was, both by natural eye, and by the training he had this way. In the end, the boy became a better shot than Captain Jat himself, who was an extraordinarily fine marksman; though somewhat unequal. Yet for all that Pibby beat him time after time, this peculiar man showed no annoyance, but persisted in the matches, as if his primary intention were to make the boy an expert with the weapon; and indeed, I have little doubt but that this was his real desire.

Now, although Pibby Tawles had tremendously confused and vague ideas as to what strangeness of mystery was concerned with the island, yet he knew perfectly that it was no chance that had brought them that way; for all the Captain's talks over his toddy had gone to show that the *true* aim of the voyage was to bring up near the island for some purpose that the lad could only guess at in a mystified way, owing to the muddling fashion in which Captain Jat had run his yarns one into another; treasure, women, monsters, and odd times a queer habit of muttering to himself about his little priestess—his little priestess! And once he had broken out into a kind of hazy ramble about the Ud, rolling his eyes at the boy strangely and gesticulating so impressively with his pewter mug that he managed to spread his toddy in an unprejudiced manner over Pibby, the table and the floor generally.

Therefore, having, as I have said, a sure knowledge that the island they approached was the real goal of the voyages, though there was an honest enough cargo below hatches, you may imagine something of Pibby's blank astonishment when Captain Jat allowed the barque to sail quietly past, touching neither brace, sheet nor tack; so that, by the morning was full come, the island lay upon the weather quarter, and presently far away astern.

Yet, as they had gone past, the lad had studied it very eagerly, and had seen in the light of the coming day that it was wooded almost everywhere, even close down to the shores, with a long, bold reef of stark rock running out in a great sweep upon the South side, so that it was plain a boat could be landed there very safely and easily under its lee. The island, Pibby had noticed, rose towards the centre, into a low, seemingly flat-topped hill, with the forests of great trees very heavy on its slopes.

All the morning the *Gallat* stood to the Southward, until they had sunk the island below the horizon. They hove-to then, and drifted until near evening, when they filled once more on her, and stood back to the Northward. By four bells that night they sighted the island, looking like a doleful smudge in the darkness away to the Northeast.

Presently, the barque was put in irons, and orders given to lower the dingy. When she was in the water, Captain Jat flipped Pibby on the ear, and growled to him to jump down into the boat. The boy climbed over, and Captain Jat followed, after having first directed the Second Mate, whose watch it was, to reach out into the open, and run in again about midnight.

The Captain took the after oar, and rowed standing up, with his face to the bows, whilst Pibby, the boy, took the bow oar and rowed sitting down.

"Easy with that oar, boy!" said Captain Jat presently, after he had pulled awhile. "Put your shirt round it." And this, Pibby had to do, and row naked to the waist, whilst his shirt muffled the sound of his oar between the thole-pins. But, after all, the night was pretty warm.

Meanwhile, the Captain had pulled off his own coat and ripped out one of the sleeves, which he reeved onto his oar, and so made it silent as the lad's. And this was the way, almost as quietly as a shadow boat in the darkness, they came in presently under the shelter of the great barrier reef, and very soon then to the uncomfortable silence of the shore under the dark trees that came down so near to the sea.

Here, before Captain Jat landed, he bid the boy lay on his oar, whilst he listened. But they could hear nothing, except the far dull booming of the sea upon the exposed beach beyond the great reef—the solemn noise of the sea coming very hushed and distant to them, and blending with the dree little sounds that came out of the near forest, as the night airs went wandering on into its gloom.

"Keep her afloat till I come, boy," said Captain Jat, as he stepped ashore. He walked a few paces up the beach, settling a brace of great double-barrelled pistols in his belt. Then he turned sharply and came back:—

"Not a sound, boy, or you're as good as dead," he said grimly, in a low tone. "Not a sound, so what you hears! Keep off there in the shadow of the reef. You'll hear me squark like a catched molley-hawk, when I come. Keep your eyes wide open, boy!" And with that, he slewed round on his heel, and went up pretty quick across the sand into the darkness of the black trees.

Pibby Tawles, the boy, stood in the bows of the boat, and stared after him, listening to the vague sounds of his passage growing ever distant and more distant, but odd-whiles sounding out clear through the dark forests, as some dried kippin snapped under his weight. Then, as Captain Jat went farther and farther, the silence of the island fell again about Pibby, save for the odd whispering of the leaves in the little airs that came off the sea, and the constant solemn booming of the ocean on the far breach that lay exposed upon the outward arc of the great reef.

And so, listening there, and full of the mystery of all the vague and muddled tales that Captain Jat had maundered through so often, over the toddy, is it any matter for surprise that the lad, Pibby, grew suddenly frightened of the loneliness and the silence, and began to think there were pale ovals, among the dark tree-trunks, that peered at him?

He thrust his hand down, inside his trousers, and eased a small double-barrelled pistol out of a canvas pocket he had stitched in there with a palm and needle, and sail-twine for thread. The feel of the small weapon gave him a degree of comfort, and abruptly he remembered that Captain Jat had told him to keep the boat off in the shadow of the reef. He jumped out over the bows, holding the pistol in his right hand, and found to his dismay that the boat was aground. He put his bare shoulder to her stern, and hove madly awhile, sweating; for he felt that Captain Jat was quite capable of knifing him on his return, if he found the boat hard ashore. With a determination, vague but dogged, to protect himself with his pistol if necessary, he made one vast, final effort, and the boat slid afloat.

He jumped in over the bows, ran aft and put his pistol on the stern thwart; then with the boat-hook he pushed out, and so came in a minute under the gloom of the reef, which rose up just there into a chaos of great rocks, weed-hidden at their bases. He thrust the boat-hook into a mass of weed, and anchored the boat temporarily.

Then, with a sudden shiver, he remembered his shirt, and, having freed it, he covered his damp back.

Pibby Tawles had been sitting quietly in the boat for, maybe, half an hour, when he heard something that made him lean forward on the thwart and listen tensely. There was something moving, in among the great rocks and boulders where the reef thrust into the shore; and the sounds were exceedingly curious:— Slither! Slither! click-click, and then a loud squelch and a great splashing, as if some huge thing scrambling over the rocks, had slipped and fallen into one of the pools left by the sea.

There was a little time of silence, and then again came the sharp, click, click, followed by a loud grating noise over the rocks. The noise frightened the boy extraordinarily, and he freed the boat-hook silently from the weed, and began nervously to punt the boat out farther from the shore; but keeping very carefully in the gloom that the shadow of the reef cast.

He held the boat again, some dozen fathoms farther out, and waited. He could hear the strange noises continuing, oddly broken by pauses of profound quiet; then again the slithering and clicking sounds. Abruptly, there was a loud crash—a huge boulder had been moved bodily and sent rolling down from the higher parts of the reef to the shore. The boulder was a big one; for Pibby could see it vaguely through the darkness, where it had bounded out into the soft sand. He thought vividly and horridly of Captain Jat's muddled yarns of grim things, and he began again silently to push the boat farther out.

Even as he loosed the hook of the boat-hook out from the weed, there came a tremendous scrambling noise among the rocks inshore, and something moved out silently onto the vague white sand of the beach. It passed over a darker patch of pebbles, and the lad heard the rounded stones grinding against each other, as if under a vast weight. The pistol seemed only a foolish toy in his hand, and he got down suddenly onto the bottom-boards of the boat and lay flat.

A long while seemed to pass, during which he heard further sounds that told him the thing was moving along the beach. He kept very still, and presently there was only silence of the quiet sea and the island about him again, with the seas booming far and hollowly on the unprotected shore beyond the reef, and the faint stirrings of the forest trees whispering oddly to him across the quiet strip of sea that held the boat off the sand.

He sat up, cautiously, and found that the boat still rose and fell on the gentle heaves of the sea close in under the gloom of the reef. He took the boat-hook and anchored her again, and all the time his gaze searched the vauge shore; but he saw nothing and heard nothing, and gradually he grew easier.

A long time passed, whilst he sat, pistol in hand, watching and listening. Everything remained quiet, and slowly he began to nod, drowsing and waking through the minutes, so that he could not be said to be either awake or asleep. And then, in a moment, he was wide awake, for there was a sound breaking the utter stillness. He sat up, gripping his pistol, and stared nervously; and as he stared, the sound came again, a far, faint inhuman howling away up through the dark forests of to the North of him. He stood up in the boat, and, abruptly, a great way off in the night, there came the sound of a shot, and once more the howling, only that now there was a strange screaming as well. There was another shot, and one single, shrill scream that came to him far and attenuated out of the night air; and then, for the best part of an hour, an absolute silence.

Suddenly, far off among the trees, Pibby saw a faint gleam of light, moving here and there, and growing bigger as the minutes passed. Presently, he saw that there were four of these gleams, and then six, and all moving and dancing about strangely; but no sound; at least, not for a time.

All at once, he heard the snapping of a twig, apparently a long way off in the wood, the sound echoing strangely in the quietness. And then, very abrupt and dreadful, the inhuman howling began again, mingled with a wild screaming, seeming to be but a few hundred paces deep in the woods. To the boy, it seemed as though something that was half a woman and half something else, howled and shrieked there among the trees; and he chilled with a very literal fright.

The six lights danced and blended and again separated, and all the time the abominable howling and screaming continued through the grim woods. Then, very sharp and sudden, the noise of one Captain Jat's double-barrelled pistols:— bang! bang! And, almost immediately, Captain Jat's voice shouting, at some distance, to bring the boat in, to bring the boat in.

The lad freed the boat-hook, and started the dingy in to the shore, and as he did so, he heard the crashing of Captain Jat's footsteps through the rotten wood and leaves; and it was plain to him that the Captain had started to make an undisguised run for the boat.

As Pibby thrust the boat inshore, he realised a number of things:— The Captain was being followed, and those lights and the strange howling had something to do with whatever followed him. The nose of the boat grounded, and Pibby picked up his weapon, and ran forrard and stood on the fore thwart, waiting.

The strange lights came nearer, moving swiftly among the trees; and suddenly the lad saw something that was plainly monstrous. He had a clear view up a long vista of dark trees, which the lights had made visible, and he saw the figure of a man, black and immensely tall against the light, running and staggering down towards the beach. He knew it was Captain Jat. The dancing lights, beyond, entered the vista, and came dancing and flaring down through the wood; and abruptly the boy got a clear view of the things that carried them. The lights were great torches, and were carried by a number of wild looking women who were nearly naked, with great manes of hair all loose and wild about them.

But the monstrous and horrid thing that caught the boy's eye was something he saw as the women came nearer, running. They had faces so flat as to be almost featureless. At first, if he thought at all, he supposed that they were wearing some kind of mask; but as they ran, the nearest woman opened her mouth and howled, the same disgusting sound that he had heard earlier that night. As she howled, she brandished both the hand that held the torch, and the other hand, above her head. But she had no hands; her arms ended in enormous claws, like the claws of a great crab. The other women began to howl, and to wave their torches and arms as they ran, and Pibby saw that some of them were like the foremost woman. He stared, with the wide-eyed acceptance of youth of the horrific and monstrous.

Captain Jat came blundering and reeling out of the wood. He stubbed his foot against something, and fell headlong onto the sand, and those extraordinary and brutish things close astern of him. Pibby saw suddenly that three of the women had knives, enormous knives, and somehow the sight of the knives made him feel better—it was more human. In the same moment, he loosed off his right barrel and immediately his left, and with each shot there fell a woman, screaming, their torches flying along the sand, and throwing up great sparks. Captain Jat staggered up, and came on at a heavy run to the boat. He reached it, and fell all his great length in over the bows.

"Put off, boy!" he gasped. "Put off!" And even as he spoke, the boat was away from the shore with the push that he had given it as he came aboard. He scrambled to his feet, seized an oar, and thrust down hard, so that the water boiled under the stern, with the way that he gave the boat. In a moment, they had the oars between the tholes, and were backing the boat madly out into the darkness of the sea; so that in a few minutes they were a good way off the shore, and the quiet and hush of the water about them.

But there danced on the beach, at the edge of the sea, those monstrous-faced and monstrous-armed women, and howled at them across the sea, and a dreadful enough noise to hear. They waved their great torches, and jigged crazily, so that the light splashed redly across the swells; and all the time as they danced, their black manes flew about them, and always they howled.

"Pull, boy!" said Captain Jat, still very hoarse with breathlessness. "Pull, Boy!" But indeed, the lad was pulling fit to break his youthful back. There passed a further time of labour and gasping silence, and presently they were out in the open water, where the quiet swells moved big and free under them in the darkness, and the reef lay between them and the shore. But they could still see the mad dancing of the lights at the edge of the sea.

Awhile later, Captain Jat eased, and they put the boat round, after which he lay on his oar, and the boy the same, for he could scarcely breathe. The lights were gone now from the shore, and there was no sound, except the far hollow noise of the breaking seas upon the exposed beaches of the island, to the Eastward.

Now, never a word of thanks said Captain Jat for the way the boy had saved him with the pistol; but presently he pulled his oar in across the boat, and lit his pipe, after which he hove the plug of his tobacco at the lad. That was his way.

"Boy," he said, after smoking a little, "I'm wondering if they knew I was whistlin' to her."

"Who, Sir?" asked Pibby.

But Captain Jat made no answer to this. After smoking a long time, he said suddenly:— "Them was the Ud-women, boy... Devil-women.... Priestesses of the Ud, that's Devil in their talk. I was here a matter of four years gone for water, and I found out somethin' then, boy, about them an' their pearl-fishin' an' devil-worshipping, an' how they've kep' it quiet from all the world. I found one of the priestesses alone one time, a little woman an' pretty, not like *them*!" (He jerked his thumb shorewards.) "I was a week lyin' off here, an' there mightn't have been anyone on the island, the way they kep' hid, boy; not till I found the little priestess down near by the spring. I knew her lingo, a bit, and we got talking. I saw her all that week, every night, secret like. She liked me. I liked her. I had her aboard once, an' she told me a heap. When I put her ashore, I took the Mate with me, Jeremiah Stimple, he was, an' we went prospecting for them pearls I'd learned about; but she'd never told me proper about the Ud an' the Ud-women. She'd never say much that way. That's how we got into trouble. We'd near got to the top of the hill, an' then come some of them devil-women. I was all cut about, an' I guess they likely sacrificed the Mate. I never saw him again.

"There must be hundreds of them devil-women ashore there in them forests. But I always meant to come back, boy. I've seen the pearls this very night. They're down in the bottom of the crater that's inside of yon hill in the middle of the island, all strung round a great carved post; an' I'm going to get 'em too, boy. You sh'd see the pearls them hag-women was dressed with. You mustn't be feared of their claws, boy. They'm only cast off claw-shells, or somethin' of that sort. Mind you, the little priestess, she said some of 'em was *real*—growed that way; but I can't think it, scarcely. But you never know what you may find in them sorts of places. What their pet Devil is, I don't know...."

"I saw somethin', Sir, after you was gone," began Pibby, interrupting. "It were a 'orrible thing...."

"I saw the little Priestess tonight, down in the crater," went on Captain Jat, without taking the least apparent notice of what the boy had begun to tell him. "I was at the top; It's not all of twenty fathom deep. I whistled soft an' gentle to her. She saw me, an' near did faint, boy, by the look of her, an' waved me to go away pretty quick. By the look of things down there, they're in for one of their Devil-Festas. They'd big torches burning—you can seethe light of 'em now." And Captain Jat nodded towards the island.

The lad, Pibby, stared away through the darkness, and surely enough there was a faint loom of light in the night above the island.

"I reck'n the festa'll be pretty soon now, boy, at the dark of the moon, an' like there'll be Chiefs from the islands round for a thousand miles, and a sprinklin' of rotten whites, I guess, and devil-work uncounted. I'm hopin' them devil-priestesses didn't see the little woman wavin' me away, or maybe she'll be in bad trouble. They come on me, just after she signed to me to clear out, an' near finished me before I'd time to slew round. They've butcher's knives, some on 'em , as long as your leg, boy, an' one of 'em near ripped me up." He opened his coat, and the lad saw dimly in the gloom that his shirt was all stained dark.

"I settled four of the brutes," Captain Jat continued, "and you outed two. That's six gone to hell, where they come from...." He broke off, and puffed meditatively at his pipe for a time, leaning on his oar, which rested on the gunnels. Pibby had never heard him talk so much before when sober.

"The native name for yon island means 'The Island of the Devil,' boy," said Captain Jat, presently. "I heard that years gone from more than one; but none of 'em could tell me anythin', or wouldn't, 'cept it was an almighty unhealthy place for a white man... or a native either, for that matter, except, maybe, as I'm thinking, when there's one of their big, secret, damn Ud-Festas on...." He broke off short, and slipped his pipe into his pocket.

"Pull, boy, an' break your damn back. There's the ship!" he said.

Ten minutes later they were safe aboard.

All next day, Captain Jat kept the barque away to the Southward of the island; but he sent Pibby aloft, time and again, with his own telescope; and when the youth came down finally in the late afternoon, to report numbers of small craft on the horizon, steering North, he nodded his head, as if the news were what he had expected.

"Native boats, boy," he said. "Keep your mouth shut, an' tell nothin' to no one. They'll hold that festa tonight, an' they'll have all their pearls strung up, an' we'll be there. You clean up all them big double-barr'lled pistols, an' load 'em nice and careful, like I've showed you. Get a move on you now!"

That night, with all lights dowsed, the barque stood again to the Northward, and dropped Captain Jat and the lad in the dingy, off the island. Captain Jat had four great pistols in his belt, and he had spent the dog-watches in mounting an old duck-gun on its swivel, in the bows of the boat. Pibby, the boy, had also two big heavy pistols tucked into his belt, not to mention his own small weapon which reposed snugly in its canvas pocket inside his trousers. They were quite heavily armed. Moreover, he had seen to it, this time, that the oars were properly muffled.

In addition to those preparations, Captain Jat had been very particular concerning the depositing in the boat of a considerable length of chain, with two stout padlocks in the ends.

Captain Jat took the boat round to the North of the island, and, presently, after pulling cautiously for an hour, he bid the lad ease up and lay on his oar a bit, and keep his eyes well skinned. For his part, the Captain lay down on his stomach on the thwarts, and spied along the surface of the quietly heaving sea, with his night-glass. And suddenly, he reached out and caught Pibby a clip with the glass.

"Down under the gunnel, boy, or they'll see you!" he muttered, and Pibby ducked and slid down under his oar, and stared away breathlessly through the darkness to the Northward.

Now that he had his eyes nearer to the surface of the sea, he discovered the thing that Captain Jat had seen with the night-glass. There was a prodigious string of native boats, within two hundred fathoms of them, paddling through the night to the island. Pibby counted them, and numbered eighty; but probably missed some in the darkness.

Captain Jat allowed these craft to get well inshore; then, taking his oar, he shoved it out through a steering-grommet, which he had fixed up in the stern, and began to scull steadily after them; but allowing nothing more than his hand and his forearm to rise above the gunnel of the boat. As the dingy crept into the wake of those silent craft ahead, the boy noticed suddenly that there had come again above the island the strange loom of light that he had seen the night before.

Presently, the heave of the sea had almost died from under the boat, and it was plain that they had come under the lee of some out-jutting "lie" of rocks. The last of the craft ahead vanished into the shadow of the island; but Captain Jat had marked the place, and followed dead on. A minute later, they saw the shore directly ahead, not a score of fathoms away; but there was no beach; only the dark trees of bushes coming right down, apparently to the water's edge. There was no heave at all now under the boat, so that they had evidently been piloted into a perfectly sheltered cove.

Captain Jat kept the boat going straight ahead. He made no attempt to slacken her way, despite the fact that they seemed to be heading straight ashore into the middle of a heavy underwood. The bows of the dingy reached the dank bushes, where they hung out over the water, and Captain Jat took both hands to his oar, and forced her in among them.

For a few moments the overgrowths seemed to smother the boat, all wet and slimy and rank. Then the boat had passed clean through, into open water beyond. Pibby, the lad, stared in front into the darkness; but could see nothing. He looked upward, and saw a narrow, winding ribbon of night-sky far above them, which told him that Capotain Jat had discovered the way into a deep-set tidal passage, the mouth of which was completely masked by the undergrowths and overhanging trees. It was, obviously, a huge crack through the side of the low crater, which the sea had turned into a creek.

Very cautiously, Captain Jat sculled ahead. It was like sculling into a pitch-black night, so black that the far upward ribbon of night-sky seemed almost to shine, by comparison. As they went, little hollow sobbing sounds, of the water in the crannies of the unseen rocky sides, came to them, dankly and somehow drearily. But Captain Jat handled the sculling oar so softly that not once did the clinker-built entry of the boat "mutter" on the water. And this way quite half an hour passed; though it seemed much longer, going utterly slow and silent and cautious in that grim dark, and steering by the winding pattern of the night-sky above, and by the odd vague sense which told the Captain when they were come over near to one side or the other, in the darkness.

Once, as they went so quiet and stealthy, there came to them indefinitely out of the night, a far howling, once and then again; and, later, an attenuated, incredibly shrill screaming, that died away and left the boy frightened and holding the stocks of his heavy pistols. But Captain Jat sculled steadily on.

Abruptly, Captain Jat ceased sculling, and stood silent. It was plain to the lad that he was either listening or staring intently; and the boy peered round, every way, nervously. Suddenly, he saw an indefinite glow of light ahead, evidently beyond a bend in the narrow creek. The glow grew rapidly into a bright light, that danced and flickered, and, in the space of a minute, there came round the bend of the creek, upon the left side, two of those brutish things that had followed the Captain the night before. They were running through the stunted trees and bushes, parallel with the course of the creek, but about twenty feet above the level of the water, winding in and out, as they went, among the trees and great bushes that grew up in the steep lower slope of the creek-side. Their agility was incredible; here and there they leaped like goats from rock to rock, their torches dripping and flaring as they ran, one behind the other.

Captain Jat stood motionless in the stern of the dingy, with his oar in one hand, and one of his pistols in the other. He watched the two beastly creatures run by, and the boy—glancing at him swiftly in his fright—saw that his face was perfectly calm; but the lights from the torches seemed to glow in his eyes, so that they shone, almost like the eyes of a wild animal.

The lad's gaze jumped back to the two running brutes. He could not see their hideous flat faces; for their great manes, all loose and wild, hung over them, damp and black and matted, as if they were fresh come up out of the sea; and indeed there was rank, wet weed, all entangled in their hair; for he saw it glisten in the blaze of the torches. Yet, though he could not see their faces, he saw their arms from their naked shoulders downward. The arms of the foremost woman ended in two monstrous claws; but the boy saw plainly that they were no more than cast-off shells of some huge sea reptile, if I may so describe it. He saw where they ended, rough and rude, just below her elbows, and that her right hand came through a hole between the mandibles of the claw, to hold her great torch.

But the second woman gave him a horrible feeling; he could not see where her arms ended and the claws began. He remembered what the little priestess had told Captain Jat. And even as he stared, frightened and horrified, the two creatures were gone past. He saw then that the foremost one had an ugly great knife, stuck naked into the back of a kind of broad belt; and the belt was all stitched with what at first he took to be big shining beads. Then, he realised that perhaps they were not beads, put pearls, as the Captain had told him. Yet it was less of that possible fortune in pearls that Pibby Tawles, the boy, thought in that tense moment, than of the fact he could not see where the arms of the second woman ended and the claws began.

Then the two running, leaping bestial things were gone away down the creek; and a minute after, they were out of sight round one of the rocky bends, and all was dark again about the boat.

The dingy began to move ahead once more in the darkness, as Captain Jat took up work again with the sculling-oar. A matter of some ten minutes of silence passed, with the water of the creek making odd gurglings and echoes on either hand among the crannies and holes in the rocks, when Pibby realised that the enormous, steep sides of the creek had joined overhead, and that they were moving forward through the complete blackness of an invisible cavern.

And then, even as he realised the fact uneasily, there showed far ahead a small, bright spot of light. The boat began to sway, and a little murmur broke out under her bows, as Captain Jat increased the speed; but he eased it at once, for the faint noise of the water under her entrance made a strangely loud sound in that silence. But still they moved ahead steadily, and that speck of light grew, until the lad saw that it was an inner mouth to the cavern, and beyond it some bright flaring light.

The boat approached, unseen in the darkness of the cavern, to within a dozen fathoms of this newly discovered entrance, and for the last minute, Pibby had been staring with a fixed and astounded interest at what he saw. The arch of the cave mouth must have been fully thirty feet high, and the width of it a little less. And through this great opening, Pibby was looking into a big circular space, apparently several hundred feet across, the walls of which went up out of his sight into the darkness above.

But what fixed both his and Captain Jat's attention was the centre portion of this extraordinary natural amphitheater; for in the centre was a small lake of sea-water, maybe about sixty feet across, and out of the centre of the lake there rose a weed-hung hump of rack, and from the centre of the hump of rock there rose a great pole, maybe fifty feet in height, black through all its length, and polished so highly that it reflected brilliantly the light of six enormous torches that burned on the tops of six great piles that stood up out of the rock all round the central pool or lake. And this pole, from its grotesquely carved head, flat-faced and repulsive, to its base, where it had been cut into the shape of a bunch of huge claws, was banded every few feet with strings of countless beads, that glimmered in a semi-luminous fashion in the flare of the torch-lights. *And every bead was a pearl.*

The water from the cavern in which the dingy floated, ran in a perfectly straight channel into the central pool or lake, and the weeded floor of the ancient crater rose a foot or so on each side, spreading away then in one level, brown, weed-covered reach to the great walls of the inside of the low mountain.

The torches showed that the bottom parts of the mountain walls were all grown with weed, to a height of about six feet above the bottom of the crater, so that it was plain that the sea, entering through the creek and the cavern, rose at high tide to at least that height, in which case there would be only the six great torches and the lofty polished black pole in the centre, with its profusion of strings of pearls, visible when the tide was up. It must have been a strange sight then, even stranger than when Captain Jat and Pibby looked out from the cavern.

And now, but not very distinctly in that light, Pibby saw where all that great line of boats had gone to; for there, so far as he could see all around the bottom of the great natural amphitheatre, were the boats, where they had been drawn up, head to stern upon the weed, and scarcely seen above the weed, out of which they rose only a little, except for their lofty head and stern timbers, which, however, had been so draped with weed as to blend with the weed-grown walls behind.

Over the sides of all these boats, and there were vastly more than the flotilla that they had followed in (for they lay side by side, apparently three or four deep), Captain Jat and the lad saw the heads of hundreds and hundreds of natives; but all vague and indistinct; both because of the uncertain flarings of the great torches, and because each native had dressed her head with a mass of weed. Indeed, it would have been easy to have entered the crater under the impression that there was no more life in it than the blaze of the huge torches.

As Pibby strained his eyes to make out the boats, wondering whether it had been hard to drag them up out of the creek and across the weed, he felt the dingy beginning to move silently back into the cavern; and, turning, he saw that Captain Jat was using his oar noiselessly, as an Indian uses his paddle, and so fetching the boat gently astern.

In this way they progressed for about a hundred yards, and then Captain Jat set the dingy in to the side, and began to grope along. Presently, he gave out a little grunt of satisfaction, and pushed the boat across to the other side; but was evidently unable to find what he wanted; for he continued to punt the boat astern with his hands, until the great opening of the cave appeared no more than a distant speck of light. Then he grunted again, and immediately sent the boat across once more to the other side. A minute later, he gave out a further note of satisfaction, and suddenly Pibby heard his voice muttering to him to pass up one end of the chain, and one of the padlocks.

He heard the Captain fumbling for a time, and the odd, slight chinking of the chain; then the dingy was thrust out again, and Captain Jat was bidding him pay out the chain gently without a sound, whilst he paddled the boat once more across. They reached the other side; and Pibby grasped his master's idea, which was obviously to put a chain boom across, slickly, so that if they had to retreat in a hurry, they would pass over it; then tauten it up, and padlock it in position, and so get away easily, whilst all of the boats of the pursuers ran foul of the boom.

The boy ran his hands in along the chain, where the Captain was working, and found that he was "anchoring" it round a huge boulder. Pibby had no doubt but that the other end was quite as efficiently secured, and he began to feel comfortable again in his mind; it was such an efficient retreat. Then, as he sat in the darkness, he fell to wondering just what those natives were waiting for, all hid with weed like they were... and the great torches... and the huge, carved and polished pole with the fortune of splendid pearls strung around it.

And then, as he worried the thought over nervously in his mind, he thrilled suddenly; for Captain Jat was once more sculling the boat ahead towards the brightly shining arch of the cavern's entrance into the arena.

Abruptly, as the boat forged ahead, there came a queer swirl deep down in the dark water, somewhere astern of the boat, that sent little waves into the sides of the gloomy cavern, breaking in the darkness with a multitudinous chattering of liquid sounds. Something huge passed under the boat, which was now approaching the entrance at a fair speed. They felt the great thing pass under them, deep below the surface, but drawing after it a wave that humped the boat up, stern first, and then the bows.

"My God!" said Captain Jat huskily, aloud.... "The UD!" His voice came back, husky and dreadful, from a thousand places in the darkness:— "My God!... The Ud! My God!... The Ud!" And in the same moment, Pibby felt the dingy begin to sway heavily, and heard Captain Jat gasp as he began sculling with a kind of mad violence, whispering:— "The Little Priestess! The Little Priestess! My God! They saw her waving! My..."

Pibby never heard any more; for they had come sufficiently near the arch now for him to be able to see again into the crater with some clearness. He stared in complete and dreadful amazement; for though the whole of the great amphitheatre was as silent as when they left it, there was now a little, naked brown woman, lashed by her neck, her waist and her ankles to the great, pearl-stringed central pole that came up out of the hump of rock in the pool. She had been brought there and made fast during the time in which they had been fixing up the chain boom. That was why the weed-hidden boats waited…. She was the sacrifice… The thing that had passed under the boat…! She had been seen waving to the Captain…. She….

The chaos of his thoughts stilled abruptly into a fearful attention. He bent forward from the forthwart, and stared, almost petrified. Something was coming up out of the water, climbing up onto the hump of rock…. Enormous legs were coming up out of the pool, scrambling at the rock, slipping, slipping, and tearing away great chunks of the weed, and finally effecting a hold. A moment afterwards, a thing like a vast, brown, shell-encrusted dish-cover, as big as an ordinary old-fashioned oval mahogany table, began to rise up out of the pool.

The boy shook as he stared; he did not know that such things existed…. A crab….! That was no word for it. It was a monster, capable of destroying an elephant…. He remembered the great thing that had slipped and slithered among the big rocks at the in-shore end of he reef. The thing was rising higher and higher. Nothing could save the woman… nothing on earth! They had better get away at once, before it discovered them. The thing was reaching out three of its great, pincer-armed legs towards the little brown woman, who began now to scream in a peculiar, breathless voice. Then Pibby was suddenly caught by the shoulder from behind, and Captain Jat dashed him aft into the stern-sheets of the dingy, out of his way. As he fell, he saw Captain Jat against the light; he had the great duck-gun in his hands. Pibby remembered that it was loaded with the thick end of a broken marlin-spike. There was a rip of fire that coincided with the flashes of light he saw as his head met the stern-thwart; there was a crashing thump of sound that added to the muddle of his fall, and Captain Jat pitched bodily backward onto the top of him, literally felled by the recoil of the big weapon. The boy screamed, and everything went grey for a moment; then Captain Jat rolled free of him, and in the same moment there was a vast thrashing of water, and the boat was cast up a yard into the air by a wave that came travelling down the cavern from the crater. The dingy slewed half round, rolled heavily and shipped several gallons; then steadied.

Pibby staggered to his feet, shaken and sick. He stared towards the pool; the water appeared to be boiling all about the hump of rock; but there was no sign of the thing that had come out of the water. The boiling motion of the water began to ease, and Pibby saw that the little brown woman sagged in her lashings against the carved black pole; but there was no mark on her to show that she had been hurt; she had become unconscious.

The next thing he knew, he had an oar his hand, and Captain Jat had another, and they were out of the great cavern, and pulling madly up the channel that cut across the floor of the crater to the pool. He noticed, with a curious inconsequence, that he could now see trees far up at the top of the walls of the crater, shaking a little in the night-wind against the stars.

The boat bumped into the masses of weed about the hump of rock, and Captain Jat gave one great spring upward, and was onto the rock, having used his oar against the bottom-boards, as a kind of vaulting-pole. His effort forced the boat away; but Pibby grabbed the boat-hook, jabbed it into a mass of the weed, and pulled her back. He saw Captain Jat sawing savagely at the lashings; and was conscious for the first time that the crater was full of wild yelling. He saw his Master pluck the little brown woman loose, and the next moment she was hove down into the boat with a crash. He did not look at her, but at Captain'Jat.... Captain Jat was reaching up, slashing at the lowest string of great pearls. The string gave, and the pearls went spraying and bounding all over the hump of rock, into the water; but Captain Jat had secured a handful.

A spear struck the polished pole, chipping it, and flew off to the side, passing through Captain Jat's sleeve. The boy glanced once now round at the arena, and saw, suddenly, that there were literally hundreds and hundreds of natives, scrambling and slipping and leaping over the weed-covered floor towards them. He saw also another thing; two of the horrible, claw-armed women were slashing at a native with their great knives; it may have been the man who had thrown the spear and chipped the post.... The post was obviously an incredibly sacred thing.

He heard his own voice shouting strangely to Captain Jat to come; but that indomitable length of man had swarmed a fathom up the polished pole, and was cutting loose another string of pearls. There came a shower of them bounding onto the rock, and into the weed and water; but again Captain Jat had secured a share. He gave one leap to the rock, and another into the boat; Then, stern-foremost, they rowed grimly for the opening into the cavern.

One of the savages, a huge fat man, had outdistanced the others, in spite of his fat. Perhaps his fat accounted for it; for he had come across the slippery weed, creeping on hands and feet, and had therefore lost no time in falling. He rose up at the edge of the channel; but as he made to spring at the boat, he slipped and fell squelching on his back, and Captain Jat pistolled him calmly as he lay.

Yet, now the danger was appalling; for scores of the natives were getting near, and a shower of spears came over the boat, four of them striking her starboard quarter, and making it look literally rather like a gigantic pin-cushion; but no one was hurt; though the Captain's clothing was cut in two places. They replied with their heavy pistols, and left a dozen of the natives dead, and so managed to ram the dingy stern first into the cavern.

Captain Jat put the boat round, as soon as they were well out of sight, and they both settled down to pull. Yet when they had gone about a hundred fathoms they heard a splash, and saw that one of the smaller native boats had already been hauled across the weed, and was now in the water of the channel. They knew that in another few minutes there would be scores of boats after them.

Half a minute later, Pibby's oar stubbed against the slack chain of the boom, and they in oars, and hauled the boat along to the side of the cavern, being now on the seaward side of the boom. Captain Jat worked desperately, and Pibby lighted the chain up to him, so as to get it as taut as possible; yet it took time; for they were in utter darkness; but the chain must be taut, if it were to act as a boom; otherwise the natives would manage either to shove their boats under or over it.

And all the time, as they worked, boats were entering the mouth of the great cavern, with torches held high over their bows to show them the way; while the boat that had been first launched into the creek was now scarcely a hundred and fifty feet away; and still Captain Jat growled to Pibby to "Light up the slack! Light up the slack!"

The small boat came on steadily, until she was not more than seventy or eighty feet away, and suddenly a great shout told Captain Jat and the boy that the light of the distant torches must have picked them out in the blackness. Immediately afterwards, all around them in the water there was *plunk, plunk,* the noise of thrown spears. There came a sharp, chinking sound, as a single spear struck the rocky side. It glanced, gashed along the Captain's face, and took away a part of his ear. He swore grimly, and gave one more pull on the chain; then closed the big padlock and locked it with a swift deliberation.

Immediately afterwards, he fetched a spare pistol out of his side pocket, and loosed off into the approaching boat, with such a good aim that one of his bullets punched a hole in two of the men, who happened to be in a line. Then, dropping his pistol into the bottom of the boat, he sprang to his oar, and a minute later they were away round the bend, bumping heavily in the darkness against the rocky side of the cavern, and listening to the fierce outcry that came echoing along the cavern, as the boom opposed all progress for the time being.

"Done 'em, boy!" said Captain Jat. "Now pull easy! We don't want the boat stove. Back water when I sings out." And therewith the two settled down to work at the oars.

Some forty minutes later, they passed through the screen of over-hanging bushes and trees that marked the mouth of the creek, and were presently out into the wholesome sweetness of the sea, with the island no more than a shape of darkness astern. Yet, when they came to look for the little brown woman, she had gone. It was evident that she had come-to, and slipped overboard in the darkness, preferring, it appears, to face any risk that the island might contain for her, than to face the facing of the unknown.

"The ship boy! Pull!" said Captain Jat, a little while afterwards. And indeed, the ship it was; and soon they were safely aboard, steering Northward, away from the island, for good this time.

Down in his cabin, with the door safely closed, yet not without more than one suspicious glance towards it, Captain Jat was presently conning over, and exhibiting to Pibby, his spoils. On the table was a jug of very special toddy, and Captain Jat was investigating it with the aid of his big pewter mug. Pibby also, it must be confessed, had adopted a fairish-sized drinking cup for the same purpose; for Captain Jat allowed him only the one, and no more.

It may be that the unusual richness of the toddy developed a latent generosity in the lean Captain; for after a lot of fingering and weighing and examining, he presented Pibby, as his share, one of the smallest of the pearls, which had been somewhat badly chipped.

Pibby Tawles, cabin-boy-deck-hand, call him what you will, took the little, damaged pearl with sufficient evidence of gratitude. He could afford to; for inside his shirt there reposed a number of pearls as fine as any that Captain Jat had brought away with him. The boy had picked them off the bottom-boards of the dingy, where they had fallen when his master cut the strings of pearls about the Sacred Pole.

In short, we may conclude, I think, that whatever else he might be, Pibby Tawles was one who had a very sound eye to the main chance; a conclusion which a further adventure of Captain Jat's has rather impressed upon me.

The Adventure of the Headland

"RUM, BOY; AN' PASS me up the spy-glass!" said Captain Jat, with-out turning his head.

"Aye, Aye, Sir," cried Pibby Tawles.

Even as he made answer, Pibby was half-way to the companion-hatch, at a barefoot run; for he had learned the need for speed during his two voyages with Captain Jat... that unabashed length of lean, pirate-hearted avarice and grim whimsies.

Pibby Tawles was back in something under sixty seconds, running, as he would have expressed it, at the rate of knots. He reached the telescope over in the front of his master, who lounged upon the rail, staring intensely at the dull gloom of the land to leeward, where it lay still and mysterious in the grey of the dawn. Captain Jat took the telescope, without a word, and Pibby Tawles put the pewter mug of rum-toddy down on the rail beside him. It may be that he set it too near to his Master; for Captain Jat adjusted the glass towards the shore, his elbow touched the mug, and the lot went to the deck, so that the rum was all squandered.

Captain Jat turned slowly and looked at Pibby Tawles; then pointed with the glass at the main t'gallant brace. Pibby knew what he meant, and knew equally well that it was no use making a fuss; so that he went over and brought the end of the brace, without a word. Captain Jat took the rope, and caught the boy three or four hard clips with it across the shoulders; after which he returned it to him, to be re-coiled. He touched the fallen pewter with his foot, and the boy said:— "'Aye, Aye, Sir," and went below with the pewter to fill it again.

He returned at a run, and put it handy for the second time; yet not, as you may think, over-near to the great protruding elbow of his Master. Then he coiled up the t'gallant brace, and went to leeward, where he rubbed his shoulders tenderly against a teak weather-cloth stanchion; for Captain Jat had laid on hard.

"Rum, boy," said the Captain again, presently. And when Pibby returned with a pewter-full, Captain Jat turned and took it from him, at the same time pushing the spy-glass into his hands, and jerking his thumb towards the land, by which Pibby knew that he was given permission to have a look. That was just Captain Jat's way.

Pibby Tawles stared earnestly through the glass at the vague shore of the great headland, past which they were running; for he knew from the half-drunken talk of Captain Jat, oddwhiles over his rum-toddy, something of what the Captain had in his mind.

"I don't see nothin' of the two rocks, Cap'n," said Pibby, after staring awhile.

"They're there, boy!" said Captain Jat with a grim conviction. "An' don't you get doubtin', or I'll break your head. That Portygee as gave me the yarn, swore to it on the cross he'd got hung to 's beads.... He wouldn't be like to lie, with him dyin' an' halfway down into hell already, as you might say."

Pibby made no reply to this; for it was evident that his Master was in one of his curious moods, when he was capable of a peculiar, though casual, sort of brutality, if angered by any difference of opinion, or by any other cause at all.

The headland was still half blurred with the indefinite greyness of the dawn, and the boy searched to and fro vainly along the crest of the cliff, for any sign of the Dago village which some of Captain Jat's oddly jerked-out remarks had given him to suppose must exist. For the Captain had often half-drunkenly explained how this village would be the thing that would prove the chief difficulty in the way of their making any proper search to test the information which he had been given by the Portuguese. Pibby doubted that "given." He knew too much of the uncomfortably remorseless note in his Captain's character.

The boy continued to stare—watching the smother of the white seas upon the beaches around the headland, and vaguely aware how they seemed to shout the loneliness and savage unknownness of the land under the barque's lee. Then, with the "tail of his eye," he saw Captain Jat raise the pewter to rap him across the knuckles; so that he knew the Captain was done his grog, and wanted the spy-glass again. He thrust the glass into his Master's hands, and caught the pewter from him; after which he went below to prepare breakfast.

Now, all the while that Captain Jat was at breakfast, the boy, who ate with him, pondered the adventure that he saw ahead. The Mate was on deck, and the bo'sun—who acted as Second Mate—was turned-in; for Captain Jat would never eat with his officers; preferring in some strange, half-sullen, half-suspicious fashion, the company of Pibby. As you know, he would never talk before his two Mates; but to the boy he would say anything that came uppermost; so that, as I have sad, Pibby was more or less (though somewhat hazily) aware of what was in his Master's mind. Yet, at present, the Captain's speech was limited to such remarks as: —

"Beans, boy!" Whereat, Pibby would ladle him a huge plate-full of his favorite dish, which consisted of beans and salt-pork, done with red pepper.

"Rum, boy!" And Pibby would refill his Master's pewter; but did Pibby make a movement to add to the one cup-full of the heave liquor that was his own allowance, the roar of Captain Jat's voice would warn him that he was watched; whereat the boy would fall-to once more upon the beans and red pepper; but the pork was a dainty that went all to his Master's plate.

"There's them Dagoes!" said Captain Jat, presently. "Yon dead Portygee made out as they was always searchin', off an' on, ever since it come out that the treasure was brought safe ashore out the *Lady Meria*. Yon devil as is dead, says they've got the yarn fixed in 'em; an' they'm terrible cranky to see strangers comin' ashore round by yon. Like as they'm thinkin' maybe, as they might be comed lookin' for the gold, or whatever it is. If we's catched, boy, they'll sure cut our throats proper."

"How did the Portygee get to know the bearin's, Cap'n?" asked Pibby.

But his master went on eating, as if the boy had not spoken.

"We'll run up the coast awhile, boy," remarked Captain Jat, after some further minutes of eating and drinking. "I'll run 'er back here after dark, so's we can land safe; an' they can't think nothin' then; for they won't see ought! You get them pistols cleaned up an' loaded after breakfas'. An' rout out them two shovels an' picks we used down in the islands."

"'Aye, Aye, Cap'n," said Pibby, well pleased at the prospect of the coming adventure. And therewith, in his delight, he refilled his Master's pewter, with rum; forestalling Captain Jat's monotonous "Rum, boy!"

For his pains, Captain Jat fetched him a clout across the side of his head, with his open fist, that sent him to the deck of the cabin.

"A drunken sailorman it is ye think I am!" roared Captain Jat, angrily; and immediately drained the pewter at a gulp; whilst Pibby got again upon his feet and began to clear the table.

"Have you got a chart, Cap'n, where to find the stuff?" he asked presently, as he went to and fro. But Captain Jat, who had now lit his pipe, puffed on silently, taking no notice of the lad.

That night, the little *Gallat* crept back along the coast, with all her lights out, or covered; and a little after midnight dropped her squat dingy under the lee of the big headland.

In the boat, there were only Captain Jat and Pibby Tawles, the boy. And both of them wore big canvas belts which the sailmaker had made, in which were stuck half a dozen big double-barrelled pistols apiece. In addition, they had each their big sheath-knives; and so were very well armed.

In the bottom of the boat, there were two picks and a couple of shovels; also a large bag, the neck tied up with a rope-yarn.

Captain Jat had the stroke oar, and rowed standing with his face to the bows. In this way (the oars having been previously muffled with parcellings of canvas and shakins) they had the boat presently inshore, under the lee of the cliff, where the foot of the headland made a "still" water. And here, in the almost total darkness, they got ashore; taking their gear with them, and drawing the boat up a few feet onto the beach, making fast her painter to a rock.

The shore about them was very dree and silent; but farther off in the darkness, there was a lonesome, eternal roar of the surf, on the unprotected coast beyond the lee of the headland, and the two of them stood for a little while, staring cautiously about them in the gloom, listening. Then Captain Jat cuffed the boy, to ease himself; afterwards cursing him because the blows sounded loud and distinct along the empty shore; and so had him shoulder the two picks, whilst the Captain himself took the two spades and the canvas bag.

They started along the shore then, towards where it slanted up into the gloom-hidden side of the great headland, all dark with heavy forest. Yet, the long, lean man appeared to have no doubt about his directions; but seemed, as it were by some peculiar instinct, to know his way; for presently he was leading along a narrow beaten track, up from the shore, which took them winding in and out, zigzagging among the trees.

In this fashion, they walked steadily for the maybe half an hour;

by which time they were gone up so high, and had passed so far in among the great trees, that they were come clear away from the noise of the sea; and all about them was the heavy, almost insufferable hush of the great forests.

At times, as they walked, there would be a low, uncomfortable rustling, as some hidden thing slid away from their path; and once, for a space, Pibby Tawles felt sure that something was keeping level with them through the darkness, a little way on the right. But presently, he lost the sounds, and ceased to be certain that he had heard anything. Oddwhiles, as they went, a crude stench, something like garlic, would assail them, as though their feet had crushed some odd, strange plant in the darkness. And so they went forward.

Three times in that first dark half hour, Pibby, the boy, stumbled heavily over the loops of rambling creeper-plants, and the third time he went headlong. The two picks he was carrying clanged loudly— the noise going strange and somehow horridly through the dark aisles that went unseen among the trees on both sides of them. Captain Jat said nothing; but turned and clouted the boy as he rose; after which they went forward once more, without a word.

Awhile later, they were come to the great brow of the headland; and here Captain Jat paused and knelt down among he roots of a big tree. He drew something from his pocket, fumbling in the darkness; then Pibby heard the strokes of a flint and steel, and saw the showers of sparks light up the face of a small compass that lay on the earth between the Captain's knees. His Master ceased to strike the flint; and rose to his feet again, pocketing the compass; after which she had slewed about to the South and East, and set off again, with Pibby Tawles astern of him.

Four times more, Captain Jat took his bearings in this rough and ready fashion; each time altering his direction slightly; and so came out, at last, free of the trees, into a kind of rocky, bush and tree lumbered plateau, upon the Western border of which glimmered and danced the flames of several fires; whilst in two places there were movements of torches.

"That'll be the Dago village, boy," muttered Captain Jat, shading his eyes needlessly, and staring. "Bear away smart to starboard; an' if you knocks them picks again, our throats is as good as cut proper; so mind you, or I'll clump ye in the lug!"

They bore away to the right now, going carefully in the darkness, and entered presently a wide belt of wood. Abruptly, Captain Jat reached back to Pibby, and dragged him in among the trees to the left of the vague track that led through the woodbelt. As he seized the boy, the Captain clapped one great hand momentarily over the lad's mouth, to insure that he would not shout or try to question the meaning of this sudden act. Then he loosed him, and peered forward, sideways, among the trees.

A moment later, Pibby discovered the reason for his master's action; there was a far off flickering of light, away amid the trees, in the direction towards which they had been going.

The lights came nearer swiftly, with a queer, dancing sort of motion; and Captain Jat backed in more among the trees on the side of the track; pressing Pibby to his rear, and swearing softly in a constant monotone of evil. Maybe a couple of minutes passed; and then Pibby was aware that he heard the swish of branches in the near distance; and, suddenly, he heard another sound, most peculiar—a kind of queer, moaning, hooning noise, very faint at first, but draw-ing nearer all the time, and growing sharper and more insistent as it neared their hiding—place.

Pibby Tawles felt for one of his pistols, and fingered it with a distinct sense of comfort; also, it was good to feel that Captain Jat's sinful length of cantankerousness and fighting-energy was close be-side him; but, for all that he had these two realities to ease him of funk, yet that sound bred in him an ever-growing discomfort and vague distress of unwordable thoughts.

And then, suddenly, the sound rose to a veritable hooning buzz, and there raced past them two sweating, breathless natives, brown and glistening in the light of the great torches they carried. They ran past along the track, towards the village maybe; and Pibby Tawles discovered the reason for that deep, insistent, threatening buzz, that had sounded so strange; for around the head of each man, there hung a moving, stupendously thick cloud of insect life, whirling round and round the men... a dancing, flickering, buzzing haze of mosquitoes, gnats, midges, beetles, and other pests of the tropic night, attracted to the men by the light of the torches they carried.

The two natives dashed past at top speed, drenched with sweat, and peering in a kind of extraordinary terror from side to side as they ran; as though expecting every moment to be faced with some horrific or terrible creature. And in this fashion, they were gone a good way off in less than a minute; so that the sound of their travel died away in the distance, along with the extraordinary noise of the huge, travelling clouds of insects that accompanied them.

"This is sure an Ud wood," muttered Captain Jat. "Devil wood, boy, 'tis sure; or them niggers 'd never carry torches like they'm doin', an' fetchin' every insec' from a mile around to feed on their thick hides!"

Captain Jat left the hiding place, and Pibby Tawles followed; and so they led off once more along the track, the Captain ahead.

"Keep an eye liftin', boy, for aught!" said Captain Jat, presently. "Them niggers may just be superstitious-like about here, or maybe as there's somthin' loose in these woods as is real dangerous. You can't never tell with them silly devils. They'd run from a pretty coloured stone, thinkin' 'twas witchcraft, an' the same time, they'd cut your blessed throat an' never stop to argy. Don't never trust 'em.... An' then, again, there *may* be somthin' queer round about 'ere...."

He broke off short, and stopped in his tracks, to listen; whipping out one of his big pistols. Pibby Tawles saw the action, vaguely, and followed his Master's lead; and so the two of them stood silent for maybe two full minutes there in the darkness among the trees.

"Sst!" muttered Captain Jat, suddenly. "Hark to that!"

Pibby also had heard it—a far away, deep, gigantic sound, that would have been somehow more familiar, had it been a noise of less dimensions. This is, perhaps, rather a peculiar way to put it; but it describes the particular fashion in which the origin of the sound eluded them.

"It's the sea, Cap'n," suggested Pibby, after a further pause for listening; during which there was an absolute silence, save for the odd, vague whisper of leaves here and there in the darkness, as the night airs stole, hushed, through the wood-belt.

"The sea be blowed!" said Captain Jat; swearing grimly in a mutter of vast contempt. "Keep your ears open, an' shut your mug! That's maybe some native devil-work, to make strangers give hereabouts a wide berth; an', again, maybe its somthin' you nor me don't understan'.... Keep your eyes skinned, boy; an' tread quiet!"

He led off again down the scarcely perceptible track; and so, in something under an hour, they were come clear out from the wood, to the great ease of Pibby, who had disliked hugely that peculiar sound in the distant night among the trees.

Beyond the wood, the track wound round the base of a large mound, which Captain Jat climbed and proceeded to take a bearing from, as Pibby could tell from the sparks of the flint and steel. The Captain came down off the mound, and led the way to the left, going slowly and cautiously.

They went forward now for a short while through a patch of

rocky country, clumped here and there with masses of heavy brush, out of which grew stunted trees. Twice during their walk across this part, Captain Jat took their bearings with the compass. And presently, Pibby Tawles realised that the Captain was listening keenly for some expected sound; going always more slowly, and at last stopping every score paces or so, to hark.

Abruptly, Captain Jat started off to the right, towards a vaguely seen straggle of trees and undergrowth, with Pibby after him. Pibby heard the sound then, the noise of falling water, and realised that it was towards this that his Master was making a way. They ploughed in among the undergrowth, and burst a path in the direction of the sound. In a few minutes, during which the noise of the falling water had grown louder and louder, they came out into a great open space, with rocks going up all about, so well as they could see in the darkness; and the noise of the water very plain now from some place to their left.

They followed up to the sound, and came to a boil of water, where a pretty big brook came tumbling down over the top of a little cliff, as they could learn, part by indefinite sight, and part by the noise of the water.

"There's them two sharp-ended rocks as the Portygee told on, boy," said Captain Jat, with satisfaction in his voice, "like as he said we should see 'em."

He pointed up through the darkness, to where, about twenty fathoms on their own side of the waterfall, the edge of the low cliff rose into two tall pinnacles of rock, black against the night sky.

"I'm thinkin' I've found it, boy, 'thout foulin' ought," continued Captain Jat, setting down the two spades and the bag upon the earth, and hauling a small lantern out of his pocket. He busied himself clumsily with flint and steel, and presently had the small lantern alight. He put the lantern on the ground, and undid the mouth of the canvas bag; out of which he took two large balls of spunyarn.

The balls were of unequal size, and he handed the larger to Pibby, telling him to climb the low cliff, and shin up the right-hand rock pinnacle; after which he was to put the bowline, in the end of the spunyarn, over the spike of the rock, and heave the ball down to him.

Pibby put down his two picks, took off his shoes, and made the ball fast round his shoulders. Then he climbed the little cliff and the right pinnacle, and put the bowline over the spiked end. He climbed down to the top of the cliff again, and called softly to the

Captain to stand from under; after which he cast the ball down into the shadows wher his master waited.

"Right, boy!" muttered Captain Jat. "Catch! Do the same on t'other." And he hove the second ball up to him. Pibby caught it, more by feel than sight, and made it fast round the top of the left pinnacle; throwing the ball likewise to his Master. Then he came down the cliff again, to give a hand.

Captain Jat led the way Eastward, unrolling the balls of yarn as he went. Pibby followed, carrying the lantern and his two picks. Presently, Captain Jat had come to the end of the smaller ball, and so veered away to the left, until the right-handed yarn had run out. Then he tautened them up, and where the ends of the two lines met, when they were taut, he set his heel down, and reached out for the lantern. He held the light down over the ground, and Pibby saw the Captain was standing on a piece of rock, covered pretty loose with blown sand and thin earth. Wind and weather had freed the edges of the earth sand, and Pibby realised that the piece of rock was thin; but near a fathom across, every way.

"Fetch them spades, boy." Said the Captain, giving him a jab in the rib with his elbow. "Smart now!"

Pibby ran for the spades and the bag. When he returned, his Master bid him hold the light down over the rock; and whilst the boy held the light, Captain Jat cleared away the sand and earth with one of the spades, and laid the rock bare.

It was a rough, natural slab of stuff, and if Captain Jat had not been remarkably strong, they would have had trouble with it. As it was, the Captain had first to split it across, with one of the picks, the sounds of the blows echoing over-far into the night; after which he forced the edge of a spade in under one end of each piece, in turn, and hove them up, whilst Pibby shoved stones underneath. Then they bent their backs to the work, and with great heaves, they had them clear, and at last were looking down into a bit of a hole in the rock beneath.

Captain Jat snatched the light from the boy, and held it down into the hole; but there was nothing in it, except an old copper cylinder, all green with verdigris, that lay half-bedded in the sand and earth that had sifted in.

"Ha! Boy!" said Captain Jat, and hove his spade down. "That's the dead spit of the one I got from the Portygee."

He crushed it under his heel, for it was too fouled with verdigris to be opened easily. When he had burst it in this way, he raked out a piece of dirty sheepskin, and had it spread flat open in a moment. Then he began to swear; and, for his ease, he knocked Pibby Tawles, the boy, over up on the rock, and kicked him a dozen times, before the lad got away from him.

Afterwards, he hove the sheepskin in the boy's face, all crumpled; and danced then all about the rock, blaspheming. He kicked the two spades, clattering enormously, one after the other, right across the hole; then he caught hold of the bag and hove it after them; and immediately came to clout the boy again; but Pibby Tawles out with one of his pistols, and he stopped at that, and burst into a sort of low laughing, reaching into the skirts of his great coat, the while. He fetched out a big flask of rum toddy, and pulled the cork with his teeth; and after that, he just squatted down, and lighted his pipe and sat drinking and smoking, with his back to the boy... muttering away to himself, and seeming regardless of any danger that the noise of his antics might have been likely to bring down upon them.

As for Pibby Tawles, after listening and peering round into the gloom for a little while, he took advantage of his Master's mood, which he had seen something of before, when the wry-natured man had been much put out. He reached cautiously for the crumpled piece of parchment, and crawled over quietly to the lantern; though he need not have bothered to go easy; for Captain Jat's sullen mood, at the moment, was such that he would hear or heed nothing; but only persist in his smoking and drinking.

When Pibby Tawles was come near to where the lantern stood upon the rock, a little to the rearward side of his Master, he spread out the parchment gently upon the rock, staring the while at the Captain to be sure the man did not see him. Then by the light from the lantern, the boy was able to discover why the Captain had been so put out; for on the old sheepskin there were just these words, which he was able to spell out slowly:—

THE EARLY BIRD HATH
    CATCHED THE WORM.
    THOU FOOL

And then, as Pibby stared at this, all mixed between grinning, and some disappointment because he had hoped to have some gain out of anything they might have discovered, he turned the sheepskin about, and found two bits of a clumsy scrawl on the back, that had at first no meaning for him.

Suddenly, however, as he stared at these, he got a sharp idea, and held the skin up towards the lantern, with the plain-written side towards him. Pibby Tawles nearly shouted then, to see what he had found; for the two clumsy scrawls upon the other side of the parchment, resolved themselves into the words "NOT" and "LOWER"; being obviously written backwards upon the back of the parchment, so that from the front, as seen against the light, they would read in with the quaint insult upon the front, entirely changing its meaning, thus:—

THE EARLY BIRD HATH
NOT CATCHED THE WORM
LOWER   THOU FOOL

Pibby Tawles looked quickly towards his Master's broad, muscular back; but the Captain was still smoking… chunnering away to himself over his pipe, in a way that showed the peculiar Vinegar of his particular Personality at work in his twisted mental arteries. From time to time, he would swig heavily at the flask of rum-toddy, and immediately again to his pipe-sucking and chunnering, hunching his shoulders in grotesque fashion, and breaking out from time to time in little snarls.

The boy stared long enough at his Master to be sure that he was not feigning unconsciousness of what was happening behind his back; for Pibby had been long enough now with Captain Jat to learn that the Captain was quite uncannily "aware" in certain of his moods; as though, at odd times, some primeval, half-faun instinct waked him to a hyper-awareness of matters around.

But this was plainly one of the Captain's obtuse hours; and Pibby slid the parchment cautiously into the breast of his shirt, and began to move back quietly again to the hole they had uncovered. He reached it, and thrust one dirty, vigorous hand down into the fine sandy earth that filled it. He worked his hand, burrowing eagerly and fiercely, and all the time, he stared at his Master's back.

Suddenly, the boy checked a gasp of amazed, half-incredulous excitement; for his burrowing hand had reached down to a hard mass, that shifted under his working fingers, and resolved into countless disks, that he fumbled for and grabbed at feverishly; and so withdrew his hand, full of dry sand and dull yellow coins that glimmered oddly in the vague light from the lantern.

"Gee!" he whispered. "Gee!" And stared at the Captain's back;

but Captain Jat was obviously unaware.

Pibby whipped off his neckcloth, and put the handful of sand and gold into it; then, thrusting his hand again down the hole, burrowed fiercely. He raked out three good fistfuls of gold coins and sand, and put them into the neckcloth gently so that they would not chink; and all the time as he worked so silently, he watched each movement of the Captain's back.

Abruptly, Captain Jat raised his hand, listening; but still with his back turned to the boy. Pibby ceased to burrow, on the instant, and gathered the neckcloth noiselessly together, the sand among the coins preventing them from chinking. He knotted the whole swiftly into a tight ball and shoved it inside his shirt, along with the parchment. Then, with a quick movement, he smoothed over the sand within the hole. And not for one moment during these brief actions did he cease to watch his Master.

The Captain continued his listening attitude; and Pibby Tawles began, himself, to listen; for it was plain to him that Captain Jat was not paying attention to any vague movement of his; but waiting for a repetition of some far sound that he must have fancied he heard out in the night.

"Hark! Boy!" said the Captain, sharply; and hove himself round upon his seat, with a single quick jerk. "that's twice this blessed minute I've heard it. Hark!"

They crouched there, listening; with the lantern casting their shadows oddly across the silence of the rocks; and the noise of the fall seeming to come to them with an almost unnatural clearness through the night about. Once, as Pibby shifted his attitude slightly, he thought he heard the faint chink of the money inside his shirt; but this was, possibly, no more than what I might term a conscience-sound; for Captain Jat's keen ears seemed to have heard nothing.

And then, long-drawn and horrible, away in the night, Pibby heard the sound that had come to them before, in the great wood-belt.

It came again... a curious, big, clamour of sound, floating oddly in the night; and, for the second time, the vague, yet frightening, familiarity of it stirred the boy's memory oddly.

He had faced round towards it, and without knowing, had drawn a pistol in each hand. The sudden indefinable terror that the sound brought to him had driven out the gold-lust; had driven out even all memory of the gold; for he had a feeling that a very real danger was roaming out there in the vagueness of the night.

He looked swiftly over his sholder at the immoveable, listening, tense, humped shape of his Master. "What is it, Cap'n?" he asked, in a low voice; with the feeling that Captain Jat *must* know. And then, even as he ventured the question, the abominable, unnaturally familiar clamour broke out again, unmistakeably nearer.

Captain Jat gave out a sudden, fierce grunt of comprehension:—

"Iils!" he said aloud, in a curious voice. "Iils! Sacred dogs, boy! They feeds 'em on the sacrifices, till they won't eat ought else. I heard about 'em once, further up this same coast. The priest sometimes lets 'em go loose at night. That's why them niggers was carryin' torch-lights, so as to frighten 'em off. They'm feared of light, same as wild beasts...."

He broke off, and snatched up the lantern. Then ran towards the water and looked down, holding the lantern low. "I guess that's why yon Portygee was so cocksure I'd not handle yon gold, when he gave me yon chart," Pibby, who had followed at a run, heard him grumbling to himself. "He grinned middlin' rum-like at me; may the devil bust him!"

The curious, tremendous clamour of sound broke out now in the woods to their back; seeming to be very near. And at the sudden noise, Captain Jat swore, and hove the lantern into the water; so that they were instantly in darkness.

"Curse them!" he muttered, with an almost incredible savagery. "They'm here a'ready! Into the water, boy; smart now! There's dozens of 'em, by the noise of 'em! An' they'm near big as donkeys, with the way they feeds 'em!"

He caught Pibby swittly by the shoulders, and swung him down through the darkness into the rush of the brook; then, with a spring like a great lean cat, he landed beside him, driving the water in all directions.

Above them, from the direction of the wood, the infernal noise burst out again, near and tremendous; and Captain Jat swore and dashed ahead through the dark, following the course of the shallow stream. Pibby kept close behind, stumbling, splashing and panting; for to his short figure, the water proved an immensely greater obstacle than to the unusually long, lean legs of his Master; who was seldom immersed above his great, bony knees.

Once, Captain Jat whipped round upon the lad, fiercely:—

"Make less your noise, boy!" he growled, stooping down almost to the level of Pibby's face. "If them Iils gets us, I'll sure clump you silly!"

Then he led on again.

Away up the stream, they heard now the clamour of the great dogs, making a threatening, broken din. By the sound of them, they had evidently come clear out from the trees, and were hunting the "scent" of the man and the boy, to and fro across the rocky plateau.

Meanwhile, the man and the boy ran on, downstream, through the darkness; the boy fighting desperately to keep up with the tremendous stride of his master. Once, Pibby lost his footing altogether on a slippery stone, and butted headlong into the stern of Captain Jat, bringing the whole lean, vigorous length of the Captain down on top of him, with the result that Pibby Tawles was sadly bruised; and, further, half drowned ruing the time that the long man sat upon the unfortunate and submerged youth, and cursed aloud into the night. And, as soon as Pibby struggled, sobbing for breath, to his feet, the Captain promptly knocked him down again, with a swinging clout; and began then immediately to go downstream once more; his anger seemingly appeased.

Now, whether it was that horde of dogs astern of them, had scent of them through the night air, or whether it was that the Captain's cursings had been too vehement for personal safety, it is impossible to say. All that is certain is that there came suddenly a fresh note into the crying of the dogs; and immediately a silence; and then, as the man and the boy paused instinctively to listen, they heard, clear and unmistakeable in the distance, the scrambling rush of padded feet coming along the bank towards them.

"They'm sure got us, boy! I told ye I'd clout you proper if they did!" said Captain Jat, and made a heavy blow at Pibby Tawles, with his open fist; but the boy dodged, and kicked his Master savagely on the knee, whereat Captain Jat swore horribly, and hopped about the bottom of the brook on one foot. He slipped, and sat down with an enormous splash, and immediately began to roar with laughter, in a great voice that could have been heard half a mile away in that sudden, threatening silence; for the only other sound was the horrid noise of the running feet, padding along the bank.

"We'll never see daylight again, boy," said Captain Jat, in an almost cheerful voice. And, without troubling to rise from where he sat in the rush of water, he loosed off with one of his big pistols at something that dashed past along the bank. "They'm here, boy! Shoot all you can, 'fore they has us!" he shouted, as he pulled the trigger.

But there was no explosion; for the priming had been wet. He cursed Pibby afresh; cursed the brook, the weapons, the powder, the dogs, and his Creator.

Meanwhile, Pibby had tried his own weapons, and found them temporarily useless.

And then, all the dark bank opposite became alive with vague, rustling, racing creatures, indifferently seen against the background of the gloomy woods beyond. There rose a deafening, hoarse, dreadful baying, gargantuan and horrible; and in the same instant the smell of the great, flesh-gorged beasts came to them. There was a sudden splash, and Pibby saw something that looked like the shadow of a huge dog in the water. Then Captain Jat was upon it, striking with his big knife; though Pibby could only guess that he was using his knife.

Pibby saw the Captain leap away from the dog in the water, and dash straight at the high, overhanging bank. The dogs above howled with bestial expectancy. Then, to his amazement, he saw a shower of sparks; and realised that his Master was striking his flint and steel into the great tussocks of the dried grass. But he could not guess that Captain Jat had half-emptied his powder-flask quickly there among the grass.

The dogs had seemed to give back, at the showers of sparks; as though afraid of the last vestige of fire. But now they made a sudden rush. And even as they rushed, the sparks fired the powder; for a vast burst of flame came out of the dry grass that sent Captain Jat staggering back, with his beard all blazing.

But it was not at the Captain that Pibby Tawles looked. In the light of the great flame, he had seen maybe a score of dogs, so enormous in size that their bodies appeared to be as large as the bodies of young donkeys. Their colour was dirty, unhealthy white, and they were hideously blotched with great sores, while their eyes showed scummy and brutishly inert in the light.

The pack of dogs had stiffened back instantly from the great blaze; and, as the fire caught the grass around, and sent up fresh spurts of flame, they gave back farther, in a curiously helpless fashion, whimpering peculiarly. Pibby Tawles saw now that the flames were flickering through the dry grass and bracken in every direction upon that side of the brook; and the dogs began to run sideways towards the wood beyond, whining as they ran.

Abruptly, the boy saw something extraordinary; for among the hinder dogs, there ran on all fours with the dogs, certain creatures that whined and snarled like dogs, yet certainly were not dogs.

The boy had climbed out of the water, onto the other bank, and had a clear view; and suddenly, he realised that the creatures that ran with the dogs were men, running with incredible swiftness upon all fours... not on their hands and knees, but upon their hands and toes. They were covered from their heads to their feet with what appeared to be great dog-skins.

"Priests, boy!" he heard Captain Jat say, suddenly, at his elbow; for the Captain had climbed up now beside him. "They'm worse nor any of them Iils, boy; if what I've heard is truth. They hunts with them at nights, sometimes, like this, so they told me down the coast; an' now I see 'tis true. An' they'm as mortal feared of light as the dogs. No use has they for flesh-meat, 'cept it be human meat, I've heard; an' well I believe it now!"

In his angry disgust, Captain Jat raised one of his pistols, and snapped it off in the direction in which the dogs and the men-brutes had disappeared. He had changed the priming, whilst he was speaking, and the report echoed dully against the hoarse roar of the fire upon the far side of the brook; but whether the Captain hit anything, or not, Pibby Tawles could not be sure; though he thought he heard a distant, half-human howling.

"Change your primin', boy," said his Master; and busied himself in reloading his discharged pistol, and replacing the primings of the others. When this was done, Captain Jat led off at a good pace downstream; a pistol in each hand, and his eyes busy with every clumping of bush, or tussock of great silver-grass they came near; for they were soon out of the strong light from the fire, which spread no very great way, on account of the rocky nature of the ground, which broke the clumpings of bush and tall grass into odd groups, and so prevented the fire from gaining to the forest beyond.

Presently, in maybe near an hour, the Captain and Pibby were gone sufficiently far from the fire for it to show no more than a dull, red glow against the night-sky to their rear; and all about them had come again the utter and dree silence of the huge, timber-grown slopes of the great headland.

"Quiet, boy!" Captain Jat growled, presently, as Pibby fouled a great root with his foot, and stumbled. A few minutes later, he stopped short in his swift, stealthy walk, and reached his hand back against the boy's chest. "Ssst!" he said. "They'm followin'. They've crost, an' they'm smellin' us out. Hark!"

For a little time of silence the two of them stood without movement; then, abruptly, far away in the forest to their backs, there rose again that strange clamouring; half-familiar, utterly horrible, and, in some peculiar fashion, unnatural.

"That's them priest swine!" said Captain Jat, grimly. "It's them that makes the funny sound to the dogs' howlin'. It's up hellum now, boy, an' run for all we're worth, or you won't never see daylight in this world again. An' don't you make a sound, or I'll clout you good an hearty!"

Captain Jat turned, and went down among the trees at a great pace. They had left the nearness of the brook sometime back; and they went downward now, blindly; yet knowing that by so doing they must eventually reach the seashore. From time to time, as they ran, there came the ugly clamour, away among the far darkness of the wood to their rear; and the trees around would catch the sound, and throw it at them, uncomfortably, from half a dozen directions in the night. And all the while, that cry of bestial hunger was steadily nearing them.

Abruptly, as they raced downward, Pibby missed his footing and went headlong; the pistol he carried in his hand, exploding with a great thud of sound, in the heavy silence among the trees. The bullet flicked between Captain Jat's legs, skinning one of his knees, and that wrathful length of man turned, cursing at the top of his voice, and clouted Pibby fiercely, right and left, as he rose.

"You damned cork-fender!" he roared. "Stay an' be eat by them devils astern!"

And with that, he turned, and continued his great stride downward through the darkness; avoiding the trees, almost as though he had some power of seeing in the dark.

Pibby got to his feet again, and followed the Captain; though his head was singing dizzily with the clumping he had received, as well as with the force of his tumble. Yet he ran desperately, managing to keep within sound of the Captain's footsteps, and slowly overhauling him; for to be left behind was to be caught by those incredible brutes in his rear.

In this fashion, they continued, and at the verge of the wood, the boy overhauled Captain Jat; but he was so breathless, and so shaken by striking himself against the tree trunks in the darkness, that he ran, gasping madly for breath, his legs numb and heavy and almost useless. It was then that Captain Jat did, for him, a surprisingly nice thing; for there broke out now a tremendous clamour of pursing dogs and men-beasts, seeming no more than a hundred fathoms or so, within the wood; and at the horrid sound, Captain Jat let out a brutal oath, and muttering:— "Cub-dunnage!" picked up the blown lad, as though he had been but a kitten, and raced away with him at an amazing pace along the beach; his great legs seeming to cover a full fathom at every stride.

Astern of them, the clamour rose now, fierce and threatening, and so clear, that it was plain the brutes had broken free out of the wood, and were stretching after them along the open shore. At that, the Captain pushed the lad higher in his arms:—

"Over my shoulder, boy!" he grunted. "Fire over my shoulder. Backen the brutes, if you can, boy, or we're sure gone!"

Pibby Tawles stared along the dark sands, and again came the clamour, very near, and sharp above the constant, wholesome noise of the sea all along his right. Then the boy saw something, many things, vague and black to their rear, that moved swiftly after them. He was, as you know, an extraordinary shot with a pistol, and he loosed off over the Captain's shoulder, nearly deafening his Master; and a fierce howl out of the semi-darkness told that his shot had hit. Time after time, he fired, and three more of his shots brought maddened yelps out of the gloom along the beach. Then he reached his hand down to Captain Jat's belt, and drew one of the Captain's pistols; for he had fired all his own. With this, he loosed off again; and there came a half human crying that was very horrible; and immediately the boy was aware that the pursuit had ceased.

From their rear, there rose now a fierce, bestial snarling, and all the time a terrible voice shrieked and shrieked, and presently died away into a dreadful silence.

"You hit one of them priest fellers!" grunted the Captain, breathlessly. "An' I guess them Iils has just turned an' eat the swine; an' serve his sort right an' proper too!"

Behind them, there rose afresh the sudden uproar of the horrid chase; which told the two of them that the brutes astern had finished their dreadful meal, and were speeding once more towards them, through the darkness.

"Put me down, Cap'n! said Pibby. "I can run all right now!"

Captain Jat said nothing; but opened his arms, and hove the boy from him, as though he had been no more than a bundle. Pibby struck the sand with a thud that sickened him; but was on his feet in an instant, and racing behind his master; whilst less than a hundred fathoms in his rear, there rose the constant, incredible clamour of the great Iils and the brute-men that hunted them.

"The boat!" said the Captain, a moment later, and spurted forward. As he did so, he must have trodden on one of the larger round stones that strewed the sands here and there, for he slid, and pitched forward with a tremendous thud onto his face. And there he lay, as still as though he had been killed.

"Get up, Cap'n!" But Captain Jat sagged inert upon the sand; for the sudden fall had knocked the senses out of him.

Behind them, the noise of the brutes swept infernally towards them through the night; and Pibby could already hear the patter of many feet, and the sharp rattle of odd stones, sent flying by the pads of the great dogs. He caught the Captain by one shoulder and arm, and hove him round upon his back, so that he could get his undischarged pistols. Then, swiftly but deliberately, the boy fired barrel after barrel along the sands, holding the heavy weapons no more than a foot above the level of shore.

With each thudding bang of the big pistols, there came ferocious yelps of pain; and then, twice in succession, a wild half-human yelling answered his shots, and the clamour of the dogs turned suddenly once more into that terrible snarling note, out of which came scream after scream, which told what was happening again.

Pibby Tawles turned then upon the Captain and slapped the big man's face savagely with his open hand. A dozen times, he struck him; and suddenly Captain Jat began to swear thickly, and then turned and sat up, blaspheming insanely.

"Get up, Cap'n! Get up, Cap'n!" said Pibby. "They'll come after us again in a tick!"

He got the man to his feet, and reeled him towards where the boat lay, not more than a dozen paces away. They reached it, threw off the painter, and pushed madly, and so had it quickly afloat. As the boat took the water, there arose again the roar of the brutes, coming towards them; and the two had scarcely got into the boat, and began to push out from the shore with their oars, when the great dogs were dashing into the shallow water all about them.

Captain Jat swung his oar round by the handle, and struck in among the dogs, and as he struck, Pibby crouched below the sweep of the great ash oar, and pushed steadily with his own against the sea bottom, and so in a few moments, the boat began to move out into deep water.

Yet even in that brief time, one of the great dogs had leapt and crooked its great forelegs in-board over the gunnel of the boat, and was scrambling furiously to climb in over; but Captain Jat beat in its head with the end of his oar, and the huge, foul-smelling beast fell back into the water.

A minute afterwards, they had the boat clear of danger, heading away out to the open sea, beyond the lee of the Headland; while astern of them, there rose the incessant, horrid clamour of the great dogs, and blending with it, a noise that was infinitely more dreadful—the disgusting, human-bestial note of the men-beasts that hunted with the dogs.

An hour later, the two of them were safely aboard; and Pibby was stowing away into his sea-chest, with infinite satisfaction, a full hundred and fifty gold pieces, out of the knotted neckerchief that he had hidden in his shirt. Then, a sudden, unusual twinge of conscience troubled him; for he remembered how Captain Jat had carried him. He thought awhile, and presently reached down to the stored gold. After which, he went into the cabin and told Captain Jat that he believed they had discovered the position of the treasure, after all.

In support of his statement, he planked down, upon the cabin table, one of the gold pieces, and explained how he had discovered it, whilst rooting among the sand in the hole.

"Boy," said Captain Jat solemnly, over the top of his fourth pewter of rum-toddy, "We'll ashore again yon next v'yage an' find yon treasure; aye! if so there's ten thousand of them damned Iils. But it won't be no manner of use now; for the whole place'll be riotin' for a month to come."

"Aye, Aye, Cap'n," agreed Pibby, and boldly ventured his cup into the toddy, a second time; for the Captain had invited him to bring his cup and join him, whilst he told his yarn. But, for his pains, Captain Jat caught him by the scruff, and poured the good liquor down his back, inside his shirt.

Which, after all, proved a very effective salve to Pibby Tawles' suddenly troublesome conscience; for Pibby went back into his cabin, and without bothering to change his shirt, turned-in and slept with the utmost vigour and satisfaction. You will remember that he had omitted all mention of the hundred and forty nine remaining pieces of gold, which lay so snug in the bottom of his sea-chest!

As I have remarked before, Pibby Tawles was undoubtedly a youth with a sound eye to the main chance.

had sunken all number of the hundred and forty-nine represents
pieces of gold, with it lay sitting in the bottom of the wrecked

D.C.O. Cargunka

The Bells of the "Laughing Sally"

"AH!" SAID CARGUNKA TO his reflection in the broken looking-glass under his office desk, "cleanliness may be next to Godliness; but I reckon good cooking *is* Godliness.... Leastaways, there's precious little Godliness in a man wiv indisgestion!"

He was sitting on a tea-chest in his office at the back of the dirty but important marine stores which fill half one side of Gallows Lane, in the town of Appledaulf, on the South coast. The marine stores belonged to him, as did the Red Lyon, public-house, next door.

He sat on the tea-chest at this particular hour every morning, and peeled potatoes; for cooking was his hobby, almost his passion. The tea-chest had been hacked down to make a low seat, and he chose it, because—as he said—it "gave to his bones"; also, though of this he said nothing, the height of it brought his face below the level of his office desk, where reposed the broken mirror that I have already mentioned, and in which, from time to time, he looked at himself with infinite satisfaction, pushing back his hair from over his shaven temples, and taking great care not to damp the hair with his wet hand; for the curls were not Nature's, but the curls of Hinde's curlers, which he wore secretly every night.

He finished peeling the last of his potatoes, and wiped his hands thoroughly on his apron. Then, he closed and pocketed the diminutive copy of Byron's *Poems* which had been propped up on the chair, at the back of the basin into which he had put the peeled potatoes. He turned to a phonograph, which stood on the top of a Tate's sugar box, and changed the wax cylinder. He wound the machine leisurely, and set it going. It was a new record, and he listened expectantly. There came a short prelude on a piano, and there burst out a splendid, rich contralto, so fine and good, that even the whir of the machine failed completely to destroy its essential humanity, which marked its quality.

443

Cargunka leaned back contentedly.

"My word!" he said; "that's good! That's fine!"

"Eight bells!
And the *Laughing Sally* sailed away,
And the sound of the bells came back to me
Across the sea
Across the sea
The sound of the bells came back to me
As the *Laughing Sally* sailed that day
Away and away with thee,
My Man,
Away with thee."

The deep contralto silenced, and there came the brief tinkle of the piano, as the phonograph ground away.

"That's sure the song they made up about old Cap'n Barstow's ship," muttered Cargunka, reflectively. "She never come back, an' that's three year, last Christmas as ever was... as ever was! Aye, they sure sail away. Like as I shall do someday, maybe.... They do say as he carried a sight of brass wiv him.... He never would trust no banks; I do know that...."

The voice broke out again:—

"And I stood on the shore and cried to thee
That day Love sailed away from me...."

And so to the end of the second stanza, which found Cargunka furtively rubbing one eye in sentimental fashion, with the corner of his dirty apron.

"Aye!" he said, "an' the bells of the *Laughin' Sally* ring across the sea... I guess that's how it'll be wiv me."

He pulled out a notebook, and jotted down the rhyme; then blew his nose. He was thinking of the two brigs that he owned, and of the periodic trips he made in them, between Appledaulf and far off San Francisco, where he owned the Dot-And-Carry-One Saloon, on the Water Front. Someday, he felt, there would be a song about one of his ships, when she went missing. As he conned over possible rhymes, the phonograph gave out the beginning of the third stanza:—

"The *Laughing Sally* sailed away
Into the Evermore that day,
And the sound of her bells came back to me
Across the deep in the evening grey...."

Cargunka wiped his eyes soberly, and made shift to jot down two fresh rhymes that had just occurred to him.

"My word!" he muttered; "that's first chop! That's mag-ni-ficent:—

"The *Happy Return*, she sailed away
And her bell ting-tinged the livelong day...."

he wrote down, labouriously. He was obviously thinking of one of his own brigs.

The phonograph began the fourth stanza of the "Fate of the *Laughing Sally*," and Cargunka lay back to enjoy it, with his eyes closed. He was interrupted in his æsthetic pleasures in an almost incomprehensible fashion; for Jensag, his quietly superior barman, ordinarily intensely silent and grave, had dashed suddenly in through the doorway that opened out of the back of the bar into Cargunka's office.

"Stop it!" shouted Jensag, in a voice of extraordinary energy. "Stop it!"

"And the bells of the *Laughing Sally* ring,
And die away forever...."

sang the phonograph.

"Stop it!" roared Jensag. "Stop it!" He barged crashing over the bucket of dirty water and peelings; then rose and kicked the bucket across the office. "Stop it!" he shouted, once more.

Cargunka rose to his full height of five feet, two, and turned upon the big, clean-shaven, white-faced, strangely tensed-up barman.

"Get—out—of—here!" he said, slowly; gritting out the words at spaced intervals.

"And the bells grow faint and lost,"

sang the phonograph.

"Stop it!" roared Jensag. "Stop it! Stop it!"

"Get out!" said Cargunka, still in a slow voice.

"I'll stop it myself!" said the bartender, in a voice that was suddenly quiet and quivering with an extraordinary, fierce suppression.

He made one swift step towards the machine, swung up a quick foot, and the phonograph flew across the office, wailing the one word:— "Bells," and fell with a crash into a ruin of broken woodwork, tin and disrupted clockwork.

"My Oath!" said Cargunka, still in that slow, quiet voice. "My old man used ter reckon we was a saved family an' he brought us up peaceful; but he always said as the Lord had no sort of use for worms...." He began to take off his coat, with a curious cheerful look shining in the back of his well-shaped, dark blue eyes.

He stepped past the still quivering barman, and thrust his head through the open doorway into the back of the bar.

"M'ria!" he shouted, "come an' take the bar!"

Then he walked back into his office, closed the door quietly after him, and spoke to the big bartender:—

"Come along out into the big room, my lad," he said, "an' take your coat off. You can come in wiv the explanations after."

The bartender said something in a queer voice, that might have been a protest; then, as if realising the futility of anything that he might say, at this tense stage of affairs, he took off his coat, and followed the halting, "dot-and-carry" step of his master.

In the big room, Cargunka wheeled round smartly:—

"Put your hands up, my lad," he said, quietly. "We'll see if you's as good at fightin' as you is at bustin' up good property."

The big barman, at this point, made an ineffectual effort to say something; but Cargunka headed him off. "Fight!" he said. "Talk afterwards! My Oath! I've not had a do for a month of Sundays!"

Then they fought.

"I'm never friends to no man!" said Cargunka, five minutes later, as he pillowed the big barman's head in the crook of his arm, and poured some very good brandy down his throat; "not till I've knocked the 'ell out of 'im."

He thrust one long, enormously muscular arm under the big man's thighs, and lifted him easily to an old cabin settee, that stood against one wall of the big room.

Chapter II

"Now, my lad, we'll talk," said Cargunka, when the big barman came round from his knock-out. "What was wiv you, to come into my office like you did, bustin' up things? You just talk to me as if I was your old man. I guess a bit of it, an' you needn't fear to tell it all straight out. Was it the lady in the phonygraft, or was she singin' your donah's song, that's dead an' gone this while back?"

With further persuasion, of a rough but kindly sort, the big barman told the whole brief tale.

"That was Stella Bavanga singing," he said, in a strange voice. "That was her stage name. 'The Fate of the *Laughing Sally*' was her big song. It was written five years ago, when the four-masted schooner, *Laughing Sally*, was given up for lost. About a year and a half later, Stella got a fit of bad health, and the doctor said she'd have to go a sea voyage. She went for a trip in a barque of the same name as the schooner that was lost. A man named Barstow was the Captain; a queer sort of man. I hated her to go. Yes, I was the husband of Stella Bavangal and I was superstitious about the name... after the song, you know. My God! I heard the bell ring, as she went down the river. You know the rest; she never came back; and I lost all interest in life. I've come down now to bartending! She made that record. She did a lot of that work...."

Dot-and-Carry-One Cargunka's eyes shone, as the sympathy and sentiment rose in him:—

"My Oath!" he muttered, gently. "My Oath! I'm glad you broke the bloomin' phonygraft! I'd a broke the old bloomin' shop up, if I'd been in your cloes!"

Chapter III

"Strike me pink!" said a burly-looking man to D.C.O. Cargunka, some weeks later. "I tell youse, old Dot-an'-Carry, I made no blame error. It was the barque herself. I recernised 'er by the skullwork round the 'house. We blew past, not twenty fathoms outside the reef. I thought we'd sure have our bottom scratched right off'n us, I did that, we was that close in. She was right in over the reef; close up agin the cliff face, as snug as a wop in a rug. However she come there, the Lord, He knows, I don't.

"No one else recernised 'er, but me; an' I kep' it to tell you. I knowed you'd play fair, an' give me the worf of the news, or a share; I don't mind so which way it comes to me. Ole Barstow carried his brass wiv him, an' there should be a pile; he didn't trust no banks; same's he didn't trust no wimmin. I've heard him say so many a time, when I sailed wiv him. Once, when it was blame calm, I heard money chinkin' down below, an' I went an' peeped down the cabin skylight; and there was the Ole Man wiv it in a bucket. Strike me! but I'm speakin' trewth. The ole devil had it in a wooden poop-bucket, all sovrins, an' he was runnin' 'is hands through it, like as you might run your fists through a bucket of peas. I guess he was just dotty on that oof of his. An' it'll be in her right this moment, if no blame thief han't got to her first; an' I doubt they'd find the cash; for she was middlin' up to her rails; so I guess she's full up wiv sea-water, an' you'll need to take a pump an' a divin' outfit. Now then, ole Dot-an'-Carry, what's it going to be?"

"Where's the island?" asked Dot-and-Carry-One Cargunka. "Give it a name, my lad."

"Not much, old D.C.O.! Not much! You fix up what it's worf to me first!" said the man.

"A quarter of all we get," said Cargunka, after thinking a minute. "That's if I decide to 'ave a go at it."

" 'Arf!" said the man. "Make it 'arf, D.C.O.?"

"No," said Cargunka. "You'll get your quarter clear. I've got to stan' all the expense. Turn up the name, or I'll drop out!"

"It's yon Three Finger Island, out to the West of the Vardee Islands," said the man. "You sign me on as the bo'sun, Dot-an'-Carry. They told me down to the wharf, as you was takin' a run out to 'Frisco, 's soon as the *Happy Return* was ready. She ain't no bo'sun; an' it won't be much off our course to run in to them Vardee Islands, an' lift the stuff. There should be a matter of thousands, by my reckoning."

And so it was settled.

Chapter IV

Cargunka stood on the lee side of the poop of the *Happy Return*, and stared away to leeward. They were a hundred and four days out from England, and had sighted Three Finger Island at daybreak.

Through the telescope, Cargunka could now see the wreck of the *Laughing Sally*, inside the reef of the island, and close in-shore. She was almost submerged; yet Cargunka had recognised her at once, by a number of details, one of which was the quaint, white-painted skull-beading round the top of her poop-deck house.

Suddenly, D.C.O. Cargunka walked away aft, and knocked three times on the deck with his heel. Immediately, as though he had been waiting only for the signal, there sprang up through the after scuttle, Jensag, Cargunka's one-time barman at the Red Lyon. Cargunka had brought him with him on this trip, for the man had heard something of the truth from Durrit, the one who had brought the news; and he had begged so hard to be allowed to come, that Cargunka had at last signed him on as steward; felling that it might be kinder for the poor fellow to realise, by an actual sight of the wreck, that it was utterly useless to begin hoping any vague hopes concerning his long-dead wife.

"Now, my lad," said Cargunka, handing his own telescope to the shaking man, "you get a hold of yourself. I told you not to get hopin'. Take a look, an' you'll see she's deep in the water. There's no more than 'er deck house and fo'cas'le-'ead deck above. It's three year since she must have struck there; and there's just no chance at all as you'll find a soul. Leastways, not humanly speakin', lad. Though the Almighty, He can do wonderful things, like. But, for all sakes! don't get hopin' anything at all. There's a dozen things that tells me already as there's no any livin' human ashore yon."

The steward said nothing in reply. He was busy, trying to hold the glass steady; but at last had to give up the attempt, because he shook so that he could not bring it to bear on any one point for more than a fraction of time.

It was late in the afternoon, when the *Happy Return* let go her anchor within the shelter of the reef, not more than a hundred fathoms away from the place where the wreck of the *Laughing Sally* lay with only her deck house top and masts in view above the water.

"You can let the men go ashore for a run, Mister," said Cargunka to the Skipper, "as soon as you've got all snug and tidied up. Tell the steward to give 'em some grub, an' they can take one of the boilers and kettle out of my galley. I'll run ashore presently an' cook them up somethin' for their picnic. Let the steward go wiv 'em. I guess he'll be easier if we let him search round a bit, poor devil."

The men put on a spurt to make all snug, when they heard from the Skipper that they were to be allowed ashore; and meanwhile, Cargunka had the little shore-punt put over the side; for he meant to make a visit to the wreck, and see how she lay. He climbed down into the punt, and sculled her over to the *Laughing Sally*. Yet he could distinguish little under the water; for the light of the sun lay now across the sea, and made it impossible to see to any depth. He could make out vaguely, however, the outline of the submerged fo'cas'le-head; and, rising from it, the dome and framework of the ship's brass bell, showing a vague green shape of verdigris, just below the surface; for the whole of the vessel was covered, as I have said, except the top of the poop-deck house and the three stumps of the masts.

Cargunka realised that he could discover nothing further that evening. The tide was at its highest, and he knew the wreck would be partially uncovered at low water, as it had been when he saw it first

though the telescope, earlier in the day. Meanwhile, as he could do
nothing, he put the punt round and sculled ashore to where the men
were making a fire on the beach.

Presently, he was indulging in his hobby of cooking, which was
so strong a need in him, that he never signed on a cook when he took
a voyage in one of his brigs; but did all the cooking himself, occupying strictly the position of cook (or "Doctor" in sea-parlance); but
claiming his rights as Owner, as soon as the second dog-watch came
along each evening; when he would shed his long apron, and ascend
to the poop; there to occupy the Captain's deck-chair, the while that
he smoked and yarned.

Cargunka kept a couple of the men by him, as temporary Cook's
Mates, as he chose to call them; but the rest, he allowed to go off at
their own will; warning them, however, to keep their ears open for the
"dinner gong." It was growing dusk, by the time that he had cooked
a meal that seemed to him worthy of the occasion, and he and his
two "Cook's Mates" were warm and perspiring. The dinner gong, he
achieved by the simple expedient of singing out to the Mate in the
brig, to strike eight bells; for it was close upon eight o'clock.

Now you must remember that it was just coming on dusk (the
somewhat brief dusk of the semi-tropics); though both the brig and
sunken barque were in plain view from the beach, and no more than a
little vague with the first shadowing of evening. Yet, despite, as I have
shown, that nothing was yet hidden by the night, a most extraordinary and quite inexplicable thing occurred. For, as the deep notes of
the brig's forrard bell died away across the water, there came, like an
answer, from the direction of the submerged barque, eight eldritch,
sharp, thin-sounding strokes on a bell.

Cargunka jumped, and swore suddenly.

"My Oath!" he said, and stared away towards the barque. He
noticed that the tide had fallen now, and the rail around the fo'cas'le
head had become unsubmerged. It was to the after part of this rail
that the barque's ship's-bell was fixed, and it showed now, a shape of
verdigris brass, dumb and immutable.

"My Oath!" said Cargunka again, and limped away from the fire,
down the beach to the water. "My Oath!" he muttered, once more,
as he stopped and stared out at the barque. "That's rum! Who the
blamed thump is playin' the blessed goat!"

He put his hands to his mouth, and hailed the brig.

"A-a-hoy there!" he sung out. "A-a-ahoy!"

Then, as the Mate's face showed over the rail:—

"Did you hear that, Mister?" he shouted. "Did you hear that? Take a look at the barque from where you are. Is there anyone there?"

The Mate ran across the deck, without a word, and stared under his hands, both at the barque's poop-deck house and her fo'cas'le head rail; for, otherwise, the whole hulk of her was still entirely submerged. In a minute, he was back again at the landward rail of the brig.

"There's nothin', Sir! Nothing at all!" he shouted back.

"Did you hear that other bell go?" roared Cargunka.

"Yes, Sir, I certainly heard something," replied the Mate, as non-committal as possible.

"You heard something! My Oath! I should say you did!" replied Cargunka. He turned to the two men behind him, where they both stood, looking in a puzzled fashion towards the wreck. "Did you men hear nothin'?" queried Cargunka.

"Yes, Sir, we bofe 'eard it," answered one of the men. "Someone struck eight bells over yon on the barque." He looked from Cargunka to the barque and back again; then scratched his head violently.

"Get into the punt," said Cargunka; and stepped in after them, in his long apron. "Pull me out round the barque!"

This was done; but though they rounded the barque twice, there was not a thing to see, beyond the top of the submerged deck house, the stumps of the three wooden masts, and the rail around the fo'cas'le head, with the bell upon it, about a foot clear of the surface of the sea. As they came opposite to the bell for the second time, Cargunka spoke to the men:—

"Shove me in, just abaft the head, as close as you can. There's plenty water over her to float the boat. I want to 'ave a look at that bell."

The men obeyed, and in a few moments, Cargunka was leaning out over the boat, feeling up inside the bell for the tongue and lanyard.

"My Oath!" he muttered, suddenly. "There ain't no striker. It's unshipped, sure!" Then, abruptly, as a thought struck him:— "Pass me over a thole-pin."

He reached out for the wooden pin, and as soon as it was given to him, he struck the bell smartly with it. The bell gave out the identical, attenuated, sharply-thin note that they had heard directly after the bell of the *Happy Return* was struck.

The men jumped unaccountably at the sound; as if it were already associated in their minds with something uncomfortably peculiar; but Cargunka merely listened intently; then struck the bell a second time, making it give out once more the thin, faraway sound.

"My Oath!" he muttered, then. "That's mighty rum! Mighty rum!"

He bent and examined the bell, with the light of a match, both inside and out; for the dusk was deepening; but it was just an ordinary ship's bell... a mere shape of solidly-fixed brass, tongueless and alone, there above the darkening sea.... And then, in a queerly effective way, it came home to Cargunka that the drowned hull of the vessel was close below them. Somehow, there in the increasing dark, the realisation came home to him, curiously clear, with something of a queer, vague, dreary, uncomfortable feeling.

"Ug!" he said. "A blessed sea-churchyard she is!" And he took his supporting hand from the dank, water-sodden rail. "She's fair got the stink of sea-slime on 'er! Back out, my lads, an' let's get our suppers. The Lord knows what we heard, or what we thought we heard. I'm middling sure, though, this bell's never 'ad a clapper in it, not these last three year, or more. My Oath! Pull, lads; there's the men all back, an' smellin' the cookin'; and small blame to 'em, though I say it! Pull, my sons!"

When Cargunka go ashore, he found all the men waiting, except the steward. Some of them had seen the man last, away up in the woods of the island; but he had seemed so anxious to be alone, that none of them had bothered him.

"Now, men," said Cargunka, "move around handy! Two of you take the punt off wiv my compliments, an' ask the Mate and the Cap'n if they'll come an' join us for a snack. If the steward don't turn up, poor devil, so much the worse for 'im. Move now!"

The men were early back with the Captain; but it appeared that the Mate had taken temporary offence at Cargunka's tone, when Cargunka questioned him regarding the bell-sounds; and so the Mate had decided to stay aboard and nurse his vanity. This, however, bothered no one; and the meal was soon in full swing, with only an occasional expression of regret that the steward was missing it all. Once, far away, through the quiet forests of the island, they heard his voice, calling.

"Poor devil!" said Cargunka; and therewith dismissed him.

After the dinner, or supper, there was plenty of watered rum, with resultant cheerfulness and songs, which were kept up until nearly midnight. About eleven-thirty, the singing was dropped, and various cuffers were spun; during which Cargunka and his Captain discussed the puzzle of the bell-sounds which he was convinced he had heard, earlier, as you know. The Captain, however, felt that there must be some simple explanation—some freakish echo, perhaps.

It was just as the Captain made this suggestion, that eight bells were struck by the Mate aboard the brig. There came a sudden expectant silence upon the men about the fire; but never a sound followed, though they waited several minutes.

"No echo there, Cap'n!" said Cargunka.

The words were not fully spoken when, clear and thin, with that curious faraway quality in the sound that Cargunka had previously noted, there came the sharp:— ting-ting, ting-ting, ting-ting, ting-ting of the bell upon the wreck.

There came a burst of exclamations from the men about the fire; and both Cargunka and his Captain jumped to their feet.

"My Oath! Cap'n, did you hear *that*?" said Cargunka. Then, without a pause:— "The boat, smart , Cap'n! Maybe that poor mad devil of a steward is playin' some fool-game. You mind the song, Cap'n?"

"Stop!" said the Captain, abruptly. "Listen!" He held up his hand; and they all heard it, then—the voice of the steward, faraway on the other side of the island, calling:— "Agnes! Agnes!" or, at least, that is how it sounded; his voice coming strange and small through the hush of the night, incredibly faint.

"Poor lad!" said the Captain. "It's not him at the bell, that's plain."

"The boat, quick!" interrupted Cargunka. "There's somethin' mighty rum in this business. Bring one of them burnin' faggots wiv you, Cap'n. Buck after me smart!"

Even as he spoke, he was racing down the strip of sand to the boats. The Captain snatched up a blazing, resinous branch out of the fire, and ran after him, the wood flaring and crackling as he dashed down the beach. The two of them leaped aboard the punt, and the men, who had followed at a run, shoved the boat out good and strong; then lined up along the shore, to watch.

Cargunka shipped a pair of the oars, and rowed, whilst the Captain stood in the bows, and held the blazing branch high over his head, as he stared towards the sunken barque. Cargunka headed the boat straight for the fo'cas'le, standing with his face towards the bows of the boat. He pushed the boat right in over the submerged fore-deck of the barque, drew in his oars, and caught at the bell. The tide had risen, and he found the water now within four or five inches of the bell. He struck a match, and examined the bell again, feeling inside it, and all round about.

"Nothin' here, Cap'n," he muttered. He reached for a thole-pin. "Listen," he said, and struck the bell, smartly. It gave back the same clear, thin sound they had heard.

"That's sure what we heard, Cap'n," said Cargunka. "Now what devilment have we run into? That's what I want to know!"

Cargunka backed the boat out from over the submerged vessel, and began to pull slowly round her, with the Captain holding up the burning, resinous branch, which cast a fitful, uneasy, flickering light over the dark water of the near lagoon, showing the strangely painted top of the deck house aft, and the green-rusted shape of the bell forrard, with the three stumps of the naked slimy masts growing up, as it were, out of the oily quiet of the water between. At times, as the light flared up, the whole of these details would spring into clear view, then, as the light fell, a comparative darkness would come.

Thrice the boat circumnavigated the long-sunken craft; but never a thing could either Cargunka or his Captain find to explain that uncomfortable striking of the bell.

Presently, Cargunka lay on his oars.

"What do you make of it, Cap'n?" he asked, in a low voice.

"I'm completely puzzled, Sir," said the Captain. "In a way, I don't like it... I mean, it's funny. It's a bit beastly, somehow, you know."

Cargunka nodded; then, as a notion seemed to strike him suddenly, he turned and paddled quietly towards the brig. When he had brought the boat quite near, he hailed the Mate, in a low voice, and told him to strike eight bells a second time. This the Mate did; but though the Captain and Cargunka waited silently in the punt for some minutes, there came no answering bells from the submerged craft.

"Now, look here," called Cargunka up to the Mate. "As soon as it's half past twelve, strike one bell, like as if we was at sea."

"What's your notion, Sir?" asked the Captain.

"I'm blest if I know, myself," answered Cargunka. "I'm half beginnin' to think things I'd not care to put into words. You noticed that blessed dead hulk yonder took no sort of notice of the *fake* eight-bells. Well, now I'm going to see if it answers just only those bells as is struck at the *proper* times. More'n that, I just carn't say, Cap'n; for I'm blowed if I know myself what I thinks or believes."

Cargunka began to paddle the punt noiselessly across again to the submerged vessel, explaining, as he did so, that he meant to go back unseen, if possible; and as the night was very dark, and the water gave out no ripples of phosphorescence under the oars, it was not difficult; for the Captain's torch had long since died out and been dumped into the water.

Very slowly, Cargunka urged the boat across, until, at last, they were lying within some three or four fathoms of the bell; though they could only know its position approximately by their distance from the stump of the foremast, which rose up into dim visibility against the night-sky, about four fathoms off their starboard bow.

Cargunka lay on his oars, keeping the boat in position, by an occasional, gentle stroke; and thus for some minutes there was an almost perfect quiet, through which came the low, constant roar of the fine-weather seas upon the outer reef, and the odd mutter of talk from the men along the beach; they being plain also to see, by reason of the fire which still burned cheerfully behind them, up the beach.

As Cargunka sat, listening for any vague sound that might come from the direction of the submerged hulk, he heard the Captain moving cautiously aft in the punt towards him; and then the Captain was whispering:— "Hark, Sir! I'm sure he's singing."

Cargunka heard it then, a voice coming far and thin through the night; one moment plain to be heard, though infinitely remote; and then, again, lost, as some eddy of the night airs carried the sounds astray.

"Poor devil!" muttered Cargunka. " 'E'll sure go barmy, if we don't corral 'im, an' bring him in, an' get 'im sensible. It's mighty strange soundin', to 'ear him singin' like that, now, away over there by his lonesome. Maybe he's thinkin' she'll hear, if she's anywheres on the island. But there's no one ashore yon. I told the men to have a good look round, while I was makin' supper; an' they none of 'em saw a thing; an' they fair covered the island wiv their noise an' singin' an' shouting. There's no castaways ashore yon, as well I knew; an' I thought maybe to get yon poor feller more settled in his mind, if I could let 'im see for himself. I wish now I'd left him to home. Hark to him now!—"

A single line was wafted far and clear and faint to them through the night upon the island:—

"The *Laughing Sally* sailed away—"

From the brig, at this instant, there came, deep and sonorous, the single stroke of the ship's bell, as the Mate struck the half past midnight, exactly to the moment by the chronometer.

"Ssdt!" whispered Cargunka, and stiffened into rigid intensity, listening, and staring unblinkingly towards the spot where he knew the bell must be. As he sat there, in a half-conscious fashion he caught a second odd line of the remote singer's, as it floated faintly through the night air:—

"And the sound of her bells came back to me—"

Even as he heard, and half comprehended the words, there came a single, incredible sound from the sunken barque—the solitary, thin "ting" of the bell; yet curiously muffled, and seeming to be no more than a couple of fathoms off the port bow of the little punt. Evidently they had come closer to the bell than Cargunka had guessed.

A strange, extraordinary thrill, that made him shiver vaguely, travelled swiftly over the back of his head. Then, without a word, he dashed the oars into the water, and drove the boat towards the sound.

"Strike a light, Cap'n…. Quick!" he whispered tensely. But instead of the Captain obeying, he backed suddenly upon Cargunka, in the darkness, with a muttered:— "Let's get out of here! Let's get out of here!"

"My Oath! Yes…. When I'M done!" said Cargunka, and crammed him down savagely onto a thwart. He drew out his own box of matches, and struck a light. He found that he had driven the punt close beside the bell, and that the bell was now partly submerged by the rising tide, which detail, he realised, had likely enough caused the sound to be muffled. The Captain had himself in hand by now, and fished out his own matches, which he struck and held, whilst his Owner examined the bell, feeling all about it, inside and out.

Presently, Cargunka stood upright, his hands and sleeves dripping sea-water.

"My Oath, Cap'n!" he said. "What sort of funny devil-work have we sure struck now!"

"I don't know, Sir," said the Captain, in a low voice. "I don't like to say what I think. I'm not a fanciful sort of man; but I don't like this; and I don't think we're being wise to be here just now in the dark. I think we ought to get away ashore right now."

"I'm wiv you, Cap'n," replied Cargunka, quietly. "It's just a peg outside my understandin'; and I don't like it, no how."

He reached for the oars, which were still lying loosely in the thole-pins, and drove the boat astern, clear away from the wreck; then headed her round for the shore, where the sailormen had grouped together, talking in low tones. Behind the men, the fire showed the gloom of the near border of the forests that covered the island. Whilst above, against the starlight, loomed vaguely the three great Peaks, from which the island had gained its name.

"The song about the bells, Sir! … and then that bell striking like that!" said the Captain, suddenly, as they neared the shore. "It's making me think along pretty rum lines."

"My Oath, yes, Cap'n," said Cargunka, and drove the boat ashore near the group of seamen, who hauled her up, questioning a hundred questions, and voicing a score of quaint superstitions, as they did so.

But it was Durritt, the bo'sun, who said nakedly the quaintest and perhaps the ugliest:—

"That's a dead man's bell, Cap'n," he said, earnestly. "Strike me! but there's no good'll come messin' round wiv *that!*"

"You go an' boil yourself, my lad!" said Cargunka. "Now then, stow all this talk, an' spread out and find the steward."

But not a man of them would budge, declaring there was something rum about the island, and Durritt was so badly scared that he offered to forgo his prospective share of any of old Captain Barstow's money that might be found, if only Cargunka would up anchor and away.

Cargunka, however, consigned him to the devil, and ordered him and all the crew aboard, with their gear; telling them to leave the punt. Then he called to the Captain, and the two of them made their way through the darkness towards where they had last heard the steward. From time to time, as they went, they would catch the faint sound of his voice in the distance, which was some sort of a guide; though puzzling, as the man appeared to be on the road the whole time. Eventually, however, they ran him down; and persuaded him to be sensible, and come aboard, which he did; though in a heavy and silent fashion, as if he were dazed with the emotions of hope and despair through which he had been passing.

Chapter V

The following morning, Cargunka sent the men ashore, with the Second Mate, to make a thorough search of the island, and he allowed the steward to accompany them. Meanwhile, he and the Mate superintended the getting of the diving gear into one of the lifeboats, which had been lowered over-side.

The bell of the wreck had been submerged, during the remainder of the night; and there had been no more of that incredible ringing in the darkness; nor had there been any uncomfortable repetition of the sound in the daylight.

Because of this, and because things of a seeming infernalness always appear less dreadful and more capable of normal explanation in the daytime, Durrit, the bo'sun, had got his courage back again, and there was no more talk of running out to sea, without even an attempt do discover the hidden money.

This was a fortunate thing; as Durrit was the only man aboard who had ever been down in a diving suit, and he alone understood perfectly the use of all the apparatus.

When everything had been got ready, Cargunka, Durrit, the

Mate and Captain Gell put off in the lifeboat to the wreck. One of the reasons for sending the men ashore, was to insure their being out of the way, as much as possible; for Cargunka thought it might be possible to get at the money readily, and so bring it safely aboard the brig, without any of the crew knowing. Therefore, he drove them all in the boat to haste, and in a very few minutes they were moored securely alongside the temporarily unsubmerged port rail of the poop; this being now above water, as was the deck of the fo'cas'le head, away forrard, owing to the tide being lower than either of the other tides they had witnessed since they approached the island.

Durrit, who had got into his gear and helmet, climbed out of the boat, and in over the port rail of the poop,. He walked knee-deep across the sodden, water-covered poop-deck, and stumped heavily aft to the companionway, which was open, and then with a wave of this hand, began to climb down the weed covered steps, backwards, sailor-fashion. The Mate was pumping, whilst the Captain and Cargunka attended the air-pipe and life-line. They watched the big copper helmet vanish with a jerky bob below the water; and then, after that, for a few seconds, there was merely the eddying of the water, growing quieter and quieter, in the mouth of the companionway, and the line and air-tube being taken slowly down.

Suddenly, there was a terrific twitch upon the life-line, dragging it clean out of Captain Gell's hands.

"Something wrong there!" said Cargunka, and leaped out of the boat, up to his knees on the submerged poop-deck, and grabbed the life-line out of the water. He raced to the mouth of the companionway, and leaped over it, while he took a strain upon the line; but though the Captain came to his aid, they could not budge it.

"I'm going down," said Cargunka, after a few seconds' pulling. He threw off his coat, and stuffed it on to the slide of the companionway; then, taking a deep breath, he ducked his head underwater, caught at the life-line, and hauled himself down, head foremost. In a score of seconds, he had reached the dank, weed-hung alleyway below; and here, not a fathom beyond the foot of the steps, he found Durrit, lying in a dimly-seen heap. Cargunka forced himself lower, and caught at the diver, to lift him; then he thought of the fouled life-line, and traced it to the point where it had fouled. He discovered that it had become hitched around the heavy, brass knob of the steward's pantry, which opened into the alleyway, opposite the bottom of the stairs. He fumbled a moment, and then had it free of the green verdigris-caked knob.

He pulled himself swiftly back to the huddled diver, and caught him up in his arms. The man was easily lifted, despite the weight of his boots and helmet; yet he sagged so inertly, that Cargunka had to drag him clumsily to the steps, slipping and staggering to resist the upsetting buoyancy of the water. At the bottom of the steps, Cargunka dropped Durrit with a thud, and made one mad dash upward for breath, bursting out through the water in the companionway, with a swirl and a gasp that made Captain Gell jump back.

"I've got him to the steps' bottom," said Cargunka, as he drew the air eagerly into his lungs. "We'll lug 'im out wiv the line."

The two of them tailed on, and in a few seconds they had the limp figure of Durrit above water. They carried him to the boat and removed his helmet, and soon the man stirred, and swallowed some of the rum that Captain Gell was trying to force into him. He was quite himself again within ten minutes, and able and willing to put on his helmet and go down again. Yet he could not explain the cause of his collapse, nor the curious hitching of his line about the door-handle. All he knew was that, when he got to the bottom of the steps, he had faced round towards the main cabin. Then, as he began to go down the alleyway, he had felt a sudden, horrible pain between his shoulder blades. That was all that he could remember, until he found himself back in the boat again.

"Are you sure you ain't got a weak 'eart, my lad?" asked Cargunka. "It may have been the pressure of the water affected you?"

But Durrit was enormously indignant at the suggestion. He was absolutely sound and fit, he insisted. He said that the pain was not an "inside" pain; but like the pain a blow might give. He wriggled his shoulders, and complained that his neck hurt low down at the back. Perhaps he had knocked himself, as he turned....

"Strip your gear off your upper half, my lad," interrupted Cargunka. "You ain't goin' down yonder, 'nless I feel sure you ain't got a gammy 'eart."

The man grumbled; but obeyed. Cargunka looked at his back, and saw at once that there was a heavy-red mark, vaguely circular, at the base of the neck, covering the lower cervical vertebrae. There was nothing more to be seen; but it was obvious that in some way the man had sustained a heavy knock or blow. It was not his heart that had been at fault.

Cargunka told Durrit he might get into the gear again, and go down as soon as he felt fit. Yet he was vaguely uncomfortable. It was a funny thing for the man to have knocked himself sufficiently hard to stun himself, without being sure even that he had knocked against anything. And then the way that the line had got itself hitched round the pantry door-handle. That was a rum sort of thing to occur.

He fell to wishing that there had been a second diving suit. He found his thoughts reverting insistently to the extraordinary ringing of the bell. And then, suddenly, he got up from the thwart on which he had been sitting, and gave himself a vigourous mental shake. They had come out to the island to get that money, and they were going to get it; and as Durrit was the only one with them accustomed to diving, it was no use putting troublesome fancies or ideas into his head, especially as he did not seem to associate his accident with the possibility of anything "queer," as Cargunka phrased it.

The Captain and Cargunka helped Durrit again into his diving-gear. The man had plainly got the gold-lust on him, and had apparently quite lost his overnight superstitions about the hulk. Moreover, as I have said, he had plainly never a thought to explain what had just happened, as being anything but a casual enough incident.

Yet, as the man's copper helmet jerked slowly below the surface of the water in the companionway, for the second time, Cargunka had an uncomfortable feeling at his heart, that he tried vainly to ridicule away. He was standing now close up to the companionway, letting the life-line carefully through his hands, whilst Captain Gell stood a fathom to his left, and did the same with the air-pipe.

Very intently, Cargunka allowed the line to go out, feeling it daintily all the time, for the least suspicion of a signal. And extraordinarily enough, the thing happened again; for once more the line was jerked with a savage, desperate sort of jerk, as if Durrit were in instant need of help. Cargunka shouted; and the Captain jumped, floundering through the water on the deck, to help him. Together they hauled; yet again the line was fast, and they could not budge it.

"My Oath!" muttered Cargunka. "What is it! What is it!"

Then, without a word, he ducked his head again straight down into the water in the companionway, still gripping the line, and so hauled himself below from the Captain's sight. As he neared the bottom of the steps, he kept glancing all about him through the water. He stared hard along the passage, and saw something upon the floor of the alley. He hauled himself to it, and found the diver lying, still and insensible. He hauled himself further along the line, and a queer little thrill of repulsion and apprehension came to him, as he realised that it was once more hitched to the knob of a door-handle—this time to the knob of the door leading into the big cabin.

Cargunka slipped the hitch hastily, with clumsy fingers; then struggled back to the body upon the floor. He caught it up in his arms, and rolled and slipped to the foot of the stairs, where he dropped the man, and dashed to the surface again.

"Haul him up! Haul him up!" he gasped, as he got his breath. After a few moments, he climbed out of the well-like companionway, and gave a hand with the line; yet the man did not come, and, with a sickening feeling, Cargunka took his breath deep, and went down into the water again. To his amazement, and real horror, he found that the bight of the line had been once more hitched by some un-natural means about the door-handle of the pantry. He cast off the line, for the third time, and lifted the man a little, so that he lay ready to be hauled up. As he did so, he had a sudden, incredible feeling of being watched—of being in danger, in some incomprehensible, deadly way. He whirled about clumsily in the water, and saw that the pantry door had been opened, showing the interior, a dank, pitch-black cavern of water and weed... and out of this, upside down, there was projected towards him an awful, sodden, bearded face, huge and horrible and blurred. With a courage that was partly a reflex of the sick, deadly fright that had him suddenly about the heart, Cargunka plunged clumsily through the water, at the thing, striking savagely, but ineffectually, with right and left; but it was gone, and only the black cavern of the long-drowned steward's pantry, showed through the gloomy, weed-fringed oblong of the strangely opened doorway.

Cargunka's head struck the deck-beams of the alleyway; for, on letting go the line, he had floated up off his feet. He grabbed up at a beam now, and threw himself backwards, and dived swiftly up through the companionway. He threw out a gout of salt water, and gasped in his breath; then shouted "Pull!" to Captain Gell. He dragged himself up onto the top step, and staggered out onto the submerged deck, and even as he did so, the Captain had hauled the inert body of Durrit clear up into the daylight.

Between them, they got the diver again into the lifeboat, and there they stripped off his diving tackle and took him aboard the ship; for it was at once evident to them that he had been badly hurt.

Here, after they had tried for an hour to bring him round, they convinced themselves that he was actually dead, and they carried him out on to the main-hatch, and left him there, with a blanket over him. Cargunka had already told what he had found and seen;

and he announced now that he was going to put on the gear himself, and go down into the sunk ship, and see what the unnatural thing was down there.

Both the Captain and the Mate begged Cargunka to drop the whole business; but this he refused to do, and told them that if they would not give him the necessary help, he would simply wait for the crew to return from their tramp ashore, and get three or four of them to work the pump and attend the line and the pipe.

Cargunka returned to the derelict, taking with him the Captain and the Mate, also the Carpenter, who had stayed aboard. He had taken careful notice of Durrit, and so had little real difficulty in getting into the suit.

Cargunka climbed heavily out of the boat, and waded across the deck to the companionway. The Captain and the Carpenter accompanied him, wading a little above their knees, for the tide was now on the rise. Cargunka stopped at the waiting mouth of the water-filled companionway, and took a slow glance round, through his three windows, at the sky and sea, as if unconsciously saying a possible goodbye.

Captain Gell took advantage of the opportunity to take something from his pocket and thrust it into Cargunka's right hand. It was a heavy Colt; but Cargunka pushed it back at the Captain. The Captain put his face up against the helmet, and shouted:— "Take it, Sir. For God's sake, don't go down there with nothing but your hands. Take it, Sir, or I'm blowed if me and the Carpenter don't hold you up here."

Inside his big helmet, Cargunka's blue eyes flashed suddenly; then softened, as he allowed the genuine affection in his Captain's voice to conquer his quick anger at the Captain's suggestion of using force. He nodded inside the helmet, and Captain Gell, who had been looking in at his front window, pushed the weapon again into his hand. Then he began to go down to the companionway; but, unlike the bo'sun, he went down frontways, not as a sailor goes, but as an average person goes downstairs.

As he reached the bottom of the steps, he saw, with an extraordinary thrill, that the door of the steward's pantry was shut again. He took a step towards it, across the alleyway, meaning to push it with his foot. But, in the very act of doing so, it began slowly to open. It swung noiselessly wide, apparently without anything visible touching it, and Cargunka found himself staring once more into the pitch-black, weed-draped cavern of the long-sunk pantry. He stared, tensely and fiercely ready, with the pistol gripped for an instant shot. Then, as he sent his gaze circling swiftly round, he saw something that set every nerve in him quivering. A great, sodden white hand was gripping the top of the door. The next instant, he saw something else, a great, water-blurred, bearded, weed-entangled face was coming down below the top of the door, into sight. As it was upside down, Cargunka backed one swift, clumsy step across the alleyway, and thrust his pistol at the thing. As he pulled the trigger, there was an enormous swirl, and something dankly-white and huge and enormously weighty dashed down at him, seemingly from the weed-grown ceiling of the pantry. Once, twice, thrice, he pulled the trigger, and the third time felt the muzzle of his pistol against the thing that was upon him. He could see nothing, for the boiling and swirling of the water. He was conscious of tremendous blows; and then, all in a moment, the boil of the water burst from him, and he was in the daylight above, with some huge thing gripped to him, thudding at him with enormous, mad, misdirected blows.

What had happened on deck was this:—

To the Captain and the Carpenter, waiting on the submerged poop-deck above, there had been a brief few moments of quiet suspense, after the big dome of Cargunka's helmet had vanished under the water. They could not see him, owing to the sky-reflection on the surface, and the complete blackness below; but they had watched the line and the air-pipe trail jerkily after Cargunka, going slowly, foot by foot down into the gloom of the water, where it lay black and silent under the shadow of the half-drawn slide of the companion-hatch. And then there had come a pause; followed, abruptly, by three dull shocks, and a great swirl and commotion below the surface.

"Pull!" Captain Gell had roared. And he and the Carpenter had lain back on the life-line, pulling like madmen. Abruptly something had "given," and they had hauled up hand over hand, and there had burst up through the water in the companionway, the rubber and helmet covered Cargunka, with an enormous, naked, sodden-looking human body, that was gripped fiercely to Cargunka, and lashed about with its great legs.

As they hauled Cargunka and the thing clear up into the daylight, the naked body ceased to thrash about and strike, and loosed away from Cargunka, who immediately staggered, splashing and rolling, to his feet. Captain Gell and the Carpenter jumped to him, and set their arms about him, to support him clear of the thing that now beat about feebly, and bleeding, in the knee-deep water that covered the poop-deck. But Cargunka pulled away from the two of them, and turned to the thing in the water.

"Don't go near it!" shouted Captain Gell, in a tone of horror. "Don't go near it!"

As he spoke, the body rolled up its great bearded face, and Cargunka let out a yell that they could hear despite his helmet.

"It's big ole Cap'n Barstow! It's big ole Cap'n Barstow!" he was shouting. And he backed away from the quietening body, even as the two others backed away, on catching what he was shouting; for it was fixed in all their minds that old Captain Barstow had been dead those three years.

Then, suddenly, Reason took hold again, and the three men jumped forward to lift the dying, drowning old man out of the water, that he was striving to keep his head above. They began to carry him to the boat, but he died on the way.

Chapter VI

They took the old man aboard the *Happy Return*, to put him beside the dead bo'sun. But here, to their delighted amazement, they found the bo'sun sitting up on the hatch, with his blanket round him, and his face full of bewilderment. They realised that they had been somewhat premature in their diagnoses; and the realisation made them re-examine the old Captain; but the three bullet-wounds made it unmistakably plain that there was no second case of temporarily suspended animation.

It was as they were attending to the bo'sun, who was still very weak and shaky, that they heard a constant murmur of shouting, from some distant place, away on the other side of the island. The shouting increased in volume, and presently it broke into a sort of deep chorus, which Cargunka recognised to be the chorus of the "Fate of the *Laughing Sally*."

With a quick, extraordinary premonition of what all this portended, he ran across to the shore side of the vessel; and there, sure enough, in a few minutes he saw all his crew come down out of the woods, singing at the top of their voices, and escorting the steward in their center, who had his arm round what might have been taken for a smallish man, dressed in a strange suit, made apparently of old ship's canvas. It was the hair, however, that told Cargunka it was indeed a woman; and the attitude of the joy-drunken steward made it very plain that the miracle had happened... that it was his "Agnes"— the phonograph contralto singer—that he had found somewhere hid on the island. Cargunka whooped madly, and raced round to where his small punt was made fast alongside. He leaped in, without a word to the others, and rowed ashore.

The men opened out for him, and stopped their singing. But the steward began to shout, at the top of his voice:— "It's her! It's her! I knew I'd find her!"

Cargunka pulled off his felt hat, and looked at the woman. He saw a pretty, piquant face, with clear, bright blue eyes, and a face extraordinarily sun-browned.

He held out his hand to her.

"The Almighty sure does wonderful things, Miss," he said, simply. "But I guess He never done a wonderfuller than this."

The girl was shaking and almost crying with excitement and joy. "Oh, yes, yes..." she began, and forthwith began to cry outright, with sheer happiness and shock.

The one-time bartender held out a big hand to Cargunka, and the little man gripped it so hard that the big man winced.

"I thank God I met you, Sir," said the big man.

"My Oath!" said the little man, confusedly. "Same here."

Chapter VII

The remainder of this tale is soon told. The girl had been found in a small cave at the far end of the island (which is about seven and a half miles long). She had lived there in hiding all the three years, so as to keep out of the way of big old Captain Barstow, who had gone very definitely mad when he saw the vessel, carrying all of his long-hoarded money, go down.

Once, when she had ventured down to the vicinity of the wreck, he had chased her for a couple of miles, screaming out mad oaths, and threats of what he would do, if ever he caught her there again. For the poor fellow, in his madness, could think of nothing but his gold, and suspected that she intended to rob him.

Often, she had watched him, from a distance, diving, diving, all day long. Indeed, she described him as seeming almost to live on the submerged craft; but whether he had ever succeeded in salving any of his gold she could not say.

In all the time on the island, there had not called another vessel;

and she had begun to feel that she might end her life there. She had grown to keep so much to her own little valley at the other end of the island, that she had actually known nothing of the arrival of the *Happy Return*, until the steward found her that morning out fishing from the rocks; and she admitted that it was possible there might have been another vessel to the island, without her knowing; but she thought it very unlikely, as she had not grown careless in watching until the latter months of her stay.

As regards the curious striking of the bell, and the attack on the bo'sun and Cargunka, these were obviously nothing more than the tricks of an obsessed mind, conceived and carried out with the characteristic cunning and remorselessness of the true monomaniac. It was plain that the last thing the madman had desired was visitors to the island. Possibly there had been some other ship called in, and he may have adopted similar means to frighten them away.

As regards the money, a large part of this, amounting to over three thousand pounds, was found in the cave which the old Captain had inhabited. A careful search of the wreck led them to a second "find," under the cemented-down iron ballast, of which the barque carried a little for stiffening. It had been this, doubtless, that had kept the Captain diving hopelessly all those years; for it was possible to trace where he had made crazy, ineffectual efforts to shift the great, shaped masses of iron, under which, at some earlier period, he had obviously placed a portion of his wealth for safety.

An examination of the fo'cas'le head, and the deck house aft, showed how the Captain had managed to breathe, whilst apparently remaining under water; for the stairs that led down out of the poop-deck house (or chart-house) led down into the steward's pantry; and as the top of the house was always above water, the Captain had been able to obtain fresh air for as long as he liked, by simply rising to the surface of the water inside the deserted and closed-up deck house.

In somewhat the same way, he had probably dived into the fo'cas'le, when he played the hanky-panky with the bell, hitting it probably with a piece of wood; for there was a quantity of imprisoned air (renewed each ebb) just under the perfectly air-tight deck of the fo'cas'le head.

Chapter VIII

Five days later, the *Happy Return* continued her voyage to 'Frisco, and Cargunka returned happily to his daily pleasures in the galley. This apparently puzzled the girl, Agnes Jensag, who knew him to be the "Owner"; but when she poked her head inside the galley doorway to ask whether she could not be of some use, Cargunka shook his head, and offered her a seat on the locker. He was peeling potatoes, and his pocket volume of Byron's *Poems* was propped up on the dresser before him.

"Wonderful man, Miss," said Cargunka, pointing at the book with his knife. He wiped his hand on his apron, and handed the book across to her, opened at the frontispiece, which was an engraving of Byron himself.

"It's said by them as knows, to be remarkable like me, Miss," said Cargunka.

The girl flashed a quick glance at him, and understood.

"Yes," she said, gravely, "I can quite see what you mean;" which was strictly the truth, and, at the same time, pleased the little man tremendously.

"An' there's my legs, Miss, just the same wiv me as it was wiv 'im. An' the same leg, too," he told her, earnestly. "An' he was a fair devil wiv the wimmin, too...."

Cargunka realised that his tongue had run ahead a bit, and he changed the talk, by asking her whether she would mind singing him the ballad of "The Fate of the *Laughing Sally*." The girl smiled and did as he wished, singing in a low, sweet contralto, that made the little man lean back in ecstasy, with closed eyes, and set him beating a slow time with the potato knife. She sang right through to the last line:—

"And the bells grow faint and lost."

And Cargunka opened his eyes and stared silently away through the open door to leeward.

"And the bells of the *Laughing Sally* ring
And die away forever."

he quoted, scarcely above his breath. "I reck'n it's gone eight bells wiv 'er for the last time. Aye!" He nodded vaguely astern. "Like as it'll be me an' one of the brigs one of these days. It's bound to come to all of us.... At sea or in bed; As I have said.... You might put that rhyme down for me, Miss. My 'ands is wet. There's pencil an' my poetry-writin' book back of you on the shelf. I writes 'em down as they comes to me," he said simply.

The Adventure with the Claim Jumpers

"YOU DON'T COME THAT over me, my lad!" said Cargunka, owner of the "Dot-And-Carry-One" Saloon, on the Water Front, San Francisco. "Eat your whack of the free lunch, and welcome; but if I catches you grub-stakin' your pockets, you'll get put out here right smart!"

"I paid for three fifteen-cent drinks, ain't I?" demanded the man on the other side of the bar, in an aggressive voice.

He had been stuffing himself with cheese, ham, fish-rissoles, backed sausages, salmon cutlets and the like, from the Free Lunch Counter, which method of obtaining a meal was quite in order; but D.C.O. Cargunka had just caught him shoving a great hunk of cheese into his pocket, which action was very much out of order, running contra to the unwritten law of the Free Lunch Counter, which says:— "Eat what you like and as much as you like, provided you keep right on drinking; but what your stomach don't want, leave right there on the Free Lunch Counter."

It's a clear and simple and easily learnt law, this Law of the Free Lunch Counter; and the owners of drinking saloons uphold it grimly, and even lustily, if need be; for if they did not, considerable human derelicts would arrive, each with a sack and ten cents. The ten cents would go into a drink, and the contents of the Free Lunch Counter would go into the sack; and, in brief, that would be the end of the Free Lunch institution, which flourishes mightily in certain places, and most vigorously in little old San Francisco.

"You had three fifteen-cent drinks sure, my lad," said Cargunka; "but that don't entitle you to hump the Free Counter away on your back. You lug that cheese hunk out of your pocket, my son, or I'll come round and do it for you."

"You'll do what!" said the man, who was a great, husky, red-faced miner, just in from the North. "Ye—. Sure now will ye say that again, so I kin get yoor meanin', ye little dot-an'-carry galoot!"

It was quite evident that the man was a stranger to that part of the Water Front, or he might have been more careful in his choice of words.

"You got a good opinion of yourself, my lad, ain't you?" said D.C.O. Cargunka, his eyes shining a little. "You got a mighty good notion of yourself, ain't you?"

"I reck'n, ye little fool, I'll jest box yoor tabs for ye, if ye say another word," said the big man. "If ye was bigger, I'd shut my fist to ye; but I'm feelin' good, I am, an' I might spoil ye worse'n God spoilt ye, ye blame little cripple—"

It was the word "cripple" that did it. D.C.O. Cargunka jumped the bar, without even putting his hands on it, and the blow he hit the big man on the jaw was heard outside in the street.

The big man sat down violently, on the weighing machine, which happened to be directly behind him; but he was on his feet in a moment, and charged the short figure of Dot-and-Carry-One Cargunka, with a tremendous bellow of rage.

"I'll pull ye out to a man's size, like a putty figger, ye crippled toad!" he yelled, as he sprang at Cargunka, and made a huge, lunging swing at his head.

Cargunka circled to the side, on his dot-and-carry leg. His movements were astonishingly quick; and the difference in the length of his legs seemed to have no effect of slowing his speed. His foot-work was perfect, almost marvelous; for, without once guarding a blow with his arms, he sidestepped, and slid under, and slipped a dozen or more vicious punches from the big, furious miner. And all the time, as he sidestepped, slipped and evaded the man's great punches, he was never once driven outside of an imaginary four-yard circle, around which the men in the bar had packed themselves in a breathless, shouting ring of mad excitement.

Suddenly, Cargunka stepped right in close to the big man, and drove in a one—two—three, bat! bat! bat! along the line of the short ribs. The big man let out a gasping yell of pain, as his head came forward. In the same instant, D.C.O. Cargunka loosed his right fist from somewhere about the vicinity of his hip, and the upper-cut he sped home to the point of the big man's jaw was a truly terribly punch. The man's chin shot up, and his elbows and knees splayed in an absurd and helpless fashion; and down he came in his tracks with a crash, like the sound of a falling bullock.

As he fell, the double swing-doors of the saloon were thrown open, and a man jumped in through, with a drawn gun in his fist.

"Put that away, my lad, 'fore you get into trouble," said Cargunka, looking over his shoulder.

"Has big Buck Kessel come in here?" demanded the man, hoarsely. "Quick now; for I'm out for bad trouble! Has big Buck Kessel come in here? They told me, up the Front, as he was boozin' in here."

"Put your gun away, my lad," said D.C.O. Cargunka again, turning towards him. "This is 'Frisco, not Denver City!"

"Stow your dam gab!" snarled the man, looking at him fixedly for the first time.... "Say!" he continued, "ain't you D.C.O.?"

"That's me, my lad," replied Cargunka. "Put the popper away, an' I'll hear what's troublin' you."

The man lowered his gun, and began to explain, in an excited voice:—

"Say, D.C.O.," he said, "I've heard of you, up the coast. You're reckoned to be a guy as is always for a square deal. Well, you hark to me, an' then I guess if you're hiding yon brasted Buck Kessel, you'll hand the white-livered swine out for me to perforate.

"You hark to me, Sir! I just come down from up the coast. I been prospectin', an' I hit gold while I was up there. Yes, Sir! You bet I hit it big—big enough to mean no more work for yours truly.

"I pegged out my claim. It was on a bit of a creek, an' then I thought I'd just put in a bit of time, washing, up an' down the creek, before I come down here to register, an' let the news go loose, that'd fill that bit of a creek up with gold-hogs as full as a squaw is of hair-bugs.

"Like the brasted fool I was, I stretched my luck too far. When I got back to my claim, that afternoon, middlin' late, there was a crowd of hard-cases, maybe a dozen of 'em, down in the creek, up to their knees, washin' my pay dirt for their bloomin' lives. Yes, Sir! An' they'd jumped my claim, an' they'd staked out the whole of the two sides of the creek, as far up an' down as made it no use to me. What you got to say to that?"

There was a growl of sympathy from the men in the Dot-And-Carry-One Saloon, and Cargunka nodded.

"Go on, my lad," he said.

"Well," continued the man, "I was that mad, I'd have tried to buck Satan if he'd come along, an' I just lugged out my gun, an' told them there'd be blue murder if they didn't vamoose my claim, right then!

"Well, the next thing I knew, someone come up behind me and I got a bash on the head. An' while I was down an' out, they took my gun and a hundred and thirty ounces of dust and small nuggets, as I'd collected up an' down the creek. What you got to say to that?

"I did my damndest. I offered to toss 'em, or fight the biggest one of 'em—Anything for fair play; but they wasn't that kind. No, Sir! They wasn't!

"They shoved me in the creek, an' held me down, till I near drowneded; an' then did gun practice stunts all round me, till I reckoned I'd do well to get away with a whole skin.

"But, one of them, this here Buck Kessel that I'm gunning for, told 'em to tie me up. He said he'd get down here and file their claims. And afterwards they could let me go, and be damned to me or anything I could try to put over on 'em.

"Yes, Sir, they tied my up like a damn shote. An' that Buck swine let off for the South. But, Lord! they didn't know me! I rolled over to where there was a bit of rough quartz stickin' up, and I just frayed out the lashing they'd put on my arms. And then I got the stuff off me legs.

"They was all that busy, washing out my pay-dirt, they never thought to bother about me. And I crept in, up at the back of their tent, and sneaked a brace of guns (this here's one of 'em!). And then I lit out for where my horse was hobbled, in a little valley, about a half mile away.

"Well, I let out, hell for leather, to see if I couldn't come up on that Buck Kessel hog, an' do him in. But he'd got clean away from me. And when I got to the offices, they told me he'd just taken out the papers; and I was too late to do anything, 'cept lodge a complaint—A fat lot of use that, hey! Me on the one side, tellin' *my* yarn, an' a dozen of them on the other, tellin' theirs! An' them with the claims *and* their papers! An' every hour that passes, they'm liftin' my dust! Yes, Sir! *My* dust. Jehu sufferin' Jehoshaphat! *My Dust!* Now then, will you turn over that Buck Kessel swine to me, so I can perforate him so his own mother won't know him? The... the... the..."

"Come here, my lad," said D.C.O. Cargunka, beckoning to him.

The man came forward, a big. rough, powerful chap he was, with a big honest-looking face.

"Now then, my lad," said Cargunka, as the man came up alongside of him. "Do you recognise the sleepin' beauty on the floor there?"

The man Cargunka had knocked out, lay quiet enough to be dead. He had not been visible from the doorway of the saloon, because the weighing machine (that frequent adjunct of the bar) had stood between.

But now, as the newcomer set eyes on the insensible man, he let out a mad oath.

"That's the—" he yelled, and without more ado he thrust his revolver down at the silent figure, crying out:— "To blazes with ye, ye rotten-hearted thief!"

The Dot-And-Carry-One Saloon boomed and echoed with the explosion of the heavy weapon, and there were shouts of horror and fright from the men in the bar.

But the man on the floor lay unharmed; for at the moment of the shot, Cargunka had struck the gunman's hand, so that the bullet had buried itself in the floor to the left of the insensible man. And now Cargunka was in the midst of a violent wrestling match, one abnormally long, enormously muscular arm being wound round the man's waist; while, with his right hand, he fought to wrench the gun away from the insanely angry prospector.

He succeeded at last in getting the revolver, and pitched it to one side. Then he bent the whole power of his short but amazingly muscular body to the conquering of this murder-mad newcomer.

Abruptly, the man weakened, curiously and unexpectedly; and before Cargunka knew what was happening, he had slid through his arms, into a quiet heap on the floor of the saloon.

"My Oath!" said Cargunka, breathlessly. "My Oath! What's that mean?"

He stared down suspiciously at the man, wondering vaguely whether it might not be some trick to catch him off his guard. Then, suddenly, he knelt on the floor, beside him, and felt his heart.

"My Oath!" he said, at last. "I b'lieve the poor devil's done out. He's starved or something, I'm thinkin'. Pass me over that whisky bottle, Bob" (this to the barman), "and I'll see what we can do wiv him...."

"When did you grub last, my lad?" were the first words Cargunka said, when the man came around.

"Blest if I know," he answered, getting somewhat giddily to his feet. "I been too busy to shunt grub. I guess I'm needin' it; but I'm goin' to fill that hog up first; so you stan' clear!"

With the word, he stooped suddenly, and twitched a second gun out of the leg of his right boot.

But Cargunka was too quick for him. He nailed his wrist with one quick grip, and tore the gun out of his fist.

"You're sure lookin' for trouble, my lad," he said. "You darn fool. My Oath! What's the use of pluggin' him! That ain't the way to do anythin', 'cept a trip the 'lectric chair.... Now you calm down, my lad, or you'll get rough-handled!"

This last was in reply to the clumsy blow which the man had

aimed at him, following an attempt to grab back the revolver, which Cargunka had just taken from him.

"You're mighty fresh, ain't you, damn you!" said the man, and aimed a second completely ineffectual blow at Cargunka's head.

"Here, Bob, and you, Andrews, hold this fool," said Cargunka. "I don't want to get hot an' hit him."

At this moment, there were several cries of:— "He's comin' to!" "The guy's opening up." "Look out for his gun, D.C.O."

Cargunka looked round, and saw that Buck Kessel was trying to sit up.

"Sittin' up an' takin' nourishment, are you!" said Cargunka. "Well, I guess you'll try some other saloon, my lad, unless you want me to let this gent loose on you wiv a gun!"

He jerked his elbow towards where the robbed prospector stood, tugging away from the two barmen, Bob and Andrews. And Kessel had no sooner seen him, that it was plain he was very willing indeed to get the other side of the swing doors.

"It's plain he's labelled you, my lad, the same kind of rat-poison you are!" said Cargunka, staring at him, grimly. "My Oath! Get out! 'fore I lamn you. You make me sick. Get out!"

And the man went out, staggering; but with very considerable haste.

Cargunka turned:—

"Now, my lad, what's your name?" he asked the prospector.

"George Monkton," said the man.

"Well, Monkton, you an' me's goin' to have a little talk," said Cargunka. "Let him go, you two. Come along in here, George, my lad, and we'll get together on this business."

Chapter II

Cargunka was walking up and down his "office," as he called the room at the back of the bar.

As he walked, he limped, owing to his dot-and-carry-one leg, from which he had received his title of D.C.O.

George Monkton was sitting at the table, eating what Cargunka described as a scramble feed, which he had cooked for the man himself, on the oil stove which filled half of the end of the narrow room.

As Monkton ate, he talked between, and even during, mouthfuls.

"Say, D.C.O.," he was saying, "who's the guy in the wall-pic'cher? He sort of favours you. Say, it ain't you now, in fancy rig—eh?"

D.C.O. Cargunka beamed, literally; and his dot-and-carry limp became more pronounced, as he walked over to the picture and looked up at it.

"No, my lad," he said, ruffling his hair back from his shaven temples, "that ain't me; but most people as comes in here, gets thinkin' it is. That's Lord Byron, the poet. A fine-lookin' man he was, my lad, don't ye think so?"

"Sure, I'd say he was some high-brow," agreed the man, Monkton.

"He'd a short leg an' a long one, same as me," continued Cargunka, looking self-conscious. "D'you ever read poetry, my lad?"

"G' Lor! Not me!" said Monkton, with his mouth full. "Guess I ain't much on readin'-gadgets."

"Well you miss a great deal," said Cargunka, solemnly; "a great deal, my lad. Now, if you've filled up proper, we'll light up, an' I'll make you a proposition. First of all, just where is this creek?"

"About seventy miles up the coast, an' about three inland," said Monkton. "The nearest place to it, is Alf Nebrech's, an' that's about fifteen miles to the West, I reck'n."

"Is there free water for a boat up to the pay-dirt?" asked Cargunka.

"Sure," replied Monkton.

"Then I reck'n I got a plan," said Cargunka. "One of my brigs, the *Happy Return*, is going up the coast next week, an' I reck'n we'll drop in on those jumpers, an' give 'em a look-in!"

"You'll sure need a mighty big posse with you," warned Monkton. "I tell you, D.C.O., they're bad men. They're gunmen that'd shoot up twice their crowd of plain diggers. You can't do nothin', b'lieve me!"

"Leave that to me, my lad," said Cargunka. "Are you game to back up my try, an' hold your mouth tight shut for evermore afterwards?"

"Sure!" said Monkton. "You show me a lead, an' I guess I'll follow. You can bet your boots on that. I'll follow you into hell an' out again, to get level with that crowd. You just show me a lead, D.C.O. That's all I asks."

"Well," said Cargunka, "I guess we'll fix the divvy right now. If I show you how to pull this thing, an' give you a hand, I'll halve up wiv you on what we get. How's that look to you, my lad?"

"It looks good enough, I reck'n," said Monkton. "I'm on!"

"Well then, I'll sign you on as A.B.," Cargunka told him. "That'll look natural enough; an' I don't reck'n never to carry no idlers in my ship. No, my lad! I works myself, an' I expects others to work too."

Chapter III

The result of Monkton's faith in D.C.O. Cargunka was well justified; for ten days later, the *Happy Return* arrived off the place where the creek came down to the shore.

Cargunka was seated in his galley, peeling potatoes, when Monkton identified the mouth of the creek; and his Captain came forrard, to ask whether he should heave the brig to.

"I reck'n, Cap'n Gell," said Cargunka, "you should know my rules by this, seein' the times we've sailed together. When I'm cook, I'm plain cook, an' you're Cap'n; an' cook I am till the end of the first dog-watch. What you got to do, you know blame well, seein' we talked it all out last night."

"Very good, Sir," said Captain Gell to his distinctly unorthodox Owner, and immediately gave orders to heave-to, whilst Cargunka continued meditatively to peel spuds; and, between whiles, he read lines from his small pocket volume of Byron's *Poems*, which, as usual, was propped up on the low dresser before him.

It is difficult to analyse with exactness just why Cargunka, who, as I have remarked before, was a man of very considerable wealth, persisted in signing-on in his own vessel as cook.

Possibly, the reasons were varied. He had, as we know, an extraordinary mania for cooking, just as some men have an invincible desire to carpenter, or to tinker with clocks, or to garden, and the situation afforded him every excuse to satisfy his natural tastes in this line. He certainly enjoyed cooking, as only the born chef can enjoy that troublesome art.

Also, it is possible that he liked the somewhat bizarre situation of occupying the position of cook, whilst he was, at the same time, Owner of the vessel. Futher, he saved the wages of a cook by doing the work himself. For, as he told Monkton, he carried no idlers in his ships; and was known to be as close in the matter of wages as any ship Owner of them all. But, to make up for this, he certainly fed his crews magnificently; so well, in fact, that when it was known that he intended to make a trip, he could have his pick of sailormen for the voyage. This speaks for itself.

Later, in the second dog-watch, D.C.O. Cargunka sat in the Captain's lounge chair on the poop, and talked:—

"No, Cap'n, we'll not go close in till well after dark. You got the name blacked out on the bow and stern?"

"Yes, Sir," said Captain Gell.

"Well, get the dingy cleared, an' fix up the rollocks an' the oars so they won't make no noise. I guess that'll be all. We'll lower her our here, and tow her in, so as not to have the sound of the falls squeaking, when we get close inshore."

"Very good, Sir," said Captain Gell.

When Captain Gell returned from giving the orders, Cargunka was lying back, reading his favourite little volume of poetry.

"Ever read Byron, Cap'n?" asked Cargunka, lowering the book on to his knee.

"No, Sir, leastways not to remember," said Captain Gell, half absently.

"Wonderful man, Cap'n," said Cargunka, and stretched out his legs in front of him, surveying them earnestly.

"Queer thing, Cap'n, I should have a long an' a short one, ain't it— A curious thing now, when you come to think Byron was the same way." He hemmed, half self-consciously. "Have you ever thought as the likeness went any further, Cap'n?"

"Very like, Sir. Very like," said Captain Gell, with unconscious indifference; for he had answered similar questions a hundred times before, in the past years.

"A wonderful fine-looking man he was, too," continued Cargunka. "And a fine athlete, too…." He paused.

"Aye, Sir," said the Captain, and he spoke now with sufficient conviction to have satisfied even Cargunka. "Aye, you're surely a fine athlete, Sir. A prettier one with the gloves, I never seen."

"It's strange as the finest bodies get blemished, Cap'n," said Cargunka, softly. He stuck out his shorter leg and looked at it for a while, in silence. "And Byron they spoiled too, an' the same leg…. My word, Cap'n, but he was a proper fine-lookin' man, too; an' a fair divvil wiv the wimmin…." He hemmed again, self-consciously. "You'd not think, to look at me, as I was gifted that way, Cap'n, would you?"

"No, Sir, I would not," said Captain Gell, firmly.

Cargunka was silent, searching round for some way in which he could convey to the Captain the truth, without seeming to boast; but he could think of nothing at the time, and so fell to reading again.

"Send Monkton aft to me in the cabin, Cap'n," he remarked, some minutes later, climbing out of the Captain's chair, and thrusting the volume of poetry into his pocket.

"Very good, Sir," said Captain Gell, and walked forrard to the break of the poop, while Cargunka limped aft to the companionway, and so down the stairs into the saloon, where, in a few minutes, he was joined by Monkton.

Chapter IV

"Now, my lad," said Cargunka, reaching up to light the saloon lamp, for it was growing dusk, "I s'pose you can pull an oar; for I don't want to take no one else ashore wiv us in the boat. The less that's known about tonight's job, the better, I'm thinkin'."

"Sure," said Monkton. "I've used boats plenty."

"Well then, my lad," said Cargunka, "it's black faces we're having tonight. It's a proper disguise, an' it'll stop us loomin' up plain in the dark. Here! Rub it in well, down round your neck and ears... That's the style!"

Cargunka had a great pot of black, greasy-looking stuff, which he first offered to the man, and then dipped into himself; and so, in a very few minutes, the two of them were as a couple of buck niggers.

"Now," said Cargunka, "here's some waste to wipe your 'ands. And you'd best button your dungarees up over your chest and wrists. That's the thing! You won't show much now in the dark, I'm thinkin'. Shove these felt socks on over your boots. Got your gun?"

"Sure," said the big miner.

"Well, don't be in no hurry to use it!" replied Cargunka. "It ain't gun-work that's going to win out tonight. It's going to be just plain brains, my lad, an' quiet feet."

Yet, for all that Cargunka was so emphatic on this point, there reposed a hefty Colt automatic in the side pocket of his coat; which suggests that he was not entirely convinced, in his own mind, that the night's work that lay ahead of them, promised to be a completely peaceful affair.

Cargunka went into his cabin, and came out with a dungaree jumper and trousers and another pair of felt socks. He pulled on the thin blue trousers over his own, and then got into the jumper, which was loose enough at the bottom to allow him to get freely at his coat pockets. After this, he drew on the pair of felt socks, over his boots, as Monkton had done; and so the two of them stood ready for the adventure.

"Up on deck with you, my lad," said Cargunka, and picked up a small, dark-coloured sack, off the cabin table. There was something in the sack, which he handled as gently as he turned and followed Monkton up on the poop.

"I guess this'll fix 'em right enough!" he muttered to himself, with a grim little laugh.

It was dark by now, and the barque's yards had been trimmed, and she was standing in for the vague shadow of the land. The wind was light, and the vessel made scarcely a sound as she ran through the water; whilst, fore and aft, not a light was visible.

Yet, so quiet was the night, that the faint creak, creak of the spars and gear (and even the low mutter of the crew's voices forrard) was plain to hear; but, except for these sounds, and the scarcely perceptible ripple of the water along the skin of the vessel, the night was just a quietness, through which came occasionally the slight noise of the water cheeping, cheeping, under the "entrance" of the clinker-built dingy towing astern; and somewhere, from far away under the dark shadow of the land, the low, hushed roar of the surf, making the quietness seem the more immense.

The land began to emerge out of the grey vague loom of shadow, into a black line that grew ever more black and definite, whilst the faint surf murmur had become a low rolling sound, hollow and deep, under the black gloom of the land.

Presently, Captain Gell came up to Cargunka.

"We're as close in as is safe, Sir," he said. "I'll have to put the hellum up in a minute."

"Very good, Cap'n," said Cargunka, and went aft to the taffrail, where he unhitched the boat's painter, and hauled her up.

"Get in quiet, my lad," he said to Monkton, who got down over the side, forthwith, into the boat, and began to ship the rowlocks.

"Hold the painter, Cap'n, while I get in," said Cargunka. "Hold her short, an' then give me the painter, as soon as I'm in. I don't want no splash."

This was done. The Captain released the painter quickly into Cargunka's hands, and the boat was suddenly alone on the ocean; for the barque had gone from them, into the surrounding darkness. Cargunka saw her a minute later, with her helm up, falling away, like a shadow ship, towards the open sea.

Then the two in the boat got out their oars, very quietly, and began to pull in towards the black cliffs of the coastline that stood up, high and gloomy, into the night.

As they drew in under the coast, the rolling grumble of the surf grew louder, and Cargunka, staring inshore, could see the white boil of phosphorescence showing vaguely, where the big slow swells burst into broken water over the coast rocks, along the bottom of the black cliffs.

Suddenly, Monkton burst into a loud laugh, as if some joke had just got home through his mental epidermis:—

"G' lor', D.C.O., what a lot of silly fools we are, sure, goin' tip-sy-toesy like this! Why, I'd go the limit, they'd not heard a sound if we was to loose off our poppers, not with the row yonder!"

"Quit that!" said Cargunka, sharply, but speaking in a low voice.

"What d'you suppose I'm troublin' about. I'm not worryin' about them hearin' me ashore yon; as you ought to know, seein' as the shack's three miles up the creek, and round the bend, at that!

"You got to understan' my way of doin' a job, my lad, before you start thinkin' me a fool. I don't do nothin' wiv me eyes shut, not if I can 'elp it! I 'ad a scout up here, three days, last week, lookin' round. You'll find some s'prisin' changes ashore yon, when we gets up the creek, I'm thinkin'!

"An' you'll like to know, maybe, my lad, as the reason we're takin' all this trouble to keep quiet, is 'cause I learnt as there's some of 'em comes down the creek, an' out here, fishin'. There's Long Dan an' Jabez Vlum an' one or two others comes out here; an' I guess you should know as they're mighty quick-eared men. An' we ain't wanting anyone to come asking questions."

"Gee!" said Monkton. "What'd you think of that now! You're sure a smart man, D.C.O. But I don't sabe what them fur-shifters is doin' out here, fishin'?"

"You will, when we get up the creek a bit, my lad," said Cargunka. "It's close on a fortnight, since you was up this way. An' as soon as that friend of yours filed his papers, there was a proper rush up 'ere. You'll find that they've got a small town spread up an' down the creek; an' fresh folk comin' in every hour, pretty near."

"Je-hosh!" said the big miner. "You sure got the wise head, D.C.O. I reckon I holds my hands to you in the wise line. I—"

"Shsss!" muttered Cargunka. "Stop rowin'! Don't move!"

The two of them froze into instant stillness, whilst the boat moved ahead, though almost soundlessly, with the way that was yet on her.... "There, turn your head to the left!" whispered Cargunka. "About fifty fathoms off the starboard bow!"

The big miner saw then what Cargunka meant. Out there, indefinite almost as shadows, were two darker shapes upon the water, some hundred feet apart. They were canoes; and, as the two of them watched, straining their eyes, they saw the sway of a single figure in each, paddling gently. Then, the two canoes passed on into the vagueness, and they could see nothing.

"Think they saw us, D.C.O.?" asked Monkton.

"I reckon not, my lad," replied Cargunka, "or we'd have had 'em singin' out to know who we was, I'm thinkin'."

"Not so sure!" muttered the big miner. "Maybe they saw us, an'll trail us in, to see what kind of outfit we is."

But Cargunka said nothing. He was staring inshore, searching the black cliffs and the phosphorescent gleam of foam at their base, for the mouth of the creek.

"I reckon that's her," he said, at last. "Pull!—Quiet an' steady now!"

Ten minutes later, they had entered the mouth of the little creek, and all about them was the quiet of the stream, and the heavy, still smell of the earth, while the scent of the pine trees made a sweet balm in the night air, with the pine needles making a constant whispering in the darkness along the nearer bank, as a light wind stole down the great gully in which the creek ran.

Chapter V

Cargunka had brought the boat close in to the Northern bank, well under the shadow of the trees; for they had rounded the bend, and the new gold-town had jumped into view—a medley of minor lights, with, about half a mile ahead of them, where the creek swung round in a second bend, the blaze of two big gasoline flares; for already a drink saloon was in full blast.

Up and down the creek (or stream as it had become here; for they were getting now about the estuary) there were spread several dozens of all kinds of shelters—tents, shacks, and cabins; and there was a hoarse, far murmur of voices on the still night.

"Je-hosh!" said Monkton, amazed. "What'd you think of that now! If it ain't a proper rush! Say, D.C.O., it's like a merrickle! Why, it was all just wood an' water when I was here less'n a fortnight gone—just that an' them damned thieves campin' on my claim—"

He broke out into a spate of insane blasphemy, at the memory of all that he had lost, his voice going rawly across the quietness of the stream.

But Cargunka turned on him like a tiger:—

"Stow that, you fool!" he said. "A fine lump you are to have wiv me. G' Lor! I'd a done better to come alone! Cussin' won't 'urt that crowd. Ain't you got sense an' guts to know that, an' do your share to get square!"

"I'm blame sorry, D.C.O.," said Monkton. "I'm sure daft to let go like that; but it just got me goat proper, to be right here, an' know I should ha' been safe for life with the gold I'd 'a pulled out of that claim of mine."

"Maybe you'll not do so bad after all, my lad," said Cargunka. "That's your claim, ain't it—away over to the right there, wiv the big-built cabin on it?"

"Sure," said the miner. "I guess you don't need me to show you round, D.C.O. I reck'n I built that, on me lonesome, before they came along. I'd reckoned I'd winter here.... Hell! What's the use of talkin'! What you goin' to do, anyhow, D.C.O.?"

"We'll pull up a bit higher," said Cargunka; and the two of them took to their oars again, keeping well over on the North side of the stream; for there were no buildings on that bank, until near the bight of the second bend, where the big gasoline flares blazed in front of the drink saloon.

"Ease a little!" said Cargunka, as they came opposite to the open doorway of the log-hut that stood at the top of the Southern bank, on the edge of Monkton's claim. "Easy wiv your oar. Back! I'm goin' to shove 'er in 'ere.... That's right! In wiv her. Catch one of them branches an' hold on while I gets the glasses."

They had put the dingy in under the shadow of a far out-reaching pine bough; and Monkton held the boat in place, whilst Cargunka drew in his oar quietly, and reached into his locker for his night-glasses.

With these, he began now to examine the cabin opposite. The distance was about a hundred and fifty feet; but the glasses showed the interior of the shanty with wonderful clearness, with the men sitting round a big packing-case, for a table.

"Lord!" said Cargunka, after staring a bit. "It couldn't be better. They'm playin' (poker I reck'n) an' they got the stuff on the table there.... Piles of it. You take a look, my lad, an' see if that don't do you good. I'll hold the boat. You pull your oar in quiet, or it'll go adrift."

Monkton pulled in his oar, silently; and put the glasses to his eyes; then he swore.

"Quit that!" said Cargunka.

"There's sure hundreds of ounces on the table, right now," said Monkton, in a strange voice. "Hundreds an' hundreds.... An' they got a lot of it in hundred-ounce bags. By the size, that's what I reck'n they are. Say, what you think of that now! That's my dust—Say—!"

"Hold tight an' keep the stopper on, my lad!" said Cargunka, under his breath. "I guess the more the better."

"Say, D.C.O., how you goin' to shape to touch all that?" asked the big miner, after a further look through the glasses. "There's six of 'em in there. An' don't you make no error! Them's bad men—They're killers, an' they got their guns right handy, as you can sure see. Say, d'you reckon we can shoot 'em up from outside, an' then rush in the stuff?"

Cargunka laughed a little, under his breath.

"You'll see, my lad, when the time comes," he said. "We got a deal to do yet though, I'm thinkin'. Hand me back them glasses. We're goin' upstream a bit to scout round, an' make sure we ain't goin' to get disturbed. Ship your oar quiet now, an' pull careful."

They went upstream for another couple of hundred yards; then Cargunka put the boat across to the South bank, and told Monkton to stand-by her, ready to shove off, whilst he went up the bank, and took a look round.

Yet, he found, as he had hoped, that there seemed to be no one knocking about. The nearest shanty (a wretched little lean-to of packing-cases and sacking) was, however, lit up, and Cargunka thought he would take a look in. He walked quietly over to it, and found that the sacking curtains which apparently occupied the place of a door, were half looped back, and he could look in.

Somewhere, farther up the stream, probably in the saloon, there began the metallic rant of a phonograph:——

"Oh, she wasn't goin' to stand it on her lone,
On her own,
No, by Joan!
She wasn't goin' to stand it on her own!"

"That's a damn rotten instrument!" said Cargunka to himself; but it was evidently "good enough," for a voice in the lean-to took up the song, drunkenly, in a tremendous bass roar:——

"Oh, she washn't goin' ter shtan' it on'er ownsh!"

And under cover of the roar of sound, Cargunka stole up, and peeped in.

He found two very drunk men sitting at an Armour's canned meat box, trying to play cards; but though this was amusing enough, in its way, the thing that attracted Cargunka's attention was the amount of the stakes, which they were risking drunkenly on simple nap hands.

"I guess this here's a rich strike, right enough," he muttered, and leant forward to get a better view. At that instant, the bigger of the two men looked up, and gave out a yell:——

"A blimy nigger, s'elp me!" he said, "or I got the jim-jams!"

But before the second man had time to turn round, Cargunka had pulled back into the shadow; and he left the man to decide the nice point, to his own satisfaction.

Chapter VI

"All clear now, my lad, for runnin'," he told the big miner, five minutes later. "Shove 'er off!"

He let the boat drift downstream silently, past the cabin that stood on Monkton's claim.

About a hundred yards below the shanty, he beached the nose of the boat gently, and made the painter fast to a spike of rock.

"Come along, my lad, step quiet," said Cargunka. "Pass me out that sack, gently now! That door opens outward, don't it? That's what my scout told me."

"Sure," said the miner. "I hung her myself. And I should know, if anyone does!"

"I don't doubt it," said Cargunka. "I never did. The chap as scouted for me, knows it don't pay none to tell me any fudge news. Now, I guess we got to hunt up a good hefty log an' bring it along. There'll be plenty around, I'm thinkin'. I guess we'll sample the wood-pile. My scout said they'd a good heap of timber stacked away at the back of the shanty. This looks like there's goin' to be two niggers in the wood-pile, in a way of speaking! I wish t' goodness yon phonygraft would shut that rotten noise!"

Yet, as it chanced, the far away rant of the phonograph proved useful enough to Cargunka and the miner; for it was screeching out again the same inane jargon:—

"Oh, she wasn't goin' to stand it on her lone,
On her own,
No, by Joan!
She wasn't goin' to stand it on her own!"

And the men in the big log-hut, took it up in a hoarse roaring chorus:—

"Oh, she wasn't goin' to stand it on her lone—"

"Now, my lad... while they're makin' that noise!" muttered Cargunka, and ran quickly and quietly round to the back of the heavily-built hut, with Monkton following.

"Here we are," whispered Cargunka. "Step easy! Lift your end!"

He slipped the bight of the small sack he was carrying between his teeth.

"Now!" he grunted, softly, through his clenched teeth. "Up wiv her!"

The two of them lifted a heavy pine-log from the wood-pile, and began to carry it noiselessly round to the front of the shanty, near to where the heavy-timber door was standing open.

"Let her rest on her end a mo," said Cargunka.

They rested the log, and Cargunka took the bight of the small sack out of his mouth, for a breather.

"We got to carry her close up to the door; an' then I've a present wiv me, as I'm goin' to heave in, gratis, my lad," said Cargunka. "Then it'll be shut the door smart, an' I'll give you a hand to get the log propped solid against it. After that, there'll be some artillery play, I reck'n. If there is, I guess we'll 'ave to move extra smart, before there's a crowd!

"Now, we'll get going again."

With infinite pains and caution, they carried the log nearer, and poised it on its end, just at the back of the open door.

Cargunka had been carrying the little sack in his teeth again. Now, he opened it, and lifted out a large glass Winchester, filled with some fluid. He took the big bottle by the neck, and swung it, once, twice, and let it fly in through the open door, where it shattered to fragments against the opposite wall.

In the same instant, he caught the door, and dashed it shut.

"Now," he gasped, in a low quick voice, and the two of them hove the heavy log nearer, and let the upper end of it fall with a thud against the outer side of the door, wedging it immovably.

"Drop!" said Cargunka; and the two of them went flat on their faces, just as a spate of cursing broke out within, following the instant of curious silence that had ensued after the throwing of the bottle. The next moment, there came a volley of revolver shots, ripping through the planking of the door; and a good thing it was for the two of them, that Cargunka had thought in time to "lie low."

Directly afterwards, there came shrieks—curious, breathless, gasping shrieks, and a loud, violent thudding against the door; and then, incredibly, an intense silence.

"What was it, D.C.O.?" asked the miner, in a somewhat awed voice. "What did you give 'em?"

"Ammonia!" said Cargunka. "They're stiff for a time, I guess; but they'll come round with fresh air. Up with you, my son, and get the door open. No, you've nothing to be afraid of. There's no room for playing possum, with all that stuff in their lungs."

They rose to their feet, and hove the log away from the door. Cargunka pulled the door open, and found that something or someone had extinguished the lamp. Yet he did not pause. He whipped open the mouth of his small sack, pulled something out and fitted it over his mouth and nose; then, with the sack in his hand, he shut his eyes and strode over a silent body into the hut. He felt for the table; touched it; and swept heap after heap of the small, heavy lumps of metal into the stout-fibred sack. As he worked, in spite of his respirator, he gasped dizzily with the fumes of ammonia that still pervaded the shack; though the night air was blowing into the hut.

He cleared the table in ten seconds, and felt all over it, to make sure that no gold remained. As he reached over, his toe stubbed against something soft and heavy. He stooped for it, and felt a small, buckskin sack, about nine inches high by three in diameter, which was leaning against the side of the big packing-case, where it had slid down, in the brief riot, after the throwing of the bottle.

He got down onto his hands and knees, fumbling round on the floor, and avoiding the insensible men, more by sense than sight. Three times, he came upon small bags of the dust; and he scraped up a double handful of fallen nuggets, cramming all, as he found them, into his sack.

Abruptly, as he groped, he heard a man sigh, and then someone stirred, and sat up, questioning. Another man moved; and another voice broke out confusedly into query, coughing and stuttering. Cargunka began to back slowly towards the door, keeping near the ground so as not to be seen against the vague loom of the open doorway. He had the sack of dust in his arms.

Suddenly, a man's voice bellowed the words:—

"The dust! Collar the dust! There's some tough in the shack! Light the lamp!"

There came a chorus of shouts, coughings and gaspings, as the men all about in the darkness began to recover; and then, like thunder in that small shanty, the bang of the heavy revolver.

"The door's open. Watch the door!" shouted the man again. He was evidently one of those in the bunks; and Cargunka heard him leap with a heavy thud to the ground. There came a scrape of a match; but already Cargunka was at the door, still creeping. He backed out, swiftly; just as the match flared. Then he was with Monkton, who had stayed at the door, as Cargunka had bid him. He dumped the small sack heavily onto the ground, and jumped at the door.

"Now," muttered Cargunka, and with one movement, they crashed-to the door, and let the log fall back against it, jamming it firmly. Cargunka caught his companion, and dragged him out of a line with the door, just as a perfect storm of revolver shots broke out inside, and the bullets burst through and through the door. Cargunka lifted the sack, and tied the mouth of it with both method and speed.

"Down to the boat," he said. "Catch hold!"

The shooting continued as they ran; and from higher up the river bank, there broke out a loud shooting in the still night. There were fresh shouts; and then the noise of feet running. And, all the time the shooting and pounding continued inside the hut.

Cargunka and Monkton kept on the steady run. They carried the small canvas sack between them, by its two strong, rope grommets; and it weighed so heavily, that they staggered in the darkness, breathless, as they ran.

Behind them, the shouting grew louder. It seemed as if the whole of the inhabitants of the new "rush" town had been roused by the persistent shooting, and were arriving at a run.

"Leg it, my lad! Leg it!" said Cargunka grimly through his teeth, as the bigger man seemed to slacken his pace under the enormous strain. "It'll be a quick lynch party if we're caught!"

The big miner's stride quickened at the remark, and as it did so, there came a dull heavy thud of a falling log, away behind them.

"They've unbottled 'em!" muttered Cargunka. "Now look out for squalls. Down here. Leg it, my lad! Leg it!... Where the devil's the boat!"

The shooting had ceased now; and there was a hoarse murmur of talk, and shouted questions and threats.

Then a voice, a huge drunken voice, that Cargunka recognised:—

"It weren't th' jim-jams! It weren't th' jim-jams! It were sure a nigger! Look around fer a nigger, b'ys. Hic! I seen 'im! Sure, don't the dawg niff 'im! Foller-on! Foller-on, Billy! Foller 'im!"

There ensued a babel of questions and further shouted talk; and then, just as Cargunka located the vague outline of the dingy in the darkness, there was a shout of:— "Get pine knots, boys, an' try down-stream, after Sandy's dawg. Coom along!"

Cargunka and Monkton came to a clumsy stop at the bows of the boat.

"Now," said Cargunka, huskily, "together!" And they swung the enormously heavy little sack of gold in over the bows.

"In wiv you, my lad!" said Cargunka; and ran to cast off the painter from the spike of rock.

"Cut it!" gasped out Monkton, who had tumbled himself heavily into the boat. "Cut the darn thing!"

"Get them oars out an' don't talk silly!" said Cargunka. "We ain't leavin' no cloos this trip; not if I knows it!"

The crowd of miners was now racing downstream towards them, along the top of the river bank. They were carrying a number of flaring pine knots. In front of everyone, a big man was running, staggering drunkenly from side to side and holding a blazing torch above his head with one hand, whilst with the other he held the end of a long piece of old lariat. The piece of the lariat was made fast to a big, pointed-eared wolf-dog, which was running along the top of the bank, with its nose close to the ground, tracking them without a whimper.

Cargunka gave just one comprehensive look, as he cleared the painter hitch. As he did so, there came the loud bang of a heavy six-shooter behind him, and the big wolf-dog flung itself up suddenly on its hind legs, its front legs pawing crazily at the air. Then it fell over on its back, kicking madly for an instant, and afterwards lay still.

"I guess that pup don't smell us out none again," said Monkton's voice, as Cargunka whirled round towards the boat, with the painter loose in his fist.

The racing crowd of men had come to an almost instantaneous halt, and there was an extraordinary moment of complete silence. Cargunka could even hear the sharp, bubbling, resinous spluttering of the burning pine knots.

"You damned fool!" he said in a fierce whisper to Monkton, as he put his shoulder against the bow of the dingy, pushed off, and jumped smartly in over the bows.

And in that instant, the crowd which had halted in that strange immediate silence about the suddenly slain dog, came to life again.

A tremendous crash of revolver-fire broke the night; and hundreds of bullets splashed into the water all about them, with ugly, hissing plop-plop-plop sounds, as the crowd fired in the direction from which the shot had come.

"Pull, you fool!" said Cargunka. "See what you got us in for, wiv your damn silly ways! Pull!"

The crowd was charging down bodily now, towards where the boat had been moored, and the shooting had eased temporarily; for most of the weapons were empty. But, already, Cargunka and Monkton were ripping the dingy downstream with fierce strokes; so that when the crowd reached the place where the boat had been, they were a good couple of hundred yards away, and going well with the current.

"Was you reckoning we'd look better as sieves, than the way we was born an' made?" said Cargunka, over his shoulder. "We'd 'a' got away wivout a shot, if you hadn't 'a gone an' done that damn silly game! What was you thinkin'?"

"I didn't reckon to have no dawgs put to trackin' me, like as if I wer' a bloomin' criminal!" said the big man, in a grim half-sulky voice.

Cargunka laughed, suddenly.

"You got spunk, my lad, all right!" he said; "but God didn't mean you to run to the brains, I'm thinkin'! Pull!"

Chapter VII

The dingy was round the bend now; and Monkton thought the chase was done; but Cargunka guessed better.

"They'll cut across the bend!" he said, "an' head us off, if we ain't mindin'. We got to pull our insides out to stop 'em!"

And he was right; for, suddenly, a clamour of shouting broke out ahead; and, turning on his thwart, he saw the flicker of torch-light, among the pine woods away on the port bow of the dingy.

"Pull!" he muttered, and bent his muscular back to a still greater effort.

The boat shot past the threatening part of the riverbank, just as the first of the crowd of men burst through into the open space, on the riverside. The flicker of the torches shone out over the water, and showed them, vaguely, on the fringe of the light.

"Got 'em!" yelled several voices; and a splatter of gun-fire broke out. But hard running through dark pine woods, by torch-light, is not conducive to good shooting, and the two in the boat passed out of range, into the darkness upon the river, without being hit; though the boat had been struck several times.

Yet the crowd was not minded even now to give up; but began to run after them, along the bank, in a determined fashion; though they seemed unable to overhaul the dingy.

"We're leavin' 'em!" gasped Monkton, at last…. "Leavin' 'em sure! They won't be able to run far, when we gets out on the big water!"

"Hold your wind, my lad, an' pull," said Cargunka, between strokes. "We, maybe, got the worst to come. You remember them two canoes!… We ain't got to be followed an' located; an' that's what they'll do, if we don't drop this bunch, before we hit the briny…. Them two in the canoes'll come monkeying round; an' I'm not out for any killin'. It ain't my way. It's ugly an' it ain't Christianlike…. You pull, my lad!"

The dingy moved fast under the tremendous efforts, and the current helped them all the time. Astern of them, on the South bank, there were the bobbing lights of the many torches, and odd shouts, with now and again a crash and a curse as some man caught his foot and tumbled headlong.

The shooting had ceased entirely; for the boat was quite out of sight of the chasing crowd, and they were making far too much noise to hear the muffled oar-roll of the padded oars in the rowlocks.

But with all their efforts, Cargunka and the big miner could not lose the men who were after them; for the boat was never more than some three hundred yards ahead, at any period of the mad chase, and Cargunka was thinking all the time of the canoes that were somewhere ahead, in the mouth of the creek's estuary.

Some of the men in the crowd astern were sure to know that a couple of the camp "providers" had come down the estuary, and the torch-light was certain to bring the men in the canoes up to see what was happening. That was, possibly, what the miners were counting on. And Cargunka knew that if the men they had seen in the canoes took a hand in the chase, it would mean gun-fighting.

"We'm there, D.C.O.!" gasped out Monkton, suddenly, after taking a look over his shoulder. "Now we'll lose 'em!"

"Lose nothin', my lad!" said Cargunka, as the boat rode out into the open sea. "Look astern! That'll bring them canoes up, in mighty quick time."

The thing that Cargunka was pointing to, was the flaring blade of the torches, as the miners rushed out of the wood, and down on to the shore at the mouth of the estuary, where they began to shout, and wave their torches.

From somewhere over the sea, came a loud "cooee," sounding strange and hollow, in all that immensity.

"There you are, my lad!" said Cargunka, in an I-told-you-so voice. "Now we got to handle that!"

"Well," said Monkton, "ain't I got me gun on me! Je-hosh! but I'd like to perforate some of 'em. I bin shot over a deal tonight."

"Hark to that," said Cargunka, ignoring the big miner's grumble; for a great voice, the drunken voice of the big man who had been so relieved in his mind about the nigger, came booming out across the ever-widening gap of water:—

"Stop 'em. Buck!... Buck Kessel!... Buck Kessel, stop 'em!... Ahoy, Buck, perforate 'em. They got your pardners' dust."

"Je-hosh!" said Monkton, "I guess that was sure that Buck swine that was in one of them canoes. I'll sure perforate him for keeps, if he's the nerve to get in my track!"

"Keep her moving good-oh, my lad," said Cargunka. "We don't want to be too near in, when the fun starts."

"Buck Kessel!" came the great voice again from the beach, sounding clear through the boom of the surf on the shores to the North and South. "Buck Kessel! Stop 'em. They got your pardners' dust. Fill 'em up with lead."

And then, suddenly, Buck's voice ringing across the sea, from somewhere on the port side of the boat:—

"Sure! I'm after 'em!"

"There's two of 'em!" came the great voice from the shore. "We've shot away all our lead. Plug 'em, Buck! Try the duck-gun on 'em!"

"Sure!" shouted Buck's voice, out of the darkness.

"Duck!" said Cargunka, and the two of them ducked their heads below the gunnel, pulling their oars in-board, just as a heavy gun roared out, from a short distance away on their port side.

There was a screaming hiss of shot all about them, and the side of the boat sounded as if it had been struck by a sudden gust of the largest and most vigorous kind of hail.

"He's peppered the boat proper," said Cargunka. I guess we don't want that to happen again, when he's any nearer, or it's going to punch the side of the boat out."

"Sure!" said Monkton, and the two of them pulled out their guns.

As they did so, the voice of Buck Kessel sounded again, apparently not more than some sixty yards away.

"I guess that peppered ye! I'll fill ye up solid with lead if ye play any hanky on me! You turn right around now, and pull for the shore."

As he spoke, Monkton loosed off his revolver at the sound, once, twice and, at the second shot, there was a little cry of pain from out of the darkness, and then a brutal spate of threats and cursing.

"Down!" said Cargunka sharply, and caught Monkton by the collar, and dragged him into the bottom of the boat. In the same instant, the big duck-gun roared out again, and the crash of the heavy duck-shot on the side of the boat was sickening. Several of the shot passed clean in through the side, and drove dangerous splinters of the hard wood in all directions, so that the two of them were bleeding in half a dozen places; but not really harmed.

"That got ye! I'll teach ye, ye damned thieves—I'll—"

But what further lesson Mr. Buck Kessel wished to instill, was not told; for both Monkton and Cargunka emptied their guns at the sound of his voice, firing low, so as to avoid killing him, if possible.

There came an ugly scream from out of the night, and then an absolute silence, broken presently by the sound of a paddle out in the darkness. There was a further space of silence, and then again the splash of a paddle, but further away.

"He ain't hit bad!" said Cargunka; "but I guess he's bad enough. He's off! Now, out oars, my lad, and maybe we'll pick the ship up before yon other chap comes foolin' round."

They pulled out into the open sea for ten minutes; and were getting well away from the shore, when suddenly Cargunka threw a low word or two over his shoulder:—

"We're bein' stalked, my lad," he said. "Watch the little twiddles of phosphor-light astern there in the water. That chap can use a paddle pretty good. He ain't making no noise—not as much as you would if you winked, my lad. I reckon that's the other canoe."

"There's the ship, away yon," said Monkton. "Maybe, if we tried, we could rush yon guy before he guessed we was wise to him. Then I reck'n we could fill him bang up to his back teeth with lead; an' we'd be right then to make our getaway, an' no one to know where we'd gone."

"Pull, my lad," said Cargunka. "I'll fix him in a bit."

He stood up and slipped off his coat.

"Now, my lad," he said, "take the two oars an' keep on pullin'; but don't sweat yourself, an' when you 'ear me whistle, come back for me."

He reached behind him, as he spoke, and pulled out his belt-knife. Then, with this in his hand, he caught the stern of the dingy and lowered himself, without a word further, into the sea.

"Well, what'd you think of that!" muttered the big miner. But he obeyed orders, listening intently, and staring hard at the faint whirling of the phosphorescence in the water, some twenty fathoms astern, where the unseen paddle plied silently in the almost complete blackness. And somewhere, as Monkton guessed, between the canoe and the boat, Cargunka trod water quietly, and waited, knife in hand.

Less than a minute later, there was a sudden yell, astern, and then a loud splash. And still Monkton pulled on, stolidly.

A minute passed, during which odd sounds came to him, vague splashings, and once a desperate gasping; and finally there was only a very complete silence; broken presently by the slight sounds of some-one swimming.

Then a whistle.

Monkton put the boat round, instantly, with savage strokes, and pulled back.

"Way 'nough!" said Cargunka's voice, softly, out of the darkness ahead. Then, in a minute, Cargunka was climbing aboard, dripping prodigiously.

"Did ye knife him?" asked Monkton, as Cargunka took his oar again, and bent his back once more to pulling.

"Not me, my lad," said Cargunka. "I ain't built blood-thirsty, like you. I capsized the canoe. We 'ad a bit of a scrap in the water, an' then I cut a tidy lump out of her side. He'll be too busy wiv this an' that to do any more stalkin' this night, I'm thinkin'."

For the first time since Cargunka had known him, the big miner laughed.

"Je-hosh!" he said. "I'd sure have liked to see the boob get his head wet."

Half an hour later, they were safely aboard the brig.

Chapter VIII

The following day, as usual, Cargunka took up his duties as cook. But that evening, as was his custom, he went aft, in the second dog watch, to enjoy the coolness of the weather side of the poop, and the comfort of Captain Gell's deck-chair.

"You know, Cap'n," he might have been heard explaining presently, "I've often thought as this dot-and-carry-one leg of mine was give to me as kind of a set-off against me other gifts. I dare bet that was 'ow it was wiv Byron. Think what he might have been, if the Almighty hadn't put the break on him, as you might say. An' even then, the ladies worshipped him. Look at me, too, Cap'n; you mightn't think it to look at me—"

"No, Sir," said Captain Gell, firmly, for the second time in this story... "What was all them lights ashore last night, Sir?" he added.

"Them," said Cargunka, still turning over in his mind how to convince the Captain of his perpetual error of opinion, without having to descend to crude self-flattery; "them, oh, I guess them was a torch-light procession as they was havin' ashore yon.... It was a s'prisin' pretty sight, Cap'n."

There was a little touch of vicious pleasure in his voice, at the look of silent unbelief in Captain Gell's eyes.

"You're an obstinate old Jew, Cap'n," he said, and sighed a little....
"Sing out for Monkton to come aft to me in my cabin."

And there, some minutes later, Cargunka shared out the gold, in the proportion of "half to you" and "half to me."

"Did you ever hear of Byron, the poet?" he asked in an earnest voice, as he concluded the division.

"Sure, he's the poetry guy, D.C.O.," said the big miner. "Didn't you tell me about him yourself?"

A Note On The Texts

WHENEVER POSSIBLE, TEXTS FOR this series have been based on versions that were published in book form, preferably during Hodgson's lifetime. The major exceptions to this rule are the stories that appear in volumes edited by Sam Moskowitz. Moskowitz was known to have access to original manuscripts and other source materials. Some stories were published only in serial form, and have been taken from those primary sources.

Over the years, many of Hodgson's story's have appeared under variant titles, which are noted below. As a rule, the titles used in this series are based on the first book publication of a story, even if it previously appeared under a different title, in serial form.

Specific textual sources are noted below. The only changes that have been made to the texts have been to correct obvious typographical errors, and to standardize punctuation and capitalization. British and archaic spellings have been retained.

The Boats of the "Glen Carrig" is based on the 1920 Holden & Hardingham edition. It was originally published by Chapman & Hall, 1907.

"From the Tideless Sea, Part One" is based on its publication in *Men Of Deep Waters* (Eveleigh Nash, 1914). It was originally published in *Monthly Story Magazine 2, No. 6* (April 1906).

"From the Tideless Sea, Part Two: More News From the *Homebird*" (AKA "The Fifth Message from the Tideless Sea") is based on its publication in *Men Of Deep Waters* (Eveleigh Nash, 1914). It was originally published in *Blue Book Magazine* (August 1907).

"The Mystery of the Derelict" is based on its publication in *Men Of Deep Waters* (Eveleigh Nash, 1914). It was originally published in *Story-teller No. 4* (July 1907).

"The Thing in the Weeds" (AKA "An Adventure of the Deep Waters") is based on its publication in *Deep Waters* (Arkham House, 1967). It was originally published in *Story-teller No. 60* (January 1912).

"The Finding of the *Graiken*" is based on its publication in *Out of the Storm* (Grant, 1975). It was originally published in *The Red Magazine No. 93* (February 15, 1913).

"The Call In the Dawn" (AKA "The Voice in the Dawn") is based on its publication in *Deep Waters* (Arkham House, 1967). It was originally published as "The Voice in the Dawn", in *Premier Magazine* (November 5, 1920).

"Contraband of War" is based on its publication in *Captain Gault* (McBride & Sons, 1918). It was originally published in *London Magazine 32, No. 5* (July 1914).

"The Diamond Spy" is based on its publication in *Captain Gault* (McBride & Sons, 1918). It was originally published in *London Magazine 33, No. 6* (August 1914).

"The Red Herring" is based on its publication in *Captain Gault* (McBride & Sons, 1918). It was originally published in *London Magazine 33, No. 1* (September 1914).

"The Case of the Chinese Curio Dealer" is based on its publication in *Captain Gault* (McBride & Sons, 1918). It was originally published in *London Magazine 33, No. 2* (October 1914).

"The Drum of Saccharine" is based on its publication in *Captain Gault* (McBride & Sons, 1918). It was originally published in *London Magazine 33, No. 3* (November 1914).

"From Information Received" is based on its publication in *Captain Gault* (McBride & Sons, 1918). It was originally published in *London Magazine 33, No. 4* (December 1914).

"The German Spy" (AKA "He 'assists' the enemy") is based on its publication in *Captain Gault* (McBride & Sons, 1918). It was originally published as "He 'Assists' the Enemy" in *London Magazine 33, No. 5* (January 1915).

"The Problem of the Pearls" is based on its publication in *Captain Gault* (McBride & Sons, 1918). It was originally published in *London Magazine 34, No. 3* (May 1915).

"The Painted Lady" is based on its publication in *London Magazine 35, No. 3* (November 1915).

"The Adventure of the Garter" is based on its publication in *Captain Gault* (McBride & Sons, 1918). It was originally published in *London Magazine 37, No. 1* (September 1916).

"My Lady's Jewels" is based on its publication in *Captain Gault*

(McBride & Sons, 1918). It was originally published in *London Magazine 37, No. 4* (December 1916).

"Trading with the Enemy" is based on its publication in *London Magazine 39, No. 2* (October 1917).

"The Plans of the Reefing Bi-Plane" is based on its publication in *Terrors of the Sea* (Grant, 1996).

"The Island of the Ud" is based on its publication in *The Luck of the Strong* (Eveleigh Nash, 1916). It was originally published in *The Red Magazine No. 75* (May 15, 1912).

"Adventure of the Headland" is based on its publication in *The Luck of the Strong* (Eveleigh Nash, 1916). It was originally published in *The Red Magazine No. 86* (November 1, 1912).

"The Bells of the Laughing Sally" is based on its publication in *The Luck of the Strong* (Eveleigh Nash, 1916). It was originally published in *The Red Magazine No. 121* (April 15, 1914).

"The Adventure with the Claim Jumpers" is based on its publication in *The Luck of the Strong* (Eveleigh Nash, 1916). It was originally published in *The Red Magazine No. 134* (January 15, 1915).

The Complete Fiction of William Hope Hodgson is published by
Night Shade Books in the following volumes:

The Complete Fiction of William Hope Hodgson is published by
Night Shade Books in the following volumes:

The Boats of the "Glen Carrig" and Other Nautical Adventures
The House on the Borderland and Other Mysterious Places
The Ghost Pirates and Other Revenants of the Sea
The Night Land and Other Perilous Romances
The Dream of X and Other Fantastic Visions